Why You Need This New Edition

If you're wondering why you should buy this new edition of *Theatre: Collaborative Acts*, here are 6 good reasons!

Theatre: Collaborative Acts continues to stimulate creative thinking and discussions of artistic, social, and ethical questions through its interwoven themes of theatre as culture, collaboration, spatial art, and a fusion of the past and present. It will help establish a firm basis of knowledge and will provide an informed perspective for a lifetime of theatre-going in appreciation and introduction courses. The fourth edition of *Theatre: Collaborative Acts*:

1. Includes new information about important professional productions, from current Broadway, Resident, and Off-Broadway productions, including *Ruined* (2009), *The Book of Mormon* (2011), *War Horse* (2007/2011), and *In the Next Room* (2009), looking critically at the ethical questions and important life messages these plays address—and the ways in which different theatrical traditions address them.

2. Gives students a varied and international perspective by featuring new artist and historical boxes on the musical as political theatre, a long run in the avant-garde theatre, a South Korean musical, the Chinese classical space, and more.

3. Provides a deeper focus on contemporary theatre and the American musical.

4. Describes additional, contemporary approaches to the analysis of play texts and to writing plays, giving students valuable perspective on the creative process.

5. Incorporates updates to the timeline of important events in theatre, which takes you through theatrical traditions and influences across cultures and time.

6. Offers 101 new, detailed captions for photographs, to help students appreciate the full significance of each visual example.

PEARSON

Fourth Edition

THEATRE

Collaborative Acts

Ronald Wainscott

Indiana University

Kathy Fletcher

Indiana University

PEARSON

Boston   Columbus   Indianapolis   New York   San Francisco   Upper Saddle River
Amsterdam   Cape Town   Dubai   London   Madrid   Milan   Munich   Paris   Montreal   Toronto
Delhi   Mexico   City   Sao Paulo   Sydney   Hong Kong   Seoul   Singapore   Taipei   Tokyo

Editor-in-Chief, Communication & Theatre: Karon Bowers
Editor: Ziki Dekel
Associate Development Editor: Angela Mallowes
Editorial Assistant: Megan Hermida
Marketing Manager: Blair Zoe Tuckman
Associate Editor: Corey Kahn
Associate Managing Editor: Bayani Mendoza de Leon
Executive Digital Producer: Stefanie Snajder
Digital Project Manager: Janell Lantana
Project Coordination, Text Design, and Electronic Page Makeup: Laserwords Private Ltd.
Manufacturing Buyer: Mary Ann Gloriande
Senior Cover Design Manager/Cover Designer: Nancy Danahy
Cover Images: The Tempest by Shakespeare Steppenwolf © by Michael Brosilow

Credits and acknowledgments borrowed from other sources and reproduced, with permission, in this textbook appear on the appropriate page within the text.

Library of Congress Cataloging-in-Publication Data

Wainscott, Ronald Harold.
  Theatre : collaborative acts / Ronald Wainscott, Kathy Fletcher.—4th ed.
    p. cm.
  ISBN-13: 978-0-205-11802-1
  ISBN-10: 0-205-11802-X
  1. Theater and society.   I. Fletcher, Kathy, 1955–   II. Title.   III. Title: Theater.
  PN2049.W26 2011
  792.09—dc23

                                           2011043278

1 2 3 4 5 6 7 8 9 10—RRD—14 13 12 11

www.pearsonhighered.com

ISBN-13: 978-0-205-11802-1
ISBN-10: 0-205-11802-X

Dedication

For Marion and Keith Michael,
who have inspired a passion for theatre
in so many students.

Brief Contents

Contents

CHAPTER 4
Understanding the Play: A Theatrical Blueprint

page 75

CHAPTER 5
Interpreting the Play:
Understanding Genre,
Reading, and Writing
page 100

CHAPTER 10
The Producer:
Coordination,
Promotion, Economics
page 237

ACT THREE: Collaboration in History   261

CHAPTER 11
Foundations: Classical
Theatrical Forms
page 262

Preface

How could we possibly describe an experience as rich and vast as the theatre in a book that would be light enough to carry around in a backpack? After spending over twenty years together seeing, producing and directing plays, teaching classes, conducting research, and writing, we needed to make some difficult choices. The task of writing this book forced us to focus on what we believe is most important to share about the theatre experience at this moment in time: Theatre is *collaboration* in the purest sense of the word—it is co-labor, working together. This co-labor exists on many levels. To participate in theatre, as either audience member or practitioner, means to be at once an individual and part of a larger whole, even part of a continuum stretching far into the past as countless people find remarkably different ways to express the condition of being human. The essence of the theatre is shared experience. As such, it holds great potential for making connections in the twenty-first century.

New to This Edition

Theatre: Collaborative Acts continues to stimulate creative thinking and discussions of artistic, social, and ethical questions through its interwoven themes of theatre as culture, collaboration, spatial art, and a fusion of the past and the present. It will help establish a firm basis of knowledge and will provide an informed perspective for a lifetime of theatre-going in appreciation and introduction courses.

The fourth edition of *Theatre: Collaborative Acts* includes new information about important professional productions throughout the text, looking critically at the ethical questions and important life messages these plays address—and the ways in which different theatrical traditions address them. The text includes examples from current Broadway, Resident, and Off-Broadway productions, including *Ruined* (2009), *The Book of Mormon* (2011), *War Horse* (2007/2011), and *In the Next Room* (2009).

The fourth edition provides new artist and historical boxes on the musical as political theatre, a long run in the avant-garde theatre, a South Korean musical, the Chinese classical space, and more, as well as an increased focus on contemporary theatre and the American musical.

An updated timeline of important events in theatre takes you through theatrical traditions and influences across cultures and time. *Theatre: Collaborative Acts* continues to provide detailed captions for photographs, 101 of which are new to this edition, as a guide to aid students in reading theatrical staging and integrating text with visual images.

New in Each Chapter

Chapter 1: Cultural Collaboration includes seven new photographs, a new historical and cultural box on the musical as political theatre, centering on *Bloody Bloody Andrew Jackson*, and updated statistics and production details on contemporary theatre practice in professional theatre.

Chapter 2: Experiencing Theatre includes five new photographs, a new historical and cultural box on the record-breaking long run of Ionesco's *The Bald Soprano* in Paris, and a focus on the audience experiencing performance.

Chapter 3: Analyzing Theatre includes seven new photographs, a new cultural and historical box on the Chinese classical versus contemporary theatre space, and various approaches to analysis of the theatrical event.

Chapter 4: Understanding the Play includes seven new photographs, a new historical and cultural box on the South Korean musical *Miso*, and a focus on analysis of play text.

Chapter 5: Interpreting the Play includes six new photographs, many new productions of plays, and more approaches to analysis.

Chapter 6: The Director includes eight new photographs and much updating of directing in the professional theatre.

Chapter 7: The Actor includes seven new photographs and approaches to the acting process.

Chapter 8: The Playwright includes eight new photographs and historical and contemporary approaches to writing and crafting plays.

Chapter 9: The Designer includes nine new photographs, a new Artist of the Theatre box on scenic designer John Lee Beatty, and many updates of new designs for the theatre.

Chapter 10: The Producer includes four new photographs and updated statistics on theatrical production from the producer's side of events.

Chapter 11: Foundations includes eight new photographs and a history and analysis of western and Asian classical theatre up to the Renaissance.

Chapter 12: Reinterpretations includes two new photographs and history and analysis of theatre from the Renaissance to c.1800.

Chapter 13: Revolutions includes five new photographs, a new Historical and Cultural box on the American Musical, and history and analysis of theatre from 1800 to the present.

The Photo Gallery on Theatre of Diversity includes six new photographs and an analysis of racial and gender diversity.

The new Photo Gallery on Contemporary Theatre includes twelve new photographs and provides a snapshot of contemporary theatre.

Organization of This Text

Theatre throughout the ages has brought different answers to the questions: Who am I? Who are we? What belongs to me? What belongs to us? What really matters?

In the first part of this book, Act One, we explore theatre and its audience. We examine the theatre as cultural activity with its many possible social functions and relationship to society in order to provide a window into the way a society views itself. We have drawn on examples from many cultures as well as the Western tradition. We also consider the collaboration of the audience with the other components of theatre-making in experiencing and analyzing plays and productions.

Act Two describes in detail the jobs and artistic contributions of theatre practitioners other than the audience—those who collaborate to prepare the theatrical event prior to the arrival of the audience: the director, actor, playwright, designer, and producer.

The three chapters of Act Three provide a brief history of theatrical collaboration. Because the past continually collaborates with the present in the theatre, we have included examples from other time periods in the chapters throughout the book. Act Three, however, provides a sense of historical continuity and chronology. The discussion in Act Three organizes theatrical events in roughly chronological order and depicts the theatre as an ongoing negotiation of the personal and the social, the individual and the communal. Selecting what to include in an overview of 2,500 years of activity is, of course, extremely difficult. In some ways the choice is highly subjective; other theatre historians could give you their own versions, which would no doubt differ from ours. And of course, what we see as important is informed by the time at which we write.

Special Features

Within each chapter we provide several series of special features to introduce students to the major themes and principles discussed in this book. Most of these boxes include illustrations.

Exploring Collaboration

These boxes contain profiles of successful artistic teams and companies and stories about their partnerships with local communities and critics. These entries feature various approaches to theatre's vital process—along with the challenges and controversy that sometimes arise.

Exploring Historical and Cultural Perspectives

These boxes provide a close-up view of critical theatrical events, terminology, and practice that have changed the field. These boxes also offer explanation and interpretation of works from different cultures and shed light on important past productions, theatrical institutions, styles, and activities that have made significant contributions to the history and development of theatre.

Artists of the Theatre

These detailed boxes about important theatre artists introduce contemporary, colorful, talented, and influential theatrical figures. Each of these figures has created outstanding work as an actor, actress, producer, playwright, director, costume designer, lighting designer, or scenic designer.

Theatre of Diversity

This Photo Gallery demonstrates a range of cultural, intercultural, racial, ethnic, gender, sexual orientation, stylistic, and topical diversity in contemporary productions. The plays represented in this feature include work from the ancient Greeks, classical Asia, and Shakespeare.

Contemporary Theatre

This Photo Gallery contains fifteen images meant to capture an emblematic snapshot of our contemporary theatre. New productions and plays almost always have important antecedents in theatre of the past.

Key Theatrical Events

Following Act Three, this timeline of selected theatrical, social, and artistic events provides readers with a global and historical context for exploring the world of theatre. The timeline also indicates the ways theatrical movements have traveled around the world and the simultaneity of important theatrical events.

Chapter Review

At the end of each chapter we offer a series of study aids. "Questions and Activities" provides a springboard for class discussions or outside projects. We arrange "Key Terms and Concepts" by topic followed by page number (the terms appear in boldface within the text). In "For Further Exploration" we suggest articles, books, videos, and websites as places for students to pursue theatre topics that interest them.

Supplemental Resources

We have prepared a package of resources to accompany *Theatre: Collaborative Acts*. The Instructor's Manual/Test Bank provides suggested syllabi, a course outline, and suggestions for using the book in an introduction to theatre course. The test questions include multiple-choice, true/false, and short essay questions for each chapter; they are available as a computerized test bank in MyTest as well as in PDF format. There is also a series of PowerPoint™ lectures available for each chapter of the book. All of these supplements are available for download at **www.pearsonhighered.com/irc** (access code required). The free website, Pearson's **Introduction to Theatre Study Site**, which can be accessed at **www.pearsontheater.com**, features introduction to theatre study materials for students, including flashcards and a complete set of practice tests for all major topics. Students will also find web links to valuable sites for further exploration of major topics.

Acknowledgments

Many people contributed directly or indirectly to the creation of *Theatre: Collaborative Acts.* This book began with a suggestion from our colleague and friend Michael Connolly to editor-in-chief Karon Bowers. Molly Taylor saw the work through the publication process. Our editors, Carol Alper, for the first edition, Jane Buchbinder, for the second edition, Jeanne Zalesky, for the third edition, and Ziki Dekel, for the fourth edition, encouraged and supported us and managed to remain both patient and good-humored while they organized, explained, critiqued, and asked stimulating questions.

   We would like to thank our friend and colleague, Charles Railsback, teacher of introduction to theatre, for sharing ideas and his experiences with the course. Other friends and colleagues generously shared materials or read and responded to portions of the manuscript at various points, including Fred M. Duer, Wes Peters, Robert Shakespeare, Linda Pisano, and David Grindle at Indiana University; Richard Finkelstein at James Madison University; and director and designer Rob McKercher at Doane College. We thank Sue Vargo and Jonathan Michaelsen at Indiana University for their support and encouragement. Graduate students and colleagues who have taught introduction to theatre and theatre appreciation have shared their problems, ideas, and concerns with us, especially DeAnna Toten Beard, Terry Brino-Dean, Eileen Curley, Heather McMahon, Heather May, Larry Dooley, Laurie Schmeling, Michael Solomonson, Andrew Hayes, Jeff Grace, Patrick Murphree, Tom Robson, Chris Hatch, Neal Utterback, Deana Nichols, Sarah McCarroll, Joe Stollenwerk, and Tom Oldham. Our many undergraduate students, especially those in our own introduction to theatre courses, have stimulated our thinking through their questions and insights.

   We appreciate the help of curators, librarians, and photographic assistants, including Ms. Michael Scott, Folger Shakespeare Library, Washington, DC; Jeremy Megraw, New York Public Library for the Performing Arts; Veronica L. Fletcher, Archivist, George Mason University; and the staff at the Museum of the City of New York.

   Many theatre companies and arts organizations have contributed numerous hours in locating and providing photographs, programs, and other materials. We would like to thank the following individuals:

   Kirsty Kaukel, Actors Theatre of Louisville
   Sara Gruber, The Shakespeare Theatre, Washington, DC
   Kirstin Franko, Arena Stage, Washington, DC
   Dave Ruark and Janet Allen, Indiana Repertory Theatre, Indianapolis
   Elizabeth Neukirch, Chicago Shakespeare Theater
   Bruce C. Lee, Utah Shakespearean Festival, Cedar City
   Dina Croce and Holly Mosiello, Huntington Theatre Company, Boston

Ellen Charendoff, Stratford Festival Archives
Erik Hansen-Hansen, photographer, Copenhagen, Denmark
John Kinzer, Indiana University
Kendra Fletcher Wainscott, Indiana University

A number of our colleagues have provided helpful manuscript reviews at each stage of development. We hope this book has benefited from their insightful comments and advice. We wish to thank the following reviewers:

Stephanie Daventry French, East Stroudsburg University
Kaye De Metz, Bergen Community College
Jeff Entwistle, University of Wisconsin–Green Bay
Ross Fleming, The University of Texas, El Paso
Kenneth Z. Kendall, Northeastern Junior College
Thomas J. Mikotowicz, University of Maine
Douglas B. Rosentrater, Bucks County Community College
Alison E. Stafford, Hinds Community College

We could not complete such a major project without the understanding, cooperation, and support of those closest to us, Jeremy and Kendra Fletcher Wainscott. The book itself is a collaborative act—the product of two authors, many colleagues, friends, and family members. We now leave it in the hands of you, the reader, to complete the collaborative process.

Ronald Wainscott
Kathy Fletcher

THEATRON (audience area) of the ancient Hellenistic Greek theatre at Delphi (2010).
Photo © Ronald Wainscott.

Act ONE

Theatre and Its Audience

"*Whereas literature is a private act of the imagination (for writer and reader), theatre happens in the present tense (fleetingly) before the eyes of an audience. In order to be theatre, it must have witnesses.*" [1]

—TRACY C. DAVIS

As a form of art and entertainment, theatre happens when audience and artists collaborate: Actors perform live for people watching, listening, and reacting. There is a certain satisfaction in the immediacy of theatre: It is always in present tense. Unlike the novel, film, poetry, and painting, which are created and then left for our experience, theatre is created anew with each performance.

Theatre is malleable—it is formed and shaped by the here and now. It shares this quality with live performance of music and dance. Theatre also shares with dance the use of the human body to create art and with vocal music the use of the human voice. Human beings use their own forms to create meaning for other human beings—an intensely personal act.

Live theatre provides two-way communication. The audience member is not just a passive observer or receiver of a message; each spectator contributes in some measure to the nature of the theatrical event. In the vast majority of cases, theatre is a group activity—theatre artists combine their talents to create an experience for a group of spectators. When individuals make the commitment to attend a performance, they become part of the entity of the audience and, to a great extent, respond as a group. It is difficult to laugh in an empty theatre; it is quite easy and enjoyable to laugh along with a crowd. A sense of unity is created when we recognize that those around us react with the same emotional intensity, whether with happiness, sadness, or anger. In the theatre, we are not alone.

IMAGE OF ACTOR GEORGE M. COHAN overlooks Time Square in New York City (2009).
Photo © Ronald Wainscott.

Cultural Collaboration

Theatre and Society

Imagine an activity at once physical, emotional, and intellectual. Imagine people creating art out of their own bodies and voices. Imagine an art form in which people can relate to each other directly, vibrantly, without the intervention of technology: no cell phones, iPods, no modems, no satellites. Imagine being able to observe, evaluate, participate in, and comment on this immediate communication. Imagine an activity that reproduces a wealth of human experience—both the best and worst our species has to offer—without physical hardship and pain.

The act of creating theatre is all of this. Theatre is human beings coming together at a particular time and place for no other reason than to practice being human, perhaps with the shared but unspoken hope that someday we will get it right!

The word "theatre" has broad usage in society from art to warfare to movies to social interaction. We talk of electronic "home theatres" and "military theatres" that denote large arenas of military operations in wartime. We observe theatre in psychology as well as anything in life experience that involves performative acts and role-playing (conscious and unconscious) in human behavior and personal analysis. Obviously, a book like this one must approach the term more narrowly in order to keep the subject from getting out of control. Here we examine theatre as two things: (1) a place of performance and (2) the process or institution of theatre, which we define as dramatic art and entertainment performed live and deliberately by one or more actors for an audience present in the same physical space at the same time. Therefore, theatre requires at least one performer, an audience, a common space, and something (often, but not necessarily a play) to be performed for that audience. Theatre can be rehearsed, scripted, or improvisational; it can be professional or amateur, but it always includes the elements noted in the previous two sentences.

Human beings can live without theatre; some societies—such as the Sumerian, Mayan, and Aztec cultures—never developed sustained theatrical activity. But in different places all over the world, theatre has been invented and reinvented many times. Theatrical productions are artistic and cultural events that function as an integral part of the community within the society that supports it. The artistic context for theatrical production is an array of arts and humanities, some of which, like literature, dance, music, painting, and architecture, bear a close relationship to theatre art. Theatre may imitate, parody, criticize, or celebrate a society's foibles and greatness and sometimes lead or incrementally alter a society's development and identity. The larger social context is usually reflected in theatre, but the theatre also interacts directly with other aspects of culture.

The span of theatrical activity in the twenty-first century is vast. Folk performances that have continued, little changed, for centuries bring people together in small villages. Tourists enjoy multi-million-dollar productions using state-of-the-art electronic equipment in metropolitan centers. Schoolchildren perform their own interpretations of historical events, and elders find a voice and camaraderie in performance. To be fair, contemporary society is fragmented, and so is the theatre art that serves and reflects that society. To talk about theatre is to talk about many theatres. In this chapter, we explore the primary purposes of theatre, the various social roles that theatre fulfills, its position in society, and North American theatre choices, both professional and amateur.

THEATRE AS ENTERTAINMENT AND ART

Theatre is a form of entertainment. It provides diversion—a vacation from reality. Like other live entertainment experiences such as concerts, dance performances, and live sporting events, theatre provides an experience that a person chooses for its own sake. Going to the theatre is not about earning money or paying bills. For a while, the audience member focuses on the world within the theatre.

Theatre that is meant strictly as entertainment concentrates on this escape from everyday routine and does not usually challenge the beliefs of the majority of its audience or push an audience beyond its comfort zone. In this way theatre serves the important social function of reinforcing values. In the nineteenth century the theatre served as a leisure activity for a mass audience in Europe, Asia, and North America. In the twentieth century that role was largely taken over by film, then radio, television, and the Internet. Many of today's comedies, thrillers, and musical comedies, however, are examples of theatre as popular entertainment. Some of the best-loved American plays fall into this category; *Harvey* (1944) by Mary Chase, *The Odd Couple* (1965) by Neil Simon, and *Mamma Mia!* (2001) by Benny Andersson and Björn Ulvaeus, advertised as "Broadway's ultimate feel-good show," and which is still running in 2011 and centers around a wedding and the bride's quest to learn the identity of her father.

Likewise, many British thrillers continue to engage audiences. New generations feel the mounting tension as suspicion shifts from one eccentric character to another in Agatha Christie's *The Mousetrap* (1952). A lot can be learned about a society by looking at its forms of popular entertainment, since these tend to reinforce currently accepted values. It is often hard to analyze objectively the entertainment of our own society, since it calls on deeply held assumptions and beliefs.

Theatre is also an art form. As such, it often challenges its audience to think harder, look deeper, confront uncomfortable truths, or come to a higher understanding. This is not to say, of course, that theatre as art is not entertaining. While it requires some effort on the part of the audience, such theatre can be exhilarating, enlightening, and life-changing. Like other forms of art, theatre can help an audience member look at life in a different way or provide a more focused version of reality than life experience.

Some of the world's greatest authors looked to the theatre as the best forum to express specific ideas as well as explore the human condition. *Oedipus the King* (c. 430 B.C.E.) by Sophocles, for example, has long stood as a remarkable examination of duty to whatever gods may exist and the necessity of adhering to important rules of conduct. Oedipus is guilty of violating human and divine law, even though he does not realize he has committed crimes until he comes face to face with his own guilt. Although he is looking for a murderer throughout most of the action of the play, he does not recognize until late that he himself is the criminal he seeks. While he has sight, he is figuratively blind. He punishes himself by putting out his own eyes and, now blinded, can at last see clearly. Although the conditions inherent in this play are extreme (Oedipus kills his father, marries his mother, and has children who are also his brothers and sisters), it still leads us to ponder the nature of humanity and our own failure to see our lives clearly. The issues in *Well* (2006) are more contemporary; playwright Lisa Kron examines our

OEDIPUS THE KING, produced by the Shakespeare Theatre, Washington, DC. Avery Brooks, as Oedipus, enters to the chorus in this production inspired by African culture and art. Notice the large central door, normally a feature traditional to Greek tragedy, but its decoration and all elements of the scenic design by Charles McClennahan are African motifs. The dark tribal costumes of the chorus stand in stark contrast to the majestic, colorful costume of Oedipus in designs by Toni-Leslie James. The staging and design leave no doubt about which character is the ruler of the city of Thebes. The 2001 production of Nicholas Rudall's translation of Sophocles' *The Oedipus Plays* was directed by Michael Kahn.

Photo © Carol Rosegg.

concept of family, of sickness and health, and our struggle to gain control over a complex and ultimately uncontrollable world. In *Time Stands Still* (2010) Donald Margulies combines the painful breakup of a long-term relationship with haunting conflicts plaguing a wounded female photojournalist just back from the war in Iraq. The play raises questions about the responsibility of reporters and photographers who record but do not interfere with or attempt to stop the suffering and deaths of others—especially the innocent. They function as witnesses to history. Like *Oedipus,* these plays ask difficult questions about the perception of reality and personal moral accountability.

THE SOCIAL FUNCTIONS OF THEATRE

Although entertainment and artistic experience are its primary purposes, theatre can serve a number of functions simultaneously. At various times theatre has been part of religious ritual, a civic celebration, a status symbol, a means of educating the young, a way of maintaining or challenging the status quo, a protest against the establishment, a means of sexual titillation, a way of raising morale and expressing solidarity, a propaganda vehicle, a profit-making venue, and a way of sparking discussion. The collaboration of actors and audience has created a powerful force in many different cultures.

Theatre and Religion

Theatre shares many important connections with religious institutions. The earliest known theatrical presentations appear to have been steeped in religious ritual and dance. In ancient Egypt priests reenacted stories of the gods, probably for an audience. Many other old societies, including those of Native Americans, Africans, and Southeast Asians, performed theatrical rituals led by a priest or shaman. The shaman celebrated the past or invoked the gods by collaborating with both the deities and the audience of believers. The performance was often very interactive in terms of impersonation, song, chant, dance, and spiritual response. Transformation was frequently a part of religious ritual. Performers not only represented another being but also believed that wearing the mask of a god or an ancestor led to a kind of possession—the spirit of the deity or ancestor inhabited the body of the performer. Ritual can be a way of connecting with other worlds and is sometimes meant to effect a change in this world. Some Native American tribes, for example, performed a particular dance ritual when rain was needed or before setting out to hunt or fight.

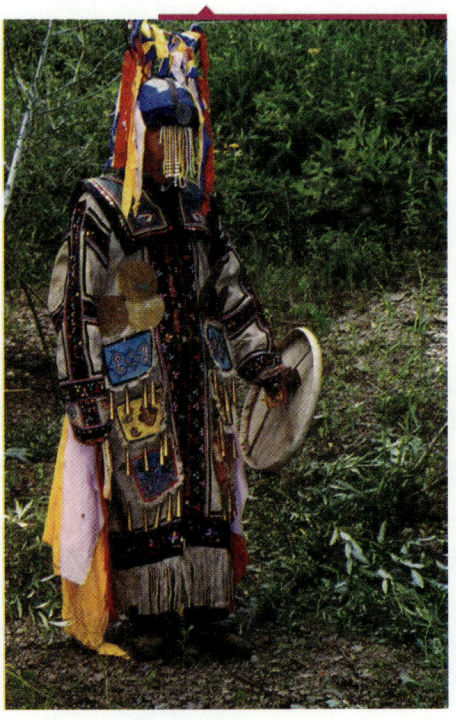

A MANCHURIAN SHAMAN in ritual regalia in 1994. The shaman often wears a mask or mask-like makeup or decoration.
Photo by Richard Noll.

The traditional view of historians is that Western theatre had its beginnings in religious ritual. Its development was associated with festivals celebrating and praising the Greek god Dionysus. Although it is difficult to say when, the Greeks moved from using theatrical performance as a part of ritual to enjoying the performance for its own sake while still using it to communicate important stories or information. Unaware of the Greek legacy, the medieval Christian church introduced theatrical activity into religious service and then recognized the potential of theatre as a means to familiarize a mainly illiterate public with biblical stories. This tradition continues in dramatizations within houses of worship (the traditional Christmas pageant, for example) as well as in large outdoor spaces. Today in India, Kathakali dance drama still enacts episodes from the great Hindu epics, the *Ramayana* and the *Mahabharata.* Some of our most eloquent playwrights recognize the cultural and dramatic importance of religious ritual. Nigerian playwright Wole Soyinka (b. 1934) uses traditional Yoruba ritual to structure many of his plays, such as *Death and the King's Horseman* (1975). Even when recognized primarily as a form of entertainment, the theatre has been used as a vehicle to disseminate and reinforce religious beliefs.

SOUTH KOREAN local and national festivals often present masked performances associated with seasonal changes, ancient celebrations, and commemorations. Much of Korea's theatrical activity is steeped in music, dance, and masking.

Photo by Kyoung-Hwan, Jang.

Theatre and Socialization

The Roman poet Horace defined the function of theatre as to teach and to please. At times the educational potential of theatre has been considered its most important asset, particularly as a way of passing on a society's rules of behavior. Generations of young people absorbed social and moral lessons by watching actors on the stage. Even at a time when attending the theatre was thought inappropriate for proper young ladies, British author Hanna More (1745–1833) wrote plays to be performed at home, specifically designed to teach acceptable feminine values. Nineteenth-century melodramas offered a host of heroes and heroines to emulate as well as villains to despise. Apprentices in eighteenth- and nineteenth-century London were encouraged to attend the theatre on Boxing Day (the day after Christmas) to see a traditional performance of George Lillo's *The London Merchant* (1731), the sad story of a young apprentice who fell into bad company, stole from his master, murdered his uncle, and suffered dire consequences. Although child- and family-oriented television programs have largely taken over the job of teaching moral standards and behavior to young people, life lessons that are acceptable to the current audience are still embedded in plays. *The Lion King* (1997)—first an animated film and then a popular Broadway musical—demonstrates that the circle of life is sacred and that in disrupting that natural balance, one risks losing everything. But if one accepts the circle of life and nourishes it, one is rewarded. The musical *Avenue Q* (2003) appeals to the audience for tolerance of different races, religions, sexual preferences, and ways of life. At its most basic, however, the play stresses the importance of accepting one's self and realizing that one's overriding purpose in life may never be found. We may compromise, but little in life is permanent.

Theatre and Politics

Theatre has frequently been used to reinforce the political status quo and build support for the government that is in power. Ruling monarchs were often praised in the plays of the sixteenth and seventeenth centuries. Popular Spanish playwright Lope de Vega, for example, frequently ended his plays such as *The King, The Greatest Alcalde* (c. 1623) not only with praise for the king but also by having the king solve the play's dramatic problem. Early American theatres staged the apotheosis of George Washington shortly after his death to honor and celebrate a cultural hero; audiences watched an actor representing the first president ascend to heaven to be welcomed by the angels. In the twentieth century the struggles of the founding fathers and mothers were memorialized in the musical *1776* (1969) as it created a lively, human background for the birth of the Declaration of Independence.

Theatrical performance has often been used to present **propaganda**—material specifically designed to advocate a particular point of view—to both support the status quo and challenge or undermine it. Before the era of newsreels and, later, television news programs, military victories (including naval battles) were reenacted and celebrated in theatres, from ancient Rome to the early twentieth century in the United States and Europe. Besides providing escape from highly stressful reality during times of war, theatre has offered patriotic support. During World War I, for example, the American theatre featured musical reviews (complete with dancing girls) such as *Doing Our Bit* (1917), which encouraged its audience to conserve war materials. Theatre has also been used to spread a negative image of enemies. *War Brides* (1915) depicted a German government forcing women to have children to populate its army. During and just after World War II, the U.S. theatre produced many adventuresome and romantic plays intended to support the war effort, bolster morale, and entertain the audience. Such a dramatized story was very popular in *Home of the Brave* (1944).

EXPLORING Historical and Cultural Perspectives

The Musical as Political Theatre

How could an audience today possibly understand the remarkable popularity and controversy surrounding an icon of early nineteenth-century politics? The creators of *Bloody, Bloody Andrew Jackson* created a dynamic theatrical conceit when they turned the former president (now featured on the twenty-dollar bill) into a rock star, played convincingly by Benjamin Walker. Writer/director Alex Timbers and composer/lyricist Michael Friedman transformed the political career of Andrew Jackson into a satirical, political musical.

Jackson's over-the-top popularity is instantly recognizable to both young and aging audiences who have grown up with rock music and the shooting stars of pop culture. Jackson the rocker is charismatic, self-serving, and wicked. Zooming through history, the play follows Jackson's rise from frontier lad to soldier to president. Out of the turmoil of the war of 1812 Jackson emerged as a populist, racist war hero who became identified with "Jacksonian Democracy," a reactionary political movement marked by xenophobia and dedicated to the removal of Indians from their ancestral lands.

Watching the rise of Jackson to political star in the theatre was akin to experiencing an unruly concert running for an unbroken 90 minutes. The trappings of celebrity and the physical excesses of the early nineteenth century were suggested by a deliberately glitzy environment punctuated scenically by stuffed dead animals (including a horse) hanging over the heads of the audience and adorning the onstage setting designed by Donyale Werle. The color red was everywhere, including myriad red twinkle lights. The effect, which encompassed the audience areas as well as the stage, was of a self-consciously cheap, rustic, and frontier-like saloon, inviting a free-for-all presentation. Portraits of nineteenth-century American political figures seemed to be everywhere, reminding us of the historical icons adorning our typical history textbooks. Deliberate anachronisms in the text abound, contributing to the outrageous humor as well as connecting the current audience to the issues of the nineteenth century. Andrew Jackson has cheerleaders, for example, in the White House.

BENJAMIN WALKER AS ANDREW JACKSON, ROCK STAR. Walker originated this dynamic role in the first performances in Los Angeles for Center Theatre Group and continued through the off-Broadway production at the Public Theater in New York and the Broadway run.
Photo © Joan Marcus.

Much of the action of the play is littered with deaths by disease and murders of Indians, frontiersmen, politicos, and the like. Although at its heart the play is replete with disturbing ideology, the satirical humor and energetic delight of the experience carry the day. Nonetheless, references to the conservative efforts of the George W. Bush administration and the "War on Terror" after the attacks on New York and Washington on September 11, 2001 punctuate or enhance some of the events taking place in Jackson's administration.

Bloody, Bloody Andrew Jackson was developed by the Center Theatre Group in Los Angeles and opened in 2008. The play moved to the Public Theater in New York and opened on Broadway in 2010. Although the production was wildly appreciated by many, a number of critics wondered if the material was appropriate for a Broadway venue because of the heavy seriousness underpinning the frivolity. The musical closed in 2011, but is likely to find new life in regional and university productions.

Theatre and Subversion

Although the theatre often supports and maintains the dominant culture, it can also be used to subvert the status quo in society. Just as the theatre can provide support for a society's values, it can also offer a public forum for challenge and disagreement.

African Americans have been using the stage to break down stereotypes since the 1950s. In Douglas Turner Ward's *Day of Absence* (1965), black actors play white characters in white makeup—a comment on the theatrical stereotype created by white minstrels playing in blackface. The plays of Athol Fugard carried an antiapartheid message far beyond his native South Africa. In *Boesman and Lena* (1969) and *Master Harold . . . and the Boys* (1982) Fugard explores the larger issues of racial relations by juxtaposing white and black characters or black and mixed-race characters struggling with the laws governing social interaction and the basic attempts to survive in a hostile world. Feminist troupes such as Spiderwoman Theatre (formed in 1975) use the stage to explore women's position in society and work for change. Theatre has provided a forum for challenging gay and lesbian stereotypes. *Cloud 9* (1979) by Caryl Churchill examines twentieth-century assumptions about gender by juxtaposing them to Victorian attitudes about sex. *The Normal Heart* by Larry Kramer (1985) advocates AIDS activism and criticizes the sluggish response to the disease by the general public.

Propaganda has been used to protest as well as support government action and to argue directly for social and political change. Women lobbied for the vote with suffrage plays during the late nineteenth and early twentieth centuries. Beginning in 1961, the Bread and Puppet Theatre combined larger-than-life puppets with human actors on the streets as well as in theatres to express impassioned disagreement with foreign and domestic U.S. policy.

Theatre has been used to protest or examine war. American antiwar plays have frequently appeared since 1915. Dramatic images of horror and violence have continued to appear in many American plays protesting war and racist violence in the Middle East and Africa. Playwright Tony Kushner sets most of the action of *Homebody/Kabul* (2001) in Kabul, Afghanistan. Written shortly before September 11, 2001, and the subsequent U.S. invasion of that country, the play is a remarkable study in cultural and linguistic chaos. Even more disturbing is the painful study of war profiteering and violence against women explored in *Ruined* (2009) by Lynn Nottage. Set in recent rebellious times in the Democratic Republic of Congo, the play, though loosely based on Bertolt Brecht's *Mother Courage* (1939), is given powerful credence by interviews the playwright and others conducted with female victims of exploitation and rape.

Specific needs have been the catalyst for theatre troupes with a clearly defined social and political purpose. The Free Southern Theatre was created in 1963 to support the civil rights movement. Luis Valdéz (b. 1940) formed El Teatro Campesino in 1965 to help change the situation of migrant workers in the United States. Believing that traditional theatre reinforces the existing class system, Brazilian Augusto Boal (1931–2009) developed the "theatre of the oppressed," an alternative way of making performance in communities designed to empower the disenfranchised.

An undercurrent of subversive thought may be introduced even in plays that, as a whole, reinforce traditional standards. In the seventeenth century, British playwright Aphra Behn wrote delightful comedies such as *The Rover* (1677) that pleased her audiences. In the midst of the fun, however, her heroines manage to protest the limitations on women's behavior. They speak very clearly about the difficult position of a woman whose entire future rested on the marriage she could make. Sometimes theatre artists have commented on politically sensitive issues by carefully selecting material to send a message yet avoid a direct challenge to the governing powers. Arthur Miller wrote *The Crucible* (1953) at the height of the McCarthy era, when many members of the performance community were being blacklisted for their real or perceived leftist beliefs. A play that is ostensibly about the Salem witch trials of the seventeenth century, *The Crucible* could also be interpreted as a comment on the anticommunist hysteria and injustice at work in the United States after World War II.

BOESMAN AND LENA by Athol Fugard. Faye M. Price and James A. Williams as the title characters struggling for existence in South Africa. Produced by the Pillsbury House Theatre in 2002 in Minneapolis, Minnesota.

Photo © Michal Daniel.

Theatre and Coercion

Recognizing its potential power, very repressive governments have entirely coopted theatre, along with the other arts, in attempts to win the hearts and minds of the people. In Germany during the 1930s the Nazi regime used highly theatricalized political rallies and forbade the production of any plays that did not seem to support its political position. Many theatrical artists fled Germany during this period. Socialist playwright and theorist Bertolt Brecht, for example, was blacklisted and was forced to work in exile until World War II had ended. After being harangued by the House Committee on Un-American Activities in 1947 due to his political beliefs, Brecht left the United States and created his most exciting theatre in East Berlin.

In China during the period known as the Cultural Revolution (1966–1980), the communist government attempted to suppress or reform all "decadent" traditional forms of theatre, replacing them with works designed to praise and justify the current ideology. To disrupt the artistic legacy, officials ordered renowned artists put to work at menial jobs or hard labor.

Similarly, for many years the only accepted style of art in the Soviet Union was socialist realism, which was judged by those in power to support and reflect the Soviet value system. Artists who insisted on voicing an opposing viewpoint or experimenting with different forms did so at their peril. In 1939 the brilliant and unconventional director Vsevelod Meyerhold (1874–1940) disappeared one night from his Leningrad apartment. After being tortured and beaten, the 66-year-old man signed a confession (later recanted) that he had participated in anti-Soviet activity. He was executed in 1940, and his actress wife was mutilated and murdered. For fifteen years the Soviet Union suppressed any mention of Meyerhold's name.

SOLDADO RAZO by Luis Valdéz, El Teatro Campesino, c. 1970. Using simple but emblematic staging in an outdoor theatre, a death figure hovers over a dead enlisted man. This company addressed the rights of the common people, especially Hispanics, while attacking the Vietnam War.

Photo by Claire Henze.

THE CRUCIBLE by Arthur Miller, directed by Richard Eyre with sets and costumes designed by Tim Hatley and lighting designed by Paul Gallo. In this 2002 Broadway revival, the black slave character Tituba and a group of Puritan girls pretend to be possessed by witches. The play reveals the duplicity of the girls yet makes their pretended possession seem real to the adult characters and moves the audience as well.

Photo © Joan Marcus.

Theatre and Empowerment

Theatrical performance can be a tool for healing, for individual growth, and for facilitating group process. A visit to the website "Arts as a Force of Healing, Building, and Empowerment" at www.artslynx.org/heal will give you an idea of the vast number of ways theatre is currently being used. The site was created for the Colorado Council on the Arts with funding from the National Endowment for the Arts after the tragic shooting of students at Columbine High School. Creators of the website recognize the role of the arts in community building and dedicate the site "not only to the healing power of the arts, but to providing access to the arts for diverse populations [so] that all humans may be empowered by the arts to be able to realize their full positive potential."[2] Links are provided to theatre organizations dedicated to fighting prejudice, to helping youth at risk, to AIDS prevention, and to special initiatives addressing the September 11, 2001, tragedy as well as those focused on learning disabilities, older adults, and blind and deaf populations.

In the twentieth century accessibility to theatre for all audience members became a serious consideration. For deaf and hearing-impaired audience members, many theatres now have sound intensification systems available and offer performances translated into sign language or captioned (with dialogue projected above the stage or in another location). Audio description provides a moment-by-moment narration of what is happening on stage for blind theatre patrons. While watching the show, a describer transmits descriptions over individual headsets.

Some theatrical organizations specialize in interactive performance designed to accomplish a specific goal. Actors develop skits to spark discussion on problems facing young people—drugs, date rape, domestic and street violence—or may help groups of people to tell and then dramatize their own stories. A good example of this kind of performance is Interact Center for the Visual and Performing Arts where artists with disability labels create, perform, earn, and help the community understand that gifts are given to all people and that vision is not lost or even impaired by a disabling condition.

BENGAL TIGER AT THE BAGHDAD ZOO (2011) by Rajif Joseph. Starring Robin Williams, who plays a caged tiger killed by an American soldier, and then the ghost of the tiger, this Broadway production brings troubling issues about the war and ensuing chaos in Iraq in 2003 to the stage. Directed by Moisés Kaufman.

Photo © Carol Rosegg.

EXPLORING Historical and Cultural Perspectives

Theatre of War

Western theatre has a long history of plays that support or attack a specific war or plays that can be interpreted as anti-war statements. The ancient Greeks left several such plays in both comic and tragic form. The outrageous *Lysistrata* (411 B.C.E.) by Aristophanes whimsically imagines a sex-strike by the women of Greece that convinces the men to cease fighting the Peloponnesian War, whereas Euripides' *The Trojan Women* (415 B.C.E.) dramatizes the horrible effects on women and children in the aftermath of a catastrophic war. Both of these plays have been regularly revived to warn the public of lamentable consequences of combat. We can only guess at Shakespeare's intent with his mixed-tone chronicle of *Henry V* (c. 1599), but this play has been regularly revived to stir patriotic fervor in Britain, or to stand as an anti-war piece, depending upon the historical moment and the interpretation of the director.

In the United States, war plays have appeared frequently since World War I. Plays and revues have supported the war effort, warned against declaring war, or explored the horrors of war. Except for the eras of Vietnam and Iraq, anti-war plays have been rare while U.S. troops were fighting, but often appeared before or after the war. As World War I was beginning in 1914, the United States tried to remain neutral, but finally mobilized in 1917. Before that date a number of anti-war plays were professionally produced in New York and on tour. Many of these plays, such as *Moloch* (1915) by Beulah Dix, were written by women. *Moloch* focuses on the senseless killing of civilians by unfeeling soldiers. After the Armistice of November 1918, anti-war plays appeared again arguing that global cataclysm must never recur. Edna St. Vincent Millay's *Aria da Capo* (1919) creates a war symbolically and poetically and dramatizes the public's awful attempt to pretend that such horrors never occurred. *What Price Glory* (1924) by Maxwell Anderson and Laurence Stallings demonstrated military ineptitude and brought a realistic but cynical view of war to the stage. Its most disturbing scene dramatizes the dying and wounded yielding to terror and denying God in the midst of cacophony. World War I was often viewed by playwrights as senseless and wasteful.

In the mid-1930s playwrights responded again when European saber-rattling recommenced. One of the new war plays was *Bury the Dead* (1936) by Irwin Shaw. Forecasting World War II, the play depicts a devastating stalemate in no-man's land reminiscent of World War I trench warfare. Shaw has his slain soldiers create a demonstration by rising like zombie corpses as the living soldiers attempt to bury them. The corpses refuse to go to their rest unless the armies will stop fighting.

The most unpopular war in U.S. history must be the Vietnam War, which inspired prolonged protest on the streets and

JOHN GALLAGHER, JR. playing Johnny, the principal anxiety-ridden young man in *American Idiot.* The setting, designed by Christine Jones, is dominated by video screens, litter, and graffiti. Seen here at the Berkeley Repertory Theatre before moving on to Broadway in 2010.
Photo © Kevin Berne.

in theatres. Megan Terry's play *Viet Rock* (1966) confronted the atrocities of war, and the musical *Hair* (1968) by Gerome Ragni and James Rado confronted the audience with a youthful counterculture overshadowed by the war in Indochina. Many playwrights in the 1970s dramatized returning soldiers unable to readjust to civilian life. David Rabe's *Sticks and Bones* (1971) poignantly and cynically created such domestic conflict by parodying the popular TV sitcom *Ozzie and Harriet.*

Since September 11, 2001, we have seen considerable consternation over terrorism and the war in Iraq. Most theatrical responses to the war have appeared in revivals of older plays like *The Persians* of Aeschylus or *Arms and the Man* by Bernard Shaw. But new works have also found an audience. The British play *Stuff Happens* (2004) by David Hare offers a strong critique of the 2003 invasion of Iraq. An array of familiar government officials speak in public with documented language and in private with clever verbiage invented by the playwright. Inspired by and blossoming from the driving music of Green Day, the musical *American Idiot* by Billie Joe Armstrong and Michael Mayer examines a lost youthful generation hooked on mind-numbing video images, the drug culture, and failure to find purpose in a post 9/11 world. This alternately humorous and distressing action also, and not incidentally, dramatizes young American men caught up in and exploited by the horrors of war in the Middle East. Although the theatrical high water mark remains the Vietnam era, it seems clear that issues of war will continue to contribute to the fabric of contemporary theatre.

The act of creating theatre, along with other arts, can have a therapeutic effect for those involved. Although such effects are useful, they remain a by-product when the focus is on creating art and entertainment. In arts therapy, however, the purpose of theatrical activity changes to individual development rather than audience communication. Drama therapy, as defined by the National Association for Drama Therapy (NADT), has the therapeutic goals of behavior change, skill-building, emotional and physical integration, and personal growth.[3] Drama therapy is practiced in many different settings, including mental health facilities, nursing homes, schools, businesses, and correctional facilities.

Theatre and Cultural Exploration

The study of theatre as a social institution is a vital method for learning about the goals and aspirations, the prejudices and blind spots—the good and the bad—of different societies. Human beings create theatre in the image of themselves—of how they see themselves or wish themselves to be. As such, the theatre mirrors the personality not only of the author of the play, the leading actor, or the famous director but also of the society in which and for which it was developed. Every theatrical performance is embedded in a particular context—social, political, and historical. No matter how far removed an audience might be from a play or record of its performance, some residue of that context remains.

As with other art forms, theatre can expand our cultural horizons. While watching Caryl Churchill's *Mad Forest* (1990), an English-speaking audience can begin to understand the despair and paranoia that were rampant in Romania during the rule of the dictator Ceauşescu and the subsequent joy and confusion after his fall. Even a play set in the audience's home country can provide a connection to a different cultural experience. Encountering the effects of racism on the south side of Chicago with the Younger family opened the eyes of white audience members who attended Lorraine Hansberry's *A Raisin in the Sun* (1959).

TARTUFFE in period costume at the Public Theater New York in 1999, directed by Mark Brokaw. The character Elmire has just escaped the attempted seduction by Tartuffe and now berates her husband Orgon who was hiding under the table. J. Smith-Cameron as Elmire and Charles Kimbrough as Orgon.

Photo © Michal Daniel.

The fact that theatre is usually a live production of a previously written play makes it particularly effective as a means for exploring life in other times. Even though a theatre performance lasts only a few hours, play texts may be preserved indefinitely. Plays still exist from ancient Greece, Rome, India, and China, and plays can be studied as literary documents in and of themselves. William Shakespeare wrote most of his scripts in the last decade of the sixteenth century and the first decade of the seventeenth for a troupe of actors (including himself) who were eager to draw an audience and outsell a rival company. Today, Shakespeare's plays are read for quite different reasons; they are examples of English poetry at its most beautiful, of thought about the human condition at its most profound. Because Shakespeare chose to write plays, however, you can watch and hear as well as read them. Although theatrical performance can never be recovered, it is possible today to witness the same play that our ancestors saw 400 years ago—or even 2,400 years ago. Certainly, the actors perform it differently, and the audience brings a very different context to its understanding of the words and the action. The very fact that it is possible to witness a human reenactment of the same story, however, creates the possibility for connection with and greater understanding of the past.

The nature of a theatrical event in society may be quite different today from that in the past. Greek tragedy, for example, developed as a dynamic element of art and competition in a multiple-day festival that was both a civic event and a religious celebration. Even though classical Greek tragedies are still revived, sometimes in surviving outdoor Greek theatres, the productions are no longer

ARTISTS of the THEATRE

National Theatre of the Deaf

For more than 40 years the National Theatre of the Deaf (NTD), founded in 1967 by David Hays in Connecticut, has combined accessibility with artistry to create an exciting new language of the theatre. From the beginning, productions have combined deaf and hearing performers. Not only is NTD an important professional producing and touring organization, but a training program for deaf artists and an important worldwide community outreach effort through workshops and educational programs. From the very first year of this company's existence, it has operated a professional theatre school. The NTD mission statement commits "to offer our work to as culturally diverse and inclusive an audience as possible," and to open the eyes and ears of the general public "to Deaf culture." In 1977 the NTD won a Tony Award for excellence in theatre.

This remarkable company has mounted more than 100 national tours and 31 internationally. It has produced and reconceived many classic works of famous playwrights such as Ibsen, Büchner, Chekhov, and Molière, and original plays by both deaf and hearing playwrights. The first NTD production that your authors witnessed was an extraordinary adaptation of the *Iliad* of Homer interpreted by deaf playwright Shanny Mow and deaf director Ed Waterstreet through U.S. football imagery. The play is entitled *The Iliad: Play by Play* (1980). At intermission of this production the company presented an eight-minute halftime show of Homer's *The Odyssey*. Then 10 years later, NTD tackled a full-length companion epic of *The Odyssey*. In 2002, NTD mounted the eighteenth-century Figaro plays of Beaumarchais adapted as an updated New York Spanish Harlem extravaganza *Oh, Figaro!*. Many of the recent touring productions have been aimed at young audiences through the NTD's Little Theatre of the Deaf, which has also appeared on *Sesame Street*. In all, the National Theatre of the Deaf has given well over 7,000 performances, earning NTD the distinction of being the oldest continually producing company in the United States.

INTERESTED? Check out

The National Theatre of the Deaf at www.ntd.org

associated with the worship of the god Dionysus, and Greek Dionysian priests are no longer in prominent attendance in the front row. Athens long ago ceased to be a cultural, political, and economic power in the world, and its current festivals have little to do with the festivals of 534 B.C.E. Much of that ancient cultural context has disappeared or is only marginally applicable to current European life. Nonetheless, people are still interested in many of the ancient Greek plays. An understanding of the cultural context surrounding their origins and first performances helps us to better understand the possibilities of the work. Surviving plays and other evidence of production such as critical reviews, letters, diaries, and ruins of ancient theatres provide clues to what happened in theatres long ago and might inspire theatre artists in presenting plays for an audience to appreciate now.

The French playwright Molière wrote *Tartuffe* in 1669. In this comedy, the main character, Orgon, is completely duped by a religious hypocrite, Tartuffe, who plots to strip Orgon of his wealth while seducing his wife. If you read this play, even in a modern English translation rather than the original French, you will see many reflections of the seventeenth century when it was written and first produced: portraits of wealthy Parisian society, that society's regard for social duplicity, the legal autocratic power of a man over his family, and a host of other conditions, large and small, that are etched into the text overtly or subtly. Unless you completely rewrite the text, much of the world of seventeenth-century French culture remains. You could choose to update the play's sets and costumes to 2012 and change the setting to a contemporary, middle-class domestic house. Nonetheless, the seventeenth century still lurks in many corners of the play.

If you produce *Tartuffe*, however, you cannot help but infuse it with twenty-first-century ideas and interpretations. Even if you slavishly recreate costumes of 1669; imitate the interior of an expensive Parisian house of the time, complete with period furniture and decorations; and teach the actors what we still know of courtly

TARTUFFE updated to the late twentieth century, produced by the University of Colorado, Boulder. The scenic design by Richard Finkelstein depicts a suburban household in Moliere, Texas, complete with poolside and interior playing spaces.

Photo © Richard Finkelstein.

AN EXAMPLE OF NONTRADITIONAL CASTING from 2008 with James Earl Jones and Phylicia Rashad playing Big Daddy and Big Momma in *Cat on a Hot Tin Roof* by Tennessee Williams. The roles were obviously written with white actors in mind, yet in this production directed by Debbie Allen, the family has been reconceived as African American. The play is still set in the deep south of the 1950s.

Photo © Joan Marcus.

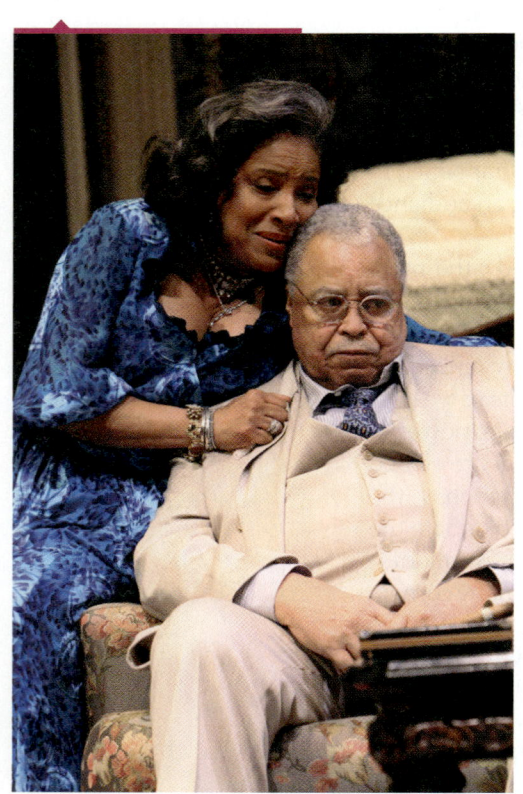

manners and movement, much of the production will smack of the twenty-first century. The cultural assumptions, values, and tastes of the moment of production always combine with the culture of the past that gave birth to the original play. This combination of past and present is one of the exciting but also daunting aspects of producing plays from other periods and cultures. As much as we might like to, we cannot really revisit history or travel to the past. We can, however, reconstruct possibilities of past cultures, somewhat like cultural and artistic anthropologists and archeologists.

The opportunity to make material from the past come alive in the present also raises interesting and sometimes difficult ethical questions. Should a theatre company present a work from the past if it contains material that would be objectionable today? Shakespeare's *The Merchant of Venice* (c. 1596), the story of a money lender who insists on extracting a "pound of flesh" as payment from a client, depicts Christians more sympathetically than Jews. American plays written before 1960 by white authors sometimes include stereotypical portrayals of people of color. Is producing such work insulting to the modern audience? Or is it important to present such material from the past as a reminder of our history and opportunity for analysis?

While theatre can be a place where different cultures meet, are there some boundaries that should be kept intact? **Nontraditional casting** (also called *colorblind casting*)—casting actors of a different race than the character as written—has slowly become an accepted practice in the theatre since the civil rights movement. Casting an actor of color to play a character written as white is one way of expanding opportunities; because of many years of exclusion, there are fewer roles in plays for actors of color. But should white actors play characters of color? Should playwrights depict cultures that are different from their own? Resurrecting pieces of the past and crossing cultural boundaries offer exciting opportunities but bring significant responsibilities. The road is not always easy to negotiate.

Between 1997 and 2005 African American playwright August Wilson challenged nontraditional casting in professional theatre as inappropriate or even detrimental to the black experience in America, which he asserted is unique and distinct.

SOCIAL CONTROL OF THEATRE

Although theatre's potential for positive contribution is recognized in many societies, in other societies this is not always the case. In some cultures and subcultures any kind of theatrical activity has been (and continues to be) thought of as a threat to morality and to the entire fabric of society and has been the target of many attempts at official control.

Theatre and the Threat to Morality

The Greek philosopher Plato found theatre disturbing and potentially dangerous. Because Plato found theatre so effective in performance, he feared that convincing acting and the powerful language of a gifted playwright could harm society if the artists decided to present subversive or morally corrupt ideas. In his view theatre is not truthful because it is based on imitation of action and character—it is not reality. Early Christian leaders (second to fifth century C.E.) invoked arguments similar to Plato's but went much further in finding the whole nature of performance corrupt, establishing a long history of opposition to theatrical activity in some branches of the church. In seventeenth-century France, it was standard practice for retired actors to renounce their profession in order to be eligible for Christian burial. In some teachings of Islam any theatrical depiction of character is prohibited along with other forms of art that represent life.

Even in societies in which theatrical activity was accepted, a deep suspicion of performers sometimes remained. In Elizabethan England an actor had to carry a document proving that he was under a nobleman's protection. Without such a document he was considered a "rogue" and "vagabond." The moral integrity of actors continued to be questioned until well into the late nineteenth century in Europe and North America. Although they might be recognized for superior artistic achievement, actors were still not welcome in middle- or upper-class social circles. In some cultures the suspicion of public performance was complicated by gender expectations. Public display was often considered inappropriate for women, and women were banned from the stage entirely in some periods. Female characters were played by men or boys in ancient Greek, Elizabethan, and various traditional Asian forms of theatre. At other times acting was one of the few professions open to women, even though it carried the threat of social ostracism for those who practiced it.

Theatre has often provided a haven for those who did not fit the current social mold. On the other hand, it has also lived up to its reputation as a morally dangerous place and has functioned as a vehicle for exploiting the less powerful members of society. Chorus girls were notoriously fair game for idle young men in Victorian England and the Gilded Age (c. 1890–1915) in New York City. Both young male and female actors in the early years of Japanese Kabuki theatre were charged with prostitution, leading to the banishment of young men from the stage temporarily and women from the stage for centuries.

Theatre Regulation

Because of the real and imagined dangers of the theatre, many societies have felt it necessary to closely monitor and regulate theatrical activity. The history of the theatre in England is an interesting example. In the seventeenth century the Puritans sought to suppress theatrical performance because of the "lying" nature of character portrayal and disapproval of the theatre's tendency to distract its audience from more devout or useful activities. All London theatres were closed during the Civil War in

EXPLORING Collaboration

Citizen Play Juries

From 1905 until the late 1920s the professional theatre in the city of New York found itself frequently under attack for promoting or depicting immoral or obscene acts on the stage. Many of the objections that were raised in this period would strike most people today as quaint and certainly reactionary, since community standards of morality are much less restrictive than they were in the first quarter of the twentieth century. Although the standards were a bit vague, the threat to artistic expression at the time was quite real, and the result was the unlikely collaboration, beginning in 1922, of law enforcement, the district attorney's office, theatrical producers, Actors' Equity (the actors' union), theatre critics, the Dramatists Guild (society of playwrights), and purity leagues, which were common in the period.

Before 1922 the New York police frequently visited and sometimes raided plays and musical revues when they received complaints from members of the public or the district attorney's office that the productions included obscene language or acts. Many of the complaints came from the Society for the Suppression of Vice. A number of productions were closed or threatened with closure, sometimes actors or producers were arrested, and sometimes a trial ensued. Even George Bernard Shaw's *Mrs. Warren's Profession* was raided in 1905; several members of the company were arrested, and the production was closed.

The collaborative solution struck by the theatre, the community, the police, and the district attorney was the creation of Citizen Play Juries made up of adult community members (male and female) who were not professionals in the theatre or members of law enforcement. From a large pool of potential jurors twelve would be selected whenever a formal complaint against a production was made to the office of the district attorney. These twelve would then see the production, meet secretly, and pass judgment on the production in terms of violation of community standards of decency. If at least two-thirds of the jury found the play indecent, it would be closed. There was no appeal from either the district attorney (if the jury acquitted) or the production's producer (if the jury condemned).

This jury system was never formulated as municipal law or statute but was an informal agreement made by all the parties involved. For some time no production was condemned by the play juries, and the district attorney's office began to get nervous about the process. In 1926 the first production closed was a musical revue that included nudity. (Nudity appeared from time to time in revues but not in plays or musicals. This barrier was not breached until 1968.) The climate grew increasingly problematic for the authorities, because the district attorney was eager to close down Eugene O'Neill's *Desire under the Elms* in 1924, Mae West's *Sex* in 1926, and *The Captive* (which

DESIRE UNDER THE ELMS by Eugene O'Neill (a reworking of the Greek tragedy *Hippolytus*) came under attack by would-be censors largely because the protagonist Eben, played by Charles Ellis (upstairs on left), falls in love with his stepmother, Abbie (on right with her husband, played by Walter Huston), played by Mary Morris. In this scene there is a wall between them, but they are imagining being with the object of their affection on the other side of the wall. Produced by Experimental Theatre, Inc., at the Greenwich Village Theatre in 1924.

By permission of Theatre Collection, Museum of the City of New York.

included a lesbian character) by Edward Bourdet, also in 1926. The play juries acquitted all of them. Despite the previous agreement, the district attorney abolished the play juries in early 1927 and promptly raided *Sex*, *The Captive*, and *The Virgin Man* (also by Mae West) and made many arrests. The shows were closed, and collaboration was over. Nonetheless, for a few years these unlikely bedfellows made the attempt to compromise and work together. Ultimately, the standards were taken out of the hands of the city's government because the New York State Legislature passed the Wales Padlock Law later in 1927. The harsh law mandated that any producer who was convicted of producing an obscene play would have his theatre padlocked for a year. This extreme measure resulted in many producers being unwilling to take risks with sexual material for some time. The censorship standards used by the courts of New York in the 1920s were not overturned until the Supreme Court did so in 1957.

Britain (1642–1660), when Puritans executed the king and controlled the government. When theatrical activity was restored in 1660, it was tightly controlled by the Crown. Charles II issued only two patents, or licenses, for producing theatre in London. In the eighteenth and nineteenth centuries the ballooning London population and passion for theatregoing demanded more performance opportunities, yet the licenses remained in effect until 1843. Entrepreneurs opened "illegitimate" theatres, and a battle began to clearly distinguish "legitimate" regular (spoken) drama (which rightly belonged to the two "patent houses") from "illegitimate" forms containing music and dance. A few British performers sought new audiences in colonial North America, but in areas settled by strict religious sects, particularly New England, theatrical performance was prohibited. Ingenious actors, however, managed to keep working. It was not unusual, for example, to see a performance of Shakespeare's *Othello* advertised as "a moral dialogue on jealousy."

Theatre Censorship

Fear of the power of the theatre as a public forum for dissent has often resulted in strict censorship of dramatic material. In England some form of preproduction censorship was in place beginning with the Elizabethan period, and from 1737 to 1968 all plays had to be issued a license by the Lord Chamberlain before production. The United States has never had a nationwide institutionalized system of censorship, but local authorities have at times halted productions that were deemed offensive to the community. In 1918 federal authorities in Philadelphia closed *The Little Belgian* because of subject matter that was deemed inappropriate during wartime. The New York production of *Sex*, a play by Mae West, ran for 375 performances before it was closed by authorities in 1926. West was performing at the time and was arrested and imprisoned along with the rest of the company.

Governments have frequently used censorship to suppress dissident political statements as well as material that is embarrassing to those in power. The entire work of Václav Havel (b. 1936) was banned in his native Czechoslovakia before the disintegration of the communist bloc. Havel served four years in prison for subversion, but clandestine theatrical performances continued. After the fall of communism, Havel was elected first president of the Czech Republic. Wole Soyinka challenged the Nigerian authorities in many of his plays, essays, and books. He was imprisoned for two years, most of it in solitary confinement, and for many years has lived away from his homeland. In 1986 Soyinka won the Nobel Prize for Literature.

In 1968 theatre practitioner and activist Augusto Boal directed a production of Bertolt Brecht's *The Resistable Rise of Arturo Ui* (an attack on oppressive government tactics) in São Paulo, Brazil. Boal was arrested, jailed, tortured, and finally driven from his own country in 1971. Obviously, Boal's government recognized that the play was being used to attack the status quo in Brazil. One of Boal's assertions was that theatre can be a rehearsal for revolution.

Subject matter that is not overtly political but considered dangerous to the fabric of society has also been restricted by censors. In eighteenth-century Japan the enormous popularity of *The Love Suicides at Sonezaki* (1703) ultimately led to a very specific prohibition. The play, written for a puppet theatre (Bunraku) by Chikamatsu (1653–1725), presented a fictionalized account of the joint suicide of two young lovers. A number of plays on similar subjects and, unfortunately, a rash of actual suicides followed. In 1722 the government banned all such plays from the stage. In the late nineteenth century realism was considered a radical movement in Europe. The plays of Norwegian Henrik Ibsen (1828–1906), for example, dared to publicly discuss social issues such as environmental pollution, gender conflict, and sexually transmitted disease. Since most existing theatres were limited by government censorship, theatrical and social reformers in Germany, France, and England found ways to circumvent the existing rules. Such "independent" theatres evaded censorship regulations by claiming to be private clubs rather than public venues.

Placing restrictions on theatre has frequently resulted in such uses of subterfuge. The theatrical impulse is remarkably widespread and tenacious. Artists want to create, and audiences want to attend the theatre. Sometimes theatre goes underground, as in Czechoslovakia before the fall of communism. Sometimes the theatre makes a place for itself on the fringes of society. The Globe Theatre, which saw the first productions of many of Shakespeare's magnificent plays, was built on the south side of the Thames River to avoid City of London restrictions. It sat in an entertainment and red-light district next to arenas that held bloody contests in which animals fought to the death.

THEATRICAL CHOICE IN NORTH AMERICA

Depending on where you are in North America, you might have many professional shows to choose from on a given night or you might get a chance to see theatre only several times a year when plays are performed at a school. Metropolitan areas tend to have a wide variety of theatre available, but there is usually some kind of theatre in small towns. Although similar categories exist in other areas of the world, the precise nature of theatre produced depends on the traditions of the region as well as performers and funds available. If there is truly no theatre available in your area, you can always make your own!

Professional Theatre

Professional theatre is created by individuals who make a living (or at least attempt to do so) in the theatre. The professional venue can be commercial or nonprofit, and many theatre artists and technicians work in both. **Broadway** and **Off-Broadway** theatres, touring shows, and major resident theatres are professional. The economic interests of artists and technicians are protected by various unions and guilds that negotiate with the producing organizations.

Commercial theatre is meant to earn a profit for investors. Typically, a commercial company is put together for a specific production. A producer or producing organization finds a show that seems to have great potential for drawing an audience. Financial

LES MISÉRABLES, the Schönberg, Boublil, musical that ran in New York from 1987 to 2003, has proved to be one of the most commercially successful musicals ever. This famous image from the finale of Act I represents a stirring presentation that reliably engaged its audiences repeatedly. *Les Misérables* was the kind of show that brought back many fans year after year. The same team also created *Miss Saigon* (1991).

Photo © Joan Marcus.

backing is usually sought beyond the resources of the producers. The hope is that money taken in at the box office and funds from foreign, film, and television rights as well as theme merchandise will at least allow the investors to break even. A long-running hit means that those who are willing to take a chance on the play receive financial reward. Global box-office receipts for the musical *Les Misérables* exceeded $1.8 billion, and on Broadway alone *Phantom of the Opera* has grossed nearly $800 million. Sometimes, however, even a failure at the box office can bring financial reward in the form of a tax write-off.

Although commercial theatres can be found in all major metropolitan areas, New York City has a particularly large concentration. The term "Broadway" refers both to a particular area of New York (the theatre district bordered by 41st to 54th Streets and Sixth to Ninth Avenues) and to the size of the house (some Broadway theatres seat as many as 1,800 patrons). Of the thirty-nine Broadway theatres in 2008, thirty-eight are located in this theatre district. The Vivian Beaumont Theatre is housed at Lincoln Center on 65th Street. The designation "Off-Broadway" dates from 1955 and refers to theatres with fewer than 500 seats in Manhattan that are not located in the Broadway district.

Companies are also put together for national (and sometimes international) tours. These companies travel across the country taking costumes, scenery, lighting—everything necessary except a space—along with them. Variations of whole-production touring have been occurring in North America since the 1850s, when so-called combination companies took advantage of the new network of railroads. Entire productions with complicated scenery and properties were transported easily and quickly throughout the United States and Canada. Like the old combination companies, modern tours are booked into various theatres, called "touring houses," for limited runs and then move on to the next city, thus expanding the audience for any show. For the 2009–2010 season 15.9 million people attended touring Broadway shows and paid $947 million in admission (an average of $59.56 per ticket).

The Broadway League, made up of theatre owners and operators, producers, presenters, and general managers, is the national trade association for the commercial theatre industry. The organization provides support for its members and aims to further the interests of Broadway theatre across North America.[4]

Nonprofit theatres may be professional but are not commercial. They share the characteristic that no individual or organization realizes a profit from the investment in production; any money that is taken in at the box office or earned from other sources is funneled back into the arts organization to support other shows and programs. Many theatres are incorporated and approved by the Internal Revenue Service as nonprofit organizations, and donations are therefore tax deductible. Like public radio and television stations, nonprofit theatres rely on annual fund drives, fundraising events, and numerous grants to survive.

Resident theatres are professional, nonprofit organizations that maintain a constant presence in a community and produce an entire season of plays. These theatres are sometimes called **regional theatres;** the oldest ones were founded to establish professional theatre in areas of the country other than New York City, but resident theatres now include professional, nonprofit companies in New York as well. Shows are produced with the understanding that they will run for a designated period of time, then will close to make way for the next selection. Typically, resident theatres hire both local artists and those from around the country. Their aim is to produce a balanced season of plays, and they hope to fill as many seats as possible with subscribers (patrons who buy tickets for an entire season of plays rather than individual shows). When the national economy is down, however, season ticket sales often decline while individual sales rise. Resident theatres often maintain a multitheatre complex and run several seasons of shows simultaneously. Arena Stage in Washington, DC, for example, offers shows in the 683-seat Fichandler Stage, the 500-seat Kreeger Theater, and The Kogod Cradle Theater, a flexible, intimate performance space seating 200 and dedicated to

A HIGHLY STYLIZED REVIVAL OF THE MISER by Molière that originated with the American Repertory Theatre and the Theatre de la Jeune Lune, but toured to other professional resident theatres. This is an unusual practice for most resident theatre companies. The production was directed by Dominique Serrand and the title character of Harpagon was played by Steven Epp.
Photo © Michal Daniel.

the performance of new works. Resident theatres offer outreach programs to further integrate the theatre with the local community, including classes, performances for local schools, play development series, after-show discussions, and tours.

The League of Resident Theatres (LORT) provides support for its members, particularly by serving as an agent in bargaining collectively with employee unions.[5] The LORT membership includes such theatres as the Shakespeare Theatre (Washington, DC), the Guthrie Theater (Minneapolis), the Alliance Theatre Company (Atlanta), and the Old Globe (San Diego). The analogous organization for English-speaking theatre in Canada is the Professional Association of Canadian Theatres (PACT).[6] Theatre Communications Group (TCG) serves nearly 700 nonprofit theatres in the United States by publishing books and periodicals and awarding grants, as well as providing management programs and advocacy.[7]

Amateur Theatre

The designation **amateur theatre** is used when the practitioners do not rely on theatrical activity for their livelihood. Amateur theatres exist for many reasons and come in all shapes and sizes. Such productions may range from highly polished and imaginative work to efforts in which the emphasis is on recreation and camaraderie rather than a finished product. Typically, amateur theatres are nonprofit organizations that combine box-office receipts with grants, institutional subsidy, and other fundraising to continue serving their clientele. Although all or most of the labor is volunteer, the expense of maintaining or renting a space, building sets and costumes, and providing the technical aspects of production is considerable.

Educational theatre may be extracurricular or integrated into classroom structure. On the elementary- and secondary-school levels, dramatic activity is used to develop student skills and widen interests. The Educational Theatre Association (EdTA) rewards excellence in student work and supports the work of theatre educators.[8] Theatre programs in colleges and universities add to these goals the possibility of professional training for students as well as the opportunity to offer a wide range of viewing possibilities to the local community. At many schools students may pursue a Bachelor of Arts degree with a major in theatre; some schools offer a Bachelor of Fine Arts with additional credit hours devoted to professional training. Graduate work in performance, playwriting, design, or technical theatre leads to the Master of Fine Arts degree and, in some schools, a Doctor of Fine Arts. Resident theatres often collaborate with colleges and universities to provide internships for students completing professional training programs. Students who are interested in the history, theory, criticism, and literature of the theatre may study for the Master of Arts and Doctor of Philosophy degrees. The Association for Theatre in Higher Education (ATHE) serves as a center for producing new knowledge, cultivating alliances with other disciplines, and promoting access and equity.[9] The University/Resident Theatre Association (U/RTA) is dedicated to professional theatre training graduate programs and associated professional theatre companies. It serves as a liaison between educational and professional theatres.[10]

Community theatre is created by residents of a particular area who come together to create theatre without being part of a larger institution. Such theatres often focus on the quality of experience for the practitioners, and audience members tend to be family and friends. Plays are often chosen with local appeal and satisfactory roles for available performers in mind and tend to be fairly traditional. Comedies and musicals, for example, are perennial favorites. Community theatres may specialize in producing

AH, WILDERNESS! (1933) by Eugene O'Neill as revived by the Guthrie Theater in 2002 in Minneapolis and directed by Douglas Wager. This romantic lakeside scene is unusual in the work of O'Neill because he creates a sympathetic, nostalgic scene between two adolescents in love. This play is frequently revived by theatres at all levels.

Photo © Michal Daniel.

for a special audience (children, for example) or involve a particular type of community member in performance (seniors, veterans, women). The American Association of Community Theatre (AACT) exists to provide networking, resources, and support for such theatres across the country.[11]

Hybrid Theatres

Many theatres do not fit neatly into either the professional or amateur category; for our purposes we will use the term **hybrid theatres.** Small resident theatres may hold a contract with Actors' Equity (the union in the United States for actors and stage managers) that allows the hiring of both union and nonunion performers. Summer stock theatres may hire well-trained students and experienced community members for seasonal work. Students who have recently graduated often form their own nonunion companies, holding down day jobs to support themselves while investing energy and time in rehearsal and performance at night. The designation "semiprofessional" is sometimes used for companies that aspire to professional status but currently are not well established enough to maintain the payroll of a professional theatre. The dedication of these artists may produce exciting shows even though the performers are not technically "professional." For example, the young actors who formed Chicago's Steppenwolf Theatre Company in 1974 and began performing plays in a church basement were committed to developing a strong ensemble while taking artistic risks.[12] The exciting productions of Steppenwolf launched the stage and film careers of Terry Kinney (b. 1954), John Malkovich (b. 1953), and Gary Sinise (b. 1955). The company is now professional and boasts a subscription base of over 20,000.

The term **Off-off-Broadway** was coined in the 1960s in New York to identify performances that occurred outside the traditional theatre spaces of Broadway and Off-Broadway. Such work was typically experimental and often occurred in alternative spaces—coffeehouses, church basements, warehouses, and private homes. As part of the 1960s counterculture, Off-off-Broadway rejected the "establishment" theatre and sought to cross both social and artistic boundaries. Today, the term "Off-off-Broadway" is used to refer to professional or semiprofessional performances with a very low budget and fewer than 100 seats. Performance runs tend to be limited and may occur only a few days a week. Production quality varies widely, but this type of small theatre can offer innovative, unusual artistic experiences. Although the term "Off-off-Broadway" originated in New York, this kind of theatre may exist anywhere. Such theatres in Chicago are known as "off-Loop" and in Los Angeles as "Equity waiver."

CULTURAL CONTEXT AND PERSONAL EXPERIENCE

Every theatrical performance is a collaboration, furnishing a place for past, present, and future to merge; for traditions to be celebrated, analyzed, and challenged; for different cultures to interact with one another. Cultural context is also part of personal memory and personal theatrical experiences. In 1963 one of the authors of this book at a young age witnessed a professional production of the musical *West Side Story* (1957) by Arthur Laurents, Leonard Bernstein, and Stephen Sondheim. It was a remarkable experience that had much to do with the author's decision to pursue a life and career in the theatre. Because of its personal importance, the theatrical memory looms large and no doubt has been colored nostalgically with the passage of time. Nonetheless, the memory of that production evokes much about the time in which it was written and composed and when and where it was produced. A 1963 production cannot be duplicated, and in an artistic and cultural sense there is no reason anyone should attempt it. The authors have both witnessed many other productions of *West Side Story* since 1963, some of which were probably more effectively produced, but for one of us that first experience was far more significant because of its personal importance and its position in time and place. It was a cultural event that was transformed into a very personal and influential event. In that recognition lies much of the potential power of the theatre.

CHAPTER REVIEW

Questions and Activities

1. Scholars disagree about where to draw the line between "theatre" and other activities that have a theatrical component. What do you consider theatre? Discuss the ways in which different public activities are theatrical—for example, parades, pep rallies, sporting events, air shows, political demonstrations, and the like.
2. Defining "art" is a difficult task and is very subjective. What do you expect from an artistic experience? Think about your experiences with theatre, painting, sculpture, dance, music. Which ones would you call art? Why? Do the same with films and television programs.
3. Choose one experience that you consider art and another that you consider strictly entertainment. Write a letter to a friend explaining why.
4. Theatre can be an important tool in crossing cultural boundaries. Are there times when it is important to keep those boundaries intact?
   Discuss the following questions:
   • Is it acceptable for an actor to play a character of a different race? If the character's race is an important issue in the play, is it still acceptable for an actor of a different race to play the character?
   • Is it acceptable for a male playwright to write about women's issues? Is it acceptable for a female playwright to explore male bonding? Is it acceptable for a white playwright to write about the experience of a black character? Is it acceptable for an Asian playwright to create a play about Native Americans?
   • Is it acceptable to produce a play that is meant to speak directly to a specific group defined by sex, race, or religion?
5. Plays from earlier periods often reflect viewpoints that are unacceptable in contemporary society. Should plays from the past be produced when those plays contain material that is objectionable because of racial, religious, or sexual stereotypes? Defend one of the following positions:
   • Such plays should not be produced. (Should they be studied?)
   • Such plays should be produced only with changes in offensive components.
   • Such plays should be produced as written but with commentary (for example, notes in the programs, panel discussions to examine the problematic material in a historical context).
   • Such plays should be produced without comment.
6. What are some other functions that theatre can serve that are not mentioned in the chapter?
7. Is censorship necessary? At what points do free speech and protection of citizens collide? What are the potential dangers of censorship?
8. Investigate the types of theatres that are available in your area. Check out your local newspaper, run an Internet search, or ask at a public library. Make a list of theatres categorized by type. Collect or print out season brochures giving the lists of plays and dates. Which shows would you most like to attend? Which ones are within your price range? Which theatres use volunteer ushers? Which theatres have student discounts or student rush? If your questions can't be answered by a web-site, call the theatre box office.

Key Terms and Concepts

propaganda, p. 6
nontraditional casting, p. 14
professional theatre, p. 18
Broadway, p. 18
Off-Broadway, p. 18

commercial theatre, p. 18
nonprofit theatre, p. 19
resident theatre, p. 19
regional theatre, p. 19
amateur theatre, p. 20

educational theatre, p. 20
community theatre, p. 20
hybrid theatre, p. 21
Off-off-Broadway, p. 21

For Further Exploration

Augusto Boal. *Theater of the Oppressed.* London: Pluto, 1998. For alternative readings of the theatrical experience.

Don Wilmeth and Christopher Bigsby. *The Cambridge History of American Theatre,* vol. 3. New York: Cambridge, 1998. For a history of American theatrical activity and dramatic literature since World War II.

Alan Sinfield. *Out on Stage: Lesbian and Gay Theatre in the Twentieth Century.* New Haven, CT: Yale, 1999; and Kaier Curtin. *"We Can Always Call Them Bulgarians": The Emergence of Lesbians and Gay Men on the American Stage.* Boston: Alyson, 1987.

James Roose-Evans. *Experimental Theatre.* London: Routledge, 1989; and Arthur Sainer. *The New Radical Theatre Notebook.* New York: Applause, 1997. For overviews and pictorial evidence for twentieth-century experimental theatre.

Helen Krich Chinoy and Linda Walsh Jenkins. *Women in American Theatre,* 3rd ed. New York: Theatre Communications Group, 2006; and Helene Keyssar. *Feminist Theatre: An Introduction to Plays of Contemporary British and American Women.* New York: Grove/Atlantic, 1985.

Errol Hill and James Hatch. *A History of African American Theatre.* Cambridge, UK: Cambridge, 2003; and L. C. Sanders. *The Development of Black Theater in America: From Shadows to Selves.* Baton Rouge: Louisiana State, 1989. For a history of black theatre in the United States.

David Krasner. *A Beautiful Pageant.* New York: Palgrave Macmillan, 2002. For the Harlem Renaissance.

John Houchin. *Censorship of the American Theatre in the Twentieth Century.* Cambridge, UK: Cambridge, 2003.

Coming to Terms: American Plays and the Vietnam War. New York: Theatre Communications Group, 1985.

Brenda Murphy. *Congressional Theatre: Dramatizing McCarthyism on Stage, Film, and Television.* Cambridge, UK: Cambridge, 1999. For an examination of coercion and censorship in theatre.

www.nytheatre.com includes a listing of New York City shows, ticket prices, and brief descriptions of plays.

Joseph Wesley Ziegler. *Regional Theatre: The Revolutionary Stage.* New York: Da Capo, 1977. For history of resident theatres.

ENTRANCE TO THE RICHELIEU THEATRE of the Comédie Française in Paris (2010). The photos above the entrance depict the actors of the company.

Photo © Ronald Wainscott.

Experiencing Theatre

Collaboration of Actor, Audience, and Space

A JAPANESE AUDIENCE gathers for a matinee program of performances of Kabuki theatre at the Kabuki-Za in Tokyo (2006). This theatre, first built in 1889, was destroyed during World War II, but rebuilt in 1951 in the older architectural style. Currently, this theatre, amid much controversy, is being torn down to be replaced by a new Kabuki-Za scheduled to open in 2013. Photo © Ronald Wainscott.

In his inspirational book *The Empty Space* (1968) director Peter Brook (b. 1925) reminds us that only three elements are necessary for theatre to exist: any empty space and a person in action in that space being watched by someone else.[1]

Whenever one person performs and another watches in the same location, theatre is created. Lots of other things *might* be present: lights, costumes, scenery, makeup, seats, a raised platform, music, predetermined words; the event *could* incorporate hundreds of actors, thousands of spectators, and millions of dollars. But the basis of theatre, the essence of the event, is a theatrical collaboration: one person "acting," one person "auding" (listening and/or watching), in the same space at the same time.

Since, by definition, the performer and the spectator (or "seer") share the same time and space, a theatrical performance can happen only once. The same actors may perform the same text with the same movement for two different audiences, but it is *not* the same event if different people are watching. Even if the same people attended both performances and the actors said exactly the same words and played the same action, the events could not be identical. An actor might inflect a word differently; the audience might laugh at a particular line, causing a performer to wait before beginning the next speech.

Every performance is different because human beings are not static. An actress's opening-night performance is not the same as her hundredth; a performer who just experienced a painful breakup plays a love scene differently than he did the night before. Every audience is different. An audience composed mostly of college students reacts differently than one composed primarily of senior citizens; a Tuesday night audience, arriving after a long day at work, is different from a Saturday night audience coming straight from bars and restaurants, ready to have a good time. The audience reaction, in turn, shapes the performance. In the midst of a comedy, actors faced with stony silence might "push"—overemphasize lines, try too hard to be funny, kill the jokes; an audience that is ready to laugh can elicit easy, polished delivery from the performers. Audience members help to shape the theatrical event, depending on what they bring along with them: familiarity with the play, with the actors; a love of action; a commitment to a specific idea; a capacity for caring; a large or small vocabulary; a short or long attention span; an annoying cough or an infectious laugh. The space makes its contribution as well. Watching a performance in an elegant, well-equipped theatre is very different from watching one in a large, empty warehouse or a small, intimate space.

Because most of us will be audience members more times in our lives than we will perform, we begin this exploration of the theatrical collaboration from the audience point of view.

THE AUDIENCE

At its most basic level, theatre provides a sensory experience for the audience; it appeals to the human senses as the audience is actively involved in perceiving, processing, reacting to, and storing a vast number of stimuli. In a complex production, you might be bombarded with the effects of light, color, form, movement, the human voice, sound effects, music, the smell of the people around you, the temperature of the air, the feel of the seats, the sense of closeness. To experience this wealth of sensory activity is exciting, often pleasant, sometimes unpleasant. But more is at work. You could have an exciting sensory experience at a laser light show. Something else takes place in the theatre.

Empathy and Aesthetic Distance

When you watch a performance, you experience two phenomena simultaneously: empathy and aesthetic distance. **Empathy** is emotional identification. In everyday life, it means the ability to put yourself in someone else's shoes. In the theatre, it refers to a sense of participation—an identification with character. It is not the same thing as sympathy, although that also might be at work. Empathy is when you feel along *with* the characters (not just *for* them).

In *The Poor of New York* (1857) by Dion Boucicault, a sea captain, alarmed by a financial panic, takes all of his savings to a bank for safekeeping. The bank's employees are corrupt and decide to steal the money. When the captain begins to suspect foul play, he is stricken by a heart attack, but the employees offer no assistance and do not call for help until it is too late. One simply counts money while the other watches with interest as the captain dies in front of them. The audience might identify with the terror and struggle of the sinking captain as well as feel anger at the corrupt employees.

In *Spring Awakening* (2006) by Steven Slater and Duncan Sheik, the adolescent love of Melchior and Wendla turns masochistic and sad. We are likely to be moved by their passion and angry at their parents for undermining their children's feelings. Our understanding of their fumbling attraction leads us to empathize with this sabotaged young love.

Marsha Norman's play *'night, Mother* (1983) focuses on the aging Thelma and her daughter Jessie. Because of many physical and emotional problems, Jessie decides, quite rationally, that she would rather be dead than alive and prepares for her suicide as she explains her reasons to her mother. Throughout the play the audience is pulled back and forth between identifying with Jessie (whose arguments make sense) and with Thelma, who desperately tries to change her daughter's mind. At the play's end Jessie exits and locks the door behind her as her mother screams and pleads through the closed door. The answer is a gunshot heard offstage. The audience's emotional participation in those excruciating moments is intense. Emotional involvement in this play is heightened also by nonstop action; the play has no intermission.

Empathy is a key component in many entertainment forms and is sometimes so strong that feeling spills over into action. Have you ever screamed at the climax of a horror film or found your body trying to run the plays while you watched a football game on television? In the theatre the fact that the actors are live and sharing the same space with the audience tends to make the identification even stronger than in film. It is not unusual for a child to stand in the theatre and shout to his favorite character, "He's hiding inside that box!" The child's actions are motivated by empathy, taken to the extreme of interference in the fictional world.

Aesthetic distance is psychological separation, or a sense of detachment. It is what keeps the audience (usually) from shouting—from trying to influence the action on stage. You understand that what you are watching is not real. When the lights come back

A FRENCH AUDIENCE in c. 1860 watching a melodrama in France. Note the strong audience response to the apparent death onstage, the large gestures of the actors, and the heroine dressed entirely in white. There is clearly audience involvement and probably empathy with the stage action. Also a stage prompter can be seen downstage center.

Original painting by Honoré Daumier. Reproduction from the Yorck Project.

A NINETEENTH-CENTURY FRENCH AUDIENCE enjoys a light, diverting comedy in 1837. Note that some audience members are focused on the stage, some have turned inward with laughter, and others are interacting with one another; the latter audience members would experience more aesthetic distance. Hand-painted lithograph by Pruche (1837).

Collection of the authors.

up, the audience members will talk and laugh and go back to their homes, and the actors will take off their costumes, put on their street clothes, and reenter daily life. The term "aesthetic distance" literally means "the distance of art"; the audience members are able to step back and view the events on stage objectively because they realize the action represented is fictional. Aesthetic distance allows you to appreciate the way something is done—to admire the skill with which an actor portrays a character, the beauty of the scenery, or the way lighting changes the mood of the play— because you realize that the effect is being crafted for you.

Another way to think about empathy and aesthetic distance is that the first appeals to the heart and the second to the head. In most theatrical events, both are present; at times audience members' emotions are engaged, and they experience the events of the play as if they were truly participating; at other times they figuratively step back, remember where they are, and admire the way the fictional world is created. Both are necessary for a complete experience. Empathy makes the event exciting and personal; aesthetic distance makes analysis possible and allows you to exercise your intellect as well as your feelings.

Much of the success of a theatrical performance depends on how skillfully the people who are creating the dramatized action are able to manipulate empathy and aesthetic distance. In a production of Shakespeare's *Othello* (c. 1604–1605), a husband filled with jealous rage approaches his innocent young wife, who is lying on the bed. If the lights dim slowly and music slips in under the action, the production elements are encouraging the audience to empathize—to surrender emotionally to the suspense of the situation on stage.

On the other hand, the audience members might be asked to step back from the dramatized world and remember that they are in a theatre. If an actor looks at the audience and addresses it directly, the audience is encouraged to relate to the actor as an actor, or perhaps a narrator, rather than as the character. In Thornton Wilder's *Our Town* (1938) the character of the Stage Manager regularly comments on events happening on stage, nearly all props are mimed, and the actors perform on a bare stage; the audience is reminded constantly that it is witnessing a performance. In *Urinetown: The Musical* (2001) by Mark Hollman and Greg Kotis, the play's narrator, Officer Lockstock, is also a corrupt cop (a villain is our guide through the dramatic action). He and others often address the audience directly and sometimes comment on the structure of the play and how much they hate the play's title.

In any play deliberate decisions are made to shift audience experience at specific moments, and depending on the effect desired, a production might emphasize empathy or aesthetic distance throughout a total performance. In *The Conduct of Life* (1985) by Maria Irene Fornes, the manipulation of aesthetic distance is closely related to physical distance. The audience observes Latin American power struggles, including torture and rape, at first in a military setting but eventually brought into the domestic life of a family. Four different locations are seen simultaneously, the living room of a home being closest to the audience (see Figure 2.1). The most horrific scenes are at first kept at a distance, but as the play progresses, the young rape victim and her military abuser come closer and closer to the audience. By the end of the play the victim of the horrors is sitting in the living room where a murder is about to take place.

Sometimes the consistent manipulation of aesthetic distance can yield surprising results. In the play *Miss Margarida's Way* (1977) by Brazilian Roberto Athayde,

OTHELLO BY WILLIAM SHAKESPEARE. In this scene between Othello and Desdemona played by David Rainey and Elizabeth Bunch, Othello will murder his wife. Production at the Alley Theatre, Houston (2008), directed by Scott Schwartz, scenic design by Walt Spangler; costume design by Alejo Vietti.

Photo © Michal Daniel.

the leading character (nearly the only character) is a vocally abusive seventh-grade teacher who berates the audience members as if they are her junior high students. The house lights remain up throughout, and the audience is encouraged to talk back to the teacher. When this play is performed, the audience often acts badly—standing, yelling at the stage, throwing things—actually taking on the role of the delinquent students. The playwright in fact includes the audience in his list of characters. In *Miss Margarida's Way* the audience is encouraged to abandon aesthetic distance to some extent and actually become physically involved in the dramatic events.

FIGURE 2.1 **Ground Plan for *The Conduct of Life* by Maria Irene Fornes.** This is a plan for staging indicated in the play text. The living room is stage level, but the dining room is 1½ feet higher. The hallway rises another 1½ feet above the dining room, or 3 feet higher than stage level, and so on. The setting has five distinct playing spaces.

URINETOWN, a satirical musical by Mark Hollman and Greg Kotis, features outrageous action at the public urinals that are controlled by the government to manipulate both the economy and the populace. Here we see public rebellion against the oppression as performed at Indiana University, directed by Danielle Howard and scenic design by Fred M. Duer in 2007.

Photo by Indiana University PhotoGraphics.

Despite the best efforts of theatre artists to control empathy and aesthetic distance, things can happen in production through no one's design or intent that have a profound impact on audience response. An actor's slip of the tongue or a noise backstage might pull an audience out of the dramatized world at an inopportune moment. A person who has experienced an event similar to one depicted on stage might identify so strongly with a character's sorrow that sadness overwhelms any possibility of analyzing the performance from an objective point of view. This audience member has little distance from his or her own sorrowful experience and therefore can create none for the performance.

As an audience member, you are probably seldom aware of the swings between empathy and aesthetic distance. You think only of integrated experience, and that is as it should be. Because these two phenomena are at work, the audience can experience great emotional intensity in the theatre with complete physical and psychological safety. In this way, the theatre provides vicarious experience; it is possible for the audience to be present in unlikely, impossible, or undesirable situations. As the audience members watch Emily in *Our Town,* they discover how it might feel to die and come back to life for one special day.

In Sarah Kane's bizarre *Blasted* (1995), the audience is bombarded with urban/terrorist warfare, replete with graphic depictions of disease, violence, rape, cannibalism, and suicide. This assault of the senses can shock audiences like real acts of terror, or perhaps desensitize some to the excesses of contemporary horror.

Theatre allows us to learn about ourselves and to come to an emotional understanding of the experience of others.

Overall Effect on the Audience

For centuries, people have speculated about the desired effect of theatrical performance on the audience, and many theories exist. The Greek philosopher Aristotle (384–322 B.C.E.) used the word **catharsis,** or emotional release; a performance was designed to engage the audience's feelings and build in intensity so that the spectator felt "cleansed" or purged of strong emotion by the end of the play. (Scholars disagree

EXPLORING Collaboration

Spatial Collaboration: *Commune* and *Pinocchio*

From time to time audiences are invited to break the actor/audience boundary and collaborate more actively in the space with the actors. In the 1960s and early 1970s this interaction sometimes occurred in environmental productions by the Living Theatre and the Performance Group. In the midst of one production in particular, *Commune* (1970) by the Performance Group, fifteen audience members were asked to leave their seats and sit in a circle onstage to represent the villagers in the Vietnamese village of My Lai (the scene of a massacre). If the number of fifteen was not reached, the performance would stop without completion. Although the audience had to participate in the performance space to finish the play, this condition was preplanned by the theatre company and was related to experimenting with audience participation and exploring the conditions of performer/audience relationships.

More than thirty years earlier a very successful production of *Pinocchio,* a children's theatre play, opened in New York. It was part of the Federal Theatre Project, a government-sponsored effort that, as part of the Works Progress Administration, was intended to put people back to work across the United States during the Great Depression. This acrobatic and circuslike production about a puppet who becomes a real boy had been performed in California and other parts of the country. In the midst of the New York run of this show, the U.S. Congress cut off funding for the Federal Theatre, which meant that all productions had to shut down. Members of the *Pinocchio* company, led by the playwright/director Yasha Frank, decided at the last minute to demonstrate in their final performance. They did so not only by altering the play but also by involving the audience in an

PINOCCHIO by Yasha Frank, produced by the Federal Theatre Project 1937–1939.

From the Federal Theatre Project Photo Collection, Special Collections and Archives, George Mason University Libraries, Fairfax, Virginia.

onstage demonstration that moved subsequently into the streets. As the production neared its end, the magically animated puppet died. It was time for Pinocchio to come back to life as a real boy, but he remained dead on the stage. The other actors plopped him into a coffin inscribed with "killed by act of Congress." Not only was Pinocchio dead, but so was the Federal Theatre. The experiment with public funding for theatre arts was over. The company and some of the audience began to tear down the scenery and create a heap on the stage. All then walked out together bearing the coffin into the urban night. The play, the children's theatre, and the Federal Theatre Project remained unfinished.

INTERESTED? Check out

Hallie Flanagan. *Arena: The Story of the Federal Theatre.* 1940; Reprint ed. New York: Limelight, 1985.

John O'Connor and Lorraine Brown. *Free, Adult and Uncensored: The Living History of the Federal Theatre Project.* Washington, DC: New Republic, 1978.

For other productions by the Federal Theatre Project, see 13,000 images of items selected from the Federal Theatre Project Collection at the Library of Congress at "The New Deal Stage: Selections from the Federal Theatre Project 1935–1939" at http://memory.loc.gov/ammem/fedtp/fthome.html.

about exactly what the term "catharsis," as applied to the theatre, meant to the Greeks. We present the most widely accepted interpretation.) Strong and consistent emotional identification with the dramatized events is central to triggering catharsis. European and North American theatre has often followed this basic premise but with variations.

In the twentieth century the German playwright and theorist Bertolt Brecht (1898–1956) rejected the cathartic model altogether and insisted that the function of theatre should be to appeal to the intellect of the audience and incite it to social action. In this view, precipitating catharsis is contrary to the very nature of what theatre could and should do. Manipulation of aesthetic distance at appropriate moments could encourage a comparison between fictional events and the real world outside the theatre. Although Brecht sometimes engaged the audience members' emotions, he would interrupt the emotional response and deny its completion. In *The Caucasian Chalk Circle* (c. 1945), for example, two lovers, Grusha, a servant, and Simon, a soldier, find each other again after a considerable separation due to war. They struggle to communicate although a stream of water separates them. This scene is painful to watch and for the audience is likely to result in considerable emotional involvement. At one point, however, a narrator intrudes to explain what Grusha is thinking but will not say to Simon. The spell is broken. After the interruption, the lovers attempt to communicate again, but the narrator intrudes a second time to reveal what Simon is thinking but will not utter. Brecht's model has been followed by many artists hoping to encourage social change through theatre.

Japanese Noh theatre embraces an end result of contemplation rather than action or emotional release. The playwright and theorist Zeami (1363–1443) described the ideal image of performance as a flower—a perfect, transitory beauty, an enigmatic and mysterious elegance. The actor should strive to create an unfading flower, despite its temporary nature. The "flower" should also surprise the audience and reveal the unexpected. Above all, the actor should maintain secrets about his art, like a magician or warrior. The slow, carefully choreographed movement, colorful costumes, and simple, open stage of Noh invite the audience to contemplate the story of the play, which is often presented as a memory relived by the central character. The reenactment of an important event takes place in many Noh plays. In *Sotoba Komachi,* by Zeami's father, Kan'ami, an old woman sits on an enchanted grave stump remembering an unpleasant love affair. She is possessed by the ghost of her dead lover and relives their agonizing relationship through the form of a dance.

OUR TOWN by Thornton Wilder, the original production. The character of the Stage Manager holds the curtain as George lies prostrate on the grave of his wife Emily. The ghost of Emily watches him as she sits among the dead in the cemetery. All is done with a few chairs on a bare stage.

Courtesy of Billy Rose Theatre Collection, the New York Public Library for the Performing Arts, Astor, Lennox and Tilden Foundations.

THE NATURE OF ACTING

At the most basic level, every human being who interacts with other human beings is an actor. Every person performs social roles for others, both consciously and unconsciously. On the face of it this is neither a good nor a bad thing but simply a part of the human condition. Psychologists and psychiatrists from Sigmund Freud onward have explored the role-playing of the human animal in order to better understand behavior, to examine internal conflicts, and to treat emotional problems. Major playwrights and other writers of fiction from Aeschylus and Euripides (fifth century B.C.E.) among the ancient Greeks to recent playwrights such as Suzan-Lori Parks (b. 1964) and Martin McDonagh (b. 1970) have continually explored the ways in which people pretend to be someone they are not or claim to believe something other than reality for purposes that are helpful or evil, economic or spiritual, comic or tragic. Playwrights often demonstrate that people perform different roles when interacting with different friends, acquaintances, family members, and strangers. People perform differently in private situations than they do in public. Social performance is a basic phenomenon of human behavior and is central to the dramatic content and conflict of the theatrical experience. Is it then surprising that an early Greek word

EXPLORING Historical and Cultural Perspectives

Brecht versus Wagner

In the early to mid-twentieth century Bertolt Brecht (1898–1956) not only took Aristotle to task for embracing the emotional purpose of drama but also attacked his more recent predecessor, Richard Wagner (1813–1883), a German composer of music drama. Wagner composed many famous operas, such as *Tannhäuser* and *Parsifal,* and was very active in their production. He published theories of drama and music and championed the idea of "total theatre," which sought to unify all the arts. Emotionality and total immersion of the audience in the illusionism of the theatrical event, or "knowing through feeling," were the keys, according to Wagner, to successful theatre and drama. Many other theatre artists embraced this approach, which was consistent with the catharsis theory of Aristotle but went much further.

Brecht, by contrast, was anti-illusionist. He wanted his audiences to engage objectively and intellectually, not merely to respond emotionally to the dramatic material. Through his plays and published theory he popularized the idea of **Epic Theatre,** which featured *Verfremdungseffekt,* usually translated as "alienation" or "to make strange." Brecht's theatre went to great lengths to call attention to the theatricality of the event: Songs were disconnected from the story of the play, narration frequently interrupted the dialogue, placards and projections delivered lyrics and political messages to the audience, and stage machinery and lighting instruments were placed or hung in full view of the audience. The plays, music, and devices of both Wagner and Brecht are frequently revived today, and they can be seen as representing polar opposite views of how theatre can function in our world.

THE CAUCASIAN CHALK CIRCLE in a production at the University of Nebraska. The heroine Grusha encounters two corrupt soldiers as the play's Singer/Narrator watches and comments on the action.
Collection of the authors.

INTERESTED? Check out

John Willett, ed. and trans. *Brecht on Theatre.* New York: Hill and Wang, 1964.

Richard Wagner. "Knowing through Feeling." In *Total Theatre,* ed. E. T. Kirby. New York: E. P. Dutton, 1969, pp. 5–8.

Byron Magee. *Wagner and Philosophy.* New York: Penguin, 2001.

John Fuegi. *Bertolt Brecht: Chaos According to Plan.* Cambridge, UK: Cambridge, 1987.

for actor is **hypokrites,** from which we glean the more negative words "hypocrisy" and "hypocrite"?

As early as the fourth century B.C.E., Aristotle identified **mimesis,** or the artist's process of imitating character and action, as so basic to humanity that it was necessary to invent theatre. Children love to play roles and often use imitation to learn to speak, to mimic grownups, and to understand the world around them. All of us probably engaged in dress-ups early in life, pretending to be adults, playing house, fighting fires, galloping across the great expanses of an American prairie in the theatre of our minds. Once we are grown, some of this activity continues, of course, but often in more controlled, private ways or perhaps during the social freedom of a costume party. Participation in theatrical production gives sanction to this sense of play.

A JAPANESE NOH PLAY, KUROZUKA, in which an old woman is transformed into a witch and is poised to attack a priest.

Hoikusha color series.

For those who choose to create theatre for an audience, the process of *mimesis* is not merely copying but creating and recreating from the observation and analysis of human models of character and action and from the exploration of self. Here *mimesis* becomes an art form to be studied, practiced, and refined by both playwrights and actors.

In the ancient Roman theatre the *persona* was the mask of the actor. We now more commonly use the word to designate psychologically the social role a person is playing or presenting in life. Both of these meanings are appropriate to the process of the actor assuming a character. The actor dons a mask, whether literal or figurative, and when the preparation is complete, the audience is asked to accept this masked actor as the character designated by the play. The mask might be a literal device placed over or on the face, thus rigidly fixing the character's expression in some emblematic moment. In Japanese Noh theatre the leading actor meditates on his mask for a long time before finally placing it over his face, almost as if trying to become one with the spirit of the mask. Makeup may be used as mask, applied to age, beautify, or distort the actor's real face. The makeup can be realistic or highly stylized like that of Kathakali performers in India, who spend hours having layered, colorful makeup applied to help them depict the supernatural figures who move dancelike through the play.

Frequently, however, the mask is figurative. Through language that was conceived not by the actor but by a playwright, through movement unlike the actor's own, by presenting action that is contradictory to the actor's beliefs or normal behavior, the identity and personality of the actor are concealed from the audience while the actor simultaneously reveals a truthful picture of the character.

FROM PLAY TO PRODUCTION

While some theatrical performances progress through **improvisation** (the performers make up the words or movements as they go along), most theatre begins with a written text. One writer (or group of writers) creates the **play or script**—a written text indicating the words the characters speak and some of the physical action. In doing so, the writer provides the basic action of the play—he or she decides the major events of the play, the basic nature of each character, and the exact words that will be spoken on stage. The play is then brought to life by a team of theatre artists—a director, actors, and designers (the composition of the creative team may change in different situations)—and theatre technicians. This team creates the theatrical **production**—the fully realized performance of the play with actors, sets, costumes, lighting, and props.

The Production Collaborators

Historically, the work of creating a production has been divided in various ways. Accounts from ancient Greece say that the playwrights staged their own work. In eighteenth-century Europe a leading performer, dubbed an "actor-manager," organized the presentation of a play. Many theatres in the twenty-first century share a basic division of artistic duties. We will refer to the following job titles many times in this book.

Typically (although by no means exclusively), contemporary production begins with a script created by a **playwright,** or author. The financial and business aspects of the production are handled by a **producer.** The producer usually negotiates the rights to a play and hires a **director,** who is in charge of the artistic aspects of production. It is the director's job to guide the transformation of the play to live production. The director interprets the play and heads the artistic team, providing a focus and organization for the creative work. In general, the director sets the tone for the production, approves its overall look and sound, sets the movement of actors, and makes the final decisions when necessary. Often, the director (although sometimes the producer) chooses the actors, sometimes assisted by a **casting director,** and the director always helps the actors to develop and refine their characterizations.

A **scenic designer** creates a visual home for the play on stage. Many people might help to build scenery, but the designer envisions and controls the visual effect. The **costume designer** creates "wearable scenery" for the actors to help define and express character, and a **lighting designer** influences the effect of all visual elements by controlling focus and mood with color, placement, and intensity of light. A **sound designer** creates acoustic and recorded sound. On some occasions, a **makeup designer** may join the production team. A musical adds a **composer** and **lyricist** (who create the music and lyrics), a **music director** (who works with singers and orchestra), and a **choreographer** (who stages dancing). In medium- to large-sized theatres the creative decisions made by this team are executed by a **stage manager** (who ensures that things run smoothly on- and backstage) and management staff, a scene shop crew, a costume shop crew, and a lighting crew.

Front-of-House Personnel

Theatre operations that deal directly with the audience are called **front-of-house.** The **house manager** is responsible for the safety and comfort of the audience members during their time in the theatre. House managers coordinate ushers, make sure the audience areas of the theatre are clean and safe, resolve any seating problems, and deal with any emergencies. In the case of a fire or other dangerous situation the house manager is in charge of getting the patrons to safety, notifying the authorities, and securing the theatre. The house manager works closely with the stage manager in starting the show and beginning again after intermissions. The **box office manager** works directly with the house manager and is responsible for organizing and overseeing ticket sales, including supervising the staff members who deal directly with the public. Front-of-house personnel act as a liaison between the audience and production and have an influence on the pleasantness of the patrons' experience.

The Rewards of Collaboration

Making theatre requires a tremendous amount of work. Although a few individuals make large sums of money in the theatre, most people who are engaged in it professionally make very little, often supporting themselves most of the time through other occupations. A vast number of people participate in theatrical production with no thought of financial reward. What is the attraction for those human beings who step out of the audience to go on- or backstage?

Perhaps most obviously, theatre provides a forum for self-expression. Many possibilities exist for artistic outlet—not only acting and directing but also designing lighting,

EXPLORING Historical and Cultural Perspectives

Makeup as Mask: Kathakali

Some of the most fascinating and complicated stage makeup in the world is fashioned for Kathakali, a form of dance-drama from southern India that is rooted in Hindu mythology. Kathakali originated in the seventeenth century and is traditionally performed in temple courtyards. Actors are all male and are trained from childhood. The actors themselves do not speak but communicate through dance and stylized gesture; their movement is accompanied by singers, drums, gongs, and cymbals. The characters they depict from the ancient *Ramayana* and *Mahabharata* are larger than life—gods and demons come to earth. The actors work acrobatically and in pantomime, often giving the impression that they are possessed by the spirit of the gods.

Costumes in Kathakali are very colorful and elaborate, including enormous headdresses. The makeup is also very colorful, and five conventionalized styles symbolize specific characters and qualities. Actors often apply makeup themselves. *Chutti* (white gill-like extensions) are then applied by a makeup artist while the actor lies on the floor. *Chutti* are built up slowly in layers on the cheeks of the face. A literal mask is not used because the performer must execute intricate and emotional facial expressions and remarkable eye movements that are said to have developed along with a strict code of gestures from ancient dance, dramatic, and ritual forms. Some actors redden the whites of their eyes with a small seed to accentuate rolling eye movements.

KATHAKALI MAKEUP is very extravagant, as evidenced in this photograph: We see paper *chutti* on the sides of the face; bright green, red, yellow, and black on the face; and an ornate headpiece, costume, and long fingernails on the actor Kalamandalam Balasubrahmaniam, who is performing a lotus hand gesture, or *mudra*.

Courtesy www.cyberkerala.com/kathakali.

INTERESTED? Check out

"Kathakali," www.cyberkerala.com/kathakali.

Phillip B. Zarilli. *Kathakali Dance-Drama: Where Gods and Demons Come to Play.* London: Routledge, 2000.

---

sound, scenery, costumes, and makeup, as well as drawing, painting, sewing, building, writing, and composing. Individuals with strong organizational and technical skills enjoy putting these to work behind the scenes in theatrical management and technical positions.

The vicarious experience of the audience in the theatre becomes more concrete in the life of the performer; the actor actually inhabits, rather than watches, the character's fictional life. All artists of the theatre, actors and playwrights especially, experience empathy with an intensity that widens their life experience and point of view. Making theatre is a way of trying on different identities—of exploring life from another vantage point, of investigating the human mystery with a unique tool. It provides a safe way of playing out conflict.

One of the most satisfying aspects of working in the theatre is collaboration—first with other artists, technicians, and administrators and finally with the audience. It is important to keep in mind that no one in the theatre creates in a vacuum. Each person contributes a part of the whole, and that part is successful and valid only insofar as it is appropriate to the success of the entire production.

SPACE

For a performance to be theatre, it must be presented in a space that accommodates both the performers and the audience at the same time. The space could be as tiny as a closet with one actor performing for an audience of one, or the space could be as large as a sports stadium with a cast of hundreds, even thousands, performing for an audience of 50,000 or more. The space could be formally designed by an architect for the express purpose of theatrical performance or could simply be a preexisting space that was never intended by the builder as a theatre. A performance space, however, need not be built at all; an open meadow or hillside might function very well. The audience might be raised above the performers, or the actors might be elevated with the audience looking up. Performers and audience could be in the same horizontal plane. There are few rules other than the one indicated by the first sentence of this paragraph.

The space must be organized with the movement of the actor and the relationship of the actors to the audience in mind. As the Swiss designer Adolphe Appia (1862–1928) reminded other theatre artists, no design for the theatre is complete without the performers. Despite the openness of the spatial possibilities of theatrical performance, several physical arrangements have become traditional in the last 2,500 years. These models have recurred in many cultures and undergone numerous variations, but the essentials of each form are repeated. All three traditional spaces—proscenium, thrust, and arena—are defined to a large degree by the physical relationship of performers and audience.

Proscenium Space

If you attend the theatre with regularity, it is likely that you have encountered a **proscenium space** frequently. Invented by the Italians in a temporary form in the sixteenth century and for permanent structures by the seventeenth, the proscenium theatre is most clearly defined by a large open arch—the **proscenium arch**—that marks the primary division between audience and performance space. A proscenium space may have an **apron,** an extension of the stage that continues toward the audience from

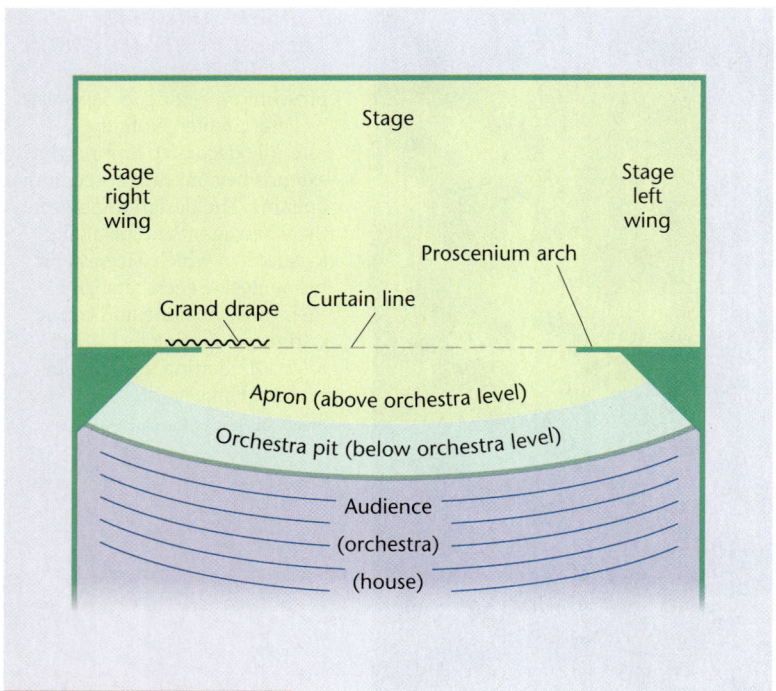

FIGURE 2.2 Proscenium Theatre Ground Plan (as seen from above).

the arch; the apron serves as an important performance space and is usually without scenery. Although some theatres have a large apron that allows freedom of movement, many proscenium spaces have a shallow apron or no apron at all. Most proscenium theatres also have **wings**—spaces offstage left and right for actors, crew, and scenery that are not in the visible performance space. The entire performance space is like a huge box (see Figure 2.2).

Resembling a big picture frame, usually rectangular rather than square, the proscenium arch frequently encloses most or all of the scenery that is traditionally placed upstage of the arch, resulting in a frame between audience and actors (see Figure 2.3). The proscenium not only serves to focus the action but also allows the use of changeable scenery with the ability to mask the offstage activity from the audience. Although there are other theories regarding the proscenium's invention, the frame appears to have been developed for this very reason: to create the effect of watching a picture in motion and in three dimensions. The proscenium's effect is enhanced by the use of a **grand drape** (front curtain) to hide scene changes or to indicate the beginnings and conclusions of acts or scenes. The use of the grand drape has diminished, however, since the mid-twentieth century because of growing sophistication in lighting and changes in aesthetic sensibilities. A proscenium theatre can become a box of illusions, and the French called it so in the seventeenth century. Its illusionary possibilities are intensified by the use of artificial light and the clear separation of the performance box from the audience area.

The audience area of any theatrical space is called the **house.** In a proscenium theatre the **orchestra** is the space immediately in front of the stage where seats are

FIGURE 2.3 Proscenium Stage from the Audience's Point of View.

FIGURE 2.4 Section View of Proscenium House.

on the floor. The theatre might also have an **orchestra pit**—traditionally a sunken area between the apron and the audience—for musicians (see Figure 2.4). Usually, the orchestra floor is gently **raked,** sloping upward from stage or pit to the back of the house. Some houses are divided by aisles running toward the stage to facilitate audience seating. A proscenium space may include seating on higher levels than the orchestra, such as private **boxes** or open **galleries** (also called *balconies* or *mezzanines*).

Proscenium spaces have been common since the Italian Renaissance, and most European theatres were using them by the late seventeenth century. Nearly every culture

THIS IMAGE OF THE DRURY LANE THEATRE in London was first published in 1808–1811 in the *Microcosm of London.* This is a proscenium theatre with an apron downstage bounded by the arch and one proscenium door on each side for many entrances and exits by the actors. This configuration was standard in British theatres in the eighteenth and early nineteenth centuries. Drury Lane Theatre could accommodate an audience of more than 3,000 members.
Collection of the authors.

FIGURE 2.5 Thrust Theatre Ground Plan.

with a theatrical tradition adopted the proscenium for at least some of its presentations, including cultures in India, Africa, Japan, and China. It was virtually the only kind of theatre space available in North America until well into the twentieth century. Nearly all the Broadway theatres in New York are proscenium spaces, and most theatres across the United States and Canada as well as in Europe are prosceniums.

Thrust Space

The **thrust space** is one of the oldest theatrical arrangements to be formalized as theatre architecture. The classical Greeks, traveling acting companies in the European Middle Ages, classical Chinese performers, some Japanese Noh and early Kabuki companies, *commedia dell'arte* (improvisational comedy) troupes in Italy, Elizabethan actors in England, and many theatre companies in Europe and North America since the mid-twentieth century have all utilized variations on the thrust space.

At its most basic the stage of the thrust is surrounded on three sides by the audience, even though a majority of the audience area is frequently facing the performance space from the "front." Put another way, the performance space extends out into the audience area so that the actors, when facing forward, or downstage, have audience members in front of them and on both sides but not at their backs (see Figure 2.5).

THE ADAMS THEATRE at the Utah Shakespeare Festival. A thrust stage, inspired by the Elizabethan public stages, was built in 1977 with an upper level, here in use for a production of Shakespeare's *Much Ado About Nothing* in 2003.

Photo by Karl Hugh. Courtesy of Utah Shakespeare Festival.

EXPLORING Historical and Cultural Perspectives

Eighteenth-Century Court Theatres

An overwhelming majority of proscenium theatres built before the age of electricity vanished because of fires, rebuilding, or urban renewal. Some were remodeled so extensively that the original structure is unrecognizable. Of the few surviving theatres, the Drottningholm near Stockholm, Sweden, is very important because it is still used for productions, most of which are staged using eighteenth-century scenery and methods except for lighting. (Originally, Drottningholm was lit by candles and oil lamps.) This small court theatre with a deep stage was built for King Gustav III in the 1760s but was closed when the king died some 30 years later. Long boarded up, the theatre was rediscovered in 1921. The most extraordinary surprise was the discovery of original scenery and stage machinery that still worked. You can visit this theatre today for a tour or a production of operas, plays, or ballets of long ago. Although still active as a theatre, it also functions as a museum of European theatre in the 1700s with its two-dimensional wing and drop scenery (flat pieces of scenery painted to look three-dimensional) and flying machines of a type rarely seen since the nineteenth century. Ingmar Bergman's film of Mozart's opera *The Magic Flute* (1975; available on DVD) begins in the Drottningholm Court Theatre. During the first few scenes you can see the eighteenth-century wing and drop scenery at work. Due to a loss of state funding in 2005, the production season has been abbreviated, but eighteenth-century plays, operas, and concerts continue. The French comedy of manners, *The Triumph of Love* by Pierre Marivaux, was produced in 2005, and in 2008 a new summer series of seventeenth- and eighteenth-century operas was introduced.

A few other court theatres survive in Europe, including a beautiful one at Krumlov Castle in the Czech Republic. Unfortunately, the Krumlov Theatre is no longer used for performances, but it has been preserved with great care. You

AN EIGHTEENTH-CENTURY INTERIOR PRISON SETTING using only original wing, drop, and border scenery surviving at the small Castle Theatre of Krumlov Castle in the Czech Republic. The Foundation of the Baroque Theatre at the Castle of Český Krumlov.
Photo by Veroslav Skrabánek.

can visit a wonderful Internet site for Krumlov Castle, including interactive, virtual tours of the spaces at www.castle.ckrumlov.cz/docs/en/zamek_oinf_sthrza.xml.

INTERESTED? Check out

The Krumlov Castle Theatre website at www.castle.ckrumlov.cz/docs/en/zamek_5nadvori_bd.xml

The Drottningholm Court Theatre website at www.dtm.se/eng

Ove Hidemark, et al. *The Drottningholm Court Theatre: Its Advent, Fate and Preservation.* Stockholm, Sweden: Byggforlaget, 1993.

Agne Beijer. *Court Theatres of Drottningholm and Gripsholm.* New York: B. Blom, 1972.

The actors then must play to the audience in an arc, since the audience is laid out before the performers like a fan. At the actors' backs might be a simple curtain, painted or constructed scenery, or a screen, but always with entrances and exits for the actors. Some permanent thrust spaces have a **façade**—a generalized standing or hanging structure, often multilevel, that may be neutral or decorated but always resides upstage of the action, creating a background that can suggest nearly any location, inside or out. A generic façade was popular in classical Greece and Rome as well as Elizabethan England and Spain in the Golden Age; in China, Japan, and India; and in more recent times in some thrust theatres in North America. Some thrust spaces allow the performers to leave the stage by aisles through the audience and/or vomitories. **Vomitories** (voms) are entrances to elevated seating for the audience that run underneath the audience

EXPLORING Historical and Cultural Perspectives

Stratford Festival Theatre

The first important thrust theatre in North America continues to be a showpiece for productions of classical plays, especially for the works of Shakespeare and his contemporaries (although the Stratford company performs modern plays as well). The stage at Stratford, Ontario, was originally designed by director Tyrone Guthrie (1900–1971) and designer Tanya Moiseiwitsch (1914–2003), who wished to produce a space appropriate for Elizabethan drama and one that reflected many of the known characteristics of the public theatres of Shakespeare's time. The Festival Theatre opened in 1957 with a production of *Hamlet* and was remodeled in 1997. It seats 1,820, but steep, two-level seating areas keep most of the audience close to the stage action and never farther away than 65 feet. On stage, part of the upstage façade, which has a central balcony and multiple doors, is removable to give variety and flexibility to the scenic possibilities. A similar but more asymmetrical thrust without the permanent façade, also conceived by Guthrie, resulted in the successful Guthrie Theater in Minneapolis, Minnesota.

The Stratford Festival in the 1970s added a much smaller and simpler thrust stage, for many years called the Third Stage but renamed the Tom Patterson Theater in 1991. The space has been modified several times over the years but is maintained for more intimate or experimental productions. The Patterson seats just under 500 audience members.

STRATFORD FESTIVAL THEATRE, viewed from house center. Note the deep thrust of the stage with the seats surrounding all three sides and the multilevel façade up center.

Photo by Jeff Speed. Courtesy of the Stratford Festival Archives.

Tyrone Guthrie. *Renown at Stratford: A Record of the Shakespeare Festival in Canada.* Toronto: Clark, Irwin, 1971.
James Forsyth. *Tyrone Guthrie: A Biography.* London: Hamilton, 1976.

INTERESTED? Check out

The Stratford Festival website, www.stratfordfestival.on.ca.

and come up to empty out into the seating area. They were invented by the Romans for theatres and amphitheatres (such as the Coliseum in Rome) and are often used today in sports stadiums.

Some thrust stages are portable or mobile to facilitate being moved from place to place by traveling troupes of actors. This kind of stage (often called a **booth stage**) was probably used by ancient Greek and Roman mime performers and was definitely used by actors in the Middle Ages. In the second half of the twentieth century, inspired especially by the theatres that were common in Shakespeare's time, the thrust space became very popular again, and many new professional and academic theatres were built, beginning with the Stratford Festival Theatre in Ontario. Other famous thrust spaces in North America include the Alley Theatre in Houston, the Mark Taper Forum in Los Angeles, the Guthrie Theater in Minneapolis, and the Vivian Beaumont Theatre in New York. It is now common for actors to train and work in thrust spaces.

Arena Space

The **arena space** is the easiest to describe but one of the most difficult to use well. Quite simply, it is a space in which the audience completely surrounds the performance area. The stage could be square, rectangular, circular, trapezoidal—in fact, any geometric shape (see Figure 2.6). A circular arena space is sometimes called "theatre-in-the-round." Typically, the performers enter and exit the space through aisles or passages that puncture the audience surround, and in most cases the passageways that serve the actors also serve the audience arriving and departing. Although arena theatres are usually associated with modern theatre, the spatial form can be found occasionally in ancient theatre such as the medieval rounds of Cornwall and the Roman amphitheatres. The arena configuration allows more people to be seated close to the action than does proscenium or thrust. Most arena spaces are small and intimate, seating fewer than 100, but some rather majestic professional spaces, such as the Fichandler Stage at Arena Stage in Washington, DC, are quite large. Many college and university theatre programs include an arena space for presentations.

An arena space discourages the use of much scenery that literally depicts a complete locale. Consequently, it is virtually the opposite of a proscenium space in terms of scenic investiture; instead of viewing the action from one side, the audience experiences it from all sides. There can be no scenic façade, no single point of view, and every audience member is facing not only the performance space but other audience members as well. Arena encourages economy in staging—both artistic and financial. To make the action clear and open to the audience in arena, actors must move more frequently than they would in other traditional spaces. Because the audience always has other audience

FIGURE 2.6 Arena Theatre Ground Plan

THE NEW FICHANDLER STAGE, Washington, DC, which opened in 2010. The renovated arena stage essentially matches the famous original in dimensions which was in need of a face lift.

Photo by Nic Lehoux, courtesy Bing Thom Architects.

FIGURE 2.7 Possible Configurations in a Black Box Theatre Ground Plan

members in view, the arena often enhances aesthetic distance by reminding the audience that it is watching a performance.

The Black Box

One type of nontraditional theatre space may be quickly becoming a traditional one. The term **black box** at one time described a simple room transformed to a theatre space, usually painted black. In the second half of the twentieth century, however, the black box became so common that some theatre companies, colleges, and universities began constructing them deliberately as smaller, flexible, alternative theatres for plays and performances that were thought to be appropriate for intimate spaces and small audiences. The traditional spatial approaches of thrust, arena, and proscenium tend to be used in a black box. The audience might be placed in an L-shaped configuration or on two opposite sides of the action, with audience members facing one another and stage action taking place in the troughlike middle. Alternatively, the audience members could find themselves in the middle of the space with the performers surrounding them (see Figure 2.7). Because the physical arrangements can be unusual or extreme, some artists call black boxes "lab" theatres, indicating a place where artists are free to experiment with new work or methods.

Found Theatre Spaces

A nontraditional theatre space is often a "found" space but need not be that exclusively. A **found space** is anywhere, indoors or out, that was never intended as a theatrical space when created or designed. A director, designer, and company of actors might discover a space that they find appropriate for a specific play or for the kind of work they wish to pursue. The space could be any room, large or small, in a public building, a house, a church, a factory. The space might be a town square, a field, a football stadium, a street corner, a gymnasium, a rooftop. In the medieval period the town square in Lucerne, Switzerland, was used for religious drama. Performances have frequently been staged at Judson Memorial Church in Washington Square and St. Mark's Church in East Greenwich Village in New York City. For example, the avant-garde playwright and director Richard Foreman has often utilized such spaces; his production of *The Gods Are Pounding My Head!*, his 2005 experimental show for his Ontological-Hysteric Theater, was staged in St. Mark's Church.

A space might be used as it is found, or it might undergo some kind of modification to make it serve the purpose. In other words, any place can become a theatre. Even traditional theatre spaces sometimes are transformed to serve a different kind of theatrical experience. For example, the stage of a large proscenium theatre might become a more intimate theatrical space by placing the audience on the stage as well as the actors, leaving the traditional house empty and ignored. German director Max Reinhardt staged *The Miracle* in the 1920s many times in cathedrals throughout Europe. In the United States he reversed the process by instructing designer Norman Bel Geddes to redecorate a large theatre throughout to resemble a cathedral. **Site-specific performance** is a term used for a production that is developed for and closely linked to a particular location. *Another Person Is a Foreign Country* (1991), written by Charles L. Mee and directed by Anne Bogart, was performed among the ruins of the first cancer hospital in the United States.

Environmental Theatre

One of the most dynamic uses of nontraditional space is often called **environmental theatre.** Although we can find precedent in older cultures, the twentieth century witnessed an explosion of environmental theatre in the 1960s and early 1970s in Europe and the United States. This approach continues to be used periodically in both professional and academic theatre. The basic principle of environmental theatre is that the audience and actors share the same space. There is little or no separation of acting and observing areas, with the result that the audience members are physically part of the performance. Consequently, the traditional qualities of aesthetic distance undergo severe modification; sometimes audience members feel put on the spot and find it difficult to locate a "comfort zone" (see the discussion of *Commune* in this chapter's Exploring Collaboration feature on page 31). Environmental theatre can occur in traditional theatre spaces or found spaces.

Many productions in the twentieth century experimented with placement of the audience even if they were not attempting to create complete environmental theatre. John Dexter's direction with John Napier's set design of the first production of *Equus* (1973) by Peter Shaffer, for example, placed some of the audience members in a fan shape at the back of the stage. This staging turned these audience members into witnesses watching a trial.

EXPLORING Collaboration

A Very Long Run

In 1947 on a side street in the Latin Quarter of Paris near Notre Dame Cathedral, a small restaurant was converted to a black box theatre that eventually was named the Théâtre de la Huchette. The theatre's identity as avant-garde was enshrined in 1957 when the company mounted two short plays, Eugene Ionesco's *The Bald Soprano* (La Cantatrice Chauve) and *The Lesson* (La Leçon). These plays had premiered briefly as amateur productions in small performance spaces with young actors in 1950 and 1951. When the pair opened professionally at the Huchette, a long run ensued, typically filling the 85-seat theatre. *The Bald Soprano* is a defining play of Theatre of the Absurd along with Beckett's *Waiting for Godot.* Ionesco subtitled his piece an "Anti-play," and it remains a masterly depiction of the failure of human beings to communicate, yet the tone of the play is comic. Even when delivering bizarre and contradictory lines, the French actors do not comment on the inexplicable language and events, but present them as if they are logical and comprehensible. When we witnessed *The Bald Soprano* in 2010 at the Huchette, the capacity audience was mixed demographically with many French students. *The Lesson* is a satirical commentary on failed education, but presented in cross-talk and hyperbolic speech. Although the experimental nature of the plays is long past, the Théâtre de la Huchette continues to present new works following the performances of the two famous plays each night. At this writing *The Bald Soprano* and *The Lesson* have been running continuously for well over 16,000 performances for more than 54 years.

AN AUDIENCE GATHERS before the Théâtre de la Huchette in 2010.
Photo © Ronald Wainscott.

NORMAN BEL GEDDES'S rendering of the New York production of *The Miracle,* staged by Max Reinhardt in 1924. Bel Geddes and Reinhardt transformed the Century Theatre, the largest at the time in New York, to an apparent cathedral. This must be one of the earliest American renovations of a theatre for a single production. The image appeared in the 1924 souvenir program for the production.

Collection of the authors.

More environmental in its approach was the first professional revival in 1974 of Leonard Bernstein's musical *Candide* with a new book by Hugh Wheeler, as directed by Harold Prince and designed by Eugene and Franne Lee. For the Broadway production in a traditional proscenium theatre, the orchestra seats were torn out so that ramps and platforms for the actors could meander all around the stools used to seat the audience. These audience members had to look in all directions to be able to see the action. More traditional audience seating, which produced a "safer," if more removed, viewpoint, was positioned around the central "environmental" area. The audience members in this traditional area looked down on the dramatic action and were free to observe the intermingling of audience and performers in the orchestra. The production created two very different experiences for the audience members depending on where they were seated: environmental for those in the orchestra and more passive, traditional viewing for those in the surrounding seats.

Experimenting with Space

Sometimes playwrights call for radically different approaches to space in their scripts. Maria Irene Fornes often experiments with space in the plays she writes and directs. In *Fefu and Her Friends* (1977) Fornes calls for five different settings in and around the house of the major character, Fefu. Five settings would not be unusual except that the playwright doesn't want five sets changing in the same space; she wants five different spaces to which the audience must move to witness the action. All the audience is together to watch the first scene in Fefu's living room; then the audience is divided into four groups who see four different scenes simultaneously but in a different order. For example, one-quarter of the audience visits the study for scene 2, but another quarter goes to the kitchen, another to the lawn, and the fourth to a bedroom. The audience keeps shifting until each group has seen all four scenes in the four spaces, then all return to the living room to view the final scene, reunited. Naturally, the production's eight actresses must perform the four middle scenes four times in a row, and all these scenes are approximately the same length. The point of this approach is not only to surprise the audience members by moving them around but also to demonstrate the effects of different spaces on how people behave, talk, and respond. When this play is produced in a traditional theatre, the production team has to choose and convert rooms that are not usually intended for performance—dressing rooms, lobby areas, prop rooms, classrooms, rehearsal studios, hallways—to achieve the number of different settings called for by the playwright.

Stage Directions

Most actors, directors, and designers use a standardized set of terms to talk about space and the use of space with a common understanding. These terms were created for proscenium stages and are based on the assumption that the audience is positioned on one side of the performance space or stage. The stage area closest to the audience is known as **downstage,** and the area farthest from the audience is called **upstage.** These terms derive from early proscenium stages that were raked—elevated much higher at the back of the stage than closer to the audience. In other words, the stage floor sloped down as the actor moved toward the audience.

Today, if an actor moves upstage of another actor or object on stage, he is moving **above** the chair or actor. If an actress moves downstage of another actor or object on stage, she is moving **below** the table or actor. All **stage left** and **stage right** directions and movements are given in terms of the actors' left and right *as they face the audience;* the space in the middle of the stage is **center.** Various combinations of these terms are used to describe different portions of the stage, such as down center, up right, down left (see Figure 2.8). A movement of any length is usually called a **cross.** Therefore, the actress playing a betrayed wife (A) crosses from center to down left below a chair to the table where she picks up a pistol, turns right and steps toward the staggering actor playing her angry, drunken husband (B) upstage right, levels the pistol, and aims it at her adversary (see Figure 2.9). When making notes in a script, most actors, stage managers, and directors use the letter X to indicate a cross, so a cross to down right would read XDR.

FIGURE 2.8 Stage Areas

C = Center
UC = Up center
DC = Down center
UR = Up right
SR = Stage right
DR = Down right
UL = Up left
SL = Stage left
DL = Down left

Some actors and directors add intermediate locations such as DRC, LC, and URC.

FIGURE 2.9 Diagram Showing Actor Movement

Some directors, designers, and actors use standard stage terms in an arena space by simply designating one side as downstage, but many artists have developed other systems, such as dividing the space into a clock face. For example, an actress might now move from center to a position at five o'clock to confront the villain waiting at eleven o'clock (see Figure 2.10).

Stage directions, physical descriptions in a play, are frequently about location and movement in space. In the late nineteenth century William Gillette was a successful playwright, actor, and director who created very detailed stage directions that leave little to the imagination in terms of movement, placement, stage business, and sometimes emotionality. The following stage directions from Gillette's thriller *Secret Service* (1896) describe the action when the hero Thorne, a Union spy during the Civil War, is seized by Confederate soldiers as he attempts to telegraph an unauthorized message. The spoken dialogue is delivered by General Randolph, who suspects Thorne of treachery:

> Hold that machine there! (*pointing at telegraph instrument. Sergeant and two men spring quickly across to right; Sergeant rushes against Thorne with arm across his breast forcing him over to right against chair and table on right—chair a little away from table to emphasize with crash as Thorne is flung against it—and holds him there. The two men cross bayonets over instrument and stand motionless. All done quickly, business-like and with as little disturbance as possible. General Randolph strides down center and speaks across to Thorne.*) I'll have you court-martialed for this![2]

THEATRE AND TRANSFORMATION

Although actors could perform for themselves alone without any intended audience, as an act of theatre the process would be incomplete. To have theatre, collaboration of artists and audience is both an opportunity and a necessity. Because the audience changes with each performance, the nature of its responses and collaboration is different each time. In the process of this interaction in a specific place, transformation occurs on many levels.

FIGURE 2.10 Use of Clock Face for Stage Areas in an Arena Stage

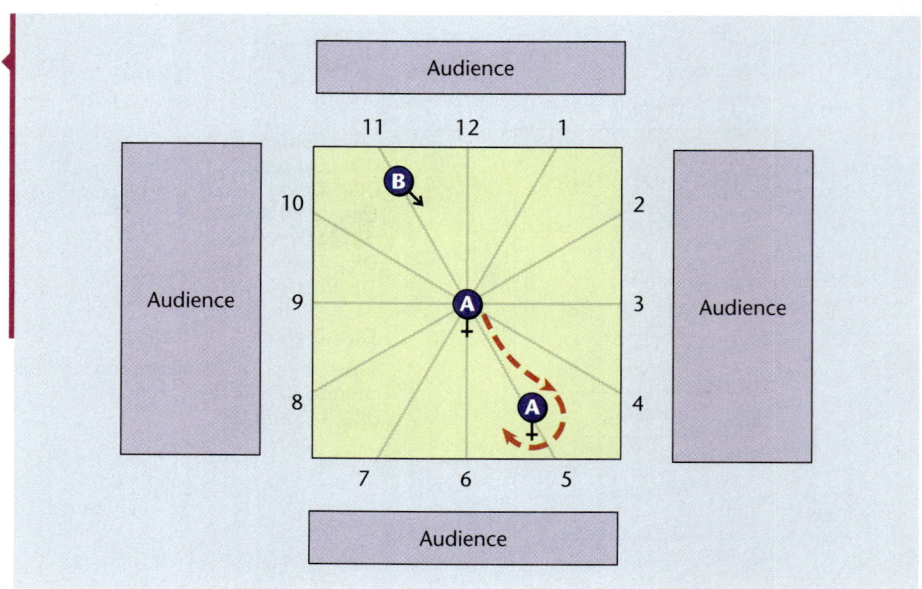

The Performing Garage

A converted garage on Wooster Street in the Soho district of New York City is a good example of a found space that was converted to a theatrical one. Founded in 1967 and directed by Richard Schechner (b. 1934), the Performance Group was inspired by the environmental work of Polish director and theorist Jerzy Growtowski (1933–1999) and the political activism of the Living Theatre, New York's most famous experimental company of the 1960s. Schechner, who wrote the definitive book on environmental theatre, and his company transformed the garage, using scaffolding and platforms to accommodate an audience that was mixed rather freely with the actors in both space and the action for each performance. Perhaps their most memorable production was the ritualistic *Dionysus in 69* (1968), which was based on Euripides' Greek tragedy *The Bacchae.* The audience entered a large space with wooden towers and platforms and could sit on either the floor, platforms, or towers. Actors were at first dispersed throughout the room but then began to congregate in groups. As performers moved through the space, they sometimes touched or spoke directly to the audience members.

COMMUNE (1970–1972), presented by the Performance Group and directed by Richard Schechner at the Performing Garage in New York. Note the audience scattered about on all levels. The performers would move among and perform with the audience members, who were also invited and coaxed to move into other parts of the performance space.

Photo by Frederick Eberstadt, courtesy of Richard Schechner. First appeared in Schechner's *Environmental Theater* (1973).

After the breakup of the Performance Group about 1980, several members, including Elizabeth LeCompte (b. 1944), Spalding Gray (1941–2004), and Willem Dafoe (b. 1955), reorganized as the Wooster Group, another experimental company that continued to use the Performing Garage. The group now describes its theatre as a flexible black box. The political and nontraditional Wooster Group has used this space in a variety of intriguing ways featuring unusual interpretations and deconstructions of famous plays. A deconstructed production begins with a well-known play, but as a pretext for a conception that is dramatized commentary on either the play itself or the values inherent in the original play. The Wooster Group created fascinating deconstructions or new conceptions of many well-known plays, such as *The Hairy Ape* (Wooster Group project, 1995), *The Emperor Jones* by Eugene O'Neill (Wooster Group project, 1993), and Arthur Miller's *The Crucible,* rechristened *L.S.D. (...Just the High Points...)* (1984). In 2007 the company created a multimedia *Hamlet,* which is performed simultaneously with the 1964 Richard Burton film version, and in 2011 opened a reconceived complex production of *Vieux Carre* by Tennessee Williams that endeavors to climb into the mind and artistic world of the playwright's developing aesthetic.

INTERESTED? Check out

Richard Schechner. *Environmental Theatre.* New York: Hawthorn, 1973.

David Savran. *Breaking the Rules: The Wooster Group, 1975–1985.* New York: Theatre Communications Group, 1988.

The Wooster Group website at www.thewoostergroup.org.

The space, for a time, is transformed through mutual agreement to a fictional world. The people watching and listening are no longer just individuals but form the collective whole of the audience. The experience of trying on a new identity for even a short time may have a transformative effect on the actor. The engagement of all who come together opens the possibility for change: in thought, attitude, feeling, and perspective.

The mythical story of the origin of the performing arts in Japan embodies both the importance of collaboration and the theatre's transformative power. The ancient gods were squabbling one day. The sun goddess Amaterasu got angry and hid in a cave, depriving the world of light and warmth. A goddess named Uzume impulsively attempted to entice Amaterasu to come out. In her emotional distress she began to move rhythmically—the creation of dance. Although Uzume's performance was intended for an audience of one, the other gods and goddesses responded approvingly to her efforts. Out of curiosity, and especially intrigued by the reaction of the larger audience, the sun goddess came out of the cave, only to be enchanted by Uzume's performance. Consequently, the birth of the performing arts arose from emotional distress, found and engaged an audience, and brought light back to a dark world.

SHOCKHEADED PETER: A JUNK OPERA. This bizarre 1999 production melded bloody folk tales and music with dynamic imagery and staging to engage a contemporary audience. This musical entertainment was created by a host of collaborators headed by Julian Bleach.

Photo © Joan Marcus.

CHAPTER REVIEW

Questions and Activities

1. Identify a play, film, or television show that led you to experience catharsis. Why do you think this experience was so emotionally intense for you? Consider both elements within the production and what you brought to the experience mentally and physically.

2. Identify plays, films, or television shows in which actors address the audience directly. What do you think this device added to the experience?

3. Identify an event other than theatre in your culture that sanctions obvious pretending or role playing. Does this event require costuming or assuming a distinct persona? Why is this event attractive to the people who participate?

4. Discuss effects that different spaces have on television viewing, movie viewing, or sports events. For example, how is watching television in a student lounge different from watching it in your family living room? Are there different types of programs that you would prefer to watch in different spaces? In what kind of

theatre space would you prefer to see a comedy? A tragedy? A large-cast musical? A two-character play?

5. Make a list of the various types of spaces where performances took place that members of your class attended (or heard about). What are some other places on your campus or in your city or town that might be interesting to use for performance? What sort of an atmosphere would each site offer?

6. Learn to give and take stage directions by practicing in a small group. Clear as large a space in a room as possible. Refer to the diagram of stage areas (Figure 2.8) and relate it to the space you have. Take turns moving each other around the space by using the appropriate terms. For example, one person gives the following directions to three other people:

To Person 1: "Begin at center, cross down right, and stand facing downstage."

To Person 2: "Enter up left, cross down right to center, and turn left."

To Person 3: "Enter from up left, cross below person 2, and stand down left facing person 1."

7. Visit an established theatrical space on your campus or in your city or town and take a tour if possible. Identify the type of space. Describe the actor/audience relationship and the feel of the theatre. How does this atmosphere change when it is full of people? Identify the different areas on stage and in the house (wings, apron, orchestra, thrust stage, façade, vomitories, etc.). Stand on stage in various positions and see what the house looks like from the actor's point of view. Practice giving and taking stage directions while on the stage (see question 6).

Key Terms and Concepts

empathy, p. 27
aesthetic distance, p. 27
catharsis, p. 30
Epic Theatre, p. 33
hypokrites, p. 33
mimesis, p. 33
improvisation, p. 34
play or script, p. 34
production, p. 34
playwright, p. 35
producer, p. 35
director, p. 35
casting director, p. 35
scenic designer, p. 35
costume designer, p. 35
lighting designer, p. 35
sound designer, p. 35
makeup designer, p. 35

composer, p. 35
lyricist, p. 35
music director, p. 35
choreographer, p. 35
stage manager, p. 35
front-of-house, p. 35
house manager, p. 35
box office manager, p. 35
proscenium space, p. 37
proscenium arch, p. 37
apron, p. 37
wings, p. 38
grand drape, p. 38
house, p. 38
orchestra, p. 38
orchestra pit, p. 39
raked, p. 39
box, p. 39

gallery, p. 39
thrust space, p. 40
façade, p. 41
vomitory, p. 41
booth stage, p. 42
arena space, p. 43
black box, p. 44
found space, p. 44
site-specific performance, p. 44
environmental theatre, p. 45
downstage, p. 47
upstage, p. 47
above, p. 47
below, p. 47
stage left, p. 47
stage right, p. 47
center, p. 47
cross, p. 47

For Further Exploration

Daniel Gerould, ed. *Theatre/Theory/Theatre: The Major Critical Texts from Aristotle and Zeami to Soyinka and Havel.* New York: Applause, 2003. David Krasner. *Theatre in Theory 1900–2000.* Malden, MA: Wiley-Blackwell, 2007. For a sampling of ideas about what theatre is and should be.

"Aristotle" in the *Perseus Digital Library,* www.perseus.tufts.edu.

"Background to Noh-Kyogen," www.nohkyogen.jp/english/english01.html. For more information about Noh and its related comic form, Kyogen.

John Harrop and Sabin R. Epstein, *Acting with Style,* 3rd ed. Boston: Allyn and Bacon, 2000. For more on acting in the production process.

Richard Leacroft and Helen Leacroft, *Theatre and Playhouse.* London: Methuen, 1984. For more detail on the history of theatre architecture.

W. Oren Parker, R. Craig Wolf, and Dick Block, *Scene Design and Stage Lighting,* 9th ed. Belmont, CA: Wadsworth, 2008. For information on the design and technical aspects of production.

TWO MEN OF FLORENCE (2009) by Richard N. Goodwin, Huntington Theatre.
Photo © T. Charles Erickson.

Analyzing Theatre

Thinking and Writing about Live Performance

Audiences in the twenty-first century are used to watching actors perform on film, television, DVD, or the Internet. The experience of theatre is different in many ways. An audience member could certainly attend the theatre with no preparation and have a wonderful time, but understanding certain concepts will make the experience fuller and richer. In this chapter we explore how to be an effective collaborator from the house. We discuss ways in which theatre differs from television and film, ways to look and listen to enhance the theatre experience, and how to analyze and evaluate performance, including an exploration of the role of the critic in the theatre and special considerations for writing about theatre.

THEATRE, FILM, AND TELEVISION

Periodically, viewers turn on their TV and hear that the program they are about to watch is "Live from New York . . . it's *Saturday Night!*" Such programs are recorded in front of an audience in a theatre or studio, and at home the viewers may be witnessing the events as they occur, although often by delay. A portion of the unexpected nature of live performance is recaptured. Of course, viewers realize that the "live" event they are witnessing is very limited because the viewers do not see nearly as much as the on-site audience sees.

Active Participation

Even a "live" broadcast does not require the kind of **active participation** that is necessary in the theatre. Watching live theatre tends to take more concentration than watching film or TV does. Even attending the theatre requires effort; you must be in a certain place at a certain time. You can't pause the performance when you feel like it; on the other hand, your viewing is less likely to be interrupted by events (a telephone call, a doorbell, a conversation in the room). In film and TV the cameras and the director who picks the camera shots are highly selective. They make the choices for the viewers. In the theatre you choose what to watch—the actor at the side of the stage playing with his hair, the flickering stage light, or the leading lady delivering a speech at center stage. Theatre practitioners try to direct your attention with movement, actor positioning, and lighting, but ultimately, the choice is yours.

TV and film images reduce the three-dimensional actor or object to two dimensions (the image is flat). The visual scale of filmed or digital images is also very different from that of live performance. Most TV images are much smaller than live performance; film images can be much larger. Theatre does not allow for a close-up shot (unless the close-up is projected on a two-dimensional screen for the audience, in which case the event is multimedia). Where you are seated in the theatre can make a difference in how you experience performance. If you are far away from the actors, it may take more energy to keep your attention focused on the stage.

Many people find that the tradeoff for more effort expended in watching theatre is an increased intensity of experience. Audience reception of film and television is typically passive (even when the entertainment is enjoyable). In the theatre, choosing to participate—taking charge of the viewing experience and listening with special attention—creates a more vivid communication event. Part of this excitement is generated by the possibility for two-way communication. In film and most television there is no shared space for the viewers and performance, so any viewer response goes unseen and unheard by the actors. In the theatre, however, actors are very aware of the presence of the audience, and the actors' performances are in turn affected by the messages they receive: laughs, gasps, silence, even rustling of programs, all communicate to the actors and in turn affect their communication on the stage.

With that two-way communication comes a certain responsibility. The people on stage are human beings; respectful and courteous treatment is important. So much entertainment is brought into our living rooms that it is easy to forget (even in the movie

AN AUDIENCE FOR JAPANESE KABUKI, with the use of two entrance ramps called *hanamichi,* which extend from the proscenium stage to the back of the house. Because the actors perform in the midst of the audience, a level of audience participation is invited, which enhances the nature of live performance and even divides the audience's visual focus.

Photo by Chiaki Yoshida. From *Kabuki* by Masakatsu Gunji (1969).

theatre) that talking, ringing cell phones, and beeping pagers disturb other audience members. In the theatre they are even more distracting to the performers on the stage.

The Nature of Live Performance

There are drawbacks to live performance. Mistakes cannot be edited as in film or television; there is less quality control. A wonderful performance cannot be saved; even a video of a theatrical performance represents only a limited record of what happened from one point of view. You can't watch a favorite live performance again and again.

But there is also a special attraction to being "live." Although mistakes can and do occur, part of the theatre's excitement is never knowing exactly what will happen next and perhaps even seeing how performers will deal with the occasional glitch. A very special performance cannot be saved, but that very fact makes the theatre intriguing. Performance is a one-time-only event—one that you have helped to create by your presence—that will never happen in exactly the same way again.

The unique conditions of live performance differentiate it from all other methods of receiving a play. A student's understanding of Henrik Ibsen's *A Doll House* performed in a university theatre must differ from the response from reading a copy of the play *A Doll House* in the library, watching a film of the play starring Claire Bloom and Anthony Hopkins in a movie theatre, or watching a DVD of the play starring Juliet Stevenson and Trevor Eve on a TV screen in a classroom. Even if the translated text of the dialogue were the same, and in performance even if the actors were the same and the director and designers the same, each would be a different *Doll House* because the audience's relationship with the performance or reading would differ markedly with each. The scale and feedback opportunities would radically differ, and audiences respond differently to various kinds of spaces. Consequently, the reception must differ as well.

A DOLL HOUSE, first Norwegian production in 1880. Notice the box set with ceiling piece and chandelier, the Christmas tree upstage, and multiple entrances, all intended to suggest a real domestic interior in the Christmas season. Nora is seen here rehearsing her tarantella dance, which she deliberately does badly in order to get her husband to help her to avoid reading the letter in his mailbox, which will reveal her forgery.

By permission of Universitetsbiblioteket, Oslo.

ANALYZING PRODUCTION

When in the theatre, it is important to be as open as possible—to take in or soak up the immediate sensory experience. At some point, however, you will probably want to analyze the event: What just happened? How did it happen? What was its effect on me? With those questions, you will begin an analysis of the performance event. Your analysis can be as simple as thinking about the performance in the car going home or talking to friends about the experience over coffee. It can be as structured as an organized paper with clear assertions and strong support.

In the minds of most audience members, reception is followed by understanding, which usually includes "the meaning" of what they are experiencing. The meaning of a play or a moment in the play can become something quite different for each audience member. Many theorists of theatre assert that meaning is fluid, based on frame of reference—the previous experiences and cultural context of individual audience members—and the intentions and skills of the actors delivering the dramatic material. Most audience members will assign or assume meaning to what they experience. Although there may be many possible meanings for what is communicated from the performance space, these meanings are authentic for individual spectators. The playwright's, actors', or director's intent might not match the interpretation reached by the audience member. This disparity does not signify failure, but the inevitable outcome of any communication or performance system that is addressing or entertaining an audience. The performance (especially including audience response and feedback) has its own unique life each time it occurs.[1]

In analyzing production, it is helpful to make a distinction between observation and interpretation. **Observation** is your recognition of what actually happened on stage: The actress playing Carol sat down heavily in the chair and held her head in her hands. A photograph or video could verify your observation. **Interpretation** is your intuitive response, your subjective experience of what the physical action communicated: Carol is depressed, sad, or exhausted. Although you and your neighbor might agree on your observation (though, of course, people may even recall things differently), you could very well have different interpretations of the behavior.

THINKING ABOUT ACTOR PERFORMANCES

In the theatre most audience responses and interpretations begin with characters and the actors who play them. Audiences are capable of believing some remarkable and impossible things when these are presented effectively on the stage. They can believe that Peter Pan flies and that Ebenezer Scrooge travels through time, space, and dreams with the ghosts of Christmas Past, Present, and Future; audiences can believe that ambushed soldiers are being strafed in a Vietnam firefight in *Tracers* (1983), that an invisible orchestra is accompanying the cowboy Curley who opens *Oklahoma!* (1943) singing "Oh, What a Beautiful Morning." As playwright Eugene O'Neill liked to tell his directors when preparing for production, audiences will believe anything if you do it well. This assertion might be overstating the case, but it is clear that excellent execution goes a long way in helping us to accept the impossible. It doesn't matter whether the play is realistic or stylized and whether it is comic, tragic, or melodramatic. The audience can suspend disbelief and accept that character as genuine, at least for the moment of performance.

If we believe an actor's interpretation of a character (even as a cat or dog), then we accept that character as existing truthfully in the theatrical world as dramatized by the production. Caryl Churchill's *Mad Forest* (1990) has a wonderfully imaginative and poignant scene between a talking dog and a vampire (but with no dog suit or vampire cape for the actors). At first the vampire tries to ignore the starving dog, which is frightened of but fascinated by the vampire. Eventually, the dog's loneliness and desperation convince the vampire to make him into one of the undead—a vampire dog. This scene is symbolic of the awful exploitation and power struggles in Romania (where the action takes place), but while the scene is playing, audiences focus on the very personal encounter of these two impossible creatures. The action comes first in creating audience response. Symbolism comes later.

MAD FOREST by Caryl Churchill. The dog (left) encounters the vampire (right). Produced at the University of Nebraska. Photo © Ronald Wainscott.

Believability

What enables the audience to accept the authenticity—or **believability**—of a character? The key might lie in beautifully written dialogue, or it could be the actor's delivery of the dialogue. Much of what is identified as character is created first by a playwright, but the actor completes the creative process and provides the key to audience belief or lack thereof. Perhaps the actor creates the illusion that the words are being delivered for the first time; the delivery of a lesser actor might sound memorized. If an actor's vocal delivery cannot be understood because of volume or articulation problems, it hardly matters how well a line is written. A fine performance by an accomplished stage and film actor such as Philip Seymour Hoffman or Meryl Streep of a weakly drawn character is not much more than an exhibition of the actor's skills. More disheartening to watch are weak performances by unprepared actors of remarkably crafted characters such as Blanche DuBois—a neurotic and sensitive woman on the verge of emotional collapse in *A Streetcar Named Desire*—or Iago, a plotting, intelligent villain trusted by all around him in *Othello*.

In thinking about how and why a production works, it is important to try to separate the character as written from the actor's performance. People often admiringly quote funny or incisive lines delivered by favorite actors in films, TV, or plays. These lines are frequently credited in the imitator's mind to the actor rather than the character. Many people tend to identify the actor so closely with the character played that objectivity is lost. People sitting at a lunch table or walking across campus might quote Tom Cruise, Judi Dench, Denzel Washington, or Cate Blanchett, or even sketchily drawn characters in commercials or animated figures such as Homer Simpson, but viewers are actually quoting writers in most cases. The personality, charisma, or vocal delivery of the actor, however, is likely to be much of what draws the imitator to repeat the dramatic or comic moment out of context.

Actor Choices

One way to isolate an actor's contribution to character is to think in terms of **actor choices.** An actor's approach to movement, for example, may be significant. Is the actor setting an appropriate tempo for the character when crossing the stage or gesturing? Is the actor leading with an appropriate part of the body—for example, does movement seem to come first from the head, chest, or pelvis? Just these choices make a remarkable difference in the quality of the movement. Do the actor's movements seem appropriate to the character's age, profession, and social background and to the nature of the dramatic moment? Does the actor's physical bearing seem consistent with the words being spoken? Does the vocal quality seem appropriate for the character? These choices may be more apparent if you see an actor perform several different characters.

An emotional life can be identified for nearly every character on the stage. Many characters are frequently given to raucous laughter or perpetual sadness. The jovial Mr. Fezziwig in stage adaptations of Charles Dickens's *A Christmas Carol* never seems to stop chuckling. Anton Chekhov's plays are filled with people who cry at the drop of a hat; Masha in Chekhov's *The Sea Gull* explains that she always wears black because she is mourning for her life. A character's depression (such as that of most of the protagonists in Woody Allen's films and plays) may make audiences laugh, or a character's inappropriate or obnoxious laughter may irritate or anger the audience. Emotionality affects audience belief, but it is also crucial to the dramatic development of a play. Suzan-Lori Parks's plays often have characters who repeatedly exhibit threatening anger. The two brothers who love each other in *Topdog/Underdog* (2001), for example, make scathing remarks to one another.

Although a character's words may define or set the tone for emotionality, non-verbal behavior usually underscores, enhances, or even contradicts the spoken dialogue. Actors and directors make choices for character portrayal and experiment during rehearsal. The audience sees only the ultimate choice. An audience member's response to a character's behavior depends on the circumstances surrounding that behavior and

HEDDA GABLER by Henrik Ibsen as a 2006 highly physical adaptation by Peter Langdon produced at the Betty Nansen Teatret in Copenhagen, Denmark. Sonja Richter as Hedda and Shanti Roney as Lovborg. Here the figurative symbolism of Hedda's pistols becomes quite literal, visceral, and contemporary. In this scene Hedda suggests to Lovborg that he should end his life "beautifully."
Photo by Thomas Petri.

what the audience is able to infer from the actor's facial expressions, body language, and tone of voice. If a character named Sue with difficulty declares her love for a character named Bill and Bill laughs at her, an audience will possibly feel sorry for Sue and angry with Bill. On the other hand, if Sue is constantly belittling and chastening Bill, an audience will possibly be glad that Bill finally gets his revenge. Then again, perhaps the audience suspects that Bill also loves Sue but is very insecure and doesn't believe Sue and so chooses to treat Sue's declaration as a joke out of self-defense. Many questions could be asked of such a scene: What was the nature of Bill's laughter? Did the actors' choices for physical communication match the words and sounds? What were the actors trying to communicate beyond obvious words and gestures?

Character Interaction

Unless the audience is watching a one-person show, it is observing actors collaborating with other actors. Working together as a team, called **ensemble** work in the theatre, is often crucial to the success of a scene. The actors should really seem to be listening to one another and reacting to one another. Dynamic and appropriate character reaction and then, in turn, the creation of new action are critical to the dramatic process. The interaction of actors as characters must be both logical and interesting to watch. An unengaged actor might appear to be waiting for his or her next opportunity to speak. Sometimes an audience sees onstage a collection of individual performances that seem virtually independent of one another. When this situation occurs, the audience is not likely to accept the world of the play as authentic.

When the actors are responding to what other actors are offering, however, the audience gets a sense of spontaneity no matter how well rehearsed the action might be. William Gillette, a popular actor at the turn of the twentieth century, was fond of describing "the illusion of the first time."[2] He strove to make the audience accept that his words had never been spoken before, that his actions were invented at that moment in response to what had immediately preceded. Of course, he rehearsed tirelessly, but his secret for success lay in that illusion of spontaneity.

THINKING ABOUT SPACE AND DESIGN

The theatrical space demands a way of looking that is not typical in everyday life. Most of what people see around them is very familiar and repetitious: their home and the routine of work or school or recreation. In a classroom, for example, students focus on an instructor or discussion group, a chalkboard or projection screen, or they simply gaze out a window daydreaming of being elsewhere. Several choices are made for the students by a professor, and students might or might not cooperate with those choices. But students seldom pay attention to the variety of details around them.

If the students or professor go to a theatre, however, and see a stage set of a classroom, they are likely to notice many details that they could ignore in their own classroom. The audience might scan the stage setting, seeking to authenticate or dispute the choices made by designer and director. Do the details seem true to previous experience? Even if most of the setting seems true to life, is there a detail or set piece that seems out of place or odd? If so, this discrepancy could be deliberate on the part of the production team or the playwright to call the audience's attention to the unusual detail. Suppose, for example, that the set seems exacting except for the fact that it has no doorway, no windows, and no entrance of any kind. The absence might seem like a mistake. Or perhaps the lack of an exit makes the characters appear to be trapped (no way in or out), which can begin to create discomfort in the audience members.

As with choices made by the actor, elements of space and design will be interpreted according to the surrounding action. If the scene escalates emotionally and it slowly becomes evident that the student characters are being terrorized by a cruel and rigid teacher, the set with no means of escape might help to create a sense of paranoia and confinement. It then becomes a symbol of unenlightened education driven by torture and inflexibility. Certain plays, such as *The Lesson* (1951) by Eugène Ionesco, deal with this very theme. In this play a professor is tutoring a single student. As the play progresses, the professor becomes increasingly oppressive, ultimately dehumanizing the student and killing her.

Seeing in Three Dimensions

Of course, nearly all people see—or think they see—real events in three dimensions. Unlike watching an image on a screen, at a live performance the audience must negotiate three-dimensionality with all of its possibilities for depth and multiple focus. Although most audiences do not consciously think of stage space in terms of its depth, they usually notice if a sense of depth is absent or if the use of depth is especially striking. For example, it is not often in a performance that an audience sees furniture or actors lined up straight across the stage. Such an arrangement would call attention to itself and would strike the audience either as amateurish, as a very formal moment in the action, or as the preparation for a chorus line. As a stage director, Ingmar Bergman (1918–2007) often used depth in significant ways. For example, he placed actors in nearly the same upstage/downstage plane but very far apart. In live performance this arrangement would create a very different image for an audience member sitting in the center of the house than it would for a spectator sitting far to the right or left. Visually, the impact of different seat locations can be almost like viewing different productions.

When examining the performance in space, it can be instructive to consider **space and design choices.** What are the director and designers attempting to get the audience to see? Where do they want the audience to look and why? What is the spatial relationship of the actors to each other and to the set?

'TIS PITY SHE'S A WHORE (1633) by John Ford produced by the American Conservatory Theater in 2008. The three-dimensional nature of the stage is accentuated by multiple levels and considerable depth as the forbidden love scene of sister and brother (played by René Augesen and Michael Hayden) takes place on a bed while a cellist plays high above and upstage of them. The depth is also reinforced by the hanging illuminated tubes and the catwalk construction. Scenic design by Walt Spangler. Lighting design by Robert Wierzel. Costume design by Candice Donnelly. Directed by Carey Perloff.
Photo © Kevin Berne.

Examining Scenery

It is no surprise that much of what an audience sees on a stage in performance isn't really what it seems to be. Walls are rarely solid and most often are made of stretched canvas or other lightweight materials so that they can be easily shifted or transported. The audience might see a wall shaking a bit when a door slams on stage. Detail that seems three-dimensional is often painted or enhanced by paint and light. The unseen portions of the scenery are unfinished—only what we see in the playing space matters. The actors in performance often see unfinished scenery, but the audience does not. An audience member knows that the scenery is fake but is prepared to believe in its reality within the world of the play.

There are two basic approaches to creating this world on stage. If the scenery is **representational,** it is crafted realistically to look and function just as the scenic location would in the real world, whether interior or exterior. The audience often wants to believe in that scenery just as it wants to believe in the actors' performances. If the scenery is **presentational,** it is not meant to resemble everyday life; it may be stylized, abstracted, or suggestive scenery. For presentational scenery, authentic appearance is not important, but the scenery should be interesting and functional. When scenery does not perform as intended, belief in the entire fictional world can be destroyed. In 1917 in the Broadway production of *Peter Ibbetson,* the actor John Barrymore was escorting the actress Constance Collier through a large scenic opera house during a moment of majestic, romantic spectacle. Unexpectedly, the scenery gave way and toppled to the floor in a cloud of dust and debris amid shrieks and curses from the startled actors. Fortunately, the actors were unhurt, but all the expectations for a beautiful illusion were spoiled, to say the least. A planned stage composition was destroyed, and it must have been difficult to recapture the tone of the play after such a disaster.

Most of the time, of course, audiences do not witness such failure, but audience members can still ask themselves, "Does the scenery seem appropriate for the action as it is played? Is the scenery consistent with the style of the play? Is the scenery attempting to suggest a specific historical period? Is the scenery an expression of a completely imaginary location? Is the presentational scenery so highly stylized that it does not suggest any locale but a mood perhaps? Does there seem to be too much or too little scenery for the action of the play? Does the performance seem overwhelmed by the scenery (critics and artists sometimes talk about overdesigned productions or a 'trial

TANGO by Slawomir Mrozek. In this production we focus on a corpse on the stage floor as two men upstage, one of whom is the murderer, dance to tango music. Produced at Towson State University.

Collection of the authors.

THE CHERRY ORCHARD by Anton Chekhov. The original representational production at the Moscow Art Theatre. The famous actor-director Konstantin Stanislavsky, as the character Gaev, addresses the bookcase in this scene. Notice the prompter's box downstage center.

Courtesy of Billy Rose Theatre Collection, the New York Public Library for the Performing Arts, Astor, Lennox and Tilden Foundations.

THE CHERRY ORCHARD by Anton Chekhov. Contrast this 1977 presentational revival, with the original. The costumes are not updated, but all of the walls are missing, and the action takes place in an open white space as if the cherry orchard and the house of the estate occupy a single space. Some of the trees of the soon-to-be sold and destroyed orchard are always present. Directed by Andrei Serban and designed by Santo Loquasto for the New York Shakespeare Festival at Lincoln Center.

Courtesy of Billy Rose Theatre Collection, the New York Public Library for the Performing Arts, Astor, Lennox and Tilden Foundations.

by scenery'). If the scenery seems appropriate to or effective for the performance, what makes it so? What seems to be the intent of this scenery?"

Imagine watching a production of a tragedy about kings set centuries ago, such as *Richard II* by Shakespeare. The stage floor is painted like a chessboard, and decorations onstage suggest chess pieces and various game imagery. When the actors enter, they are all dressed in either black or white, as if they are game pieces themselves. Such a scheme is more than a little obvious, but the heavy-handed point is likely to make itself evident very quickly, perhaps leading you to think of the entire play in terms of gamesmanship, which is probably what the director and designers wanted you to consider when seeing this play. In most cases scenic messages will be much more subtle.

Set properties (usually large additions to the setting such as furniture) also become part of the scenery. Chairs, for example, are frequently recurring set props, and they often blend in with the surroundings. At times, however, they take focus and communicate meaning. We see many, many chairs in the aptly entitled French play *The Chairs* (1952) by Eugène Ionesco. The playwright calls for the actors to steadily fill the space with chairs that remain empty throughout the performance. This presence and absence is part of the point of the play, in which the aging characters anticipate a great moment that never comes. On the other hand, a 1982 modern-dress British production of *Bérénice* (1670) by Jean Racine placed a single imposing chair on stage and no other furniture. Not only did the chair catch the attention of the audience, it also became a focus of tension because no actor ever sat in it or used it until the play was nearly over.

CURSE OF THE STARVING CLASS by Sam Shepard in a 2008 production directed by Peter DuBois at the American Conservatory Theater in San Francisco. This prop-heavy play explores the plight of a struggling, dysfunctional family. The center of their obsession is the refrigerator, which here is being plundered by the mother, played by Pamela Reed, while her son, portrayed by Jud Williford, looks on. Artichokes are flung all over the stage.
Photo © Kevin Berne.

Once the actress playing the title role finally sat in the chair, the action carried dramatic weight because the tension was finally released.

After viewing a performance, you could ask yourself, "Are the set props merely sittable/standable units that are meant to indicate place and provide conversational units for the actors, or do they contribute more? Are the set properties communicating thought or symbolism?"

Examining Costumes

It is easy to take costumes for granted and associate the choices strictly with the character being observed, almost as if the character were a real person who pulled these clothes out of the closet that morning. Audiences are sometimes stunned or surprised if the costumes are particularly attractive or detailed or are dismayed if they seem inappropriate to character or to the period in which the play or its production is set. But all costumes are a product of specific choices made by the costume designer and director.

Costumes can be important to locating the play in space and time. Most audience members have an idea of dress in famous periods such as Imperial Rome, Elizabethan England, or "Roaring Twenties" New York, and often recognize the period or location simply by costumes. In many productions, however, the play has been shifted in time or place, or perhaps historical periods are combined or even invented, as often happens in

EXPLORING Historical and Cultural Perspectives

The Effect of Audience Space on Angels in America

Space has a profound effect on an audience member's experience of production. It is not only a question of being able to hear or see better. The relationship of an audience member's position to the performance area can affect the level of emotional involvement with the action. A good illustration of this dynamic is our experience with Tony Kushner's *Angels in America: A Gay Fantasia on National Themes* (1993–94).

Two plays make up *Angels in America: Millennium Approaches* and *Perestroika.* Together they explore the impact of AIDS on the gay community as well as the personal struggles of several gay men with religious backgrounds that are intolerant of their choices, family disapproval, and the underground nature of alternative lifestyles in conflict with modern marriage and the workplace. Real, fictional, and fantasy characters appear in the plays, and they present both representational and presentational scenes in settings ranging from park benches to offices and living rooms, from public restrooms to heaven. An angelic visitation to the bedroom of a dying AIDS victim is contrasted with the fantasy action on an arctic ice floe.

When we saw the Broadway production of *Angels in America,* we saw both plays, *Millennium Approaches* and *Perestroika,* on the same day (one at a matinee and the other in the evening). For *Millennium Approaches* we sat in the front row and felt as though we were virtually thrust into the action, which seemed very immediate and vital. In the evening, however, we sat about halfway back in the orchestra and felt somewhat isolated, as if the play's emotional import had difficulty reaching us there. On the other hand, the staging, images, and artistic composition of the production were

ANGELS IN AMERICA by Tony Kushner. Produced by Indiana University, Directed by Jane Page in 2011.
Photo by Indiana University PhotoGraphics.

much easier to comprehend with distance. In retrospect we were much more excited about *Millennium Approaches* and more objective about *Perestroika.*

works of fantasy or plays set in the future. In this case audiences are completely free to accept or reject the designer's vision of how things might look in Los Angeles in 2534.

Perhaps the most effective assessment an audience member can make of costumes is appropriateness to character. Questions might be raised about appropriate color and texture, the costume's relationship to the costumes of other characters in the play, or the character's social position, economic status, occupation, age, and gender. Of course, many designers hope that the audience will not leave the show thinking about the costumes or lighting or the sound or settings, but will simply accept the designs as authentic manifestations of the world of the play as interpreted by the production team.

UNDERSTANDING STYLE

"Style" is a complex term, and people use it frequently with a variety of meanings and intents. Some people mean it in a superlative sense, such as "she has style and grace," without providing modifiers for the word "style." Such uses of the word "style," however, tell us little about things theatrical. We will use **style** to suggest manner of expression and methods of onstage behavior as they affect composition and performance. It is not the content that dictates style, but the way in which that content is packaged and delivered to the audience. Style is dictated by language—poetry, prose, and dialects. Style is identified by character movement and social manners, by changes and fashions in architecture, clothes, furniture, and decoration (on both low and high economic scales). Style is expressed by music, painting, and dance. In short, style is heavily reliant on the period of history, the economic status of the characters, cultural values, and the geographical region or specific locality of the world that the style reflects or suggests. It is common to talk about a Restoration style (1660–1700 in England) or a Greek classical style, but such labels alone may suggest much or little depending on one's acquaintance with those periods of history.

Style can be a method of "authenticating" a place or time. A production of *The Weavers* by Gerhart Hauptmann could suggest rural Germanic Silesia in 1892 (the place and time of the play as written) through representational setting, costumes, properties, manners, and movement. This approach would require hundreds of peasant costumes (many in rags) because there are hundreds of starving workers exploited by the weaving industry. The audience would see the hovels of the weavers because a big part of the play demonstrates their suffering. It would also see some of the rich industrialists and a house of the rich exploiters, which in turn is wrecked by the workers in revolt. To be representational with this play requires much detail and probably expense. On the other hand, a production team may sometimes impose a style that is quite different from the original on the material to be performed. For example, the hundreds of peasants might be used as a stylized chorus presenting the woes of the downtrodden, or a production could present just a few actors representing a much larger group. They could be costumed accurately but placed on a bare stage to avoid all of the scenic detail and at the same time underscore the austerity of the weavers' situation.

Playwrights also indicate stylistic shifts within the play's text. For example, in 1928 Bertolt Brecht rewrote an eighteenth-century British ballad musical, *The Beggar's Opera* by John Gay. In his German-language *Threepenny Opera*, Brecht kept the London location but moved the action to the nineteenth century. Composer Kurt Weill threw out all the old music and inserted funky 1920s jazz tunes. Brecht called for the characters to be dressed in one historical style but speak and sing as if in another. Such shifts are by no means unusual in the theatre, and similar incongruities have been used in varying degrees in many different periods. Sometimes a style is actually invented, as we see in work that is meant to suggest the future. *R. U. R.* (1920) by Josef and Karel Čapek, which introduced robots to the stage and the word "robot" to our language, was set futuristically in the 1950s and 1960s. Once we are well past the time of creation

PEER GYNT (1867) by Henrik Ibsen. In this 2008 production at the Guthrie Theater, the mythical figure of the Button Molder (a symbol of death and reuse of the useless) played by Jim Lichtscheidl surprisingly climbs out of a Norwegian stove to encounter the title character on his meandering sojourn through life. Many plays dramatize impossible encounters of the spectral with the everyday events of the living, asking the audience to suspend their disbelief. Stylistic choices made by the production team often enlighten or challenge their audiences. Directed by Tim Carroll, scenic and costume designs by Laura Hopkins, lighting design by Stan Pressner.

Photo © Michal Daniel.

R. U. R. by Josef and Karel Čapek, Theatre Guild. *R. U. R.* introduced the word "robot" to languages in this, the first American production in 1922. See how the director and designer at the time envisioned an army of robots in the 1960s. Directed by Phillip Moeller; designed by Lee Simonson.

Courtesy of Billy Rose Theatre Collection, the New York Public Library for the Performing Arts, Astor, Lennox and Tilden Foundations.

of such a style, however, we can usually see that the invented style is heavily indebted to the period in which it was created.

The style of the original play can also be altered in production. Many plays from the past that were originally written in poetic form have, in the twentieth century and beyond, been translated into prose. This factor alone radically changes a play's style. When Carlo Goldoni's situation comedy *A Servant of Two Masters* (1743) is produced outside of Italy, the Italian regional dialects are often replaced by local dialects.

MACBETH by William Shakespeare in a 2010 modernized treatment with Erik Heger as the title character and Michelle O'Neill as Lady Macbeth. Both costumes and furniture bespeak the contemporary nature of the production and thrust the medieval-like material of the play into our own era. Produced at the Guthrie Theater, Minneapolis. Directed by Joe Dowling; scenic and costume design by Monica Frawley; lighting design by Frances Aronson.

Photo © Michal Daniel.

Working-class dialects of England or New Jersey, for example, are more recognizable to English-speaking audiences. The British play *Coriolanus* (c. 1608) by Shakespeare is a violent tragedy originally set in classical Rome and other parts of Italy. Some modern productions of the play have reset it in 1930s fascist Italy to underscore the political and social corruption running through the play.

A production team may borrow a performance style from one culture and apply it to the plays of another. A production team in the United States or France, for example, might borrow the performance style of Japanese Kabuki and apply it to Western plays. Over the last several decades the West has seen nearly all the famous Greek and Elizabethan tragedies performed in such a borrowed style. Of course, this has also worked in reverse. Japanese directors, for example, have in turn adapted Western plays to their own classical styles or in some cases have drawn from several sources to come up with invented styles. Chinese, Indian, and other Asian and African theatre companies have also adapted Western plays to one of their own performance styles and have adopted Western realistic or stylized methods from the twentieth century, sometimes with great success.

In examining a production, it is helpful not only to recognize the style or styles being used but also to assess how such styles seem to help or hinder the theatrical event. Does the selection of a new style seem to make older material more accessible? Does the strangeness of an old style allow the audience more objectivity in analyzing action that is set in the past? If different styles are used in the same production, does the conflict or contrast make the experience confusing or does it make it more exciting?

SHAKESPEARE'S THE MERCHANT OF VENICE is here updated from the late sixteenth century to the late eighteenth century. In this 2007 version of the play's famous casket scene, the chests are suspended in the air as Bassanio (played by Ron Menzel) must select the correct casket in order to win his beloved Portia (Michelle O'Neill). Directed by Joe Dowling at the Guthrie Theater in Minneapolis.
Photo © Michal Daniel.

EVALUATING PRODUCTION

Audience members tend to evaluate a performance event. It seems natural to affix the terms "good" or "bad" to a production, to recommend the show to others or pan it. Word of mouth is often a powerful tool for getting audiences to see a show, and every performance deserves a fair examination. In deciding what worked and what did not, you can learn a tremendous amount about the theatrical process as well as clarify your own preferences and values.

Considering Context and Artistic Intent

To appreciate a show at any one of the myriad theatrical venues available, it is important to consider the **context of performance.** If you attend a professional show such as *Wicked* (2003) or *Spring Awakening* (2006) in a major city such as New York, Boston, Chicago, Atlanta, Montreal, or San Francisco, your major objectives might be to have a social evening out of the house and to experience an enjoyable performance. The purpose of the show in that venue is commercial; producers expect to make money from the performance, or it would not exist. You have paid a considerable amount of money for a ticket, and you come expecting the highest level of professionalism in design, execution, and performance.

Even within the same city, no more than ten blocks away, you could attend a performance by a troupe of young actors aspiring to professional careers but currently making their living at other pursuits during daylight hours. Through sheer commitment, force of will, and inspiration, the performers have managed to stage a play in a church basement, a warehouse, or the corner of a coffeehouse. When you choose to attend this theatre, you do so with different expectations. The space will not have the glamour or the comfort of Broadway; you do not expect expensive sets or costumes or glossy performances. You can, however, hope to see inspiration, talent, imagination, ingenuity, and commitment.

Perhaps you need not go even ten blocks. You could exit from the commercial theatre only to encounter street or guerilla theatre. Often geared to political or social agendas and akin to public demonstration, such productions are typically mounted improvisationally with little or no preplanned staging, but some of the speeches,

SWEENEY TODD: THE DEMON BARBER OF FLEET STREET, a 1979 musical by Stephen Sondheim and Hugh Wheeler, has proven a popular piece in revival due in part to its stunning amalgamation of humor, horror, and melodrama—an unusual combination for a musical. This production was directed and choreographed by George Pinney in 2003 at Indiana University.

Photo by Indiana University PhotoGraphics.

images, props, and placards are formulated in advance and used to confront the audience directly. The issue could be abortion rights, Middle East turmoil, immigration reform, U.S. troops in Iraq, civil war in Libya—any number of contested issues that are disturbing to the activists. The performers are in your face, making demands, challenging your beliefs or lifestyle. This too is theatre—one in which the cultural context can have a sense of irony, since you are witnessing it just outside a commercial theatre building, with a mostly well-heeled crowd of theatre patrons who had no preparation for the rough theatre they are now encountering. Therefore, you can choose to attend theatre, but sometimes the theatre chooses you.

Beyond the general context of the production, it is helpful to try to articulate the **artistic intent** of a production. Do you believe that the show was meant to entertain you, shock you, comfort you? In establishing the intent of the artists, you can more effectively evaluate how well the production achieved its goals and ask, in the end, whether those goals were worth attempting.

Taste

We will define **taste** as the personal inclination and preferences of the beholder of an aesthetic experience. Taste is inextricably tied to our previous experience with all aspects of culture: leisure activity including sports and the fine and performing arts, television and all types of popular culture, decoration, architecture, reading, fashion, advertising—nearly everything around us that is created by human beings rather than occurring naturally. You might look at a new TV show, music video, painting, film, or play and find yourself alienated; perhaps it lies outside your previous knowledge or experience, and you feel unprepared to process the new stimuli. On the other hand, you could be excited, even though you find the new work alien, because through previous experience you have often encountered new or experimental material. The response could be intellectual, emotional, or both.

Some argue that in theory regular exposure to many different kinds of theatrical events is likely to broaden appreciation of an array of styles, methods, and genres of performance. This notion of acquired tastes is not always true, however. No matter how much theatre a person experiences, that person might always prefer a specific genre, style, or period of work. Someone's list of theatrical preferences could begin and end with American musicals—or thrillers, or Greek tragedies, or Shakespearean comedies. After all, most historians and theorists of the theatre have specializations that are likely to be related to their preferences.

"I Don't Know Why I Like It . . . I Just Do"

Active examination of personal theatrical experience is likely to heighten not only your understanding of your own tastes but also your ability to express your opinions and formulate meaningful argument. Carefully executed analysis (both written and oral) is likely to improve problem solving, powers of observation, recognition of structure and design, understanding of symbolism, and analysis of cultural correspondences. It is important therefore that examination of performance does not include only positive (or negative) comments but reflects the writer's understanding of why a performance was successful or not. It is difficult but instructive to be objective about one's own emotional responses to a production—after the fact, of course.

If you are moved by an actor's portrayal, by a particularly poignant speech, or by a powerful song, try to determine why the moment was so successful. Do particular visual images come to mind? Was the success related to

ALL-MALE ROMEO AND JULIET produced in 2008 by the Shakespeare Theatre in Washington, D.C. Although all productions of Shakespeare's plays in his lifetime were cast with men and boys, only forty-four years after his death women began to play Juliet and the other female roles in his canon. When occasionally men return to these roles, they usually draw attention and are sometimes disturbing or challenging to the expectations and taste of some audience members. Others, of course, are intrigued by the shift. James Davis as Juliet and Drew Eshelman as the Nurse. Directed by David Muse; costume designs by Jennifer Moeller.

Photo © Scott Suchman.

belief in the character? Was the emotional response triggered by the spoken text, by the mimetic action of the actor, by the music underscoring it, by the character isolation created by the lighting? Perhaps this action was very close to the audience or safely removed. What do you remember that could have triggered the emotional response?

"I Just Don't Like It"

"I just don't like it" is the too-easy response to a play or performance that confuses, offends, bores, challenges, or mystifies an audience member. A spectator can grow frustrated by an event or simply dismiss it as unimportant. Sometimes audiences give up quickly on an artistic experience, or they might struggle with it for hours or even days. If a production does not appeal to you, it is important to think about why. Were you bored? Offended? Confused? What caused this response? Were the production choices inappropriate? Was the material uninteresting to you?

Different plays and works of art are likely to appeal to you at different ages or levels of experience. Was the production style completely new to you? If a student watches action thrillers full of fast-paced chases, fights, and violent language almost exclusively, the first response to a Japanese Noh performance might well be negative. Noh would probably seem impossibly slow, almost like watching a performance in slow motion. Noh is keyed not just to music, colorful costumes, and demonic possession; it is interpreted through silence and reflection and ghostly memories. Unlike the pace of contemporary life, which is often relentless in the rush to get things done, Noh is in no hurry at all.

TRAVESTIES (1974) by Tom Stoppard, directed by Carey Perloff in 2006 at the American Conservatory Theater in San Francisco. The topsy-turvy setting reflects the confused memory of the narrator of the play who mixes an old production of *The Importance of Being Earnest* with his life and the real events of 1917 in Zurich, Switzerland with Lenin, James Joyce, and the creation of Dada. Scenic design by Douglas W. Schmidt.
Photo © Kevin Berne.

THE ROLE OF THE CRITIC

A few people make a career out of experiencing and evaluating production and sharing that viewpoint with the public. **Theatre critics** have a difficult job. They work with one foot in the theatrical community and the other in the public arena. They serve as arbiters and entertainers simultaneously. The ideal theatre critic provides a fair yet interesting critique of a very complex event, usually under a deadline. People who write about theatrical productions often have a complicated relationship with the arts community. In the past theatre critics were sometimes closely connected with a particular theatre or performer and used their reviews as a forum to build public support. William Winter, for example, was a good friend of nineteenth-century star actors Edwin Booth and Richard Mansfield and wrote biographies of them along with newspaper criticism. Today we have an expectation of impartiality from our critics; we expect an unbiased evaluation of the shows that they write about. Particularly in the commercial sector, a review in a major newspaper can have a strong influence on the outcome of a production. Broadway producers frequently close a show if opening night reviews are poor, believing that it will be impossible to draw enough of an audience to offset the costs of the production.

The Critic and the Audience

Critics have a responsibility to the readers, listeners, or viewers they serve. Newspapers, radio, television, and Internet sites employ critics to cover entertainment events and pass along information to their audiences. Ever-rising ticket prices make consumers very careful about choosing where to spend their entertainment dollars. Many people use reviews to help them make difficult choices.

The simplest **review** gives information about the show: where, what, when, and ticket information. An effective review gives the consumer enough information about the show to make an intelligent decision given personal tastes and priorities. If the review includes **criticism**—in other words, analysis, interpretation, or evaluation of what was done—it is important that the writer support any judgment about the production with description.

The job of a critic is not only to judge a production. When exciting things are happening onstage, the review helps to spread the word. The critic serves as a link between the theatrical production and its potential audience. The successful review of a production, whether written for publication or as a class assignment, should collaborate with the reader. Besides being clear and accurate, the review should encourage the reader to visualize parts of the performance and understand the writer's point of view. As a reader you can then decide whether you are likely to agree with the writer's viewpoint. Critics are also expected to produce copy that is interesting to read. This need sometimes conflicts with the desire for evenhanded evaluation and leads to an emphasis on humor or a cleverly biting tone. The critic owes the audience a fair and interesting review; whether a production is poorly or beautifully done, it must be honestly described and evaluated.

The Critic and the Artists

Some theatre artists who have been hurt by negative reviews understandably look on critics with suspicion or even contempt. It is disheartening to invest the enormous amount of time and energy required by production only to have such efforts spoken of harshly in public. Given the potential damage from a negative review, it is important that critics do their best to provide balanced coverage, praising good work as well as pointing out aspects that were below par. A conscientious critic also cultivates sensitivity to the nature of the production and its aims (professional or amateur, large or small budget).

A fine critic can provide an informed perspective on the artist's work that few audience members can offer, setting a production in a historical context and providing a comparison with contemporary work. The very best writers can pass on a vision for changing theatre, pointing out current needs in the community that the artists may fulfill. Before 1918 many theatre critics in the United States lamented the state of theatrical entertainment, which many critics called "show-shop," meaning entertainment devoid of meaningful content cranked out for the so-called tired businessman. After the horrors of World War I, a few critics began to suspect that surviving the cataclysm of a world war might alter the theatrical landscape, and they were correct. In the late 1910s a handful of intrepid playwrights such as Eugene O'Neill and Susan Glaspell, designers such as Robert Edmond Jones and Lee Simonson, and directors such as Arthur Hopkins and Philip Moeller raised the artistic and intellectual standards of commercial theatre, and many critics rallied around them instantly. O'Neill's first commercially produced full-length play, *Beyond the Horizon* (1920), had a very uninspired production, was poorly cast and cheaply designed (not by any of the artists listed above), and was ineptly rehearsed, yet many critics recognized that it was an important play. This poorly produced but well-written modern tragedy won the Pulitzer Prize for drama that year.

The Critic and the Historical Record

Although criticism is often considered nearly as ephemeral as production—it is often produced for immediate consumption and is discarded with the daily newspaper—a piece of criticism essentially becomes part of the historical record. Students of the theatre rely on reviews, for example, to reconstruct productions from the past and learn about preferences in different time periods. The Internet has provided easy accessibility to many newspapers and periodicals that were previously considered obscure. A daily critic must first satisfy the more immediate needs of the contemporary audience and media, but it is important to keep in mind the possible reach of a review and write with as much accuracy and thoughtfulness as possible.

Theatrical reviews are also regularly published in magazines such as *The New Yorker* and *American Theatre,* as well as scholarly journals such as *Theatre Journal.* Unhampered by daily deadlines, critics are able to spend more time evaluating a small number of productions. This kind of criticism is not as timely as daily reviews but is often better able to examine a production with greater consciousness of its importance to the historical record.

A Second Look at Production

Professional critics sometimes return to a production to see whether their original rave or pan review still seems justified or to see how a production might have grown or diminished. Critics sometimes back off from their original positions or clarify them and declare an even greater admiration or contempt for the production in question. It is clear, however, that these critics, who make their living by reviewing live performance and often have remarkable abilities to analyze incisively after seeing new material just once, still notice many things that they apparently missed the first time.

EXPLORING Historical and Cultural Perspectives

Classical versus Contemporary Space

In December 2010 in Beijing we were struck by the impact of theatrical space on performance. We witnessed, on consecutive days, the same two classical Chinese plays performed by different companies, first in a small classical space, Huguang Guildhall (pictured in this box), and then in the Liyuan Theatre, a large proscenium space. The western style proscenium configuration has replaced most of the traditional theatres in the People's Republic of China. A domestic light comedy about a pretty, frivolous girl being courted by an older man, *Picking Up a Jade Bracelet* was followed by *Presenting a Pearl on the Rainbow Bridge,* an acrobatic, dance-like performance replete with supernatural figures and stylized military battles.

In the traditional spaces (dating to the thirteenth century) all is played under a canopy surrounded by a low railing, and all entrances and exits are made through cloth doorways opening onto a square, carpeted stage. Since the early twentieth century, rectangular proscenium spaces have replaced most of the traditional ones and all exits and entrances are made from the wings, although the carpeting and simple set properties are maintained. In the traditional space the musicians are visible stage left, but they are invisible in the proscenium space.

Although both companies had similar costumes, choreography, makeup, gesture, and artistic skills, the traditional arrangement seemed more organic and intimate, and the acrobatics were more impressive there because the smaller space required greater precision by the performers. The larger theatre required more performers to fill the space; the company expanded the spectacle and presented more of the story of the play than the smaller company. The loud,

HUGUANG GUILDHALL (2010), a traditional Chinese music drama theatre in Beijing, People's Republic of China, built in 1807. It is one of the few remaining classical theatre spaces. Note the red tea tables for audience seating.
Photo © Ronald Wainscott.

engaged audience behavior we have read about from centuries ago seems to fit the smaller space where all of the audience is much closer to the action. Interestingly, the larger theatre clearly caters more to foreign tourists than does the older Huguang Guildhall. This dual experience provided an unusual opportunity for writing critically about performance from a historical point of view.

Seeing a production a second time can be a valuable learning experience for anyone. If you return to a theatre to see a second performance of the same production, the experience must be a different one. The audience members with whom you are in company will differ from the first audience. Some of their responses will vary and will, in turn, affect actors' performances. A full house engages the performers more effectively than a sparse one does, regardless of the capacity of the house. If you are a part of a very responsive audience at your first performance but the second is very quiet, your experience is likely to differ significantly. Such "second sight" can be even more dynamic if you sit in a different part of the theatre for the second performance.

At a second viewing of a production you are likely to notice many details that you missed the first time. Your focus is likely to shift (as it should), and you are now in a state of expectation because you know what is supposed to happen next. You can be more objective, less emotionally engaged perhaps but probably more intellectually engaged. You can "see" better, you have increased aesthetic distance, and you are better equipped to understand the performance. It is easier the second time to figure out the mechanics of the presentation that might have fooled you the first time through surprise and the power of the unexpected—not unlike a magician's illusion.

We are not implying that you should always see a performance at least twice to examine it effectively, but we are suggesting that it is helpful to do this from time to time (when practical) to raise your own awareness of your skills and limitations. The more practice you get, the more acute your abilities are likely to become.

WRITING ABOUT PRODUCTION

People have probably been writing about theatre as long as they have been going to see theatre. In his comedies Aristophanes wrote about the plays of Greek tragedians. We're writing about plays and productions in this book. You will probably be asked to write about theatre as a student. Writing about theatre encourages personal exploration. Sometimes one of the great pleasures of experiencing a play is talking about it afterward with friends or colleagues—learning what others saw and what they thought, crystallizing your own reactions, and reaching a greater depth of understanding in trying to communicate with someone else. Writing goes a step beyond talking. It forces you to recognize what you feel and think; it encourages you to verbalize a point of view in a very specific way and requires you to organize your thoughts. Writing about theatre, as about other things, is a way of thinking; it leads the writer to make concrete decisions. Precision of thought is necessary to communicate on paper. When writing, a person must connect in a very personal way with the experience, and in producing a document, the writer is encouraged to support assertions with evidence. Your piece of writing is meant to convey your ideas about the theatrical experience to the reader, and in creating it, you expand the chain of communication that began with a notion in the playwright's mind.

Once you have made arrangements to see a performance, you need to decide whether to read the play in advance if it has been published. This choice is a matter of personal preference. Reading the play ahead of time will make you better prepared to analyze the production, but surprise value could be lost. Your choice might be different depending on the play.

When you arrive at the theatre, take note of the theatre space, if it is new to you. What kind of audience are you a part of on this particular evening? Check out the program and be sure to take it home with you. It will give you information that you need about theatre personnel, spelling, and dates. Many theatres provide program notes that are designed to deepen the audience experience. These notes often include chronologies, short biographies, criticism of the play or previous productions, production histories, or related graphics.

When the show begins, turn your full attention to the stage; let yourself become involved in the world of the play. Don't try to analyze or figure out the play or production yet, and *do not take notes during the show!* We know that this is a common practice, but we firmly believe that it is not a good idea for two reasons: It is very often distracting to the audience members seated around you, and if you are writing, you are not experiencing the performance—you have pulled yourself out of the artistic experience as it is meant to occur.

If you feel panicky that you will not remember enough to write a paper, it is perfectly acceptable to take notes furiously during intermissions, and we highly recommend doing so immediately after the performance. Trust yourself: If you are focusing on the experience, you will retain far more than you ultimately need to analyze the production. It is important to record your impressions as soon as possible after witnessing the performance, however. Take notes quickly (brainstorming); don't worry about sentences or grammar. First, briefly describe your own feelings during and after the show; then analyze what made you feel or react in specific ways. Record what you remember: images, lines of dialogue—anything that stood out for you. Write down sensory impressions: colors, sounds, light, and dark. Make lists of adjectives to describe particular parts of the production.

Although the theatre is a subjective experience, it is important to be as objective as possible in supporting what you say about production by providing evidence. You will describe the way in which the production elements created (or failed to create) the world of the play. Perhaps you believe that the production did a fine job of creating an eerie, suspenseful mood. Your support might be that the dark atmosphere with patches of isolated light and the music that crept in at the most tension-filled moments helped to create a threatening mood.

The following is a short list of tips for writing about production:

- Always identify the play, playwright (or equivalent), theatre or place of performance, and date you saw the production.
- Identify the event precisely.
- Use your program to credit the artists whose work you are discussing. "The lighting designer" and " the actor playing Hamlet" have names; please use them.
- Avoid using the words "good" and "bad." They don't tell the reader anything useful. Use descriptive adjectives instead. Was the acting, for example, believable, stylized, overblown, subtle? Why? Was the set colorful or efficient?

If you have trouble getting started, ask yourself what the production made you feel or think about, how the production accomplished this, and whether your experience was what the director or playwright intended.

Writing about a transitory experience is both challenging and exciting. It requires that you be attentive and present in all senses of the word during the event, that you exercise your skills of observation and interpretation, and that you create symbols (words) that will in some way reproduce your experience for others. Writing about theatre will develop and tune skills that will serve you well far beyond the walls of the theatre or classroom.

WHEN IT ALL WORKS

Even when we have read the play and/or seen previous productions of the script, we can still be taken emotionally by a production. It is exciting when this happens. We saw a production of *Much Ado about Nothing* by the Royal Shakespeare Company that seemed so complete in its emotional and comic presentation, so precise in its technical skill, so graceful in its scenic beauty, and so engaging in its acting performances that our immediate response after the applause finally subsided was a wish that it could start all over again, despite the fact that we had been watching in the theatre for some three hours. No matter how sophisticated your analytical skills may become, there is always the possibility of complete immersion—always the chance that you can yield completely to the power of the theatrical event.

CHAPTER REVIEW

Questions and Activities

1. Explore the difference between describing (objective) and interpreting (subjective). Choose one scene in a play that you have seen (or a film if a play is not possible). Make a list of terms describing elements of the scene, for example, "red light, screams from offstage." Now add interpretive words for what you saw, for example, "red light—hot, evil, frightening; screams from offstage—startling, bloodcurdling, disturbing."

2. If your class members (or even a small group of them) have seen the same production, choose one scene to discuss. First, have each person make a list of words that convey emotions generated by that scene. Compare your lists. Choose some similar words from different people. Explore what made these people feel that way (elements of performance—actors, set, costumes, lighting, sound)? If there are very different responses, find out why. See whether you can express why people responded differently to the same scene.

3. Discuss productive ways to give criticism (both negative and positive). If you are on the receiving end, what do you think works well? What is counterproductive?

4. Choose a play that has been recently produced by a professional company. Run a search on Lexis/Nexis (or another database that can connect you with newspaper and periodical articles). Use the playwright's last name with an important word from the title as search terms. Choose several reviews of the same production, print them, and read them. Did the critics give a clear description of the play and production? On the basis of the reviews, do you think you would like the show? Highlight the main points of the review in one color and the support for that idea in another color. Are the main points well supported? Do you get a strong mental image of what is happening on stage? Do the reviews present different opinions? Is there one review that you believe is stronger than the others? Explain why.

Key Terms and Concepts

active participation, p. 53
observation, p. 55
interpretation, p. 56
believability, p. 57
actor choices, p. 57
ensemble, p. 58

space and design choices, p. 59
representational, p. 60
presentational, p. 60
set properties, p. 62
style, p. 64
context of performance, p. 67

artistic intent, p. 68
taste, p. 68
theatre critic, p. 69
review, p. 70
criticism, p. 70

For Further Exploration

David Ball. *Backwards and Forwards: A Technical Manual for Reading Plays.* Carbondale: Southern Illinois University, 2003.

Robert Benedetti. *The Actor at Work,* 10th ed. Boston: Allyn & Bacon, 2009.

Vicky Ann Cremona, et al. *Theatrical Events: Borders, Dynamics, Frames.* Amsterdam: Rodopi, 2004.

Willmar Sauter. *The Theatrical Event: Dynamics of Performance and Perception.* Iowa City: University of Iowa, 2000.

Richard H. Palmer. *The Critics' Canon: Standards of Theatrical Reviewing in America.* Westport, CT: Greenwood, 1988.

Kalina Stefanova-Peteva. *Who Calls the Shots on the New York Stages? The New York Drama Critics.* New York: Routledge, 1994.

ELEKTRA adapted from Sophocles (2010), Betty Nansen Teatret, Copenhagen.
Photo by Ulrik Jantzen and Marijana Jankovic.

Understanding the Play

A Theatrical Blueprint

There must be a plan for most theatrical performances. With few exceptions, someone has decided before the audience gathers, even before the actors are selected, basically what will happen on stage. The "play" is a plan or blueprint for the total production. In most cases this means a printed text, which typically contains **dialogue** (words spoken by the characters) as well as **stage directions** (written descriptions of physical or emotional action or physical appearance). The play is to some degree an outline that must be finished by the production team; it is two-dimensional until the artists make it three-dimensional. A wonderfully written play cannot ensure a fine performance but may provide a strong foundation for the successful collaboration of a team of artists.

Theatre, film, and television are very different media, but they share many storytelling techniques. Because most people have seen more film and television than live theatre, we will sometimes use examples from these forms.

In *The Poetics* (fourth century B.C.E.), an early examination of dramatic literature, Aristotle identifies the components of a play. There are other approaches to studying plays, but we have chosen to present Aristotle's ideas because they are very basic and useful for understanding and analyzing many types of plays. Even though this list is thousands of years old, it is still a useful place to begin. Aristotle identified six **elements of a play:** plot, character, thought, language, music, and spectacle. It is important to understand the definitions of the six elements because we will use them throughout this book, and because they are used as a kind of shorthand by many people who work in, talk about, and write about the theatre. You will find somewhat different interpretations as you continue to read about and study the theatre. Each of Aristotle's six elements is defined in the following sections and applied to Shakespeare's play *Romeo and Juliet* (1594–1595).

PLOT

Plot, according to Aristotle, refers to the organization of the action of a play. Playable action is vital to a good play, but plot is not action. Plot is not a story or list of events, but an organizing principle: Plot is what gives a play its unity. Without plot, a dramatic performance would seem to be a series of random events with no observable connection. Aristotle believed that plot is the most important element because it organizes all the rest. Another term for plot is **structure.**

Causal Structure

Plays can be unified in a number of ways. The traditional Western (European and North American) drama is often organized in a linear and causal fashion. **Linear plot** means that the events of the drama progress forward and sequentially in time; **causal** (or "cause-to-effect") **plot** indicates that one event causes the next: Event A leads to event B, which leads to event C, and so forth. Without A and B, there is no C. Most thrillers and comedies on film and television have a linear and causal structure. Playwrights and critics after Aristotle have looked carefully at the causal plot and established specific terms to describe its function, which we use to examine *Romeo and Juliet.*

The action of *Romeo and Juliet* could be described as the attempt of two young lovers to come together in the face of tremendous odds. If the lovers were immediately successful, *Romeo and Juliet* would be a very short play, but all kinds of obstacles present themselves. Romeo and Juliet meet and fall in love; their attempts to be together are thwarted by the enmity of their families, the Capulets (Juliet's) and the Montagues (Romeo's). A desperate attempt to escape together ends in their deaths. The causal relationship of one event to another in the play is complex, and sometimes there are multiple possible causes for any one event, but the existence of causality is always clear. The action continually progresses forward in time in the world of the play, beginning shortly before Romeo and his friends crash the Capulets' party and ending with the suicides of the lovers and the discovery of their bodies in the Capulet tomb. At no time does the audience see action that had occurred previously (although it is often described). We can say, then, that the plot or organization of *Romeo and Juliet* is linear and causal.

At the heart of causal structure is the **conflict** of opposing forces: Two or more characters (generally) want the same thing (money, power, a kingdom, love) or want different things to happen (escape or justice, revolution or consolidation of power). The forces work against each other until, in some way, the outcome is decided. The central conflict in *Romeo and Juliet* is Romeo and Juliet versus their families and friends. The lovers wish to be together; the old feud between the Capulets and Montagues keeps them apart. Although conflict between characters is the easiest to identify, a complex play will often locate conflict in a number of areas: moral conflict (good versus evil), for example, or conflict between two ideas. Typically, though, the conflict of larger forces is embodied in the characters themselves.

Point of attack refers to the point in the story at which the playwright chooses to start dramatizing the action. Plays are highly selective in terms of the events that are included in performance, and these selections lie at the heart of the play's structure. The story of the play might stretch far into the past, but the playwright selects one moment in that story to begin actually showing (rather than telling about) the progress of events. When *Romeo and Juliet* begins, the feud is already well established, but the lovers have not met; indeed, Romeo begins by professing his adoration for Rosaline. After the lovers meet, the action stretches over a number of days; we witness many events in the struggle of the lovers, including their secret marriage and Romeo's banishment and return to Verona. The play therefore has a relatively early point of attack—the playwright chooses to dramatize most of the important incidents in the story. A play with an early point of attack is often said to be **episodic:** Selected dramatized moments in the story are separated by breaks in the action, as in Tony Kushner's *Angels in America*. The playwright sometimes indicates a passage of time between scenes through dialogue.

ROMEO AND JULIET, the 2005 Chicago Shakespeare Theater production. The inciting incident is the party scene at the Capulets' home. Romeo and Juliet meet and fall in love, having a private moment in the midst of reveling. Juliet is played by Julia Coffey. Romeo is played by Carman Lacivita. Directed by Mark Lamos.

Photo by Liz Lauren courtesy of Chicago Shakespeare Theater.

In contrast, when a play has a late point of attack, most of the events in the story have already happened, and we see only the last few episodes or only one episode dramatized. If *Romeo and Juliet* had a late point of attack, for example, the last few hours of the lovers' lives would be dramatized in great detail and the early events such as their first meeting would only be described. Marsha Norman's play *'night, Mother* (1983) has a late point of attack. The actual time that elapses for the fictional characters is the same amount of time that the audience is in the theatre—only 90 minutes. The clock is ticking in full view, underscoring the real time of the play. The audience shares the last hour and a half of Jessie's life as she prepares for death.

As a play opens, the playwright usually sets up the dramatic situation for us by using **exposition,** or information that is needed to understand the play. Although exposition may be introduced throughout the play, a great deal of information is typically conveyed in the first few scenes. Character and setting must be established; crucial past events of the story (those occurring before the point of attack) must be described so that the audience can follow the causal connections as the play progresses. Exposition can be conveyed visually; we see two opposing groups of people, for example, in the opening scene of *Romeo and Juliet* and learn immediately of the battle lines drawn between the Capulets and Montagues. Most exposition, however, is conveyed through

ROMEO AND JULIET.
Part of the rising action
is the balcony scene,
here performed on the
architectural ruins of a
Roman theatre near Ankara,
Turkey. Note the rope ladder
for access to the "balcony."

Courtesy of Billy Rose Theatre
Collection, the New York Public
Library for the Performing
Arts, Astor, Lennox and Tilden
Foundations.

dialogue. Juliet's father plans to marry her to the wealthy Count Paris. The two men are heard planning the engagement early in the play, so the audience is prepared, late in the play, when the father insists on the wedding, unaware that Juliet is secretly married to Romeo.

However it is presented, the exposition creates a situation in which an uneasy balance of forces exists; nothing major is happening yet, but the audience soon recognizes the potential for conflict. When the Prince breaks up the initial street brawl, he not only gives the history of the feud but also announces an extreme consequence for another eruption of violence: "If ever you disturb our streets again, / Your lives shall pay the forfeit of the peace," a consequence that later will apply to Romeo.

The **inciting incident** is an event that destroys the uneasy balance and sets off the major conflict of forces. From this point on, the conflict is clearly defined and will build throughout the play. The meeting of Romeo and Juliet is the inciting incident of Shakespeare's play. They fall in love at the Capulet party without knowing each other's identity. When Romeo learns Juliet's name, he characterizes his danger in financial terms: "Is she a Capulet? / O dear account! My life is my foe's debt." When Juliet learns Romeo's identity, she exclaims, "My only love, sprung from my only hate! / Too early seen unknown, and known too late!" The conflict of the lovers versus the ancient grudge is now clearly defined.

Following the inciting incident, small units of action are dramatized that build in emotional intensity; this section of the play is called the **rising action.** The major forces in conflict gather information, lay plans, and pursue their own objectives (or goals). As they encounter obstacles, they must try something new. Audience empathy with the characters becomes stronger; as the stakes get higher for the characters, the audience becomes increasingly involved in the action. Romeo and Juliet meet surreptitiously and declare their love in the famous balcony scene. The stakes are raised as the Friar secretly marries Romeo and Juliet and Romeo kills Juliet's cousin Tybalt in anger over the death of his friend Mercutio. Romeo's subsequent banishment and Juliet's desperate attempt to avoid a forced marriage by drinking a sleeping potion set the stage for the climax.

The **climax** of a play is the emotional high point of the action; the conflict has reached a critical stage, and the outcome is finally decided—often, one side wins and the other loses.[1] All has been leading up to this moment on stage. Playwrights understand that their climactic scene is the most important one of the play. The dual suicide of the lovers is the climax of *Romeo and Juliet.* Hearing of Juliet's supposed death, Romeo returns from exile and kills himself at his lover's side. Juliet awakens too late to prevent his death and kills herself with his dagger. The lovers have chosen death over separation. The outcome of the conflict is decided; in *Romeo and Juliet* neither side wins. The lovers are together for eternity but only in death. The Capulets and Montagues are no longer fighting, but the families have lost a son and daughter; Tybalt, Mercutio, and Paris have been slain as well.

Emotional intensity drops during the **falling action**—the events from the climax to the end of the play. Loose ends are tied up for the audience, and balance is restored, although something clearly is different from at the play's beginning. Falling action is also sometimes called the play's resolution or dénouement. In the falling action after the death of Romeo and Juliet, the families arrive at the tomb, Friar Lawrence explains the tragic series of events, and the Prince makes his final pronouncement.

In the simplest causal plots, emotional intensity can be graphed as a kind of lopsided pyramid (see Figure 4.1). We can see the emotional intensity established at a relatively low level, begin to rise at the inciting incident, rise slowly, climax, and fall rather quickly. (Once the climax is over, things must be wrapped up speedily, or the audience will lose interest.) Many plays will not fit this graph. Some plays do not rise neatly to the climax but have dips in intensity and secondary climaxes in the rising action.

Other plays may include **subplots,** or secondary lines of action, in which different conflicts are developed. A subplot may be entwined with the major line of action and reach its climax in the same scene, or it may develop independently and climax at another time. In Shakespeare's *A Midsummer Night's Dream* (c. 1595), the main line of action concerns four lovers lost in the woods and the fairies who interfere in the lovers' affairs. A secondary line of action develops around a group of workers who gather in the woods to rehearse a play for the king's wedding. The two strands of action intersect when one of the workers, Bottom, becomes magically involved with the fairies. Both lines of action culminate in the final scene as the workers perform their play at the king's wedding while the lovers watch. Anton Chekhov's full-length plays always include several simultaneous plot lines. In *Three Sisters* (1901), for example, we not only follow the combined and separated lives of the elegant title characters but also witness the smarmy manipulations of their crass sister-in-law, who plots to supplant the sisters in their own home.

Aristotle identified two more terms that are useful in understanding plot: discovery and reversal. **Discovery** occurs when something important is found, learned, or realized during the action of a play. The discovery might be of an object (the murder weapon is found, for example) or a piece of information (the detective is actually the murderer). The most meaningful discoveries are often those that a character makes about himself or herself or about the nature of the human experience. Powerful discoveries happen in *Romeo and Juliet* when the lovers learn each other's true family identity, when Juliet realizes that she can no longer trust her nurse, and late in the play when Juliet awakens to find her lover's lifeless body beside her.

ROMEO AND JULIET. The balcony scene interpreted in 2010 by Laura Esposito as Juliet and Sonny Valicenti as Romeo. Both balcony photos stress not only the yearning, but the physical distance and danger demanded by the scene. The Acting Company/Guthrie Theater co-production, directed by Penny Metropulos.

Photo © Michal Daniel.

ROMEO AND JULIET. In part of the climax, Romeo is now dead and Juliet is about to be awakened by Friar Lawrence descending the stairs. The character Paris can be seen dead stage right of Juliet's head. British production by Henry Irving (c. 1882), who also played Romeo.

From the *Illustrated London News.*

FIGURE 4.1 **The Emotional Effects of Causal Structure** Graph (a) represents the rise and fall of emotional intensity in the simplest causally constructed plot. Note that the action is not uninterrupted in its rise; each episode or unit of action may have its own rise and fall. Most plays will not fit neatly into the single pyramid structure. Graph (b) represents a play in which the emotional intensity reaches a high point, then falls slightly, only to build again rapidly to its true climax. A play with a subplot (secondary line of action) is represented by graph (c). The development of the subplot begins after the major action has been established and continues independently until both conflicts are resolved in the climax.

Reversal occurs when a line of action veers around suddenly to its opposite. The prime suspect in a murder investigation turns up dead, for example, and the detective must look for another solution to the crime. A good example of reversal in *Romeo and Juliet* is Romeo's slaying of Juliet's cousin Tybalt. Until this event the love affair has been clandestine, but there is still some hope that the couple, married in secret, might be able to reconcile their families. Tybalt's murder and Romeo's subsequent flight from Verona lead directly to the play's tragic climax. Aristotle thought that Sophocles' tragedy *Oedipus the King* (c. 430–425 B.C.E.) was perfectly structured because at the play's climax, discovery and reversal happen in the same moment: When the tragic hero learns that he is, in fact, the very murderer he has been seeking (discovery), he goes from being the most powerful man in Thebes to an exile, shunned by humankind (reversal).

European playwrights of the nineteenth century perfected the use of causal structure in a type of drama called the "**well-made play.**" The term can be confusing, since, of course, *any* type of play can be written or constructed well. This particular theatrical term (*pièce bien faite* in French) refers to a category of drama in which a meticulous and involved plot takes precedence over all other elements. As perfected by French playwright Eugène Scribe (1791–1861), the well-made play featured an intricate pattern of causality, carefully controlled suspense, and misunderstandings and reversals, leading to an emotionally satisfying climax followed by rapidly falling action.

If you are able to apply the structural terms previously defined to a causal play and create a graph reflecting its emotional rise and fall, you have a good start toward understanding how the play works. Sometimes it is difficult to decide how to apply the terms; there might be debate, for example, on which moment is actually the climax of the play, and good arguments could be made for alternative choices. The identification of the climax then becomes a question of interpretation; the choice that you make will have an effect on how you view the play as a whole.

Variations on Linear, Causal Structure

Playwrights understand that a familiar structure is comfortable for the audience. Years
of watching the dramatization of stories in film and television have developed audience
expectations for outcome. Think about how strong your expectations are for what will
happen as you watch a play, film, or teleplay (script for television). Writers can play *with* or
against this expectation. Any challenge to an established pattern can be very powerful on
stage. A play that does not include falling action after the climax, for example, can be very

EXPLORING Historical and Cultural Perspectives

Deus Ex Machina

In ancient Greece theatre artists developed a scenic machine called the *mechane,* which was a crane-like apparatus that was capable of "flying" an actor or set of actors into the performance space for special effects. We have no surviving images or specific descriptions of this device, but we know that it was popular and used in both comedies and tragedies. It was used, for example, in the surviving comedy *The Clouds* by Aristophanes in order to satirize the rhetorical system of the philosopher Socrates. The actor playing the philosopher was raised up in the air by the *mechane* to suggest that Socrates had his head in the clouds. In many of our extant Greek tragedies, we have definite and possible uses of the *mechane* in order to effect a dynamic conclusion to the conflict dramatized in the play. Euripides was apparently criticized harshly for his overuse of this device to solve the problem of a play; a god or goddess flies in near the end to create a cosmic discovery or reversal of fortune that resolves the conflict. Many people found that Euripides too easily defaulted to this contrivance. We can see it in use in his *Medea,* for example, as she flies away on a magic dragon to escape what would be certain death. More typically, however, Euripides includes a god, such as the sudden appearance of Apollo near the end of *Orestes,* who reverses events (including a death), or the goddess Athena who stops the king's pursuit of the heroine at the conclusion of *Iphigenia in Tauris.*

The Romans gave us the Latin phrase *deus ex machina* (god from the machine) to describe this dramatic device, which over time came to stand for any contrived conclusion for a play or other forms of literature that told stories. Therefore, long after the literal god machine was no longer in use, the phrase was attached to manipulated climaxes, including reversals and discoveries. In weak plays, *deus ex machina* might be an act of desperation by the playwright to solve an impossible dilemma. It is, however, sometimes used deliberately for satirical effect or some kind of commentary on the characters or world of the play. In *Tartuffe* (1669) by Molière, for example, the playwright boxes his protagonist, Orgon, into a corner from which he would be unlikely to escape. Left to the likely conclusion, the play's titular villain would be victorious at play's end. In order for the comedy to end happily, Molière sends an improbable emissary from the King to catch the villain, Tartuffe, and save the duped Orgon. Shakespeare likewise creates climactic contrivances in the

TARTUFFE by Molière. The use of deus ex machina is the arrival of the king's messenger who unbelievably saves the day. This 1999 production at the Public Theater in New York, directed by Mark Brokaw, satirizes the moment by having the messenger arrive on a carousel horse mounted on wheels. The messenger is played by Patrick Garner.
Photo © Michal Daniel.

romantic *Cymbeline* and *A Winter's Tale.* Melodrama often has such endings, and the *deus ex machina* continues to appear from time to time in very diverse plays such as *Angels in America* by Tony Kushner and the musical play *A Funny Thing Happened on the Way to the Forum.*

INTERESTED? Check out

Peter Arnott. *Greek Scenic Conventions in the Fifth Century B.C.* New York: Greenwood Press, 1978.
Michael Halleran. *Stagecraft in Euripides.* New York: Rowman and Littlefield, 1985.

disturbing. A **cliff-hanger** stops at the climax; the outcome of the conflict is not shown. Television series sometimes end their seasons with a cliff-hanger episode to encourage viewers to tune in next season. In 1935 playwright Clifford Odets used the cliff-hanger structure to advocate social action. Written during the Great Depression, *Waiting for Lefty* tells the story of cab drivers struggling to unionize against oppressive management. The play ends at the climax as the newly motivated drivers leave the auditorium shouting,

"Strike!" In Henrik Ibsen's play *Ghosts* (1881), Oswald, the son of Mrs. Alving, suffers from inherited syphilis. He experiences an attack or seizure that leaves him in a vegetative state. Earlier in the play, in anticipation of this occurrence, Oswald had begged his mother to administer a lethal dose of morphine pills if such a thing ever happened. The play ends with the visual image of Mrs. Alving holding the box of pills, standing by her unfortunate son. The audience does not learn whether she will fulfill his wish.

Western playwrights of the early twentieth century introduced the **flashback** variation to linear structure; although most of the play progresses forward in time, occasional scenes actually dramatize events that occurred in the story before the point of attack. Sometimes a play or film begins and ends in the present while the vast majority of the action dramatized is from the past; the "present" scenes serve as a frame for a long flashback. In Tennessee Williams's *The Glass Menagerie* (1945), the narrator, Tom, begins and ends the play by speaking to the audience in the present, but most of the play dramatizes his past life with his mother and sister as he recalls it.

One of the finest uses of the flashback technique is in Arthur Miller's *Death of a Salesman* (1949). By intercutting present and past scenes, the playwright both tells the story of the aging salesman Willy Loman and recreates the confusion in Willy's mind for the audience. In Harold Pinter's *Betrayal* (1978) linear structure is reversed. The first scene in the play is actually the last to happen in the story chronologically; the play begins with the end of an adulterous love affair. As the play continues, nearly all scenes are set progressively farther back in time. In the last scene of the play the audience sees the characters' first confession of love and listens to their declaration of mutual affection with the poignant knowledge of all the pain to come. Caryl Churchill's *Top Girls* (1982) begins with a fantasy sequence in which the main character, Marlene, meets with famous women from the past, then moves to present reality, and finally flashes back to the past; Marlene, her sister, and her niece interact in a scene that occurred before the original point of attack. The last scenes shown in both *Top Girls* and *Betrayal* are actually the earliest in time.

Situational Structure

Although many plays are organized by causal plot, playwrights frequently use other effective organizing principles to present and unify dramatic action. Dramatists may choose a plot based on idea, image, mood, or character. Japanese Noh dramas, for example, frequently treat a past event, and emphasis is on deepening revelation rather than progressive action. In *Aoi No Uye* (c. fourteenth century and attributed to Zenchiku) a princess, Aoi No Uye, lies very ill and unconscious. She is not played by an actor but is represented by a folded kimono down center. A witch is brought in to help the ailing princess, but the witch conjures up a ghost that turns out to be a manifestation of the intense jealousy of Rokujo, a living enemy who is in love with the princess's husband. Rokujo has tried to hurt the princess in the past, and these attempts are reenacted in the present time of the play by the ghost of her embodied jealousy. Rokujo's spoken words (actually delivered by a chorus) are in the past tense even though Rokujo's body (now transformed into a demon) is threatening the princess with a mallet. Ultimately, a holy man banishes the evil through a kind of exorcism, and peace is restored. So the action is played out in both present and past tense at the same time.

Indian Sanskrit plays do not seek an emotional release or catharsis but create pleasure for the audience through a harmonious balance of moods (**rasa**). The plays imitate a condition, not action as is typical in Western drama. There is no tragedy in *Shakuntala* (c. fifth century) by Kalidasa or in any other Sanskrit plays, which assiduously avoid death on the stage. This play explores the situation in which Shakuntala, the heroine and title character, finds herself. Most of the action in the play is created by magic and divine intervention. The heroine and a king fall in love but find themselves separated. The king is placed under a curse that causes him to forget pregnant Shakuntala, and they are never reunited in the earthly world. When Shakuntala is facing complete abandonment, she is saved by a nymph, who spirits her away to a holy

WAITING FOR GODOT (1953) by Samuel Beckett is an excellent example of situational dramatic structure in a Western play. This production was directed by Carey Perloff at the American Conservatory Theater in San Francisco with nontraditional casting. Vladimir and Estragon (the two tramps) attempt to reason with Lucky while Lucky's master Pozzo looks on. Actors left to right: Steven Anthony Jones, Peter Frechette, Frank Wood, and Gregory Wallace.

Photo © Kevin Berne.

mountaintop, the home of the gods. Years later a charioteer of the gods takes the king to the mountain, where, with the curse broken, the lovers are reunited (now with their son) and can return to the king's earthly kingdom. A happy ending (even if it is only cosmic) seems to be the reigning expectation of Sanskrit theatre.

Substitution of condition for traditional action also sometimes finds its way into modern Western drama, as in *Waiting for Godot* (1953) by Samuel Beckett. Here two tramps on a road imitate the process of waiting. Very little of consequence happens in the way of action: They bicker, suffer, complain, and make no effort to accomplish anything important. They are waiting for something to come to them. Yet the play is funny, sad, and fascinating in its exploration of the human condition. The same is true of the best surviving Sanskrit plays.

Structure by Idea, Character, and Image

Plays can also be unified by idea, character, and image. In *The Blue Room* (1998), David Hare's adaptation of Arthur Schnitzler's *La Ronde* (*The Circle,* c. 1900), the scenes are not causally linked at all, and the action cannot be graphed in the traditional manner. The play dramatizes a string of sexual encounters that cross economic and class boundaries. The first scene is between a Girl and a Cab Driver; the second scene is between the same Cab Driver and a Nanny; the third is between the Nanny and a Student; and so on. In the final scene an Aristocrat has an encounter with the Girl from Scene 1. The play, then, has a circular structure (from which Schnitzler took his title). Unity is provided by idea and character repetition rather than by causation.

Swedish author August Strindberg experimented with providing unity through image. *A Dream Play* (1907) follows the journey of a goddess who visits the earth. The action progresses as dreams progress, not through logical connection but by repetition of character and image. One scene dissolves, and another replaces it; characters appear

A DREAM PLAY (1902) by August Strindberg, adapted and staged here in a 2007 postmodern interpretation by Katrine Wiedemann at the Betty Nansen Teatret in Copenhagen, Denmark. Scenography by Maja Ravn.

Photo by Natascha Thiara Rydvald.

and disappear, images reappear in new places, and characters reappear in strange guises. Strindberg's stated objective was to create a play organized in a way familiar to the human subconscious rather than the conscious mind. Similarly, the French Surrealists of the 1920s and beyond harnessed aspects of the dream world to make ordinary, everyday events occur in impossible ways, just as they do in our dreams. Jean Cocteau, for example, created *Wedding on the Eiffel Tower* (1921), in which the bizarre is mixed with the prosaic. Even though the action is supposedly taking place on an upper level of the Eiffel Tower in Paris, at one point, without comment or explanation, a girl rides by on a bicycle. Even though there are many actors in the play, all of the lines are delivered by two narrators, who are both dressed as Victrola-style phonograph machines.

One of the most intriguing plays from the Arab world, the Egyptian play *The Tree Climber* (1962) by Tewfik al-Hakim, takes a fluid approach to time and place. Time is not linear and space changes instantly and without explanation; the action is not causal. The play is a thoughtful murder mystery, but the events and spatial shifts are impossible in the real world. A Western-style inspector attempts to solve the crime but is incapable of entering the spiritual and quirky world of the protagonist, who is also the chief murder suspect. Known only as the Husband, the protagonist communes with the earth, obsessing with his garden. Only the Dervish, a religious figure who is representative of traditional Arab culture, seems to understand the disappearance of the wife and the import of the mysterious events.

Many plays and performances after the nineteenth century (especially experimental works) have attempted to defy, disrupt, or free dramatic structure from its traditional or reigning position. Audience expectations are often undermined (the playwright might deny a dramatic climax, for example). Form may become fluid and not representational of anything recognizable such as a real or logical progression of events. Time may be negated. In Adrienne Kennedy's *Funny House of a Negro* (1964) there is very little story, but the central character, Sarah, an African American, is bombarded by voices and images of the white world (especially Queen Victoria), Africa, Christianity, death, rape, suicide, and confused memories of her own family background. She desires to escape the tortures

SUBJECT TO FITS: A RESPONSE TO DOSTOYEVSKY'S "THE IDIOT" (1970) by Robert Montgomery. Produced in 2007 by the Alley Theatre, Houston. This play is laced with much repetition along with grotesque imagery to imitate the dysfunctional workings of a deranged mind. Although the title character actually has epilepsy, he is surrounded by eccentrics and madmen, one of whom is portrayed here by Chris Hutchison. Directed by Gregory Boyd. Scenic Design by Takeshi Kata.

Photo © Michal Daniel.

of a severely conflicted life, but she also wishes to free herself from the past and her heritage and become a writer. She is trapped in her mind, which becomes a disturbing "funny house," a nightmare from which she cannot awake.

Repetition as Structure

An event, action, or line of dialogue may be repeated with or without variations and provide a kind of unity for the play. German playwright Heiner Müller's *Hamletmachine* (1978), for example, uses Shakespeare's *Hamlet* (1600–1601) as a jumping-off place to comment pessimistically and violently on social and political failure in the modern world, especially Europe. The play repeats distressing images and lines that become a denial of the conceptions audiences are likely to have of Hamlet and Ophelia. Hamlet even claims that he is not Hamlet, and Ophelia violates all of Shakespeare's presentation of her as soft, compliant, gentle, and chaste.

Repetition is even more dynamic and frequent in *America Play* (1994) by Suzan-Lori Parks. The play deconstructs the assassination of Abraham Lincoln and creates a disturbing view of the icons from the U.S. Civil War and racial issues from the point of view of an African American woman at the end of the twentieth century. A revisionist of history, Parks presents the assassination of Abraham Lincoln as if it were a sideshow act. For a fee, people can participate and play the assassin. This action is repeated many times in variations as if burning the images into the brains of the audience. Parks seems to ask, "Where is African American history in a field of sacred white icons?"

Poststructuralism

Dramatic work created after World War II that breaks down traditional causal structure is often identified as **poststructuralism.** Many plays and performances of the last several decades are somewhat like negative photographic images of what were once positive dramatic events. The perception of concrete space becomes negative or impossible space, and events are so negotiable or ambivalent as to be indefinable or so contradictory as to be adrift among definitions. It is sometimes impossible to figure out a logical story, since none is presented. The last three plays mentioned have no story per se but are rich in dramatic event, images, and disturbing problems.

Much of this work is also metatheatrical, that is, self-conscious in its presentation of theatre as a theatre. There are many antecedents for **metatheatre,** from the simplest "play within a play," such as that found in Shakespeare's *A Midsummer Night's Dream* (1595–1596). The workers (called "rude mechanicals") perform a silly play for the wedding of the monarch (so the audience watches a play about characters watching a play). In the German romantic metatheatrical extravaganza *Puss in Boots* (1797) by Ludwig Tieck, all of the action is set in a theatre. The audience members (some of whom are actors with scripted lines) watch a play break down and never reach completion. At the same time Tieck demonstrates why audiences should reject the old-fashioned neoclassicism of the eighteenth century and replace it with the modern drama of romanticism. In one of many wonderful moments from this hilarious play, the audience rejects the play and the actors they are watching and calls for an encore by the scenery. When the setting is revealed again (without actors), the audience greets it with tumultuous applause.

Structure in the Twenty-First Century

The theatre at the end of the twentieth century was characterized by great diversity, and the structural experiments suggest where dramatic structure is going in the twenty-first century. Playwrights both called on and defied tradition, used and broke rules, pushed boundaries of structure, experimented with emphasizing various dramatic elements, and shattered audience expectations. The early twenty-first century has seen a continuation of traditionally structured and long-running musicals such as *Aida* (2000), *Mamma Mia!* (2001), *Hairspray* (2002), *Wicked* (2003), *Jersey Boys* (2005), *Mary Poppins* (2006), and *Billy Elliot* (2008). Fortunately, however, nontraditional structure or radically reconceived staging methods have also appeared, especially in *Spring Awakening* (2006), *American Idiot,* and *Bloody Bloody Andrew Jackson* (both 2010).

Playwrights such as Caryl Churchill defied traditional dramatic structure to question contemporary social structure and gender limitations. The first act of Churchill's *Cloud 9* (1979) takes place in British Colonial Africa during the Victorian period. The second act begins in 1979 London, but the stage directions state that 25 years have passed for the characters. In the next century, Churchill began to simplify and strip away the obvious theatricality and returned to one-acts, but continued to chip away at sociologically and politically charged material. In *A Number* (2002) she addresses human cloning, and in *Drunk Enough to Say I Love You?* (2006), she presents a political allegory on British and U.S. governments in the guise of two male lovers who discuss terrorism, invasion, and overrunning the rights of citizens while involved in flirtations and sexual innuendo. Her *Seven Jewish Children* (2009) takes on the Palestinian problems.

The Pillowman (2003) by Martin McDonagh is essentially linear in structure but is so steeped in storytelling that many of Katurian's (the protagonist) stories are dramatized like flashbacks, in a colorful, cartoonlike, mimetic style, while Katurian narrates. This method creates a dynamic contrast to the bleak and almost colorless reality of the police interrogation rooms of most of the play's action. The mimed stories also raise questions regarding Katurian's real past and the creations of his imagination—often blending the two.

Experimentation since the late twentieth century has led us to question the nature of the word "text" itself. Beyond the spoken words, the descriptions of mimetic action become crucial to many contemporary plays. Beginning with Samuel Beckett, many playwrights have used physical action to express human singularity and frustration. Robert Wilson (b. 1941) and Richard Foreman (b. 1937) have created performances in which images take precedence over language. Wilson's *The Black Rider: The Casting of the Magic Bullet* (created in 1990, but reconceived in 2004), follows the path of a lowly clerk who sells his soul to the devil for magic bullets. All is expressed with remarkable, colorful imagery set to music. Foreman's Ontological-Hysteric Theatre,

IN THE NEXT ROOM OR THE VIBRATOR PLAY (2009) by Sara Ruhl. A recent comic commentary on Victorian morality and the treatment of women. The action centers around a doctor's use of an electric vibrator to treat perceived hysteria in women. People now think of this implement in a very different way. Broadway production by Lincoln Center. Directed by Les Waters. Scenic design by Annie Smart; costume design by David Zinn.

Photo © Joan Marcus.

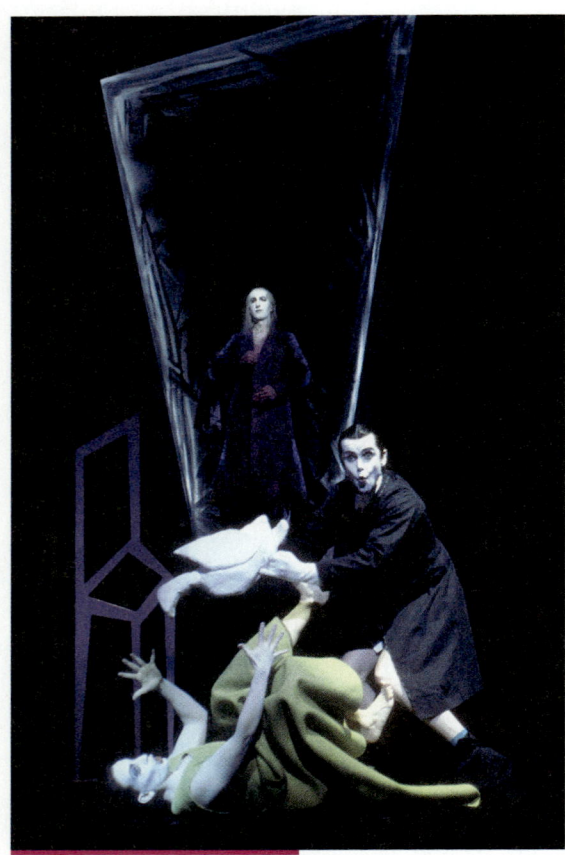

THE BLACK RIDER: THE CASTING OF THE MAGIC BULLETS (2004), a very dark-toned, postmodern musical presentation by Robert Wilson with music by Tom Waits. The actors are Richard Strange, Matt McGrath, and Mary Margaret O'Hara.

Photo © Brinkhoff/Mögenburg, Hamburg.

which he continues to reinvent through such plays as *Deep Trance Behavior in Potatoland* (2008), approaches the abstract in theatre (a tall order). In this multimedia production, Foreman combines live actors with radically angular, but contemporary scenery with century-old images projected on large screens also askew, and all is reminiscent of séances of long ago. The result is deliberately anachronistic and artistically challenging.

Despite exciting experimentation, in the United States many playwrights of nonmusical plays have been led by producers to create small-cast plays often for economic reasons. Also **performance art** (usually one-person/first-person shows that purport to make the artist the subject of the performance), propels much of the avant-garde. In Britain, however, successful large-cast, scenically diverse productions continue to appear, but most notably in the plays of Tom Stoppard such as the nine-hour *The Coast of Utopia* (2002), which explores the nineteenth-century run-up to revolution in Russia with an ensemble of some 38 actors. Stoppard's *Rock 'n' Roll* (2006) combines Czech politics from 1968 to 1990 with rock music of the same era. At its root, this episodic play explores the nature of political and artistic freedom. Both of these intriguing plays first appeared in the United States in 2007.

In analyzing nontraditional plays, it is helpful to think about how the playwright challenges our expectations of traditional structure. What kind of experience does the play create instead, and what might be the purpose behind offering such an experience to the audience? Rejection of traditional dramatic structure often coincides with political or social rebellion and commentary and might represent an artistic response to gender issues, to cultural or artistic conflict, or to political strife. Nontraditional structure sometimes reflects a despairing reaction to horrors and fears generated by the Holocaust, the nuclear arms race and lingering atomic arsenals, waves of worldwide terrorism, racial and ethnic cleansing, and the ever-shrinking global community and ever-expanding and geographically shifting population. Playwrights, like much of the rest of the world, are asking but also dramatizing, "Where are the boundaries?"

CHARACTER

Character refers to the persons that are created to perform the action of the play. Character is the element of drama that most people find the easiest to understand, probably because human beings constantly observe and interpret human behavior in everyday life. It seems natural to look beyond surface reality and probe for someone's reasons or motivation, try to understand the true meaning behind a statement, or attempt to reconcile two seemingly incongruous actions. Unlike some other types of literature that utilize imaginative creation of character, a play does not usually have a narrative voice explaining what the character feels or thinks. The audience must watch, listen, and interpret. It is sometimes easy to imagine characters as having a life outside the world of the play, but for the purposes of understanding drama, character exists only within the action and words of the play as supplied by the author.

An accomplished playwright will develop a character only to the extent needed to fulfill its function in the play. We usually learn a great deal about a play's **protagonist,** or central character. *Romeo and Juliet* has dual protagonists; both are young, impulsive, and loyal to friends and family. The intensity of their love for each other is fully and magnificently developed in the course of the action, as are the changes in character that this love brings about. We know less about Romeo's friends Mercutio and Benvolio,

Juliet's cousin Tybalt, the lovers' parents, Juliet's nurse, or Friar Lawrence, who is instrumental in moving the action. We know as much as we need, however, to understand the play and to have a clear idea of the essence of each character. To spend more time characterizing secondary or minor characters would detract from the unity of the play as a whole. The play is about the struggle of the lovers, not about the problems of their families and friends.

Character Credibility

Information about character is given in three basic ways: (1) what characters say about themselves, (2) what others say about them, and (3) what the characters do. Characters do not always tell the truth. As in life, the audience evaluates the accuracy of character information by considering the circumstances. Tybalt (a Capulet) calls Romeo (a Montague) a "villain." The audience is unlikely to believe Tybalt, given the historical enmity between the families. At the other extreme, when Juliet calls Romeo "the god of my idolatry," we know that her vision is colored by new love. Action, or what the character actually does, is the most important way of defining character. Romeo shows his impulsiveness by scaling his enemy's balcony in the dead of night. Juliet is loyal and determined; these qualities lead her to take the sleeping potion, even though it means that she will be shut up alive in the family burial vault.

Levels of Characterization

One way of understanding how characters are developed in a play is to consider five **levels of characterization:** biological, physical, psychological and emotional, social, and ethical. A minor character may be developed only through the first two levels; a full and complex character will draw on all five.

Biological traits include the species of the character. Usually, of course, plays are written about human beings, but important plays have included fairies, demons, monsters, animals, spirits, gods, and even robots. Typically, such nonhuman characters are depicted with human characteristics. Another important biological trait is sex. Whether characters are male or female usually has a profound effect on their behavior in the play and may dictate their social position and range of activity. Similarly, a character's race may influence social position in the dramatic environment. The title character in Suzan-Lori Parks's play *Venus* (1996), an African woman with unusual anatomical features, both fascinates and repels early nineteenth-century Londoners by her "otherness." She is labeled a freak.

A biological trait that has often been used for comic effect is the creation of twins. In Roman comedy Plautus produced considerable confusion and mayhem when twins are mistaken for one another in *The Brothers Menaechmus* (c. second century B.C.E.), which Shakespeare in turn adapted as *Comedy of Errors* (c. 1592). Shakespeare further complicated the misunderstandings by adding a second pair of twins, who are servants to the leading characters.

Physical traits include stature, weight, hair and eye color, and facial hair. In the theatre, such traits are filled in automatically by the actor playing the role and by changes made with costume and makeup. Sometimes a physical trait is central to a character's personality. Shakespeare's villain Richard III is a hunchback; his revenge is partly motivated by his anger at this physical disfigurement. In Tennessee Williams's play *The Glass Menagerie* (1945), Laura's painful shyness is magnified by her limp. Helen of Troy's stunning beauty brings an entire nation to ruin in Euripides' tragedy *The Trojan Women* (415 B.C.E.), and Rapunzel's magnificent golden hair brings a union with a prince in the Stephen Sondheim and James Lapine musical *Into the Woods* (1987). Sometimes the authenticity of the physical traits is not so obvious. David Henry Hwang created a stunning clash of cultures in *M. Butterfly* (1988). Both his protagonist, Rene Gallimard, a French diplomat in China, and his audience are fooled

M. BUTTERFLY by David Henry Hwang. Rene Gallimard, played by Mark Capri, falls in love with a Chinese music drama actress named Song Liling, who is really a cross-dressing male played here high on the ramp by Francis Jue in this Theatre Works production in Palo Alto, California, in 2006. Directed by Robert Kelley.
Photo © David M. Allen.

by an apparently beautiful Chinese actress who turns out to be a young man in drag. Hwang successfully manipulated perceptions of biological and physical traits simultaneously.

Psychological and emotional traits develop the character's basic internal makeup. Richard III is angry, vengeful, clever, and ruthless. Laura is sensitive and withdrawn and lives most happily in her imagination. Juliet's nurse is sympathetic but foolish. Shakespeare's Hamlet is intelligent, thoughtful, and melancholy. As in reality, a character's psychological and emotional life has a great impact on physical action. It provides the motivation for the action of the play. How the character relates to others is important. Is a character an extrovert or an introvert? Gregarious or withdrawn? Joe Pitt, in *Angels in America: Millennium Approaches* (1991) by Tony Kushner, is a frustrated federal legal clerk who is gay but denies it. He is stuck in a bizarre marriage and confused by his religious background, but finally, with great trepidation, he enters the sexual world he has been avoiding. Sir John Falstaff, by contrast, seems secure with his life choices and jokes, drinks, and cavorts his way through three of Shakespeare's plays. A character can be abrasive or helpful to others, as unselfish as Willy Loman's faithful wife, Linda, or as self-serving as Argan in *The Hypochondriac* by Molière (1673), whose vision does not extend beyond his own imagined ailments. Cases of maladjustment, however, often end in disaster. *Topdog/Underdog* (2001) by Suzan-Lori Parks has two African American brothers who compete with one another. Booth is an unemployed shoplifter, and his older brother Lincoln (they are named for president and assassin) works as a whiteface Abe Lincoln impersonator at a cheap arcade. For years, however, Lincoln was a street hustler dealing three-card monte. Both brothers have created fantasy lives for themselves with regard to sexual prowess and street skills but continue to suffer (although in denial) about their awful past. They were abandoned and betrayed by their parents when adolescents. The violence and displacement of their wrecked lives finally erupt into fratricide over money as Booth kills Lincoln.

Social traits may include a character's job or profession, socioeconomic status, or religious or political affiliation. It is significant, for example, that Romeo and Juliet are from powerful, upper-class families. Both households have many servants, friends, and relations, many of whom are actively engaged in perpetuating the old feud. It is important to the parents that their children make a "good" marriage; in forcing Juliet to marry Paris, Juliet's father believes that he truly has his daughter's best interests at heart. Hamlet is a prince of Denmark; his social position puts him in the thick of a dangerous power struggle at court. Willy Loman's job is of prime importance in *Death of a Salesman* (1949); Arthur Miller uses Willy's position in society to explore the conflicts inherent in the American dream. Gerhart Hauptmann's *The Weavers* (1892) features a group protagonist: impoverished characters united by their common working-class status. In Alan Bennett's *The History Boys* (2004), the action focuses on a set of well-educated adolescent boys in an English boarding school. At the same time that we experience the youthful antics and problems of the boys, we are asked to consider the antithetical sexual and intellectual positioning of teachers and teaching methods (especially of history) in the development of promising students. The result is a conflict of generations, not only between the students and the teachers, but among the teachers themselves. From a very different sphere in the social fabric comes *Fences* (1985) by August Wilson. The protagonist, Troy Maxson, is a struggling garbage collector in 1957. He has a background of prison and baseball in the Negro League, but he was passed over when integration finally came to major league baseball. While trying to keep his family afloat, he undermines his son's dreams and betrays his faithful wife with another woman. In the pre–civil rights days he is a victim of racist employment practice; white men are not onstage in the play, but their oppression is felt throughout.

Ethical traits are the moral standards held by a character. Although the audience is frequently given clues to a character's integrity by other means, an ethical or moral choice is often a defining moment for a protagonist, particularly in a tragedy. In Arthur Miller's *The Crucible* (1953), John Proctor, on trial for witchcraft, chooses death rather than incriminating other innocent people. The results of grasping for power are even more ominous in the Chinese play *The Orphan of Chao* (fourteenth century), attributed to Chi Chün-hsiang. The villain General Tu-an Ku not only kills his political enemy, but also murders every member of his family and extended family—men, women, and children—to ensure that Ku will remain in power. Of course, he misses one infant, who, when grown, learns the truth and exacts revenge from the evil general. All three characters in Michael Frayn's *Copenhagen* (1998) are obsessed with ethical choices posed in the scientific community during the creation of the atomic bomb. Frequently, a character's choice in a time of moral dilemma has a profound effect on the play's action. Sister Aloysius, a school principal and nun in *Doubt* (2004) by John Patrick Shanley, wages a relentless campaign against a priest who she believes is sexually abusing her students—even though she has no evidence to confirm her suspicions. A profound but enigmatic ethical choice is made at the conclusion of *Conduct of Life* (1985) by Maria Irene Fornes. The wife of an oppressive and criminal military officer pulls out a pistol and kills him. Then, without explanation, she places the gun in the hands of a 12-year-old girl who had been repeatedly sexually abused by the officer.

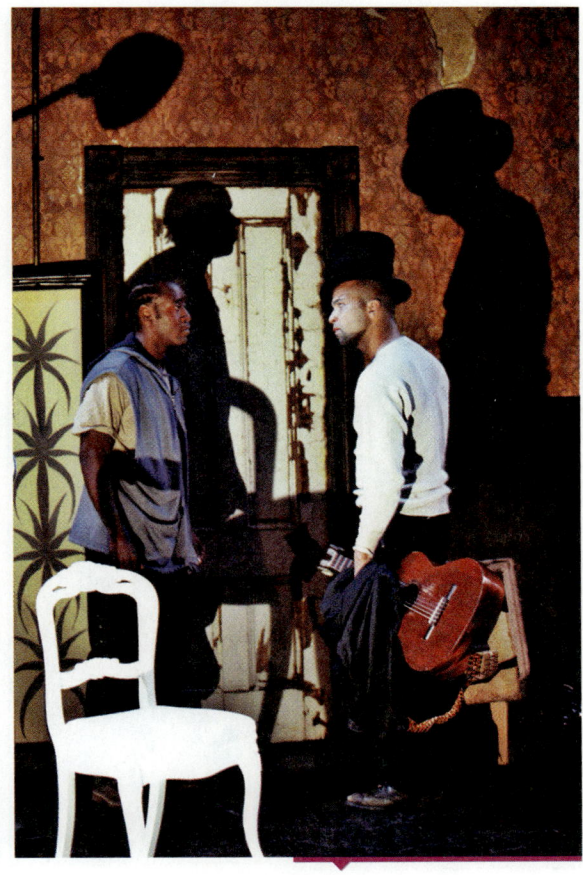

TOPDOG/UNDERDOG by Suzan-Lori Parks. Lincoln, in the top hat, is played by Jeffrey Wright. His brother, Booth, who will kill him, is played by Don Cheadle. Directed by George C. Wolfe. The Joseph Papp Public Theater, New York.

Photo © Michal Daniel.

Understanding Character Relationships

Much of our enjoyment in the theatre is derived from watching the interaction of characters. As in life, the audience comes to understand character by observing the impact human beings have on one another and the ways in which characters behave in different situations.

It is helpful to look at the entire network of relationships established in a play. Any past relationship, usually presented through exposition, will be important to understanding present conflict. Romeo's love for his friend Mercutio fires his desire for revenge against Mercutio's murderer, Tybalt. John Proctor's prosecution in *The Crucible* is due in part to the machinations of young Abigail, who hopes to rekindle an adulterous affair.

August Wilson's *The Gem of the Ocean* (2004) is set in 1904 Pittsburgh in the house of a mysterious woman, Ester, who claims to be 285 years old. She lives at the center of this play, which uses outcasts and struggling post-Civil War black characters, some of whom were former slaves, to explore the spiritual cleansing of Citizen Barlow, a troubled young man who is at war with himself and the controlling white world. In an exotic ritual journey, Ester, using a fascinating quilt as a map, guides Citizen to the bottom of the "ocean" to the "city of the bones" (a symbol of the thousands of unknown black slaves killed in transport to the new world). By encountering this mystical part of his unexplored past and heritage, Citizen can be reborn to face the present and the future of his race.

Relationships may have a wide impact. The brother/sister relationship between Tom and Laura in *The Glass Menagerie* is full of love, understanding, and compassion; the mother/son relationship between Amanda and Tom is characterized by misunderstanding, impatience, and conflict. The ultimate failure of the mother and son

RUINED (2009) by Lynn Nottage, challenges human ethical choices in disturbing ways as an enterprising madam tries to profit on the wages of war, and her women struggle to survive in the midst of violence and rebellion, pillage and rape. 2011 production of La Jolla Playhouse, directed by Liesl Tommy; scenic design by Clint Ramos. This play won the Pulitzer Prize in 2009.

Photo © Kevin Berne.

to establish a means of communication (or at least a peaceful coexistence) leads to Tom's abandonment of the family. Tom's relationship with his sister is doomed, not internally but by the dysfunction of the mother/son relationship.

THOUGHT

Thought refers to the ideas in a play and can be generated in a number of different ways. Sometimes a playwright will actually write a speech for a character explicating a particular idea or arguing a point. The famous "To be, or not to be" speech from *Hamlet* (1600–1601), for example, is an exquisitely worded argument of the most basic human question: Should I choose life or death? At the end of *Romeo and Juliet,* the Prince reminds the bereaved families that their own enmity has brought about their sorrow: "Capulet, Montague, / See what a scourge is laid upon your hate, / That heaven finds means to kill your joys with love." The British playwright George Bernard Shaw was a master of working specific ideas into dialogue, often featuring an argument or debate prominently in the action. In *Mrs. Warren's Profession* (1902), a debate occurs between Mrs. Warren and her daughter Vivie. The mother explains the logic of her background as a prostitute and then a madam to pull herself out of the gutter of poverty and servitude. Vivie seems to understand but cannot accept how her mother funded the wonderful education that Vivie has received. With an impossible divide between them, mother and daughter will continue their lives in separate spheres. In stressing intellect over emotion, Bertolt Brecht made many choices as a playwright to support thought. Shen Te, the heroine of Brecht's *Good Person of Setzuan* (c. 1940), finds herself in a dilemma. She is such a compassionate and selfless woman that she allows everyone to walk all over her. To save herself, she creates a male alter ego, Shui Ta, and performs this role to regain control with demanding, even ruthless, treatment of the people who have been taking advantage of her. In other words, Shen Te must be bad to protect her own goodness.

Use of Imagery to Create Thought

In a complex play, meaning exists on many levels. A concept might be developed through a visual image or expressive language. The youthful, muscular language of *Romeo and Juliet* is made manifest in the actor's climb up the balcony, only to be replaced in the end by the vision of two corpses enveloped by the sounds of mourning. In *Hamlet,* thoughtful speeches on mortality are reinforced by verbal images of death and decay ("something is rotten in the state of Denmark"), concrete visual images of skulls and bodies, and the physical action of dueling, poisoning, and stabbing. The characters' dread, guilt, and fear are given physical presence by the appearance of the ghost of Hamlet's father.

In looking for the ideas that are expressed in a play, it is important to take the play as a whole into consideration. Characters have conflicting viewpoints, neither of which might actually communicate what the playwright thinks. Wole Soyinka's *Death and the King's Horseman* (1976) demonstrates the failure of alien cultures to understand one another but, more important, the destruction of sacred parts of native culture by arrogant, uncomprehending British colonial authority. Nigerian Yoruba culture celebrates the beauty of life through a ritual of death, but this is disrupted by both the British and natives, with catastrophic results.

THE CAUCASIAN CHALK CIRCLE by Bertolt Brecht. In the second act, Brecht communicates some of his most important thought about the evil nature of the world when left to its own devices. The corrupt judge Azdak makes ridiculous but curiously appropriate judgments. Produced at the University of Nebraska.
Photo © Ronald Wainscott.

Contribution of Plot to Thought

Plot is most instrumental in creating thought. What actually happens in the play—what the playwright chooses to include or exclude, how the playwright chooses to begin and end the play—has a profound effect on ideas that are communicated by the play. *Romeo and Juliet* would be a very different play if the events did not lead to the protagonists' deaths. If the lovers managed to run away and live happily ever after, the play might be seen as a celebration of the power of young love over unreasonable opposition. Instead, the tragedy dramatizes the terrible costs of prejudice and vengeance and the failure of authority figures to provide appropriate counsel and understanding to the young. In *Antigone* the title character is entombed alive and hangs herself. Her beloved Haimon follows her into the tomb, where he falls on his father's sword. In response, Haimon's mother, Eurydice, also commits suicide. Because the violence is kept offstage, the audience can focus on how the deeds affect the living rather than on the horror of the physical acts. On the other hand, sometimes the stage is full of dysfunctional action. *The Lieutenant of Inishmore* (2001) by Martin McDonagh places horrible, senseless carnage in the face of the audience. Some of the most horrific violence one is likely to find in any play, ranging from torture to corpse mutilation, appears onstage. Amazingly, the playwright is able to create outrageous humor in the midst of an onstage bloodbath of people and cats as he deconstructs the excesses of civil and religious war in Ireland. In the end all of the horror turns out, as if in sitcom, to be the result of mistaken identity.

Use of Allusion

Many times thought in plays is communicated by **allusion**—references to previous art, literature, historical event, geography, and culture. When audience members recognize these references, they are likely to find parts of the play opening up in unexpected ways. Allusion is a method of layering and texturing the play, enriching it for those who are prepared for the recognition. In some cases the entire play can function as something of an allusion. *A Tempest* (1969) by West Indian Aimé Césaire, for example, revisits and reconstructs Shakespeare's *The Tempest* to refashion the nature of colonization in the action of the play. Caliban, a literal monster in Shakespeare's play, in Césaire's becomes more clearly a victim of the powerful Prospero, who in turn decides at play's end to remain on the island and continue his struggle with the native Caliban. In the final moments of the play, Prospero appears to have sunk into madness. It is much easier now to see the awful consequences of European colonization on native peoples than it was in Shakespeare's time. Or a playwright might turn a play inside out, so to speak. Tom Stoppard took a traditional play—Shakespeare's *Hamlet*—as a point of departure but told the story from the viewpoint of two minor characters. *Rosencrantz and Guildenstern Are Dead* (1967) shows the offstage action between Shakespeare's scenes. The play can be understood and enjoyed by someone with no knowledge of the older play, but such knowledge offers an extra level of enjoyment as the audience member understands Stoppard's clever use of the original as well as his comments on how our view of the world has changed since the seventeenth century.

LANGUAGE

Language refers to the playwright's choice of words in a play. Unlike that in a poem, novel, or essay, language written for the stage must be capable of being spoken aloud. It is usually a heightened version of human speech. For many centuries the standard language of the theatre was poetry; a play written in **prose** (language similar to everyday speech) would have been considered inartistic and unworthy of production. The language of plays from the past sometimes seems artificial and strange at first, but an audience can become accustomed to it fairly quickly when it is accompanied by lively staging and clear performances.

Dialogue written in **verse** (poetry) may have a rhyme scheme or just a specific rhythm. In seventeenth-century France, Molière wrote comedies (such as *Tartuffe,* 1664) and Racine wrote tragedies (such as *Phèdre,* 1677) in rhyming couplets. Shakespeare's plays are written largely in **blank verse;** the lines are not rhymed but have a specific, set rhythm. This rhythm is often **iambic pentameter,** which means that there is a stress on each second syllable and five stresses per line. Shakespeare frequently varies this pattern, however. Sometimes the stresses fall in unusual places or extra beats are added; sometimes the ends of lines rhyme; sometimes the characters speak in prose. When plays in verse are translated into another language, it is usually impossible to reproduce the effects of the original poetry. By the eighteenth century in comedy and by the nineteenth century in melodrama and realism, prose had become the theatrical standard. If actual speech were transferred to the stage, however, it would seem boring and repetitive. Even the most authentic-sounding dialogue has been sharpened and shaped by the playwright.

The use of figurative language often enriches dramatic dialogue. When Romeo declares, "Juliet is the Sun," he uses a **metaphor** (equating two unlike objects to suggest a similarity between them) to convey the importance Juliet has assumed in his life. Juliet uses a **simile** (comparing two unlike things using *like* or *as*) to link the depth of her love to that of the ocean. **Sensory imagery** brings the physical world of the play alive for the audience and helps to convey the character's experience of environment, as when Romeo describes the dawn: "Look, love, what envious streaks / Do lace the severing clouds in yonder east." Juliet's use of **hyperbole** (overstatement) suggests her impatience when she insists that "'Tis twenty years" until the next morning.

In most plays dialogue moves back and forth between characters. When one character speaks for an extended period the speech is called a **monologue.** If the character is alone on stage or if the other characters are not supposed to hear the words, such a speech is called a **soliloquy.** A brief remark by a character meant to be heard by the audience but not the other characters is called an **aside.** Asides and soliloquies appear frequently in presentational plays.

When the words of a play are not planned ahead of time and written down but are made up on the spot by the actors, we call the creation of the text **improvisation**. Often, some rules or givens are established before the actors begin to make up words and actions, but the important quality of improvisation is that the text is, at least in some measure, based on impulse and is reactive to and dependent on the audience response. Historically, the best-known type of theatre based on improvisation is *commedia dell'arte*.

Contribution to Character

Language can communicate a great deal about character and situation. Even knowing the general idea to be conveyed, a playwright must make specific choices about how a character should express that idea. There are many ways to say "no," for example; a character who says, "Negative, sir" is very different from one who says, "Nah, I don't think so." We often infer social class and regional affiliation solely on the basis of how a character speaks. Many of Tennessee Williams's characters are clearly products of the southeastern United States, Neil Simon's of the Northeast. Shaw's play *Pygmalion* (1912) and its musical adaptation, *My Fair Lady* (1956), explore the dynamics of language and social class: Henry Higgins passes off a young Cockney girl as a duchess primarily by altering her dialect.

A playwright's choice of words can also give us important clues about a character's intelligence and emotional state. Is a character's language simple or sophisticated? Straightforward or obtuse? Does the character use many negative or positive words? Words with highly emotional connotations? Once Romeo has seen Juliet, his language reflects the profound impact: "O, she doth teach the torches to burn bright!" He develops his description of Juliet's beauty with a series of strikingly original images of light against dark: "The brightness of her cheek would shame those stars / As daylight doth a lamp." Later, carefully chosen language makes real for the audience Juliet's fear of waking in a tomb "Where bloody Tybalt, yet but green in earth, / Lies fest'ring in his shroud."

Any change in the pattern of language may signal another kind of change: heightened emotion, change of tone, or alteration of circumstance. Even when dialogue is not written in poetry, rhythm still plays an important part in creating mood and establishing a character's state of mind. For example, in Harold Pinter's *Betrayal*, Jerry is talking to his best friend, Robert. Jerry has been having an affair with Robert's wife, and he has just learned that she has confessed everything to Robert. Punctuation in the speech indicates a specific rhythm. The character does not speak in smooth, finished sentences, but haltingly, in disconnected phrases. Words are repeated, and pauses occur between thoughts. The rhythm suggests that the character is having difficulty deciding what to say; he is thinking, coming to realizations even as he speaks. On stage, pauses are often just as important as words—sometimes more so. A silent character is often one who is undergoing an intense inner struggle, and this can be reflected in the actor's face and body.

Establishing Mood and Environment

Language can also be used to describe the characters' environment and set the mood of the play. Even the general quality of the world of the play can be established through language. Hamlet compares his home to "an unweeded garden that grows to seed. Things rank and gross in nature / possess it merely." The murder of Hamlet's father has turned the court of Denmark into a place of evil, and the language of the characters reflects that transformation. Conversely, in Oscar Wilde's late Victorian comic universe, language is a tool to be manipulated and enjoyed. *The Importance of Being Earnest* (1895) is full

THE IMPORTANCE OF BEING EARNEST (1895) an iconic comedy of manners replete with verbal sparring by Oscar Wilde as revived by the Guthrie Theater in 2009. Algernon, played by John Skelly, flirts with Cecily played by Erin Krakow. Directed by Joe Dowling; costume designs by Matthew T. LeFebvre.

Photo © Michal Daniel

of important words applied to trivial things and vice versa. Gwendolen is "devoted" to bread and butter, but Lady Bracknell tells an orphaned young man, " To lose one parent can be regarded as a misfortune; to lose two looks like carelessness." The misapplication of language reflects the topsy-turvy values of the play's upper-class characters.

The two final elements of a play can only be indicated in a printed text. The production team fleshes out suggestions from the playwright and brings its own creativity to the creation of the two elements that appeal most directly to the audience's senses: music and spectacle.

MUSIC

Music has been very important in the theatre of most cultures, and in many cases it has been vital. At the time that Aristotle made his analysis, some dialogue and many choral passages in the Greek theatre seem to have been chanted and/or sung, accompanied by instrumental music. In later centuries theatre in the West became highly oriented toward spoken dialogue. This tendency was solidified in the late nineteenth century, when realism was in fashion, since dialogue seemed to be a more accurate depiction of everyday life than song. Music tended to be relegated to specialized forms, such as opera or musical comedy. In contrast, traditional theatrical forms in Asia and Southeast Asia kept music fully integrated into production, with song and musical accompaniment serving important functions in performance. For example, in the forms of Noh and Kabuki in Japan, and music drama in China, music serves song and dance and underscores dramatic action. Most Noh plays, such as *Hagoromo,* and many Kabuki plays are dance dramas that culminate in a dance performance by the protagonist. Arias are a common convention in Chinese music drama, and the characters often sing the dialogue. In most productions of these forms, the musicians and singers are prominently displayed onstage. The actors often sing, but sometimes a narrator or a chorus will sing their dialogue for them. Inspired by such Asian forms, Bertolt Brecht created many plays with music; *The Caucasian Chalk Circle* and *Mother Courage* are two examples in which major characters sing their lines. Brecht was also fond of staging such plays with the musicians onstage with the actors.

Music is a powerful tool for encouraging emotional identification; it can increase suspense, excitement, sadness, and happiness. In Western musical theatre, song is frequently used to express heightened emotion, but, following the model of Brecht, song is sometimes used to interrupt the story or emotional development and present ideas about class struggles, corruption in the palaces of power, and the plight of the poor. Shakespeare frequently calls for music in his plays, but we know little about the type of music that was used. For example, Capulet calls for music and dancing as his party begins. The music here may be used both to create the atmosphere of a public gathering and to underscore the first meeting of the protagonists. Even in realistic plays, a limited amount of music can serve important functions. In *A Raisin in the Sun,* traditional African music and jazz coming from a phonograph and radio set the mood in the Younger household and help to establish the family's cultural roots. Tennessee Williams's *A Streetcar Named Desire* (1947) has so much offstage music coming from the French Quarter in New Orleans that much of the dramatic action of the play is underscored.

It is sometimes useful to expand the definition of "music" beyond traditional song or instrumental underscoring and include the use of other sound. Offstage sound effects can contribute to mood, give important information, or cause action, as when the noise of the approaching watchman hurries Friar Lawrence from the Capulet tomb, leaving Juliet alone to join Romeo in death. The gunshot at the end of *'night, Mother* not only is startling, but also signals the end of Jessie's life. One of the most famous offstage sounds comes at the end of Henrik Ibsen's *A Doll House* (1879) when Nora leaves her husband. We hear only the front door slamming shut.

EXPLORING Historical and Cultural Perspectives

Korean Mime Musical

Music finds many uses in plays from the Greeks to the present. Plays endowed with the label of "musical" typically include many songs with lyrics and recitative. In South Korea, however, for several decades musical storytelling has taken a form with little or no dialogue. A series of musical plays performed in Seoul under the umbrella title of *Miso* (beautiful smile) incorporate traditional Korean stories, music, and extensive dance and stylized movement. The 2010 edition of *Miso* at the Chongdong Theatre presents the story of the love affair of Chunhyang (a beautiful young girl) and a young man, Mongryong, who are divided by a powerful magistrate, Byeon Hakdo, who wants Chunhyang for himself. Of course, she will not yield to the villain who throws her in prison, but all ends happily with Mongryong studying hard and becoming a secret inspector of the crown who returns to his village in disguise, outwits the villain (who is himself committed to prison), and marries Chunhyang. Interestingly, Mongryong overcomes the villain without violence. All ends in celebration with the wedding and village dance.

The play opens with a dance depicting a harvest and purification ritual led by a female shaman. Midway through the dramatic action of the play, a sword dance occurs with much martial twirling reminiscent of traditional Chinese performance. An acrobatic interlude is presented by juggling and drumming clown-like entertainers who even encourage audience participation—a remarkable shift from the style of the rest of the performance.

A high point of the musical is a drumming number in which hero and villain express their desire for Chunhyang

MISO (2010). The Five-Drum dance in which the protagonist and villain express their attraction to the heroine and contempt for each other through exuberant drumming.

Photo from program. Collection of the authors.

and their contempt for one another through powerful beating on large drums. No dialogue is ever spoken in this play, and the principals never sing, although two brief songs are sung by a narrative character. A plot summary was also projected on the screen before the dramatic action began. This musical tragicomedy is a bit like *Romeo and Juliet* with a happy ending.

SPECTACLE

Spectacle refers to the visual elements called for in a play. It could include scenery, costumes, props, lighting, actor physicality, and movement and can offer a satisfying sensory experience. The intense colors used in Indian Kathakali dance drama and the beautiful, detailed costumes and sets of Japanese Kabuki theatre have appealed strongly to generations of audience members. In addition, visual elements can convey mood, furnish excitement, and convey meaning. Many choices regarding spectacle are left up to the production team, but the play often calls for or implies important visual elements. The opening brawl between the Capulet and Montague factions gets *Romeo and Juliet* off to a rousing start and clearly establishes the feud between the families. The image of Romeo and Juliet touching each other's palms is clearly indicated in the dialogue and has become a familiar symbol of young love. The Capulet party offers opportunity for colorful costumes and dancing—a scene of gaiety—in sharp contrast to the tableau of the lifeless young lovers at the play's end.

Many Western plays open with a description of setting. The playwright defines the world inhabited by the characters as it exists in that playwright's mind. Frequently, this physical description is filled with information about the play's geographic location, about the social and economic position of the characters, about the characters' tastes. Susan Glaspell's one-act play *Trifles* (1916) begins with a description of the deserted farmhouse of a murder victim:

> *a gloomy kitchen, and left without having been put in order—unwashed pans under the sink, a loaf of bread outside the breadbox, a dish towel on the table—other signs of incompleted work.*[2]

Spectacle, in this case, becomes central to the action of the play, as the female characters, Mrs. Hale and Mrs. Peters, solve the crime by reading the past from small domestic clues—"trifles" overlooked by the male law enforcement officers.

Even when a setting is abstract or minimal, it makes an important contribution to defining the dramatized world. Samuel Beckett's *Endgame* (1957) takes place in the aftermath of some kind of unspecified holocaust. The barren reality of the characters is encapsulated in the set. The interior is free of any decoration. The light is described as gray. The windows, too high to be reached without a ladder, suggest an unseen world outside.

In any given play the six elements—plot, character, thought, language, music, and spectacle—work together to create a special world on the stage. The relative significance of the different elements varies considerably from play to play. In *Romeo and Juliet,* for example, plot and character are stronger than thought. In Kathakali dance drama, spectacle and music are of prime importance. The weight of each element can change according to the time and culture in which the play was written and in which it is performed as well as the preferences of the individual playwright. It is the combination of elements that creates the experience for the audience, but a careful analysis of components can often reveal a great deal about how a play functions in the theatre.

PERICLES by Shakespeare. A remarkable spectacle was created in a small space in a revival in 2005 at the Guthrie Theater in Minneapolis. Actors Lee Mark Nelan and Kate Eifrig. Directed by Joel Sass.
Photo © Michal Daniel.

CHAPTER REVIEW

Questions and Activities

1. Choose a television series that you know well and analyze its structure. How is exposition delivered? Is there more than one line of action in each episode? What kind of climax does it typically use? When do the commercial breaks occur? Try several different types of shows (cop show, sitcom, soap).

2. Read a linear, causally structured play (for example, Susan Glaspell's *Trifles,* Lorraine Hansberry's *A Raisin in the Sun,* or Henrik Ibsen's *A Doll House* or *Ghosts*). Create a graph that reflects the emotional rise and fall of your play from an audience's point of view. It won't look exactly like the diagrams in this chapter; each play will be somewhat different. Choose specific moments in the play for inciting incident and climax. If your choices differ from those of other students, discuss how the choice of climax affects interpretation of the play.

3. Read a play that is not causally structured (for example, Ntozake Shange's *for colored girls who have considered suicide when the rainbow is enuf,* Tom Stoppard's *The Invention of Love,* or Eugène Ionesco's *The Bald Soprano*). How would you describe the plot of this play—in other words, what provides its unity? What holds it together?

4. Discuss the advantages and disadvantages from a writer's point of view of writing for a continuing series versus a single two-hour play or film.

5. Choose a character from a play, film, or television show. List as many character traits as you can think of, putting them in the five levels of characterization. Then discuss *how* these character traits are conveyed.

6. Choose a play or film in which thought is very important. What ideas were conveyed? *How* were these ideas conveyed?

7. Write a critical analysis of a play. Begin by reading and experiencing the play. Think about which of the six elements is most important in this play. Read the play again. Pay particular attention to and take notes on the particular element(s) you have chosen as your focus. (See also the sections "Reading a Play" and "Writing about a Play" in Chapter 5.)

Key Terms and Concepts

dialogue, p. 76
stage directions, p. 76
elements of a play, p. 76
plot, p. 76
structure, p. 76
linear plot, p. 76
causal plot, p. 76
conflict, p. 77
point of attack, p. 77
episodic, p. 77
exposition, p. 77
inciting incident, p. 78
rising action, p. 78
climax, p. 78
falling action, p. 78
subplot, p. 79
discovery, p. 79
reversal, p. 80

well-made play, p. 80
cliff-hanger, p. 82
flashback, p. 83
rasa, p. 83
poststructuralism, p. 86
metatheatre, p. 86
performance art, p. 88
character, p. 88
protagonist, p. 88
levels of characterization, p. 89
biological traits, p. 89
physical traits, p. 89
psychological and emotional
    traits, p. 90
social traits, p. 90
ethical traits, p. 91
thought, p. 92
allusion, p. 93

language, p. 94
prose, p. 94
verse, p. 94
blank verse, p. 94
iambic pentameter, p. 94
metaphor, p. 94
simile, p. 94
sensory imagery, p. 94
hyperbole, p. 94
monologue, p. 94
soliloquy, p. 94
aside, p. 94
improvisation, p. 95
commedia dell'arte, p. 95
music, p. 96
spectacle, p. 97

For Further Exploration

J. L. Styan. *The Elements of Drama.* Cambridge, U K: Cambridge University, 1960.

Ronald Hayman. *How to Read a Play,* 2nd ed. New York: Grove Press, 1999.

James Thomas. *Script Analysis for Actors, Directors, and Designers.* Oxford, UK: Elsevier, 2005.

John Russell Taylor. *The Rise and Fall of the Well-Made Play.* London: Methuen, 1967.

Viola Spolin and Paul Sills, eds. *Improvisation for the Theater: A Handbook of Teaching and Directing Techniques,* 3rd ed. Chicago: Northwestern University, 1999.

JANET McTEER as the title character in a rainstorm in the tragedy *Mary Stuart* (1800) by Freidrich Schiller, adapted by Peter Oswald, Broadway production (2009).

Photo © Joan Marcus.

Interpreting the Play

Understanding Genre, Reading, and Writing

In this chapter we discuss a useful tool for analyzing and comparing plays: dramatic genre. Because a play is meant as a blueprint for production, it needs to be read differently from other literature. To help develop these skills, we discuss effective strategies for reading a printed text as well as writing about plays, which can lead you to new levels of understanding and interpretation.

DRAMATIC GENRE

A culture that creates or sustains theatrical activity often finds a way to classify its plays; putting plays in categories is one way of talking about which ones are similar and discovering how they work. In the ancient Indian Sanskrit drama, a play was classified according to the mood, or *rasa,* it evoked. Japanese Noh divides its plays into five categories according to character and subject matter: gods, warriors, women, supernatural beings, and miscellaneous characters. As far back as the Greeks, plays in the Western tradition were classified according to genre. **Genre** relates to the kind of emotional response a play creates in the audience. One genre is not better than another; different types of emotional reactions serve different purposes in the theatre. We will discuss four major genres here: tragedy, comedy, tragicomedy, and melodrama, as well as some of the subgenres that have been used to identify plays at various times. In the twentieth century genres became so combined that many recent plays defy generic identification.

Tragedy

While the terms "tragedy" and "tragic" are frequently used in everyday speech to mean "sad" or an event including unexpected death, in the theatre these terms refer very specifically to a particular type of drama. If a play is serious and ends unhappily, it may be a **tragedy.** Traditionally, "serious" and "unhappy" are not the only characteristics of tragedy, however. Aristotle believed that tragedy evoked the emotions of pity and fear in its audience—pity because the audience sympathizes with the protagonist and fear because the audience empathizes with the character who is facing a difficult problem.

Audience members in most periods have expected a certain dignity and importance from tragedy. The nature of this importance—often translated as **magnitude** in Aristotle's definition of tragedy—has been debated for centuries. What makes a play "important"? For the ancient Greeks and for many societies to follow, "importance" was closely related to the social class of the characters. Tragedy was about people of noble birth. Today, many people object to the notion that social class has any relationship to the "importance" of a person's life or story, but it is at least understandable that when something happened to a royal family, the entire kingdom was affected. In *Oedipus the King* (c. 430–425 B.C.E.) Oedipus has been a very successful ruler of Thebes, for example, and his fate is inextricably tied to that of his people. Magnitude might also refer to the importance of the issues treated in the play. The action of tragedy raises serious and difficult questions—the nature of justice for example, or free will versus predestination.

The protagonist in a tragedy frequently faces an **ethical choice,** or choice about a moral issue: Should I kill the king who murdered my father? Should I implicate other people to save my own life? Sometimes a character's ethical choice brings about the character's own downfall. In Sophocles' play *Antigone* (415 B.C.E.), the title character faces a difficult ethical choice. Both of her brothers are dead. The king, her uncle, has ordered that one brother, who fought in a rebellion against the state,

MEDEA by Euripides. In this 2002 production by the Theatre de la Jeune Lune, Minneapolis, note the central door, open space, and architectural façade, which are traditional in interpretations of Greek tragedy and are based on our understanding of Greek space and plays. Medea (on the ground) is played by Barbara Berlovitz. Chorus by Isabell Monk; Creon by Allen Hamilton. Directed by Steven Epp; scenic and lighting design by Dominique Sarrand; costume design by Sonya Berlovitz. Photo © Michal Daniel.

should remain unburied. The body must be allowed to rot. Antigone's religion and family loyalty tell her that she must give her brother a proper burial. She follows the dictates of her conscience and buries her brother, disobeying the law of the state. Antigone makes her choice with full knowledge that her uncle has declared any violation punishable by death. The conflicts of personal conscience and obedience to authority, of loyalty to state or religion, of following the dictates of love or honor, have tremendous resonance in the twenty-first century, regardless of when the play was written.

The Greeks saw tragedy as a way of explaining why bad things happen; if terrible things happened to a good person for no reason, it would suggest chaos rather than order in the world. Protagonists were often basically good people who made mistakes. Later critics have pointed out that tragedy often depicts a complex moral universe: Things are not just good or bad. As such, tragedy is a true reflection of the world we live in. No one is perfect, and good can be found in "bad" people, just as bad qualities can be found in basically "good" people.

Theorists have wondered about the popularity and longevity of a dramatic form that ends unhappily. What compels human beings to create and seek out this kind of empathic experience? For the ancient Greeks, **catharsis** was one answer—it was healthy to evoke strong emotions and then let them ebb away. Certainly, the ability to experience extreme emotion vicariously is an intriguing part of tragedy. Other commentators have found a teaching value in tragedy; the advice of some tragedies seems to be "Don't make the same mistake." One of the most enduring explanations of tragedy, however, is that the form demonstrates nobility of the human character. Our attention in tragedy is not so much on *what* happens but on *how* it happens and how the people involved deal with adversity. The audience often knows the outcome of tragedy from the beginning. The ancient Greeks knew the legends and myths on which their tragedies were based before they entered the theatre, but the playwrights retold these tales and altered emphasis. Shakespeare tells us in the opening of *Romeo and Juliet* (a romantic tragedy, 1594–1595) that the lovers are "star-crossed" or unlucky; we know that their story will not end happily. We are interested in the strength of character that is demonstrated and the kinds of choices the characters make on their journey. *Romeo and Juliet* was also adapted as a modern urban musical tragedy, *West Side Story*, in 1957.

Although tragedy as a genre is not a focus of most traditional Asian theatre, a number of Japanese Kabuki plays feature situations that are recognized as tragic. *The Scarlet Princess of Edo* (1817), for example, includes complex, violent, and erotic action. Princess Sakura falls into poverty and prostitution and loses her child amid many murders and suicides as well as a visit from a ghost.

In the eighteenth century, as more democratic forms of government became a reality, playwrights began to write tragedies about middle-class characters. George Lillo's *The London Merchant* (1731) depicts the downfall of a shopkeeper's apprentice. By the mid-nineteenth century, Georg Büchner in Germany was at work on *Woyzeck* (1836), a tragedy with a working-class protagonist. Woyzeck, a poor soldier, is victimized by both the military and a corrupt doctor who uses him as a guinea pig in his scientific experiments. Woyzeck finally snaps and repeatedly stabs Marie, his promiscuous lover, to death.

Tragedy is less common in new work beyond the nineteenth century, but it has occasionally appeared in plays such as Eugene O'Neill's *Desire under the Elms*

WOYZECK (1837), a working-class tragedy by Georg Büchner, as reconceived and directed by Robert Wilson, who has created some of the most carefully choreographed and magnificent postmodern images in recent theatrical production. Jens Jørn Spottag as Woyzeck, Kaya Brüel as Marie at the Betty Nansen Theatre, Denmark.

Photo © hansen-hansen.com. Courtesy of Eric Hansen-Hansen.

ALL MY SONS (1947), a modern, realistic, American tragedy by Arthur Miller. This 2010 revival by The Huntington Theatre Company featured Will Lyman as the guilt-ridden protagonist, Joe Keller, who agonizes over his unethical decisions that contributed to the deaths of American airmen during World War II. He is depicted here unable to sleep at night being comforted by his wife, Kate, who is oblivious to his past deeds and is played by Karen MacDonald. The play concludes with Keller's suicide. Directed by David Esbjornson; scenic design by Scott Bradley.

Photo © T. Charles Erickson.

(1924) and *Mourning Becomes Electra* (1931), two dark explorations of family life that were based on the Greek tragedies of Euripides and Aeschylus. American playwright Maxwell Anderson used historical British figures to depict the clash of political responsibility and personal emotion in *Anne of a Thousand Days* (1948), about Anne Boleyn, and *Mary of Scotland* (1933), about Mary, Queen of Scots. Artists and theorists have speculated about the difficulty of writing modern tragedy, pointing out that a tragic viewpoint is difficult to achieve, since playwrights can no longer assume shared religious or moral beliefs in the audience. Some argue that in this age of fragmentation it is difficult to find a person whose fate is of great enough significance to be considered of tragic importance. In 1949 Arthur Miller wrote his essay "Tragedy of the Common Man," advocating a redefinition of "importance" and defending his use of an ordinary protagonist in *Death of a Salesman* (1949). The title of the play is significant; Miller examines the suicide of a salesman, not a king or a queen.

Since the last several decades of the twentieth century, some feminist critics have found the traditional structure of tragedy (based on stimulating catharsis) to be an inherently male construct, evolving from a male view of reality. Women playwrights, they argued, tended to see human events in less linear terms and often implied the possibility of change and growth in their plays, rather than inevitability.

Comedy

Of course, if a play is basically humorous, it is probably a **comedy.** Although comedy is a tremendously popular form, the genre of comedy is more difficult to pin down than tragedy. If tragedy creates the emotions of pity and fear, the genre of comedy might be defined through its *lack* of such emotional involvement. If you feel very strongly about something, it is often difficult to laugh. When you find something funny, you are looking at the situation more objectively; sometimes, no matter how bad things get, it is possible to step back and laugh because of the ridiculousness of the situation.

SPAMALOT by Eric Idle and John DuPrez was the Broadway musical hit of 2005. The production presents big splashy numbers full of anachronistic elements such as the Lady of the Lake and her Laker Girls who sometimes act like cheerleaders. The spirit of Monty Python is alive and well in this show directed by Mike Nichols.
Photo © Joan Marcus.

The audience can laugh in comedy because any threat to the characters is much less serious than in tragedy. In comedy there is seldom a sense of impending doom because the stakes in the conflict are lower. Rather than death, a character might be threatened with discovery in an embarrassing situation. Rather than ethical choice, characters typically make expedient choices—not *whether* something should be done, but *how* it should be done: How can I sneak out of this room before my husband finds me here? How can I convince the rich lady to give me the money that I need? How can I meet this attractive woman? How can I steal that delicious pie? Because the stakes are lower, our emotional engagement tends to be less intense than it is with tragedy.

Comic action sometimes diverts an audience by taking it out of itself. *Anything Goes* has been one of the most popular musical comedies since its premiere in 1934. It has spawned numerous professional revivals, feature films, and countless amateur productions. The Broadway versions of the libretto have been rewritten regularly since the first one by Guy Bolton and P. G. Wodehouse, and the famous Cole Porter music has been rearranged often, with a new version of book and score for the 2011 Broadway show. The silly but diverting action revolves around lovesick principals, disguises, misunderstandings, and crazy adventures aboard a trans-Atlantic ocean liner. Along with its title song, the tune "I Get a Kick Out of You" probably best represents the escapist adventures of this play.

Some comedy uses laughter to render a serious problem less dangerous. The audience is invited to objectify a problem by ridiculing it. In *Volpone* (1606), Ben Jonson treats the subject of greed in a humorous way. The villains at the center of the action, Volpone and Mosca, are so successful that they can be caught by no one but themselves. Often, the conflict in comedy results from a social norm being violated—an old man wants to marry a young girl, for example, or two characters want to carry on an extramarital affair. Usually, the social norm is reestablished at the end of the play: The appropriate people are paired up, and all is right with the world. The return to social order is often celebrated festively with a dance or a marriage, and most or all of the characters are reunited in the final scene.

Comedy has a broad appeal, and its development has taken a number of different directions in the last two thousand years. Some critics have found it useful to subdivide the genre into at least five types. Some you will find very familiar; others you might not yet have encountered.

Situation comedy, as the term suggests, emphasizes the humorous qualities of the situation in which the characters find themselves. The type is usually traced back to ancient Roman comedy, which treated the affairs of typical middle-class people. *The Phormio* (161 B.C.E.), by Terence, is a situation comedy about the ridiculous manipulations of a wily servant who helps two young men win the brides they seek. The play was so successful and influential beyond its time that Molière adapted it (but changed the name of the servant hero) as the hit comedy *The Tricks of Scapin* (1671). Playwrights from many periods have adapted the major servant character under various names—Phormio, Scapin, or Scapino—and continue to use the role as a wonderful vehicle for a comic actor. Shakespeare based *Comedy of Errors* (1592–1593), the crazy exploits of two sets of twins, on the Roman situation comedy *The Brothers Menaechmus* (c. second century B.C.E.).

Neil Simon has been very successful in writing situation comedies for the U.S. stage. *Rumors* (1988) is a spoof of a murder mystery. Farcical plot dominates the array of quirky, often paranoid characters who are all wealthy and sparring friends. Coincidence complicates most of the action at a dinner party that is missing its hosts. Although Simon's recent plays have usually maintained a basic situation comedy format, they often contain serious and contemplative moments, creating a bittersweet tone. The TV "sitcom" is the most prevalent example of the situation comedy in current society. *Gary Unmarried* and *The Middle* are family-based situation comedies, although the former is a divorced family that continues to interact. Many sitcom families are comically dysfunctional. Sometimes the "family" of sitcoms is actually a work environment as appears in *The Office* and *30 Rock*.

Farce is a type of comedy that emphasizes broad physical action. In this case the term "broad" means large or exaggerated action. The performers of *commedia dell'arte* (an improvisational form from Italy) specialized in this type of comedy. Use of the term **slapstick** to designate broad comic action originated with *commedia* actors and their use of a long, flat paddle with a flap that literally made a loud slapping sound when used for comic beatings. The *commedia* legacy can be traced through the Marx Brothers, the Three Stooges, and into animated cartoons. Coincidence and mistaken identity occur frequently in farce, and the characters are put in situations that require specific physical action. Japanese Kyōgen plays serve as comic interludes for the more somber Noh drama, *Tied to a Pole* (c. 1350), also adapted for the Kabuki theatre, revolves around two servants. To prevent them from stealing his liquor, their master binds one servant's hands together and lashes another servant to a pole. Despite this incapacitation, the servants try to drink their master's wine and ultimately succeed. The physical comedy that results is communicated clearly to the audience members, regardless of whether

COMMEDIA DELL'ARTE
farcical stock character Capitano, a braggart soldier and would-be lover type, who is ineffectual in both roles. He typically wears a half mask and high plumed hat, and carries a very long sword to compensate for his erotic and pugilistic deficiencies.
Illustration by Maurice Sand (c. 1860).

TIED TO A POLE In this Japanese Kabuki farce, the two servants are chided and threatened by their master before he leaves the house. The master has bound his two servants because he doesn't trust them while he is gone, yet they acrobatically manage to raid his supply of wine without using their hands. Kabuki world tour.
Photo Grand Kabuki Program (1982). Collection of the authors.

they share a language with the performers. The French medieval farce *Pierre Pathelin* (c. 1470) dramatizes a lawyer tricking a merchant, then a supposedly stupid peasant in turn tricking the lawyer. *Pierre Pathelin* was popular in France for centuries. In fact, farce is frequently associated with France. Molière wrote many farces in the seventeenth century, such as *The Flying Doctor* (c. 1650). At the end of the nineteenth century Georges Feydeau created some of the most enduring farces; in *Hotel Paradiso* (1894), as in many farces that have followed, there are many doors on stage because characters are constantly running in and out, just missing each other, just barely escaping discovery. Feydeau's characters typically pursue clandestine affairs and are forced to hide under beds, in closets, and in trunks, afraid that they will be caught in a compromising position. British playwright Alan Ayckbourn capitalized on this sexually suggestive situation by entitling one of his comedies *Bedroom Farce* in 1977.

Farce provides the opportunity for highly physical actors to display their technique. *A Funny Thing Happened on the Way to the Forum* (1962), a musical farce by Stephen Sondheim, Burt Shevelove, and Larry Gelbart cobbled together from bits and pieces of Roman comedy, has utilized the talents of comic actors Zero Mostel (in 1962), Phil Silvers (in 1972), and Nathan Lane (in 1996). *Noises Off* (1982) by Michael Frayn follows the antics of an out-of-control theatrical company. The play ends with a fast-paced scene in which the characters onstage perform a play, and everything that can go wrong does. Some favorite "classic" TV shows are farces; *I Love Lucy*, for example, was created around Lucille Ball's talent for physical comedy.

Comedy of character is driven by the eccentricities of its major figure. Molière also specialized in this subtype, often playing the major roles himself. The action of *The Hypochondriac* (1673) revolves around a man who imagines himself ill with a variety of ailments; Harpagon in *The Miser* (1668) is blinded by his own greed. A musical example of comedy of character is *Hello, Dolly!* (1963), based on Thornton Wilder's *The Matchmaker* (1954). Dolly Levi is a colorful and persistent character who drives the action of the play. Based on a comic strip from the 1930s, the musical comedy *Annie* (1977), by Charles Strouse, Martin Charnin, and Thomas Meehan, is unified by its focus on a precocious orphan girl searching for her parents. Beth Henley's *Crimes of the Heart* (1979) features three eccentric sisters who are reunited during a time of family crisis.

NOISES OFF by Michael Frayn. The Act I setting for this farce depicts the interior setting for the production of a play. The audience watches the characters rehearsing a play. Notice the plentiful doors on different levels, which encourage farcical chases, hiding, and near discoveries. Directed by Risa Brainin; scenic design by Nayna Ramey; costume design by Devon Painter.

Courtesy of Indiana Repertory Theatre.

Reckless (1988) by Craig Lucas is a black comedy of character that includes a parade of eccentrics surrounding a transformative female protagonist on the run from her husband.

Comedy of idea is focused on thought rather than character or situation. The plays of the Greek author Aristophanes are comedies of ideas. During the years of a real war between Athens and Sparta, Aristophanes staged *Lysistrata* (411 B.C.E.), in which women take over the fortress of the city and refuse sex to all their mates until the men decide to stop fighting. George Bernard Shaw is the master of comedy of idea in English. *Arms and the Man* (1894) debunks the concept of heroism, and *Man and Superman* (1905) predicts the next wave of human evolution: newly emancipated, independent, and modern men and women who will replace the obsolete, frail human beings of Shaw's time. George C. Wolfe's *The Colored Museum* (1986) uses the musical revue form (songs and short scenes tied together by a theme) to satirize stereotypes from black history, ranging from an experience in a slave ship to a lampoon of *A Raisin in the Sun*.

Comedy of manners, as the term suggests, explores the behavior of a particular segment of society. Characters frequently find that their own desires are at odds with social expectations. Historically, comedy of manners has focused most often on upper-class society to both celebrate and poke fun at its pretensions. The English Restoration period (1660–1700) is known as the golden age for comedy of manners and produced plays in which the idle rich entertain themselves with sexual intrigue and clever dialogue. In William Wycherley's *The Country Wife* (1675), the major character, Horner, circulates the rumor that he is incapable of having sex in order to gain access to other men's wives. Oscar Wilde's frequently revived *The Importance of Being Earnest* (1895) is a fine example of comedy of manners from the Victorian period; in it two young ladies vow that they can only love and marry someone named Ernest. The play seems to make fun of the new movement of realism, including some of Wilde's own plays, such as *Lady Windermere's Fan* (1892). George Bernard Shaw's *Pygmalion* (1912), a comedy of manners that was later adapted by Lerner and Loewe as the musical *My Fair Lady* (1956), explores the relationship between social class and speech.

In 1845 Anna Cora Mowatt created a comedy of manners with American characters; *Fashion* makes fun of the newly rich who mimic the fashions of Paris. In the end truthfulness and integrity triumph over social pretension and hypocrisy. American playwright Philip Barry developed a distinctive style of comedy of manners in the 1920s and 1930s with plays such as *The Philadelphia Story* (1939), which features a vivacious young heroine (originally played by Katharine Hepburn) who has rejected but is later reunited with her true love. Stephen Sondheim and Hugh Wheeler's musical *A Little Night Music* (1973) follows this tradition by exploring the erratic behavior of upper-class society with both a satirical and sympathetic eye. Many comedies of manners include a large dose of satire, and *The Little Dog Laughed* (2006) by Douglas Carter Beane is no exception as it explores the vicissitudes of media fame in American culture replete with sexual confusion, con artists, and failed attempts at secrecy in a world that allows none.

Romantic comedy follows the attempts of lovers to get together. It shares this basic structure with many situation comedies, but romantic comedies more often produce a feeling of well-being and sympathy at the end, rather than strong laughs. Shakespeare's *Much Ado about Nothing* (1598–1599) is a good example, as avowed enemies Beatrice and Benedick end up confessing their love for each other as the result of a trick orchestrated by their friends. The perennially popular musical *The Fantasticks* (1960, which had a first run of almost 42 years), by Tom Jones and Harvey Schmidt, is a romantic comedy in which the lovers weather misfortune and hard experience before ultimately satisfying their fathers' hopes of union.

Most comedies combine elements of several different subtypes. Farcical action is an important part of *Much Ado about Nothing* and *The Fantasticks*, even though the main thrust of action in these plays is romantic. In categorizing a play, it is important to think about what drives the major action: the situation, a character's eccentricities, an idea, social behavior, romance, or perhaps a different element.

Tragedy and comedy treat the two poles of human experience, and their symbols, the tragic and comic masks, have come to denote the theatrical experience in its entirety. Although most societies have recognized the importance of encompassing both the tragic and comic in theatre, they have differed in their viewpoint of what the relationship between the two genres should be. In the ancient Greek theatre and the classic Noh theatre, tragic and comic action were kept separate and were seldom combined in the same drama. The serious plays were also separated from the comic plays by being performed on different performance days in Greece or in different parts of the program in Japan. The Elizabethans did not mind combining genres and indeed used humorous scenes as **comic relief**—action created to ease emotional tension or contrast with a major event—at strategic points within a serious play. In *Macbeth* (1605–1606), Shakespeare brings on the comic character of a drunken Porter just as the title character and his wife have killed King Duncan (an excruciatingly tense scene). The Porter makes sexual jokes that have nothing to do with the tragic action, and he never appears again. In spite of occasional comic moments in serious plays or serious moments in comic plays, a play is categorized by its overall emotional effect. Few people would call *Macbeth* a comedy on the basis of the Porter scene. *The Caucasian Chalk Circle* by Bertolt Brecht includes outrageous comedy in the midst of a serious story. In the second half, a corrupt imposter becomes a judge who helps the poor and downtrodden by passing judgments in violation of the laws created by the rich and powerful.

SCHOOL FOR WIVES (1662), a French character comedy by Molière, the plot is driven by the eccentricities of Arnolphe, who insists that the only way to keep wives faithful is to bring them up in ignorance of the world. This he does with Agnes so that he can marry her, but of course his ridiculous plan backfires. A 2009 production by the Shakespeare Theatre of New Jersey directed by Bruce B. Crowe. Arnolphe is played by Bruce Cromer and Agnes by Erin Partin.

Photo © Gerry Goodstein.

Tragicomedy

When the tragic and comic tendencies seem equally mixed, a play is often called a **tragicomedy.** During the Italian Renaissance, tragicomedy came to mean a middle form that incorporated serious action, everyday (rather than noble) characters, and a happy ending. The Elizabethans created plays with serious action but happy endings, as in Shakespeare's *The Winter's Tale* (1610–1611), which ends with a repentant husband discovering that the wife he thought was dead is actually alive. This middle or third form had many manifestations in the eighteenth and nineteenth centuries. In France Denis Diderot theorized the need for a serious play without a tragic conclusion and

ENDGAME (1957) by Samuel Beckett depicts a bleak existence in a gray, nebulous, bunker-like space with time running out for the characters. Nonetheless, much of the action is comic and clown-like, just as it is in the playwright's *Waiting for Godot.* Produced at the Court Theatre in Chicago in 2005. Hamm and Clov (played by Allen Gilmore and Joe Foust) perpetuate a master/servant relationship as they move toward their end. Directed by Christopher Bayes. Photo © Michael Brosilow.

called the form *drame.* His own versions of this type were dull, but he inspired many others to experiment with the idea. In the early nineteenth century, German romantic playwright Heinrich von Kleist insisted on calling any of his serious plays, such as *The Prince of Homburg* (1811), simply *spiel,* or "play," and many who followed him have done the same. In the twentieth century many playwrights called their mixed-tone efforts "plays," and since the 1950s television has grown fond of identifying serious teleplays as simply "drama."

In the late nineteenth and early twentieth centuries, Russian playwright Anton Chekhov perfected the drama of mixed tone: Comic and tragic points of view are presented almost simultaneously. A typical Chekhovian stage direction is "laughing through tears." In *Uncle Vanya* (1899) a well-meaning, middle-aged man comes to realize that he has spent his entire life supporting a priggish and pretentious fraud. Mid-twentieth-century playwrights took such tragicomedy in different directions. Tennessee Williams wrote with mixed tone but tended to emphasize the serious in plays such as *A Streetcar Named Desire* (1947). Samuel Beckett explored the dark side of the human condition using traditional comic turns in *Waiting for Godot* (1953). In *A Raisin in the Sun* (1959), Lorraine Hansberry depicted both the strength and the tensions within a family as its members pursue different and sometimes conflicting routes to escape poverty. Although the tone differs remarkably in the Pulitzer Prize-winning *August: Osage County* (2007) by Tracy Letts, a domestic situation creates a comic but distressing landscape as a dysfunctional extended family in rural Oklahoma alternately faces or evades alcoholism, drug addiction, suicide, incest, and racism in the midst of petty squabbling and a reordering of the family leadership. Many contemporary artists find tragicomedy an appealing form, since it seems to reflect the ambiguity in modern life.

Melodrama

If the action of a play is serious but ends happily and if the focus is more on *what* happens rather than *how,* the play can be classified as a **melodrama.** Although melodrama shares the combination of seriousness and happiness with tragicomedy, certain characteristics set it apart; because of its enormous popularity, melodrama is often thought of as a separate genre. In everyday speech, we often use the term "melodramatic" in a belittling way to mean "overemotional." In theatrical terminology, however, "melodrama" refers to a specific genre of play with recognizable characteristics. Melodrama tends to rely on fast-paced action and suspense, and the audience's main concern is whether something will happen rather than how the characters will react: Will the cops arrive in time? Will the beautiful woman kill her lover? Sometimes the action may be highly emotional rather than physical, as in the television subgenre of soap operas, or "soaps." Will John divorce Mary? Will Harry discover his son's true identity? Discovery and reversal

THE STREETS OF LONDON is Dion Boucicault's British version of his *Poor of New York* shifted deftly to a different location to make the melodrama topical. The spectacle of the burning building was part of the draw of this play, regardless of the title or city indicated by the title.
Victoria and Albert Museum, UK.

play large roles in the action of melodrama: The murder weapon is discovered, the old friend is revealed to be a traitor (discovery), the villain lifts a key from the jailer and escapes (reversal).

The climax of a melodrama is usually a scene in which spectacle plays a major role. Exploding mines, fiery steamships, heroines teetering on cliffs, and car chases have all been used to raise dramatic tension to the breaking point. Westerns have shoot-outs with pistols, science fiction adventures have shoot-outs with lasers. In some subgenres of melodrama the climax is less dependent on spectacle, but the emphasis is still on suspense. Murder mysteries, such as the many dramatizations of the Sherlock Holmes stories, rely on revelation of the killer (discovery) for the climax.

Traditionally, the conflict in melodrama is between the forces of goodness and evil. A hero or heroine is usually pitted against a villain, and the play ends with **poetic justice:** Good is rewarded; evil is punished. Melodrama shares with tragedy the emotion of fear but also stimulates hate. The clarity of moral definition in melodrama is quite different from that in tragedy.

Melodrama may or may not deal with serious issues. It has been a favorite way of advocating social and political causes. *Uncle Tom's Cabin* (1852) was trumpeted as an important contribution to the abolition of slavery, and the temperance movement used melodramas such as *The Drunkard* (1844) and *Ten Nights in a Bar-Room* (1858) to depict the dangers of drunkenness and the possibility of redemption. The clear-cut definition of good and bad makes melodrama a useful tool for encouraging and discouraging various types of behavior while holding out the possibility of reward.

Twentieth-century melodramas include murder mysteries such as Agatha Christie's *The Mousetrap* (1952) and thrillers such as Frederick Knott's *Wait until Dark* (1966), in which a blind woman is terrorized in her home by two men. Television and film quickly adapted melodrama. Most story-based television series that are not sitcoms are melodramas of one type or another. The spectacular action of melodrama is especially well suited to special effects films. One of the best-known and finest examples of twentieth-century melodrama is George Lucas's *Star Wars Episode IV: A New Hope* (1977), the first of the *Star Wars* films to be released. It pits the (good) rebels against the (evil) empire. Darth Vader is a perfect villain (evil through and through). Luke, Leia, Han, and Obi-Wan team up as a collective hero. Luke destroys the Death Star in the spectacular climax, and the final scene shows the heroes receiving medals and applause. In subsequent *Star Wars* films, Lucas kept the basic form but began playing against audience expectations in selected scenes: Darth Vader is revealed to be Luke and Leia's father and later redeems himself to some extent by saving Luke from the emperor. The enormous popularity of the *Star Wars* films (as well as the steady stream of those featuring superheroes) is a testament to the satisfaction that audiences derive from melodrama that is done well.

Departures from Traditional Genre

Many plays, particularly from the twentieth century on, do not seem to fit neatly into a traditional genre. It is not necessary to declare unequivocally that a play belongs in one genre or another. In trying to decide, however, you will often discover some important qualities. Playwrights sometimes work against our traditional expectations. In Calderón de la Barca's tragicomedy *Life Is a Dream* (c. 1636), the playwright startles his audience by suddenly killing off the clown near the end of the play.

In *Rock 'n' Roll* (2006) by Tom Stoppard, we may be surprised to see the worlds of rock music mixed with the geopolitical conflicts of the Cold War, especially in England and Czechoslovakia. Furthermore, the action sometimes includes disparate locations or even periods of time simultaneously onstage. A play that seems like a comedy at the beginning and then becomes serious is often very disturbing. A taboo subject treated in a comic tone makes us uneasy; such a play can make us question our own value system. Joe Orton's play *What the Butler Saw* (1969) makes farce out of the taboo subject matter (at the time the play was written) of homosexuality and incest. *Copenhagen* (1998) by Michael Frayn does not correspond to any of the traditional Western genres but is structured much like a traditional Noh play: The dead reflect on the past, trying to find meaning. Some playwrights find the whole notion of genre irrelevant and take advantage of the freedom to craft plays without the restrictions of a label. Others use or adapt genre to serve their own purposes. Many plays do not fit neatly into the generic box, but identifying *why* they do not is often enlightening.

READING A PLAY

When you read a play, you are not seeing the finished product as imagined by the playwright; it will not be complete until it is staged as a production and living actors are speaking the lines and moving through space. Reading is not the ideal way to experience a play. However, if you limit your knowledge to only those scripts that you can see produced, you will never experience many beautiful, funny, and inspiring plays. If you choose to become a theatre practitioner, you will read and interpret many plays in order to create production.

ROMEO AND JULIET (1899) Maude Adams and William Faversham in the balcony scene. This is a traditional nineteenth-century interpretation of this scene from the most famous romantic tragedy of Elizabethan theatre.

By permission of the Folger Shakespeare Library.

A RADICAL DEPARTURE Just 22 years after the Maude Adams production, this Russian expressionistic interpretation of the *Romeo and Juliet* balcony scene (1921) broke with tradition. Directed by Alexander Tairov. Designed by Alexandra Exter.

From Konstantin Rudnitsky, *Russian and Soviet Theater 1905–1932.*

It is therefore important for everyone who has an interest in theatre to develop the skill of imagining the play in three dimensions while reading. When you experience an actual production, the directors, designers, actors, and technicians have already done much of the work for you. When you read a play, you take on all of these roles in your own imagination.

Visualizing the Action

As you begin to read a play, try to create a mental picture of each of the characters and the space that they inhabit. Sometimes a writer will give you very complete descriptions; sometimes a writer will provide almost nothing. David Mamet, for example, sets parts of *Glengarry Glen Ross* (1983) in a Chinese restaurant. There is no description. You can imagine the space as spare and monochrome or filled with color. The intensity with which you "see" the action of the play will have a strong effect on your emotional reaction to it.

It is important to understand the action of the play as immediate, even when reading. If we think of the play as something that has already occurred, it loses much of its power. Imagine that the action is happening in real time, just as it would occur with action in a theatre. Watching the drama unfolding before you, even within your own mind, is the most fruitful way to experience a dramatic text.

To get the broad sweep of action and most immediate emotional impact, it is best to read a play for the first time in one sitting without stopping. Once you have a sense of the play as a whole, you can begin to analyze the play to increase your understanding of how it works. The most important thing to grasp as you read a play is the basic action: What is happening? It is usually not difficult to answer this question for a fairly simple play with five or fewer characters; it is more of a challenge in a play with several lines of action and many characters. Making a diagram in which character relationships are represented spatially can help you to keep things straight. We have included a diagram for *Romeo and Juliet* that illustrates graphically how the characters are related to each other (see Figure 5.1). When you look at the diagram,

FIGURE 5.1 Character Relationships in *Romeo and Juliet.*

Shakespeare's symmetrical use of character becomes apparent: Each side (Capulet and Montague) is represented by one young lover, a servant attached to that person (Nurse, Balthasar), two parents, one nephew of a parent, and a kinsman of the Prince. In other plays, Shakespeare organized the character relationships differently to facilitate a different kind of action.

Most of the text of a play is dialogue; the playwright's primary means of communication is through the words of the characters. When reading a play, however, it is important not to overlook stage directions, which can give important information. A character's physical movement, posture, or gesture may be significant. A particular visual image as described by the playwright may be essential for a complete understanding of the text. Indeed, the climax of a play may occur in a moment of action, unsupported by dialogue. Much of the hysterical comedy in the last act of *Noises Off* is furnished by event: Props appear, disappear, and fall apart, and three different "burglars" break onto the stage set in a matter of minutes. At times dialogue and stage directions may contradict one another. At the end of both acts of Samuel Beckett's *Waiting for Godot,* the two tramps agree to leave, but in the final (and very significant) stage direction, the reader is told that the characters do not move. It is important to visualize the action as you hear the dialogue so that you are aware of the discrepancy. Research into human communication indicates that when verbal signals (words) and nonverbal signals (such as posture, gestures, facial expressions, tone of voice) seem to contradict each other, people tend to believe the nonverbal. In the theatre as well, an audience tends to interpret visual cues as "truth"; a reliance only on dialogue as you read may lead to confusion about the play's action.

It is also important to be aware of action suggested in the dialogue. Some playwrights, either through artistic choice or because of expectations during the period in which they wrote, have kept the use of stage directions to a minimum. Elizabethan plays, for example, usually contain few and sometimes cryptic stage directions. In such cases it is important for the reader to look for implied stage directions—actions suggested by the dialogue. The "kiss" of the lovers' palms in *Romeo and Juliet* is suggested not in a stage direction but in a verbal exchange. Two sets of twins separated at birth encounter each other for the first time at the end of Shakespeare's *Comedy of Errors.* Their initial shock as each character encounters "himself" is a wonderful visual moment that is implied only by the dialogue.

Understanding Cultural and Historical Differences

Because a play is always the product of a particular time and place, certain assumptions were made when the play was written—assumptions about how the play would be produced, who would or would not be reading or seeing the play, how certain characteristics and ideas would be viewed by the potential audience. Shakespeare's plays change location often and rapidly because he took for granted the use of a flexible, bare stage with minimal set pieces that could be easily changed. His plays were not meant for publication; the only people reading them would be members of his company who were actively involved in the staging and with whom Shakespeare had continuous contact. There was no need for many stage directions; the action would evolve during rehearsal.

The term **convention** refers to an agreement between the production personnel and the audience. A widely used convention in the twenty-first century is the dimming of the house lights, which tells the audience that the performance is about to begin. In seventeenth-century France the house and stage remained fully lit by candles throughout the performance. The audience was called to attention by a theatre employee pounding on the floor with a large staff three times. The fact that characters

EXPLORING Historical and Cultural Perspectives

"Exit, Pursued by a Bear": Those Problematic Stage Directions

In Shakespeare's *The Winter's Tale* Antigonus lays a baby on the seacoast of Bohemia, only to be chased offstage (and apparently devoured) by a bear. The cryptic stage direction "Exit, pursued by a bear" tells us little about how the playwright imagined the bear or how his company made such a completely unexpected device (the animal appears out of nowhere) work on stage.[1]

Such problematic stage directions can drive directors crazy. Unimportant ones may be cut, but some (like the bear) set up important situations later in the play. Each production team must do its best to come up with an imaginative solution. The history of *The Winter's Tale* is littered with different approaches to "Exit, pursued by a bear," including realistic bear costumes, stylized bears, and shadow bears shown on stage.

In *Jet of Blood* (1925) a violent, surrealistic play by Antonin Artaud, the playwright provides intriguing and bizarre stage directions that seem more akin to film than to live theatre, such as architectural structures falling from the sky in slow motion, an army of tarantulas swarming out from under a character's skirt, people eating each others' eyes, and body parts of characters suddenly swelling up and bursting.

Less of a problem, but still a challenge, are terse stage directions such as "They fight." Each director (often aided by a fight choreographer) who takes on the challenge of *Hamlet*

MACBETH Shakespeare's stage directions in such scenes as this one are usually cryptic. The First Folio, for example, reads: "fight, and young Seyward slaine" and "enter fighting." It is up to the performers, director, and fight master to create a usually protracted, exciting combat. Liev Schreiber as Macbeth in 2006. The Public Theater. Directed by Moisés Kaufman.

Photo © Michal Daniel.

must carefully stage an exciting, convincing fight to meet the demands of the play's climax. As you read such a script, it is important to remember all that might be implied by the simple direction "They fight."

---

speak in poetry in some plays is accepted as a convention, as are characters bursting into song (with orchestral accompaniment) in a musical. Different kinds of theatre have different conventions attached to them. In classical Chinese music drama a table becomes a mountain when used as such, and in Noh drama a fan can symbolize many things. Sometimes a playwright or director will establish a convention to work only within a particular play or production. Perhaps there are no doors in the set, but the actors perform as if there were. The audience figures out that the doors exist, even without seeing them.

Conventions are often so much a part of our experience that we don't even think about them. What does it mean to you when on television you see a closeup of an actor's face and his lips are not moving but you hear him speaking? You probably assume that you are hearing the character's thoughts. You learned this convention at some point in your viewing experience; it seems second nature now.

Conventions change from culture to culture and are developed, modified, and abandoned through time. A Western audience member watching Japanese Kabuki theatre for the first time might be startled to see an actor strike and hold a pose and exaggerated facial expression with his eyes crossed. This pose is a ***mie*** and is accompanied by a burst of wooden percussion in performance. It is a heightened expression

GEM OF THE OCEAN by August Wilson. In this play Wilson combines the residue of slave culture with early twentieth-century urban African American community and economic struggles. The quilt is actually a map suggesting the mystical, ritualized journey that the young man is about to take with the guidance of Aunt Ester played by Phylicia Rashad. This production was directed by Kenny Leon at the Huntington Theatre Company in Boston in 2004.

Photo © T. Charles Erickson.

of emotion and exhibits the skill of the actor. Audience members who are familiar with the convention look forward to a *mie* with anticipation and call out to the actor in the midst of performance, encouraging him to sustain the *mie*.

When reading a play, you may be confused at moments because you are unfamiliar with a convention. If you are reading for emotional response and to get a basic sweep of the action, you might want to mark such passages to investigate later. Conventions are sometimes explained in editorial notes, you can ask someone familiar with the period or culture, or you can do some research about theatre of the time period.

Playwrights are often unaware of many cultural assumptions they make while writing a play, since these are so deeply embedded in the particular culture. The Greeks did not explain the significance of their gods; the Elizabethans did not explain the symbolism of herbs and flowers; the Neoclassicists did not explain contemporary medical procedure; the Japanese did not explain the use of fans. Yet all these made their way into plays that we still read and perform today. Sometimes the audience perception of the play's basic action changes through time. Henrik Ibsen's plays were highly controversial in the late nineteenth century. He could assume that his audience would be shocked by the idea of divorce; Nora's decision to leave her "doll house" was radical, frightening, and, to some, immoral.

A radical confrontation of art and culture occurred in 1983 when playwright Arthur Miller directed the Chinese premiere of his *Death of a Salesman* at the Beijing People's Theatre with an all-Chinese cast. Miller had misgivings about communicating such a quintessentially American play to an audience from such a different culture

EXPLORING Historical and Cultural Perspectives

Juliet Was a Guy in Drag? Changing Theatrical Conventions

How important are the theatrical conventions with which a play was first produced?

Audiences in the Elizabethan period were used to males performing female roles. Seeing a woman perform in one of Shakespeare's plays would have been shocking to them; such public display by a female was considered inappropriate and dangerous. The tragic heroines of ancient Greece were also performed by men. Juliet, Cleopatra, Beatrice, Ophelia, Cassandra, Hecuba, Clytemnestra—all the great female characters from Elizabethan England and ancient Greece—were first created by male performers.

From the historian's perspective, it is fascinating to speculate about how cross-gender casting might have influenced a play's meaning, even though we can never recreate for ourselves the mindset of the original audience. Because we are used to performers playing characters of the same sex, our response to the convention would be quite different, and use of the original convention might change or distort the meaning of the play. From time to time modern directors have returned to cross-gender casting for classical plays, with both fascinating and ludicrous results.

There have also been experiments in reconstructing original stage conditions, settings, and costumes: a replica of the Globe Theatre (as it was understood at any given time) for Shakespeare and his contemporaries, wing and drop scenery for Restoration comedies, the use of masks for Greek tragedy. Learning about historical performance conditions can help us to understand the way a play was meant to work, but each new production must be reconceived for the present audience. Practitioners today do not feel an obligation to reproduce a period's performance conditions. However, research often provides a starting point for design and helps theatre artists to conceive an environment that supports the needs of the text.

INTERESTED? Check out

The National Theatre of Great Britain's production of the *Oresteia* by Aeschylus, including three plays, *Agamemnon*,

ELLEN BATEMAN as Richard III c. 1853. Child stars were abundant on the nineteenth-century stage and many of them cross-dressed in terms of both gender and age. Ellen Bateman did both, for example, by playing Richard III as early as the age of eight!
Collection of the authors.

Choephori (The Libation Bearers), and *Eumenides (The Furies)*, English version by Tony Harrison, directed by Peter Hall, 1983 (available on DVD). The production successfully adapted a number of conventions from Greek tragedy (masks, male actors for female roles, extensive use of the chorus) for a modern audience.

Stephen Orgel. *Impersonations: The Performance of Gender in Shakespeare's England*. Cambridge, UK: Cambridge University, 1996.

and political system, to say nothing of directing actors who shared no language with him. It was a huge success anyway, but the play became a very different theatrical presentation.

Whether you are reading for enjoyment or as preparation for staging a production, a lack of familiarity with the playwright's culture can sometimes cause confusion or even lead to misinterpretation. It often takes extra effort to come to a clear understanding of a play from the past or from a different contemporary culture. The most important tool in interpreting plays from the past or plays from a different culture is an open mind—a realization that physical environment, customs, and values change over time and from place to place. In seeking a full understanding of any play, we need to consider its place and time of origin. Any background that we can discover in the time we have available will be helpful.

Research

Often, the easiest way to acquire such background is through introductions and notes provided by editors that share the knowledge of experts in language, literature, and history, often reinforced by significant research. If you embark on your own search, you might look for information on the playwright, the society, and, specifically, the theatre of the time and place. When you know that Shakespeare's female roles were played by young male apprentices, it gives an added level of humor to plays such as *Twelfth Night* (1600–1601) and *As You Like It* (1599–1600), in which female characters (who were actually male actors in female costume) disguise themselves as men. When you understand that married women could not own property and had no rights to their children, it makes Nora's decision in *A Doll House* (1879) to leave her family even more frightening and poignant. Without an awareness of the repressive power of the state, it is not possible to understand the fear and paranoia depicted in plays set in Eastern Europe before or during the disintegration of the Soviet Union, such as Caryl Churchill's *Mad Forest* (1990). For a production or analysis of the musical *Spring Awakening* (2006) it would be very useful to explore not just the original nineteenth-century source play by Frank Wedekind, but the world of education and the plight of teenagers in Germany of that period. The musical combines the cultural sensibilities of the present with the repressive past.

An appreciation for the background of a play and the theatrical conventions that were current at the time of its composition will make reading more pleasurable and allow a more informed interpretation. Our reaction will never be exactly like that of the first audience who saw the play, and we might choose not to stick strictly to the conventions of the past, even in our imaginations. To be freed as much as possible from our own (often unconscious) assumptions, however, gives us greater freedom of choice and therefore a wider imaginative scope.

WRITING ABOUT A PLAY

As part of your study of theatre, you might be asked to write a critical paper that analyzes a play in order to come to a deeper understanding. A work of criticism (as we are using the term) does not necessarily judge the quality of the play (although it may), and it is not merely a summary of the action. In a critical paper you are sharing your ideas about how the play works with your reader.

If you find it difficult to begin this kind of project, try the following procedure. After you have finished an initial reading of the play, take notes. Record quickly (not worrying about how it sounds) how the reading made you feel, what it made you think about, what particularly struck you in the play. When you have cleared your mind onto paper, take a break if possible, and when you come back, look over your notes for correspondences. Which things seem to belong together? What ideas or images seem related or keep recurring? You might want to rewrite and organize your notes.

With these ideas in mind, read the play again. Look for words and visual images suggested by either dialogue or stage directions that helped to create your feelings or thoughts about the play. How did the playwright create these impressions? What, specifically, made you react in the way you did?

You will need to narrow your discussion of the play, depending on the scope of paper you plan to write. A thorough analysis of all aspects of a play (as a director would do in preparation for production) would create quite a long document. If you are writing critical essays for class, it is more likely that you will focus your discussion on one aspect of the play that interests you.

You might examine the play on the basis of structure, character, thought, language, or spectacle or a specific part of one element, such as the use of animal imagery in Shakespeare's *Othello*. You might focus on how one aspect of the play is developed through several different elements (e.g., how the images of death and decay are worked out in the language and spectacle in *Hamlet*). You might do a comparative paper on two plays (e.g., the use of the past in Maria Irene Fornes's *Fefu and Her Friends* [1977] and Tom Stoppard's *Arcadia* [1993]). There are many avenues to reaching a better understanding of a script. Your method of analysis should be chosen to suit the play you are dealing with.

It is often necessary to go beyond your own responses and limited frame of reference to find more information about a play and inform yourself about other people's interpretations. A **critical research paper** must include the ideas of others as well as your own conclusions. The purpose of the research is to aid your understanding of the script. You are presenting your analysis of the play, but the paper should be an informed interpretation, drawing on previously published works. If you are dealing with a well-established play or author, you will need to be selective and deal with the most important sources. For recent or more obscure work you will probably be reading articles or entries and reviews in online newspapers or periodicals, typically in data bases through your library such as JSTOR, Google Scholar, or LexisNexis Academic. The ideas of other people that you mention must be clearly documented (with footnotes, endnotes, or parenthetical documentation) so that it is clear which ideas in the paper are your own.

Reading and thinking about plays can be fun and enlightening. When you read actively and imaginatively, a play jumps to life. Comparing that play to others by thinking in terms of genre can lead you to notice interesting things you might have missed before. As a reader of plays, you collaborate with a playwright from the past (whether the play was written two thousand years ago or two months ago) to create present meaning.

CHAPTER REVIEW

Questions and Activities

1. Make a list of the four major genres. Think of the plays and films you have seen recently. How would you categorize them according to genre? Explain why you made each choice. Do the same for your favorite films and plays from any period.

2. Make a list of the subtypes of comedy. Take the comedies from your list in question 1. Decide how you would categorize each play or film and explain why you made the choice.

3. There is a long tradition in theatre and then film of burlesque—making fun of popular genres and subgenres by imitation. Some examples in theatre and film are Richard Brinsley Sheridan's *The Critic*, Charles Bush's *Psycho Beach Party*, and the films of Mel Brooks. Choose one such play or film to read or watch. What did the burlesque point out that is true (although usually exaggerated) about the original genre or subtype?

4. Choose a contemporary play and analyze it according to genre. What characteristics does the play share with the traditional genres? If you had to categorize the play, what would you call it? If you feel you could not place the play in a genre, explain why.

5. Identify conventions at work in different types of entertainment events: theatre, film, TV, sports events, rock concerts. What happens if the convention is broken?

Key Terms and Concepts

genre, p. 101
tragedy, p. 101
magnitude, p. 101
ethical choice, p. 101
catharsis, p. 102
comedy, p. 104
situation comedy, p. 106

farce, p. 106
slapstick, p. 106
comedy of character, p. 107
comedy of idea, p. 108
comedy of manners, p. 108
romantic comedy, p. 109
comic relief, p. 109

tragicomedy, p. 110
melodrama, p. 112
poetic justice, p. 113
convention, p. 116
mie, p. 117
critical research paper, p. 121

For Further Exploration

David Ball. *Backwards and Forwards: A Technical Manual for Reading Plays.* Carbondale: Southern Illinois University, 1983.

Arthur Miller. *Salesman in Beijing.* New York: Viking, 1983, a published account of Miller's remarkable cross-cultural experience, based on a diary he kept during the rehearsal process of *Death of a Salesman* in China.

James Thomas. *Script Analysis for Actors, Directors, and Designers.* 3rd ed. Oxford, UK: Focal Press, 2004.

David Scanlan. *Reading Drama.* Mountain View, CA.: Mayfield, 1988.

Theatre of Diversity

Theatre is often a meeting place for past and present—a meeting place for different cultures. Theatre of diversity suggests many theatres, many cultures, and cross-cultural efforts. The term suggests diversity in subject matter, in style, in relationship to the past, as well as diversity of race, gender, and sexual orientation. The photographs presented here are only a sample, but they demonstrate in visual terms the vast offerings of the theatre of our time.

Reinterpretation through Race

In 2009 a new production of *Death of a Salesman* (1949) by Arthur Miller opened at the Yale Repertory. Here we see the character Willy Loman portrayed by Charles S. Dutton with his wife and sons played by Kimberly Scott (Linda), Billy Eugene Jones (Happy), and Ato Essandoh (Biff). Dutton has a long history of playing important roles on stage as well as in film and television. This is certainly not the first commercial revival of a famous American play to be produced in this manner. We have seen Tennessee Williams's *Cat on a Hot Tin Roof* (pictured in Chapter One) and Eugene O'Neill's *Long Day's Journey into Night*, for example, plays originally written with white actors in mind, reinterpreted as a black experience. More

frequently in western culture this has occurred with revivals of Greek tragedies, such as the Oedipus plays at the Shakespeare Theatre Company in Washington, DC, or musicals like an all-black *Hello Dolly!*, and the plays of Shakespeare, of course. More typical, however, are mixed cast revivals such as the 2008 *Come Back Little Sheba* (1950) of William Inge, or *The Country Girl* (1950) of Clifford Odets. The results are usually fascinating or moving in ways that make the theatrical experience a very different one, even for those audience members who may know the plays very well. Such revivals often draw a significant multicultural audience as *Playbill* reported in 2008. This production was directed by James Bundy with costume designs by Katharine O'Neill.   Photo © Joan Marcus.

African American Theatre

Fences (1985) by August Wilson remains this playwright's most successful play, winning both the Tony Award and Pulitzer Prize. It was launched at the Yale Repertory Theatre under the direction of famed African American Director Lloyd Richards and starred James Earl Jones as the frustrated baseball player cum garbage collector Troy Maxson in the 1950s. This production went on to Broadway and the play subsequently has been produced more frequently and successfully than any other Wilson play in resident theatres across the country. In this 2007 revival directed by Jonathan Wilson at the Hartford Stage, Troy is played by Wendell Wright (at left) sharing a bright moment with his friend Jim Bono (Don Mayo) while Troy's wife Rose (Wandachristine) looks on in delight. Wilson's plays are typically played with detailed realistic settings like this one designed by Scott Bradley. No other playwright of color has found such a broad-based audience as Wilson, while providing a host of wonderful characters to be portrayed and engaging plays to be interpreted by African American actors, directors, and designers. When we saw the first Broadway production of a Wilson play, *Ma Rainey's Black Bottom* in 1984, few audience members of color were present, but in subsequent Wilson productions in New York and across the country, that dynamic has changed. Wilson created a new audience for the theatre. Photo ©T. Charles Erickson.

Period and Racial Diversity

Julius Caesar by William Shakespeare in a modernized treatment with Denzel Washington as Brutus with the bloody knife and William Sadler as Julius Caesar under attack by Brutus and his conspirators. This racially mixed interpretation of the Shakespearean tragedy, directed by Daniel Sullivan, is a striking example of casting against expected type for roles and creates new tensions in a play already laden with intrigue, betrayal, and violence. This 2005 Broadway production is updated to the present or near-present.

Shakespeare himself updated his rendition of the ancient Roman history to Elizabethan times in language and costume. Curiously, the play was never done in the period indicated by events until the nineteenth century when some theatre practitioners grew interested in historical accuracy. In the twentieth century and beyond, many productions have shifted to modern eras just as Orson Welles, for example, changed the period and place to a fascist location in 1937 in response to the rise of totalitarianism in Europe. These kinds of historical shifts go full circle, taking us back to the production expectations and sensibilities of Shakespeare's day. Everything then was modern dress. Costumes designed by Jess Goldstein; scenic design by Ralph Funicello. Photo © Joan Marcus.

Musical of Diversity

Ragtime (1998), like most American musicals, is based on material developed in another medium. Loosely based on the 1975 novel by E. L Doctorow of the same title, and driven by ragtime music, the play presents a cross-section of American development in the New York area in the early twentieth century. Central to the play is the need for a large, racially mixed cast as the economic and social separation of races and ethnicity is made evident in the staging in this photo. The director placed the races in segregated spheres and on different levels, but all action and characters (many generically named by familial type such as Mother, Father, Little Girl) are driven by the black rag musician (Coal House Walker). We see the musician at center stage in this 2009 Broadway revival directed and choreographed by Marcia Milgrom Dodge. Characters based on real famous people such as Houdini, Emma Goldman, and Booker T. Washington also appear throughout. Perhaps aside from the dynamic music written by Stephen Flaherty and the wonderful storytelling of Doctorow adapted by playwright Terence McNally, audiences continue to be fascinated with and challenged by America's ongoing struggle with racial issues. This musical play is emblematic of the convoluted and often volatile fabric of American society. The issues of more than a century ago continue to be topical and engaging. Scenic design by Derek McLane and Costume design by Santo Loquasto. Photo © Joan Marcus.

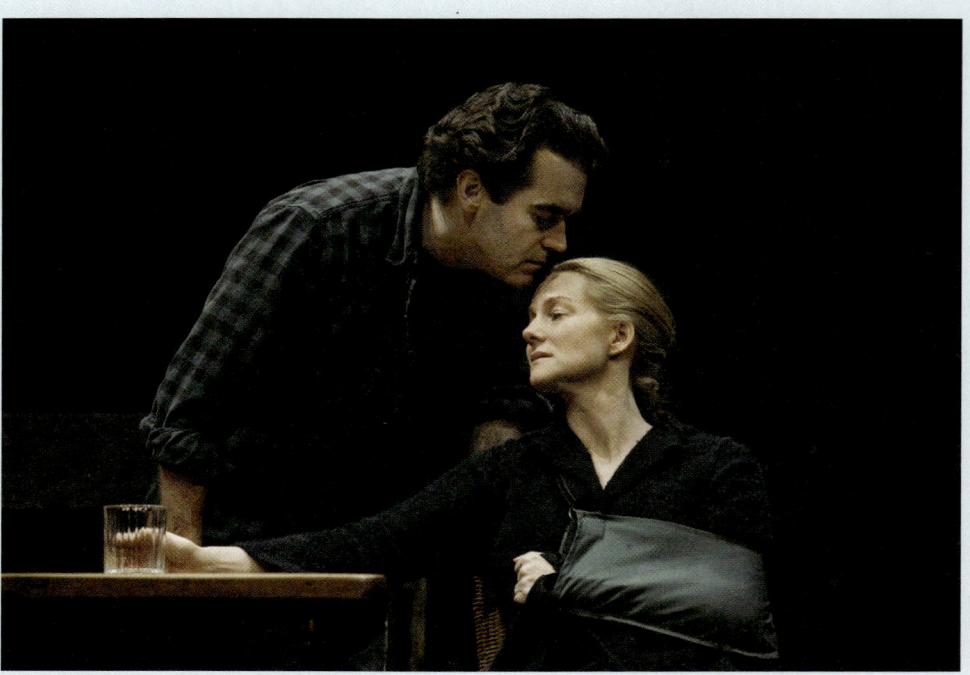

Physical Impairment

Aside from the long history of wheelchairs on the stage (going back at least as far as *The Hypochondriac* of Molière in 1673), and blindness and deafness (*The Miracle Worker* being the most famous example), severe visible physical impairment does not frequently make its way onto the mainstream stage. Unusually, the ancient Greeks left us *Philoctetes* by Sophocles centered on a lame warrior with a horribly festering leg. The number of plays dealing with severe physical impairment escalated, however, in the second half of the twentieth century along with a renewed onslaught of onstage violence. Sometimes the plays are essentially about the effects of the impairment as in *The Elephant Man* (1977) by Bernard Pomerance, but more frequently such plays focus on a character caught up in another problem that is complicated by the impairment. Such is the case with *Time Stands Still* by Donald Margulies. Depicted here is a moment from the 2010 production in New York starring Laura Linney as Sarah Goodwin, a professional photographer who has made a career of photographing war and dangerous activity around the globe. As the play begins, she is returning home after a near-death experience from an explosion in Iraq that has disabled her and damaged her face, which is covered with scars. As the play progresses across some eight months, the scars slowly diminish and some of her mobility returns (an interesting task for the actress), but the real issues of the play focus on her facing the ethical issues of remaining journalistically neutral in the face of ongoing violence, death, and destruction. Brian d'Arcy James as Sarah's domestic partner James Dodd; directed by Daniel Sullivan. Photo © Joan Marcus.

Unexpected Diversity in Sheridan

The Rivals (1775) by Richard Brinsley Sheridan is a comedy of manners set in the resort city of Bath, England. It examines foibles of society and pretensions to advancement while playing out two different love affairs (one revolving around mistaken identity and the other around sentimentality). In this 2006 production a black actor, Gregory Wallace, is playing Faulkland, a sentimental lover almost always at cross-purposes with Julia, the woman he loves, played by Stacy Ross. Such nontraditional casting can be read in several ways, such as casting the best actor in the role regardless of race, or as casting in this way to underscore the lack of communication between the attracted characters in an unexpected way. Audiences are likely to be mixed in their interpretations. Directed by Lillian Groag at the American Conservatory Theater.   Photo © Kevin Berne.

Kabuki Women Played by Men

The classical Kabuki theatre of Japan fascinates audiences in both Eastern and Western cultures. Kabuki is exotic even in Japan because most of its plays and performance styles are centuries old. Of all the Asian theatrical forms and styles, Kabuki is the most accessible to North American audiences because Kabuki tours internationally and shares a number of characteristics with traditional Western forms while providing elements that are alien to the West. Kabuki includes melodrama, comedy, and tragedy, violent physical action, and both presentational and representational performance. The *onnagata* (male actor who performs female characters) seems completely transformed into the image of a woman in costume, makeup, and movement. Yet he speaks with an obvious falsetto voice that alters our reception of the female character. Although some of the characters and action are extravagant and supernatural stylizations, some of the action is literal in its presentation. The Kabuki style has inspired playwrights, designers, and directors in the West to borrow or adapt many of its methods and images. In this photo the *onnagata* actor Tamasaburo carries the character with amazing grace and sometimes movement very difficult to execute. Many *onnagata* characters perform dances or find themselves in emotional distress or danger. If the character dies, she is expected to die beautifully.   Collection of the authors.

Updating a Modern Classic

A Doll House has undergone many radical changes since it first appeared in 1879. Most productions follow the received text reasonably closely, but from the very beginning directors and actors adjusted the text to meet their own sensibilities and prejudices or to update the play for their contemporary audiences. Many early productions changed the ending so that Nora would stay with her husband and children rather than walk out. This of course perpetuates inimical injury on the integrity of the text if maintained as realism. Many productions have cut the scene with the three children to avoid having to deal with wrangling the little tykes. Unfortunately, we know much less about Nora's sacrifice if we have not seen her playing with her children. More positively, however, the play has frequently been updated in setting and costumes, rewritten to reflect contemporary language, or in the case of *Dollhouse*, an adaptation by Rebecca Gilman pictured here, the behavior of Nora and Torvald is updated in a way that would be unthinkable to the late nineteenth century. It has the advantage, however, of transporting gender issues and behavior from more than a century ago into the present, yet holding onto the realism that drives the original text. Here Sarah Agnew as Nora sexually teases her husband Terry (instead of Torvald) portrayed by Peter Christian Hansen. Directed in 2010 at the Guthrie Theater in Minneapolis by Wendy C. Goldberg, scenic design by Alexander Dodge, costume design by Anne Kennedy.   Photo © Michal Daniel.

Reinterpretation of Gender Power Structure

Lee Breuer with Mabou Mines radically reconceived Henrik Ibsen's *A Doll House* in 2003 in a production that continues to be performed around the country and abroad. Breuer made a film of it in 2008. This postmodern deconstruction and partial parody of the original play is entitled *Dollhouse*, and the production becomes quite literally that with a miniaturized playing space with tiny doors. At its conclusion, the action opens up to a miniature opera house with marionettes in the audience boxes. Much of the action

is underscored by live music on piano, and the action is surrounded by or uses toys and toy furniture. Sometimes the gesturing of the actors is melodramatically large, and sometimes the voices of the women are babyish. The most striking aspect of this interpretation, however, is the casting of tall women approaching six feet in height, but adult little people for the men. This is evident in the photograph in which a three- to four-foot actor, Kristopher Medina, plays Krogstad to the tall Nora of Maude Mitchell. The deconstruction of the power of gender roles becomes a visual metaphor. All of the stage properties are appropriate for the size of the men, but inappropriate for the women. The men can enter and exit freely through the doors, but the women must stoop or crawl through. The resulting action is sometimes disturbing, sometimes fascinating, and sometimes comic.   Photo © Richard Termine.

Asian Puppetry

Since the eighteenth century, Bunraku puppetry, also referred to as doll theatre, has been very popular in Japan and is now considered an important classical form of Japanese theatre. Many of the plays present serious stories, combining tragedy, melodrama, and comic action. Sword fights and battle scenes are common, as are love stories and domestic conflicts that often revolve around gender issues and unrequited love. Each major puppet is carefully crafted in beautiful costumes and presents dramatic action in either a highly stylized manner or in a reality-based style as is seen in this photo. Each major role puppet is presented by three silent puppeteers: a master who controls the puppet's head and right arm, a second assistant who controls the left arm, and a third who controls the legs and feet. A storyteller stage left narrates and delivers all of the dialogue. The earliest stage revolve in history was developed for Bunraku, and Chikamatsu, one of Japan's premiere playwrights, wrote primarily for Bunraku. His love-suicide plays remain popular. Pictured here are two puppet characters from *The Sushi Shop*, a domestic play performed by the National Bunraku Theatre, a professional company in Osaka on tour in Tokyo in 2006.   Collection of the authors.

Western Puppetry

The theatre of both East and West has a long tradition of puppetry that is often given a reality base as in Bunraku, but more commonly is highly stylized whether hand puppets, shadow puppets, or marionettes are used. We see the latter here in a nineteenth-century version of medium-scale puppets performed at the Théâtre de Seraphin in Paris. The male and female puppeteers present in a scaled-down proscenium theatre with only one wing position. Footlights and sidelights are in evidence, and in this period they would probably be gas lit. The use of gas is also underscored by the presence of a fireman seated to the left since gas fires were prevalent in the period. Notice the assistants who prepare the puppets for use and pass them to the seven puppeteers, at least one of whom is operating two puppets at once. Many cultures have developed popular puppetry alongside human actors, but some cultures, especially in the middle east and southeast Asia, have in some periods allowed only puppetry.   Collection of the authors.

Women in Chinese Music Drama

Although actresses were a major part of Chinese classical theatre from the beginning, they were banished from the stage in the 1700s and not allowed to return until 1912. In the early years women were often the stars of troupes and sometimes were managers of companies. Because men developed techniques for playing women during their banishment, many of the conventions we still see on the stage were probably developed by or at least modified by male actors. The convention of falsetto voice, for example, was then taken up by women when they returned. Cross-dressing, however, had always been a part of Chinese classical theatre and still is. Many female characters cross-dress as boys or young men to take part in intrigues and adventures—just as we see in Elizabethan comedies. In this image from *The Legend of the White Snake*, we see the Green Snake (unaccountably costumed traditionally in blue) in human female form on a quest to steal silver from a magical storehouse. A guard attempts to stop her, but she will of course succeed. Photo from 2010 program of Liyuan Theatre, Beijing. Collection of the authors.

Hispanic Culture Cross-Examining Itself

Many poignant Hispanic plays have emerged in North America since the mid-twentieth century. José Rivera has been widely produced, especially in resident theatres. His *Marisol* depicts a Puerto Rican woman attempting to suppress her ethnic identity and blend in with the commercial world of New York. In this production the title character's paranoia in an unfriendly environment in New York is exaggerated by an impassable door with multiple locks—a dynamic symbol of her insecurity in the world in which she desperately wants to belong. Marisol is played by Karina Arroyave. Directed by Marcus Stern; scenic design by Paul Owen; costume design by Laura A. Patterson. Courtesy of Actors Theatre of Louisville.

Gender and Gay Issues

Since the 1960s many new plays have appeared both in avant-garde and mainstream theatres exploring gay and lesbian issues in the contemporary world. The most commercially successful of this work must be *Angels in America* (1991) by Tony Kushner. Simultaneously, many older and classical plays have been reinterpreted to reflect gay and lesbian issues by rewriting or even deconstructing them. More frequently, however, all or most of the text is left intact, but the play's action is reset or the play is cast in ways that refocus the world of the play in terms of gender or sexuality. In this production of Molière's *The Misanthrope* at the Betty Nansen Teatret in Copenhagen, Denmark, the male roles were recast as female, creating sexual tension between women, rather than the male/female conflict of the original play. This treatment, of course, demands that the audience receive the play in a new way. Directed by Peter Landal. Designed by Karin Betz. Ghita Nørby (left) as Alceste, Lotte Anderson (with fan) as Célimène, Bodil Udsen as a rival.
Photo © hansen-hansen.com and courtesy of Eric Hansen-Hansen.

Changing Roles of Women in the Workplace and Home

Top Girls (1982), by Caryl Churchill, explores the changing roles of women in the workplace and in the home. The character in this photograph is Pope Joan, a semimythical figure from the distant past. Pope Joan was a woman masquerading as a man who headed the Catholic Church before her sex was discovered, resulting in her murder by an enraged mob. In this production at the University of Nebraska, Pope Joan was played by an African American actress. Such nontraditional casting is intriguing for an audience because it contradicts expectations and further complicates the power and gender issues raised by the play.   Collection of the authors.

DOSTOYEVSKY'S CRIME AND PUNISHMENT adapted by Marilyn Campbell and Curt Columbus at The Jungle Theater in Minneapolis (2009). Directed by Joel Sass.

Photo © Michal Daniel.

Act TWO

Collaboration in Art and Practice

" *[The] author, director, scene designer and actor must . . . resist every temptation to score personally. Each must make himself a free, transparent medium through which the whole flows freely and without obstruction. No one at any moment can say, 'Ah, this moment is mine!'* " [1]

—ARTHUR HOPKINS (DIRECTOR)

A small community is created through work on theatrical production. Artists, craftspeople, and technicians shape the event to be shared with an audience. Although each individual may take pride in his or her own creation, the work of each of these practitioners is complete only when combined with the work of all the others. Creating theatre is truly a "co-labor." The work has been divided many ways. The different jobs as we describe them here are based on standard practice in many theatres, but there are no rules about division of labor in the theatre. In this book we first discuss the director (and some of the director's collaborators), and then the actor, playwright, designers, and producer. Even when we talk about a norm, in the following chapters you will also find examples of practitioners who follow a different pattern because that type of collaboration suits them and produces the kind of event that they value. Although a standard division of responsibilities helps to ease the difficulty of diving into the creative process, the nature of collaboration is to some extent created anew with each theatrical venture. The practitioners not only create the art to share but also redefine the nature of the collaborative process.

MAJOR BARBARA (1905) by George Bernard Shaw (2007) at the Guthrie Theater. Directed by Lisa Peterson; scenic design by Neil Patel. Photo © Michal Daniel.

The Director

Vision and Leadership

The **director** in the theatre has a job similar to that of the conductor of an orchestra or the coach of a basketball team. The director is a leader. Although many individuals contribute to the group effort, the director must galvanize the collection of assorted personalities and temperaments into a functioning whole, must inspire as well as unify. As it exists today, the job of director incorporates a number of different types of activities—textual interpretation and artistic conceptualization, coordination of all visuals, and actor coaching. As we discussed in Chapter 2, it is certainly possible to have theatre without a director, but in current practice a director is usually considered indispensable. How did the director's job come to be? The development of this position in the theatre provides a fascinating study in the shifts of power as the interests and values of cultures change.

HAS SOMEONE ALWAYS BEEN IN CHARGE?

At the turn of the twentieth century the director emerged as the most powerful artistic figure in theatrical production. The director's authority was the result of considerable artistic struggle, sweeping technological development, the movements of romanticism and realism, and monumental changes in playwriting and acting techniques that swamped the theatre in the nineteenth and early twentieth centuries. Some jobs of the modern directors have always been executed by someone, but there are many tasks and responsibilities taken on by modern directors that are unique to the position as it developed after the mid-1800s.

Actor-Playwrights and Company Leaders

In many periods playwrights or actors were in charge of the production of plays. In the classical Greek theatre (the time of Aeschylus) the playwrights (who at first were also actors) appear to have made various production decisions, selected supporting

DIRECTOR ROBERT WILSON demonstrating for principal actors during a technical rehearsal of his adaptation of Georg Büchner's *Woyzeck* at the Betty Nansen Teatret in 2001. Wilson is very specific regarding physicalization with his actors.

Photo © hansen-hansen.com and courtesy of Eric Hansen-Hansen.

actors, and coordinated the chorus (although there were also choral trainers). By the time of Sophocles, however, most or all of the playwrights had stopped acting, and contests for actors were added to the Dionysian festival. By the time of Aristotle in the Hellenistic era, guilds of professional actors headed by an artist/priest were in charge of production. There was no separate position of director (other artists, most likely the leading actors, filled the bill).

In ancient Rome acting troupes usually had a leading actor or manager, but we know little of this person's responsibilities beyond management of the company and making arrangements with government officials for festival performances. Leaders for acting companies in India that performed Sanskrit plays had some stage management and directorial duties, but the record is vague. Actors, both male and female, appear to have been in charge in ancient China and Japan, but again little detail survives. The openness of the stages and the minimal scenery and properties of Asian classical forms suggest that directing in the modern sense was not necessary or desirable. Most of the extant clues to performance concern acting and dramatic text.

Medieval Play Masters

The first indication of the position we today call the director occurred in medieval Europe. In response to the often extravagant, expensive, and crowded productions of the **cycle** plays (biblical dramas), a number of **play masters** (who were sometimes called "prompters" and "ordinaries") appeared. Records still exist regarding play masters from French, Germanic, and English territories. These men coordinated and staged the cycles of their communities. Very good play masters, such as Jean Bouchet in France, found themselves in demand and began traveling to stage the cycles of other communities as well. Does this make the play masters the first touring stars? To organize and document the production process, play masters kept **promptbooks** that might include the play

'TIS PITY SHE'S A WHORE by John Ford. A page from a late twentieth-century promptbook early in the play. The handwritten notes indicate additional entrances marked "E," light cues number 13 and 14 marked in a box "L," and the stage direction written on the left side of the page "work L to number 5 & 4." The numbers refer to different levels of platforms. Beginning at line 129, the arrows indicate the continuation of the line by other characters.

Collection of the authors.

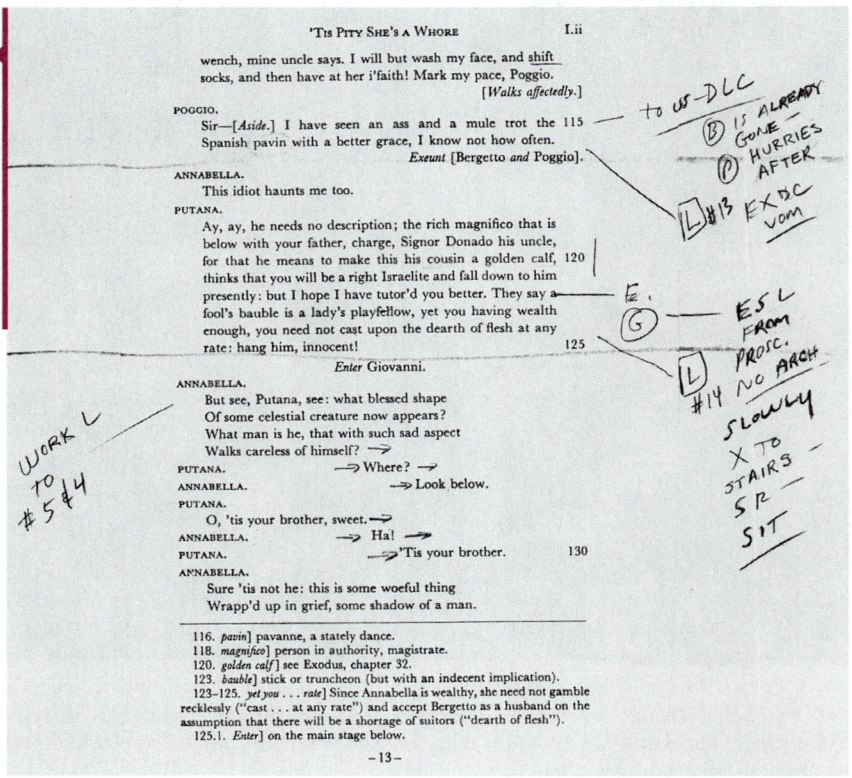

text, drawings of sets, ground plans, stage directions, and various production notes. Important surviving promptbooks include one from Valenciennes in France dated 1547, and one dated 1583 from Lucerne, in what later became Switzerland. The Passion Play at Lucerne was staged by Renward Cysat, a city government employee.

Many of these medieval "directors" combined some of the duties we now associate with directors, stage managers, technical directors, and house managers. After the extinction of the religious cycle plays due to Reformation and Counter-Reformation edicts, there is no evidence that such directorial control and promptbook work appeared again until the nineteenth century.

Actor-Managers

By the seventeenth and eighteenth centuries most Western professional theatre companies were led by actor-managers such as Molière in France and Caroline Neuber (one of the earliest female managers) in Germany. **Actor-managers** made financial decisions, selected the repertory of plays, hired the actors, and performed (some were leads, and some played secondary roles), but they seem to have had little to do with staging. Following traditional patterns, most actors controlled the space themselves. Typically in the West, leading actors took center stage, with others standing left and right of them or in a semicircle downstage on the apron. Stage business for a particular role, such as the handling of props, was often set by popular performers and passed down to actors who followed. Asian actors also followed staging and characterization choices that were inherited. When an actor took over a role made popular by an established company member, he was expected to reproduce the favorite physical moments while adding his own touches to the performance. The lucky actors were the first to do important new roles and thus launch the traditional lines of performance.

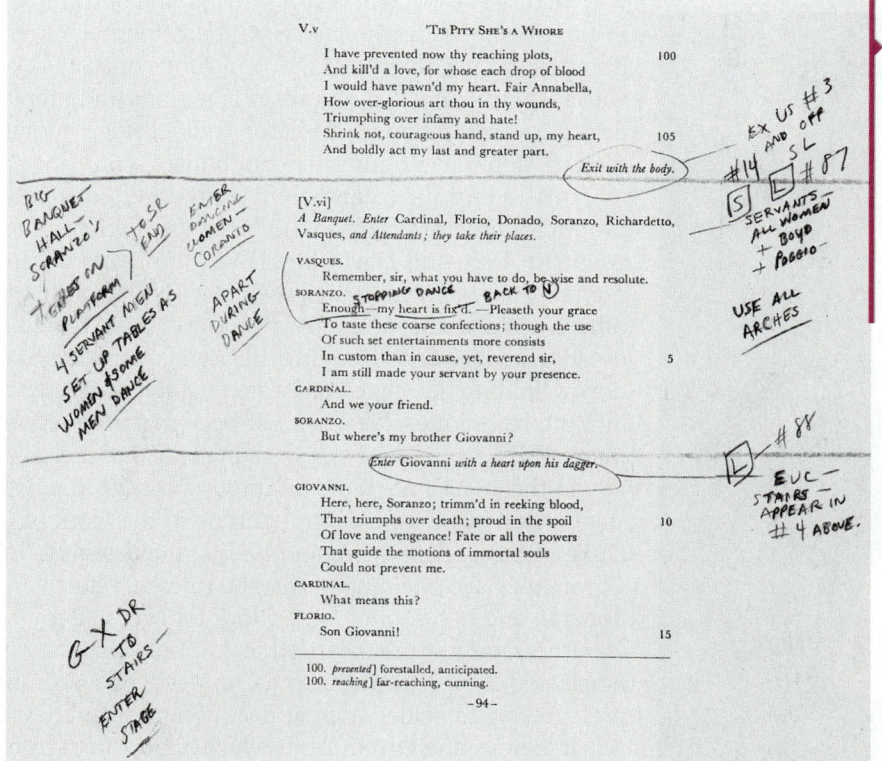

'TIS PITY SHE'S A WHORE by John Ford. A page from the same promptbook late in the play. At this point in the play, we have the 14th sound cue and the 87th and 88th light cues. This is the scene in which one of the protagonists, Giovanni, enters with the heart of his sister impaled on his dagger.

Collection of the authors.

In the nineteenth century in the West the rules changed with the coming of **antiquarianism** (historical accuracy), three-dimensional scenery, local color, very detailed stage directions, and complicated scenic effects demanded first by romantic melodrama and then realism. The situation was further complicated by numerous long runs of single plays by the 1850s rather than the traditional rolling repertory system (different plays performed on alternating nights). **Combination companies** (full productions rather than individual stars) began touring throughout Europe and North America. To keep track of complex productions and record their work, some actor-managers created detailed promptbooks complete with historical research. Charles Kean and William Charles Macready in England applied this technique primarily to revivals of Shakespeare's plays in which they starred. Dion Boucicault took similar care with the staging of melodrama in the United States, England, and Ireland and was so successful on both sides of the Atlantic that all three countries claim him. Many nineteenth-century promptbooks survive in rare book collections such as the Folger Shakespeare Library in Washington, DC, and some have very detailed stage directions. Productions following these promptbooks must have required careful attention to staging and ensemble acting. Throughout the twentieth century and up to our own time, most professional directors and their stage managers have continued to work with very detailed promptbooks.

The Emergence of the Modern Director

As long runs of single plays became the norm, scenery, costumes, and acting techniques were developed for specific productions. Artistic power shifted from star actors and managers to people who were masterful at interpreting plays and convincing actors to take direction in order to coordinate the stage effects and acting ensemble. From the ranks of managers, actors, and prompters (who fed actors forgotten lines from offstage) came a number of directors who at first concentrated on coordinating the theatrical event and organizing stage pictures. Over time, however, many directors, most of whom were not actors themselves, took charge of the artistic vision. In the early years especially, such artistic centralization often led to a dictatorial style in working with actors and designers. This stringent control is evident in the directorial work of W. S. Gilbert, the playwright and librettist of the Gilbert and Sullivan comic operettas. Gilbert was all-powerful in staging his productions and preplanned actor movement using a miniature model stage, moving his "actors" about like figures in a dollhouse.

In the late nineteenth and early twentieth centuries producer-directors took total charge of their productions. Augustin Daly and David Belasco in the United States, for example, not only wrote their own plays and rewrote those of others, but also cast and rehearsed the actors, created scenic detail, and oversaw all staging. Belasco gave so much attention to lighting the stage that he is considered an innovator in lighting techniques. Nearly all of Belasco's productions and many of Daly's productions were in service to melodrama.

In the 1870s and 1880s an important shift in power and stage detail came from central Europe in the work of Georg, Duke of Saxe-Meiningen, and his staging assistant, Ludwig Chronegk. Saxe-Meiningen was the ruler of a duchy (a small domain) and had a lot of money for production. Because they were running a court theatre that was subsidized by a royal household, Saxe-Meiningen and Chronegk felt no commercial pressures and wielded a great deal of authority. They built a remarkable acting ensemble in which all leading actors were also required to take walk-on roles. With unlimited time for

THE OLD READING ROOM at the Folger Shakespeare Library in Washington, DC. A first Folio of the plays of Shakespeare appears on the table. This is a wonderful room in which to conduct theatre research when rare, original, and unpublished materials are needed.

By permission of the Folger Shakespeare Library.

rehearsals Saxe-Meiningen designed sets and costumes exclusively according to historical accuracy, and Chronegk worked out staging in meticulous detail. The resulting productions—especially the innovative crowd scenes—stunned European audiences when the troupe toured with classical and romantic plays. A new standard was set.

Many young directors throughout Europe, especially in France, Germany, Russia, and England, were inspired by the Saxe-Meiningen troupe. As playwrights created realistic scripts, André Antoine in Paris and Konstantin Stanislavsky in Moscow further developed a production style for the new generation of plays. Antoine (beginning in 1887) created the model for independent theatres (small theatres run without the intervention of local authorities) that were dedicated to realism and naturalism. Antoine often placed furniture along the curtain line and directed his actors to frequently turn their backs to the audience, thus creating **fourth wall staging**—treating the stage space as if it were an enclosed room. The effect for the audience was that of peering in on an actual event rather than witnessing a theatrical performance. Stanislavsky focused on the acting ensemble and actor training in his remarkable productions of the naturalistic plays of Anton Chekhov and Maxim Gorky. By the twentieth century in the West, directors were fully in charge.

INTERPRETATION

From a preexisting text, the artists of the theatre (directors, designers, and actors) create a construction from all that they recognize as implied or suggested by the text. **Interpretation** is creating meaning beyond what is literal or obvious in the text. The modern director could be defined as an interpretive artist who attempts to

THE MERCHANT OF VENICE by Shakespeare, the Rialto exterior scene. Directed by Augustin Daly in the late nineteenth century. Note the attention to detail in the treatment of the stage floor to imitate a stone plaza, the Venetian canal, sailing craft, buildings, and pillar—all imitating real architecture and boats from Venice.
By permission of the Folger Shakespeare Library.

unify the production by coordinating the work of all theatrical artists as they make decisions about possible meaning and signification of dialogue, character action, scenic location—all aspects of the world of the play. The director might endeavor to interpret a script carefully and accurately, trying to champion the intent or perceived intent of the playwright. On the other hand, the director may use the script more as a pretext in order to present the director's own vision or ideas that are inspired or supported by the script. Either approach requires that the text be interpreted through analysis, research, brainstorming, intuition, and experiment. Theoretically, there are many valid interpretations of any play, especially one that is rich in ideas or complicated in dramatic action.

Varying interpretations of ideas and characters result in wildly different audience receptions of a play. Shakespeare's *Hamlet* presents an interesting challenge to interpretation: Is Hamlet's madness real or pretense? If Hamlet is really losing his mind after confronting the ghost of his father, then his deliberations over the nature of suicide and what lies beyond death must be taken very differently than if he is only pretending madness in order to pursue his revenge. The Chinese music drama *The Orphan of Chao* includes a parade of violence—murder, suicide, hanging, and throat cutting—throughout the play. A director who is horrified by the cruelty of these events will interpret the play very differently from a director who sees the violence as clan fighting, only to be expected in the struggle over control of an empire. The former director will be intent on shocking the audience; the latter will be more philosophical about the corruption of power.

Even specific physical action in a text can be interpreted differently. In *Romeo and Juliet,* Mercutio is mortally wounded by Tybalt in a street fight. It is clear from the dialogue that Romeo attempts to stop the young men from fighting and comes between them. In that moment Tybalt stabs Mercutio with his sword. What is not clear is whether the deadly thrust was deliberate or accidental on the part of Tybalt. Directors have interpreted this moment in a variety of ways, most commonly as deliberate (taking advantage of Romeo's intrusion to put an end to Mercutio). But the stabbing might also be interpreted as accidental, caused by confusion resulting from Romeo's good-intentioned interference. The fight can be staged as adolescent posturing by Mercutio and Tybalt or as a deadly battle with intent to kill. The choice is a critical one. It dynamically alters the emotional import of the scene as well as the nature of Romeo's subsequent challenge and slaying of Tybalt, which results in Romeo's banishment.

OUR TOWN (1938) by Thornton Wilder typically is done with no scenery or set properties other than chairs. In this 2010 interpretation at Williamstown Theatre Festival (Massachusetts), a host of wooden chairs and tables becomes a sculptural and emblematic scenic environment. The character Emily Webb (Brie Larson) plays up to her father portrayed by Dylan Baker while the narrative Stage Manager (Campbell Scott) watches. Directed by Nicholas Martin. Scenic design by David Korins; costume design by Gabriel Berry.

Photo © T. Charles Erickson.

Interpretation cannot be avoided. Every director, just like every other reader of a play, interprets either consciously or unconsciously. There is no such thing as doing a play "straight"—of allowing the text to be neutral for whatever interpretation an audience member might wish to give it. Because of the nature of the job, a director should be very conscious of interpretation and find ways to express it to actors and designers as well as receive interpretations of the collaborators. Because plays must be interpreted, no two productions can be the same.

Critics and historians over the years have placed a high premium on directors who have shared remarkable interpretations of famous plays. In his 1906 staging of Henrik Ibsen's *Hedda Gabler,* for example, Russian director Vsevolod Meyerhold recognized the play's symbolism and emotional framework and discarded the representational setting that is called for in the well-known realistic play. Instead of the traditional box set (representing an enclosed room), a wide, shallow shelf surrounded by draperies thrust the action into the face of the audience. Rather than sitting in a parlor chair, the self-centered Hedda sat on a symbolic white, furry throne. Instead of a stove for the burning of her would-be lover's manuscript, the audience saw only a red pool of light. The play became an entirely new experience, yet the essence, if not the style, of Ibsen's play still reached an audience.

DEVELOPING CONCEPT

As is suggested by the example of Meyerhold's staging of *Hedda Gabler,* interpretation leads to concrete choices in production. A **concept** is made up of the artistic decisions meant to communicate a specific interpretation to the audience. The development of concept can begin well before a director has assembled an artistic team. As the director reads, studies, and analyzes a play, a **dramaturg**—a literary and historical advisor assigned specifically to the production—might serve as a consultant and conduct research on the play, author, or historical period. As the director makes specific interpretive choices, these choices begin to suggest concrete ways of presenting the play. On the other hand, the director can make no conceptual choices until conferences with the designers. Out of their discussion and sharing of vision, the concept begins to emerge. Concept is created visually and aurally; it is made manifest in scenery, costume, lighting, tempo, line readings, movement, and composition—the very things that a director creates, coordinates, or approves. Although an audience is not always certain of a director's interpretation, the audience can always receive the sensory results of concept.

Different concepts produce radically different productions. Three twentieth-century productions of Shakespeare's *A Midsummer Night's Dream* demonstrate the variety of concepts possible for a given play. When Herbert Beerbohm Tree directed it in 1901, he saw the play through the eyes of a late Victorian enamored of sentimentalized realism. The forest setting was depicted with scenery cut out and painted to resemble real trees. Audience members reported seeing live rabbits and real grass on the stage. The fairy characters sported the gauzy wings and gowns of Victorian children's books. In 1914 Harley Granville-Barker startled viewers with a more austere, simplified world on the stage. On a mostly open stage, scenery was presentational: Scenic designers Norman Wilkinson and Albert Rutherston created stylized hills and valleys painted on green translucent draperies. Fairies were given an eerie quality, with skin painted entirely in gold except for brilliant red mouths. Despite Granville-Barker's experiment, traditional productions continued with variations on the more realistic approach through the first half of the twentieth century.

Peter Brook began the conceptual work for his 1970 production of *A Midsummer Night's Dream* by deciding to strip away not only the details of forest and palace, but also much of the sweetness and airiness found in so many previous productions. He placed all of the action in a simple white box designed by Sally Jacobs. Trees were suggested by squiggles of plastic tubing, and a catwalk around the top of the set allowed performers who were not on stage to watch the action below in full view of the audience.

A MIDSUMMER NIGHT'S DREAM as directed by Harley Granville-Barker, using open space, low platforms, and translucent draperies. A strong movement away from the literal and toward the simplified and sometimes emblematic stage is reflected here.

By permission of Victoria & Albert Picture Library.

Inspired by Chinese acrobats, Brook approached the play like a circus with acrobatics and trapezes but without the garishness and glitz. Fairies were suspended in the air on trapezes. The result was a restoration of magic, wonder, and sexuality to the play. The fairies were clad in simple, brightly colored robes; the human lovers wore tie-dyed garments popular in the 1960s. The mischievous Puck delivered a speech while swinging upside down on a trapeze toward the audience. The differing concepts of Beerbohm Tree, Granville-Barker, and Brook produced memorable but wildly different sensory experiences for their respective audiences.

The most startling or challenging concepts usually arrest the attention of audiences and the notice of historians and critics. In 1919 German director Leopold Jessner staged much of the action of *Richard III* on a large flight of stairs to make concrete Richard's rise to kingship and subsequent fall. Before Jessner, productions of this play had largely focused on interpretation of character. Jessner's production was more about the logistics of power than the seductive actions of the villainous hero. His concept made the audience view the play differently.

In an effective interpretation of *Richard III,* directed by Brian Kulick and Michael Cumpsty in 2007, the staging was imaginative and simple. In a black box arranged in thrust, three walls of mirrors loomed aloft, and the upstage reflective panel often glided to the floor. Some six or eight crystal chandeliers hung above, but were often lowered close to or on to the floor and reflected in the mirrors, creating the illusion of many more chandeliers. One long metal table on rollers plus rolling chairs became the only set props, used in myriad ways. For the persuasion of the masses scene, all of the audience was given little boar flags to wave. Thus, the audience became humorously complicit in the rise and crowning of the villainous Richard.

In 1990 French director Ariane Mnouchkine revitalized *The Oresteia* of Aeschylus under the title *Les Atrides* and created one of the most important cross-cultural experiments of the twentieth century. Her exploration of gender strife came to the center in this production, which added dramatic text from Euripides and combined Greek

RICHARD III directed by Leopold Jessner. Note the high staircase on which much of the action takes place. The color red was dominant for the power of Richard, who usurped the throne and ruled until the "white" forces overwhelmed him at the end of the play. This image was drawn and painted by the designer Robert Edmond Jones after he saw the production in Germany. It first appeared in the book *Continental Stagecraft* by Jones and Kenneth Macgowan in 1922.

From *Continental Stagecraft* by Kenneth Macgowan and Robert Edmond Jones (1922).

and Indian theatricality, especially Kathakali-style costumes and makeup. Unlike the Greek and Asian sources, Mnouchkine's production used an international cast of both men and women but suppressed gender identification within the costuming. By the late twentieth century innovators such as Brook, Mnouchkine, and others discussed in this chapter had developed international and multicultural concepts associated with poststructural and postmodern theory and practice.

RICHARD III by William Shakespeare, with Michael Cumpsty in the title role. Directed in 2007 by Cumpsty and Brian Kulick at the Classic Stage Company off-Broadway in New York. Scenic design by Mark Wendland, lighting design by Brian H. Scott, costume design by Oana Botez-Ban.

Photo © Joan Marcus.

COMMUNICATING AND MANAGING THE ARTISTIC VISION

PERICLES by William Shakespeare in a visually dynamic interpretation directed by Joel Sass at the Guthrie Lab Theater in 2005. This fairy-tale-like play invites much mystery and abstraction with its scenes of magic, raising the dead, and the strong narrative voice of Gower (played by Shawn Hamilton foreground), who has an omniscient presence in the play. Ron Menzel plays the romantic title character in the doorway. Scenic design by John Clark Donahue, costume design by Amelia Busse Cheever, lighting design by Marcus Dilliard. Photo © Michal Daniel.

If the artistic vision of a production typically rests with the director in the twenty-first century, how is that vision communicated to the show's artistic staff, and how in turn is that vision enriched and modified by the collaborating artists? Most directors strive to communicate clearly with all designers and make certain that the separate contributions result in a unified work of art, but the methods for doing so are dynamically different.

Meyerhold in Russia was an example of the master artist—the creator or "author" of the production—called for by some designers and theorists at the turn of the twentieth century. The word **auteur** is sometimes used for directors who operate with almost total control. Although this way of working is often dictatorial, it does not mean that designers or actors are unimportant. Lyubov Popova, an important early female designer, created a remarkable **constructivist set** for Meyerhold's *The Magnanimous Cuckold* (1922). It consisted of exposed beams, supports, and movable parts and was not meant to represent anything from the world outside the theatre. Meyerhold wanted an abstracted, multilevel space on which the actors could work athletically in a highly choreographed style. Popova's work precisely met the vision of the director.

In a very different vein, German director Peter Stein approached his 1971 production of Ibsen's *Peer Gynt* (1867) in a fully collaborative way. The actors and other members of the company conducted historical research together to create a vision for the production. Stein obviously coordinated the approach, but many discoveries were made by the actors, who functioned somewhat like a collective dramaturg to prepare the remarkable production. *Peer Gynt* is structured like a folk tale, changing location frequently and occurring in vastly different real and imaginary spaces. The company's work resulted in a complete renovation of the theatre (most of the orchestra seats were removed), making the space look more like a warehouse with playing spaces spread throughout the resulting arena on various levels. The title role was shared by a number of actors, and much of the sexual and commercial corruption of the nineteenth century was exposed and explored through the epic wandering of the title character.

Julie Taymor had many talented collaborators for *The Lion King* (1997) but perpetuated her vision not only by directing the production but also by conceiving and designing puppets combined with actors, masks, and costumes. Consequently, her exploration of the world of the play was very hands-on as she sculpted and built models for the masks and puppets. Her codesigner for masks and puppets, Michael Curry, concentrated especially on technical design and operation. Scenic designer Richard Hudson and lighting designer Donald Holder worked with Taymor to create a sense of the African environment. Taymor asked for a presentational set that did not hide the way the mechanized set pieces or puppets functioned but revealed the ways in which theatrical magic was created. Tony Meola created the sound design, which included the installation of large speakers under the seats of the New Amsterdam Theatre to create the sound and

THE MAGNANIMOUS CUCKOLD by Fernand Crommelynck, directed by Vsevelod Meyerhold, designed by Lyubov Popova in 1922 in Russia. Here we see the constructivist setting, which functioned as an acting machine for the athletic performances of the actors trained in biomechanics.

From *Russian and Soviet Theater 1905–1932* by Konstantin Rudnitsky. Thames & Hudson.

THE LION KING directed by Julie Taymor. A dynamic moment in which giraffes and a cheetah are created by the actors with puppet extensions and stilts. The actor becomes one with the costume but can still be recognized as performer as well as animal.

Photo © Joan Marcus.

ARTISTS of the THEATRE

Peter Brook

The 1970 production of *A Midsummer Night's Dream* is only one of the many startling theatrical experiments of British director Peter Brook (b. 1925). Brook began directing in his teens and achieved a reputation for fine, carefully staged productions remarkably quickly. In the 1950s and early 1960s his reputation for unusual productions grew, primarily because of his interpretations of Shakespeare. His 1962 production of *King Lear* was a significant turning point in his career. He abandoned the set (which he had designed himself) during rehearsals for a spare, nearly empty stage. Brook increasingly turned his attention to developing actor performances and striking, simple designs.

In 1964 Brook participated in an experimental season at the Royal Shakespeare Company. Inspired by the theory of Antonin Artaud, Brook and his fellow artists developed techniques designed to act directly and forcefully on the audience's senses and emotions. The powerful, raw imagery of Brook's production of contemporary German author Peter Weiss's play, *Marat/Sade,* set in an early nineteenth-century insane asylum, shocked and excited the theatre world. The Roman tragedian Seneca is rarely revived in the modern theatre, but Brook's production of Seneca's *Oedipus* successfully dealt with the play's horrific violence in a way that seemed to speak particularly strongly to the world in 1968. Brook's book *The Empty Space* was published in 1968 as well. It still serves as an inspiring, provocative examination of the nature and purpose of theatre.

After directing many productions in some of the world's finest theatres, Brook felt the need to push the boundaries of his art even further. In 1971 he founded the Centre for International Theatre Research in Paris (later renamed the Centre for International Theatre Creation). Putting together money from many sources, Brook intended the Centre to be an environment for making theatre free from commercial pressure. He assembled an international company, hoping that the combination of many different backgrounds and theatrical conventions would enhance creativity. The Centre allowed Brook to use extended development and rehearsal periods impossible in most theatre venues. His work focused on preparation of the actor for performance using many techniques: physical, vocal, spiritual exercises, improvisation, and shared cultural experience. An extended trip to many areas of Africa brought the entire company into contact with different cultures and performing traditions. Brook alternated periods of research, rehearsal, and self-discovery with public presentations, often taking theatre to audiences (such as prisoners and hospital patients) who would never attend traditional theatre. Material was developed by writers and actors based on a wide variety of source material. In 1971 the company performed in Persepolis, Iran, as part of an international arts festival. The piece, entitled *Orghast,* was an exploration of ritual and was played in a language developed specifically for that piece by poet Ted Hughes with input from the company.

In 1974 the Centre opened a permanent performance space, Bouffes du Nord in Paris. The building had been constructed as a theatre in 1876 but partially destroyed by fire and abandoned in 1952. The French Ministry of Culture provided money to make the repairs absolutely necessary, but the ruined appearance of the auditorium was maintained, complete with gaping holes, charred walls, and crumbling nineteenth-century decorations—a reminder of the historical richness of the space.

In 1982 Brook directed and headed the development of *The Tragedy of Carmen,* a new work based partially on the famous nineteenth-century opera by Bizet and on the original novel by Merimée. Brook sought to divest the raw, emotional story from the many years of tradition and spectacle associated with the opera. The setting was a simple sand-covered circle suggesting a bull-ring. Perhaps Brook's most gigantic undertaking to date was an adaptation of *The Mahabharata,* the ancient Sanskrit epic poem central to Hindu religion and culture. The text was adapted by Jean-Claude Carrière, but the production evolved over several

vibrations of a wildebeest stampede. An account of Taymor's period of conceptualization with her fellow artists is published in *The Lion King: Pride Rock on Broadway* (1997).

In 2007, director Will Pomerantz with the Epic Theatre Ensemble (a group dedicated to performing plays grappling with serious social, ethical, and political issues) revived a 1992 war play by Howard Barker entitled *A Hard Heart* Off-Broadway, in the American premiere. A three-level scenic design by Narelle Sissons that suggested a large metal freight container, opened up to reveal a bunker under siege (the battle noise was often frightfully loud), where an unnecessary and futile religious and territorial war was being planned and coordinated by an arrogant female military genius called Riddler, who is treated as godlike by her countrymen. The variety and precision of the staging in a small space was a remarkable achievement and underscored the claustrophobic nature of terrorism and siege war.

years of work. The adaptation took over nine hours to perform and included an enormous cast from 16 countries. In 1988 Brook returned to an established classic of the stage with a production of Anton Chekhov's *The Cherry Orchard.* A nearly bare stage with only Persian rugs, a cabinet, and screen served as the family estate about to be sold. Audience members were mesmerized by the emotionally full and dynamic performances of the cast, which included English, American, Swedish, and Czech actors. In 2000 Brook mounted a world tour of his *Tragedy of Hamlet,* a streamlined version of Shakespeare's famous tragedy; in 2005 he launched *Tierno Bokar,* which Brook calls an African story exploring the power of tolerance.

Brook's passion for theatre has taken him to many places, both literal and figurative. His art is at once intensely connected to the time in which he lives and deeply personal. The ensemble work of his company is legendary, and although his pieces are often developed collaboratively, the final presentation is often highly focused and breathtaking in its simplicity.

In 2007 Brook revisited a 1972 apartheid play by Athol Fugard, *Sizwe Banzi Is Dead.* In Australia, this South African play was performed with black actors (one of whom is a Congolese rap artist), in French with English subtitles. Brook continues to explore intercultural frontiers. In 2011, at the age of 86, he stepped down from his position at the Centre, but continued to direct with new productions of Mozart's *The Magic Flute* and short pieces by Samuel Beckett.

A MIDSUMMER NIGHT'S DREAM as directed by Peter Brook for the Royal Shakespeare Company. In the setting designed by Sally Jacobs, Brook placed all of the action in or on top of a white box augmented by trapezes and a floating feathery red bower. Puck, Titania, and Oberon played by John Kane, Sara Kestelman, and Alan Howard.

By permission of the Royal Shakespeare Company.

INTERESTED? Check out

David Williams, compiler. *Peter Brook: A Theatrical Casebook.* London: Methuen, 1988.
Peter Brook. *The Empty Space.* New York: Atheneum, 1996.

Peter Brook. *The Shifting Point: Theatre, Film, Opera 1946–1987.* New York: Theatre Communications Group, 1994.
Michael Kustow. *Peter Brook: A Biography.* London: St. Martin's, 2005.
Official website for Peter Brook. www.peterbrook.net

Michael Kahn's production of *The Oedipus Plays* (2001), adaptations of Sophocles at the Shakespeare Theatre in Washington, DC, was conceptualized as an African rather than Greek trilogy of the Oedipus cycle. Most of the actors played multiple roles. Even Avery Brooks as Oedipus also played a messenger in *Antigone.* Using African music and design as well as full choruses, the plays became a celebration of tribal culture and community action while at the same time exploring the tragic destruction, suffering, and redemption of Oedipus, Antigone, and Creon.

The work of Stein, Taymor, and Kahn demonstrates a fully collaborative spirit and working method, but even in the work of a more autocratic director such as Meyerhold, it is necessary for the director to unify the vision through inspiration, suggestion, and persuasion, not just authority.

COLLABORATING WITH THE PLAYWRIGHT

A director often prepares and presents a play with no input from the playwright who created the script. The director's job can be quite different when the playwright is present for preproduction preparation and rehearsals, as frequently occurs with the premier production of a play by a living author. A personal relationship with the playwright can be forged that evokes trust and mutual respect for the text, which is the artistic child of the dramatist. American director Elia Kazan certainly understood this and cultivated a close relationship with two of the most important playwrights of his generation: Arthur Miller and Tennessee Williams. He eventually fell out with these artists over both political and artistic conflicts, but for many years he interpreted numerous modern classics such as Miller's *Death of a Salesman* (1949) and Williams's *A Streetcar Named Desire* (1947). Kazan often talked his playwrights into making changes, both major and minor, to lines, action, or structure. Sometimes improvements were made, such as the use of a fluid single space for *Salesman* rather than a series of realistic sets. When directing Williams's play *Cat on a Hot Tin Roof* (1954), Kazan suggested the very positive change of bringing a major character, Big Daddy, back in the last act of the play, but other changes damaged the play's structure. Under Kazan's direction, Williams changed a very ambiguous and unsettling conclusion to one of certainty and sentimentality. When Tennessee Williams later published the play, he included both his own version of the last act and "Kazan's version." In 1974 Williams created yet a third version (and probably the best), which combined parts of one and two plus new material. It was directed by Michael Kahn.

When playwrights find a director they trust, they sometimes want to work exclusively with that director. Director Harold Clurman's realistic kitchen sink style with the legendary Group Theatre championed a revolution in American acting and perfectly suited Clifford Odets's working-class, Depression-era plays such as the family drama *Awake and Sing!* (1935) and *Golden Boy* (1937), the story of a young man who gives up his aspirations as a violinist to make it big in the violent world of professional boxing. Both Odets and Clurman sought ensemble acting, in which remarkable levels of unspoken meaning could be revealed through subtle physical changes. On the other hand, the Nobel prize-winning British playwright Harold Pinter and director Peter Hall both reveled in ambiguity of character, event, and meaning. Hall directed the first production of *The Homecoming* (1965), in which Teddy inexplicably leaves his wife Ruth with his father, uncle, and brothers to serve as a surrogate mother and prostitute. By the mid-1980s, however, Pinter (also an actor) was usually directing his own plays. Playwright Michael Frayn and director Michael Blakemore have collaborated on four Broadway shows since 1983 as well as a number in Britain. Important milestones include *Noises Off* (1983), *Copenhagen* (2000), and *Democracy* (2004).

Sometimes playwrights and directors come to loggerheads, as occurred with JoAnne Akalaitis's 1984 production of Samuel Beckett's famous *Endgame* (1957). The play had been produced many times with the setting called for in the text—an undecorated, nondescript but stark interior. Akalaitis reset the play in a highly recognizable, rundown subway passage. Beckett was so distressed by the resetting that he not only attacked the production but also tried to have it stopped. Akalaitis had not altered any of the dialogue, but Beckett argued that the production's specificity denied the play's ambiguities and thus undercut its potential for expressing the universality of the human condition. Akalaitis argued for the director's necessary freedom of expression and the right to conceptualize the theatrical event in whatever way the director chooses. The question is not just who owns the rights to a play but whether anyone owns the rights to interpretation. Such controversy over artistic license, concept, and artistic integrity has been very active for several decades now, with directors sometimes under the critical microscope.

On the other hand, Beckett had complete confidence in the interpretations of Alan Schneider from the 1950s until the director's accidental death in 1984. Schneider was dedicated to the texts and intentions of playwrights he admired.

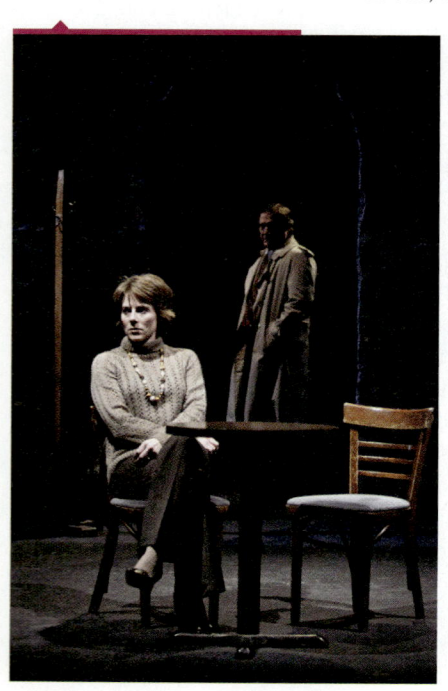

BETRAYAL (1978) by Harold Pinter. A 2006 production of this psychological exploration of adultery. It is a tricky play to perform and direct since Pinter reverses chronological order yet builds to a climax. Michelle O'Neill as Emma and Bob Davis as Jerry. Directed and designed by Bain Boehlke. Jungle Theater, Minneapolis.

Photo © Michal Daniel.

EXPLORING Historical and Cultural Perspectives

Who Owns the Work?

Directors sometimes run afoul of living playwrights or "play purists" who believe that famous works should not be tampered with or far removed from the original intent. Such positions, however, beg such questions as How can one really know the intent of any playwright not still living? Is the intent sacred? and How can the original intent address new audiences some ten, fifty, or hundreds of years after composition? Aside from paying royalties for plays protected by copyright, who really owns a text in performance?

In 1982 the Wooster Group in New York began working on *L.S.D. (. . . Just the High Points . . .)*. Director Elizabeth LeCompte and the company developed the piece collectively. As the work emerged, it came to be about two decades in the United States and the impossibility of creating definitive history. Material from the 1960s focused on the drug subculture; the 1950s were represented by excerpts from *The Crucible*, Arthur Miller's play about the Salem witch trials. The play is an indictment of Joseph McCarthy, the House Committee on Un-American Activities, and the persecution of U.S. citizens.

In the hands of the Wooster Group *The Crucible* was deconstructed. Pieces of Miller's text were integrated into a performance collage, and the company sought permission to use excerpts from the play. The Wooster Group was treating the text as a social document that served as a starting point for raising new questions outside the author's intentions. After seeing a performance of the work in progress, Miller directed his agent to refuse permission to the Wooster Group. He stressed that he wanted his play produced only in the way he intended. He was concerned that the production would be viewed as a parody of his play, which could negatively influence future productions of *The Crucible* in New York.

A very different approach to dramatic text and ownership is taken by Charles L. Mee, a prolific playwright widely produced by resident theatres such as the Berkeley Repertory Theatre, Actors Theatre of Louisville, the Public Theater in New York, and the Steppenwolf Theatre Company. His plays are popular both in avant-garde circles as well as with audience members who have a keen interest in new interpretations of classical theatre. Mee has collaborated with some of the most inventive and successful directors in contemporary American theatre including Martha Clarke, Anne Bogart, and Gordon Davidson.

Many of Mee's plays are radical and fully modernized (post-modernized?) adaptations of classical work, sometimes familiar in title, such as *The Trojan Women: A Love Story* (1996), adapted from Euripides, as well as a new *Orestes* (1992), inspired by the same Greek tragedian. On the other hand, the Greek source is not so obvious in *Big Love* (2000),

HOTEL CASSIOPEIA (2006) by Charles Mee is one of his most successful investigations of American artists in mediums other than Mee's own. Based on the boxes and collages of Joseph Cornell, the play becomes a simultaneous somber yet playful presentation of the life of a remarkable recluse who seems to long for the beautiful but never leaves his box. Directed by postmodern artist Anne Bogart with the SITI Company; scenic design by Neil Patel.

Photo © Michael Brosilow.

a retelling of *The Suppliant Women* by Aeschylus, or *Snow in June* (2003), based on ancient Chinese theatre combined with American popular culture such as vaudeville. In 2008 Mee worked in collaboration with scholar Stephen Greenblatt creating a play loosely based on what is known of a lost play by Shakespeare and John Fletcher entitled *Cardenio*. He has explored the creativity of several American artists, most recently in *Under Construction* (2009), which is structured like a collage. It is not surprising that Mee's website, where his plays are made available, is called "The (Re)Making Project."

Mee believes that there is no such thing as an original play since authors always are inspired by and borrow from each other. He points out that even the ancient Greeks retold pre-existing myths and encourages others to use his plays in developing new work, but cautions that the plays as he has written them are under copyright and any performance requires permission.[2] Mee's point of view is rather different from Miller's. The controversy over control of artistic material has reached a critical point in the development of contemporary theatre. It may be that resolution of the issue is impossible.

INTERESTED? Check out

David Savran. *Breaking the Rules: The Wooster Group*. New York: Theatre Communications Group, 1988.

Charles L. Mee's "the (re)making project," www.charlesmee.org, for a fuller development of his viewpoint of the play as historical document.

Schneider directed at least fifteen different plays by Beckett (some of them several times), including the American premieres of *Waiting for Godot* (1953) and *Endgame* (1957). Schneider had a similar artistic relationship with American playwright Edward Albee and directed most of his work, including *Who's Afraid of Virginia Woolf?* (1962) and *A Delicate Balance* (1966), two domestic dramas that are brutal in their revelation of hidden truth. Because of Schneider's insistence on the primacy of the writer's vision, some critics and historians consider his interpretations of these playwrights' work to be the definitive ones.

DIRECTORS AND ABSENT PLAYWRIGHTS

It is more common for directors to create radical concepts when interpreting plays that are no longer under copyright or under the control of the playwright's estate. Directors Tadashi Suzuki and Anne Bogart, like Giorgio Strehler before them, frequently revive older work with startling, even remarkable results. Italian director Strehler, for example, who is often identified as an exponent of poetic or lyrical realism, created an interpretation of Shakespeare's *The Tempest* in the 1980s that was **metatheatrical**—that is, the production used the play to comment on the nature of performance and the world as theatre, ending with a complete collapse of the theatrical scenery.

In 1995 postmodern director Anne Bogart reconceived *The Adding Machine* (1923) at Actors Theatre of Louisville. From this expressionistic play depicting early commercialism and the dehumanization of humanity, Bogart explored the victims of technocracy as seen through the eyes of the computer age. Bogart continues to develop new works as well as adapt old texts. She and director Tadashi Suzuki cofounded the Saratoga International Theatre Institute (now the SITI Company) in 1992 to facilitate international cultural exchange and collaboration in American theatre. As artistic director of SITI, Bogart launched a new production of Shakespeare's *A Midsummer Night's Dream* (2004) set in 1930s California, and a Shakespeare play within a radio play within a staged play called *Radio Macbeth 2007*. Suzuki, who leads the Suzuki Company of Toga in Japan, has successfully combined traditional Western and Eastern work into a stunning approach to theatricality. As a Japanese director and teacher of acting, he has drawn on classical forms such as Kabuki and Noh, but his casts are international, and he mixes modern images with ancient ones in usually open, austere, but beautiful spaces. He has shared these startling cultural and artistic explorations with audiences

THE MASTER BUILDER (1892) by Henrik Ibsen. This 2009 Yale Repertory Theatre production directed by Evan Yionoulis, with scenic design by Timothy Brown, seems to turn vertical architecture (so important in this play about an architect), into a horizontal playing field. Ibsen's master architect Solness, played by David Chandler, is fascinated with a young woman, Hilda (Susan Heyward), who personifies youth knocking on the door of the aging artist.

Photo © T. Charles Erickson.

throughout the world. Many of his productions are reconceptions of Greek classical plays such as *Oedipus the King* in 2001; *Clytemnestra* (1983) has material from at least four different Greek tragedies, and *Dionysus* (1993) uses the Greek god of ecstatic celebration to investigate the relationship of government and religion.

COLLABORATING WITH DESIGNERS

Many directors and designers conceive theatrical space, costumes, lighting, and sound through healthy give-and-take and full collaboration. Typically, the director begins meeting with designers well before casting or rehearsals. The director often brainstorms with designers both separately and together, sharing interpretation, ideas, and images. The director focuses the work of the designers and inspires them to make their own artistic contributions while shaping all of the work into a single, unified concept. The artists may take inspiration from many places, but as a whole, the settings, lighting, costumes, and sound combine to produce a style that is unique to that production.

Successful Collaborations

Elia Kazan's production of Arthur Miller's *Death of a Salesman* in 1949 was a hybrid of realism and presentationalism. The setting, designed by Jo Mielziner, resembled the skeleton of a small house set against the backdrop of a cityscape. There were few walls and little furniture, and downstage of the floor of Willy's house was an open playing space. Yet the selective pieces of furniture were realistic and usable, the costumes were realistic, and the acting (as in nearly all of Kazan's productions) was realistic, following the system of Stanislavsky and the Group Theatre, of which he had been a founding member. The lighting was selective, and in Willy Loman's flashbacks in time the lighting became bizarrely yellowish. This production of *Death of a Salesman* was indicative of much of the work of Kazan and Mielziner together; they were clearly a successful team.

Similar observations could be made of the director/designer team Arthur Hopkins and Robert Edmond Jones before Kazan, and of Peter Hall and John Bury or Trevor Nunn and John Napier afterward. For more than ten years, beginning in 1916, Hopkins and Jones led the way in New York with simplified staging often called the **new stagecraft** in plays by Shakespeare such as *Richard III* and *Hamlet* and modern plays such as O'Neill's *Anna Christie.* Hall and Bury, as well as Nunn and Napier, worked together almost exclusively for many years in London at the National Theatre, the Royal Shakespeare Company, the commercial West End theatres, and in the United States on Broadway. Hall and Bury produced many Shakespeare plays and most of Harold Pinter, as well as the landmark *Amadeus* (1979) by Peter Shaffer that combined elaborate eighteenth-century costumes with a sleek, simplified set. Nunn and Napier were comfortable staging both Shakespearean plays and contemporary musicals such as *Cats* (1982) and *Les Misérables* (1985). Once directors and designers find a collaborator in whom they have complete trust and understanding, they are often reluctant to sever that relationship. Such collaborative compatibility is a key to the long-term success of many well-known directors and designers of the last century.

Seeing in Three Dimensions

The ability to see theatrical space three-dimensionally is critical for a director. During the planning stages of a production—whether sitting in a theatre, examining a set model, or studying a two-dimensional ground plan for the set or sketch for a costume design—the director needs to see in three dimensions. Once a set or costume has been constructed, it is usually too late to change it without great expense and loss of valuable time. Directors must be able to see the potential of a design as it will be used in production. They are concerned not only with how a set looks, for example, but also with what kinds of entrances and exits and traffic patterns it provides for actor movement. In the planning stages, the director and design team make decisions that will shape the entire audience experience.

EXPLORING Collaboration

Metamorphoses

Director-playwright Mary Zimmerman of Lookingglass Theatre Company in Chicago brought back a device that was used by the ancient Romans and was popular in the nineteenth century but used it in a decidedly twenty-first-century way. For her adaptation of *Metamorphoses* by Ovid, a rectangular water tank designed by Daniel Ostling filled most of the stage. The tank looked like a shallow swimming pool. It was the primary acting space, and nearly every character had to negotiate the water in reenacting the ancient tales and myths with a contemporary twist. Confining most of the action to a body of water suggested primordial existence, yet Zimmerman's language and images addressed the experiences and values of contemporary society preoccupied with technology and speed.

Zimmerman's method of developing theatrical material is untraditional and highly collaborative. She begins with an idea for developing a piece from a particular text (such as *The Arabian Nights*, the notebooks of Leonardo da Vinci, or in this case, the ancient Greek myths as told by Ovid). She then selects a cast who will help to develop scenes and writes text in between rehearsal periods. Zimmerman works with designers Ostling, Mara Blumenfeld (costumes), T. J. Gerckens (lighting), and Andre Pluess and Ben Sussman (sound) before the script is written or the characters are developed. Because the play is both written and staged within a traditional rehearsal period, the construction of the sets must be under way while the show is rehearsing. In this method of working, the designers influence the entire development of the show. In the case of *Metamorphoses*, the presence of the pool of water, a symbol in many cultures of change, influenced the selection of myths to dramatize and images to explore. Zimmerman called the water the eleventh performer

METAMORPHOSES (2001), as directed by Mary Zimmerman and produced at Second Stage in New York.
Photo © Joan Marcus.

and explained the many ways that it reflected actor images, interacted with light, and created an entirely new visual dimension on stage.[3]

Metamorphoses, originally produced by the Lookingglass Theatre Company, Chicago, was brought to Second Stage in New York City in 2001 and moved to the Circle in the Square Theatre.

Zimmerman has followed *Metamorphoses* with other fascinating productions: *The Notebooks of Leonardo da Vinci* (2003), also produced at Second Stage; *The Secret in the Wings* (2004), a dark revisitation of fairy tales; the visually stunning retelling of Jason and the Argonauts in *Argonautica* (2006); and, in 2010, Leonard Bernstein's musical *Candide*, for which she returned to the original eighteenth-century novel to create a new book.

Many masterful and innovative directors, with their designers, have found ways to transform space and challenge or delight their audiences with the spatial results. In the 1910s Jacques Copeau and his assistant, Louis Jouvet, created a permanent architectural space that could accommodate any play and place all the focus on the actors and the spoken text without the "distraction" of specific scenery. In Germany in the 1920s Erwin Piscator was the first to combine the new media of film with live actors onstage. The audience for *Sturmflut* (1927) watched actors interacting with film images of battleships attacking them. In both Europe and America since the 1970s Robert Wilson has emerged as a leading director, designer, and auteur. His productions such as *Einstein on the Beach* (1976), *The Knee Plays* (1984), *Woyzeck* (2001), and *The Black Rider* (2004) offered remarkable visual feasts of images; choreographed, repetitive movement; and minimalist music by Philip Glass and David Byrne. In his adaptation of *Crime and*

Punishment (1976–1984), Russian director Yuri Lyubimov used the shadows of furniture on the stage walls as if they were the objects themselves. In the same production a wooden door became a symbol of oppression and seemed to take on a life of its own as it moved about the stage. The ability to imagine the way a costume, set, or lighting effect will work on stage is critical to the director's work with designers.

COLLABORATING WITH ACTORS

Despite the importance of interpreting and conceptualizing as well as negotiating the performance space, the director's work with actors is central to making a show artistically successful. Ultimately, it is the actor with whom the audience will identify, and the director's job is not only to choose the actors but also to help them achieve a successful characterization while working together effectively.

Casting the Show

Casting, or selecting the actors for each role, is a crucial responsibility for the director. A **casting director,** or specialist in finding actors for specific roles, assists the director in some professional productions. The standard tool for casting is the **audition.** Auditions vary considerably, but many directors and casting directors want to see unfamiliar actors deliver a prepared audition piece: one or two monologues (speeches from plays), a few bars from a song. In some cases this initial audition may be done via video. Directors sometimes have actors do unrehearsed ("cold") readings from the play being auditioned or other material. Other times directors prefer to interview actors or will consider only actors they have seen perform previously. Once the choice of actors has been narrowed, actors may be invited to attend more extensive auditions, or **callbacks,** for the director to make specific casting choices.

In casting a show, the director considers physical and vocal characteristics—not only whether an actor seems to fit a role, but also how the actor looks and sounds in relation to other actors available. If the actress playing Juliet is cast first, for example, there might be three actors who could perform Romeo well, but one of them might be the best choice for this particular Juliet. Actors are often asked to read together in various combinations. A physical resemblance could be a consideration when actors are to represent a family. The director also must assess more intangible qualities such as talent and range. Will an actor be believable in the specific type of role? Can the actor achieve the intense emotionality, comic timing, or sustained physical activity called for in the script? Finally, the director will consider how the actor works with others. An otherwise talented performer who is not a team player can be devastating to the developmental process. Will the actor take direction or be unwilling (or unable) to implement suggestions? It is difficult to predict success from a brief acquaintance. Directors often rely on actors they have worked with previously as well as talking to other directors to have the best chance of putting together a cast with the right chemistry to produce an effective working atmosphere as well as exciting relationships on stage.

Developing Character and Ensemble

Most directors help actors to develop characterizations. The challenge is to create a unified style for the production while still allowing each actor to explore a role psychologically and emotionally. Coaching the actors often includes discussion of character background and motivation. Some directors use improvisation to help actors make discoveries about their characters; for example, leaving the text behind, the actors, as characters, might improvise a scene related to but not actually dramatized in the play. Directors may work with masks in rehearsal, even if they will not be used in performance, to explore different qualities of movement and heightened emotion.

ARTISTS of the THEATRE

George C. Wolfe

One of America's most important directors is also a playwright. George C. Wolfe came to the theatre as a writer, most notably a new African American voice heard loud and clear in *The Colored Museum* (1986) and *Jelly's Last Jam* (1991). Since that time, he has evolved as a talented, visionary Tony and Obie award-winning director with some of his era's most important plays such as *Angels in America* (1993) and *Top-dog/Underdog* (2001). Between 1993 and 2005, Wolfe served as Artistic Director of the Public Theater in New York and the New York Shakespeare Festival, where he successfully promoted a series of plays, not only by Shakespeare but also by an array of contemporary African American, Latino, and Asian as well as white playwrights. Many of these writers have emerged as important voices in the contemporary theatre: perhaps most notably, Tony Kushner, Suzan-Lori Parks, José Rivera, and Diana Son. It seems appropriate that he would serve so admirably at the Public, because his first success, *The Colored Museum*,

CAROLINE, OR CHANGE by Tony Kushner and Jeanine Tesori, as directed by George C. Wolfe (2004) for the Broadway production. Simultaneous action and singing are spread across the stage.
Photo © Michal Daniel.

was produced there by Joseph Papp, who founded the venerable New York institution. Wolfe returned to the Public Theater in 2006 to direct Meryl Streep in a revival of *Mother Courage and Her Children* by Bertolt Brecht.

Wolfe's commitment to diversity (he uses the word "inclusion" to describe his approach) is related to what he calls "cultural collision," which he is fond of promoting in the theatre that he creates. He aims to spark not only controversy but also meaningful collaboration and interaction that results in theatrical events that cannot be ignored—that demand response, discussion, and, it is hoped, personal or group action. In a 2005 interview he asserted that "the potency of language and your commitment can transform people." He sees the theatre as not just a form for images and language, but "an art form of ideas. We can surrender to an idea."

Caroline, or Change (2003), with book and lyrics by Tony Kushner, music by Jeanine Tesori, and directed by Wolfe, is a musical of serious ideas. This rhythm and blues show is set in 1963, in Louisiana, in the midst of the civil rights strife, the assassination of John F. Kennedy, and economic

hardship for the protagonist. Yet the heart of the play is also a personal and domestic struggle that Wolfe modulated beautifully. In 2011 Wolfe co-directed (with Joel Grey) a revival of *The Normal Heart,* Larry Kramer's play from 1985 about the devastating effects of AIDS and the slow response of society to the crisis.

Wolfe's work with the playwright is critical. The playwright must find his or her own voice, and Wolfe is determined "to find the urgency and intimacy in the play." The playwright surely *had* to write the play. It is the director's function to discover why. As a director bringing the whole production together, Wolfe realizes that keeping a cool head in a room full of artists is not only difficult but also crucial. He sees himself as the "designated driver."[4]

INTERESTED? Check out

George C. Wolfe. *Two by George C. Wolfe: The Colored Museum and Spunk.* New York: Fireside, 1991.

George C. Wolfe. *Jelly's Last Jam.* New York: Theatre Communications Group, 1993.

As individual characterizations develop, the director modulates the performances in relation to one another. Some directors are very successful at molding an acting **ensemble,** a cast that functions seamlessly together as a unit rather than as individual performers. As the director of many of August Wilson's series of plays on the African American experience in the twentieth century, Lloyd Richards created with his actors a wonderful sense of family and community in plays such as *The Piano Lesson* (1989), which explores the struggle between two grown siblings. Ensemble is created not only by intelligent casting decisions, but also by the tone set by the director in rehearsal and the skill with which the director can unify the actors in a common performance style.

Directors have different ways of relating to performers. Some are very hands-on in guiding the actors. David Belasco, for example, early in the twentieth century, would dictate all movement and often act out the roles for the actors. This amount of control may be extreme, but José Quintero, a sensitive director of the mid- to late twentieth century, in directing the plays of Williams and O'Neill, often took on the persona of a character as he talked to the actor playing that role. Other directors leave the actors free to make most major discoveries and selections on their own. Arthur Hopkins in the 1920s was masterful at noninterference, giving the actors considerable room and only gently guiding them through very difficult problems. Rather than providing answers, Hopkins preferred to ask questions of the actors regarding character, motivation, and action that inevitably led to appropriate decisions for the production at hand. He believed that his most important responsibility with the actors was in casting brilliantly so that the actors were not only appropriate for the roles, but also able to work together creatively. This model is still followed by many directors.

A sensitive director will deal with different actors in various ways. Some performers need a lot of reinforcement and encouragement; others respond better to a more businesslike approach to criticism. A director may give an experienced actor a freer rein than an apprentice performer. The ability to sense what help the actors need at different stages of character development is an invaluable skill for directors.

COLLABORATING WITH THE STAGE MANAGER

Working closely with the director through the entire production process is the **stage manager.** Stage managers coordinate a show during rehearsal and performance and keep the director's artistic choices intact during its run. It sounds simple when stated succinctly, but the stage manager is usually the busiest person in the theatre, organizing, setting schedules, enforcing rules, solving problems, and generally making sure everything stays on track. Depending on the show's complexity, the stage manager may bring one or several assistants on board.

A good stage manager takes care of practical matters so that the director can focus on artistic development. If secured early enough in the production process, the stage manager will organize and run auditions. The stage manager is in charge of preparing the rehearsal space, often unlocking and setting up, including taping out the ground plan of the set on the rehearsal floor and acquiring suitable rehearsal props and furniture. The stage manager maintains order and discipline among cast and crew and takes care of the mountain of paperwork generated by a production, including the promptbook. A modern promptbook typically includes a copy of the script marked with all cuts and text changes (these must be minimal if a play is under copyright), blocking notes, and all **cues** (changes in sound, lighting, or set). Professional stage managers are also responsible for keeping records on attendance and health benefits as well as reporting accidents, injuries, and any infraction of the rules to Actors' Equity.

Beginning with the last week or so of rehearsals through final performance, the stage manager serves as the nerve center of the production, calling the show over a headset, giving a warning and "go" cue for lighting, sound, and scene changes as well as warning calls for actors' entrances. When a show runs seamlessly from the audience's perspective, an accomplished stage manager has prepared, rehearsed, and developed a sensitivity for the pace and rhythm of all production elements as they are established by the director. After opening, the stage manager is responsible for keeping the show as the director intended, which might include calling corrective rehearsals and preparing cast replacements. The stage manager is responsible for onstage and backstage activity and must be prepared for any kind of emergency.

Besides having superior organizational skills, a stage manager must be able to work with all kinds of people. The relationship between stage manager and director is often the key to a smoothly functioning production company. Stage managers deal directly with designers, actors, and all technical staff, including **run crews** (workers who maintain and execute cues for props, costumes, set, lighting, and sound during the run of a show). The stage manager must maintain discipline as well as keep up morale, be able to think quickly, stay calm, and act decisively. Because of the wide variety of skills involved, good stage managers are highly prized. The Stage Managers' Association is a professional organization created as a network for support; for sharing problems, ideas, and stories; and for supporting education.

The responsibilities of the modern stage manager probably developed from the old prompter's position of the nineteenth century and earlier. In the days of rolling repertory, when the actors performed in different shows every night, the **prompter** sat at the side of the stage or in a special box down center to call out any forgotten lines or stage business. The advent of electric lighting and electronic sound as well as long rehearsal periods and long runs helped to create the stage manager's role as it now exists.

Sometimes also called a production stage manager, a **production manager** is usually employed by a theatre company with multiple performance spaces such as a resident theatre company or a large university theatre. The two most important jobs of a production manager are usually scheduling (spaces, rehearsals, and production meetings) and coordinating stage managers for the productions, especially when two or more productions are running and/or rehearsing simultaneously. In an educational environment the production manager is also likely to teach stage management courses and train new stage managers on the job.

Like a good stage manager, a good production manager is highly organized, a good listener, and an enabler. Some production managers work out overall production budgets and mediate personnel problems in consultation with the artistic director of the organization. The production manager can provide important frontline responses to the artistic director and alleviate some of the logistical nightmares facing the artistic director of a large theatre company.

THE REHEARSAL PROCESS

After a show is cast, it goes into **rehearsal**—the period of work in which the show is made ready for the stage. A four- to five-week rehearsal period (six days a week, seven hours a day) is typical for professional productions. Educational and community theatres tend to take four to six weeks (five or six days a week, three to four hours a night). The director decides how to use the rehearsal period, and each show may be somewhat different. There are, however, many rehearsal techniques and practices that are customary. For most of the rehearsal period the play is worked in small parts; one day's rehearsal might be spent entirely on one scene or part of a scene.

Read-Through and Analysis

Many rehearsals begin with the cast reading the play aloud followed by a discussion. In some cases, however, the director or playwright might read the play to the cast. Typically, the cast spends at least one or perhaps many days together reading and discussing the play. Other directors prefer to get a play "on its feet" immediately and begin staging right away.

Staging Rehearsals

The director is ultimately responsible for **staging**—combining all elements to bring the text alive in three dimensions. As rehearsals progress, the director sets the **blocking.** Some directors dictate predetermined blocking to the performers; others encourage actors to find appropriate character movement while rehearsing a scene, then adjust or refine that movement. The director looks for blocking that makes sense for the characters and environment but also creates an interesting visual image for the audience. The actors' bodies and all other visual elements work together to create a composition. The director considers the width, height, and depth of the stage or other playing space.

Staging choices can help to create focus on a particular actor or area. If a crowd of people on one side of the stage is turned to face a lone actor on the other side of the stage, the lone actor usually takes focus. An actor standing in an open doorway tends to be in a powerful visual position, since the line of the doorway acts as a frame. The position of actors may also suggest power relationships. If two actors are seated and a third is standing, the standing actor not only tends to take focus but will also seem to dominate the seated actors. Such power relationships can be altered by the actors' body language, however. If the standing actor is staring off into space, for example, and the seated actors are leaning toward each other, it might seem as if the seated actors are conspiring against the standing actor.

Staging can help to tell the story of a play. Even in a wordless scene a character mounting a series of steps and receiving a crown is clearly assuming a royal position. A balanced or symmetrical stage picture tends to suggest harmony or rigidity. An unbalanced or asymmetrical arrangement can convey the impression of discord or uneasiness. A director also uses staging simply to create interesting compositions. Part of the sensory pleasure of theatre for the audience is the experience of watching shapes in a changing relationship to one another. A triangular composition, for example, is effective in the theatre, with the most significant person or thing making up the apex of the triangle. Whether beautiful or desolate, the visual images on the stage should be interesting and evocative. Of course, some directors have little interest in composition and simply develop movement on the stage that seems logical and motivated, choosing to spend rehearsal time on extensive character and ensemble work.

ARCADIA (1993) by Tom Stoppard poses interesting challenges for directors by calling for a fluid approach to time in a single location. He juxtaposes different historical periods, overlapping scenes in which one set of characters is oblivious to another, yet all are united thematically, intellectually, and emotionally. This Broadway revival of 2010 transplanted from London was directed by David Leveaux with scenic design by Hildegard Bechtler, lighting design by Donald Holder, and costume designs by Gregory Gale.

Photo © Carol Rosegg.

In the musical theatre, staging is closely related to choreography. Some of the most successful directors have served as both director and choreographer, a combination that not only is helpful in achieving unity of production but also enables the director to work with the actors in nearly every aspect of their creative process. Bob Fosse served in both capacities for many productions such as *Chicago* (1975), in which his distinctive seductive style imbued both acting and dance with energy and sexuality. In more recent times director-choreographer Susan Stroman has received accolades, including at least five Tony Awards, for her stylish, inventive ensemble work and staging in productions such as the musical triptych *Contact* (1999), subtitled "three short stories," *Oklahoma!* (2002), and the farcical Mel Brooks musicals *The Producers* (2001) and *Young Frankenstein* (2007). Beginning as a choreographer in the 1990s, Kathleen Marshall has specialized in both directing and choreographing revivals of famous musicals such as *Grease* (2007) and *Anything Goes* (2011).

Development Rehearsals

During the middle weeks of the rehearsal period the director works with the cast on developing characterization and refining movement. Usually, the set and costumes are being built. While still working most of the time on small pieces of the script, directors often schedule periodic run-throughs in which an act or the entire play is performed without stopping. Run-throughs give actors a sense of the play's dramatic development and rhythm and allow designers to see emerging movement patterns on stage.

As the company approaches the end of the development period, the cast begins to run through the entire play consistently so that the actors gain confidence in their work while the director can adjust the pace, rhythm, and continuity of the show. The director must sometimes modify the tempo of scenes and, when appropriate, orchestrate a buildup to the climax of the play. Because a production is rehearsed most of the time in pieces, putting the pieces together at the end is often a daunting task. This period is often the most nerve-wracking portion of rehearsal for all involved and requires both objectivity and sensitivity and sometimes diplomacy on the part of the director.

PERICLES by Shakespeare produced at the Public Theater in New York in 1998. This epic fairy-tale romance, stitched together by a narrative figure, follows the wanderings, loves, and dangerous exploits of an ancient hero. The design used here underscores the variety and exoticism of events and locations called up by both the action and narrative presentation. Scenic design by Mark Wendland; lighting design by Mimi Jordan Sherin; directed by Brian Kulick.

Photo © Michal Daniel.

Technical and Dress Rehearsals

Near the end of the rehearsal process, light, sound, and set changes are added to the show during **technical rehearsals.** The director, designers, and technical staff experiment with changes and finalize lighting and sound levels as well as timing for all technical elements and communicate these in detail to the stage manager. Costumes are finally added for **dress rehearsals.** Some changes in set, lighting, sound, or costumes may occur up to opening night.

OPENING THE PRODUCTION

By the time a production reaches opening night, the director's work is done. The stage manager coordinates the actors and crews as they prepare to do their work in front of the audience. The director (if all has gone well) is left with little to do. Unlike a film director, the director in the theatre has no absolute control over the final live performance. Unlike an orchestra conductor or a sports coach, the director must ultimately let go of the production and trust the actors and stage manager to do their jobs. Once a professional production has officially opened, the director is supposed to step aside and allow the actors to share the play with an audience without any more adjustments, note giving, or changes. If a problem arises, it must be addressed by the stage manager. Directors in educational theatre often look upon the run of the show as a chance to continue the students' learning process and choose to watch performances and give notes to help the actors improve, but the tweaking by this point should be minimal. Letting the production go can be a very difficult but also exciting shift for the director, who has spent so much time with preparation, analysis, and rehearsal.

Professional directors are members of the Society of Stage Directors and Choreographers. Successful directing requires many skills: the ability to read and analyze written work, to see in three dimensions, to "read" people and decide how best to help them in their own artistic journey, as well as the ability to lead and organize. It is a demanding and stressful profession, since the director ultimately takes responsibility for the success or failure of any production. Directors are individuals and tend to be strong in a certain area: interpreting text, creating visual images, encouraging ensemble, using space imaginatively. There may be as many directing styles as there are directors, and each one touches the lives of everyone involved in the theatrical experience.

CHAPTER REVIEW

Questions and Activities

1. Discuss the respective strengths and weaknesses of the dictatorial approach and the hands-off approach to directing. For the sake of the discussion, assume the extreme of both styles. What advantages and disadvantages can you foresee for each type?

2. The work of a director who creates startling visual images is often more noticeable than that of a director who concentrates most of his or her attention on nurturing believable performances and ensemble work. What criteria would you use to "discover" the work of the latter director? What sorts of things would you look for in evaluating the director's work?

3. Because of the importance of leadership in the position, directors must often negotiate delicate issues of power and authority. For example, college students sometimes have a hard time directing their peers. Discuss various situations in which leadership might prove problematic. Brainstorm about ways in which a director might deal with the situations.

Key Terms and Concepts

director, p. 135
cycle, p. 136
play master, p. 136
promptbook, p. 136
actor-manager, p. 137
antiquarianism, p. 138
combination company, p. 138
fourth wall staging, p. 139
interpretation, p. 139
concept, p. 141

dramaturg, p. 141
auteur, p. 144
constructivist set, p. 144
metatheatre, p. 150
new stagecraft, p. 151
casting, p. 153
casting director, p. 153
audition, p. 153
callback, p. 153
ensemble, p. 155

stage manager, p. 155
cue, p. 155
run crew, p. 156
prompter, p. 156
production manager, p. 156
rehearsal, p. 156
staging, p. 157
blocking, p. 157
technical rehearsal, p. 158
dress rehearsal, p. 159

For Further Exploration

Gabriella Giannachi and Mary Luckhurst, eds. *On Directing: Interviews with Directors.* New York: St. Martin's Griffin, 1999.

Toby Cole and Helen Krich Chinoy, eds. *Directors on Directing: A Source Book of the Modern Theatre.* Indianapolis: Bobbs-Merrill, 1979.

Francis Hodge and Michael McLain. *Play Directing: Analysis, Communication and Style,* 7th ed. Boston: Allyn and Bacon, 2009.

Brenda Murphy. *Tennessee Williams and Elia Kazan: A Collaboration in the Theatre.* Cambridge, U K: Cambridge University, 1992.

Harold Clurman. *On Directing.* New York: Simon & Schuster, 1997.

Lawrence Stern and Alice R. O'Grady. *Stage Management,* 9th ed. Boston: Allyn and Bacon, 2006.

David Richard Jones. *Great Directors at Work: Stanislavsky, Brecht, Kazan, Brook.* Berkeley: University of California, 1986.

Paul Allain. *The Art of Stillness: The Theater and Practice of Tadashi Suzuki.* New York: Macmillan, 2003.

Marvin A. Carlson. *Theatre Is More Beautiful Than War: German Stage Directing in the Late Twentieth Century.* Iowa City: University of Iowa, 2009.

Society of Stage Directors and Choreographers website, sdcweb.org.

Stage Managers' Association website, www.stagemanagers .org.

Actors' Equity Association website, www.actorsequity.org.

Literary Managers and Dramaturgs of the Americas website, www.lmda.org.

FENCES (1985) by August Wilson. 2010 Broadway production, starring Denzel Washington and Viola Davis. Directed by Kenny Leon.

Photo © Joan Marcus.

The Actor

From Mask to Contemporary Performance

The late actor Jason Robards was fond of reminding interviewers of the difference in acting live in the theatre and film acting. In the theatre no one can cut the scene and reshoot because it has to be played to its end.[1] The actor always feels the presence and response of a living audience: a condition that is simultaneously exciting and frightening—a journey into the unknown. Robards (who died in 2000) had a long, successful acting career in both theatre and film. Many critics and fellow actors called him the perfect actor for Eugene O'Neill's realistic plays. His performances in *Long Day's Journey into Night* (1956), *The Iceman Cometh* (1946), and *Moon for the Misbegotten* (1947), among many others, were unforgettable for those who witnessed them. Although Robards is celebrated for his acting abilities, his realistic, introspective style would have been very out of place in any period before the late nineteenth century. His wonderfully rough and gravelly voice (even when young), which made him distinctive to audiences, would probably have kept him off most stages before his time. It is clear that acting styles, tastes, and methods have changed dramatically and altered many times since the Greeks and Asians developed dramatic forms and early techniques for the art of acting. We should avoid the common assumption that performance has somehow evolved to more sophisticated and superior levels of achievement. It has simply changed with the times and cultural shifts, and it will change again. Yet Robards's words speak to acting of all periods. Even if armed with the words of a playwright and the guidance of a director, ultimately the actor is in the performance space engaging a living audience that is waiting to be moved and entertained.

DEVELOPMENT OF THE ACTOR

From its beginning the art of acting has been one of imitating and representing specific or imaginary human beings and their actions through intellectual, psychological, and emotional exploration. Of course, actors don't represent only people. They might play animals as in *The Lion King* or abstract concepts such as Good Deeds in the medieval morality play *Everyman*. Whatever the nature of the character, however, the actor's instrument is only him- or herself—the voice, body, and mind. From our distant vantage point we know more about the early actor's external expression than his emotional work. The historian's clues about performance before the invention of photography and sound recording come from actors' memoirs or written descriptions by audience members or critics regarding powerful voices, unusual movement, and decoration or adornment of the actor's body. Most of this information, however, dates from the late seventeenth century or later. From earlier eras we have surviving images of actors in paintings, drawings, sculpture, mosaics, and various decorations but little information about how the actors approached performance.

Masks

In the case of the Greeks and many other early performers, historians have given extensive attention to the use of masks. Greek actors played multiple roles by changing masks and costumes; it is assumed that actors also altered voice and gesture when changing roles. The masks and costumes were no doubt especially important when male performers took on roles of females, gods and goddesses, or bizarre manifestations such as birds, frogs, and clouds in the comedies of Aristophanes.

The use of masks and the size of Greek theatres—even the smallest surviving theatres were large by modern standards—suggest a carefully

THE MASK is the oldest known device for expression of character to an audience. No Greek or Roman classical masks have survived, but we have many images of masks on vases and walls, in mosaics, and carved in stone or cast in metal or clay. This replica of a Greek mask of comedy is cast in clay from a Hellenistic or Roman sculptured rendering of a mask discovered in a dig in Athens at the site of the Roman Agora (market) in Athens. The original can be seen in the Ancient Agora Museum in Athens, Greece. The wide open mouth and emotional expression, which seem to be typical, are in keeping with the Roman name for mask, which is *persona*.

Photo © Kendra Fletcher Wainscott.

selected system of gestures. Hand and arm movements were perhaps emblematic (communicating a specific idea), as in surviving Asian performance styles (such as Noh, Kabuki, Chinese music drama, and Kathakali). Such gesturing is consistent with the dancing, singing, and stylized movement that surely were part of the masked choral acting in Greece as well. There is also every indication that Roman mask acting was broad to fill the huge theatres and serve the farcical plays. Likewise, the masked actors of *commedia dell'arte* in Renaissance Italy were expansive, grotesque, highly physical, and full of clowning.

Masked acting is not confined to antiquity; actors in many African and Asian cultures have continued to use masks all along. Over the last hundred years or so, Western actors and directors frequently have returned to masks and found that when wearing masks, actors must select larger and more simplified gestures to harmonize movement with the mask. Playwrights such as Luigi Pirandello and Eugene O'Neill experimented with masks as an acting device. In *Six Characters in Search of an Author* (1921), Pirandello called for masking his six title characters, who are abstractions, but all other characters—the human actors, director, and others—were performed without masks. In *The Great God Brown* (1926), O'Neill used masks to represent social and family roles, but more important, the masks were devices for hiding the characters' psychological anguish from other characters. The action gets more complex, however, when one character dies and another character takes up the dead man's mask, puts it on, and pretends to be his deceased friend.

Contemporary directors have utilized masks to help establish style of production. Peter Hall adapted the Greek convention of masks for his all-male production of *The Oresteia* at the National Theatre in Great Britain in 1981. To create the world of the jungle for her production of *The Lion King* (1997), Julie Taymor combined masks, puppets, and imaginative physical work. Often the masks also revealed the actor's face so that the mask became an extension, like a puppet controlled by the puppeteer. A similar dynamic is at work in *Avenue Q* (2003) in which the puppeteer and actor are one. When watching the performance the audience member tends to shift focus from actor to puppet and vice versa, while sometimes taking in both at once. Modern directors have found that when working with masks, casual, offhand movement looks silly or insignificant. Movement with masks therefore becomes dancelike, something more akin to choreography, as we see in Julie Taymor's productions. The mask is powerful, dynamic, and iconic. It can represent a fixed moment, a psychological motif, or an emblematic emotional state. Even a mask, however, can seem to change depending on the angle of presentation by the actor or the way in which lighting illuminates the mask.

THE GREAT GOD BROWN by Eugene O'Neill. One of the two major characters, Billy Brown, finds himself torn between his own personality and life and those of his best friend, Dion. After the death of Dion, Brown assumes the persona of Dion. In this scene, he agonizes over his own mask and the mask of Dion. Produced at Towson State University.
Collection of the authors.

The Actor's Face

Historians know little about nonmask acting until the medieval religious cycle performances, and even then masks were used to depict devils. It is clear, however, that many medieval actors used their own faces to portray biblical characters. From about

A CHINESE ACTRESS making up for the role of Sun Yü-ch'iao in *Picking Up the Jade Bracelet* by Shih Yü-cho, a traditional comedy focused on a coy young girl being pursued by a young man who tries to bribe her with a jade bracelet for her love. Makeup in classical Chinese theatre often becomes mask-like with traditional designs for makeup as well as costume styles for every role. This production was performed at the Liyuan Theatre in Beijing.

Photo © Ronald Wainscott.

the thirteenth century in the West, the unmasked face became the norm, although masks would periodically return.

What new demands or opportunities for the actor accompanied exposing the actor's face? Historians get clues from the surviving plays and occasional private accounts but must still guess at some parts of changing acting styles. One obvious dynamic change is a new focus on the attractiveness of the performer. Renaissance and later accounts frequently laud the beauty of actresses and the charisma of both genders. Although makeup (sometimes very elaborate) became a standard for actors, audiences began to more clearly recognize their favorites on sight, and such recognition might have launched the beginning of fascination with performers in the public social arena. From the eighteenth century onward, evidence for this attraction to performing personalities survives in published biography and autobiography. The cult of personality escalated in the nineteenth century as a part of the movement of romanticism and remains a strong feature of our own cultural landscape.

Today, many audience members respond with strong affirmation to physical beauty and to highly skilled performers whose visage undergoes remarkable transformation. It is easy to see the importance of facial expression in the work of modern **pantomime** artists who rely only on physical expressiveness and do not use their voices in performance. Dynamic facial alteration was used brilliantly by Marcel Marceau (1923–2007), the most famous contemporary pantomime artist. His routine of the mask maker, in particular, demonstrated instantaneous and emotionally charged change of expression as he portrayed both the maker and the masks. Facial antics play an important role in the success of film stars such as Jack Black and Robin Williams, TV actors Lucille Ball and Dick Van Dyke, the master stage comics Nathan Lane and Bill Irwin, and the queen of contemporary musical theatre, Bernadette Peters. Such facial transformation is associated with clowning and farcical plays, but audiences are also mesmerized by the facial power and mutability of Anthony Hopkins, Helen Mirren, James Earl Jones, and Judi Dench when they are playing villainous or dramatically intense characters.

The Actress Enters

The actors in institutional theatre in Greece and Rome were strictly male, but women were not always absent from acting. Although we have sketchy information that women might have performed in Greek **mime** (a kind of variety entertainment), actresses certainly acted frequently in Roman mime. This kind of performance was undoubtedly entertaining, but was not taken seriously by those who left a record of it. The Roman mime was a speaking actor, but also a variety performer working improvisationally and with script. Both genders were often unmasked and barefoot and performed bawdy scenes laced with satirical comment. Numerous accounts survive attesting to women mimes appearing nude and performing simulated or actual sex acts onstage. Although mimes were very popular during the Empire, they were held in low regard socially and morally and categorized with prostitutes.

TYPICALLY AVOIDING MASKS and extravagant makeup, western actors reveal much of their own countenance, not only when performing in realism, but in plays from the classical repertory as here in *King Lear* by Shakespeare in a 2007 revival at the Public Theater in New York. Kevin Kline as Lear laments the death of his daughter, Cordelia, played by Kristen Bush.

Photo © Michal Daniel.

Nonetheless, Theodora, a mime actress, married the Emperor Justinian. Once Rome was Christianized, the church attacked mimes who had often satirized Christianity and excommunicated them.

Women in medieval Europe (especially France) performed in the religious cycle plays, but historians know little about them. As professionals women became more prominent in Italy with *commedia dell'arte,* in Spain during the Golden Age, and in Restoration England. In Italy (and to some degree internationally, since some of the *commedia* troupes toured or took up residence in other European countries) some actresses became popular favorites. In the late 1500s Isabella Andreini was celebrated in poetry throughout Europe. She was repeatedly praised euphorically for her skills and beauty as a *prima donna* and young lover in the I Gelosi company, which she led with her husband. We could consider Andreini the first superstar actress.

In Spain, despite repressive social and religious conditions for women, professional actresses abounded after 1587, but they often encountered censure from the authorities. They appear to have been the first actresses to have plays and major roles written specifically for them. During the English Restoration (beginning in 1660), women first became professionals on the English-speaking stage, and their presence undoubtedly led to the creation of very different kinds of female roles for women in comedies of manners and intrigue. Although such shifts were breakthroughs for women in the European performing arts, actresses as a class were still regarded as morally suspect and socially unacceptable. In both Japan and China women as actresses held the stage from the beginnings of performance, but they lost their permission to perform in the seventeenth century (Japan) and eighteenth century (China) and were reinstated only in the late nineteenth and early twentieth centuries. Many of the new Asian actresses, however, were more interested in performing in modern plays than in the classical forms.

THE CHERRY ORCHARD (2007), showcasing Kate Burton as Ranevskaya at the Huntington Theatre Company in Boston. Since the British Restoration, the English-language theatre has enjoyed a remarkable parade of talented actresses. Directed by Nicholas Martin.
Photo © T. Charles Erickson.

ARTISTS of the THEATRE

Bernadette Peters

Bernadette Peters (b. 1948) is arguably the best-known actress on the American stage. Although she has performed successfully in television and film, her natural home seems to be the Broadway theatre. She is small in stature, but her energy on stage is breathtaking.

Her powerful, flexible voice and charismatic stage presence won her the opportunity to create two roles in Stephen Sondheim/James Lapine musicals. In the first act of *Sunday in the Park with George* (1984), she played Dot, the practical yet caring mistress of artist Georges Seurat (played by Mandy Patinkin). Peters brought a down-to-earth quality to the young woman who loves an artist but understands that life must go on and that her unborn child must be provided for in a way that Seurat's bohemian lifestyle will not support. In the second act she played Marie, a grandmother who helps a young artist (Patinkin) connect with his past and find renewed energy to create. As the Witch in *Into the Woods* (1987), Peters was both funny and heartbreaking. The diversity of her vocal talent was showcased in music as diverse as a comic rap song and the achingly beautiful "Stay with Me." Her split-second transformation from hideous crone to sexy bombshell was a delightful stroke of theatricality. (Both musicals are available on DVD.)

Peters's career began at age 3½ with spots on popular TV game shows. She made her Broadway debut in 1967 in *Johnny No-Trump,* but her career took off with a stellar performance in the Off-Broadway musical spoof *Dames at Sea* (1968). Other career highlights include two Tony Awards. The first was for *Song and Dance* (1985), a musical about love and loneliness in New York City by composer Andrew Lloyd Webber. The first act tells the story of Emma (Peters) in song, and the second act tells the story of one of Emma's lovers in dance. Peters's second Tony was awarded in 1999 for *Annie Get Your Gun.* This Irving Berlin musical was created in 1946 for the Broadway star Ethel Merman, who has always been strongly linked with the role of Annie Oakley. Peters managed to make the character her own, however, and delighted audiences for two years with well-loved songs such as "You Can't Get a Man with a Gun" and "There's No Business Like Show Business." In the spring of 2003 Peters took on another role made famous by Merman: Mama Rose in *Gypsy.* Returning to Broadway after a six-year absence in 2010, Peters enchanted critics and audience members with her performance of Desirée in a revival of Sondheim's in *A Little Night Music,* and in 2011 she performed in a revival of *Follies* (also by Sondheim and James Goldman) at Kennedy Center in Washington, DC, and on Broadway.

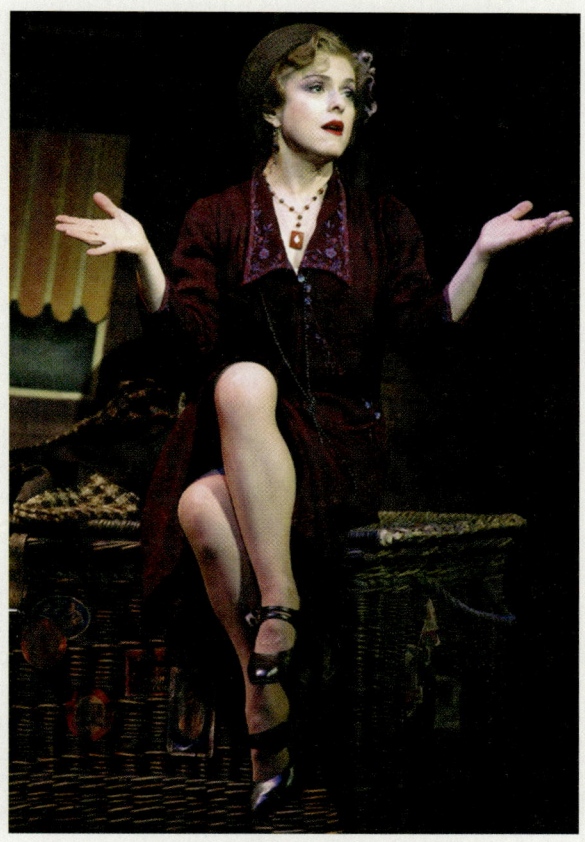

BERNADETTE PETERS as Mama Rose in the 2003 Broadway revival of *Gypsy.*
Photo © Joan Marcus.

INTERESTED? Check out

Bernadette Peters's film performances in *Impromptu* (1991), directed by James Lapine, with Mandy Patinkin, Hugh Grant, and Emma Thompson; *It Runs in the Family* (2003); and *Pennies from Heaven* (1981) and *The Jerk* (1979), both with Steve Martin.

www.bernadettepeters.com.

The 1999 Broadway revival cast recording (CD) of *Annie Get Your Gun.*

Peters's solo albums, including *Bernadette Peters Loves Rodgers and Hammerstein* (2002).

The Tradition of Cross-Dressing

Before women were allowed to join acting companies in Britain, men and boys performed female roles, as had previously been the case in Greece and Rome. The use of male performers for female roles is still traditional in some Asian forms, such as Noh, Kabuki, Chinese music drama, and Kathakali. Although Shakespeare and his contemporaries sometimes used masks for obvious disguises, the actor's own face was the norm, even with cross-gender casting. Shakespeare wrote roles in which boys would portray women who disguised themselves by dressing as boys before having the character's "real" gender revealed at the play's end, as in *As You Like It* (1598–1599) and *Twelfth Night* (1600–1601). Historians believe that male actors costumed themselves as women and engaged in vocal changes and movement to present the female persona but that the audience was very aware that it was observing cross-dressing. You can see modern interpretations of such conventions in the film *Shakespeare in Love* (1998) and in many revivals of the farcical-tragical interlude "Pyramus and Thisby" in *A Midsummer Night's Dream* (1595–1596).

Cross-gender performance has never left the stage in fact and has maintained an important role in theatrical entertainment. Even after actresses became a common sight throughout Europe by the seventeenth century, many of these women began to engage in gender-switching roles, and some men continued to play older female roles. In **breeches roles** for women an actress played a male character or a female character disguised as a male. For some audiences this presentation was erotic, but cross-dressing also pointed up the social perceptions of what was appropriate to each gender's sphere. Cross-dressing roles were common in Spain in the late sixteenth to mid-seventeenth centuries. A good surviving example is Rosaura in Calderón's *Life Is a Dream* (c. 1636), in which the character first appears as an intrepid young man searching for his father and intent on restoring the family honor but midway through the play switches to female attire. At the end of the play she takes to a horse again in a hybrid costume reflecting both male and female attributes. English Restoration comedies, such as *The Country Wife* (1675) and *The Rover* (1677), are full of female characters (played by women) who dress as boys to advance an intrigue or to improve their public mobility. If accepted as male, the women could travel nearly anywhere unaccompanied. Thus cross-dressing continued in a new guise even when both sexes could perform on stage.

Nineteenth-century comedy and melodrama perpetuated the practice of cross-dressing, often with women playing roles not as women in disguise but as characters who were meant to be accepted as male yet reveal the femininity of the actress. The opportunity for both sexes to "try on" the behavior of the opposite gender has been recognized as an intriguing device and has been used in a number of ways by contemporary artists. Cross-dressing continues today as a challenge to actors of both genders who must seek to either fool their audience into accepting the transformation or use the gender switch to comment on gender issues while maintaining recognition of their real sex.

ACTING STYLES AND METHODS

Today, descriptions and explanations of acting methods fill many volumes; new how-to books on the acting process seem to appear every month or so. For many centuries, however, actors typically guarded their methods like a magician's secrets. Zeami discussed acting for the Japanese Noh theatre in detail but meant his writings to be revealed only to members of his acting family and to be kept unavailable to the public. From the early eighteenth through the nineteenth centuries European actors revealed some of their methods and approaches in

EXPLORING Historical and Cultural Perspectives

Contemporary Cross-Dressing

With a rage of cross-dressing plays or older plays reconceived with cross-dressing since the 1970s, the British and U.S. stages have enjoyed a generous helping of feminist as well as gay and lesbian plays that feature cross-dressing characters serving a variety of functions in comedy and tragicomedy especially. One of the most celebrated of such plays is *Cloud 9* (1979) by Caryl Churchill. In the first act of this play, a Victorian mother is played by a man, and her son is played by a woman to reveal commentary on sexual stereotypes of the period. Betty, the mother, tells the audience in direct address that she is the creation of men and therefore wishes to be what they wish her to be. The "son" Edward says the same thing about his father.

Then in the second act, set in 1979, a young girl is played by a grown man to again underscore how stereotyping and the impact of Victorian values lived on in the late twentieth century.

The Ridiculous Theatrical Company, led by Charles Ludlam, not only deconstructed nineteenth-century plays such as *Camille* (1973 and 1990), in which Ludlam took the leading female role himself, but also created new cross-dressing plays such as *The Mystery of Irma Vep* (1984). Two actors (one was Ludlam) played eight roles, doing lightning-quick costume changes in a parody of Victorian melodrama. In hilarious fashion Ludlam attacked our foibles and pretentious silliness in everyday life as well as in our famous theatrical works of the past. Charles Busch has created many cult hits, typically featuring himself in female roles, such as *Vampire Lesbians of Sodom* (1984) and *Psycho Beach Party* (1986), which satirically examine gender roles through absurd parody.

His *Die Mommie Die!* (1999), revived off-Broadway in 2007 with Busch playing the title role, hilariously satirizes 1960s Hollywood and mystery murder films and plays, as well as sexual and gender stereotypes and repression.

Split Britches, a feminist theatre company that explores lesbian lifestyles, received considerable attention beginning in the 1990s with its satirical and political material punctuated by cross-dressing. Led by Peggy Shaw, Lois Weaver, and Deb Margolin, the company has deconstructed famous plays and novels and satirized societal fear of alternative sexuality in *Lesbians Who Kill* (1992), *Belle Reprieve* (1991), *Salad of the Bad Café* (2000), and *Miss America* (2008).

CLOUD 9 (1979) by Caryl Churchill opens in the nineteenth century, as we see in this photograph. A sexual affair is struck up between Harry Bagley, a British explorer, and Betty, the wife of Harry's friend. The irony is that Betty is played by a man, so a heterosexual relationship is represented on stage as homoerotic. Produced at Towson State University.
Collection of the authors.

INTERESTED? Check out

Laurence Senelick. *The Changing Room: Sex, Drag and Theatre.* New York: Routledge, 2000.

Lesley Ferris. *Crossing the Stage: Controversies of Cross-Dressing.* New York: Routledge, 1993.

Sheila Rabillard, ed. *Essays on Caryl Churchill.* Toronto: Stoddart, 1997.

Elaine Aston and Elin Diamond. *The Cambridge Companion to Caryl Churchill.* New York: Cambridge University, 2010.

www.splitbritches.com.

published "confessions" and "apologies" (as the memoirs of popular actors were often called). The earliest surviving indicators of actors' methods usually focus on vocal delivery. Although acting styles frequently shifted and actors continued to experiment, most periods of history clearly placed a high premium on the actor's voice. Much of what historians know is based on the rhetorical methods of a given

HAMLET, with the French actor Talma playing to the Gertrude of Joséphine Duchesnois in the early nineteenth century (1807). This image, published in an early French translation by Jean-François Ducis of Shakespeare's play demonstrates the flamboyant style in which actors often presented romantic leading roles. We would find the physicalization very ostentatious and the speech rhetorical.

Bibliothèque National de la France, Paris.

era. **Rhetorical delivery** in ancient accounts, and well into the nineteenth century, was the art of oratory and of any public verbal communication, including physical interpretation through gesture, posture, movement, and facial expression.

The Rhetorical Tradition

It is not likely that actors in classical Greece or Republican Rome would have had success in the huge theatres of their era without powerful voices and clear articulation. Most or all of these actors probably had to have effective singing voices as well, since music was an important part of the performance. There is little to be found in the evidence surviving from these periods that suggests any sort of reality-based, psychological approach to acting (even though actors can develop these roles realistically today if they choose). Given what is known about ancient performance conditions, the acting was presumably highly **presentational** (not an attempt to imitate "real life"). The actors delivered poetry across vast spaces to large audiences outdoors, under the sun, wearing masks, in or near a circular orchestra, underscored by music. The male actors switched roles (and sometimes gender) throughout the performance. Although this style might seem artificial today, the approach to performance was obviously successful since the Greeks held onto these performance essentials for centuries and inspired the Romans to do something similar.

European actors in subsequent periods shared a reliance on rhetorical theory that was based on an understanding of how the passions affected the human body.[2] Before the twentieth century, actors and orators adopted a widely understood system of physical attitudes and gestures that were deemed appropriate for any conceivable emotional state. As limiting as such a mechanized system sounds to us, it is clear that the finest actors were capable of transcending such a system to captivate their audience and engender belief through their uncommon talents and charisma.

Audiences of any period come to the theatre with expectations and the need to understand the performance. The most successful actors fulfill most of these expectations, but they give the audience something more, something that separates them from the "uninspired" actor. David Garrick, for example, in the eighteenth century startled and delighted his audiences with his remarkable mimetic abilities that communicated volumes to his audience beyond the language he spoke. Consequently, critics singled him out for his "natural" acting even though he was still a part of the traditional rhetorical approach to performance. The actor's emotional restraint and the need to repeat roles in multiple performances led many actors to rely on craft—repeatable vocal delivery, gestures, movements, and expressions—rather than on emotion.

With the romantic rebellion at the end of the eighteenth century and the first half of the nineteenth century, however, many actors yielded to a flamboyant overflow of emotionality and eccentricity. Onstage sudden physical and emotional transformations became even more pronounced with actresses such as Sarah Siddons in England and Rachel in France. Actors Edmund Kean and Charlotte Cushman stalked the stage menacingly, even when not playing villains, and Edwin Forrest filled the stage with his athleticism and powerful voice, which was once described as "the falls of Niagara."[3] In the age of melodrama and touring stars, much of what the actor performed was punctuated by an exclamation point. This emphasis on emotional display does not mean that carefully developed craft disappeared, but many actors sought the appearance of unrestrained emotionality and enjoyed arousing their audiences the way many rock and pop stars do today.

Contemporary Realistic Performance

The movement of realism was so remarkably successful after the 1870s that it continues to dominate playwriting, screenwriting, and performance for theatre, film, and television. The actor's approach to a character was also profoundly affected by the emergence of psychoanalysis at the turn of the twentieth century. Psychoanalysis inspires actors to study character action not just in dramatic terms but also through close examination of human behavior. Perhaps the most significant watershed for the acting process, however, was the work of Konstantin Stanislavsky at the Moscow Art Theatre beginning in 1898. This actor-director did not invent realistic (or **representational**) acting, but through his experimentation, direction of realistic plays, training of actors, and books describing his methods, he reached out to most of the theatre world in the twentieth century. Stanislavsky created a common language for sharing the acting process and stressed the importance of psychological exploration of character, a detailed study of human behavior, and the use of self in ways that continue to resonate with contemporary actors.

A DOLL HOUSE by Henrik Ibsen in a 1902 revival. Both this play and the actress Minnie Maddern Fiske as Nora are early exemplars of realism in plays and acting. She also directed and co-produced many of her productions in which she insisted on detailed, realistic box sets. Fiske was noted for her naturalistic delivery of lines and onstage activity that appeared to be spontaneous and believable as authentic human behavior. She often turned her back on the audience and was especially adept at presenting conflicting emotional responses such as tears and smiles.
By permission of the Museum of the City of New York.

THAT CHAMPIONSHIP SEASON (1972) by Jason Miller is a reality-based all-male ensemble piece that explores the ravages of memory, pipedreams, disappointment, and loss on a once glory-seeking high school basketball state championship team. Some twenty years later they reunite for one night with their aging, terminally ill coach, who once inspired them but now reveals his mean-spirited bigotry. The reminiscences of the men are fueled by alcohol. This 2011 Broadway revival was directed by Gregory Mosher with scenic design by Michael Yeargan.

Photo © Joan Marcus.

Stanislavsky's methodology has been adopted and adapted over the years and has become the center of most realistic approaches to acting performance. Rather than focusing directly on how to express an emotion vocally and physically, an actor using the realistic method of Stanislavsky concentrates on physical and playable action: on obtaining what the character wants or needs at any moment in the play. Playing an action rather than a state of being involves the actor mentally and physically, creating an appropriate environment for emotion to evolve, resulting in a natural and subtle physical and vocal expression. Actors analyze the script in detail and, in particular, identify the **given circumstances** that include everything about the character written by the playwright that is not a matter of interpretation or opinion: where the character is from, for example, or the fact that he or she is highly educated, recently divorced, or terminally ill.

Actors seek out the basic action to be played and not only perform it but also justify it. One of the reigning assumptions is that actors can know more about the characters than the characters do about themselves. Actors play **character objectives** (or goals) that are important, logical, even vital to the character's action, needs, desires, and state of mind (as if the character were a real person). The actor must modify or shift objectives when encountering obstacles created by other characters, when confronted with changing circumstances, or when entering a new stage environment. In *A Streetcar Named Desire* (1947), for example, Blanche DuBois is a stranger to New Orleans and the run-down section of the French Quarter where she is seeking her sister. Her opening objective is to find Stella, but she becomes so terrified of the strange and threatening urban location that her objective shifts to securing a safe haven from a threatening world. Actors may further identify **subtext,** or the actual meaning behind the words spoken. A character might say, "no," for example, with the subtext of "you're crazy" or "ask me again and I might say yes"—which would produce very different line readings.

Actors explore the physical, social, and psychological aspects of their characters and may draw on their own experience to connect viscerally with the experience of the character. Exercises in **sense memory** help actors to recall sights, sounds, touch, and smells from specific past events, to "remember" what something feels like. **Affective memory,** or the reexperience of past emotion, can be harnessed to solve moment-to-moment

ARTISTS of the THEATRE

James Earl Jones

James Earl Jones was born in Mississippi in 1931 and moved to Michigan at age 5. His parents separated before his birth, so he was raised by his maternal grandparents. As a child, Jones's communication was hampered by a stutter and extreme self-consciousness; he hardly spoke from age 6 to 14. Jones credits an English teacher with helping overcome his difficulties. Donald Crouch was a retired college professor who taught English at the rural school Jones attended. Having learned that the young man wrote poetry, Crouch challenged him to recite one of his poems aloud to the class. Jones credits Crouch as responsible not only for his career in acting but also for much of his development as a human being.

After attending the University of Michigan on a scholarship, Jones moved to New York City to pursue an acting career, establishing contact with his father, the actor Robert Earl Jones. The young man's first role on Broadway was as a houseboy in *Sunrise at Campobello* (1958), based on the life of Franklin D. Roosevelt. Jones had three lines. His breakthrough came in 1961 with an Off-Broadway production of *The Blacks* by Jean Genet that also launched the careers of Billy Dee Williams, Louis Gossett, Jr., Maya Angelou, Cicely Tyson, Roscoe Lee Browne, and Godfrey Cambridge. *The Great White Hope* (1968), at Arena Stage in Washington and then Broadway, brought him world renown, as well as a Tony Award for Best Actor. For the film of the play he earned a Best Actor Oscar nomination. Thereafter, Jones performed regularly on Broadway—seven shows between 1968 and 1983—including Eugene O'Neill's *The Iceman Cometh,* a one-man show on Paul Robeson, *Othello,* and two plays by South African playwright Athol Fugard, *A Lesson from Aloes* and *"Master Harold" . . . and the Boys.* Jones was awarded his second Tony for his role as Troy Maxson in August Wilson's *Fences.* After seventeen years, he returned to Broadway as Norman in *On Golden Pond* (2005) and was again nominated for a Tony. In 2008 Jones opened as Big Daddy in an all-black revival of *Cat on a Hot Tin Roof* by Tennessee Williams.

Along with his stage work, Jones has maintained a prolific and varied film career, including Stanley Kubrick's *Dr. Strangelove* (1964) and Kevin Costner's *Field of Dreams* (1989). He is probably best known to the public as the voice of Darth Vader in *Star Wars* (1977–2005, a voice-over role that he recorded in two and one half hours), and Mustafa in the Disney film *The Lion King* (1994). His many television appearances have ranged from *The Guiding Light* (1952) to *Will and Grace* (2003). His deep, resonant voice has allowed him to pursue a lucrative commercial voice-over career.

INTERESTED? Check out

James Earl Jones and Penelope Niven. *Voices and Silences.* New York: Limelight, 2004.

DRIVING MISS DAISY (1987) by Alfred Uhry in a 2010 Broadway revival with James Earl Jones as Hoke Colburn, the driver to Daisy Werthen, played by Vanessa Redgrave. These two giants of the acting profession faced off each night in an evocative exploration of complex character set in the midst of the civil rights movement. Directed by David Esbjornson.

Photo © Carol Rosegg.

DOUBT (2004) by John Patrick Shanley. Cherry Jones as Sister Aloysius and Brian F. O'Byrne as Father Flynn. The standoff between these characters is not only an exciting acting challenge, but a challenge to our ethical assumptions regarding the educational environment, the role of the church in education, and verification of sexual misconduct. Directed by Doug Hughes.

Photo © Joan Marcus.

problems that arise when interpreting and fleshing out the character. To find the emotional expression for a particular moment, such as coping with the death of a loved one, an actor might remember in detail an event from his or her own life that produced a similar emotional reaction. Typically, however, the actor doesn't think, "What did I feel when my uncle passed away?" but "What did I do? What did I see?" When on stage, the actor doesn't play emotion but appropriate action. The actor must listen and respond to what he or she is given by other cast members. If an actor alters the delivery of a line, it is likely that another actor's delivery in response will have to be altered as well. The goal is often to create an organic **ensemble** that pretends to live spontaneously—to act and react—authentically in the stage world as defined by the play.

Another goal of contemporary realistic acting methods is the creation of a "complete" and open actor—one who is highly versatile vocally and physically and not limited by personal habits—to create believable characters that the audience can accept as genuine. An actor working in the mode of realism should be equipped to create an "honest" interpretation of a character as if breathing and interacting in a real world. The illusion of spontaneity should be absolute. A realistic ensemble wants to create believability among the actors in performance as well as to inspire believability in the audience who witnesses the presentation.

One can see many such performances on the American stage. Audiences were particularly struck by a production of Sam Shepard's *True West* (1982 production) as performed by the Steppenwolf Theatre Company in Chicago. Actor John Malkovich as the derelict character of Lee appeared especially spontaneous and threatening. His physical violence when attacking a typewriter with a golf club, very close to the audience, created anxiety in some audience members as if they, not the typewriter, were threatened. Again with Steppenwolf in 2007, Deanna Dunagan, as the mother of a dysfunctional family in *August: Osage County* by Tracy Letts, plays a flamboyant and angry woman strung out on drugs in a theatrically dynamic but realistic fashion that overwhelms the members of her carping brood. By contrast, Cherry Jones as Sister Aloysius in *Doubt* (2004), by John Patrick Shanley, delivered an unusually controlled, introspective, and emotional performance. Nonetheless, the character was embroiled in a conflict that could lead to the destruction of careers and children's welfare.

Contemporary Presentational Performance

Although realism seems to be the touchstone for most contemporary acting, presentationalism is alive and well in the theatre. The Asian classical forms provide examples of centuries-old techniques emphasizing stylized movement, gestures, facial expression, and use of the voice. Plays in the Western repertory with devices inspired by the Asian forms (such as those by William Butler Yeats and Bertolt Brecht and his followers) call on actors to go beyond the techniques of realism. Contemporary directors and playwrights feel free to draw from many different traditions for any given show, and actors must be ready to meet this challenge.

The most obvious arena for presentational acting in Western theatre is the musical. Although musicals can be of any genre and mood, the musical actor is often a singer and dancer as well and must express character through painstakingly choreographed movement and dance and through rhymed song and recitation as well as dialogue. The resulting performance is very lyrical. The presentational devices of the musical form clearly separate the preparation and performance from reality. (How many of us carry an orchestral accompaniment in life?) Nonetheless, many musical actors include techniques and devices of psychological realism in their rehearsal and character study even though the product must go beyond the conventions of such an approach. An accomplished musical actor can still make the audience believe the moment—especially the emotionality of the character's presentation. Such performances demonstrate vividly that an actor's work need not be realistic to move or engage the audience. Nathan Lane's performances in *A Funny Thing Happened on the Way to the Forum* (1996 production) and *The Producers* (2001) are good examples. Both plays are very exuberant, presentational musicals, full of silliness. Nonetheless, Lane engendered belief. In the musical *The Light in the Piazza* (2005) Victoria Clark, a mother who must deal with her developmentally challenged young daughter in love, created an understated, emotionally torn, nearly realistic presence through it all. The entire cast of adolescents in *Spring Awakening* (2006) must alternate between realistically drawn scenes and characters in nineteenth-century Germany and contrast this with sudden explosions of exuberant or angry singing, yelling, stomping, leaping, and dancing as the play shifts back and forth between contemporary alternative rock and poignant, smothered lives of the confused and abused youths. The impression one might get is that adolescents of a previous century are channeling the future. And the future is now.

Since the 1890s, experiments of the **avant-garde** (cutting-edge theatre) have fascinated and inspired as well as confused audiences throughout the world. Acting performances in some of this work lie far outside typical realistic practices. When performing in symbolist plays in France in the 1890s, for example, actors spoke their lines in a deliberate monotone while performing before draperies. German expressionism in the 1910s called for choruses to speak in a mechanized, robotic fashion. The 1960s experimental theatres were filled with actors taking on generic characters who presented Everyman-like images,

SPRING AWAKENING (2006) by Duncan Sheik and Steven Sater. Note the vibrant stomp dancing and leaping of the boys around and above Jonathan Groff as Melchior, who attempts to concentrate at the same time. Directed by Michael Mayer and choreographed by Bill T. Jones.
Photo © Joan Marcus.

specters of the dead, or plant and animal life. Characters shifted through planes of existence and time. In writing for alternative theatres, one playwright, Megan Terry, in plays such as *Calm Down Mother* (1965) even calls for "transformational" acting, whereby actors instantly shift from one character to another without any exit, costume change, or other realistic device.

Throughout the last 120 years or so, many playwrights and directors have experimented with alternatives to realistic acting. In Russia a Stanislavsky-trained actor and director, Vsevolod Meyerhold, broke away from the Moscow Art Theatre to pursue his own dreams and led the development of **biomechanics,** a highly energetic, mimetic approach to physicalization that abstracted human movement and created a very athletic actor. Antonin Artaud's **Theatre of Cruelty** (developed in France between the world wars) emphasized a breakdown of causality and stressed emotionality over intellect. German playwright and director Bertolt Brecht developed politicized acting theory (as part of his total concept of **Epic Theatre**) that is still vital to much contemporary acting in nonrealistic productions. He popularized ideas such as the actor observing the character from the outside and commenting on it through performance. For example, a Brechtian character often interrupts the action to sing—not as a character getting so worked up that he or she must burst into song but singing to comment on ideas in the play. The actor can in turn sing the song not as the character in the play but as an outsider. For Brecht the primary argument of a scene and the social action of the characters were far more important than story and psychology. A presentational acting style in today's theatre may call on all the resources of the actor, including movement as strenuous as acrobatics and vocal technique (even for spoken words) akin to singing. Some theatre artists, such as Tadashi Suzuki, have developed rigorous training methods for preparing the voice and body to meet demands beyond those of psychological realism. Drawing on his training in classical Asian forms, Suzuki's goal is to create an integrated and highly expressive actor freed from the mind/body dichotomy that is so familiar in Western cultures.

Many aspects of these presentational theories and practices, once radical and confusing to many audience members, are now accepted with relatively little adjustment. Even the musical has borrowed from such work with *The Adding Machine,* a musical adaptation of Elmer Rice's 1923 expressionistic modern classic. In this 2008 reincarnation by Joshua Schmidt and Jason Loewith, we experience the bleak world of an unpleasant loser named Mr. Zero as he journeys from his mind-numbing workplace, to his awful home life, to a hell-like heaven that is no better than what he left on earth.

THE CAUCASIAN CHALK CIRCLE by Bertolt Brecht. Two grotesque characters in half masks. These characters are simultaneously evil and comic. There are times in Brecht's Epic Theatre when he uses evil characters to create good. Produced at the University of Nebraska.

Collection of the authors.

THE ACTOR'S WORK

Whereas a master pianist or violinist searches for a well-made and expressive instrument with which to perform, the actor seeks to develop his or her own body, voice, and mind to the fullest extent. As the needs of the theatre change, the expectations of the actor do as well. In contemporary theatre practice, an actor may be called on to perform in a different style of play and production with each new job.

Actor Training

Before the early twentieth century most acting methods were taught within an apprenticeship system (as were many other trades). A young person accepted into a theatre company began playing walk-on roles or roles with few lines and learned by watching other actors perform and receiving instruction on a need-to-know basis. This basic approach is still alive in Asian classical forms such as Kabuki, in which actors begin training as children, learn a particular type of role, and graduate to increasingly difficult parts as they mature and demonstrate their proficiency.

By the nineteenth century in Europe many state-subsidized theatres had schools attached, but these were basically an extension of the apprenticeship system, with experienced company members instructing and demonstrating for younger performers. In France Françoise Delsarte (1811–1871) created a system for studying plays, observing human behavior, and finding emotional expression through detailed analysis that became enormously popular in actor-training schools throughout Europe. It was brought to the United States by the actor-inventor-playwright-teacher Steele Mackaye in the 1870s. The Delsartian system of learning movement and gesture was ultimately rejected with the coming of realism, since it relied on a standardized scheme for expressing emotion. Delsarte's systematic approach to preparing actors that relied on training the body, voice, and intellect, however, set the standard for actor training programs as they currently exist in universities and conservatories (schools dedicated specifically to development of performance skills).

Today actors develop their bodies by taking movement classes specifically designed for actors as well as dance, stage combat, and martial arts instruction. Excess tension inhibits free expression; breathing and physical relaxation exercises are therefore important in freeing both the body and the voice. Vocal training, integrated with the physical development, focuses on breathing and voice production (the actual making of sound). Voice and breath are connected to the actor's understanding of the body and all of its possibilities, as well as the actor's imagination. Actors are trained in **projection** (making the voice loud enough to be heard but still sounding conversational) and **articulation** (forming all the sounds of words so that an actor can be understood). Learning the **International Phonetic Alphabet**—a system of specific symbols representing individual sounds—helps actors to both analyze their own speech and reproduce different dialects and accents.

Actors usually learn techniques of script analysis and character exploration developed by Stanislavsky and his followers, such as the great acting teachers Stella Adler,

Uta Hagen, and Sanford Meisner. They may be taught detailed analysis of text and given practice speaking verse. Students are trained in careful observation of human beings and other animal life. Exercises in improvisation such as the theatre games developed by Viola Spolin help actors learn to respond immediately with their voices and bodies to changing situations. Although many actors today begin their professional lives with training from a college or university theatre program or a conservatory, most actors continue to develop their craft through classes, coaching, and individual work on voice and body throughout their lives.

The Actor in Rehearsal

Memorizing lines is only a small part of the acting process. Actors will analyze the script using techniques they have learned and found effective. If the action of the play takes place in an earlier time and will be performed in costumes and a set of that period, the actor might read about social conditions of the time in addition to other background information provided by the director or dramaturg. At early rehearsals actors usually have scripts in hand and record **blocking** or other notes as the work proceeds. Soon, however, at a date set by the director, actors must be "off book," with lines and movement memorized. A movement coach might teach period manners and movement or provide any specialized training necessary for the show as well as watching the actors' work and suggesting ways to enhance physical characterization. Rehearsal clothes that approximate the special challenges posed by period costumes (for example, corsets, hoopskirts, or togas) are often worn throughout the rehearsal period. When stage combat is required, the movement coach or a separate fight master will teach the actor carefully choreographed routines that must then be practiced daily with partners, first in slow motion and gradually working up to performance speed. A vocal coach often assists the actor in finding an appropriate vocal quality for the character, learning dialects, and clarifying speech.

Rehearsals always include many struggles with the play text. Actors experiment, try many different readings and interpretations, and sometimes argue and persuade as the director encourages discovery and guides the actors through the possibilities for realizing the text and its characters. Although actors bring a great deal of themselves to a role, an important quality is the ability to take direction—in other words, to be flexible enough to implement the director's suggestions. Sometimes a great deal of discipline is needed to focus concentration on the work to be done. In early rehearsals directors start and stop a scene many times to ask questions, suggest alternatives, explore motivation, adjust positions, or discuss timing. Actors learn to play what they are given by other actors—to respond to new line readings and physical action from others onstage. Much of the rehearsal period is dedicated to learning to trust and depend on the other actors. A strong rapport among performers can add a spark of energy and spontaneity to production, and a character is fully developed only when it seems to live within the same world as the others on stage.

As rehearsals proceed, the actors find themselves frequently modifying or severely changing choices made early in the process. Every change almost always evokes different choices. As opening approaches, actors use the **run-throughs** to create a sense of continuity and learn the shape of their roles. The actors discover when they have down time, when they need to prepare to go onstage, the energy level needed for emotional or physical high points in the action. Typically, directors give notes to actors after a run-through; it is the actors' responsibility to implement the changes at the next run-through, which might require study or preparation outside of rehearsal.

Frequently, the actors do not rehearse in the theatre in which they will perform for an audience until technical rehearsals or shortly before. The delay is usually due

AUGUST: OSAGE COUNTY (2007) by Tracy Letts. The family ensemble at a dysfunctional post-funeral dinner. Deanna Dunagan as the mother sits up center in white pearls. Directed by Anna D. Shapiro, scenic design by Todd Rosenthal, costume design by Anna Kuzmanic.
Photo © Joan Marcus.

to economic constraints or limitations of available theatre spaces. Once the actors move into the real space, however, there are always adjustments. Acoustics sometimes change dramatically; the performance space is often considerably larger than the rehearsal space. Actors must adjust to the finished sets, which might include some surprises. Except during fittings, the actors rarely wear the costumes until **dress rehearsals** several days before opening, so appropriate rehearsal clothes are important. Despite careful planning, it is sometimes necessary to modify actor movement for the costumes or vice versa. The same is true for hand and set properties and the addition of lighting and sound. Adjusting to the stage lighting, especially if there is abundant movement in the lighting and many blackouts, can be a considerable task.

Problems are worked out in **technical rehearsals** and dress rehearsals (and **previews** if the company uses them). Before going onstage, actors typically go through a warmup, or series of physical, vocal, and mental exercises. Like athletes and singers, actors depend on their bodies and voices and take care to prepare them before a performance. After all the preparation, collaboration, and rehearsal the actor finally interacts with an audience, not just other actors and the director. With the addition of an audience, there is a jump in engagement and energy from the actors, and the collaboration between actors and audience commences.

Stage versus Film Acting

In today's entertainment world, most actors work in film and television as well as in the theatre. There are important differences between acting on stage and acting for the camera. When acting in the theatre, an actor builds a role gradually over the rehearsal period and works up to emotional high points as the show proceeds. Sustaining the performance over several hours is an important consideration. Movies and TV shows are frequently shot out of sequence, so the actor does not build a performance over time. Instead, the actor must be able to reach an emotional high point on cue with little preparation and must be able to repeat the performance for different filmings, or takes. Only one is selected. Lines are usually learned in advance only for the scenes being shot on a particular day, and rehearsal for each scene is often limited. During a 2010 presentation at Indiana University, actor Martin Sheen, with a long history of film and television acting, told his audience that when he returned to the stage in a revival of *The Subject Was Roses* in 2010, he was astounded at how physically and mentally exhausting he found the rigors of performing an entire role night after night.[4]

The level of vocal projection and articulation necessary for the stage would seem highly exaggerated when filmed. Most film work requires a subtle style of acting appropriate to the closeup shot, which can reveal minute changes in facial expression. The slightest whisper can be amplified to an appropriate volume. An important aspect of acting for the stage is the ability to repeat a performance night after night yet still retain the vital sense of spontaneity. Actors who are lucky enough to be engaged in a long-running show constantly look for ways to keep their performance fresh without changing aspects clearly set by the director. Although each kind of acting has its own problems and rewards, acting on stage has the advantage of immediate communication with the audience during the performance.

The Professional Actor

KOREAN TRADITIONAL HAHOE DANCE-DRAMA MASK. The character is known as Yangban, the Aristocrat. The design for the wooden mask with flexible mouth dates from the twelfth century.

Photo © Kendra Fletcher Wainscott.

The life of a professional actor can be exciting and precarious, emotionally overwhelming, or exhilarating. The professional actor needs to be steeled for the possibility that he or she might always have a "day job." Most actors frequently find themselves unemployed or between gigs—or "at liberty," as actors called it in the 1920s. For example, for the 2009–2010 season, Actors' Equity Association, the labor union that represents professional actors and stage managers in the United States, reported that 58.6 percent of its members in good standing (25,516 out of 42,475 Equity actors) were unemployed for the entire season. Of the 16,959 actors who worked, only 5,540 were working in an average week. The median income from stage acting for all Equity actors that season was only $7,475, a figure slightly better than the report of the 2008–2009 season. Only 7 percent of all working actors earned more than $75,000 in the season from acting. Forty-two percent of working actors made $5,000 or less.[5] These bleak figures demonstrate how risky the profession can be, since the calculations include the income of actors who are doing well financially.

The profession is often filled with promises that require endless resume, head-shot, and website updates, live and video auditions, callbacks, interviews, and lunches with producers and agents, rather than real job offers. All of this activity is both time-consuming and costly; financial matters are additionally strained for actors because agents receive a percentage of all their earnings—no matter how low they are. Sometimes the actor feels like a commodity rather than a person. In the musical *A Chorus Line* (1975), which was developed from the actual experiences of performers, a character sings a lament, wondering whether his resume is the sum of his identity. Sometimes the acting profession is more about getting an Equity card (union membership), securing an agent, or trying to get cast than it is about art.

For the actor who is talented and lucky enough to work regularly, however, life beyond rehearsals and performances is filled with travel, adjusting to new locations and working methods, and changing media. In addition to the

EXPLORING Collaboration

Actors as Collaborators

The interaction that is most visible to an audience is that of the actors. A show can succeed or fail on the basis of whether actors truly collaborate with one another. At the most basic level, actors must rely on each other for the show to progress. A moment's lapse could mean a missed entrance, a blown cue line—any number of mistakes that could be catastrophic for the other actors, the technical crews, and the show as a whole. Professional integrity and the knowledge that colleagues are depending on them (as well as an instinct for self-preservation) lead actors to develop intense powers of concentration and a kind of split consciousness. They are focused simultaneously on character material (thinking/responding as the character) and technical considerations, such as whether the audience is able to hear the lines, how to hold an important prop, how to find an exact spot on the stage when entering in the dark, and sometimes whether a fellow actor needs help.

Mistakes are inevitable in live performance. Even the most experienced actor may occasionally "go up" (forget a line). An alert actor can often save a fellow performer by altering or repeating a line or ad-libbing stage business. The mistake might even go unnoticed by the audience, particularly if the actor is sensitive to the body language of the partner in a scene and senses distress. This kind of subtle, nonverbal communication flows regularly on stage between performers. Actors tend to feed off one another's energy. Flat and slow interaction can often be energized by an actor who enters the scene with higher energy.

On the level of artistic decision, actors collaborate in developing characterization. Any choice an actor makes will have an impact on the other performers. If the actress playing Juliet decides that her character is terrified of being caught by her nurse or family during the balcony scene, the actor playing Romeo might need to work all the harder to keep her from fleeing into her bedroom. When an actor gives something new while performing a scene, the partner must respond to that change appropriately for the character. One of the worst situations for an actor is a partner who gives nothing or very little. Finding a way to respond to an expressionless face or line reading is the worst kind of acting challenge.

Some directors even go so far as to send actors away to work on a scene with the vague challenge "Come back and show me something new." A highly imaginative team of actors might return with various ways to play the scene, allowing the director and actors to take the scene to a higher level.

When a show is going well (and sometimes even when it's not), actors forge strong relationships with each other. When they are able to work together repeatedly, actors learn each other's strengths, weaknesses, and preferred

HAMLET by William Shakespeare at the Public Theater in New York (1999). Although we tend to remember duels in terms of the two principals, this is really an ensemble activity that requires carefully modulated and focused group activity if the scene is performed well. Combat scene between Laertes and Hamlet. Left to right, the actors are Diane Venora, Hamish Linklater, Robin Weigert, Francis Jue, and Live Schreiber as Hamlet. Directed by Andrei Serban.
Photo © Michal Daniel.

methods, making the development process speedier and (sometimes) less painful.

Some actors are so attuned to one another that they make special efforts to perform together. Occasionally, they may even be married, as were Alfred Lunt and Lynn Fontanne, who performed together frequently in the 1920s and then exclusively through the 1930s and beyond. Audiences were fascinated by their onstage/offstage union. Centuries earlier, in seventeenth-century France, fascinated but gossipy responses greeted the performances of Molière and his much younger wife, Armande Béjart. In our own time another inspiring married acting couple, Ruby Dee and Ossie Davis, worked together both as actors and social activists until Davis's death in 2005.

INTERESTED? Check out

Jared Brown. *The Fabulous Lunts: A Biography of Alfred Lunt and Lynn Fontanne*. Bloomington, IN: AuthorHouse, 2005.
Autobiographies of actors are usually full of firsthand accounts of performer relationships and anecdotes. For example:
(An eighteenth-century actor) Colley Cibber. *An Apology for the Life of Colley Cibber*. 1740. Reprint, Mineola, NY: Dover, 2000.
(A nineteenth-century actor) Emma Stebbins, ed. *Charlotte Cushman: Her Letters and Memories of Her Life*. Boston: Houghton, Osgood, and Company, 1878.
(A twentieth-century actor) Alec Guinness. *Blessings in Disguise*. Pleasantville, NY: Akadine Press, 2001.

stage, film, and television programs, many successfully employed stage actors also work in commercials, industrials (live advertising shows for companies and products), modeling, recording voice-overs, audio books, and radio. Through it all, many actors continue their own training in private studios and teach younger actors. Actors must read (and not just submitted play scripts), engage in observation of people, and go to the theatre when not performing. The actor who has not yet reached the level of consistent employment might ask, "How much time do I give myself to make it?" The question is tricky because most actors spend years trying to get in the proverbial door. Professional acting is a crowded business with many casualties. Only the determined and the talented should apply. As things now stand, there is no shortage of young actors willing to make the sacrifices and take the risks.

CHAPTER REVIEW

Questions and Activities

1. Choose a character and scene in a play that you have read. Identify an objective for the character. In other words, what do you think the character is trying to accomplish in the scene? Avoid states of being (such as "I want to be happy") and look for active wants and needs (such as "I must convince my mother to give me the $100"). How would different choices of objective change the way you played the scene?

2. Recall a scene from a play you have seen on stage. Imagine the actors playing the same scene for a film. Assuming that the dialogue stayed the same, what might change about their performances?

3. Discuss the acting in a show you have seen. Did the cast take a representational or presentational approach? Why do you think this choice was made? Were the performances believable within the world of the production? Did the actors seem to be performing in the same style? Did they function smoothly as an ensemble? Why or why not? How did the actors use body and voice to create specific characters?

Key Terms and Concepts

pantomime, p. 164
mime, p. 165
breeches role, p. 168
rhetorical delivery, p. 170
presentational, p. 170
representational, p. 171
given circumstances, p. 172
character objective, p. 172
subtext, p. 172

sense memory, p. 172
affective memory, p. 172
ensemble, p. 174
avant-garde, p. 175
biomechanics, p. 176
Theatre of Cruelty, p. 176
Epic Theatre, p. 176
projection, p. 177
articulation, p. 177

International Phonetic Alphabet, p. 177
blocking, p. 178
run-through, p. 178
dress rehearsal, p. 179
technical rehearsal, p. 179
preview, p. 179

For Further Exploration

Richard C. Beacham. *The Roman Theatre and Its Audience.* Cambridge, MA: Harvard University, 1992.

W. Beare. *The Roman Stage.* London: Methuen, 1964.

George Duckworth and R. L. Hunter. *The Nature of Roman Comedy,* 2nd ed. Norman: University of Oklahoma, 1994.

Stella Adler. *The Art of Acting.* New York: Applause, 2000.

Robert Cohen. *Acting Professionally: Raw Facts about Careers in Acting,* 7th ed. New York: Palgrave Macmillan, 2009.

Toby Cole, ed., et al. *Actors on Acting: The Theories, Techniques, and Practices of the World's Great Actors, Told in Their Own Words,* 4th ed. New York: Random House, 1995.

John Harrop and Sabin R. Epstein. *Acting with Style,* 3rd ed. Boston: Allyn and Bacon, 1999.

Actors' Equity Association website at www.actorsequity.org/home.html.

Robert Benedetti. *The Actor at Work,* 10th ed. Boston: Allyn and Bacon, 2009.

Peter Brook. *The Open Door: Thoughts on Acting and Theatre.* New York: Theatre Communications Group, 1995.

Constantin Stanislavsky. *An Actor Prepares.* New York: Routledge, 1989.

Uta Hagen. *Respect for Acting.* New York: Macmillan, 1973.

THE TEMPEST by William Shakespeare. Produced by the Steppenwolf Theatre Company, Chicago in 2009. Directed by Tina Landau; scenic design by Takeshi Kata.

Photo © Michael Brosilow.

The Playwright

Imagination and Expression

In his preface to *Six Characters in Search of an Author,* Luigi Pirandello claims that the six title characters of his play suddenly appeared to him, as if they had invaded his consciousness, even his life, suddenly and without explanation. Pirandello's description of his creative process is similar to that of many playwrights: a manifestation so powerful that the characters seem to take on a life of their own. Authors report that some plays begin with a visual image "seen" or a conversation "overheard" within the writer's mind. The catalyst for a play might be a newspaper article (Peter Shaffer's *Equus*), a previous play (Tom Stoppard's *Rosencrantz and Guildenstern Are Dead*) or novel (Alain Boublil and Claude-Michel Schönberg's *Les Misérables*), a place (Susan Glaspell's *Trifles*), a historical event (Shakespeare's *Henry V*), a visual artist's work (Charles L. Mee's *bobrauschenbergamerica*), a specific painting (Stephen Sondheim and James Lapine's *Sunday in the Park with George*), a comic strip (Charles Strouse and Martin Charnin's *Annie*)—the possibilities are endless.

We do not understand a great deal about the creative process, but one thing seems clear: Writers use both the subconscious and conscious mind, dredging up material from a place that is not consciously under their control, then using intellectual, critical faculties to organize, shape, and edit. Playwright David Henry Hwang has noted that writing is a process of discovery, of revealing knowledge to the writer's conscious mind.[1] Much of what we call "talent" in a writer may be the strength of the original vision, but such inspiration is useless without the ability to transform that raw material into words that can be communicated to other people. Dialogue must be represented precisely on the page to give the performer clues about how to deliver it; a comma in the wrong place or a poorly chosen word can drastically affect the actor's interpretation of a line.

CABARET (1966), by Fred Ebb, Joe Masteroff, and John Kander, is a good example of a play adapted from other sources. This musical was adapted from *The Berlin Stories* by Christopher Isherwood and the play *I Am a Camera* by John van Druten exploring pre-World War II Berlin. This stunning 1997 revival was directed by Sam Mendes and choreographed by Rob Marshall, with scenic design by Robert Brill.
Photo © Joan Marcus.

Writing for the stage is quite different from writing a novel, short story, or poem. The playwright must be aware of creating a blueprint—a document that is not complete in itself but is rich and full enough to inspire visual and interpretive artists and artists of the body and voice (actors) to create an aesthetic whole. The spelling of the English word "playwright" holds a key to its special meaning. In the medieval period the term "wright" was used for a craftsperson: a shipwright built ships, a wheelwright made wheels and wheeled vehicles. A *playwright,* therefore, is not just a writer, but a *crafter* of plays. The written document is not an end in itself, but the beginning of a three-dimensional aural and visual experience to be built and shaped. In the case of a musical, a composer, lyricist, and playwright (or librettist) might collaborate extensively to develop a workable blueprint. For most of theatrical history, the most convenient way to communicate such a plan to others or to preserve its essence was through written text, and we are fortunate that documents survive to give us an inkling of our theatrical legacy.

THE CHANGING POSITION OF THE PLAYWRIGHT

At times, crafters of plays have been anonymous, their identity consumed by the producing organization; at other times, playwrights have been celebrated as individual artists. The position of the playwright in the complicated web of theatre-making changes according to how theatre fits into society as a whole and according to the role of the text in production.

Playwriting as Civic Contribution

We are told that the earliest Greek playwrights performed and staged their own plays, thus functioning as what we would now call playwright, actor, and director. Thespis and Aeschylus were actors as well as playwrights. Playwriting was not a profession—people who wrote plays earned their livings in other ways—but theatrical activity was considered a significant civic contribution. It was an honor to be selected to compete and an even greater honor to win a prize for the best set of plays. The theatre became professionalized in the late Greek and Roman periods, but the strong sense of civic connection resurfaced in the Middle Ages. Although a few of the medieval play texts identify the playwright, we do not even know the names of most of the authors of the cycle plays based on biblical stories. Groups of cycle plays are identified by the name of the community that presented them: the York Cycle, for example, or the Wakefield Cycle. Participation in the religious and civic event was apparently more important than individual identification or ownership. Playwrights remained anonymous or nearly so in Asian forms as well. With the notable exceptions of early Noh and the celebrated playwright Chikamatsu in the Bunraku theatre, we know little about the authors of classical Japanese theatre or the creation of the remarkable plays of the Yüan period in China or Sanskrit plays in India.

The Play as Commodity

Identity of the writer became more important as professionalism increased during the Renaissance. In Elizabethan England, for example, a script was a potentially valuable commodity. Early Greek plays may have belonged to the state. Cycle plays belonged to the cities, but an Elizabethan writer could sell plays to competing theatrical troupes. In general, a playwright sold a play for a flat fee to a company, which usually chose not to publish the text, since to do so would make it available to competitors. In consequence, some of the first publications of Shakespeare and his contemporaries were pirated editions; someone in the audience, or perhaps a disgruntled actor, scribbled out dialogue from memory and sold the copy to a printer. Even though Shakespeare's plays were very popular, they were not revered as great literature until much later. The first collected edition of his work was not published until 1623, seven years after Shakespeare's death. Sometimes an author was attached to, or a member of, a specific

ARTISTS of the THEATRE

Suzan-Lori Parks

Playwright Suzan-Lori Parks (b. 1964) revels in the creativity that her colleagues (both on stage and in the house) bring to theatre. When she records the dialogue of her characters on paper, she thinks in terms of music, even putting in the stage direction "rest" (as in a short period of silence). For a moment of silence between two characters just before an important emotional change occurs, she alternates the characters' names on the page with no dialogue indicated; she calls this technique a "spell." Parks understands that she is turning responsibility over to the actors and director to fill these essential silences. The rests and spells can be a full stop of action and sound, or can be filled with action— just no dialogue. The way to fill these rests and spells is up to the director and actors. As a playwright, she does not try to control these periods. The giving up of control in this way is exciting for Parks. She is willing to trust the other artists to finish the work after she is in rehearsal. In this, Parks is unusual, since many playwrights do not share such collaborative trust in the production team. She extends this trust and collaboration in finding meaning to the audience as well. Like many contemporary theorists of theatre and literature, Parks recognizes the importance of drawing many different interpretations from the same play or production.

THE PLAYWRIGHT SUZAN-LORI PARKS working with her director Michael Greif at the Public Theater in 2006 on her remarkable nationwide project *365 Days / 365 Plays.*
Photo © Michal Daniel.

In 2002 Suzan-Lori Parks became the first African American woman to win the Pulitzer Prize for Drama with her play *Topdog/Underdog,* the story of Lincoln and Booth, two brothers caught in an intensive love/hate relationship. George C. Wolfe, artistic director of the New York Shakespeare Festival and the Public Theater in New York City, directed *Topdog/Underdog* at the Public and in its subsequent Broadway run. Parks credits Wolfe with championing her work early in her career. Writer James Baldwin had an important influence on Parks when she was a student in his creative writing class; in fact, he was the first to suggest that her personality as a writer was suited to the theatre.

Parks explores the impact of history on the lives of her characters and examines the effects of racism in plays that are varied in style. *The America Play* (1993) features an African American man who impersonates President Lincoln in a sideshow (also the career of the character Lincoln in *Topdog/Underdog*). *Venus* (1996) is based on the true story of an African woman who was exhibited as a sideshow phenomenon in early nineteenth-century London. The central character of *In the Blood* (1999) is the homeless mother of five children.

Her monumental experiment in community and exploration of the experience of the artist, writing a short play every day for a year, emerged as *365 Days/365 Plays.* The plays were produced in 2006–2007 at more than 600 theatres nationwide (each theatre doing a week of the plays). Parks's recent projects include directing the first production of her family play, *The Book of Grace,* at Zach Theatre, Austin, Texas (2011); a new adaptation of the Gershwin musical *Porgy and Bess* (American Repertory Theatre 2011); and a continuing performance piece, *Watch Me Work,* during which the audience is invited to watch the writer work on a current project or write themselves, followed by a question-and-answer session on the creative process.

As part of an army family, Parks lived in many different places while growing up and attended high school in Germany. She received a B.A. from Mount Holyoke College in 1985 and currently heads the Audrey Skirball Kenis Theater Project's Writing for Performance Program at CalArts. In addition to the Pulitzer Prize, Parks has been honored with two Obie Awards for Best New American Play produced Off-Broadway (for *Imperceptible Mutabilities in the Third Kingdom,* 1990, and *Venus,* 1996) and numerous other awards and grants. Her first novel, *Getting Mother's Body,* was published in 2003.

INTERESTED? Check out

Deborah R. Geis. *Suzan-Lori Parks.* Ann Arbor: University of Michigan, 2008.

Philip C. Kolin, Ed. *Suzan-Lori Parks: Essays on the Plays and Other Works.* Jefferson, North Carolina: McFarland, 2010.

Kevin J. Wetmore, Jr. and Alycia Smith-Howard, Eds. *Suzan-Lori Parks: A Casebook.* New York: Routledge, 2007.

CORIOLANUS, a difficult play by William Shakespeare that combines military history from the Roman era, myth, and tragic action. This play is frequently updated to accommodate the military action and make it relevant to the present, as occurred in this production played in the round with action coming out of the blackness. Produced by the Oregon Shakespeare Festival, Ashland in 2008. Directed by Laird Williamson.

Photo © Michal Daniel.

acting troupe and intimately involved in its success; Shakespeare wrote many plays for the Lord Chamberlain's Men, later renamed the King's Men, a company in which he was a shareholder. A profitable production meant more money for the shareholders, so the popularity of a play had important financial consequences.

Until the late nineteenth century most authors received only a flat fee for their plays, with occasional extras added for successful scripts. Playwrights in eighteenth-century England, for example, were given the profits from a "benefit night" on the third, sixth, and twentieth nights of the play's first run of performances (if the show ran that long—a run of twenty nights was rare). On some occasions playwrights received only benefit payments; therefore, a play that closed after the first or second performance night might render a playwright no revenue at all. In 1791 the French National Assembly passed the first law giving **royalties** (a fee for each performance) to playwrights. The writer's heirs were entitled to collect payment up to five years after the author's death. It was some time before other countries followed suit.

Social Position of the Playwright

In the seventeenth and eighteenth centuries neoclassicism encouraged a more literary approach to text, setting specific standards for playwrights to follow in composition and honoring those who did so. Such critical praise often meant little at the box office, however, and any involvement with the stage made a writer, particularly a woman writer, morally suspect and socially unacceptable. The notion that the writer's talents were sold to the highest bidder led to a comparison with prostitutes. Despite the popularity of her plays, Aphra Behn, the first professional woman playwright in England, was frequently vilified and dismissed as an immoral and unnatural phenomenon. Writing for the theatre remained a tenuous means of earning a living for both sexes; the playwrights who did not maintain other jobs in the theatre such as acting or management were novelists, journalists, poets, and editors. The playwright Molière was both an actor and the company manager; similarly, playwright Richard Brinsley Sheridan was a theatrical manager and politician. The coming of romanticism in the late eighteenth century led to a growing emphasis on individual talent and originality. Shakespeare was at that time elevated to near divine status, but such reverence did not usually extend to contemporary playwrights.

In the early nineteenth century dramatists were frequently referred to as "hacks." The rapidly growing middle- and working-class audience called for a great amount of new material, which writers often furnished by translating and loosely adapting preexisting works (often without crediting the original author) and cobbling together highly theatrical but often derivative melodramas and fantasy plays. In the last quarter of the century the social position of the playwright began to improve, along with the rest of the theatrical profession. The work of Henrik Ibsen and the playwrights who followed his example led to an increased emphasis on the theatrical text as literature. Because of the controversy surrounding production of the early plays of realism, such as *A Doll House* and *Ghosts*, the public often was first introduced to those works in printed form. Ibsen's plays were frequently discussed, attacked, and praised by readers long before they were seen in production.

Copyright Regulations

Late nineteenth- and early twentieth-century international copyright laws brought recognition of the play as a writer's intellectual property. England passed its first (rather limited) copyright law in 1833. The first International Copyright agreement was created in 1886, but it took some countries a long time to sign; others never did. Today, in most countries, an author retains all rights to the play except for those specifically sold or assigned to someone else. No theatre may produce a play, no publisher may print it, without first receiving the permission of the writer and (usually) compensating the writer financially. To violate this standard is unethical as well as illegal; a playwright should be paid a royalty each time a play is produced. For work created after January 1978, current U.S. copyright law gives the author ownership of the work for life and to the author's estate for seventy years after the author's death. Most works published between 1964 and 1977 are under copyright (depending on the circumstances of publication); works published between 1923 and 1963 may be under copyright if the original term was renewed. Works published before 1923 are considered in the public domain and can be produced freely, although to be ethical, it is important always to acknowledge the author of the play in all production information. Even when a play is in public domain, however, a translation might well be under copyright. Molière's plays may be produced freely, for example, but when an English version created after 1923 is produced, permission must be obtained and a royalty paid to the translator. In 1920 the Dramatists Guild, Inc., was formed as part of the Authors League of America to safeguard writers' interests. The Guild now offers a standard contract to members for both commercial and nonprofit theatres.

Still, only a very few writers today make their entire living writing for the theatre (or even for theatre and film). There are many more scripts in existence than there are production opportunities, and most playwrights spend many hours after the writing is completed in copying, mailing, and otherwise marketing their work to theatres, publishers, agents, and play contests. Publications such as *Dramatists Sourcebook* (Theatre Communications Group) and *The Resource Directory* (Dramatists Guild) list organizations that accept new plays for consideration.

THE PLAYWRIGHT AND PRODUCTION

In most traditional models, the playwright is responsible for the initial vision of the play, for crafting the words to be spoken and suggesting important action or visual images. There are many ways in which the relationship between writer and production team can be organized.

Writing with Actors in Mind

When a writer is connected to a company or at least familiar with actors who are likely to perform the roles, a special connection exists between the written text and the first production company. Aristotle complained that Hellenistic playwrights were catering to the whims of actors. Shakespeare and Molière wrote parts for people they worked with on a daily basis and for themselves; Shakespeare was an actor; Molière was a lead, playing Argan in *The Hypochondriac* and Harpagon in *The Miser.* Zeami and Kan'ami were actors as well as leading Noh playwrights, and in the case of Zeami, we have not only a body of plays but also a critical text on the acting process. In the nineteenth century it was common for authors to create a work for a specific star. The American actor Edwin Forrest even sponsored contests for the best play with a leading role for him, a process that resulted in some of his most famous characters, such as Metamora in a play by that title by John A. Stone. Contemporary playwright Tracy Letts is also an actor and an ongoing member of the ensemble of the Steppenwolf Theatre Company. He wrote the Pulitzer Prize-winning play, *August: Osage County* (2007), with this company in mind, and most of the principals came from that ensemble when it opened in Chicago and then continued on to Broadway.

In such cases the playwright can tailor a character to the strengths of particular actors. An actor's appearance, personality, or history can help to shape the fictional character, and a stage-wise playwright would of course take into account the various levels of talent available in the company and any specialties: comedy, tragedy, singing, dancing, acrobatic ability. Shakespeare's characters sometimes changed significantly when an actor joined or left his company; the clown roles, for example, altered dramatically when William Kempe (Dogberry in *Much Ado about Nothing*) was replaced by Robert Armin (Feste in *Twelfth Night*). Mark Hollmann recalls that the casting of actor John Cullum in *Urinetown* ten days before starting rehearsals Off-Broadway led to a new song in the musical.[2]

Of course, writing for a specific company imposes some limitations as well. It might restrict the number or type of characters to be created; it might dictate the space into which the play must fit. Because of production conventions, playwrights of the seventeenth and eighteenth centuries used settings for their plays based on stock scenery already owned by the theatre. Today, experienced playwrights are keenly aware of theatre production budgets as they consider settings and casting requirements.

RICHARD II as written by Shakespeare, who knew that Richard Burbage would be playing the title role. With this in mind, he could write to the strengths of his actors. Richard, played by Michael Hayden, is here delivering his famous "hollow crown" speech in which he laments the ordinariness of his humanity despite his royal position. This revival was produced by the Shakespeare Theatre Company in Washington, DC in 2010. Directed by Michael Kahn. Costume design by Jennifer Moeller. Photo © Scott Suchman.

Writing with a Theatre in the Head

Many plays are written with no prior knowledge of when, by whom, or even if they will be produced. In such cases the writer's imagination is freer to roam, but there will necessarily be a wider gulf between the initial vision and its concrete manifestation on the stage. For some authors this inevitable transformation is exciting; for others it is problematic. Eugene O'Neill, for example, created detailed physical descriptions of his characters, no doubt based on the vivid pictures in his mind. The possibilities were slim, however, of finding an actor who could perform the role as well as match O'Neill's precise depictions, and he was continually disappointed in the gulf between the scene in his head and the one on the stage. In O'Neill's mind, Anna Christopherson, the lead in the play *Anna Christie,* was tall and blonde. In the first production the actress Pauline Lord was a short redhead, yet her performance was electrifying and considered definitive by her generation. Long after O'Neill's death, the portrayals of Anna by Liv Ullman in 1977 and Natasha Richardson in 1993 were much closer to O'Neill's image.

ANNA CHRISTIE by Eugene O'Neill. Pauline Lord as the original Anna Christopherson. The first act of the play takes place in a bar, and some of Anna's past involvement with prostitution makes itself evident to the audience but not to her father.

Courtesy of Theatre Collection, Museum of the City of New York.

A basic awareness of the physical aspects of theatre is important for writers who wish to see their work produced. A writer who participates in production in other ways gains the advantage of practical knowledge. Someone who attends and studies the theatre regularly as an audience member can also develop a strong sense of dramatic feasibility. A writer who is completely unconnected to the theatre in any way might have a difficult time satisfying the needs of the stage. Many beginning playwrights, for example, think in filmic terms, imagining visuals that are not possible in live theatre (such as a close-up), or write in a style that is more appropriate for silent reading than oral delivery. Such writers often benefit from involvement as a volunteer in theatrical production. Participating at a theatre that produces new scripts is particularly valuable. Playwrights learn great lessons from hearing their plays read aloud by actors or colleagues. Playwrights themselves can read their dialogue aloud to test the readability and sound of the lines. An understanding of the limitations as well as the imaginative possibilities of the live theatre is essential for someone who is planning the skeletal structure on which many contributing artists will build.

Collaborating with Actors, Directors, and Dramaturgs

In current theatrical practice, it is typical for the playwright to collaborate with the creative team on the first production of a play. This collaboration may range from occasional long-distance consultation by phone, fax, and email to daily onsite participation in building the production. The playwright can serve as a valuable resource for unlocking a play's possibilities and may offer interpretations, explain development, and give opinions of performances and designs. The relationship between the author and a play's first director can be productive and exciting or painful and destructive. The potential for conflict over power is great, since the playwright enters the process with a prior sense of ownership, and the director feels responsible for the final production. If actors and designers get different messages from the playwright and director, personal and artistic confusion can be the result. Wise directors often discuss the working relationship and procedures with the writer in advance, before dealing with the entire company. Some directors prefer that the playwright not speak directly to actors and designers but route all feedback through the director. Others cultivate a more free-wheeling approach to sharing ideas but insist on serving as the clearinghouse for any major conceptual or interpretive discussions.

The way in which playwrights and directors interact varies greatly. Some writers need reinforcement and careful questioning; others thrive on a more adversarial relationship in which conflict with the director pushes them to new creative places. There are as many successful ways of working as there are successful teams; no one approach will work for everyone. The choice of certain directors, playwrights, and actors to work together repeatedly suggests both the difficulty of finding a combination that works and the artistic value of that combination once it is established. At the turn of the twentieth century, Stanislavsky was the first director to recognize that a new, more subtle style of acting was necessary to make the plays of Anton Chekhov work. In the early twenty-first century the highly visual, physical style of director Anne Bogart is an appropriate match for the plays of Charles L. Mee, which venture past psychological realism and linear construction. Opening in 2006 and continuing in repertory is Bogart's multimedia production of Mee's *Hotel Cassiopeia,* a magnificent exploration of the illusive world of reclusive artist Joseph Cornell. The staging imitates Cornell's art while exploring the sadness and isolation of his personal life. Often, a **dramaturg**—a specialist in dramatic literature and theatre history—is available to help the playwright. A dramaturg typically reads the script, attends readings, attends rehearsals, and offers suggestions to the playwright and director. A playwright might consult the dramaturg on issues of structure, characterization, or dialogue to get informed advice on solving problems the play may have. As with the director, the playwright's working relationship with a dramaturg can take many forms, depending on the situation and the personalities involved.

THE GOVERNMENT INSPECTOR (1836) by Nikolai Gogol. This Russian satire on governmental and provincial corruption and stupidity is frequently revived since it is easily adapted to other times, cultures, and governments. It has been produced in both a realistic manner as well as highly stylized ones. In this 2008 revival by the American Conservatory Theater in San Francisco, the costumes are essentially realistic, but the staging is very presentational. This party scene resembles staging for a musical. Gregory Wallace as the lead Khlestakov is at the highest point in the center. Directed by Carey Perloff.

Photo © Kevin Berne.

EXPLORING Collaboration

The Sondheim/Lapine Collaboration

The highly successful collaboration of Stephen Sondheim and James Lapine began when Lapine contacted Sondheim about the possibility of working together. After agreeing on the idea of theme and variations as a starting point, the two artists hit on the Georges Seurat painting "Sunday Afternoon on the Island of La Grande Jatte" as the focus for their musical. *Sunday in the Park with George* (1984) was the result. Lapine wrote the book; Sondheim wrote the music and lyrics. After two years of development, *Sunday in the Park with George* opened on Broadway on May 2, 1984, under the direction of Lapine, whose production choices further extended the ideas of the play into the visual realm.

The two men bring different strengths to the partnership. Sondheim's focus is aural; he is attuned to rhythm, language, pitch. Lapine's early career as a graphic artist developed a strong visual sense. Together, they produced an innovative theatrical experience. *Sunday in the Park* explores the position of the artist in society and the relationship between art, emotion, and human connection.

SUNDAY IN THE PARK WITH GEORGE in a 2008 Broadway revival that used lighting projections on white walls instead of the scrims and scenic units of the original production. Directed by Sam Buntrock, scenic and costume design by David Farley, projection design by Timothy Bird. Photo © Joan Marcus.

Soon after *Sunday in the Park* opened on Broadway, Lapine and Sondheim decided to collaborate again, this time focusing on a fairy tale or adventure. Lapine began charting story lines of various tales and reading modern commentary on their meaning. *Into the Woods* (1987) explores the themes of community and responsibility by intertwining familiar folk tales. Whereas the language and music of *Sunday in the Park* were inspired by the painter Seurat's technique of pointillism (tiny, self-contained dots of color, which at a distance merge to create a complete image), *Into the Woods* utilized several styles of songs appropriate for the wide variety of characters. Lapine again directed the first production. Bernadette Peters, who had originated the role of Dot in *Sunday in the Park with George,* returned in the important role of the hideous-turned-sexy witch of *Into the Woods.*

The two writers pursued independent projects but came together again for *Passion* (1994), a story of a man's relationship with two women that explores the irrational, consuming nature of love. Lapine wrote the book based on the 1981 movie *Passione d'Amore* and directed the first production. Sondheim created a full romantic score and lyrics to reflect the heightened emotions of the characters.

Into the Woods was revived and redesigned on Broadway, again under the direction of Lapine, in 2002, but for the Broadway revival of *Sunday in the Park with George* in 2008, the show had a whole new production team and a very different look.

The history of the Sondheim/Lapine collaboration illustrates the exciting possibilities that can be unlocked when talented artists combine forces to produce a product bolder, more brilliant, and with more depth than either might have achieved on his own.

INTERESTED? Check out

Sunday in the Park with George (1999) available on DVD.
Into the Woods (1997) available on DVD.
Passion (2003) available on DVD.

Text or Pretext?

One of the thorniest artistic and ethical issues in the theatre of our time is the relationship of the text (and therefore playwright) to the rest of the production. In the first half of the twentieth century the director was frequently looked on as an interpretive artist whose job was to come to as complete an understanding of the playwright's intent as possible and then serve that intent in all aspects of production. The words of the play usually were considered set in stone whether the play was ancient or modern. Judicious cutting of the play was considered acceptable for time considerations, and directors usually did not feel bound to reproduce all stage directions indicated in the script. Any addition or rearrangement of the text without the playwright's permission, however, was considered inappropriate, since the playwright was the final authority.

As early as the first decade of the twentieth century, however, a different point of view began to surface in theatrical circles. When designers Gordon Craig and Adolphe Appia began to focus attention on the director as the master artist of the theatre, the stage was set for regarding the script as a pretext for production—as one element of equal weight with design and performance. Antonin Artaud declared that there should be "no more masterpieces," discouraging reverence for the text in favor of a visceral, sensual experience. The shift in paradigm had a profound effect on the perceived status of the playwright. Today it is possible to find practitioners who embrace either position, as well as those who fall on a continuum somewhere between the two extremes. Directors JoAnne Akalaitis, Peter Sellars, and Anne Bogart are current examples of theatrical **auteurs**—directors who, in building the three-dimensional performance, feel responsible for creating meaning for the audience, and when the play is in public domain, may use or reconstruct the playwright's text to serve the director's purpose in managing the theatrical whole. Here the director, rather than the author, is the primary creative force. When the playwright is living, a difference in how author and director regard the relationship of text to production can result in artistic and even legal conflict.

THE NOTEBOOKS OF LEONARDO DA VINCI (2003), conceived and directed by Mary Zimmerman. Although dominated by visual imagery, here we see a melding of playwright, director, and to some degree, designer, not unlike some of the work of Robert Wilson, and frequently identified with the postmodern. *Notebooks* reconstructed images, science, and philosophy from the great artist and combined images and ideas while translating all to three-dimensional art, often in motion. Scenic design by Scott Bradley.
Photo © Joan Marcus.

Revision in Rehearsal

When the playwright is able to collaborate in the production process, she or he has a valuable opportunity to see and hear the play "on its feet." Some playwrights make few revisions once the play is in rehearsal, but others use the experience to continue shaping the play. Early in the rehearsal process, structural problems may become apparent, and the author may move scenes around, cut, or add material. When dialogue is not working, it can be refined or eliminated. Frequently, during the rehearsal process a playwright may rewrite a scene repeatedly, attempting to fix a problem identified by the director, dramaturg, an actor, or the playwright. Valuable comments from directors and actors can lead to changes or improvements in the script. It is not unusual in a musical for entire songs to be added or cut. A speech was turned into "The Rape Song," a pivotal number in *The Fantasticks,* fairly close to opening to take advantage of the singing talents of Jerry Orbach.[3] The original run closed in 2002, but the show was revived in 2006 with a number of politically correct alterations made by the original lyricist, Tom Jones. All along "The Rape Song" was really about a fake abduction; for the revival, most of the dialogue and lyrics were altered using words such as "abduction, raid, masquerade," to replace the word "rape."

As the rehearsal process continues, actors need a set script to rely on and changes tend to become fewer and less drastic. In the high-stakes world of commercial theatre, however, changes may be made at the last minute, even after the show is in front of an audience. In the first half of the twentieth century, shows bound for Broadway used to be performed "out of town" for a period of revisions and adjustments before officially opening in New York City. New plays now are usually developed in small theatres before they are produced on the main stage of a resident theatre or adopted by a commercial producing organization. With the current practice of **previews,** professional productions often play for weeks with a paying audience at a somewhat reduced ticket price before the official opening to which critics are invited. Some established nonprofit theatres offer special programs to showcase new plays.

When the Playwright Is an Actor or Director

At times the playwright also serves as a member of the production team. The precedent for directing and/or performing in one's own work goes back at least as far as the ancient Greeks in the West and Noh theatre in the East. Modern writers are divided on the advisability of doing such double duty. In the 1910s and 1920s Rachel Crothers both designed and directed some of her own plays. Edward Albee has taken to directing much of his work such as *Zoo Story* (1959) along with his much delayed sequel *Peter and Jerry* (2007) at the Off-Broadway theatre Second Stage in 2007. After being disappointed by a number of premieres, Sam Shepard began directing the first productions of his plays, feeling it necessary to complete his vision in physical form in the theatre.

The advantage to directing one's own play, of course, is increased control of the final product. When the writer also has the skills to realize the vision on stage, either through staging or performance, the production is most likely to get as close as possible to the original idea of the play. Playwright-director Emily Mann notes that when directing her own work, she can determine whether a problem is caused by the acting, writing, or directing and has the power to fix a writing problem immediately.[4] Such intense involvement has its limitations, however; a playwright who is also functioning as an actor cannot listen objectively to the dialogue. A playwright who also directs the show does not have the benefit of a separate director's viewpoint. Playwrights who have had their work directed and acted successfully by others frequently point out that the energy and vision of the artistic team enhanced the production in ways previously unimagined. An insightful director, actor, or designer may discover qualities in the script of which even the playwright was unaware. In an ideal production the company does not just realize the playwright's vision but transcends it.

ARTISTS of the THEATRE

Michael Frayn

British writer Michael Frayn has written news stories and columns, novels, plays, and screenplays. His first professional play, *The Two of Us,* was produced in 1970, but *Alphabetical Order,* set in a provincial newspaper library, brought his first theatrical success in London in 1975. Five more plays followed between 1976 and 1980; then came *Noises Off* (1982). This fast-moving farce won Evening Standard and Laurence Olivier awards in Britain before moving to Broadway in 1983 and earning a Tony nomination for best play of 1984. *Noises Off* (which means "sound effects offstage") is set behind the scenes of a theatrical touring company and reveals both the public and offstage behavior of the company members. It has been produced worldwide and was revived at the National Theatre in Britain in 2000 and on Broadway in 2001. With this play his reputation as a comic writer was firmly established.

Benefactors was produced in London in 1984 and on Broadway in 1985. This play, which explores the relationship between two couples over fifteen years, was also a great success on both sides of the Atlantic. After that, Frayn turned to translating the plays of the Russian playwright Anton Chekhov. These translations were published between 1985 and 1990 and have been widely and successfully produced. In 1998, Frayn surprised the theatrical world with his original work, *Copenhagen,* a deeply thoughtful and complex play exploring an encounter in 1941 between two physicists, the German Werner Heisenberg and Niels Bohr (Heisenberg's Danish mentor). In a spare and highly theatrical style, Frayn dealt with the intersection of human relationship and personal responsibility in the context of the development of nuclear power and atomic weapons. Although the facts discussed in the play are true and the conversation is based on an actual event, the writer imagined the interaction between the two men and Bohr's wife, Margrethe. The play opened on Broadway in 2000 and won the Tony award that year for best play.

Another of Frayn's plays based on historical incident, *Democracy* (2003), was very popular in Britain and received critical acclaim on Broadway (2004) but did not prove as successful at the box office in the United States. The leading characters in *Democracy* are Willy Brandt, the West German chancellor from 1969 to 1974, and Gunter Guillaume, a communist agent who worked as a personal assistant to Brandt while spying on him for East Germany. Again, Frayn explored the ethical and emotional ramifications of this highly complicated situation. *Afterlife* (2008) focuses on the life of Austrian theatrical director Max Reinhardt and incorporates the medieval morality play, *Everyman,* which Reinhardt often directed.

Michael Frayn's serious plays are influenced by his interest in philosophy, which he studied at Cambridge. His clever, often humorous, dialogue entertains the audience at the same time it challenges their intellects. Frayn is also a successful novelist; *Spies* won the Whitbread novel of the year award in Britain in 2002.

INTERESTED? Check out

Many of Frayn's plays have been published singly. There is also a three-volume collection of his plays entitled *Plays 1, 2, and 3.* London: Methuen.

His major translations of Chekhov are collected as Anton Chekhov. *Plays.* London: Methuen, 1988.

Also see his satirical account of game-playing during the rehearsals of *Copenhagen:* Michael Frayn and David Burke. *The Copenhagen Papers: An Intrigue.* London: Picador, 2003.

COPENHAGEN. The three principals, Philip Bosco (as Niels Bohr), Blair Brown as (Margrethe Bohr), and Michael Cumpsty (as Werner Heisenberg). Directed by Michael Blakemore, set and costume design by Peter J. Davison.

Photo © Joan Marcus.

MA RAINEY'S BLACK BOTTOM (1984) by August Wilson was the playwright's first commercial success and continues to be revived professionally as here at Actors Theatre of Louisville in 2011. Set in 1927, this play examines the role of early jazz music, but especially the black musicians who wrote and performed it while being treated as second class citizens, if not worse. All of the action takes place in a Chicago recording studio. *Ma Rainey* joins nine other plays by Wilson in exploring the African American experience in the twentieth century. He finished his cycle not long before his death in 2005, the same year his last play *Radio Golf* was first produced. Actors Theatre of Louisville and Milwaukee Repertory Theatre production directed by Ron OJ Parson. Photography by Alan Simons.

By permission of Actors Theatre of Louisville.

DEVELOPMENT OF NEW PLAYS

The playwright's collaboration with directors and actors is sometimes extended earlier into the development stage of the script. Play readings offer a chance for the writer to hear the play come alive without the large investment of a production. A reading may be private and very informal, may be presented to the public or an invited audience, may be rehearsed, and may sometimes even be minimally staged but with the actors keeping scripts in hand. Often the audience for a reading is invited to comment and give suggestions to the playwright. New plays sometimes also undergo a workshop process in which a director and actors work with the writer to develop the script using reading, discussion, and improvisation. The playwright then uses the discoveries from workshop in revising the script.

Many theatres currently offer programs dedicated to helping new work along. In addition to its regular season, Center Stage in Baltimore offers Play Lab, a series of readings of new plays. Some theatres specialize in developing new work. The New York Theatre Workshop and Chicago Dramatists, for example, exist to develop and produce new plays and foster the development of playwrights. Many musicals are now developed in workshop—*Avenue Q* and *Spring Awakening,* for example. Stephen Sondheim often chooses to develop shows in workshop for a long time prior to public performance. The B.M.I. Lehman Engel Musical Theatre Workshop (New York) offers musical theatre development programs for composers, lyricists, and playwrights.

Nontraditional Play Development

Since the 1960s some theatre artists have chosen to disrupt the boundaries of responsibility between playwright, director, and actor by creating scripts in innovative ways. Some artists prefer to write and perform their own work, which leads to a very personal, complete production. Solo artist Spalding Gray developed material in front of an audience in a very intuitive way and mined his own experience to produce

EINSTEIN ON THE BEACH (1976) stands as one of the most innovative theatrical creations of the twentieth century. An exemplar of nontraditional play creation by Robert Wilson, it is a defining moment in his work, which typically involves startling design, postmodern, often minimalist and repetitious music, carefully choreographed movement, and unified artistic vision. Much of the play examines the evolution of transportation. Music and lyrics by Philip Glass. 1992 revival.

Photo © T. Charles Erickson.

monologues such as *Swimming to Cambodia* (1985), *Monster in a Box* (1990), and *It's a Slippery Slope* (1996). Anna Deavere Smith chooses to develop material not from her own life, but from interviews with a wide variety of Americans. For *Twilight: Los Angeles, 1992,* she conducted research in the wake of riots over the beating of Rodney King by Los Angeles police. Smith, who is African American, performed characters as different as a white Hollywood talent agent, a Korean grocer, and police chief Daryl Gates. She conducted over 300 interviews as research for *Let Me Down Easy* (2009), an exploration of attitudes toward the human body, the state of the healthcare system, and the experience of death.

Some companies choose to develop the play from the beginning in a workshop setting. Playwright Moisés Kaufman developed *The Laramie Project* with Tectonic Theater Project and members of the community of Laramie, Wyoming. Through interviews and workshops, the collaborators explored the horrific, homophobia-inspired murder of Matthew Shepard in 1998. Ten years later they returned to Laramie to re-interview citizens and explore what effect the event had on the community. *The Laramie Project: 10 Years Later* debuted simultaneously in theatres across the country, an approach borrowed from the Federal Theatre Project from the 1930s. Sometimes a playwright is involved in the actual scripting process and retains control and copyright. Caryl Churchill wrote *Cloud 9,* for example, after participating in a workshop on sexual politics with the Joint Stock Theatre Company. Although Churchill actually composed the play alone, it was inspired and guided by collaborative exploration in workshop. *Tracers* (1980) by John DiFusco, Vincent Caristi, Richard Chaves, Eric E. Emerson, Rick Gallavan, Merlin Marston, Harry Stephens, and Sheldon Lettich was created by a group of veterans from the Vietnam war—actors, director, and writer. The play's authorship comprises the names of all those who participated.

Issues of Ownership

The collaborative process of script development as it is currently practiced raises difficult issues of intellectual property. Ultimately, the playwright has control of any play he or she has written—but who "owns" the moment that was developed by actors

EXPLORING Historical and Cultural Perspectives

The Humana Festival of New American Plays, Actors Theatre of Louisville

For six weeks in the early spring, producers, directors, critics, playwrights, designers, actors, theatre lovers, and tourists from around the world converge on Louisville, Kentucky. The occasion is the Humana Festival of New American Plays. Actors Theatre of Louisville (ATL), a nonprofit, professional theatre, was founded in 1964 and began presenting a festival of new plays in 1977. The event has grown in the number of plays it produces and uses all three stages of the ATL complex. Actors Theatre states that approximately 3,000 scripts are received annually for consideration in the New Play Program. Nearly 75,000 plays have been submitted since 1976. Over three-fourths of plays produced at the Humana have been published in individual acting editions as well as Actors Theatre anthologies, making scripts widely available for reading, study, and production. *Getting Out* (Marsha Norman, 1977), *Crimes of the Heart* (Beth Henley, 1979), *Agnes of God* (John Pielmeier, 1980), *Keely and Du* (Jane Martin, 1993), and *Hotel Cassiopeia* (Charles L. Mee, 2006) are just a few of the plays premiered by ATL that have gone on to be widely produced and highly acclaimed.

BIG LOVE (2000) by Charles Mee was originally performed at the Humana Festival and has since been revived all over North America, especially in universities. This image is from a 2007 production at Indiana University. Photo courtesy of Indiana University PhotoGraphics.

INTERESTED? Check out

More about the Humana Festival, Actors Theatre's regular season of plays, and its other innovative programs at the ATL website at www.actorstheatre.org.

---

in a workshop improvisation and later written into the script? If the director comes up with an important piece of action or a major visual image or a dramaturg suggests a successful idea for restructuring, should the contributing artist share in the intellectual ownership (and therefore any monetary rewards)? This volatile issue has been and continues to be debated by individual artists and the guilds or unions that represent them (Dramatists Guild, Actors' Equity, Society of Stage Directors and Choreographers, and Literary Managers and Dramaturgs of the Americas). At times disagreements over artistic ownership end up in court.

Freedom and Limitations

In today's theatre a "crafter of plays" may choose to write alone, with collaborators, or in workshop and to build a script that is unfettered by questions of personnel and production budgets or specifically tailored to the needs of a company or theatre. There are no artistic rules for playwrights to follow; they are free to choose models from the past, establish new conventions, let their imaginations soar. Ironically, escalating production costs create a different kind of limitation. Given the handcrafted aspect of live theatre, companies can afford to produce only a limited number of scripts. Competition is fierce, and aside from musicals, marketing a large-cast, big-budget

EXPLORING Collaboration

The *Rent* Controversy

The collaborative nature of theatre, particularly the methods of script development now in use in many theatres, can have stunning artistic results but can also produce legal confusion. The musical *Rent* went through a long process of development with many people contributing to its growth. Inspired by the story of the opera *La Bohème*, the show began as an idea from Billy Aronson, who worked on it with Jonathan Larson in the early 1990s. The two agreed that Larson would continue alone on the project. In 1992 Larson made contact with the New York Theatre Workshop (NYTW), a nonprofit Off-Broadway theatre designed to workshop and present new dramatic material. NYTW encouraged the development of *Rent* and in 1994 mounted a studio production of the script at that stage. Those in charge at NYTW agreed that the musical was promising but needed a lot of work before a full production could be mounted. NYTW hired Lynn Thomson as a dramaturg, and she worked closely with Jonathan Larson on rewriting the script during the summer and fall of 1995. Most of the work took place in Larson's apartment with no one else present. Just before the Off-Broadway opening in 1996, playwright and composer Jonathan Larson died suddenly and unexpectedly at the age of 35. *Rent* went on to become a hit, moved to Broadway, won numerous awards, and became the center of a highly controversial lawsuit.

Thomson claimed to have contributed a considerable amount of the writing and asked Larson's heirs for credit as coauthor and 16 percent of the author's share of royalties. She maintained that, had he lived, Larson would have made sure that she received adequate compensation. Of course, Jonathan Larson was not available to substantiate or refute her claim.

The case went to court. During the trial, luminaries of the American theatre testified for both sides. Tony Kushner, author of *Angels in America*, noted that he voluntarily assigned 15 percent of his royalties to two dramaturgs

RENT by Jonathan Larson. The full cast in the Broadway production. Directed by Michael Greif; set design by Paul Clay, costume design by Angela Wendt, lighting design by Blake Burba.
Photo © Joan Marcus.

who helped to create the final version of that script. In July 1997 Judge Lewis A. Kaplan ruled against Thomson because there was no legal proof that Larson intended Thomson to be a coauthor, but Kaplan noted that there was considerable merit to Thomson's case. An appeal was filed and dismissed. Thomson filed a lawsuit seeking to keep the material that she had created from being used in the musical. In 1998 Thomson settled out of court with the Larson estate, the terms to remain confidential.

The legal battle over *Rent* emphasizes the difficulty of assigning rights to intellectual property when the process of making art is characterized by intensive collaboration. Alisa Solomon wrote in *The Village Voice* that the case revealed the conflict of theatrical collaboration with the principles of copyright law. While collaboration requires a free exchange of ideas and unselfish commitment to the work, the copyright process requires precision and documentation.[5]

play is next to impossible. Theatrical producers tend to look kindly on plays with few characters and minimal set requirements.

The economic restrictions currently placed on playwrights may be of short or long duration. We know, however, that historically, theatrical conditions are not permanent. It is impossible to know, but exciting to imagine, what new expectations await our future crafters of plays.

CHAPTER REVIEW

Questions and Activities

1. Discuss the advantages and disadvantages of playwrights directing their own work. Make a list of all the things that would be easier and all the things that would be harder to accomplish. How are writing and directing different activities?
2. Choose a story from a newspaper, magazine, or the Internet. Discuss how it could be turned into a play. Describe the setting and the major characters. How would the play begin? How would it end? The article is only the inspiration; determine whether there are several different ways in which the play might be developed.
3. Like painters, playwrights construct a creative reality that is based on how they view the world. Take a picture of a person from a magazine or Internet article. Write a description of the picture as a starting point for a character. Go beyond the description to specify imagined character traits. Compare your version to others' versions.

Key Terms and Concepts

royalties, p. 188
dramaturg, p. 192

auteur, p. 194
previews, p. 195

For Further Exploration

Toby Cole, ed. *Playwrights on Playwriting.* New York: Cooper Square Publishers, 2001.

David Rush. *Building Your Play: Theory and Practice for the Beginning Playwright.* Carbondale: Southern Illinois University, 2010.

David Savran. *In Their Own Words: Contemporary American Playwrights.* New York: Theatre Communications Group, 1988.

Michael Mark Chemers. *Ghost Light: An Introductory Handbook for Dramaturgy.* Carbondale: Southern Illinois University, 2010.

Website for the Dramatists Guild of America at www.dramatistsguild.com

Website for Literary Managers and Dramaturgs of the Americas at www.lmda.org

THREESIXTY'S PETER PAN under a tent in a modified thrust; promoted as being in the round due to 360 degrees of dynamic CGI effects. A touring British production directed by Ben Harrison; scenic design by William Dudley; Lighting design by Mark Henderson.

Photo by Kevin Berne © Threesixty Entertainment.

The Designer

Materializing Conception and the World of the Play

One night, after audience members have taken their seats in a theatre, they see a dimly lit stage. The stage floor is **raked** (not flat but set at an angle), and towering structures made of metal pipe surround the playing space. Rays of intense light shoot through the metal structures, creating oddly shaped, ominous shadows and pools of red on the floor. Music fills the space. It is in a minor key with a pronounced, driving rhythm.

On a different night, the audience members enter to the sounds of fast, melodic piano music. The scenery depicts a courtyard. The outside of several stucco buildings can be seen, with stone patio areas filled with tables, chairs, and pots of red geraniums. The colors in the set are warm earth tones—oranges, warm browns, yellows. There are no obvious lighting effects, but the scenery seems to emit a warm glow. The mood is one of happiness and well-being or reassurance.

Before even seeing an actor, perhaps without even knowing what the play is about, the audience members have been prepared for a specific experience. The first night they anticipate something "heavy"—a tragedy or serious play—something that might end unhappily. The second night they are ready for a comedy—something light, fast moving—perhaps with many complications but turning out well in the end.

The designers' job in the theatre is to control environment. Scenic, lighting, and costume designers contribute effects that the audience sees; sound designers create effects that the audience hears. These sensory impressions not only communicate information to the audience in an efficient way, but also influence the audience's emotional involvement with the play. The designers help to shape the audience experience; their individual contributions become part of the whole and affect the work of the rest of the company. Effective designers in the theatre today must be both inspired artists and collaborators.

THE DEVELOPMENT OF THE DESIGNER

In the long history of the theatre the prominence of designers is somewhat new. Of course, someone has always designed or decorated scenery or the performance environment. Someone has always designed, purchased, made, or selected costumes and masks. Someone has always provided properties. Once theatrical activity

BEIJING TRADITIONAL MUSIC DRAMA. Costume of a female general (Mu Guiying) in combat. Scenes from the eleventh century are depicted. Costumes and makeup from such traditional forms are very colorful and detailed. Beijing Opera postcard.

Collection of the authors.

moved indoors, someone had to find a way to illuminate it. From the earliest Greek performances someone was writing and performing music and working on offstage sounds (in other words, designing sound). Few names of theatre architects or scenic designers before the seventeenth century are known to us, but someone had to design and build all of those remarkable theatres in Greece, Rome, and their colonies and territories.

Before the Italian Renaissance and in many cases long after, most of these designers and technicians were invisible—or at least are so to today's students of theatre. While the remains of some of their remarkable work can be appreciated, little is known of their relationship to productions of plays and the ongoing activity of theatre companies. Before the nineteenth century, few designers were publicly credited. Even with the appearance of well-known designers, many designers continued to be anonymous until the twentieth century. Creators of sets, costumes, and properties were usually considered an adjunct to the "real" business of the theatre, which was carried out by actors, playwrights, and managers. Now, of course, designers are usually recognized and sometimes well compensated for their contributions to the professional theatre. Designers are usually at the heart of production preparation long before actors begin rehearsing a new production.

What precipitated the change? Perhaps the two biggest factors were the rise of the modern director and the advent of electric lighting (both in the late nineteenth century).

As early as the fifth century B.C.E. in Greece, the playwright Aeschylus was credited with providing some kind of "skenographia," or decoration of the **skene** (stage house) upstage of the **orchestra** (circular performance space), at the Theatre of Dionysus. Many translators over the years have interpreted this term to mean scene painting, but the exact reference is uncertain. Aeschylus also supposedly introduced machinery and scenic elements that indicated tombs and altars. If the surviving descriptive passages are true, then the classical Greeks had some interest in designing for particular productions, not just general decoration. A late classical account of theatre architecture in Greece and Rome refers to **pinakes** (flat, painted scenery) and **periaktoi** (prism-shaped, three-sided scenic units) that could be painted and revolved. Exactly how any of these items might have been used or how often is unknown. Actors depicted in vase paintings wear traditional robes and footwear. Masks apparently covered the entire head, but little is known about how they were made. An ancient anecdote from an anonymous biographer included in the marginal notes of early copies of Greek tragedies tells us that the chorus of furies in *The Oresteia* of Aeschylus was terrifying to the audience; the masks and costumes surely had something to do with instigating the fear.

The Romans used curtains and floor traps in some of their theatres, and a few Greek theatres had an underground tunnel extending from the skene to an opening in the orchestra. The possibilities are intriguing. The plays that survive from both Greece and Rome suggest that properties were frequently used, but perhaps some action was mimed rather than executed with properties. In Chinese music drama, for example, characters are often depicted on horseback, but the actor rides without the presence of either real or property horses. Actors use mimetic action and a symbolic system of gestures to replace many properties.

In the medieval period designs were created for cycle plays (based on biblical stories) that often incorporated spectacle such as transformations, rainstorms, and fire effects emanating from the mouth of hell. Despite a number of written accounts from the period, not many details remain about methods and designs. Few helpful medieval paintings or drawings survive, and as intriguing as they are, they raise more questions than answers. Promptbooks and written eyewitness accounts from around 1200 to 1550, however, underscore a popular attraction to and probable expectation of stage spectacle, both literal and symbolic. Some costumes seem to have been symbolic as well. Adam and Eve, for example, were dressed in white leather to indicate nakedness.

ASTLEY'S THEATRE in London c. 1804. This theatre was obviously catering to the novelty of combining equestrian events with melodrama, comedy, and sometimes tragedy. Because a proscenium performance stage was used in conjunction with a performance ring like a circus, the design challenges could be daunting. For some productions, a ramp crossed over the orchestra pit to allow horses to ride back and forth from arena to stage as when, for example, a castle on stage was under siege from the ring.
From the *Microcosm of London,* collection of the authors.

Devil costumes and masks could be quite imaginative in their expression of evil and the grotesque. Most characters wore medieval dress, even though many characters were biblical; historical accuracy did not become an issue in the theatre until the nineteenth century.

In Japan, China, and India, formalized, generic stage space dominated the theatrical forms. We do not know who is responsible for the standard painted pine tree background for Japanese Noh; the curtained, carpeted space of Chinese music drama; or the columned open space of early Indian theatre, but clearly someone designed remarkable, suggestive theatre spaces for these forms that became the norm for performance in each of these cultures. Costumes for the classical Asian forms were often colorful and splendidly decorated. Over the centuries the spaces and standardized designs continued to be replicated; costumes, masks, and makeup became virtually fixed for particular characters in particular plays, and Kabuki in the eighteenth century adapted the Noh space to serve its own purposes.

An important shift in the West arrived during the Italian Renaissance with innovations in perspective drawing and painting. Flat painted scenery often dynamically recreated detailed and accurate images of palatial buildings, town squares, and sylvan glades. This type of scenery, called **wing, drop, and border scenery,** included flat painted panels on either side of the stage (wings), a large expanse of painted fabric upstage (drop), and strips of cloth or panels hung horizontally across the tops of the wings (borders). Wing, drop, and border scenery became the standard first in Italian court entertainments and opera and then in the professional theatre and was ultimately framed by the proscenium arch. Such pictorial representation became the standard in Europe and the Americas and remained so until well into the nineteenth century.

Wings, drops, and borders are still used in variations from time to time, although since the nineteenth century, three-dimensional scenery and properties have been combined with flat scenery. The pictorial, illusionistic, literal depiction of theatrical locale remains one of the standards for scenic design.

Italian designers such as Giacomo Torelli and Giuseppe Bibiena achieved fame throughout Europe for their scenic designs and theatre architecture in the seventeenth and eighteenth centuries, but most of their work was in the service of court entertainments and opera, neither of which followed the strict guidelines of neoclassicism, the ruling system of the theatre. Neoclassicism, the Renaissance interpretation of Greek and Roman models of plays and theory, called for a play to take place in only one location. This restriction was a stumbling block for designers and playwrights working in the theatre because it did not usually allow for changes of settings within a play. Also, because they staged a rolling repertory of plays and did not have long runs of single plays at the time, professional theatres could not afford different settings for every play. The building and painting of new scenery was an extravagant expense.

Consequently, the generic design approach that was popularized by Sebastiano Serlio in the sixteenth century became the standard. Each theatre company had a handful of settings that could serve many different plays: a standard urban exterior or domestic interior for comedy, a generic palatial exterior or interior for tragedy, and a wooded exterior or domestic interior for tragicomedy. Accordingly, few audience members paid attention to the designs and often took them for granted. The sets were usually background indicators for the play. About the only time any excitement for scenery was generated was when a theatre manager announced that his theatre had expended much money to have new scenery painted for a new season of plays. The painters often remained anonymous. No artist made his living solely or primarily as a scene designer. Theatre designs were supplemental, a source for extra money to be made on an occasional basis. Designers in the seventeenth and eighteenth centuries were more like consultants or adjuncts than collaborators. Actors were in charge of acquiring and maintaining their own costumes (a major professional expense), and the focus was on looking attractive rather than the more modern considerations of appropriateness to character and situation.

BLUE JEANS (1890), a popular melodrama by Joseph Arthur performed in a typical box set. Note that the heroine is about to attack the villain in order to save the bound hero from certain death from the whirling saw blade.
Courtesy of Museum of the City of New York.

By the mid-eighteenth century a few theatre managers had decided it was time for a change. In London, actor-manager David Garrick decided to remove the audience members from onstage seating and create a new focus for the stage environment. From France he hired Philippe De Loutherbourg, an innovative designer who created many new settings for the repertory of the Drury Lane Theatre. De Loutherbourg used **ground rows** (low, flat painted scenery at stage level that extended the line of the wing out toward center stage). This development invited the audience to focus on the floor and playable environment, not just on scenery above the floor. He also experimented with transparencies for transformation scenes as well as color media for candlelight and oil lamps. Early on, he understood the importance of lighting to the theatre. Convinced that audiences would be fascinated by the latest technology, De Loutherbourg created a miniature theatre for exhibition halls using scenery without an accompanying play. Audiences came to watch his tiny scene shifts and innovative special effects, which suggested what full-size stages would support in the nineteenth century.

Meanwhile, in Italy, the family of Bibienna designers, although working in opera and court entertainment, began creating settings that featured multiple vanishing points for perspective drawing and moved toward asymmetrical views of interiors and exteriors. This work, however, confined itself to two-dimensional scenic units. Nearly everything was done with paint.

It was in the nineteenth century that three-dimensional scenery changed audience expectations of the possibilities for scenic design. The **box set,** an enclosed set with walls and sometimes ceiling, became a standard for interiors after 1830. This innovation invited designers to decorate the stage floor as in a house or palace, for example, increased the numbers of set properties (such as furniture) in imitation of contemporary interiors, and coaxed actors to move upstage off the apron and inside the box.

In 1823 James Robinson Planché designed historically accurate costumes for a revival of Shakespeare's *King John.* He followed this design with historically accurate costumes and scenery for another of Shakespeare's plays, *Henry IV, Part I,* in 1824. Called **antiquarianism** at the time, such practice inspired many designers to research authentic styles of dress, architecture, and interior design from the past and incorporate

STICK FLY by Lydia Diamond. This design is a good example of a box set with ceiling, harking back to the nineteenth century, but evoking a contemporary African American apartment. Produced in 2010 at the Huntington Theatre Company, Boston. Directed by Kenny Leon. Scenic design by David Gallo.

Photo © Scott Suchman.

or adapt accurate historical images when producing plays written or set in the past. Within a few decades most stage design in the West favored literal depictions of recognizable locations, often utilizing three-dimensional elements. Historical accuracy has remained a standard practice for some productions up to our own time.

At the turn of the twentieth century, another shift occurred that continues to inspire design in our own era. Attracted to Asian theatrical and decorative forms, intrigued by the use of open space as a design element, and troubled by the excesses of realistic and literal detail in popular theatre, designers Adolphe Appia from Switzerland and Gordon Craig from England launched a design movement that returned to simplicity and suggestion rather than detailed evocation of the real. In the first quarter of the twentieth century their designs and those of many followers such as Robert Edmond Jones in the United States and Ernst Stern in Germany swept over stages in Europe and America. In turn, many Asian forms borrowed from the West (Kabuki, for example, adopted the proscenium arch). Such cross-fertilization created many new hybrids in theatrical design, a trend that continues in contemporary production.

By the second decade of the twentieth century, many audience members expected each production to have a unified style that was appropriate for the play. Costumes were designed considering both individual character traits and the total look of the show. Set, lighting, and costumes were carefully coordinated. Perhaps the most dynamic designer of the twentieth century, Josef Svoboda, created remarkable experiments with space and lighting and worked on an international stage. Beginning in 1958 in what was then Czechoslovakia, he combined platforms, three-dimensional scenery, and open space with projection screens; mixed film with still projections; and mastered the art of projected scenery. Sometimes he completely transformed space with lighting alone. In the wake of Svoboda and with the aid of modern computer-generated imaging for

TWO JOSEF SVOBODA DESIGNS The action for Josef Svoboda's design of *Oedipus the King* (left) was played on a huge staircase that extended from the orchestra pit below the stage and disappeared into the fly space. Actors could enter from many locations—left, right, and below. This "impossible" architecture was not only stunning in the theatre but also suggested the classical origins of the play while locating the theatrical event in the twentieth century. Svoboda's design for *As You Like It* (right) used low platforms suggestive of both architecture and an almost magical scenic environment completed by projected scenery that suggests a forest. Changing the projections could alter the location and mood completely. Only the platforms were constant.

Photographs by Dr. Jaromir Svoboda. From *The Scenography of Josef Svoboda* by Jarka Burian.

both lighting and sets in creating designs as well as executing the designs onstage, the possibilities for theatrical design seem nearly limitless. Such computerized imaging is at its busiest in Las Vegas shows such as Cirque du Soleil and Broadway musicals such as *Wicked* (2003) and *Young Frankenstein* (2007), but it adorns small, intimate performances as well. Costumes currently range from the realistic and everyday to highly stylized

EXPLORING Historical and Cultural Perspectives

Development of the Revolve

The **revolve** (also called revolving stage and turntable) was invented in Osaka, Japan, in 1758 for use in Bunraku (puppet theatre) and soon after, in Kabuki theatre. Its creation is attributed to a Bunraku playwright, Namiki Shozo. Although small in scale for Bunraku and at first resting on top of the stage surface (a temporary measure), the revolve as adapted to Kabuki became a large revolve that was set permanently into the stage near the end of the eighteenth century. By 1827 this scenic device had become very complicated, with the invention of an inner revolve that was somewhat smaller than the larger one (like concentric circles). The inner revolve was capable of moving with the larger one or in the opposite direction, creating the possibility for extraordinary scenic changes. The revolve continues to be a mainstay of Kabuki production and the device often measures about sixty feet across, usually set at center stage. Early on, Japanese artists recognized both the practical and spectacular possibilities of revolves, which can hold two entire settings at once or bring tableaux and actors into place while other elements remain stationary.

The revolve was not used in Western theatre until the turn of the twentieth century (in 1896 for opera at Munich, Germany). At about the same time that many European playwrights and practitioners started discovering Asian theatrical forms, German directors and designers recognized the possibilities for revolves and began designing their own versions and incorporating them into the productions of classics, especially Shakespearean plays that have many changes of location. Director Max Reinhardt with his designer Ernst Stern made very effective use of the revolve in many revivals of Shakespeare such as *Henry IV* (a chronicle), *Othello* (a tragedy), and *The Merchant of Venice* (a tragicomedy). Their 1905 production of *A Midsummer Night's Dream* featured a central revolve for all of the forest scenes (all but the opening and closing scenes of the play). Most of the large revolve was covered with trees, resulting in myriad entrances and exits and a variety of views effected by simply rotating the revolve a few feet at a time. At midcentury Bertolt Brecht was especially fascinated by the revolve and built its usage into the composition as well as the direction of his plays such as *Mother Courage* and *The Caucasian Chalk Circle*, particularly

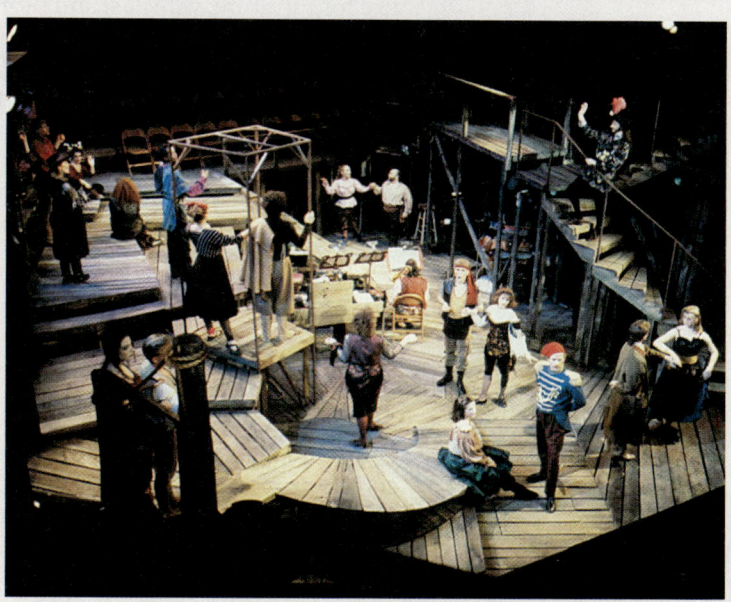

THIS CONSTRUCTIVIST SET for *Candide,* by Leonard Bernstein and Hugh Wheeler, not only filled the stage but also extended well out into the house for this production with many levels, platforms, ramps, and stairs—all of wood. Notice the small revolving stage that was propelled by the actors, not by machinery or electronics. Scenic design by Lori Bush, University of Nebraska.

Collection of the authors.

for journey scenes as well as scenic changes. Of course, revolves in many variations have frequently adorned the productions of multiset plays and musicals such as *Noises Off, The Lion King,* and *Thoroughly Modern Millie* (2002) throughout the twentieth century and up to the present.

INTERESTED? Check out

Earle Ernst. *The Kabuki Theatre.* Honolulu: University of Hawaii Press, 1974.

W. Oren Parker, R. Craig Wolf, and Dick Block. *Scene Design and Stage Lighting,* 9th ed. New York: Wadsworth Publishing, 2008.

Walter Rene Fuerst and Samuel J. Hume. *Twentieth-Century Stage Decoration.* New York: Dover, 1967.

flights of fancy. In the early twenty-first century, theatrical design has reached a very sophisticated level of achievement, yet it is clear that there is much more to come. No doubt, many current designers would say, "You ain't seen nothin' yet."

THE DESIGNERS' CHOICES

Designers have a wide variety of styles to choose from in today's theatre. Audiences might see onstage only a few chairs and tables in front of a simple curtain or an elaborate fabrication of an entire room, complete with all walls, ceiling, and decorations. The stage could be cluttered with multicolored plastic cubes that the actors seem to use for furniture, vehicles, and props; or the space might be empty, a highly polished wooden floor with no attempts to hide stage walls or lighting instruments. Audiences might observe abstract images creating a stylized environment for performance, as if witnessing a bizarre dream, or the actors could mime everything as they ask the audience to imagine the presence of objects in their hands. The actors themselves might even pretend to be scenery, suddenly becoming trees blowing in the wind or the doors of a palace swinging open. Thus, the designers face many opportunities and challenges in creating an environment for the play.

Representational and Presentational

Representational scenery, costumes, lighting, and sound imitate precisely the kind of environment and details in which the action of the play would occur in real life. At its most extreme, in the movement of naturalism at the end of the nineteenth century, representational scenery appeared to be a real location in every detail with all the appropriate props and decorations. A domestic interior might include books, magazines, lamps—all three-dimensional objects that could be handled by the actors. If the setting is an exterior, one might see dirt, rocks, grass, fallen leaves— every element one would expect to find in a natural environment. Dressed in clothes looking just like those of the period in which the action takes place, the actors probably move and behave in the set as if it were actually the room represented. They do not acknowledge the presence of the audience, and the actors' behavior suggests an imaginary **fourth wall.** Often audiences are fascinated by how close to reality the scenic pictures seem to come. Occasionally, audience members applaud representational scenery because they recognize its details and approve its authenticity. Such scenery, or simplified versions, most often appears in realistic plays written since the nineteenth century, such as Lillian Hellman's *The Children's Hour* (1934), which is set in a house converted to a school for girls, or *Long Day's Journey into Night* (1956) by Eugene O'Neill, set in an unfriendly living room in 1914. The texts of these plays specify considerable scenic detail in their descriptions of interior settings.

Representational scenery can also be applied to plays of any period if the artists so choose as long as the artists' choices suggest literal reality. Although representational scenery and costuming are often elaborate, this is by no means a necessity. Nonetheless, labor-intensive construction and decoration as well as expensive building materials and set props often provided for complete representational settings and costumes (especially indicating earlier historical periods) are found prohibitive for theatre companies that must economize. Notwithstanding the opinion of some critics and artists that representational designs are confining and limiting to creativity, representational interpretations often reveal imagination, skill, and extraordinary artistry.

ROUND AND ROUND THE GARDEN (1974) by Alan Ayckbourn, the third play of his Norman Conquests. Although this is a British sex farce, scenic designer Ralph Funicello created a very literal representational exterior complete with artificial grass surface—a practice not often seen onstage since the early twentieth century. A 2010 production of the American Repertory Theater in San Francisco directed by John Rando.

Photo © Kevin Berne.

A **presentational** approach to design offers many possibilities. Presentational scenery, costumes, and lighting can suggest, distort, or even abstract reality. The scenery is often deliberately incomplete or presents an environment that would be impossible to find in life. Such designs may rely primarily on mood, color, shapes, or visual symbols implied by the text of a play or born in the imagination of the director or designer. Unfortunately, the presentational setting is sometimes a choice of expediency due to economic and temporal limitations placed on the theatrical artists. More significantly, it is often an artistic choice that asks the audience to receive the theatrical event in unexpected or challenging ways. The presentational setting may expose the building's permanent architecture or ask us to fill a void with our own imaginings prompted only by scenic suggestions. Presentational costumes can comment on the characters or color-code them or suggest the whole by a mere piece.

Many plays as written call for presentational designs or performance styles. The basic approach to creating the environment of the play will be established early in the design process as designers communicate with the director and with each other. While obvious in some plays from most historical periods, the call for presentational scenery has been particularly evident in stage directions since about 1890, in plays such as *Ubu Roi* (1896) by Alfred Jarry, with its grotesque but childlike approach to space and time, or *Waiting for Godot* (1953) by Samuel Beckett, set in a bleak exterior marked only by a scrawny tree. Presentational settings are also typical of nearly any musical play. For example, *Spamalot* (2005) by Eric Idle and John Du Prez features contemporary game show imagery and cheerleaders added to the medieval world. Design aspects of some productions combine the presentational and representational, however. The basic setting in the musical *Avenue Q* (2003) appears at first to be a representational residential street front in the New York borough of Queens (although slightly miniaturized). The first visual images of the show, however, appear on large video screens on each side of the proscenium opening, and the scenery quickly opens up to a presentational style as actors appear with large puppets, and tiny rooms pop out from inside the façade or "float" in space downstage of the row houses.

WAITING FOR GODOT by Samuel Beckett as performed at the American Conservatory Theater, San Francisco. Directed by Carey Perloff.

Photo © Kevin Berne.

Historical versus Imaginary

With any new production the designers, collaborating with a director, always confront the decision of whether to create a stage environment or costumes that are abstract or highly stylized or literal in terms of the historical period and precise location of the action of the play. If the production team wants the historical period to be recognizable to the audience, it needs to decide whether to change the location or time period in which the play is set. For example, *A Doll House* by Henrik Ibsen is set in an upstairs multiroom apartment in Norway in the 1870s. The design team might decide to reset the action in 1920s America or 1980s Tokyo with a focus on commercialism or in 2012 South Africa with an all-black cast struggling with the residue from apartheid. In shifting periods or locations, of course, some of the local details would need to be altered.

Alternatively, the desire might be to abstract the space. The famous final moment of *A Doll House* is a slamming door. The play has been produced with symbolic settings that would not exist in a real apartment: a space dominated by a multitude of doors or a gigantic door to symbolize the significance of the final moment. The action could also be set on a large, open, reflective floor surrounded by mirrors; everywhere Nora turns, she is faced with images of herself that might distort or magnify as she increasingly becomes dissatisfied with who she is and how she does not understand her place in society. Perhaps the mirrors are large enough and angled to allow the audience members to also see themselves; when they watch Nora looking at herself in the mirror, they see themselves with her. There are no rules limiting the possibilities of designing and staging the play. The only limitations are those of imagination and economics.

ARTISTS of the THEATRE

John Lee Beatty

John Lee Beatty (b. 1948) has been very active in the professional theatre as a scenic designer since 1973 and continues at an accelerated pace. Educated at Brown University and the Yale University School of Drama, trained by the legendary designers Ming Cho Lee and Jo Mielziner, Beatty soon emerged as a leading designer for Broadway, Off-Broadway, and resident theatres across the country. Over the years and up to the present moment he has been nominated many times for Obie, Tony, and Drama Desk Awards and won at least seven times. Even his first solo effort on Broadway, the satirical comedy *Knock Knock* (1976) by Jules Feiffer, was nominated for a Tony.

He designs settings in many styles from realism like *A View from the Bridge* to musicals like *Chicago*, but some of his most memorable are reality-based and amazingly detailed in bringing together the essence of the world of the characters we are watching on the stage. On numerous occasions we have witnessed audiences applauding his settings, yet it is soon evident that the spaces serve the movement of the staged action and provide a logical and often fascinating environment for the playwright's and director's vision. His beautiful design for Edward Albee's *A Delicate Balance* in 1996 captured authentically the upscale family of the household, but its coldness underscored the problems in this troubling play. His 2010 design for *Time Stands Still* by Donald Margulies seemed like an authentic loft environment for the photographer and journalist who live there, but it was very dark and colorless, almost sinister, suggesting the trouble to come. It was not an inviting space.

On the other hand, Beatty's work is sometimes unexpectedly simple and streamlined in his choices when such an approach serves the play well, as it did in the 2010 *Driving Miss Daisy* by Alfred Uhry or *Doubt* (2004) by John Patrick Shanley. Much of the action of the first takes place in a car suggested

TALLEY'S FOLLY (1979), a Pulitzer Prize-winning play by Lanford Wilson. John Lee Beatty designed the original production and then this 2008 revival for the McCarter Theatre Center in Princeton, New Jersey. Directed by Marshall Mason, who also directed the original production.
Photo © T. Charles Erickson.

by highly polished wooden chairs and a steering wheel and column. Nothing more. In both plays a few objects or partial scenic elements suggested the whole and allowed the character studies that drive these plays to get our full attention.

We have observed him offering workshops for students of design, and it is evident that his flexible approach to dramatic texts and his patient handling of students make him an extraordinary teacher in his discipline when the opportunity arises. To thrive and remain at the top of his profession as long as he has bespeaks the enduring admiration and trust that producers and directors, including some of our best like Daniel Sullivan, Marshall Mason, and Jo Mantello, have for his remarkable artistic gifts.

Interpreting Space

Some theatrical spaces, such as the proscenium theatre, are clearly designed for scenery. Nevertheless, many directors and playwrights have deliberately used little or no scenery in the proscenium space—a choice that calls the audience's attention to the permanent features of the theatre, suggests simplicity, and lends a generic sense to the artistic proceedings. Performances under such circumstances are often referred to as **metatheatre,** or productions that self-consciously comment on the play as taking place in a theatre. Sometimes plays are written in this way. In *The Comic Theatre* (1750) by Carlo Goldoni, for example, the action is set in an eighteenth-century Italian theatre where a rehearsal is about to begin. The front curtain begins to rise but is stopped by the company manager (a character), and an argument ensues over whether to rehearse with the curtain up or down.

In her play *Well* (2006), Lisa Kron combines the aesthetics of performance art with traditional play structure. The play proceeds as if the actors are self-consciously aware of performing roles in a play that is really about the life of the playwright who is also onstage. The play's structure incorporates interruptions by the actors as if the action is getting out of control. More frequently, a director or production team interprets a play metatheatrically even if the playwright never had such a thing in mind.

Designers must give considerable attention to the ways in which theatrical space affects the audience experience. Consider a large auditorium versus a small, intimate arena, for example. Imagine the same play being performed in both. Intricate detail will not be noticed by anyone beyond the first few rows in a large theatre. In the small space, however, there is greater opportunity for subtlety. Many conditions and spatial relationships can manipulate or alter the theatrical event. Is the audience truly sharing the space with the performers, or is there a clear separation? A separation is defined by most theatre architecture, but the production techniques employed may try to break down or minimize that barrier. Designers today might find themselves designing for the audience space as well as the stage space.

Collaborating with Space

Obviously, theatre artists cannot literally collaborate with space, since space cannot negotiate, but the space that is available or deemed "necessary" for a production receives much attention from the director and set designer when they are planning, rehearsing, and performing a play. There are many things about a given space that cannot be altered. Many features, however, can be changed, hidden, eliminated, or adapted. Sometimes practitioners find themselves "lost in space," unable to gain control of it and feeling victimized by what is considered inflexible. The space ends up controlling the production rather than the other way around—a situation that is unfortunate but not uncommon. On the other hand, imaginative, talented, and lucky theatre artists can make clever use of what might otherwise seem a limitation or liability. Working with or around an unusual feature sometimes produces a fine theatrical moment that would otherwise have remained undiscovered.

A university production of Brecht's *Threepenny Opera* in Baltimore in 1986 was housed in a theatre that featured an unusual single vomitory that opened from below the audience seating onto the downstage apron of a proscenium stage. This feature often seemed to get in the way of stage action. On this occasion, however, the set designer William J. Pierson found a novel way to use it. He built a bridge from the stage out over the vomitory and concealed it; the bridge functioned as an extended thrust stage, allowing the action to spill out into the audience. The designer also placed a trapdoor at the downstage end of the bridge with access through the hidden vomitory beneath the bridge. When it was time for the antihero Macheath to appear in jail, he suddenly popped up through the trap, only to be incarcerated in the midst of the audience.

Many professional resident theatre companies, university, and community theatres have a home space—one or more theatres that they rent or own and in which they produce many different productions with varied needs and demands. Therefore, when selecting plays to produce in their familiar theatres, they know precisely what many of the problems are likely to be in fitting a play to the available space. The artists in such circumstances often feel as though they have a relationship with the home space. Other production companies have no home. They must plan productions for a space that is new to them or in some cases unknown until near the time of opening.

Seeing Beyond the Playwright and Director

When a designer joins the artistic team for a new production, he or she will most likely read the play first and then listen to the ideas or concept of the director, or perhaps director and designer will conceptualize together. Whatever the method, the designer is faced with many clues and directions from the written play and many more from the director. Designs are often at their most exciting and imaginative when the designer can not only be true to the intent or spirit of the playwright's creation and the director's vision, but also see and realize things that verify and enhance, going beyond the scope of playwright and director. If this were not true, then most playwrights and directors could simply dictate exactly what they want to an accurate draftsperson and skilled carpenters, painters, dressmakers, and tailors. Sometimes this has occurred, of course, but the resultant settings and costumes are more craft than art. The talented designer is an artist with whose creative work the production concept takes on evocations of space, or body, or sound that complement and fulfill the play and direction. Design dynamically serves to establish style, emotional tone, and location of the action of the play. Design enables the audience to see what should be seen.

COPENHAGEN by Michael Frayn. A shot of the three principal actors performing in the ellipse. The image was probably taken from the elevated on-stage seating area. Designed by Peter Davison; directed by Michael Blakemore.

Photo © Joan Marcus.

At their best, designs become ideal space, illumination, and character identification serving the movement and action of the play at that time. For director Michael Blakemore's 2000 production of *Copenhagen,* Peter Davison designed both set and costumes. The play recreates real events surrounding the race between the Allies and Germans to develop the atomic bomb, but it does so in a stylized, impossible manner. The three characters are former friends, and two are scientists who ended up working for opposing causes. They are dead yet remember and reenact events. Because memory is not certain and the events dramatized are contested, there are often several variations of the same story. The performance space for *Copenhagen* was essentially empty (three straight-back chairs were sometimes used) but formed as an elliptical shape. The intent as stated by the designer was for the actors' movement within the space to imitate atomic particles moving about. But the design did more than this. On the upstage side a neutral-colored wall followed the line of the ellipse and incorporated two tiers of seats for audience members. The effect of the high wall was of unfeeling enclosure and governmental or military presence—like expressionless halls of power. The effect was also like a courtroom: The audience members were witnesses to the action; they were not just observing the action but judging it.

With the entire setting a presentational space that was bathed in light, neutral colors, Blakemore and Davison put the characters in dark, realistic clothing of the postwar period, lending authenticity. The lighting by Mark Henderson and Michael Lincoln sometimes flooded the space intensely as if "exposing" the troubled characters but also isolated the character "particles" at times, allowing the audience to zero in on each crisis facing the characters. Just as the characters frequently moved about the space, the lighting also moved.

THE SCENIC DESIGNER'S WORK

The scenic designer creates a home for the action. The shape of the acting space and the look of any scenery or set props are the scenic designer's responsibility. While reading and analyzing the play, the scenic designer pays particular attention to any practical considerations (the need for actual doors, for example, or for a certain number of entrances/exits) as well as atmosphere or image that might be reinforced visually.

What Does the Play Demand?

When thinking about space and design for a specific play, many designers strongly consider what the playwright seemed to have in mind (when that is possible). Other designers dismiss that notion and conceive the production almost exclusively in their own terms. In either case a designer must take into consideration a play's **given circumstances** (what the play text specifically calls for).

The Ghost Sonata (1907) by August Strindberg is a fascinating and difficult play about death and decay. It takes place in four locations, but the fourth is visited only briefly; the first three are dealt with extensively. In the first location the action takes place in an exterior setting, just outside a strange apartment house. Through the windows (if the design is literal) the audience can see glimpses of the interior. Throughout the first scene the interior of the house and its inhabitants are discussed extensively. The second scene takes place inside the house (the round room), but through an open door the audience can see a portion of the hyacinth room. The third scene is set in the hyacinth room, which provides a view back into the round room and at the end opens up briefly to the "isle of death." Consequently, most of the play is spatially structured by a journey into and through the house. This play has been produced with representational, highly detailed realistic scenery, but it has also been performed in presentational settings that are more related to mood than location. Some productions have used four separate sets; others have built a single setting that moves and transforms. Some artists see Strindberg as calling for scenery that literally opens up and draws us inside the awful house of death step by step. All of these approaches are valid responses to the play, but the uses of space are remarkably different when experienced in a theatre and elicit very different audience responses.

Communicating with the Production Team

After reading and analyzing the play and meeting with either the director or the entire design team, the scenic designer will usually produce a series of quick sketches. These are shown to the director as a way of communicating the ideas that have been developing in the designer's head. Through brainstorming and conferencing, the director and designers move toward acceptance or modification of the designs or sometimes find themselves starting all over. When the designer and director feel that they are on the same wavelength, the designer will execute the following:

- A **ground plan**—a drafting of the plan of the stage as seen from overhead. A ground plan shows where any scenic pieces or perhaps set props (such as furniture) are to be placed. The director can see the potential for blocking in the ground plan; the lighting designer can see how the acting area will be shaped and what set pieces need illumination.
- A **section**—a drafting showing the vertical elements of the space and their relative positions (for example, the height at which scenery, lighting, and masking are to be hung).
- A **rendering**—a picture of the set, drawn in perspective from the audience's point of view. The rendering shows most clearly what the stage will look like from the house. It is usually done in color and depicts the appearance of the set under lights.
- A **model**—a three-dimensional miniature version of the set, built to scale (usually one-quarter or one-half inch to the foot). A model has the advantage of allowing the director to experiment with spatial possibilities.

Some designers choose to do both renderings and a model; some choose one or the other.

When the design receives final approval from the director, the designer (or sometimes a designer's assistant) generates a series of working drawings to show how the scenery is to be built. These draftings may include the following:

- A **front elevation**—breaking the set into units to be built and showing each piece of scenery from the front.
- A **painter's elevation**—(in color) showing the plan for painting each piece of scenery.
- A **rear elevation**—showing each piece from the back. Rear elevations are particularly important in constructing the scenery, since a rear view may show how each piece of scenery is to be built.

DESIGNER'S RENDERING FOR SUDDENLY LAST SUMMER, which matches the ground plan. Here you can see the effect of the canopy, angled walls, and the decorations, which make it a gardenlike setting.

EXPLORING Collaboration

Robert Edmond Jones with Arthur Hopkins

In 1915 young Robert Edmond Jones had a design project for a forgettable one-act play entitled *The Man Who Married a Dumb Wife,* which appeared in an exhibition of new stagecraft designs in New York. Harley Granville-Barker, a visiting British director who was dedicated to principles of the new stagecraft, happened to see Jones's rendering. Granville-Barker was so taken by the set design that he decided to add a production of this play as a curtain-raiser for the season of plays he was bringing from England featuring work by Shakespeare and George Bernard Shaw. He hired the unknown Jones to design the set and costumes he had suggested in his rendering. This unplanned production set in motion a remarkable instant celebrity for the work of Jones, which sometimes outshone the plays he was designing.

Granville-Barker's production caught the attention of another innovative director, Arthur Hopkins, an American who was fascinated with European experiments. Hopkins quickly established a long-term artistic relationship with Jones, beginning later in 1915 with a production of *The Devil's Garden* by Edith Ellis. From this point until 1934, these two masterful theatre artists collaborated on at least forty-one productions. Jones always designed the sets and usually lighting and costumes as well. Although Hopkins and Jones often worked with other people, they clearly had an affinity for one another's methods and complete trust in their artistic collaboration.

The glory years were the 1920s, when they collaborated on realistic plays, fantasies, expressionism, modern comedy, and classical tragedy; they might have set a Broadway record in the period for the number of plays they produced written by women playwrights, such as Sophie Treadwell. Their production of Treadwell's *Machinal* (1928) was the last important presentation of American expressionism before the decline of that strident style that always featured a chronically disturbed central character on the brink of psychic disaster.

In their presentation of comedy of manners and intrigue, they had no equals as they presented glib, character-driven whimsy and social commentary such as *Good Gracious, Annabelle* (1916) by Clare Kummer and *Holiday* (1928) by Philip Barry. They presented these plays realistically, but the realism was always simplified and streamlined, without the more typical approach to extravagant detail for interior scenes. This simplified realism was also used in their interpretations of Ibsen's plays such as *Hedda Gabler* and *The Wild Duck* (both in 1917) starring Alla Nazimova just as this Russian actress was emerging as an American star. The Hopkins/Jones production of Eugene O'Neill's *Anna Christie* (1921) was one of the most successful commercial

RENDERING OF HAMLET by William Shakespeare designed by Jones for a 1922 production starring John Barrymore and directed by Arthur Hopkins. This multilevel space suggests the grandeur of a vast palace, but it also creates dynamic silhouettes and multiple playing levels. Huge curtains could be drawn to close off the archway when desired.

From *The Theatre of Robert Edmond Jones.* Collection of the authors.

productions of early selective realism in the history of the American theatre. Although audiences and critics marveled at the perfect evocation of a pre–World War I barroom, many of the details that are so common to realistic staging were simplified and replaced by atmospheric lighting and gritty interior walls and windows. Jones and Hopkins managed to make dirty and grimy space look alluring.

Perhaps their most famous work occurred with their revivals of Shakespeare featuring the famous Barrymore siblings: John in *Richard III* (1920) and *Hamlet* (1922), Lionel in *Macbeth* (1921), and Ethel in *Romeo and Juliet* (1922). All of the settings for these multilocation plays were variations of a **unit set** (a single scenic unit used to represent many different locations). These productions were inspired by unit-set experiments in Europe, but Jones and Hopkins gave them personal interpretations that have remained important to the history of American theatre.

INTERESTED? Check out

Ralph Pendleton. *The Theatre of Robert Edmond Jones.* Middletown, CT: Wesleyan University, 1958.

Ronald H. Wainscott. *Staging O'Neill: The Experimental Years, 1920–1934.* New Haven, CT: Yale University, 1988.

Arthur Hopkins. *Reference Point.* New York: Samuel French, 1948.

Robert Edmond Jones. *The Dramatic Imagination.* New York: Theatre Arts, 1941; New York: Routledge, 2004.

These documents allow the designer to communicate his or her vision to others on the production staff. Traditionally drafted by hand, the drawings can now be generated with greater accuracy, efficiency, and flexibility for changes by using computer imaging. While creating the draftings, the designer establishes **sight lines**—in other words, determines what the audience can and cannot see. Anything that is visible but should not be (the top of a piece of scenery, for example, or backstage space) is hidden with **masking**—black velour draperies or flats that can be hung or placed vertically and horizontally across the stage.

Executing the Scenic Design

The set designer develops plans and makes the artistic choices but relies on technical staff for execution. Throughout the building of the set, the designer communicates frequently with the technical director. The **technical director** is responsible for the safety of the theatre space, for scheduling, for construction and equipment installation, and for making sure designs are executed according to the designer's specifications. As someone with a great deal of technical and practical knowledge, the technical director serves as problem solver. The technical director oversees the transfer and setup of scenery and props into the stage space.

When sets are built onsite, a **scene shop foreman** oversees their construction by a crew of carpenters, scenic painters, and other craftspeople. Commercial productions without a home theatre send designs to special scene shops for construction and then transfer the items to the performance space just before technical rehearsals. The **props manager** organizes the collection or building of all properties in the show.

The scenic designer keeps in close touch with the technical staff during the building process and participates actively in technical rehearsals—watching how the set functions, taking notes about changes that need to be made, and conferring with the technical director.

A DESIGNER'S WHITE MODEL FOR LITTLE WOMEN, an intimate opera by Mark Adamo. Models are very useful for the director and other designers to see the space in three dimensions as the prerehearsal preparations are taking place. This is especially true of multilevel spaces like this one. Some directors also like to have a model present in the rehearsal room where it can be helpful to the actors until they have the real setting. Scenic design and model construction by Fred M. Duer for a production at Summer Opera Theatre, Washington, DC, and Opera Delaware, Wilmington, DE (2007–2008). Originally directed by David Grindle.

Design and photo by and courtesy of Fred M. Duer.

THE COMPLETED SETTING FOR LITTLE WOMEN in performance. Compare the model with the finished production set.

Design and photo by and courtesy of Fred M. Duer.

The union for professional designers is United Scenic Artists of America. In the professional theatre, technical positions are staffed by members of the International Alliance of Theatrical Stage Employees, Moving Picture Technicians, Artists, and Allied Crafts of the United States, Its Territories and Canada, the labor union representing technicians, artisans, and craftspeople in the entertainment industry. Strict rules about working time and job descriptions protect the livelihood of these professionals. A carpenter, for example, is not allowed to refocus a lighting instrument; an electrician may not hammer a nail. In amateur theatre, where the rules are less stringent, volunteers typically pitch in to do the work, often supervised by a professional. Students working for class credit and experience are directed by faculty and staff in educational theatres. Many people who are not interested in performing find fun and fulfillment in working behind the scenes.

THE LIGHTING DESIGNER'S WORK

DUET BETWEEN PERFORMER AND COMPUTER generated lighting and projection. We see a live performer being recorded digitally with the image somewhat abstracted and projected behind the performer with a slight delay. The audience sees the performer in real time with a projection of the essence of what the performer executed a moment earlier. *The Nature of Human.* Interactive video and lighting design by Robert Shakespeare. Ruth N. Halls Theatre, Indiana University, 2008.

Design and photo by and courtesy of Robert Shakespeare.

To a casual observer, the work of the lighting designer is sometimes the least noticeable in a production, yet all the other visual elements depend on it. Lighting, at its most basic, provides visibility and manipulates that visibility by supporting the moment-to-moment action of the play. Much of the lighting task is about revealing. Lighting the actors is crucial in most productions; audiences can lose interest quickly if they cannot see the faces of the performers. Because lighting can radically change the mood of a production and the look of costumes, set, and properties, lighting designers must work very closely with all of their colleagues.

The installation of gas lighting in the early nineteenth century made systematic control of theatrical lighting possible; a technician could change intensity on the stage or in the house by moving one lever. The open flame of the gas and the possibility of explosion, however, made gas a dangerous addition to theatres. A fireman became a part of the theatre's staff, meant to remain on duty in case of emergency even when the theatre was empty. The invention of the long-lasting incandescent light bulb by Thomas Edison and others by 1879 and its subsequent refinement for the theatre made the concept of actually designing lighting possible. Early electric lighting systems were still dangerous and caused numerous theatre fires, but perfection of the technology led to increased safety and flexibility for the theatre artists. Many early directors took full charge of lighting, as did many scenic designers in the early days of electric light. By the 1920s directors and scenic designers often argued over the right to light the production. As technology developed and the many possibilities became evident, lighting became a design component in its own right. Most lighting designers today tend to specialize in lighting alone, and a number of lighting teams have emerged in the last few decades.

Changing Space with Lighting

Aesthetic distance and spatial relationships are manipulated by uses of light or the absence of light. The sun was the only light for theatre in classical Greece and Rome, and the sun does not necessarily cooperate with human artistic plans. Indoor theatres of the seventeenth and eighteenth centuries used candles and oil lamps, which established mood and general illumination, but provided little variety despite many attempts by artists to manipulate it. Gaslight generated an enormous amount of heat and discomfort for the audience, especially in the balconies. Through all of these periods, however, until late in the nineteenth century, the audience was always lit. A major shift occurred when theatre practitioners began dimming the house lights, accentuating the separation between performance and viewing space. We are so accustomed now to sitting in the darkened house watching a brightly lit stage that many outdoor theatres are used at night so that the audience can be in darkness and the stage can be lit. This dynamic does as much as any other element of the theatre space in terms of manipulating aesthetic distance.

Creating Movement and Mood with Lighting

Lighting designers have many tasks. One of the most important, of course, is lighting the actors and the action so that they can be seen clearly, but this is not a simple matter. Lighting must be used to mold the human face and figure. In a stage flooded with light, it may still be difficult to see the actors clearly unless shadows in some areas make the three dimensions of the face and body apparent. Lighting can make the human form and face look ugly or beautiful, flat or three-dimensional. Low-angle lighting set below the horizon (such as footlights) can create stark, disturbing images or ghostly faces (shadows rise from below). Likewise, high-angle or "down light" can suggest mystery or anonymity in the face with shadows moving downward from an actor or object.

Lighting can create primary and secondary focus. Actors are nearly always lit with more intensity than the scenery. On an otherwise dimly lit stage, an actor in a spotlight will attract the gaze of the audience members. If an empty area is suddenly illuminated, the audience expects something to happen in that space soon. Lighting can set objects and actors in relief—pull them out of the stage picture—or blend them in. Lighting also hides or minimizes some stage elements until they become the focus of the dramatic moment. A particular chair might have been visible during an entire scene, but just before a murder takes place at that chair, the lighting could grow brighter on that piece of furniture and dimmer on the rest of the stage. A traditional way of making a performer seem to appear out of nowhere is actually a lighting effect. The performer stands behind a **scrim**—a translucent piece of fabric. When lit from the front, the scrim appears opaque (solid). When the scrim lighting is extinguished and the actor behind it is lit, the scrim seems to disappear, and the performer becomes visible.

Lighting helps to create mood, and the orchestration of lighting can modify, sustain, or eliminate the mood. A dimly lit stage can create a somber atmosphere, whereas pleasingly bright lighting suggests happiness or stability. If the lighting becomes very intense, however, it can suggest an institutional setting, sterility, or perhaps threat or unseen power.

Sometimes lighting is used as a representational tool that heightens the sense of reality. Stage lighting can imitate sun or moonlight, depending on its color. Audiences tend to read blue lighting as moonlight. Even though the light of the moon is not really blue, the color suggests moonlight on stage. Light at noon seems to come from directly overhead. In late afternoon the angle of light is nearly horizontal: Objects can be brightly lit on one side and dark on the other, throwing them into relief. These effects can be suggested onstage by adjusting the angle and intensity of the lighting instruments. Producer-director David Belasco spent much of his production preparation time in the early twentieth century perfecting realistic lighting effects, some of which became famous. In *Madame Butterfly* (the play in 1900, not the opera), Belasco

ARTISTS of the THEATRE

Jules Fisher and Peggy Eisenhauer

Jules Fisher as a very young man in 1963 found himself creating lighting designs for Broadway productions. He lit five Broadway shows in his first season, beginning with *Spoon River Anthology,* and has continued to light over 200 Broadway and Off-Broadway productions. Since 1985, most of those have been in collaboration with his lighting partner Peggy Eisenhauer, under the name Third Eye, Ltd. Fisher was lured to lighting through his fascination with science and magic; Eisenhauer first found the theatre through dance. Both designers were educated at Carnegie-Mellon, although many years apart. In fact, Eisenhauer was first influenced to follow the path of lighting design when she witnessed Fisher's stunning work for the musical *Pippin* (1972)—when she was but 13.

Before their collaboration ensued some of Fisher's most famous productions included *The Subject Was Roses* (1964), the first production of *Hair* (1968), *Jesus Christ Superstar* (1971), and *La Cage aux Folles* (1983). Together their highlights include the Tony award–winning *Angels in America* (1993), *Ragtime* (1998), *Gypsy* (2003), *Assassins* (2004), and *A Free Man of Color* (2010).

BRING IN 'DA NOISE, BRING IN 'DA FUNK (1996), a musical sensation by Reg E. Gaines et al. Conceived and directed by George C. Wolfe; scenic design by Riccardo Hernandez. Winner of Tony awards for Fisher and Eisenhauer.

Photo © Michal Daniel.

For lighting of the musical *Jane Eyre* (2000) they created one of their most complex and intriguing designs. It required full mechanical integration with a large revolving stage, flying and gliding scenery, and a circular light bridge that turned with or sometimes independently of the stage revolve. Many projections were shot through multiple scrims, creating fascinating distortions that corresponded to the emotional distress of the leading characters.

In a *Playbill* interview in 2005, Fisher and Eisenhauer explain that their main task as lighting designers is to climb inside the director's head and discover a visual expression of the director's interpretation and intent. They assert that their work is a complete act of collaboration without any claims of who accomplished what; they are a successful and unselfish, albeit very busy, team. Together they have lit at least thirty-four Broadway productions—not counting numerous lighting projects in other kinds of theatres, as well as TV, film, and concerts.

INTERESTED? Check out

Mervyn Rothstein. "A Life in the Theatre: Lighting Designers Jules Fisher and Peggy Eisenhauer," *Playbill,* June 2005. Also at www.playbill.com/features/article/93707.html

created an extended lighting sequence that imitated the passage of early evening through night to dawn as the protagonist sat on the stage waiting in vain for her lover to return.

Light can be combined with shadow and color to imitate a specific place. It often finishes the job begun by the setting, but lighting alone can alter the set in remarkable ways. At the turn of the twentieth century, designer Adolphe Appia was especially influential in describing and rendering possibilities for light and shadow. Utilizing open spaces, especially platforms and elevations, Appia created designs that featured strong contrasts, and he experimented with ways to create shadow dynamically in the theatrical space. Most of his work was on paper, since few theatre producers were ready at the time to pursue and finance Appia's vision, but the Swiss designer had many disciples in the decades after his work.

Like the other designers, lighting designers sometimes study and adapt techniques from the past. Footlights were standard equipment throughout the eras of candles, oil lamps, gas, and early electricity. They were positioned on the stage floor at the edge of the apron and were focused upward to light the actors. Early in the twentieth century, many designers started eliminating footlights; they were considered garish by many innovators and tended to cast strange shadows on the actors' faces. Footlights returned (often selectively for low-angle effects) late in the twentieth century. Kevin Adams, lighting designer for *Spring Awakening,* went far beyond harnessing lighting techniques from the past and combined nontheatrical elements from the environment as well as abstract elements. During the songs, the stage was filled with neon, bare bulbs, shafts of harsh light, and what the designer calls "sculptural light objects." In stark contrast, the nineteenth-century domestic scenes were lit very simply.[1]

The Lighting Designer's Tools

Lighting designers work with four basic elements:

- **Intensity** (how bright the lighting is)
- **Color**
- **Distribution** (how light is spread over the stage: angle and texture)
- **Orchestration** or **movement** (changes in any of the first three elements)

Intensity is controlled by the number of lumens pumped onto the stage, which depends on the number of lighting instruments used. *Color* is created by filtering the light with color media or color filters—translucent sheets of plastic (high heat polyester) or dichroic filters (tempered glass with metal coating) made in a wide range of colors and placed in front of lighting instruments. *Distribution* of light is determined by where lighting instruments are placed as well as the type of instruments used. Angle is an important part of distribution because it affects the mood and appearance of the actors as well as suggesting time of day. The location of each instrument (both horizontally and vertically) determines the angle at which its beam hits the stage, actors, or objects illuminated.

In controlling distribution, today's lighting designers can choose from a wide variety of instruments that are designed to do different jobs. The type of instrument that is used most frequently is a **spotlight.** Glass lenses create a focused and controllable beam of light, and various shaped metal and glass reflectors affect the quality of light and the shape of the beam. A **Fresnel** spotlight, for example, uses a lens adapted from nineteenth-century lighthouses (and takes its name from the man who invented it). This lens creates a beam of light with a soft edge, and the beams from different instruments can be easily blended to create the appearance of an even area of light. An **ellipsoidal** spotlight, in contrast, creates a hard-edged beam and includes four shutters around the circular lens to further control its focus; a shutter can be moved in to keep light away from a set wall, for example. **Par lamps** (parabolic aluminated reflectors) create parallel rays. Newer automated instruments can change all of the elements electronically; a single instrument may be able to change color, distribution, and intensity instantly.

Orchestration of lighting in today's theatre is accomplished by using the **lighting console,** a control board with a memory system. Many instruments can be hung on

CRIME AND PUNISHMENT adapted by Marilyn Campbell and Curt Columbus at the Berkeley Repertory Theatre in 2009. The shadow of the imaginary pursuer dwarfs the protagonist played by Tyler Pierce whose claustrophobic room is defined by walls and ceiling of doors. Scenic design by Christopher Barreca; lighting design by Stephen Strawbridge. Directed by Sharon Ott.

Photo © Kevin Berne.

stage and turned on or off only when they are needed. Intensity can be changed in any area throughout the show by adjusting one or any number of instruments. Color can be changed by intensifying instruments with one particular color filter and dimming others. With the creation of dimmers and lighting consoles in the twentieth century, designers developed complicated **crossfades,** which can be rapid or slow. Lengthy changes transform the space so subtly that the audience often doesn't notice until the change is nearly complete. A room growing dark near the end of the day, for example, might take twenty minutes. With the advent of lighting consoles it became possible to preprogram all of the **cues** (timed changes) sequentially (there are often hundreds in a busy show) so that mistakes by the console operator are minimized, and the cues can be precise each time.

Projections are often included in current lighting designs. A **projection** is an image thrown onto the stage using light. The simplest kind of projection uses a metal cutout like a stencil, called a **gobo** (also called a pattern or template). The gobo is inserted in a gate on an ellipsoidal spotlight, and the solid areas block the light, casting shadows on the stage. In this way, leaf patterns can be thrown on stage creating the image of a forest, bars suggesting a prison, or abstract shapes to create any number of effects. Some gobos are also combined with color filters and provide full-color images, not just shadow patterns. Photographs or abstract images on slides and transparencies can be projected on the stage, screens, and objects. At times projectors have even taken the place of or supplemented painted or three-dimensional scenery. Gobo rotators can create motion effects with the projected light.

DON JUAN GIOVANNI (2007), adapted from Molière and Mozart by Stephen Epps and Dominique Serrand, who also directed and created the scenography with lighting design by Marcus Dillard. Here we see a performed scene being captured simultaneously by video from another angle and projected on a screen behind the actors. Essentially, the audience sees two points of view at once.
Photo © Michal Daniel.

Lighting instruments themselves, as well as the consoles, have been improved markedly in the last few decades: more powerful and sophisticated lamps, automated instruments that can be refocused or set in motion while in the air, improvements in projectors enabling additional movement in the light thrown from the instruments, and laser lights. Peter Kaczorowski, who also designed *The Producers*, created almost continuous comic but dynamic laser and other lighting effects in *Young Frankenstein* (2007). In *The 39 Steps* (2008), a comic spoof on the Hitchcock thriller, Kevin Adams suggested film noir and the 1930s period with highly selective streaks of lighting to illuminate minimal settings along with strong silhouettes. In *The Pillowman* (2005), lighting designer Brian MacDevitt created unusual projected lighting imitating cartoonlike stained glass images. This illumination was combined with distorted and miniaturized scenic elements designed by Scott Pask for very colorful, humorous, but violent stage effects in the flashbacks and storytelling of the play. New developments appear each year, just like improvements in computer hardware and software.

Communicating and Executing the Lighting Design

When analyzing the play, the lighting designer will pay particular attention to the play's structure, mood, and all possibilities for orchestration of lighting. If the design is realistic, he or she will consider how the lighting can contribute to establishing time and place, as well as any practicals needed. A **practical** is a visible light source onstage that is often enhanced by unseen lighting instruments. For example, when a desk lamp or overhead chandelier onstage is turned on, light usually emanates from the practical, but accompanying instruments may punch up the effect and help to imitate and perhaps intensify the light thrown by the practical on the stage.

The lighting design process begins at the same time as other designs; the lighting designer meets with the director and production team regularly, and the lighting design evolves with the costumes, sets, and the director's staging, all of which usually continue to be refined until the production is ready to open.

The lighting designer faces a great challenge in trying to communicate his or her vision to the director and production staff, since lighting is the most ephemeral of the theatrical elements. Computer imaging now gives the designer a chance to preview the effectiveness of the lighting and share the effect with the whole creative team. Although not providing a perfect facsimile of the onstage effect, the computer allows the designer to provide a very good idea of what he or she plans to do. Sometimes lighting instruments are set up in a lighting lab to show actual effects in miniature. A costume designer, for example, could check the look of a fabric under the correct stage lighting.

The designer creates a technical drawing or **lighting plot** showing where each instrument is to be hung, along with the type of instrument and color filters to be used. Before technical rehearsals, a **master electrician** works closely with the lighting designer and directs a lighting crew to hang, focus, and filter the lighting instruments and to set up circuitry, the lighting console, and sometimes sound equipment also. In the early days of electric light, most designers sought to conceal the lighting instruments from the audience to create realistic effects (most people don't have stage lights in their living room). Throughout the twentieth century, especially when lighting musicals and presentational productions, many designers began to hang instruments in full view (from the balconies, sides of the house, or, as in Bertolt Brecht's theory, deliberately low above the stage) to call attention to the fact that the audience is in a theatre. Such practice has become so commonplace, however, that it no longer makes a statement. Frequently, a lighting or sound booth is erected in the house rather than

OEDIPUS THE KING by Sophocles employs a computer-generated lighting concept dominated by large shadows and grim mood. This is a moment in the play when the chorus on stage is awaiting the return of Oedipus from the palace since he learned the truth of his birth. Directed by Howard Jensen, Indiana University.

Lighting design by and courtesy of Robert Shakespeare.

OEDIPUS THE KING. The lighting concept image a few moments later in the play—the entrance of Oedipus after he has blinded himself—has switched to back and down light, framing him in the doorway. The lights focus on Oedipus, but the lighting also spills forward onto the stage, picking up the figures of the chorus as all of the actors and the lights focus on Oedipus.

Lighting design by and courtesy of Robert Shakespeare.

using a built-in booth, probably influenced by the practice in touring rock concerts where the operators have an audience view of the stage and can hear better than they could in a glass-fronted booth.

During tech week (the week of technical rehearsals), the director and designer sometimes choose to have a lighting rehearsal, in which the cues (changes in lighting, sound, or set) are constructed and run with no actors present. The director and designer can then look at the lighting onstage together and make adjustments. Stage management and technical staff often stand in for actors when it is important to see the effect of light on a human body. Actors are present for a **cue-to-cue** technical rehearsal, in which only the parts of the play that include cues are run; any dialogue or action in between is skipped. The stage manager organizes and runs the cue-to-cue. The designer and director then make adjustments, particularly in the timing of the cues, until the desired effect is achieved. A **technical rehearsal** (or tech run) follows, in which the stage manager, actors, and run crews practice putting all elements (except costumes) together in a complete run of the show. The lighting designer continues to work with the director, stage manager, and technical staff through **dress rehearsals,** refining and perfecting the contribution of lighting to the total production.

A successful lighting designer is a sensitive artist with a mastery of lighting technology. He or she must know the fundamentals of electricity but above all must be an artist who sculpts and paints with light and has a thorough understanding of the other design positions. Obviously, a good lighting designer must keep abreast of technological change. Computer skills are an important and fast-growing requirement for technicians in many of today's theatres. When budgets allow, automated lighting instruments, projections, and laser graphics may be added to more traditional technology, and designers must have an understanding of the full range of possibilities to serve the production well.

THE RIVALS (1775) by Richard Brinsley Sheridan. This light-hearted comedy of manners as produced by the Huntington Theatre Company in Boston in 2005 sets all of the action before a selective and emblematic façade suggesting the crescent architecture of Bath, England, where the play is set. The costumes use an eighteenth-century silhouette, but are color coded to match the prevailing moods of the characters, and feature simplified decorative detail which modernizes the costumes, giving them something of a cartoon-like presentation. Costumes designed by Michael Krass; scenic design by Alexander Dodge. Directed by Nicholas Martin.

Photo © T. Charles Erickson.

THE COSTUME DESIGNER'S WORK

Designing costumes became important when the theatre embraced historical accuracy and an overall artistic vision for production became the norm. The production team, rather than individual actors, then became responsible for providing costumes that harmonized with the other designs. Costumes can work with lighting and setting to establish the time period and location of the play. The designer must be conversant with various historical styles and forms of dress and have the necessary skills for research. Depending on the concept of the production, period costumes may be altered or abstracted. If historical accuracy is not a part of concept, the designer is free to create an imaginary style appropriate to the concept.

Beyond expressing concept and establishing the world of the play, costumes become a critical part of the audience's reception and understanding of the characters. A character who first appears in a red satin gown will suggest a different set of associations than one who appears in a ragged homespun dress. In analyzing the play, a costume designer pays particular attention to the physical needs of the character. If one character must dance the night away, the design choices are different from those made for a character who sits rigidly on a wooden stool most of the time. The designer analyzes character as well. Socioeconomic status is an important consideration in how the character dresses, as well as basic personality. An outgoing character might wear bright colors and unusual styles; a retiring character might choose dark colors and conservative styles. Changes in social status or psychological state can be expressed graphically through changes in costume.

THE WAY OF THE WORLD (1700) by William Congreve is here interpreted with historically accurate costumes to evoke the rich fabrics and busy designs of the Restoration era in England. Costume design by Jane Greenwood; directed by Michael Kahn in 2008 for the Shakespeare Theatre Company of Washington, DC. Photo © Carol Rosegg.

The Costume in Space

The costume designer communicates from the beginning with the other designers as well as the director, although costume choices may evolve as other design elements evolve. When it comes to colors, textures, fabric choices, and finishing details, designers and director often negotiate so that the furniture, for example, does not clash with the costumes or, in some cases, does not erase the costumes, since the color and texture nearly match. The costume designer must also be acutely aware of lighting, because the stage lighting could severely alter or destroy the image a costume designer is seeking. It is important that the costume, scenic, and lighting designers communicate frequently about choices.

Distance on the stage is also critical to costume design choices. If the designer is creating a costume that will never be closer to the audience than thirty feet from the front row, the choices will be considerably different than if a costume will be seen mostly on the apron or down center. Directors must communicate such staging to the designer, and most designers periodically attend rehearsals to see such distances as well as the physical action of the actors. If a director has an actor rolling about the floor in an expensive wedding dress, as could occur in the Polish play *Tango* by Slawomir Mrozek, or several actresses in wedding dresses who must kill their bridegrooms with daggers and get very bloody in the process as in Charles L. Mee's *Big Love,* the designer needs to know.

Communicating and Executing the Costume Design

A costume designer begins by showing the director quick sketches that are meant to express basic ideas and offer choices. The director may approve, reject, or ask to see additional development. When the designer and director seem to have reached agreement as to basic approach, the designer produces costume **renderings**—pictures of the costumes on the actors. Ideally, a rendering is done for each costume in color, often with appropriate swatches of fabric attached.

In creating each design, the costume designer works with four variables:

- **Silhouette.** Silhouette or line is the outer shape of the costume. It is easy to understand silhouette if you think of a costume as a shadow on the wall; no color and no detail are visible, just the basic shape. Silhouette is particularly indicative of time period and culture. The draped and gathered cloth of the Indian sari creates a particular female silhouette. A tight-fitting bodice, tight waist, and skirt flaring out, stopping midway between knee and ankle, make up a typical silhouette from the United States in the 1950s. The profile of an upper-class woman from Europe or the United States in the 1860s to 1880s would reveal a floor-length skirt with a bustle (large protrusion) over the rear end.

- **Color.** Different colors tend to create different emotional responses in human beings. The designer thinks not only about the effect that a particular color will have on the audience, but also about the message that it sends about the character who chose to wear it. The designer must also understand that symbolic associations with color are culturally specific; white (symbolizing purity) is traditional for weddings in the United States, but red (symbolizing good luck) is appropriate for weddings in China.

- **Texture.** Texture is the "feel" of the fabric. Even if an audience member never touches the cloth, the sense of sight gives information about how a fabric feels. Fine, smooth fabrics such as thin silk and satin tend to suggest sophistication. Soft, rich fabrics such as brocade and velvet suggest wealth. Rougher fabric—homespun, for example—can suggest low status or hard times. Associations with texture are also culturally specific; in the United States during the 1930s and 1940s denim was considered a working man's fabric and was associated with manual labor; denim is currently fashionable for many people no matter what the activity or social status.

- **Accent.** Accents are details to finish or set off a costume. Buttons, lace, piping along edges, embroidery, and jewelry are all examples of accent. A woman's dress in a peach color might be accented with large black buttons down the front or a single rhinestone brooch at the shoulder. A single red rose in the lapel of a man's black jacket is a striking accent.

Commercial or touring productions without a home theatre send the designs to a professional costume shop for construction. For productions in an established theatre, the costume designer will choose to build costumes from scratch, buy them, rent them, or pull them from stock (i.e., choose from items that already exist in the theatre's costume collection). Availability of funds and building time are critical, and the costume designer must consider the expense of fabrics and other materials. The size and experience of the staff influence the designer's choices, especially in educational theatre, where students are largely responsible for costume construction.

The costume designer works closely with the **costume shop manager,** who coordinates the efforts of cutters, stitchers, and other costume personnel. Items

WHIMSICAL COSTUME for the character Feste in *Twelfth Night* by William Shakespeare. Compare the costume rendering to the realized costume, shown on the completed setting. Produced at Iowa State University. Costume design and photos by and courtesy of Linda Pisano.

pulled from stock must be altered to fit specific actors and might be dyed or changed to achieve the appropriate look. Building a costume from scratch is a labor-intensive process that involves taking the actor's measurements, drafting a pattern, cutting, sewing, and fitting the garment on the actor. The designer often works closely with the costume shop personnel to achieve the look reflected in the original rendering.

Costume designers are sometimes responsible for more than clothing. They design makeup and masks unless a separate designer is assigned those duties. Purses, hats, and shoes must be found or created to coordinate with each costume. The craft area of a costume shop is often a busy place, with shop personnel making or trimming hats, constructing masks, making armor, and fashioning jewelry.

Early in the design process the designer creates a **costume plot,** a chart that records items of clothing worn by each actor in each scene of the play. For small shows it is fairly simple, but for large-cast shows with multiple or quick costume changes, the costume plot is especially important for organization. Finished costumes are usually the final visual element added to production. During tech week some directors like to have a costume parade: Actors are dressed in costumes and appear under the appropriate stage lights. The director and designer discuss any changes that ought to be made. At the first dress rehearsal the actors wear and use all the items created for them while performing the entire play. Ideally, actors will have used substitutes during rehearsals for any items that would cause major

ARTISTS of the THEATRE

William Ivey Long

William Ivey Long grew up in the theatre. Both of his parents were active in the theatre in Chapel Hill, North Carolina, and he spent many hours with the artists of the Carolina Playmakers, the repertory company of the University of North Carolina. William Ivey Long studied American history at the College of William and Mary and later architectural history at the University of North Carolina. He returned to theatre by enrolling in the Yale School of Drama to study costume and set design.

Long has designed over fifty Broadway shows, including both plays and musicals. His first Broadway design was for a 1978 revival of the nineteenth-century Russian play *The Inspector General;* after that, he designed the musical *The 1940s Radio Hour* (1979). Since the 1980s he has designed many of Broadway's most successful musicals. He won Tony awards for *Nine* (1982), *Crazy for You* (1992), *The Producers* (2001), and *Hairspray* (2002). In 2005 his costume designs for the revivals of the play *A Streetcar Named Desire* (2005) and the musical *La Cage aux Folles* (2004) received Tony nominations. That same season Long had six shows running at the same time on Broadway. His recent projects include *Pal Joey* (2008) and *Catch Me If You Can* (2011).

Long's style of costume varies widely with the type of show and the concept of each director. The look of sleek black leotards in the revival of *Chicago* (1996) is quite different from the atmosphere he created for *Hairspray* (2002), with its brightly colored 1950s costumes. In Sam Mendes's 1997 revival of *Cabaret,* Long created ratty, sexually suggestive costumes that became almost scenic in the shabby chic of the Berlin club environment designed by Robert Brill. Frequently, both settings and costumes were dominated by grays and blacks, which prepared the audience

SKIMPY, CRUDE COSTUMES designed by William Ivey Long for the cabaret girls in the Roundabout Theatre Company production of *Cabaret* (1997) directed by Sam Mendes. Depicted here is Natasha Richardson as Sally Bowles with members of the chorus singing directly to the audience (many of whom were sitting at cabaret tables).

Photo © Joan Marcus.

for the Holocaust image at production's end. These deliberately ugly costumes were a stark contrast to Long's flashy, stylish costumes in the musical *Contact* (1999) and his playful designs for *The Producers* (2001) and *Young Frankenstein* (2007). Yet in all four productions he helped to create different levels of the erotic—from the dangerous and forbidden in *Cabaret,* to the steamy and sensual in *Contact,* to the farcical and silly in *The Producers* and *Young Frankenstein.*

changes in movement. Rehearsal skirts, for example, are frequently used to approximate long skirts of earlier periods; if corsets are to be worn, the actors must work with them early to learn how to adjust breathing and movement. Actors who are unused to wearing shoes with high heels must learn to walk in them. Despite the best planning, there are always some surprises related to costumes when they are put in the context of the total production and adjustments need to be made. The designer, director, actor, and costume shop collaborate to solve problems and ensure costumes that are both appropriate to the concept and workable for the actor before opening night.

ARABIAN NIGHTS (1994), conceived and directed by Mary Zimmerman and reworked for more than a decade. Produced here at the Berkeley Repertory Theatre in 2010. Playful, cartoon-like costumes and performances highlighted parts of this production with costumes designed by Mara Blumenfeld.

Photo © Kevin Berne.

Meeting the Challenge

Costume designers must contribute to concept and sometimes find dynamic ways to either call attention to the costumes or lead the audience to accept them as a natural part of the entire environment and period suggested. For *The Oedipus Plays* (2001), directed by Michael Kahn at the Shakespeare Theatre in Washington, DC, designer Toni-Leslie James drew on traditional African tribal costume, especially in fabric patterns, and maintained earth tones throughout. The three choruses were distinct as types but included variety among the participants. The design for *The Oedipus Plays* was a remarkably different task from James's design for *Angels in America* (1993), which featured late twentieth-century dress or the funky costumes of *Jelly's Last Jam* (1992). Catherine Zuber has regularly designed successfully for musicals and plays that call for radically different design tasks. She created the understated clerical costumes for *Doubt* (2004), the lyrical but authentic 1950s costumes of *The Light in the Piazza* (2005), as well as the flashy period costumes of *Dracula, the Musical* (2004), and colorful, period-inspired costumes for Shakespeare's *Twelfth Night* (1998) at Lincoln Center.

Realistic plays or plays evoking periods from long ago often present interesting challenges, especially if the cast is large. Designer Andreane Neofitou is quite adept at both period and large-cast challenges, having worked often for the Royal Shakespeare Company and created the costumes for *Les Misérables* (1985) and *Jane Eyre* (2000). Especially when working on these and other productions with set designer John Napier, who often creates high-tech environments with minimal historical detail, Neofitou must suggest the visual sense of period with costumes. By contrast, Oana Botez-Ban, the costume designer for *Richard III* (2007) at the Classic Stage Company, created costumes with a period silhouette, but little of the fabric detail that would occur in real clothes of the period. The title character always wore black, while bright, jewel-toned costumes for the surrounding characters were color-coded to indicate family relationships and political alignments. Without help, such character identifications can be very confusing in this play, especially when nearly all of the cast is doubling.

For some shows, costume designers must create a fantasy period—either a futuristic vision, a hybrid of different periods, or a completely fabricated past that never existed. The latter is what designer Norman Bel Geddes, for example, created for the *The Miracle* (1924), an imaginative medieval epic. Tim Hatley designed a Monty Python take on the medieval period for *Spamalot*. By contrast, Hatley also designed realistic Puritan costumes for the 2002 revival of *The Crucible.*

THE SOUND DESIGNER'S WORK

Until just before the Great Depression, sound effects and music in the theatre were created live by technicians or musicians. Some well-equipped theatres from the Elizabethans to the nineteenth century featured machines such as thunder runs, wooden troughs in the floor above the stage level or even over the house into which heavy balls could be rolled to create the rumbling effect of thunder. A more traditional approach was the thunder sheet—a large sheet of metal that a stagehand could strike or shake to mimic the rolling and crashing of thunder.

A COSTUME DESIGN by Norman Bel Geddes for Max Reinhardt's 1924 production of *The Miracle.* The rendering represents the executioner. Although the executioner is a sinister character, Bel Geddes's cartoonlike approach mellows the threat of the character. The eye motif on the costume is repeated in other characters as well.
Collection of the authors.

Recorded sound was first used in the production of Elmer Rice's *Street Scene* in 1929, which featured the nearly constant sound of a busy New York street. Obviously, recording and playback methods since that time have become very sophisticated thanks to high-speed techniques, audio mixing and editing, computerized sound consoles, and digital recording. Productions still use live music of course, and sometimes sound effects are created live, but aside from musicals, most sound in the theatre is now recorded. Even the dance musical *Contact* used recorded music, although this was unusual for commercial musical theatre.

Many theatre companies used to relegate sound design and sound engineering to the lighting design area, but since the 1980s sound design has emerged as an independent and dynamic part of the design process. When analyzing the script, the sound designer looks particularly for any ambient sound that is suggested (crickets chirping, music from a nearby carnival) as well as effects that are important to the action of the play (an offstage car crash, a train passing, gunfire). The director and designer sometimes decide on effects that are not called for in the script to support mood or suggest action happening offstage. Many prerecorded sound effects have long been available on records, tapes, and compact disks. Computer software now allows designers to retrieve, create, and digitally modify various kinds of sound effects.

Music is frequently called for in scripts that are not considered musicals, and directors sometimes add music as background, underscoring, or as bridges for scene changes or to prepare the audience before the action begins on stage. Music can establish time period and can be a powerful tool in creating atmosphere. If reviving a realistic play from the 1940s, such as *A Streetcar Named Desire* (1947) by Tennessee Williams, or the 1950s, such as *Picnic* (1953) by William Inge, the designer may compile underscoring or scene shift pieces from period pop music to instantly connect the audience to the time of the action. Alternatively, a composer may be hired to work with the sound designer to create music that sounds like music from the era represented in the play. In the simplest model for this kind of sound work, the director and designer often work together in selecting appropriate music for a show; the designer finds and records the music. Some sound designers are also composers.

For many musicals since the 1960s actors wear wireless body mikes (microphones) and sometimes headsets, as in *Rent* (1996). In most cases body mikes are hidden from view in costumes, but usually close to the face. In *Avenue Q,* for example, mikes were attached to hair, hats, and wigs. Such an amplification system must be created or adapted by the sound designer. Especially with the advent of rock musicals and the introduction of electronic musical instruments not only to rock but also to many styles of music, the electronic control of sound became vital to performance. The theatre's debt to the rock music industry is great in this regard. Sound designers of rock musicals with impressive results include Bart Fasbender in *Bloody Bloody Andrew Jackson* (2010), and Brian Ronan for *American Idiot* (2010), perhaps the loudest theatre musical we have ever encountered. Accomplished sound designers are in demand for nearly any kind of play. Tony Meola, for example, has designed sound for radically different styles of plays such as *The Lion King* (1997), *Copenhagen* (2000), and *Wicked* (2003). Paul Arditti's sound design, combined with the music of Paddy Cunneen, was effectively creepy and mood-setting in *The Pillowman* (2005). Brian Ronan's sound design for *Spring Awakening* (2006) was especially impressive due to the rapid and frequent stylistic shifts throughout the production.

A RENDERING OF THE CHARACTER MERCUTIO in a production of *Romeo and Juliet* as designed by Linda Pisano at the Indiana Repertory Theatre in 2004. The production period is obviously updated. Note the fabric swatches attached to the design. This is typical in order to share textures and fabric choices with the director, other designers, and the actors as the production is being prepared. The seals on the bottom right of the rendering indicate that the designer is a member of the IATSE union. The director was Priscilla Lindsay.

Design and photo by and courtesy of Linda Pisano.

INTEGRATING ALL THE DESIGNS

Designers work closely with the director to meld their contributions into an artistic whole. The task becomes increasingly complex yet exciting as technology opens up new possibilities. The pursuit of increased specialization and continued reading and learning in the field must be balanced with the need for the designers to communicate and negotiate with other production personnel. Besides the give-and-take required with directors, designers must consider the actors; no design choice is successful if it is not functional for those who are walking on the set, dancing in the costumes, or delivering a speech while facing a bright light. Sometimes the lines of design responsibility are blurred; a special lighting effect (such as a neon sign) might form an important element in set design; a property sometimes becomes a costume, or a costume becomes a property. In *Mad Forest* (1990) by Caryl Churchill, for example, a large Romanian flag with the crest cut out is pulled down and worn by a character. In *Long Day's Journey into Night* (1956) by Eugene O'Neill, an old woman enters the room at the climax in a morphine stupor, carrying her faded wedding dress. Such events often lead to interesting discussions in design meetings about whose responsibility it is to create such a costume/prop. The skills necessary to communicate consistently and unambiguously are as important to successful design as are visual or aural sensitivity and talent.

In some cases when integrating the designs, one person might try to do it all. In 1924, for example, one of America's most talented designers, Robert Edmond Jones, not only directed the first production of Eugene O'Neill's *Desire under the Elms* but also designed the sets, costumes, and lighting. Sound designers had not yet come onto the scene. One could imagine whimsical design conferences at which Jones sat at a table talking to himself.

CHAPTER REVIEW

Questions and Activities

1. Discuss the set design for a show you have seen. Was the approach representational or presentational? Did it depict a particular location? How did the set contribute to the mood or atmosphere of the show? What did it tell you about the setting or characters?

2. Discuss the costume designs for a show you have seen. What did the costumes tell you about the individual characters? Did the costumes suggest a time and place? How did they contribute to the mood or atmosphere of the show? Were costumes and makeup representational or presentational?

3. Discuss the lighting design for a show you have seen. What did you notice the most about the lighting onstage? Did it seem to come from a realistic source? Did it seem to suggest location? Did the lighting change as the action of the play progressed? How did it affect the mood or atmosphere of the show?

4. Discuss the sound design for a show you have seen. Was there preshow music or sound (while the audience was being seated, before the show started)? How did it affect your expectations? Were there sound effects or music in the play? Did it/they serve a realistic purpose? Was sound used to help the flow of the show? Was there music under the actors' curtain call? What mood did it suggest?

Key Terms and Concepts

raked stage, p. 203
skene, p. 204
orchestra, p. 204
pinakes, p. 204
periaktoi, p. 204
wing, drop, and border scenery, p. 205
ground row, p. 207
box set, p. 207
antiquarianism, p. 207
revolve, p. 209
representational, p. 210
fourth wall, p. 210
presentational, p. 211
metatheatre, p. 213
given circumstances, p. 216
ground plan, p. 216
section, p. 216
rendering, p. 216

model, p. 216
front elevation, p. 217
painter's elevation, p. 217
rear elevation, p. 217
unit set, p. 218
sight lines, p. 219
masking, p. 219
technical director, p. 219
scene shop foreman, p. 219
props manager, p. 219
scrim, p. 221
intensity, p. 223
color, p. 223
distribution, p. 223
orchestration or movement, p. 223
spotlight, p. 223
Fresnel, p. 223
ellipsoidal, p. 223
par lamp, p. 223

lighting console, p. 223
crossfade, p. 224
cue, p. 224
projection, p. 224
gobo, p. 224
practical, p. 225
lighting plot, p. 225
master electrician, p. 225
cue-to-cue, p. 227
technical rehearsal, p. 227
dress rehearsal, p. 227
rendering, p. 229
silhouette, p. 229
color, p. 229
texture, p. 229
accent, p. 229
costume shop manager, p. 229
costume plot, p. 230

For Further Exploration

Joslin McKinney and Philip Butterworth. *The Cambridge Introduction to Scenography*. New York: Cambridge University Press, 2009.

Oscar G. Brockett, Margaret Mitchell and Linda Hardberger. *Making the Scene: A History of Stage Design and Technology in Europe and the United States*. San Antonio, TX: Tobin Theatre Arts Fund, 2010.

J. Michael Gillette. *Theatrical Design and Production,* 6th ed. New York: McGraw-Hill, 2007.

W. Oren Parker, R. Craig Wolf and Dick Block. *Scene Design and Stage Lighting,* 9th ed. New York: Wadsworth Publishing, 2008.

Arnold Aronson. *American Set Design*. New York: Theatre Communications Group, 1985.

Ronn Smith. *American Set Design 2*. New York: Theatre Communications Group, 1991.

Richard Pilbrow. *Stage Lighting Design*. New York: Quite Specific Media Group, 2000.

Richard H. Palmer. *The Lighting Art: The Aesthetics of Stage Lighting Design*. 2nd ed. Englewood Cliffs. NJ: Prentice Hall, 1994.

Lynn Pecktal. *Costume Design: Techniques of Modern Masters*. New York: Back Stage Books, 1999.

Deena Kaye and James LeBrecht. *Sound and Music for the Theatre,* 3rd ed. New York: Focal Press, 2009.

Robert Viagas, Ed. *The Alchemy of Theatre—The Divine Science: Essays on Theatre and the Art of Collaboration*. New York: Applause Books, 2006. Essays by theatre artists, including designers.

The International Alliance of Theatrical Stage Employees website at www.iatse-intl.org

Website of practicing designer, Fred M. Duer: www.indiana.edu/~fmdesign

MONUMENT erected by Lysikrates, a producer (choregos) of prize-winning plays in the Dionysian festival in Athens, Greece (c. 334 B.C.E). It is the only such monument surviving from the hundreds that once adorned the city of Athens. 2010 photo © Ronald Wainscott.

The Producer

Coordination, Promotion, Economics

All of the artists of the theatre might create a wonderful play and production, but providing the funding, getting all of these artists together, finding an appropriate audience and performance space, and promoting the productions usually falls to a producer, a collection of producers, or a producing and promotional organization. This chapter examines the work of the producer, the process of getting the audience and the production together, and the economics of the theatre in the United States.

EARLY PRODUCERS

Just as someone has usually been in charge of the performance of a play, someone has typically been in charge of producing a play, or managing a theatre company. In ancient Greece the civic government and religious priests coordinated the production of plays with an annual spring festival honoring the god Dionysus. Rome often had a manager (*dominus grex*) in charge of the acting company, and many professional companies from the sixteenth century on in Europe, America, China, and Japan had a company manager who was sometimes an actor (like Molière in France), a financial manager (like Philip Henslowe in England), or a playwright (like Li Yu in China). These managers did not just make artistic decisions, but hired and fired, controlled the financial fortunes of the company, and promoted either specific productions or a season of plays. Such managerial, funding, and economic responsibilities in the contemporary theatre usually fall to a producer, artistic director, or executive director (other labels are sometimes used for them as well). The most well-known producers typically work in the commercial professional theatre, but they are also usually necessary in nonprofit resident theatres, community theatres, even some academic theatres.

THE ROLE OF THE PRODUCER

The person who is most responsible for getting an audience and show together is the **producer**—the person in charge of all financial aspects of production. In nonprofit theatres the job title is often **managing director.** Whatever the title, the producer must collaborate with theatre artists as well as the general public. The job requires finely developed organizational and persuasive skills as well as a thorough understanding of finance. Producing responsibilities may be taken on by one person, or they may be shared by a group.

Producing in Commercial Theatre

An independent commercial production such as a Broadway or Off-Broadway show typically begins with a producer. This position has a long history, but the current commercial producer is often based on a nineteenth-century model. In the late nineteenth century producer-directors such as Augustin Daly and David Belasco created powerful organizations dedicated to careful, detailed single productions of plays that were intended to turn a profit. By 1896 a collection of businessmen who were not artists organized the Theatrical Syndicate to control haphazard professional touring and did so very effectively. The Syndicate, however, also created a monopoly with theatre ownership and control of actors and playwrights, who were not yet organized as a union or guild. The monopoly was broken in 1915 but was replaced by a rival organization, the Shubert Brothers, which created its own monopoly. Through government action and internal reform, the monopolies are long gone, but the role of the producer as a nonartistic agent of oversight and fiscal responsibility is still very much in place. The Shubert Organization still produces plays and operates theatres, but it is one of many, including the very successful Nederlander Producing Company.

A commercial producer finds a play. Sometimes a playwright or director working on a script actively seeks out a producer. If the producer believes in the play and thinks it likely to make a profit, he or she may secure production rights to the play. Money

WICKED (2003) by Stephen Schwartz and Winnie Holman, and directed by Joe Mantello, with scenic design by Eugene Lee, has proved to be a remarkable Broadway and touring success. It has been running since opening at the George Gershwin Theatre, a Nederlander theatre, and was produced by Marc Platt, Universal Pictures, the Araca Group, Jon B. Platt, and David Stone.
Photo © Joan Marcus.

must then be raised to cover the cost of staging the production. Many backers may be brought on board, each contributing a significant amount, to fund the preproduction work. Backers must be convinced that the show is likely to run long enough to earn back the initial outlay. The producer must find both rehearsal and performance space. Some modern producing organizations own their own theatres, but many rent available commercial spaces. The producer hires (and can fire) all personnel connected with the show but normally collaborates with the director in engaging leading actors and designers. Negotiations must take place with different unions for each aspect of production. The producer must weigh the cost of talent needed to produce a fine show against the need to keep the production costs as low as possible.

The producer hires the show's director, sometimes through a theatrical agent. Agents usually represent directors, actors, and other theatre artists and can serve as an important connection between artists and producers. Although most artistic control rests with the director, the producer controls the purse strings and therefore maintains a certain amount of artistic power. The producer is answerable to the backers and so must try to keep the production within budget as well as meet payroll and keep adequate financial records. Ultimately responsible for creating an audience for the show, the producer oversees marketing and publicity. In commercial theatre the producer typically works with a public relations firm. Marketing and publicity include designing websites, posters and billboards, writing and distributing news releases and direct mail campaigns, producing TV and radio commercials, and serving as a liaison with the media.

Given the enormous financial risk, producers often look for shows that have been highly successful at an earlier time or in other countries. The cost of mounting a play in New York, for example is four to five times that of London.[1] In the 1980s the blockbuster musicals *Cats, Les Misérables,* and *Phantom of the Opera,* all produced by Cameron Mackintosh, were imported from British to American stages. In 1996 *Rent* moved from a successful Off-Broadway production to Broadway, as did *Avenue Q* in 2005 and *Spring Awakening* in 2006. In 2003 *The 25th Annual Putnam County Spelling Bee* started as a nonmusical play Off-off-Broadway; shortly thereafter, it was reconceived as a musical. In early 2005, it played so successfully Off-Broadway, at Second Stage, that only months later it became a Broadway hit at Circle in the Square.

A successful Broadway show runs as long as it is making money. For the 2010–2011 season, 12.53 million people attended Broadway shows in New York and paid $1.8 billion in admission. As a typical Broadway week in 2011, for the week ending May 22, there were thirty-five Broadway productions that grossed $24,911,281 with an attendance of 288,757. Six of the thirty-five productions ran at capacity attendance: five were musicals; the sixth was a British import (*War Horse*). A new musical, *The Book of Mormon* (by the creators of *South Park*), ran to standing room.[2]

The producers often have a close relationship with theatre owners in the Broadway sphere. In fact, they are sometimes part of the same organization. As of June 2011, there were forty active Broadway theatres. Of this number, the Shubert Organization owns seventeen, the Nederlander Organization (now for three generations in the same family) owns nine, and Jujamcyn Theaters owns five.[3] All three organizations produce, but their theatres also present plays produced by others. Some individual producers over time have created large organizations of their own. For example, Cameron Mackintosh in London has produced many blockbuster musicals since the 1970s, such as *Cats, Phantom of the Opera, Les Misérables,* and *Mary Poppins,* that originated in Britain before arriving on American shores. In many cases Mackintosh has produced alone, but sometimes he collaborates in production, as he did with Disney Theatrical Productions for *Mary Poppins.* Macintosh owns a number of West End theatres in London, but none in the United States. Although he only produces musicals, his theatres often feature classical and modern spoken-word plays.

Sometimes film companies get involved with theatre producing in the hopes that a successful show will then become a movie. New Line Cinema, for example, produced *Hairspray,* and Universal Studios co-produced *Wicked.* A number of individual producers rose from press representation organizations as did Jeffrey Richards, who still has his press company, but has produced with other individuals for a number of years, most notably with *August: Osage County, Spring Awakening,* and *Bloody, Bloody Andrew Jackson.*[4] Of course, professional resident theatres also produce or co-produce productions that began in their own theatres before transferring to commercial theatres.

Tony Awards (Broadway) and Obie Awards (Off-Broadway) for an entire show are presented to the producers, since they are the ones who get the ball rolling in the commercial arena. In their book *The Producers: How We Did It* (2001), Mel Brooks and Tom Meehan include an entertaining account of getting producers and artists together to launch their remarkably successful musical.

Producing in Nonprofit Theatre

Some directors, typically having worked in the field for a period of time, assume the great responsibility of heading up an entire producing organization. Most professional nonprofit resident theatres (those that have a permanent home and produce a season of plays) are led by an **artistic director,** who has primary responsibility for the artistic life of the theatre. In the late 1940s and early 1950s artistic directors founded organizations that are still a vital part of the theatre scene in the United States. Theatre 47 in Dallas was founded by Margo Jones, the Alley Theatre in Houston by Nina Vance, and Arena Stage in Washington, DC, by Zelda Fichandler.

Although in nonprofit theatre the artistic director is responsible for the theatre's artistic mission, he or she usually works closely with the managing director. This team must focus on the continuity of the organization rather than a specific show. Casting and design choices must take the entire season into consideration, and although all shows will have a particular budget assigned, the entire season must stay within a larger budget as well. Along with taking care of publicity and marketing, an audience development staff may also coordinate special outreach programs to bring in new audience members and to help current patrons stay involved in the life of the theatre. Tickets are often sold at reduced rates to large groups, special backstage tours are arranged, guest speakers are provided for group functions, and special promotions may be offered for specific shows or days of the week.

In a resident theatre the artistic director frequently makes the final decision on plays to be done and directors and designers to be hired. Whereas the director of a production is responsible for the outcome of a particular show, the artistic director must think about the season as a whole. Is there variety? Is the theatre serving its constituency well? Are the productions meeting the artistic goals of the theatre? Artistic directors may work closely with a board of directors—a committee of artists, civic leaders, and businesspeople from the community who are typically generous supporters of the theatre. The artistic director spearheads fundraising activities with help from the board and support staff. Such activities include grant writing to public and private agencies and foundations as well as direct appeals to theatre patrons for donations. Although most artistic directors have some responsibility for overseeing the business aspects of the organization, these duties may be shared with a managing director and/or **executive director** or **company manager.**

Artistic directors usually direct one or more of the productions each season; many artistic directors achieve national and international renown by sharing important productions beyond their home theatres. Robert Falls of the Goodman Theatre in Chicago, for example, brought actor Brian Dennehy to New York in *Death of a Salesman* in 1999, *Long Day's Journey into Night* in 2003, and *Desire under the Elms* in 2009. Many artistic directors such as Michael Kahn (at the Shakespeare Theatre Company in Washington, DC) and Joe Dowling (at the Guthrie Theater in Minneapolis) direct in commercial and resident theatres throughout the country. Artistic direction can be very demanding and frustrating over time, and many successful artistic directors such as Daniel Sullivan (formerly of the Seattle Repertory) and Mark Lamos (formerly of the Hartford Stage Company) have returned to freelance directing. Some have taken faculty positions in university theatres.

Periodically, productions from resident or summer theatres, such as the Goodman shows above, move into commercial houses. The Pulitzer Prize–winning play *Doubt,* by John Patrick Shanley, was first produced in 2004 by the Manhattan Theatre Club, a resident theatre in New York, before moving to Broadway in 2005 with the same cast and artistic team. Similarly, *August: Osage County* (2007) originated at Steppenwolf Theatre Company in Chicago before moving to Broadway in 2008. Nonprofit theatres sometimes collaborate on a production, continuing development at each presentation and sometimes moving the play to a commercial venue. In this way the production is given a wider audience, and the theatres share the cost of development as well as increased national visibility and potentially any profits from the commercial run. *Hedda Gabler* (2001), with Kate Burton and directed by Nicholas Martin, began at Williamstown Theatre Festival in Massachusetts. When a production moves, the originating theatre may become one of the commercial producers mounting the venture. In the case of *Hedda Gabler,* the production began at Williamstown but was also developed at the Bay Street Theatre in Sag Harbor, New York, and the Huntington Theatre

TIMES SQUARE in New York City has been transformed in the twenty-first century by creating a pedestrian and lounging section in a large area of what used to be congested streets. While still attracting huge crowds to theatres, hotels, and restaurants, the Broadway theatre district is now more user-friendly and comparatively "park-like" than ever before.
2010 Photo © Ronald Wainscott.

ARTISTS of the THEATRE

Harold Prince

The most famous producers in theatre history have also worked as artists, usually as directors. As both producer and director, Harold Prince (b. 1928) has had a powerful influence on American theatre, particularly the musical. He began coproducing shows at an early age for the celebrated director George Abbott, including the very popular *The Pajama Game* (1954) and *Damn Yankees* (1955). In 1957 he coproduced *West Side Story*, a musical reworking of the Romeo and Juliet tale. The show was directed and choreographed by Jerome Robbins, was later turned into a film, and has become a favorite musical to revive in both professional and amateur venues.

In the 1960s Prince produced some of the decade's most successful musicals, including *A Funny Thing Happened on the Way to the Forum* (1962), which was inspired by ancient Roman comedy, and *Fiddler on the Roof* (1964), the story of a Jewish ghetto in Russia. He began directing in the 1960s as well and in 1966 both produced and directed *Cabaret,* which follows the loosely woven story of the romance between a nightclub singer and a writer in 1930s Germany. The basic story, however, is intercut with scenes set in the nightclub or cabaret, during which the performers dance and sing, not to advance the story but to depict the decadence of German society and creeping influence of Nazism. Prince's production was surprising not only for the ultimate seriousness of its subject matter but also for the highly presentational (not realistic) style of the cabaret sequences. The set (designed by Boris Aronson) featured a mirror that reflected and distorted a view of the audience, encouraging a link to be drawn between the degeneracy of 1930s Germany and contemporary America.

In the 1970s Prince teamed up with composer and lyricist Stephen Sondheim to break new ground in musical theatre. In 1970 Prince produced and directed *Company*, which was widely acknowledged as the best example to date of a concept musical—one that was organized more by theme than story. *Company* evolved from related playlets about marriage. Boris Aronson designed a chromium and glass set, complete with working elevators. Both the look of the show and the blend of music and dialogue to investigate human psychology and relationships were startling at the time.

Company was followed by *Follies* (with Stephen Sondheim, 1971), produced by Prince and codirected with Michael Bennett (who later went on to direct *A Chorus Line,* 1975). Inspired by a picture of actress Gloria Swanson standing in the remains of a demolished theatre, *Follies* depicts the reunion of two aging showgirls, their husbands, and a theatrical impresario in a theatre about to be demolished. The past is explored through song and dialogue and represented visually by ghostly apparitions of the female characters' younger selves. Prince's production was a visual feast, featuring a massive set and extravagant costumes. It was a financial failure, losing $665,000, perhaps suggesting poor decisions on the part of Prince as a producer. Prince, Bennett, and many who saw it, however, considered *Follies* an artistic triumph. The production has become legendary among musical theatre buffs.

Prince directed and recovered his reputation as a producer with *A Little Night Music* (1973), an elegant, bittersweet comedy about sexual role-playing, based on the film *Smiles of a Summer Night* (1955) by Ingmar Bergman. His next collaboration with Sondheim again broke new ground. *Pacific Overtures* (1976) told the story of the opening of Japan to the West, focusing on the subsequent erosion of Asian tradition. The cast was all-Asian (a rarity in the United States at that time). Prince incorporated traditional Japanese Kabuki theatre techniques in staging. The production again was a financial failure but, like *Follies,* is now believed to have been ahead of its time and is considered an artistic milestone.

Prince directed but did not produce the Sondheim show *Sweeney Todd: The Demon Barber of Fleet Street* in 1979. The piece is a musical thriller featuring extremely complex music by Sondheim. The story was taken from another unusual

Company in Boston before opening on Broadway. All theatres were listed as producers. The artistic director at Huntington became the Broadway director of record.

Resident theatres are very concerned about the "graying" of American audiences as electronic media preoccupy potential young audiences. The Cleveland Play House in Ohio is addressing this situation by offering an impressive array of classes and workshops for youth and children, student matinees of regular productions, children's theatre performances, even playwriting workshops for high school students.[5] A number of resident theatres have become proactive in expanding theatre education and building theatre audiences for the future.

CABARET as originally produced and directed by Hal Prince in 1966.
Courtesy of Billy Rose Theatre Collection, the New York Public Library for the Performing Arts, Astor, Lennox and Tilden Foundations.

source: an adaptation of a nineteenth-century British melodrama about a barber who kills his patrons and sends the bodies to a woman who bakes them into pies.

Another important Prince contribution from the 1970s (without Sondheim) was the revival of *Candide* (1974). The musical had failed in the 1950s; believing that the show would be more successful if it were truer to the original novel (by the eighteenth-century writer Voltaire), Prince contacted the artists of the 1950s version and received their permission to remake the musical. Prince directed the revised version at the small Chelsea Theater Center in Brooklyn. The Chelsea then produced the play on Broadway in conjunction with Prince. Broadway traditionalists were again shocked by the renovation of the Broadway Theatre to accommodate

environmental staging (intermingling audience and actors without a clear separation of space), but the energetic production won a following.

Prince went on to direct (but did not produce) two blockbuster musicals from the British composer Andrew Lloyd Webber: *Evita*, which opened on Broadway in 1979, and *Phantom of the Opera* (produced by Cameron Mackintosh), which opened on Broadway in 1988 and was still running in 2011. In 1993 Prince directed *Kiss of the Spider Woman*, and in 1994 he opened a stunning revival of *Show Boat* on Broadway. He has continued directing (with some producing); he served in both capacities for a revival of *A Little Night Music* in 2009.

At last count, Prince had been awarded twenty Tony awards for Broadway productions. His collaborations with other gifted artists have changed the face of the American musical numerous times, and his career is a fascinating study of the tensions of artistic versus financial decisions in the theatre. Although Prince began in commercial theatre, he now (like most theatre artists) tends to develop new works at resident theatres before subjecting his shows to the high-stakes world of Broadway.

INTERESTED? Check out

Carol Ilson. *Harold Prince: A Director's Journey.* New York: Limelight, 2000.
Foster Hirsch. *Harold Prince and the American Musical Theatre,* expanded edition. New York: Applause, 2005.
See the Internet Broadway Database, www.ibdb.com (maintained by the League of American Theatres and Producers), for a complete list of credits for the shows mentioned above.

Producing in Amateur Theatre

In amateur theatre the producing duties are often shared by a number of people. In a large educational theatre department or community theatre, producing may be primarily the responsibility of an administrator (the department chairperson, for example, or an executive director). In those theatres the producer's major concern is for the overall health of the organization. In smaller theatres the duties are assumed by a number of people, many of whom may be volunteers. Working on publicity, fundraising, or public relations committees is a way for people with strong organizational and communication skills to support the theatre.

THE ECONOMICS OF THEATRE

The live nature of theatre creates one of its biggest challenges: financing. A film can be copied thousands of times and distributed to movie theatres, video stores, private homes, or streamed via the Internet; it begins earning its money once the creative work is complete. A theatrical performance, however, must be recreated every night for a particular audience. The show needs its actors, technicians, and other staff until it closes. Unlike film, the product cannot be resold; it is intangible and cannot be held in the hand but constantly must be created anew. Consequently, the immediacy of the theatrical experience sometimes comes at a high price.

Production Costs

In amateur theatre, the initial outlay for a production includes a royalty fee paid to the playwright, the cost of materials for sets and costumes, the cost of technical equipment that must be purchased or rented, advertising costs, as well as the salaries of professional staff hired to lead and guide the volunteers. In addition, a professional production must pay all company members: directors, designers, technicians, actors, ticket sellers, and others, most of whom are unionized. Any organization that has its own space must pay for upkeep and repairs as well as all utilities. A show with no home base will need to pay the owner of the performance space for its use.

Not surprisingly, professional theatre is expensive, especially in first-run houses in cities such as New York and Chicago, where property values and taxes are exorbitant.

THE SADLER'S WELLS THEATRE in London, managed by Charles Dibdin, is an excellent example of producers seeking novelty and new theatrical entertainments to attract large audiences—in this case "aqua dramas." This early nineteenth-century theatre was typical of public theatres then with proscenium arch, apron playing space, and proscenium doors for actors' entrances and exits, as well as a large pit and three tiers of galleries and boxes for the audience. The stage, however, covered a huge water tank, which was always uncovered for the last act to depict sea battles and whatever could be envisioned for exciting, but wet, melodramatic action.

The Microcosm of London (1808–1811) from collection of the authors.

The owner of a theatre must pay taxes and upkeep on the building regardless of whether the theatre is empty or the current show is successful at the box office. In rented spaces this expense is passed on to the show's producers and ultimately to the audience. Weekly theatre rental, for example, may run $25,000 plus a percentage of the weekly gross ticket sales, which is usually a five-figure amount.[6]

Since the early twentieth century, production costs have escalated much faster than the rate of inflation. In the 1920s most first-run professional productions of Broadway plays could be staged for about $10,000 to $20,000, but many were done for much less. A typical outlay for a nonmusical with three or more sets was about $14,000. *The Straw,* a failure by Eugene O'Neill in 1921, closed after twenty performances, but the producer George Tyler lost only $9,000 on the venture.[7] In the early twenty-first century, however, even a simple, single-set show with two or three actors can cost from $1 to $2 million to get to opening night on Broadway (the most expensive of the professional venues). Musicals are even more expensive to produce, because of typically large casts, multiple sets, hundreds of costumes, more extravagant lighting, and payment for additional personnel: music director, composer, lyricist, choreographer and musicians. *Spring Awakening* (2006), in moving from Off-Broadway to Broadway, cost $4.2 million to open, and *The Book of Mormon* (2011) came in under budget at $9 million, but larger-scale musicals cost much more. The musical *Wicked* (2003) reportedly cost $14 million to stage, the troubled *Spiderman: Turn Off the Dark* (2011) over $70 million, twice that of any Broadway show before it. Running costs for musicals are exorbitant, typically running $250,000 to $800,000 per week; *Spiderman* cost $1 million.[8]

Off-Broadway musicals are obviously less expensive, but still risky. *Playbill* estimates that most of these smaller musicals cost about $1 million to open and $50,000 to $100,000 per week to keep running.[9] Theatres in smaller cities with lower overheads still struggle with climbing production costs. Out of 180 nonprofit theatres that participate in an ongoing Theatre Communications Group survey, more than half operated in the red in 2008 and 2009.[10]

A hit show, particularly a musical (which tends to tour more extensively than a spoken-word play), can be extremely lucrative. By 1997, when *Cats* (produced by Cameron Mackintosh) set the record for the longest running Broadway show, it had been seen by an estimated 8 million people on Broadway and 50 million worldwide and had sold 390,000 T-shirts, 130,000 sweatshirts, and 1.14 million souvenir books.[11] When it closed on Broadway in September 2000, it had played 7,485 performances over eighteen years. When *Les Misérables* (also produced by Mackintosh) closed on Broadway in 2003, it had played 6,612 performances over sixteen years and had been seen by 9 million people. Worldwide, the show has been seen by over 50 million people and has been produced in thirty-four countries in twenty different languages.[12]

Unfortunately, most theatrical productions do not earn a profit. According to Patrick Healy of the *New York Times,* most commercial shows never turn a profit on or off-Broadway; they do better making money through licensing for regional and touring productions.[13] A more likely scenario is for a show to close before it has time to recoup the producers' original investment; eight out of ten shows on Broadway fail.[14] Perhaps the most infamous Broadway flop is the musical *Carrie,* based on the novel by Stephen King, which closed after only five performances in 1988 and lost $8 million.

Producers, artistic directors, and managing directors in all professional theatres must deal seriously with labor relations, which often means not just maintaining appropriate workplace environments and conditions, but negotiating with unions, guilds, and societies. Often, group negotiations are necessary in hammering out contractual agreements, such as the League of Resident Theatres or the League of American Theatres and Producers working out contracts with Actors' Equity or the Dramatists Guild. Individual negotiations with high-profile actors, directors, and designers, however, can be a challenging task as well. Failure in such negotiations can result in strikes, walkouts, closed or postponed productions, even the closure of theatres and theatre companies, as in the 2007 Stagehands Union strike in New York.

Effect on Types of Plays Produced

Because of prohibitive production costs, many commercial producers are hesitant to invest money in a show that might close quickly, so they opt for what they believe will prove to be a major box-office draw. The result has been a narrowing of material on Broadway and other commercial venues to mostly safe plays that are likely to appeal to a mass audience. Large-cast, spoken-word plays are very difficult to get produced, since the chances are great that the show will not earn a profit or break even. A big exception to this practice is the Broadway success of *August: Osage County,* opening in 2007 with a cast of thirteen.

Producers sometimes sign on recognizable film and television actors (who also may have extensive stage experience) in an attempt to ensure full houses, but this practice often limits the show's run. The 2011 revival of *That Championship Season,* for example, had a limited run due to film and TV commitments of most of the cast. Although O'Neill's most famous play, *Long Day's Journey into Night,* had already enjoyed four Broadway productions, the splendid revival of this play, directed by Robert Falls in 2003, also had a limited run of four months in order to secure the services of Vanessa Redgrave and Brian Dennehy.

In the 1920s it was not uncommon for an amateur production to catch the attention of critics and find itself in a Broadway house within the year. The Provincetown Players, for example, staged the first productions of the modern classics *The Emperor Jones* (1920) and *The Hairy Ape* (1922) by Eugene O'Neill in a converted stable in Greenwich Village, seating only about 200 people, yet both productions moved into Broadway houses less than two months after opening. Such a move is inconceivable in today's high-stakes entertainment world.

In effect, commercial theatre tends to consist of musicals (which, if successful, produce a high return on investment), comedies, and the occasional unusual serious play (usually with one set and a small cast) that has proven successful in other venues. *Time Stands Still* (2010) for example, a four-character show with one set, opened on Broadway and played successfully after performances at the Geffen Playhouse in Los Angeles. Similarly, *Doubt* in 2005 moved from the Manhattan Theatre Club to Broadway with a cast of four and a simplified unit setting. The successful 2005 revival of Edward Albee's *Who's Afraid of Virgina Woolf?* also included a cast of four and a single set. For the most part, production of pre–twentieth-century dramatic literature presents too high a risk in the commercial world and is carried on by resident theatres and educational theatres. Artistic experimentation happens in resident and educational theatres as well as Off-off-Broadway and some nontraditional companies scattered across North America but is increasingly difficult to fund. Nonprofit theatres find that programming traditional crowd-pleasers is important if they are to bring in the funds to keep the theatre functioning. In difficult economic times the number of such shows that are necessary to pay the expenses often crowds out more difficult, but exciting, work.

Theatre Funding

A dependence on box-office receipts severely limits the options available for an audience. Many important, thought-provoking plays have been artistic but not commercial successes. In many European countries theatres are subsidized by the government as cultural institutions of equal importance with art galleries, museums, and libraries. Government funding for the arts has been more difficult to sustain in the United States. The **National Endowment for the Arts (NEA),** founded in 1965, is a public agency of the federal government created to support the arts and art education as well as widening the audience for the arts in the United States.[15] As the largest single funder of nonprofit arts organizations in the United States, the NEA supports arts education and preservation as well as the development of new projects. Although the NEA's budget is quite small in comparison to other government expenditures, the Endowment has been frequently attacked for its grants to artists whose work is objectionable to some segments of the tax-paying public. Since the 1950s, nonprofit theatres have increasingly sought corporate sponsorship to help with escalating production costs. This financial contribution might take the form of underwriting a season of plays, a specific production, or even an actor's performance. Not surprisingly, corporate gifts evaporate quickly in a slow economy.

EXPLORING Historical and Cultural Perspectives

Stagehands Union 2007 Strike

On November 10, 2007, after months of failed negotiations, the Stagehands Union, Local 1 of International Alliance of Theatrical Stage Employees (IATSE) in New York City, went on strike to protest what they saw as unfair treatment by the League of American Theatres and Producers. This strike of nineteen days affected only Broadway productions, at least twenty-seven of them, since a few of the theatres and productions, such as Lincoln Center and *Young Frankenstein,* had already negotiated separate contracts with the union. The rest of the League would not budge, so the stagehands went on strike and were supported immediately by Actors' Equity, the box office workers who are also unionized, the musicians union, and several others. Obviously, none of the affected productions could possibly perform. This show of support from separate but artistically allied unions extends back at least as far as the first actors strike of 1919 when the already organized stagehands supported the fledgling actors union. The stagehands had frequently supported other unions, but 2007 was the first strike in their long history. Mutual labor support was critically important in helping the striking union to success.

STAGEHANDS UNION STRIKERS picketing in front of the production of *Legally Blonde* in New York, November 15, 2007. The flyers that the strikers were handing out in front of the theatres had the Stagehands message on one side and a statement of support from Actors' Equity on the reverse. Both unions have always supported each other.

Collection of the authors.

The Stagehands passed out flyers on the street laying out their arguments, but on the flip side of those flyers, Actors' Equity produced a document that not only talked about the professionalism and dedication of the stagehands, but their vital role in maintaining safety, and a statement that is central to the thesis of this book: collaboration of artists and professionals, many of whom work behind the scenes, are essential for the theatre.

Ultimately, compromises were made by both management and the stagehands, but for nineteen days strikers were seen in the theatre district in front of theatres still lit up as if a performance was imminent. We found the strikers accessible and forthcoming with their individual assessments of what was happening. We encountered only civility, no hostility or anger, but a determination to work out a fair

settlement with management and get back to work. And many gave us permission to photograph them for this book. As in any strike, there were many rumors, but none that seemed to create problems for the process.

Of course, other parts of the New York economy were affected by the strike, and estimates for losses in tourism, restaurants, hotels, and the like were about $2 million per day. Losses to the theatre are estimated at about $40 million. This strike also affected Thanksgiving travel and shopping, a big economic time for New York. When performances recommenced on November 29, most of the productions recovered, and several new productions that were scheduled to open during the strike period had been postponed. Obviously, the unions and management, as well as theatregoers and the city government, were relieved.

Effect on the Audience

Rapidly rising production costs have driven ticket prices up. In 1920 the highest-priced Broadway ticket for spoken-word productions was $2.00. Musicals usually charged no more than $2.50 per ticket. By the end of the economic boom of the 1920s the top price was still usually under $4.00. By contrast, a ticket to a Broadway show in 2011 might range from $20–40 for standing room, student or general rush or day-of-show lottery, to about $150–300 for the best seats. Even nonprofit theatres find themselves passing unsubsidized costs on to the consumer. A theatregoer in 2011 might have expected to pay anywhere from a low of $18–45 to a high of $75–110 to see a show at a major resident theatre. When you read this, ticket costs may be even higher.

A regrettable by-product of high ticket prices is a narrowing of the potential audience to those individuals with discretionary income. An awareness of the prohibitive nature of ticket prices has led to a number of steps, even in commercial venues, to make tickets affordable to a wider audience. The Theatre Development Fund (TDF), a nonprofit organization dedicated to supporting new productions and broadening

EXPLORING Historical and Cultural Perspectives

The Federal Theatre Project

During the height of the Great Depression, the federal government created the Works Progress Administration, which in turn developed many thousands of jobs in a variety of sectors using federal funds. One of these sectors was the **Federal Theatre Project** (FTP), a nationwide effort representing the first time that the U.S. government directly subsidized theatre (an idea that was controversial then and continues to be as Congress regularly challenges decisions of the National Endowment for the Arts).

Between 1935 and 1939 thousands of theatre artists were taken off the relief rolls in some forty states and put to work creating new plays, unusual productions of classic plays, children's theatre, Yiddish and African American companies—all with inexpensive ticket prices. Some of these productions were dynamic experiments such as Orson Welles's production of *Doctor Faustus* (1937) and the all-black production of Gilbert and Sullivan entitled *The Swing Mikado* (1939). In a remarkable national project, an antifascist play by Sinclair Lewis entitled *It Can't Happen Here* (1936) was produced simultaneously by at least twenty-one companies in as many cities from coast to coast. Some shows were tough examinations of widespread poverty, such as *One-Third of a Nation* (1938), and at times they were critical of government policies, as in *Triple-A Plowed Under* (1936).

Federal authorities were often in distress over the content in FTP productions. In 1937, reacting to rumors that some new plays were highly critical of the government, the authorities announced an immediate halt to all new productions for two months. The now famous musical *The Cradle Will Rock* (1937) was just about to open. Finding their theatre padlocked, the actors rebelled by staging the play anyway in an empty theatre without settings, technical support, or an orchestra. The only accompaniment was the composer Marc Blitzstein at a piano. From this rebellion emerged the experimental Mercury Theatre, headed by Orson Welles and

THE TENEMENT FIRE in *One-Third of a Nation* (1938) by Arthur Arent as produced in New York by the FTP.
From the Federal Theatre Project Photo Collection, Special Collections and Archives, George Mason University Libraries, Fairfax, Virginia.

John Houseman. This event is memorialized in the 1999 Tim Robbins film, *Cradle Will Rock*. Although FTP continued to operate beyond *Cradle*, the House Un-American Activities Committee began hearings on FTP in 1938, and by June 1939, Congress had pulled the plug on the Federal Theatre Project, calling it left-wing and a haven for communists.

INTERESTED? Check out

Barry B. Witham. *The Federal Theatre Project: A Case Study.* New York: Cambridge University, 2009.
Hallie Flanagan. *Arena: The Story of the Federal Theatre.* 1940; New York: Limelight, 1985.

the audience for the performing arts, offers discount programs to increase the number of potential theatregoers in New York City. Its popular "TKTS" booth in Times Square, for example, sells Broadway and Off-Broadway day-of-show admissions at 20 to 50 percent reductions. TDF also sponsors a voucher program for Off-off-Broadway theatres and nontraditional performance spaces to help build audiences and subsidize admissions.[16] Many nonprofit theatres offer special discounted rates for families and students.

Still, the cost of professional theatre (whether commercial or nonprofit) makes it unavailable to many people. How can live theatre be made more accessible to a wider audience? The question is difficult, but answering it will be vital to the theatre's future.

Theatre and the Community

Besides the more intangible contributions that theatre can make to a community, studies have shown that a lively arts scene is healthy for a city's economy. According to the Theatre Communications Group, in 2009 there were 1,825 not-for-profit professional theatres in the United States that mounted 187,000 productions seen by 30 million people. Also, nonprofit theatre employed 128,200 artistic, administrative, and production personnel, and contributed $1.9 billion to the economy.[17] Looking at the broader economic impact on an area, for 2008–2009 the Broadway theatre industry alone contributed $9.8 billion to the economy of New York City and created 84,400 full-time jobs.[18] Theatre audience members tend to patronize restaurants and bars, parking facilities, and public transportation. Performance events serve as major tourist attractions and can even be a part of urban renovation designed to bring people back to the city after working hours.

The New 42nd Street, a nonprofit development created in New York between 1995 and 2000, is a successful collaboration of theatre artists, government, and corporate America. A decrepit neighborhood in Times Square was renovated, resulting in several

TKTS BOOTH on 47th Street in Times Square is marked by bright red signs that list the Broadway and Off-Broadway shows available for reduced price tickets. Several hours before the tickets become available for both matinee and evening productions, long lines begin to snake around the area. The bank of bleachers is a waiting area for the crowds although many people use the benches to rest, eat, or meet friends at almost any time. This photo was shot early in the morning before the crowds are active.
2010 Photo © Ronald Wainscott.

HUGUANG GUILDHALL THEATRE in Beijing. For centuries in the commercial theatre of many nations, producers have used the names and faces of actors and actresses to attract audiences to plays. Playbills and posters have been common in the West since the eighteenth century, but images of performers for advertising have been typical in many Asian theatres as well. This theatre entrance in 2010 is typical with its large placard on the left listing all of the plays in their classical repertory with images of actors and actresses in famous roles.
Photo © Ronald Wainscott.

new theatres, the New Victory, the New Amsterdam, and the American Airlines Theater emerging from rundown ones. The result was new homes for family and children's theatre and for the Roundabout Theater Company, as well as rehearsal studios and a much safer, revitalized entertainment block in New York. Such community collaboration benefits not only the urban environment, but the performing arts in a vital way. This block has emerged as a magnet for young audiences.[19]

The relationship between any society and its theatre is complex and ever changing. A frequently repeated argument for arts funding is that societies of the past speak to us today mainly through the works of art that they left behind. Theatre leaves only clues— but important ones: play scripts; reviews; theatre buildings (whole or in ruins); personal accounts in letters, diaries, and periodicals; stories handed down by word of mouth; paintings; and, more recently, photographs and videos. The reconstruction of theatre from the past gives us a fascinating perspective on the culture that produced it. Theatre in the present serves its community in many ways. No matter what the venue, no matter what the ticket price, it can serve as a vibrant means of human communication.

CHAPTER REVIEW

Questions and Activities

1. How much are you willing to pay to see a live theatre performance? A rock concert? A sports event? Does it make a difference whether the people you are watching are amateurs or professionals? Why or why not?

2. Assume that you or a small group from your class is going to produce a play on your own with students from the college or university acting classes. Select a play that you have read. Make a list of all the specific things that need to be done on your end. The artistic side is being taken care of by another group. What will you need to do?

3. Go a step further in your imaginary production. Choose one of the jobs and do whatever is necessary—for example, create a budget, decide on a space, and so on. Do any research necessary to complete the task. Report back to your group or class. You are answering the question, "What would it take to get a show up in this time and place?"

Key Terms and Concepts

producer, p. 238
managing director, p. 238
artistic director, p. 240

executive director, p. 241
company manager, p. 241
National Endowment for the Arts (NEA), p. 246

Federal Theatre Project (FTP), p. 248

For Further Exploration

Stanley Green. *Broadway Musicals, Show by Show,* 6th ed. New York: Applause, 2010 ; and Andrew Lamb. *150 Years of Popular Musical Theatre.* New Haven, CT: Yale University, 2000. For a history of American and British musicals.

Larry Stempel. *Showtime: A History of the Broadway Musical Theater.* New York: W. W. Norton, 2010.

David M. Conte and Stephen Langley. *Theatre Management: Producing and Managing the Performing Arts.* Hollywood, CA: Quite Specific Media Group, Ltd., 2007.

Duncan M. Webb. *Running Theaters: Best Practices for Leaders and Managers.* New York: Allworth, 2004.

Donald C. Faber. *Producing Theatre: A Comprehensive Legal and Business Guide,* 3rd ed. New York: Limelight, 2006.

Mary C. Henderson. *The New Amsterdam: The Biography of a Broadway Theatre.* New York: Hyperion, 1997.

Ken Davenport. www.theproducersperspective.com/ my_weblog/10-questions-for-broadway-pros/. Broadway producer interviews theatre practitioners.

Contemporary Theatre

Attempting to capture an emblematic snapshot of our contemporary theatre is always problematic since new developments are not always indicators of trends, and new productions or plays almost always have important antecedents in theatre of the past. Nonetheless, this gallery suggests one overview of contemporary theatre practice.

Contemporary Thrust Theatre

Thrust theatres have their sources in Classical Greece, Chinese classical theatre, Japanese Noh theatres, medieval cycle plays, and Elizabethan public theatres. But this staging form vanished with the success of proscenium theatres and did not make a major reappearance until the mid-twentieth century in Europe and North America. It is now a common arrangement in the United States in resident theatres, Shakespeare festivals, and universities. The Courtyard Theater, the main-stage space of Chicago Shakespeare Theater (CST) on Navy Pier opened in 1999. This thrust stage is very deep, and most of the seats in the 500-seat house face the long side, rather than the stage front downstage. The CST reports that the theatre was inspired by the design of the Swan Theatre of the Royal Shakespeare Company in

England. This arrangement is not only dynamic and keeps much of the action close to much of the audience, but it also requires creative staging on the part of directors, scenic designers, and lighting designers to use the space effectively. It is an exciting space in which to witness theatre.   Photo courtesy of Chicago Shakespeare Theater. Photo by Steinkamp/Ballogg, Chicago.

Revisiting Familiar Tales

Historically in the theatre, fairy tales and children's literature have been revisited regularly since the nineteenth century. Especially since Sondheim's *Into the Woods* (1987), however, many tales from the past have been radically reconceived, often visiting famous old stories with a satirical, deconstructed or postmodern approach. This is especially evident in the work of Mary Zimmerman, but many other playwrights and directors have delved into the psychological possibilities of dreams and fable. *Alice's Adventures in Wonderland* and *Through the Looking Glass* by Lewis Carroll have been especially intriguing. It is clear that many reconceptions are consciously undermining or liberating the much safer interpretations of the Disney version so keenly fixed in people's minds. This version is *Lookingglass Alice* as produced by the Lookingglass Theatre Company at Actors Theatre of Louisville in 2010. Samuel Taylor as the Mad Hatter and Lindsey Noel Whiting as Alice find themselves in a mirror exercise. Written and directed by David Catlin.   Photography by Harlan Taylor and by permission of Actors Theatre of Louisville.

Popular Literature as Theatre

The novels and stories of Charles Dickens found their way on the stage even when they were new. His work has been adapted frequently for the Broadway stage since at least 1860. This is not surprising since his characterizations are often so theatrical, to say nothing of his abiding fascination with the theatre in which he sometimes dabbled. While film and television continue to rework his novels, often quite faithfully, the theatre continues to restage him, perhaps most famously in *Nicholas Nickleby* by the Royal Shakespeare Company in 1980, but often in musicals as well, such as *Oliver, A Christmas Carol*, and *The Mystery of Edwin Drood*. *A Tale of Two Cities* (2009) by Jill Santoriello deals with the era of the French Revolution. Late in the play, a wicked woman, Madame Defarge, played by Natalie Toro, commits suicide in a dynamic if macabre scene. Directed by Warren Carlyle; lighting by Richard Pilbrow; costume design by David Zinn.   Photo © Carol Rosegg.

Women's Voices

Women as playwrights were once nonexistent (unless anonymous), or very occasional such as Hrotsvitha (tenth century) and Aphra Behn (seventeenth century). The numbers increased after 1660 with periodic waves in the eighteenth and nineteenth centuries. Since the early twentieth century, however, and in the wake of Women's Suffrage and increasing property and social rights, many women have entered the ranks of professional playwriting. African American women have made a stunning mark since Lorraine Hansberry in 1959 with *A Raisin in the Sun*. No woman of color has generated more theatrical excitement in the present than Lynn Nottage, whose plays such as *Intimate Apparel*,

Fabulation, *Crumbs from the Table of Joy*, and *Ruined* (pictured here) have been produced widely in professional resident theatres and Off-Broadway. Clearly Nottage does not only write excellent plays, but provides an unusual voice and point of view in presenting problems and issues unique to women and women of color in ways that intrigue, disturb, and enlighten us. This production of *Ruined* was presented by the La Jolla Playhouse and directed by Liesl Tommy in 2011.   Photo © Kevin Berne.

Intimacy in the Midst of Satire

Candide, a satirical musical with a delightful score by Leonard Bernstein, first appeared in 1956, but has been rewritten and produced with new books many times, including this new one adapted from most of the earlier books and lyrics, but reconceived and directed by Mary Zimmerman. All are based on the rollicking eighteenth-century cynical novella by Voltaire, but this newest adaptation attempts to more accurately revisit the educational, social, and political world sent up by the novelist. As the world-wide travels of the title character get him in one scrape after another, he remains steadfastly in love with the same young woman

for no apparent reason. He seems oblivious to much of the violence, usury, and greed about him, but marches on to a tongue-in-cheek happy ending that has such glorious music that we can be fooled by its near sincerity. This image presents a happy, intimate moment between Candide (Geoff Packard) and his love Cunegonde (Lauren Molina), but most of the action is cacophonous and diverse. Produced at the Goodman Theatre, Chicago in 2010.   Photo © Liz Lauren.

Popular Musical Revival

No matter how many new musicals appear on the American stage each year, some continue to be revived (sometimes many times), both on Broadway as well as in resident theatres, universities, and community theatres throughout the country. *Anything Goes* (1934) with some of the best music of Cole Porter, repeatedly finds an audience despite a frivolous book that has repeatedly been rewritten, but remains innocuous and silly in plotting and language. Clearly audiences find this play fun to watch with its pure escapism, while being attracted to the familiar music and furious display of tap-dancing choreography. Depicted here is

the 2011 production directed and choreographed by Kathleen Marshall. The show won a Tony Award as Best Musical Revival, and we see actress Sutton Foster (also awarded with a Tony) as the principal character Reno Sweeney, leading the company in "Blow, Gabriel, Blow."   Photo © Joan Marcus.

Pushing the Boundaries of Expectations in a Musical

The producers and creators of *The Book of Mormon* (2011) took a big risk in bringing satire on religion to the mainstream musical theatre, but they were rewarded with an armful of awards and a blockbuster hit. Undergirding the success was a loyal audience of fans of the TV cartoon satire *Southpark*. Principal *Southpark* writers, Trey Parker and Matt Stone, along with Robert Lopez of *Avenue Q* fame, created the new musical. Yet the play quickly found a new audience that seemed surprised that the subject matter could be so entertaining without

being mean-spirited. Here we see Mormon missionaries singing and dancing in Uganda. Co-directed by Trey Parker and Casey Nicholaw.   Photo © Joan Marcus.

Pushing Realism into an Impossible World

This production of the modern classic *The Master Builder* (1892) by Henrik Ibsen, converts the realistic interior of much of the action of the play (originally done in box sets) to an architectural facade that becomes the playing surface of the actors. Consequently, we constantly see the house, yet the characters do not become elements inside the setting; they almost seem to float on the surface that represents the world of the central character, Solness (played by David Chandler). This architect is struggling with what he perceives as failed artistry and feels trapped in a loveless marriage. His wife Aline is played by Felicity Jones. The result is realism performed in a stylized setting that becomes symbolic of, rather than environmental for, the protagonist's world. Since the mid-twentieth century, many directors and designers have rejected reality-based settings for realistic plays—thus opting for performance spaces that are very much of the theatre, rather than film or television. Produced in 2009 by Yale Repertory Theatre. Directed by Evan Yionoulis; scenic design by Timothy Brown.   Photo © T. Charles Erickson.

Creating Impossible Space and Event

The Notebooks of Leonardo da Vinci (2003), at Second Stage, an Off-Broadway theatre in New York. This theatrical piece was conceived and directed by Mary Zimmerman, who created a host of bizarre and fascinating images drawn from the sketches and inventions of Leonardo and reinterpreted and made concrete on the stage. Much action was set to music, and many passages from the famous notebooks were delivered in English and Italian. What we see created is an amalgam from Leonardo's workshop of art, science, technology, and philosophy. To try to visually express the workings of such a fantastic mind was a challenge, and Zimmerman's work can be mesmerizing even if one cannot always interpret the product with effective analysis and exactitude. The image here suggests flying, floating, and simultaneous, impossible acts. It is as if magic is combined with science.   Photo © Joan Marcus.

Defining with Lighting

Since the advent of electric lighting, the use of high and low-angle lighting and dynamic uses of shadow have become frequent occurrences in the theatre. In this production of *The Great God Brown* by Eugene O'Neill at Towson State University, we see a dynamic use of high-angle back light. We can see the silhouettes and a few details of costumes and positions of the actors' bodies, but no faces. Because all is surrounded by darkness, the characters are isolated, not only from their surroundings but also from one another. Form is more important here than character. Lighting designed by Scott Rosenfeld; costumes designed by Georgia Baker. Collection of the authors.

Uniting Lighting and Scenic Design

The magical world of *The Tempest* by Shakespeare invites contemporary designers and directors to explore imaginary spaces with both lighting and scenic investiture (often combining them with projections and evolving lighting sequences as we see here in this 2010 production at the Illinois Shakespeare Festival). The image appears to be isolated in space, but it is really a part of stairs and platforms that can become a mystical place with isolated lighting and transforming projected imagery. Scenic design by Fred M. Duer. Directed by Deb Alley from a concept by Joel Fink. Lighting design by Julie Mack. Courtesy of and photo by Fred M. Duer.

Dynamic Designs

Sometimes a straightforward play such *Shadowlands* by William Nicholson (1989) can become a fascinating theatrical journey. Nicholson created the work from his earlier television play that examines his experience with the life, illness, and death of his wife. Clearly inspired by the popular and imaginative world of the children's books of C. S. Lewis, who is also the central character of the play, this 2008 revival at the Guthrie Theater in Minneapolis brings some of the imagery of a child's world into the theatrical exploration of adult problems. Directed by Joe Dowling; scenic design by Patrick Clark; lighting design by Marcus Dilliard. Photo © Michal Daniel.

Children's Theatre/Theatre for Children

Since the early twentieth century, much of the world, east and west, has witnessed an explosion of children's theatre. Some of the earliest known children's theatres were opened in Russia, but by the 1920s, many such projects could be found throughout North America and well beyond. The impetus might be to involve children actively in the arts for educational purposes while teaching aesthetics and "good taste," to provide alternatives to sports, or to build future audiences. Whatever the early reasons, a new focus was created for children in the arts early in the century, and it has become important in many parts of the globe as demonstrated by this well-designed children's theatre in

Beijing, China. Some such theatres are oriented toward training and developing children in the theatrical arts. In some cases, a company may be mostly adults who perform for children, rather than with them. Some such theatres are amateur, and some are professional. Consequently, children's theatre is an active part of the contemporary theatre, and is likely to continue to be so.

2010 photo © Ronald Wainscott.

Realism Persists

Once the novelty and sometimes shock value of realism wore off in the last part of the nineteenth century, it soon dominated the mainstream. For several decades theatre artists most frequently practiced realism. Although the avant-garde after c. 1890 fought against realism, it became clear that realism in both playwriting and acting were to dominate the commercial theatre. By the mid-twentieth century, a dual focus of stylized versus realistic, presentational versus representational, suggested an ongoing split in styles that still persists. Some artists and critics argue that film and television can execute realism better than theatre because of such things as location shooting and the close-up. Whatever one's position, however, much live theatre is still realism, and preferred by some theatregoers. In this 2011 production of *The Diary of Anne Frank* at the Indiana Repertory Theatre in Indianapolis, we see realistic setting and costumes clearly suggesting a historical period and domestic activity meant to be accepted as real. Directed by Janet Allen; costume design by Linda Pisano; scenic design by Bill Clarke. Courtesy of Indiana Repertory Theatre. Photo by Jim Poyser.

New Puppetry

Few theatre productions have ignited audiences the way that *War Horse* has since it opened at the National Theatre in London in 2007. It had similar success when it opened on Broadway in 2011. Of course, the play's World War I story brings home the sacrifices and awfulness of that first global war, but much of the focus is on a boy who must give up his beloved horse. Most of all, however, audiences are fascinated with the remarkable life-size horse puppets brought to life majestically by a talented team of puppeteers who must work both inside and outside bodies of the see-through horses. It will be interesting to see if this extraordinary experiment will inspire a host of new stage puppetry. Photo © Paul Kolnik.

HELLENISTIC GREEK THEATRE at Delphi. Part of a complex in the precinct of Apollo.

2010 photo © Ronald Wainscott.

Act THREE

Collaboration in History

When we look at the ways in which different cultures have created and defined theatre, we see how people thought about life and sometimes the afterlife, what they valued, what they feared, and how they made sense out of the events around them. Studying theatre of the past is a fascinating activity. What we are struck by, however, is the way in which the past does not remain the past. Theatre artists of each "present" look backward to the creations of their near and distant predecessors. They revive, adapt, reinterpret, reconceive, and deconstruct. Some of the most innovative approaches to theatre were born when artists reacted against the status quo; in other words, the "new" defined itself in opposition to what was already in place, and artists made a conscious attempt to push established art into the "past." Sometimes reacting to the status quo meant resurrecting a much older viewpoint or device. We also see interconnections between different cultures, often distant from one another in geographical location as well as time. Theatre artists have always been creative borrowers. Artists do not necessarily steal the ideas of others (although that has occurred more than a few times). Theatre artists often discover or rediscover inspiration and solutions both far away and close to home. They adopt, change, and revitalize the borrowed elements. Shakespeare, who was not subject to copyright laws, and the German playwright Bertolt Brecht, for example, were great borrowers, but they also reveled in originality and novelty. The theatre artists' roots run deep and far in the history of theatre.

In this section we hope to convey the sense of a dynamic process. Because of our belief that the past is still a vital element in the life of the present, we have chosen to present information about previous theatrical events throughout this book. We realize, however, that you need some sense of historical continuity and chronology. We hope to provide an overview for you in these three chapters and the accompanying timeline, "Key Theatrical Events." Selecting what to include in an overview of more than twenty-five centuries of activity is, of course, extremely difficult. In some ways the choice is highly subjective; other theatre historians could give you their own versions, which would no doubt differ from ours. And, of course, what we see as important is informed by the time at which we write. Ten years ago, portions of this section would have been written differently. We hope that you will take the following chapters as a basis on which to build your own knowledge of the theatre, adding to it as you continue to read plays and experience productions.

ENTRANCE AND EXIT CURTAIN of classical Chinese theatre, Huguang Guild Hall in Beijing.
2010 photo © Ronald Wainscott.

Foundations

Classical Theatrical Forms

No one knows how the theatre really began, but at least since the fourth century B.C.E. many theories have been offered to explain its appearance and rise to prominence. Religious ritual appears to be a likely major source, but theatre was almost certainly preceded historically by music, dance, storytelling, oral history, and ancestor veneration, all of which contributed dynamically to the models theatre took in its earliest forms. It can be argued that the first performers in history were shamans—priests in ancient Asia, Africa, the Middle East, North America, and parts of Europe—who communed with their gods and ancestors to heal disease and affect natural events through ritual and dance. Surviving hieroglyphics in Egypt indicate that religious theatre existed there as early as 2500 B.C.E. and continued to be performed at Abydos in honor of the god Osiris for many centuries. What we know about these theatrical events is sketchy at best (short descriptions of what a priest performed). The Greeks in Athens created the earliest theatre that has left us the texts of plays and theatre architecture. The efforts of the Greeks, although grounded in religious ritual, are generally accepted as the oldest surviving dramatic studies of humanity as part of an ongoing public institution.

CLASSICAL GREECE

In 534 B.C.E. the city of Athens added contests for tragedy to its annual city festival honoring Dionysus, the god of wine, fertility, and ecstatic celebration. Subsequently, all theatre presentations in Athens for over a century were produced only in honor of this god. Like the famous Olympic games, theatre for many years was a contest, at first among playwrights for the best set of tragedies, but later for best comedy and best actor, among other competitions.

Nearly all of the Greek plays that have come down to us were first produced in the fifth century B.C.E. We have thirty-one tragedies by three playwrights (plus one anonymous tragedy) and eleven comedies by one playwright. Although we are happy to have these remarkable plays, it is sad that probably a thousand or more plays have vanished from such a dynamic period of theatre activity. If current estimates of Greek

HELLENISTIC GREEK THEATRE at Epidaurus. Note the vast seating area (theatron), full circular orchestra (rare in Hellenistic Theatres), and entrance/exit gates (paradoi) for the chorus and sometimes actors. Only partial remains of the skene foundation have survived.

2010 Photo © Ronald Wainscott.

output are roughly accurate, we have no more than three percent of the Greek plays produced between 534 and 404 B.C.E.

Theatre was occasional, and one could not earn a living as a playwright or actor; all practitioners technically were amateurs, although they were highly skilled. Contributing talent or money to the theatre of the festival was an important civic responsibility. Later Greek theatre professionalized when touring actors organized into guilds (The *Technitae* or Craftsmen of Dionysus) by the late fourth century B.C.E. Many fragments but only one full play, a domestic comedy by Menander (c. 342–291 B.C.E.), have survived from that era, which is called Hellenistic (named for the spread of Greek culture beyond Greece).

At the beginning of the process in 534 B.C.E. the actor and playwright were the same person. The early tragic playwrights, such as Thespis (sixth century B.C.E.), performed their own plays, which featured one actor and a **chorus** (a group of singer/dancers who interacted with and responded to the actor). Later a second and then a third actor were added, but all of the surviving tragedies were written for three actors who performed multiple roles with a chorus whose size is usually estimated at twelve to fifteen. The chorus, however, might have begun with fifty performers, since that was the size of the traditional **dithyramb** (a choric presentation sung and danced in homage to Dionysus). The dithyramb is older than tragedy and is claimed to be a source for it. All actors and chorus members were strictly male (even though many characters and choruses represented females), and they performed in a large, typically circular performance space called an **orchestra** (dancing place). The chorus entered and exited through the **parados.** At some point a retiring space called a **skene** (our source for the words "scene" and "scenery") was added upstage of the orchestra, and the audience of many thousands watched the action from a large **theatron** (seeing place) on a hillside to which seats were eventually added (see Figure 11.1). All parts of the theatre, though temporary at first for each Dionysian festival, were set in stone permanently by the fourth century B.C.E. Although a few theatres held only a few thousand spectators, most of the surviving theatres are so large that they remind many people of stadiums. The extant architecture creates a dilemma for modern historians, since nearly all of the surviving plays are from the fifth century B.C.E. but extant Greek theatres are from the fourth century B.C.E. or later. Therefore, because the theatres and plays were created in different eras, the theatrical spaces that still exist may not be good indications of the staging that was originally used for the plays.

The action of tragedies, comedies, and other theatrical forms was performed with music and dance, singing, chant, and speech. All actors and chorus members wore full masks covering the entire head, and actors surely performed with dynamic movement and large gestures to reach such large audiences. The vocal and physical skills needed by the actors would have been impressive indeed.

At the Dionysian festival, Greek tragedies, once fully developed, were performed by three actors in three groups of three plays by three competing playwrights. After all the performances a group of judges, chosen from the ten tribes of Athens, selected the set of plays they found the best. Sometimes a playwright told one story through all three plays (a **trilogy** that can be read as one three-part play today), but other playwrights presented three different stories in their three tragedies. All Greek tragedies that we now possess except one are based on myths that were ancient even when the plays premiered. The famous stories were familiar to many in the audience, but it is clear that playwrights retold them in a variety of ways. The story of Electra, a princess who conspired with her brother to murder her mother and the mother's lover, survives in tragedies by Aeschylus (c. 525–456 B.C.E.), Sophocles (c. 496–406 B.C.E.), and Euripides (c. 480–406 B.C.E.), and each tragedy has a very different focus and point of view. These three playwrights won numerous Dionysian contests, and some of their plays continue to inspire us in modern **revivals** (any productions of a play occurring after the original production).

The only surviving trilogy of plays, *The Oresteia* (458 B.C.E.) by Aeschylus, is still performed, translated, and adapted and has proven to be one of the most enduring dramatic presentations in theatre history. The three plays that make up *The Oresteia*

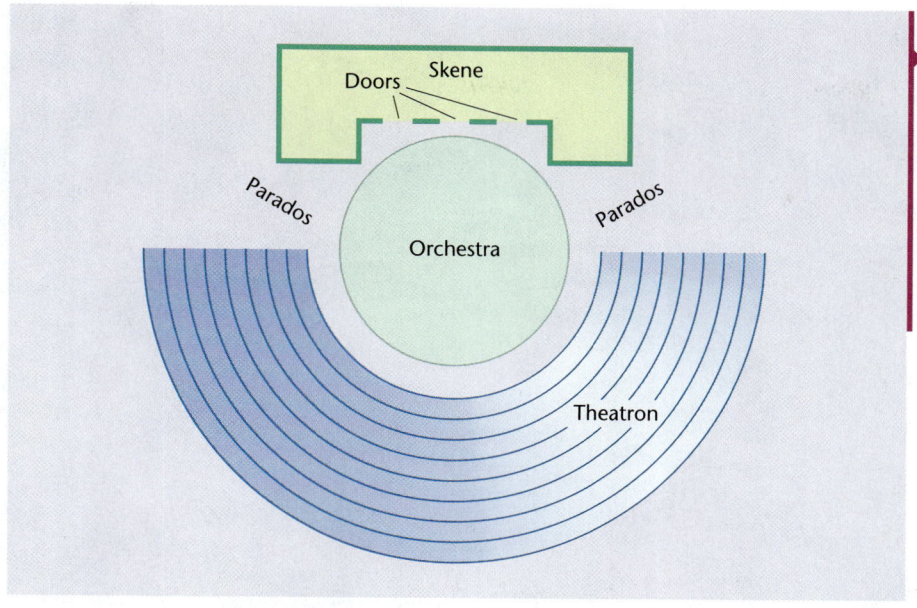

FIGURE 11.1 (a) Greece: Classical Theatre Ground Plan
(b) Greece: Audience View

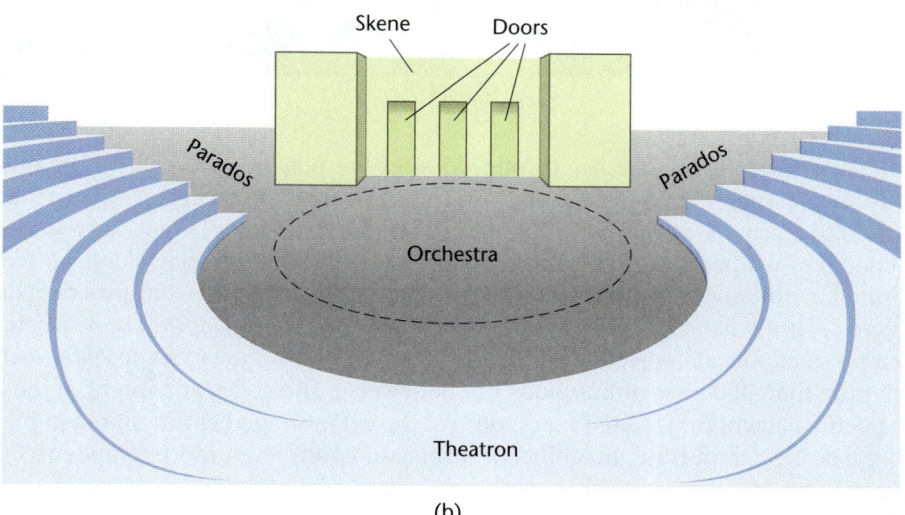

(one of which dramatizes the story of Electra) explore personal vengeance and the creation of a standard for criminal justice. Aeschylus also wrote the only Greek tragedy we have that was based on events in the playwright's own time rather than mythology: *The Persians* (472 B.C.E.) examines with sympathy enemies of Greece whom the playwright had fought a few years earlier.

Some of the plays of Sophocles, especially *Oedipus the King* (c. 430–425 B.C.E.) and *Antigone* (c. 441 B.C.E.), both explorations of guilt and crimes against divine law, are often studied as perfect examples of Greek tragedy and are frequently revived and anthologized for courses in dramatic literature. Although written and first performed at different points in the career of Sophocles, *Oedipus the King*, *Oedipus at Colonus* (406 B.C.E.), and *Antigone* in our own time are sometimes performed together as if they are a trilogy. All three plays deal with the family of Oedipus.

Euripides left us many poignant depictions of suffering and domestic conflict, perhaps most notably in *Medea* (431 B.C.E.), a tragedy of revenge in which the title character kills her children in order to punish her adulterous husband, and *The Trojan Women* (415 B.C.E.), an examination of the victims of war and the horror of its aftermath.

THEATRE OF DIONYSUS in Athens, Greece. This is the most famous theatre in the history of Greek theatre. Unfortunately, this space where the plays of Aeschylus, Sophocles, Euripides, and Aristophanes were first performed was severely remodeled in the Hellenistic period and again by the Imperial Romans after they took control of Athens. The shape of the orchestra, the wall around the orchestra and the remains of the skene are all from much later periods than the classical era of the sixth and fifth centuries BCE. The space is such a ruin that it is no longer useful as a performance space.

2010 photo © Ronald Wainscott.

Euripides also wrote *The Bacchae* (produced after the playwright's death), the only tragedy still surviving in which the god Dionysus appears as a character. *The Bacchae* continues to fascinate audiences with its conflict of mortals and the god surrounded by a chorus of women possessed by Dionysus. In 2002 Euripides' play *Hypsipyle* was performed in outdoor Greek theatres for the first time since the fifth century B.C.E. This play was lost until major fragments were discovered in 1906. Most of the reconstructed text for production was conjectural, but audiences for the first time in some 2,400 years heard more than 400 lines of Euripides' dramatic verse. The styles and intent of these three poetic playwrights differed markedly, yet the extant tragedies are united in presenting a searing, mournful, magnificent display of agony, endurance, grandeur, fall from greatness, and a remarkable human spirit that rises in the face of despair.

The Greeks also left us comedy. The satirical, ridiculous extravaganzas of Aristophanes are infused with fantasy and bawdy jokes. His attacks on contemporary people whom he found corrupt, governmental practices he found misguided, or artistic endeavors he found inferior abound in his lyrical plays full of choric songs and impossible events. Often a political and social reactionary in his plays, Aristophanes staged *The Clouds* (423 B.C.E.) as an attack on the philosopher Socrates. He placed an actor wearing a Socrates mask high in the air in a basket (head in the clouds) hanging from a crane and surrounded him with a bizarre chorus of singing and dancing clouds. In *The Frogs* (405 B.C.E.) Aristophanes dramatizes a mock competition between the real but deceased playwrights Euripides and Aeschylus in the underworld. Aristophanes favors the more conservative Aeschylus, who could save Athens from its woes, it is said, if only he could return from the grave. This fantasy becomes the first important document of dramatic criticism. It is unfortunate that we have no comedies from any other playwrights who preceded or competed against Aristophanes, but his eleven plays still leave a vivid picture of Athenian social, political, and cultural life.

Despite the importance of the plays and the significance of Greek theatre in the Western theatrical tradition, we really know very little about Greek classical theatre production, since the playwrights left no stage directions and most of the surviving information is sketchy. We are intrigued, for example, that some "pass the hat" street

EXPLORING Historical and Cultural Perspectives

Rediscovering Menander

After several thousand years, scholars are grateful that any texts from the ancient world survive. What we know about ancient Greek theatre depends on what people at the time and in subsequent periods valued, recorded, and saved—either purposely or by accident. Most of the Greek plays that still exist are available because people through the centuries thought they were worthy of study or production, copied them by hand (before the invention of the printing press), and taught them in schools.

The twentieth-century rediscovery of the work of the Hellenistic comic playwright Menander is an exciting story of archaeological and detective work. Menander lived from about 342 to about 291 B.C.E. There are records of his having written over one hundred plays, eight of which won first prize in contests. Menander's work was highly thought of in the ancient world; his reputation grew in stature in the centuries after his death. His plays were known until late antiquity, but during the Middle Ages, any surviving texts were lost. At the beginning of the twentieth century only a few papyrus fragments of Menander's plays were available to read and study. Papyrus (from which our word "paper" is derived) is a plant material that was used to write on in ancient Egypt. Other bits and pieces of Menander's work were saved because they were quoted by later critics, grammarians, and other authors. Otherwise, Hellenistic comedy was known only by what people had said about it and by some Roman comedies that were known to use Hellenistic comedy as a source.

In 1905 an excavation in Egypt turned up part of a papyrus book, or *codex*, dating from the fifth century C.E. These fragments, called the *Cairo Codex*, were published in 1907. Large parts of three plays by Menander were now available, as well as smaller pieces of two other plays. Half a century later, the *Bodmer Codex* (named for the European collector who bought it) was discovered in Egypt. This papyrus, dating from the third century C.E., contained one nearly complete play, *The Dyskolos* (often translated as *The Grouch* or *Old Cantankerous*), which had first been performed in 316 B.C.E. Published in 1959, this comedy about a grumpy old father who gets along with no one revolutionized the study of Hellenistic comedy. The *Bodmer Codex* also contained parts of *The Girl from Samos* and *The Shield,* which were published in 1969. The dry climate of Egypt is credited with allowing the papyri to survive for such a long time.

Other fragments of Menander have turned up in surprising places: in the outer wrappings or cases of mummies. A material called cartonnage, made from papyrus or linen and plaster and then painted, was often used to decorate or enclose mummies. The Egyptians made cartonnage with recycled pieces of papyrus (to use new papyrus would have been extremely expensive). Painstaking stripping of mummy cartonnage has resurrected a number of valuable papyri. Pieces of another Menander play, *The Sikyonian,* were found

A DOMESTIC SCENE from Roman comedy. Many Roman comic plays were adapted from or inspired by Menander, a Hellenistic Greek. The two figures on the left are older male figures. A flute player is at center, and a girl and slave are at right.

By permission of Bridgeman Art Library.

in Egypt in 1906 in part of the cartonnage of a mummy case. Almost sixty years later, large pieces of the missing sections of *The Sikyonian*—from the *same document*—were found in two mummy cases in a Paris museum. These fragments were published in 1965. Together, these discoveries produced about 500 lines of the play. Scholars are still hopeful that some day the missing 300 lines of *The Sikyonian* might be rediscovered. Even once a papyrus fragment has been found and identified, it is often damaged and difficult to reconstruct. Its publication and translation are painstaking processes calling on years of expertise and research.

INTERESTED? Check out

Menander. *The Plays and Fragments.* Translated by Maurice Balme; introduced by Peter Brown. Oxford, UK: Oxford University, 2001.

Stanley Ireland. *Menander: Dyskolos, Sami and Other Plays: A Companion to the Penguin Translation of the Plays of Menander by Norma Miller.* London: Bristol Classics, 1992.

For more on papyri, see the Duke Papyrus Archive at http://scriptorium.lib.duke.edu/papyrus, especially "From the World of the Papyri" (http://scriptorium.lib.duke.edu/papyrus/texts/world.html) and "Writing in Egypt under Greek and Roman Rule" (http://scriptorium.lib.duke.edu/papyrus/texts/rule.html), which includes a picture of a papyrus fragment of a play by Euripides.

ROMAN THEATRE OF HERODES ATTICUS. After the Romans took over Greece, they modified but were dissatisfied with the Greek theatres and started building their own, such as this one in Athens, which is still used for performances. In this photo the theatre is being prepared for a concert. The complete enclosure, half-circle orchestra, five entrance doors, and low stage (pulpitum) are typical of Roman design. The top of the scaena façade is only slightly higher than the top of the cavea (seating area). Note that the doorways dwarf the people onstage.

2010 Photo © Ronald Wainscott.

performers called **mimes** seemed to include women in their companies (Plato records an example), but the institutional theatre never allowed women to perform. Unfortunately, we know little about Greek mimes. Nonetheless, the plays and ideas that are evident in Greek theatre are replete with exciting possibilities. Greek plays continued to be written and performed in Greek-controlled territory long after the fall of Athens in 404 B.C.E. It was well after the Athenian decline that the Hellenistic philosopher Aristotle wrote his influential *Poetics* (c. 335–323 B.C.E.), which stands as the first important examination of the tragic form. When combined with the remarkable philosophy, art, and architecture of the Greeks, the legacy of their theatre inspires many play revivals, new plays, dramatic theory, uses of masks, theatre architecture, and contemporary scenic design.

CLASSICAL ROME

The Republic of Rome conquered all Greek territory by 146 B.C.E., but nearly a hundred years earlier Romans had begun performing plays based on and inspired by the tragedies and comedies of Greece. Like their forebears, the Romans performed plays at religious festivals but differed by dedicating the productions to any of their gods as long as the festivals honored one god at a time. Legend credits Livius Andronicus (third century B.C.E.) with the first plays and acting performances, but no plays survive until the comedies of Plautus (c. 254–184 B.C.E.) and Terence (c. 195/185–159 B.C.E.). Roman comic playwrights adapted Greek comedies, like those of Menander, but eliminated the chorus (a major departure). Although heavily influenced by Greek theatre, the Roman theatricals should not be seen as strictly derivative. The Romans made many stylistic and content changes, and when we are able to compare fragments of the work, it is clear that the Romans provided numerous original touches that reflected their own values and culture.

Roman theatre spaces and production techniques also built on the Greeks, but the results were very different. Instead of using hillsides, the Romans erected freestanding theatres that surrounded the audience and performers while remaining open to the sky for light. These were the first theatres to focus the audience's attention strictly

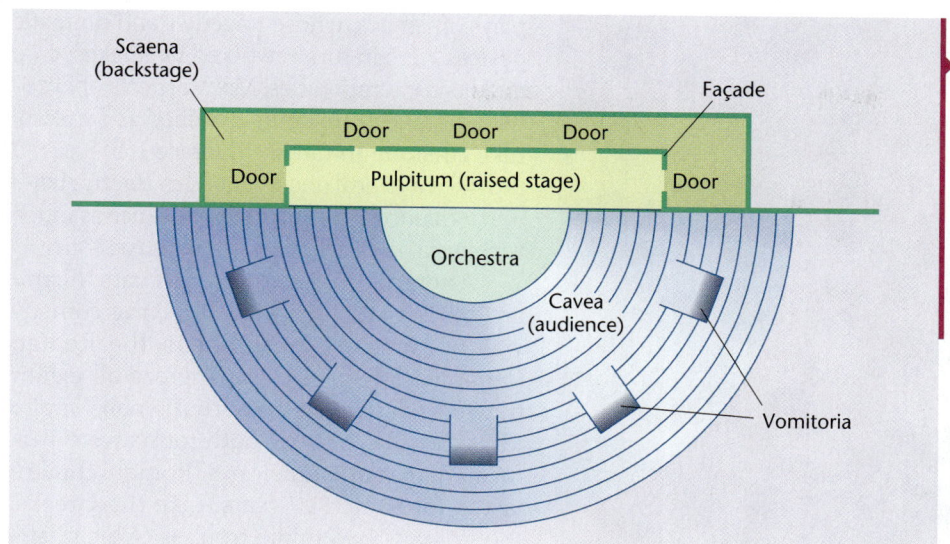

FIGURE 11.2 Rome: Theatre Ground Plan

on the stage without distractions from the surrounding environment. Roman architects exploited the arch to extend their structures high into the air. Because some of these imposing theatres have survived remarkably intact throughout Europe and North Africa, we can reconstruct the Roman structures more authoritatively than we can the Greek ones (see Figure 11.2). Romans introduced many devices that continue in modern usage such as stage **traps** (openings in the stage floor for ascents and descents) and **vomitories** (stadium-like entrances for the audience) as well as a front curtain. Roman Latin also contributed many words permanently to our theatre vocabulary such as *actor, auditorium,* and *histrionics.*

Like the Greeks, the Roman actors were males who performed in masks in large open spaces backed by a stone **façade** (architectural background) punctuated by a series of doors. A half-orchestra still remained in the space, but it was no longer used by the actors. The orchestra became a place for special audience seating or sometimes water shows. The Romans added walls to the orchestra so that they could flood it with water when the occasion arose. A few names of actors have survived, and one of them, Roscius (c. 131–62 B.C.E.), became synonymous in the popular mind with great acting. Until the twentieth century, when the term faded from common usage, a talented actor was often referred to as a "Roscius."

The comedies of Plautus and Terence are rollicking farcical situation comedies focused on domestic trivialities, pratfalls, misunderstandings, and mistaken identities. These plays (which were really musical comedies, although the music vanished long ago) influenced many playwrights beyond their time, especially in the European Renaissance. Plautus created the definitive mistaken identity play in *The Brothers Menaechmus* (c. 205–184 B.C.E.), wherein twin brothers are reunited after much confusion. The model of the masterful trickster is enshrined in *The Phormio* (161 B.C.E.) by Terence. A wily servant tricks two stodgy fathers into accepting their sons' romantic choices. Roman sitcoms and their form have continued into the present adapted as musicals (*The Boys from Syracuse,* 1938; *A Funny Thing Happened on the Way to the Forum,* 1962), movies (the Marx Brothers, Mel Brooks), and television shows. The antics of Roman comedy are still very familiar to audiences of nearly all ages and cultures, and they seem much more modern than do the surviving Greek comedies.

Roman tragedies, although rarely revived any more, also influenced later periods. The tragedies of Seneca (c. 4 B.C.E.–65 C.E.) have Greek sources but are extensively reconceived adaptations of *Oedipus, Medea,* and others. In Seneca's interpretations, the violence escalates. Seneca was fascinated by revenge as a motivation, and only he (at least in surviving plays) maintained something of a chorus. Supernatural figures also stalk the

A MOSAIC OF TWO ROMAN MASKS. On the left is a male slave mask from comedy. On the right is a female mask from tragedy. Like the Greek masks, these fit over the head, not on the front of the face. Behind the female mask is a pair of flutes used in performance.

From Museo Capatolini, Rome. By permission of Scala/Art Resource.

plays of Seneca, whose tragedies and dramatic devices were in turn reworked by Shakespeare and his contemporaries. Many aspects of Elizabethan tragedy are often identified as Senecan. Like Aristotle in Greece, Horace (65–8 B.C.E.) provided a critical document—his ***Poetic Art***—that influenced the Italian Renaissance as much as Seneca and perhaps more than Aristotle.

Attempts to generalize Roman theatre are problematic, since all surviving comedy was written and produced in the Roman Republic (509–27 B.C.E.), whereas all extant tragedies date from the early Roman Empire (27 B.C.E.–476 C.E.). Yet both forms were performed in both eras, and Roman theatre lasted for some 800 years. Like the Greeks, the Romans had mime troupes (which definitely included women). The mimes, along with musical pantomime performers in the late years of the empire, became more popular than the regular theatre. Some mime troupes even included sex acts and scatological parodies of early Christian ritual. It is not surprising that with the conversion of Rome to Christianity as a state religion and the fall of the Roman Empire, the institution of the theatre crumbled and disappeared in Europe for a considerable time.

MEDIEVAL EUROPE

Well before the fall of the Roman Empire, imperial leadership had converted to Christianity, which ultimately dominated both religion and government in Europe after 500 C.E. New church leaders such as Tertullian in c. 200 C.E. stringently attacked theatre, acting, spectacle, and any kind of secular, imaginative literature such as plays. Although there is evidence to support ongoing itinerant theatrical activity in Europe during the so-called Dark Ages (500–900), there is no evidence of any formal, legal theatre until the tenth century. Ironically, accepted theatre practice was reborn in the church itself. Inspired by reading the Roman comedies of Terence, Hrotsvitha, a tenth-century German canoness (associated with a nunnery), created fascinating Christian plays featuring dynamic heroines. Hrotsvitha's plays might not have been performed in her lifetime, but celebrations of famous stories from the Judeo-Christian Bible proliferated throughout Europe.

Tropes were presented as early as around 925. In these exchanges of dialogue in musical form, the singers or chanters represented characters from the Bible, such as the three Marys at the tomb of Jesus in a trope called *Quem Quaeritis* ("Whom Do You Seek?"). For centuries these and other types of **liturgical dramas** (plays included as part of the worship service) were performed in Latin by the clergy in many monasteries and cathedrals. The clerics also established an approach to staging that used an open space (*platea*) in front of an emblematic background (**mansion**). This system remained the chief model for nearly all medieval staging practices both inside the church and in the community (see Figure 11.3).

Although liturgical plays continued to be performed, after around 1200 many extravagant religious **cycles,** or collections of plays, were performed outdoors and were not confined to cathedrals and monasteries. Cycles were performed in the vernacular (the local language) rather than Latin and appeared throughout Europe. The plays in these cycles, often called **mystery plays,** were based on biblical stories and ranged from the creation of the world to the last judgment. These collections of mysteries, such as the Wakefield Cycle in England and the Valenciennes cycle in France, remained the cornerstone of medieval theatre because they were so popular, plentiful, and vividly theatrical.[2]

Mansion (symbolic scenic unit behind platea)

Platea (open playing space)

FIGURE 11.3 Medieval Mansion / Platea

One of the most famous religious dramatic forms of medieval Europe was the **morality play,** which depicted humanity's struggle with good and evil. Structured as a journey, most morality plays followed a generic character through his lifetime. *The Castle of Perseverance* (c. 1425) and *The World and the Child* (c. 1520), for example, follow the central character, Mankind (representing all humanity), from cradle to grave. The most famous morality play, however, *Everyman* (c. 1500), dramatizes only the final hours of a man facing his death. All morality plays were peopled with symbolic allegorical characters such as Good Deeds, Pride, and Gluttony, giving human characteristics to abstract ideas.

Like the theatre of Greece and Rome, the cycles were performed as part of religious festivals, most frequently in association with the holidays Corpus Christi, Easter, and Christmas. Famous mysteries depicted Cain killing his brother Abel; Noah and the

SCENIC MANSIONS lined up on an open stage (*platea*) at Valenciennes in France c. 1547 for a cycle of biblical plays. The mansion representing Heaven is on the far left, and Hellmouth is on the far right emitting flames, smoke, and demons. In between are locations associated with the life of Jesus: Nazareth, a temple, the gates of Jerusalem, the palace of King Herod, and the Sea of Galilee.
Painted by Hubert Cailleau. From Bibliotheque Nationale. By permission of Bridgeman Art Library.

EXPLORING Collaboration
The Community, the Church, and the Feast of Corpus Christi

In 1311 Pope Clement V instituted a new holy day (holiday). Corpus Christi ("body of Christ") was meant to be a day of thanks and celebration for the sacrifice and redemptive power of Christ, symbolized by the Eucharist (Communion). The Roman Catholic Church had recognized the power of theatrical performance as a means of spreading its doctrine. By the end of the fourteenth century, cycles of plays were an integral part of the midsummer Feast of Corpus Christi. Although it began as a single day, the holiday grew over the centuries to three or four days in some places and a week, two weeks, or almost a month in others. Not surprisingly, the most elaborate productions occurred in population centers—market towns with a fairly large number of residents and ample resources. These towns developed complex cycle plays to honor and celebrate the holiday. The massive undertaking required the collaboration of many different parties.

Guilds became well established in the medieval population centers as a means for people in the same field to support each other and further their professional interests. Merchant guilds became prominent in the civic arena as growing towns replaced the old feudal way of life. Craft guilds provided a way for artisans and craftsmen (such as weavers, painters, and bakers) to set standards, train new workers (using an apprentice system), and regulate competition. The craft guilds came to play a vital role in the Corpus Christi festivities as individual guilds took responsibility for staging specific plays. In some instances the type of guild was matched to an appropriate story. The York Cycle, for example, included nearly fifty plays. The shipbuilders produced the play about the building of the ark; the fishers and mariners produced the story of Noah and the flood; the bakers produced the Last Supper. In a rather macabre pairing, the butchers produced the torture, crucifixion, and burial of Christ. The goldsmiths took charge of the coming of the three kings (magi) bearing gifts, perhaps displaying their handiwork on stage. Some guilds were established for the express purpose of funding and organizing plays.

Plays for the cycles were written for and became the property of specific towns. There was work to be done in preparation for the festival, including construction of scenic units and props, making or borrowing costumes, finding and rehearsing actors and musicians, erecting viewing or performance platforms, and selling tickets. Crowd control had to be organized, and housing had to be provided for the flood of audience members from nearby villages and farms.

The production of plays for Corpus Christi served many functions. The clergy saw an opportunity for bringing the stories of the Bible vividly to life in the language of the people when church services and the Bible were in Latin and

MEDIEVAL ACTOR IN DEVIL COSTUME, holding his mask, probably for a cycle play. Note that he holds a clawed pitchfork, but wears a contemporary sword.
Manuscript image from Bibliothèque de l'Arsenal, Paris.

the public was largely illiterate. Community leaders saw an opportunity to build prestige; merchants benefited from the influx of potential customers; craftsmen were able to perform a community service and raise awareness of their professional organization simultaneously. The creative activity was no doubt a welcome change from the rigors of medieval life for performers, technicians, and audience members.

INTERESTED? Check out

Glynne Wickham. *The Medieval Theatre.* 3rd ed. Cambridge, UK: Cambridge University, 1987.

Visit http://english/cua.edu/toronto/york98.cfm to read about a revival in 1998 of the entire York Cycle at the University of Toronto, the first production of *all* the surviving plays since the final performance in York in 1569.

See also the website for Poculi Ludique Societas in Toronto at www.homes.chass.utoronto.ca/plspls/intro

great flood; and the trial, crucifixion, and resurrection of Jesus. The most famous and one of the finest of the mysteries is *The Second Shepherds' Play* from the Wakefield Cycle. This mixed-tone play ends with a solemn presentation of the nativity of the Christ child, but most of the play is given over to comic action about shepherds trying to outwit a sheep thief. The action is full of ironic parallels between a fake birth (using a lamb) and the birth of the "lamb of God."

Some communities also presented **miracle plays** (or *saint's plays*) such as *Mary Magdalene* (c. 1500) that recounted the real or apocryphal lives of saints. The cycles drew on the community for actors and sometimes had a version of a director (called **play master**); the scenic support was often spectacular and full of wondrous events depicting transformations and miracles. The cycles and miracle plays grew in number and complexity (lasting from one to twenty-five days) until conflict over the Protestant Reformation led the Catholic Church to reconsider some of its practices; Protestant countries banned the cycles and all religious plays as corrupt in the 1500s. Despite the official bans, some cycles continued for a while, but only Spain continued to perform them until the eighteenth century.

Most playwrights and actors of medieval Europe remain anonymous to us, but we know much about staging practices because of many detailed accounts and **promptbooks** (books containing scripts, detailed stage directions, and production practices). The promptbook from the Lucerne (Switzerland) cycle also includes drawings of the setting laid out in the town square. Such staging usually had the mansions of heaven and hell as the boundaries. All other mansions and dramatic action took place between these poles of biblical redemption and damnation. Some productions used **processional staging:** Moving wagons or **pageants** (think of floats in a parade) traveled through the streets carrying actors and scenery to perform in various locations.

Secular plays (nonreligious dramas) began to be written and performed again by the 1200s. Some of these farces are still produced. *Johan, Johan* (1533), which was written by John Heywood in England, follows a credulous husband as he gets revenge on his wife who betrays him with a lustful priest. Some intriguing secular musical plays, such as Adam de la Halle's *Robin and Marion* (c. 1283, from France), have a mixed tone. Often presented between courses at a banquet, such plays were called **interludes.** Through narration and direct audience address, the characters in medieval drama frequently move between the world of the play and the spectators' reality. A famous interlude, *Fulgens and Lucrece* (1497), by Henry Medwall, features two narrators (named "A" and "B"), who at one point stop narrating and join the action of the play's story because one of them is attracted to the heroine. The interlude and the morality play, both of which were often performed by professional acting companies, are the most important indications of a European return to institutional theatre outside religious drama. Aspects of the interlude are often evident in Shakespeare's plays written for professional companies. Unlike the classical European forms that preceded and followed medieval practice, medieval Europe produced no tragedy. Mixed tone in medieval mystery cycles, moralities, and interludes, however, appears to have influenced Renaissance theatre in England and Spain.

CLASSICAL INDIA

Before the medieval Europeans rediscovered theatre, **Sanskrit plays** appeared in Hindu culture and suggested directions that later Asian theatre would take. A detailed document by Bharata, **The Natyasastra** (sometimes translated as "Doctrine of Dramatic Art"), which appears to predate the most important surviving Sanskrit plays, outlines the principles of performance, staging, and dramatic form as practiced in India and applied to Sanskrit plays. Theatrical origins are associated with the priest caste and the form is closely

THE MARTYRDOM OF SAINT APOLLONIA, depicted in a miniature painting by Jean Fouquet, c. 1445. This is thought to be a performance or rehearsal of a medieval miracle play played in the round. Scaffolding representing mansions and/ or seating areas appears in the background with many people in costumes of angels, demons, and so forth. The figure in a blue robe holding a book and baton is sometimes interpreted as the play master conducting and prompting the actors, but he could just as well be a performer.

From Lauros/Giraudon. By permission of Bridgeman Art Library.

KATHAKALI PERFORMER with extravagant makeup and costume. The stylization is extreme in this dramatic dance form. Note the long fingernails on the left hand, the mask-like approach to makeup, and the unusually wide skirt. The performer is always barefoot and the use of eyes and hands is critical to this style of performance.

2009 photo taken in Cochin, Kerala, India by Qnonsense at en.wikipedia.

tied to religion, but lower-caste actors soon joined in. Performance was very presentational and included colorful costumes, music, dance, and a complicated emblematic system of hand gestures. The type of theatre space varied, but it was decorative and symbolic rather than scenic. The actors performed on a mostly open stage. Unlike the Greek and Roman theatre, women often participated as actors in Sanskrit plays and performed prominent roles.

Most of the stories of Sanskrit drama are based on epic Indian literature such as the *Mahabharata* and the *Ramayana,* which featured heroic adventures of gods and mortals. The dramas are structurally organized around *rasas* (moods or sentiments), rather than action and event as we see in typical Western plays. All the plays end happily after a nearly free-form journey through time and space. Of the surviving plays, most are dated to the fourth and fifth centuries. Most famous among these are *Shakuntala,* the travails of an abandoned young mother, by Kalidasa, and *The Little Clay Cart,* the narrow escape of a virtuous courtesan from a jealous villain, attributed to King Sudraka. By the 1200s and hastened by an Islamic invasion of India, the creation of Sanskrit plays ceased, but Sanskrit contributed important drama that is still regularly studied and occasionally performed in both India and the West. Like Roman comedy, Sanskrit now exists primarily on paper, but early Indian performance styles cast a long shadow, which can still be glimpsed, often breathtakingly, in two related forms: Kutiyattum and Kathakali.

Before the decline of Sanskrit plays, another religious theatrical form based on ancient epics appeared in India called **Kutiyattum**, which was performed in temples and can still be seen by modern audiences. It appears to combine elements of the *Natyasastra* (including using actresses) with folk traditions. The visual and aural manifestations of Kutiyattum correspond to early Indian practice, using music, open space, and colorful costumes but without the philosophical texts of its Sanskrit predecessor. By 1700 or so, another remarkable dance-drama, **Kathakali**, appeared and is now often identified as the dominant classical theatre of India. This all-male epic theatre features some of the most incredible makeup and costumes found in any theatrical experience, and its complex system of gestures bears resemblance to the performance descriptions in the *Natyasastra*. Although little text exists in Kathakali, singers provide a narrative. The actor-dancers sometimes enact violent scenes, which were supposedly absent from the Sanskrit plays. Unlike the legacies of Greece and Rome that survive as a small collection of plays and influences, one can still see performances in India that reflect ongoing connections with ancient practices.

CLASSICAL CHINA

Although some kind of theatrical activity in China seems to have been brewing as early as the eighth century C.E., there is no evidence of professional theatre before the tenth century, after which differing forms of plays and theatrical styles developed in both northern and southern China. By the thirteenth century, as mystery cycles were flourishing in Europe, the first great Chinese plays appeared, identified as Yüan plays, since they were written during the Yüan Dynasty (1280–1368). Many of these plays fascinated the public and continue to be read and adapted in both Asian and Western culture. Most of the surviving plays remain anonymous or are credited to playwrights about whom we know little or nothing. *The Orphan of Chao,* an episodic adventure keyed to family revenge, made its way to the French stage in adaptation by the mid-eighteenth century. The wonderfully lyrical *Romance of the Western Chamber* by Wang Shifu is as long as a novel but still charms through its host of songs and the lightly erotic tale of two secret lovers. *The Circle of Chalk* (about a battle for custody of a child) by Li Xiandou is one of the most famous in the West through its adaptation by Bertolt Brecht as part of *The Caucasian Chalk Circle* (1944).

Chinese culture apparently produced no tragedy for the stage, but most of the plays feature a mixed tone like Sanskrit and might end either happily or sadly but with a sense of **poetic justice:** Virtue is rewarded; evil is punished. Instrumental music of strings, flute, and percussion was important, and many of the plays included solo singing. Unfortunately, as with Greece and Rome, the original music has not survived. Plays from the north were traditionally organized into four parts or acts and an additional scene called a *wedge* as either prologue or epilogue. Southern plays, in contrast, were written in many acts— up to fifty in some cases— and were more often comic or melodramatic.

CHINESE MUSIC DRAMA
Havoc in Heaven (Journey to the West), one of many Monkey King plays performed throughout China, but here at the Liyuan Theatre, Beijing, China (2010). The Monkey King actor on the right is wearing mask-like makeup and usually is involved in shenanigans, in this case because he is distressed by the treatment he receives from his queen mother.

Photo from Liyuan program, Beijing. Collection of the authors.

What is perhaps most striking about classical Chinese theatre, however, is the approach to performance, which was highly stylized with movement, dance, chant, and music. Different Chinese regions developed individual styles. In the early 1800s Chinese artists combined many of them to form what is now known as **Chinese music drama** (or *Beijing Opera*). The earliest known stages were nearly bare thrusts except for a carpet, a table, and two chairs; this configuration remains traditional for music drama. A performance could be indoors or out, but the stage was sometimes roofed. The traditional space had only two doorways upstage: one for entrances, the other for exits. The musicians and stage attendants remained onstage with the actors throughout (see Figure 11.4).

Music drama still tells epic and domestic stories, but the literary qualities of the earlier work are substantially diminished and replaced with remarkable acrobatics and various kinds of spectacle created by the actors themselves or through their ornate and colorful costumes and masklike makeup. Although both men and women performed in the early years of Chinese theatre, by the eighteenth century women were banished from the stage; they were not restored until 1912. Before banishment actresses often cross-dressed as males and sometimes led the acting troupes. Once women were removed, however, male cross-dressing featuring falsetto voice was established as a convention when music drama was being defined. Women have now returned to many of the

FIGURE 11.4 China: Yüan Playing Space

Backstage

Entrance   Exit

Stage

Carpet

Musicians

Audience

EMPRESS ZHANG, a famous character in Chinese music drama is now typically played by a woman, but for centuries the female characters were enacted by men. This beautiful character appears in many plays, but ultimately is killed in a military coup. She wears a dress decorated with a dragon and phoenix, emblems of imperial rank, and her white water sleeves are important elements of expression, emotion, dance, and beauty. Many characters, male and female, use water sleeves.

Beijing Opera postcard. Collection of the authors.

FIGURE 11.5 Noh Theatre

female roles. Through contemporary performance we can still see many traditions inherited from a sophisticated professional theatre that flourished in China at a time when Europe saw little but religious dramas performed by amateurs.

CLASSICAL JAPAN

Toward the end of the Yüan Dynasty in China, the first great classical theatre of Japan, **Noh** theatre, developed in the court of the shogun in the feudal samurai system of the late fourteenth century. Noh has always maintained music and dance as part of the dramatic presentation. Two early master actor-playwrights created and perfected the Noh theatre. Kan'ami (1333–1384) is credited with defining Noh's essential form, and his work is represented well by *Sotoba Komachi,* a play in which an aging woman is possessed by the spirit of her dead lover. *Sotoba Komachi* and nearly all the Noh plays are products of reflection as practiced in Zen Buddhism. Typically, the play is in the past tense, recalling painful events of long ago. Kan'ami's son Zeami (1363–1444) is considered the most important figure of Noh, not only because he wrote hundreds of plays, many of which are still performed, but also because he wrote theory of performance and composition. His **Kadensho** presents the central image of Noh, *yugen,* which means the creation of temporary beauty—likening the Noh performance to a flower: elegant, lovely, transitory.

Noh theatre traditionally presents a varied program of plays, reflecting different moods and styles. A favorite play is *Hagoromo* (attributed to Zeami). It depicts a goddess who removes her magical robe to bathe in a stream, only to have the robe taken by a fisherman. She must enchant him with a dance to get him to return the robe. This climactic dance is an expected event in Noh structure. All is performed on a templelike, open, semithrust stage with a highly polished floor. The audience is seated on two sides (downstage and stage right). On the upstage wall is a large painted pine tree, and the main square of the stage is outlined by four pillars supporting a roof. A railed bridge (*hashigakari*) leads from the backstage mirror room (a space for actor preparation) to the acting area (see Figure 11.5).

The leading character (*shite*) is masked, but most other characters are not. The actors perform in front of onstage musicians playing flute and percussion, and a chorus, which often speaks for the *shite,* although we also hear the *shite's* voice. Actors are traditionally male (even though most *shite* roles are female) and assisted onstage by neutrally costumed stage attendants whom the audience pretends are not visible. The gestures of actors are highly stylized and often accentuated by remarkable uses of fans.

Noh continues to be performed, and new audience members are struck by the colorful costumes, enigmatic masks, and slow, stately, ritualistic approach to performance.

The most popular classical Japanese form is **Kabuki,** which began in 1603 through the dancing performances of the priestess Okuni. Although Kabuki was begun by a woman and the form was dominated by female performers for over twenty-five years, the government banned women from Kabuki in 1629. It has been traditionally performed by men ever since, with female roles, or **onnagata,** performed by men who specialize in this form of cross-dressing. Kabuki features original plays as well as many adapted from Noh and puppet theatre (**Bunraku**), which includes some

Mirror room

Painted pine tree

Hashigakari

Hurry door

Three pine trees

Audience

Four pillars

Audience

of the most famous plays of Japan. The most celebrated playwright, Chikamatsu (1683–1725), wrote for both Kabuki and Bunraku and has been widely translated. One of his most famous plays is *Love Suicides at Sonezaki* (1703), which explores social and domestic problems. Two lovers kill themselves because they are unable to realize the marriage they desire. For the most part, however, the playwrights are not considered nearly as important as the actors in Kabuki. It is first and foremost an actors' theatre; the best actors are given names associated with great actors of the past who performed the same roles. Danjuro XII, for example, performed for many years as Ebizo X before he was "promoted" in 1985 to Danjuro, the most famous acting name in Kabuki.

As in Noh, music, dance, and colorful costumes are significant in Kabuki. It was originally performed on stages adapted from Noh, but ultimately Kabuki took a very different direction. Kabuki actors do not wear masks, but the makeup is often intricate and masklike. Typically, Kabuki performance is spectacular, using a revolving stage (the first in the world, created in 1758), huge elevator traps, and special effects that delight audiences with a mixture of realism and stylization. In *Masakado* (*The Demon Princess*, 1836), for example, the princess creates a magical dance that causes an earthquake, and the play ends with all the scenery collapsing. Kabuki is a great borrower and added the proscenium arch after encountering it in the late nineteenth century. The most dynamic element of the performance space, however, is the **hanamichi,** a stage-level ramp that passes directly from the stage apron down right center to the back of the house. This narrow path, which places the actor in the midst of the audience, is used for many important entrances and exits (see Figure 11.6).

Many Kabuki plays feature betrayed romance, eroticism, and military themes. In *Kumagai's Camp* (1751) a samurai warrior must confront the severed head of his own son and pretend that it is the head of his enemy. Any display of emotion would be seen as betrayal by Kumagai's shogun. The actor's remarkable skill with **mie** (a showy pose and facial expression suggesting sustained emotion) must reveal his grief to the audience while concealing it from his lord. Kabuki tends to be the classical form most accessible to Western audiences who are first encountering theatre in Japan.

Most of these Western and Asian classical and seminal forms continue to be performed and adapted in theatrical production, deconstructed or revised by experimenters, and studied by scholars and students of the theatre. Much of what we continue to pursue in the theatre and its scholarship has either built on this work or rebelled against it; the plays and styles and approaches to production developed so long ago by the Greeks, Romans, Medieval Europeans, Indians, Chinese, and Japanese make up our artistic legacy—inspiration to those who followed and the foundation for the theatre's ongoing journey with audiences of the twenty-first century.

OUTDOOR NOH THEATRE at Yasaka Shinto Shrine in Kyoto, Japan (2006). A temple-like canopy rests on four pillars over the main stage, laid out in a square. The stage adjoins a ramp on the stage-right side (*hashigakari*) that in turn is connected to the mirror room from which the protagonist (*shite*), will emerge in every Noh play.

Photo © Ronald Wainscott.

FIGURE 11.6 Kabuki Theatre

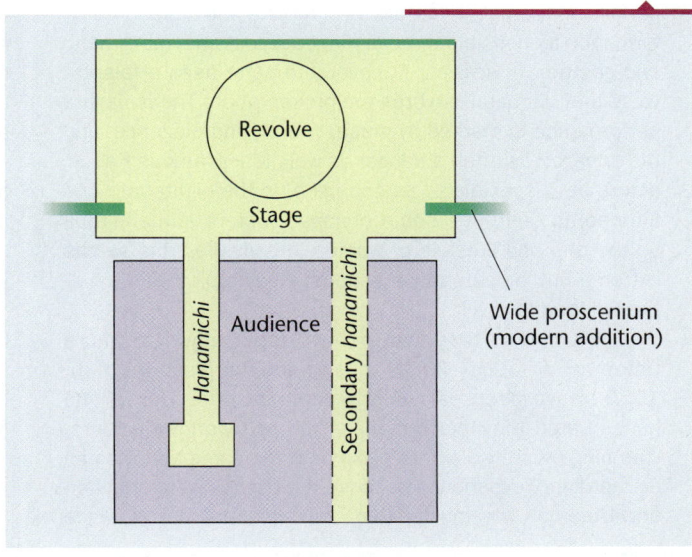

Revolve

Stage

Hanamichi   Audience   Secondary hanamichi

Wide proscenium (modern addition)

EXPLORING Historical and Cultural Perspectives

Kabuki Cross-Dressing: The *Onnagata*

TWO ONNAGATA PERFORMANCES: On the right is Tamasaburo as Princess Taema in *The Thunder God* with Ebizo as Narukami. On the left is Utaemon as Princess Takiyasha in *Masakado.* He is seen here in a dance reflecting both graceful presence and demonic possession. Note the spider web motif on his costume, which is important imagery for his character.

Kabuki grand tour of the United States. Photo by the Japan Society. Kabuki Grand Tour program (1982). Collection of the authors.

Although the Japanese classical theatre form called Kabuki was created by women, it was taken over by men in 1629 according to government decree. *Onnagata* is the Kabuki term for the actor who is a female impersonator. The male performer attempts to create as complete and literal a transformation as possible through makeup, costume, movement, and gesture. In speech, however, the actor uses a falsetto voice that ultimately stylizes the presentation. The *onnagata* performance is marked by grace, charm, and elegance, and the *onnagata* is often a dancer as well. Many famous Kabuki actors have specialized as *onnagata.* In the eighteenth and nineteenth centuries some *onnagata* actors actually took up the role and lifestyle of women in daily life. This seems extreme but indicates how seriously they took their work—they wished to live it.

In our own time two actors especially, Nakamura Utaemon VI (1917–2001) and Bando Tamasaburo V (b. 1950), have been particularly popular and effective and have shared their performances through worldwide tours. Watching these two actors perform at the same time was an extraordinary experience because their styles were so different. Utaemon was much older than Tamasaburo. His dance

and gestural work were subtler, and he seemed very vulnerable, although he often suppressed emotionality except for extreme moments of tension. Tamasaburo, by contrast, seemed more direct. His physical work was more dynamic and at times flashier. Both actors, however, despite the falsetto voice, were very convincing as women. When watching them, one thought of "she," not "he."

Tamasaburo continues as a star not only in Kabuki but also in film and dance. He has played Shakespeare's Lady Macbeth, for example, and has choreographed and danced to classical music by Bach as it was played live by the sensational cellist Yo-Yo Ma.

INTERESTED? Check out

Samuel L. Leiter, ed. *A Kabuki Reader: History and Performance.* New York: M. E. Sharpe, 2002.

Iwao Kamimura. *Kabuki Today.* Tokyo: Kodansha, 2001.

Masterpieces of Kabuki. Shochiku Home Video, a division of NHK in Japan. Distributed in North America by marty-grossfilms.com. A 33-DVD series of Kabuki performances in Japanese with English translation and commentary.

CHAPTER REVIEW

Questions and Activities

1. Theatre was an important part of religious and civic celebrations in ancient Greek and medieval communities, involving the entire town, even the region, in the event. Do we have an equivalent today?

2. Noh is the product of a time and place very different from ours. The first time an audience member sees Noh theatre, it is often necessary to adjust his or her approach to time: Noh proceeds at a slow, ritualistic, and meditative pace. Do your perceptions change as you participate in different types of activities or experience different forms of entertainment? Do you prepare yourself in different ways, mentally and/or physically? Do you think people who grew up playing computer and video games perceive the world in a different way from those who did not?

3. How do you think the different theatre spaces of Greece and Rome would affect an audience's viewing experience? Both were open air, but the Greek theatres were built into a hillside (the audience was often facing a magnificent landscape), and the Roman theatres were freestanding.

Key Terms and Concepts

chorus, p. 264
dithyramb, p. 264
orchestra, p. 264
parados, p. 264
skene, p. 264
theatron, p. 264
trilogy, p. 264
revival, p. 264
mime, p. 268
Poetics, p. 268
trap, p. 269
vomitories, p. 269
façade, p. 269
Poetic Art, p. 270

trope, p. 270
liturgical drama, p. 270
platea, p. 270
mansion, p. 270
cycle, p. 270
mystery play, p. 270
morality play, p. 271
miracle play, p. 273
play master, p. 273
promptbook, p. 273
processional staging, p. 273
pageant, p. 273
interlude, p. 273
Sanskrit play, p. 273

The Natyasastra, p. 273
Kutiyattum, p. 274
Kathakali, p. 274
poetic justice, p. 275
Chinese music drama, p. 275
Noh, p. 276
Kadensho, p. 276
Kabuki, p. 276
onnagata, p. 276
Bunraku, p. 276
hanamichi, p. 277
mie, p. 277

For Further Exploration

See the list of sources at the end of Chapter 13 on page 320.

ROMEO AND JULIET in 1753. Reconstructed version with David Garrick and Miss George Anne Bellamy in the tomb scene.
Photo by permission of the Folger Shakespeare Library.

Reinterpretations

Europe Rediscovers the Western Classics

Following a few precedents in nondramatic literature, by the sixteenth century European artists and scholars were seriously revisiting classical thought in playwriting and theatrical practice. Europeans at this time had little or no awareness of the Asian theatrical forms; serious melding of East and West in theatre would not occur until the late nineteenth century. For some 200 years or more, however, Europeans rejected medieval thought and practice and attempted to create a new classicism inspired by what they could learn about the Greeks and Romans. After remarkable experiments in Italy, England, Spain, and France, the European theatre settled into a nearly uniform approach to theatrical practice and dramaturgy (we will note the important variations). This uniformity, in plays at least, is usually called **neoclassicism**: a systematic approach to playwriting based on interpretations of classical Greek and Roman models of plays and theory.

THE ITALIAN RENAISSANCE

Between the Japanese eras of Zeami and Chikamatsu, Italy launched its Renaissance of art and literature. This rebirth of classically inspired creativity produced few plays that are still revived, but Italy's contributions to the theatre between about 1500 and 1700 were enduring achievements. Of course, Italian art looked back to the humanistic art, literature, and philosophy of the Greeks and Romans. This ferment at court and in the academies led directly to the Italian inventions of perspective painting of scenery and easily changeable scenery for the stage. Italians also invented the **proscenium arch** (picture frame) theatre, and because Italian theatre moved indoors, theatres standardized artificial illumination using candles and oil lamps. The Italians created opera as an attempt to understand and reconceive Greek tragedy, developed neoclassical principles for the writing of plays, and launched the vibrant, improvisational *commedia dell'arte.*

Italianate scenery was developed in part through inspiration from developments in perspective drawing and painting but also out of a keen desire to provide scenery for specific types of plays (tragedies, comedies, and pastoral tragicomedies) as well as spectacular scenic effects for court entertainments and opera. Perspective scenery for plays appeared as early as 1508, and standardized approaches to such scenery were popularized in the designs and writings of Sebastiano Serlio in 1545. Although Serlio and others experimented with a variety of methods for transferring perspective to the stage, the standard became two-dimensional, changeable **wings** or **flats** that could be pulled quickly on- and offstage in grooves on the floor and at the top of the tall wings. This system, fully implemented by Giovan Aleotti by 1606, eventually became the standard for all of Europe and North America. Consequently, there was great international demand for Italian designers such as Giacomo Torelli, who in the 1640s developed the chariot and pole system (winch, line, and tackle machinery that could change all the scenery simultaneously) (see Figure 12.1).

Italianate scenery was at first presented on platforms in halls without any kind of framing. After experiments with temporary

SIXTEENTH-CENTURY DESIGN for tragedy during the Italian Renaissance. Designed by Sebastiano Serlio. Note the single central vanishing point and that all scenery is drawn and painted to appear much farther away from the audience than it actually is. This became the standard visual approach to theatrical scenery in Western countries as they adopted the proscenium theatre and changeable scenery.

From *Serlio's Architettura, Book 2,* 1569 edition. Courtesy of Fine Arts Library, Indiana University.

Shutters or drop

Second wing position

First wing position

Stage

Apron

Audience

Proscenium arch

(a)

Proscenium arch

Drop (or shutters)

Borders

Wings

Apron

(b)

FIGURE 12.1 (a) Italian Renaissance Changeable Scenery (Wing, Drop, and Border), Ground Plan (b) Wing, Drop, and Border, Audience View

prosceniums, new theatres dedicated to court entertainments, opera, and theatre began to appear with permanent frames separating the audience from the scenery. The oldest proscenium theatre surviving to the twentieth century (reconstructed after being destroyed in World War II) is the Teatro Farnese in Parma, which was designed by Aleotti in 1618. By the late 1600s nearly every European theatre had a proscenium, and this kind of theatre architecture is still the most common throughout most of the world.

Italian neoclassicism began to develop early in the 1500s. By the late 1600s it was standard practice throughout the Western world and remained so until the early nineteenth century. Although playwrights from other countries wrote more significant plays using neoclassicism, the system was developed by Italian playwrights and theorists. Neoclassicism, which had accumulated all of its principles and rules by 1570 in a treatise by Lodovico Castelvetro, was an attempt to justify secular literature (including plays) and to get official and church sanction for the creation of nonreligious plays. The new method was inspired by the classical writings and plays of Greece and Rome as well as the authoritative treatises on drama written by Aristotle in Greece and Horace in Rome.

Once established, neoclassicism no longer needed to justify its existence, but the standards became rather inflexible rules against which the romantics finally rebelled in the late 1700s. Three basic tenets were central to neoclassicism: reality, morality, and universality. Reality did not mean realism but what the Italians called **verisimilitude,** which established that theatrical events as written and staged should be reality-based (events that could really occur in life). Some aspects of verisimilitude were drawn from the classics, some were not, and what often seemed a tendency in Greek and Roman plays became rules for the neoclassicists. The **three unities,** for example, can be found in some of the classics but were by no means rules in Greece. These were the unity of time (the action of the play should take place in twenty-four hours or less), unity of place (action should occur in one location), and unity of action (no subplots unless fully integrated with the central conflict). One of the most entertaining Italian comedies, Niccolo Machiavelli's *The Mandragola* (c. 1520), for example, takes place on a street in front of several houses in Florence. The events of the play span one day and night. All of the action is geared to an intrepid young man's successful seduction of a young wife and his trickery at the expense of her credulous old husband. The unities were meant to enhance believability of the action and scenic presentation while unifying the artistic integrity of the play. The pursuit of reality also led to avoiding onstage violence and supernatural events (no one would believe or accept them, it was thought).

Neoclassicism also demanded that plays should teach a moral lesson, at first to help justify secular subjects and receive the sanction of church and political authorities. Sometimes the moral lesson was stated at the conclusion of the play, or it was clearly implied throughout. Typically, the conclusion states the importance of not foiling true love, the rewards of remaining virtuous, or the idea that peace and human understanding only come after significant suffering. The early *Mandragola* did not follow this rule, but most Italian plays did. The neoclassicists also strove for an idealism and universality in morality and characterization, which led to much stereotyping of character. Known as **decorum,** this universality of character led playwrights to draw characters according to current notions of appropriate behavior, values, and language in terms of age, sex, social class, occupation, and economic condition.

Another unifying device was standardizing dramatic form by insisting that all plays be written in five acts, mostly based on the idea that appeared in Horace and the five-act division of Roman plays as received in the Renaissance. Even though the Italians reached a consensus with tragedy and comedy, they also experimented with tragicomedy and popularized it, especially through pastoral (rural and idyllic) mixed-tone plays such as *The Faithful Shepherd* (1590) by Giambattista Guarini. This play, dominated by romance and the failed efforts of villainy, along with Guarini's published theories, had a huge influence on tragicomedy in Spain and England.

From the early Renaissance in Italy and for centuries thereafter throughout Europe, most royal courts supported, subsidized, or commanded acting troupes, dancers, and musicians and sometimes enjoyed plays and special court productions created specifically to honor or please the royalty. From the 1400s to the 1600s in Italy such court entertainments were often called *intermezzi* and were spectacular pageants full of symbolism and allegory frequently performed between other entertainments or during the intervals between acts of a play or opera. England's version of court entertainment in the sixteenth and seventeenth centuries was the **masque,** a poetic extravaganza with dancing, often celebrating the monarch (particularly King James I or Charles I) or a royal visitor to the court.

When not working with fully scripted plays, the Italians ventured far from the restrictions of neoclassicism. Professional Italian **commedia dell'arte** (improvisational comedy) also became an international phenomenon whose import outlasted neoclassicism, but *commedia*'s origins are less certain. It appears that by the mid-1500s popular professional *commedia* companies were performing throughout Italy, and some had moved to other countries such as France by 1548. Because of similarities in character types, scenarios, and style, some historians surmise that *commedia* had its origins in the Greek and Roman mimes. However these actors might have developed their art, they found a huge following for their improvisational methods, acrobatic clowning, farcical plots, and attractive lovers. Many characters wore masks; for example, the servant clowns (**zanni**) such as Arlecchino and Brighella carried out foolishness and intrigues against ridiculous older masters such as Pantalone (a miser) and Capitano (a braggart soldier). But many unmasked characters were central to the action. Actresses played unmasked types such as the leading lady (**prima donna**) and young lover (**innamorata**), supposedly to reveal the beauty of the actresses. Of course, young male lovers (**innamorato**) were also unmasked for similar reasons. Actors followed a scenario or plot outline. Although the story of each scenario was fixed, the actors improvised much of the dialogue and action with each new performance.

Commedia dell'arte predated and worked outside the conventions of neoclassicism until the mid-1700s, when neoclassical playwrights in Italy and France convinced many *commedia* actors to start performing fully scripted plays, eliminate masks, and soften the broad humor. This neoclassicized *commedia* spelled the end for *commedia* as a continuing improvisational and farcical acting style. Because *commedia*'s characters, costumes, and the idea of improvisational style still fascinate us, many theatrical companies frequently revive plays based on *commedia*. Ironically, many plays that brought traditional *commedia* to an end are revived and performed in what is intended as a *commedia* style. In fact a multitude of contemporary "commedia" acting troupes have attempted to reconstitute the style and methods, and they frequently perform throughout Europe and North America.

ELIZABETHAN ENGLAND

Beyond doubt, the period of theatre history that tends to fascinate most contemporary Western theatregoers is that of William Shakespeare, who is usually lionized as the preeminent playwright of the English language, if not the world. Regardless of whether his importance is exaggerated, he is clearly the most famous playwright of Western civilization. What other playwrights can claim so many theatre festivals dedicated to them? Who does not know about *Hamlet* even if he or she has never read the play? Although most people today view the Elizabethan period of theatre through Shakespeare's work, Shakespeare's fellow Elizabethans would not have done so.

This period of greatness in English theatre took place between 1587 and 1642, a short era that coincided with British exploration, conquest, and nationalistic fervor. During the reign of Queen Elizabeth I, professional theatre in London forged a union between acting companies and a host of writers (mostly university-educated). The all-male companies (women's roles were played by boys or young men) often attracted noble patrons, but the box-office receipts were vitally important to the success of the players.

The English at first showed little interest in Italian neoclassicism or changeable scenery, although they would adopt both in 1660. Instead, the actors performed in three-story, polygonal **public theatres** that were open to the sky. All action transpired on a thrust stage fronting a façade with probably two doors and sometimes a curtained discovery space between them. The façade also had a second level for such things as the balcony scene in *Romeo and Juliet* (c. 1594). The audience stood in the pit or yard surrounding three sides of the elevated stage or sat in galleries or boxes extending three stories into the air (see Figure 12.2). The most famous of these structures was the Globe Theatre created by Shakespeare's company, the Lord Chamberlain's Men, who were led by actor-manager Richard Burbage. These companies also used indoor "private" theatres, but the standard of performance seems to have been established in the public theatres. The companies doubled many roles and performed with a **rolling repertory** (a system of daily changes of plays) with more than thirty plays a year. A popular play reappeared throughout the season.

Also inspired by classical models, especially the Roman tragedies of Seneca, English playwrights returned to tragedy as well as comedy, tragicomic romances, and historical chronicles. Most of these plays were written in **blank verse** (unrhymed **iambic pentameter**), but the playwrights also made extensive use of prose and rhymed verse, which were often mixed with the blank verse as "home base." Elizabethan drama is typically marked as beginning with Thomas Kyd's *The Spanish Tragedy* (1587), a study in vengeance, madness, and grotesque onstage violence, which long stood as a model of tragedy of revenge.

Although many important plays and playwrights are identified with the Elizabethan theatre, several playwrights are of paramount importance and enjoy frequent revivals. Christopher Marlowe was the first to master blank verse, and he created significant models of heroic, antiheroic, and historical tragedy. His *Doctor Faustus* (c. 1588) was the first important play on the recurring subject of selling one's soul to the devil; *Edward II* (c. 1592) was the first important **chronicle** (a dramatic adaptation of historical events dealing with kings and frequent struggles for the crown) of a deposed English king; *Tamburlaine* (c. 1587) was apparently the first play whose popularity inspired a sequel, *Tamburlaine II* (c. 1588). We have been suffering with sequels ever since. Most of Marlowe's tragic heroes were first performed by Edward Alleyn, the leading actor of the Admiral's Men (Richard Burbage's chief competition). About the time Marlowe was murdered at the age of twenty nine, Shakespeare's playwriting career was catching fire.

Unlike Marlowe, Shakespeare was an actor and was not educated at a university. He fully understood the company for which he was writing and must have performed some of his roles himself. Most of Shakespeare's tragic heroes were first performed by Burbage. Also unlike Marlowe, who specialized in tragedy, Shakespeare created masterpieces in nearly every major dramatic form of the era. From situation comedy such as *Comedy of Errors* (c. 1593) to romantic comedy such as *Much Ado about Nothing* (c. 1598) to fantastic comedy of the supernatural such as *A Midsummer Night's Dream* (c. 1595), Shakespeare created lasting renderings of romance, foibles, and

(a)

(b)

FIGURE 12.2 (a) Elizabethan Public Theatre, Ground Plan (b) Fortune Theatre, Ground Plan (Based on Seventeenth-Century Builder's Contract)

THE NEW GLOBE IN LONDON near the site of the original Globe. It has many features considered typical of Elizabethan public theatres, including a raised stage with two levels of performance space. A stage with a roof (shadow) supported by columns, set in a thrust arrangement in the pit (yard) with three levels of galleries for seating beyond the pit. We see the space here just after a rehearsal in 2007.
Photo © Kendra Fletcher Wainscott.

mistakes in both the seen and unseen world. His tragicomic romances such as *The Winter's Tale* (c. 1610) and *The Tempest* (c. 1612) are laced with supernatural wonders and include a dark mood that tempers the comic structure. His chronicle plays have been so effective that many people confuse his renderings in *Richard III* (c. 1593) and *Henry V* (c. 1599) with genuine history. He is most frequently noted for his tragedies, however, especially the rise-and-fall action of *Macbeth* (c. 1606), the study of jealousy in *Othello* (c. 1604), the forestalled revenge in *Hamlet* (c. 1600), and the domestic tragedy played out in public in *King Lear* (c. 1605).

The one popular type of play that Shakespeare did not master became the specialty of Ben Jonson, another actor-playwright, who created some of the most biting satire of his time and sometimes got in trouble with the authorities for his barbed tongue. His *Volpone* (1606) creates a comic villain surrounded by fools and a manipulator so masterful that he cannot be overthrown except by himself. He must ridiculously overreach to be overwhelmed by the **wheel of fortune** (the notion that fortunes change if we wait long enough). In fact, most of humanity in Jonson's plays, such as *The Alchemist* (1610) and *Every Man in His Humour* (1598), is shown as foolish, stupid, and easily duped. Recalling the Greek Aristophanes, Jonson was an acidic commentator on his times.

After the death of Queen Elizabeth in 1603 and the ascension of James I, many playwrights created plays filled with terror and a host of malcontents. Similar to today's horror movies, *The Duchess of Malfi* (1613) by John Webster and *The Revenger's Tragedy* (c. 1606) by Cyril Tourneur created a pessimistic tone with sensational scenes of torture, poisoning, strangulation, sword fights, and runaway vengeance. All was enacted

EXPLORING Historical and Cultural Perspectives

Rediscovery of the Rose and Globe Theatres

In 1587 the Rose Theatre was the first theatre built across the Thames River from London (the Bankside) by manager Philip Henslowe and actor Edward Alleyn, the chief competition for Burbage and Shakespeare's company. Some of Shakespeare's early plays, such as *Henry VI,* and famous plays by Marlowe, such as *Doctor Faustus,* and Kyd's *The Spanish Tragedy* were performed at the Rose. The site of the Rose is close to that of the later Globe Theatre. Both theatres, however, were destroyed during the Commonwealth (1642–1660), when theatre was outlawed and many documents relating to the theatres were destroyed. For centuries scholars tried to piece together the nature of the Elizabethan public theatres with the remaining evidence: building contracts for the Fortune and Hope Theatres and a collection of images of interiors and exteriors that are woefully incomplete and out of scale and raise as many questions as they answer.

Little was known about the construction of the Rose until more than 60 percent of the foundations were uncovered during a new construction excavation in 1989. This discovery provided important evidence to support or negate speculation about the structure and size of the Elizabethan public theatres. Although not all Elizabethan theatres can be extrapolated from the architectural remains of the Rose, its excavation certainly lifted part of the veil shrouding Elizabethan theatre construction. The Rose foundation demonstrates that this theatre was polygonal in shape (some thirteen or fourteen sides) and had a thrust stage about fifteen feet deep, later extended to sixteen, which was trapezoidal in shape surrounded on three sides by a yard and elevated galleries for the audience. The interior was nearly fifty feet wide, and the exterior was about ninety feet. Eventually, a new building was placed over the site (as was originally planned), but it was built to protect the remains of the Rose.

A bit later in 1989 a smaller part of the foundation of Shakespeare's famous Globe Theatre was also excavated. (Most of the site is covered by an early nineteenth-century building, which is protected as a historical monument.) On the basis of these remains the Globe was estimated to be also polygonal but larger, about one hundred feet wide, with perhaps twenty sides. The new Globe Theatre in London (intended to be modeled on what is known about the original Globe and used for performances of Elizabethan plays) was already designed and partially constructed at that time, but some changes were made after the 1989 discoveries. Today you can visit the site of the Rose, which is still being prepared for permanent preservation, as well as the fully functional new

SEVENTEENTH-CENTURY IMAGE of a London stage that resembles what we know and surmise of the Rose Theatre: a trapezoidal stage with a low railing, a curtained upstage discovery space, and a second level for actors and possibly audience members. Audience members are standing in the pit. "Roxana Tragaedia" drawing.
By permission of the Folger Shakespeare Library.

Globe nearby, which gives regular performances. The film *Shakespeare in Love* (1998) includes a set representing the Rose Theatre, based on an interpretation of the remaining evidence.

INTERESTED? Check out

Andrew Gurr. *The Shakespearean Stage 1574–1642,* 3rd ed. Cambridge, UK: Cambridge University, 1992.
Christine Eccles. *The Rose Theatre.* New York: Routledge, 1990.
The Rose Theatre Trust website at www.rosetheatre.org.uk.
The Shakespeare Globe Centre (USA) website at www.sgc.umd.edu, maintained by the University of Maryland.

HAMLET in 2001 at the Theatre de la Jeune Lune, Minneapolis, MN, with Steven Epp in the title role. Many iconic images of the character of Hamlet focus on his fascination with death emblemized by his presence at a grave and holding the skull of Yorick, a jester important to him in his youth.

Photo © Michal Daniel.

in the midst of remarkable, hard-edged poetry, however. Toward the end of this era, John Ford created *'Tis Pity She's a Whore* (c. 1630), which combines beautiful lyrical poetry with scenes of crime, incest, and suicide. Perhaps its most poignant image, a brother interrupting a banquet with the heart of his sister impaled on his dagger, is a telling image for the tragedy of this age. Officially, this remarkable period ended with the closing of the theatres in 1642 at the outbreak of a horrendous political and religious civil war. For eighteen years of Puritan control, there was no monarch, theatres were dismantled, acting companies were outlawed, and aside from a few underground performances, public theatre in England was dead.

THE SPANISH GOLDEN AGE

Developing simultaneously with but independent of the Elizabethan theatre, Spain's professional theatre entered what is called a Golden Age that lasted from c. 1580 to 1680. Professional actors had been working for some time before 1580, however, in both religious (***autos sacramentales***) and secular plays (***comedias***) with companies made up of both men and women. The actors performed in temporary spaces, often courtyards, until professional public theatres were built in Madrid, Seville, and elsewhere beginning in 1579. The public theatre, called a ***corral***, resembled the Elizabethan public theatre in many ways: a raised, roofed stage backed by a façade with doors and a discovery space; a second balcony level; three levels of galleries and boxes for the audience; and a pit (*patio*) for standees open to the sky. The stage was not a thrust, however, and limited seating was provided in the *patio* close to the downstage edge. As indicated in surviving plays, the performance space also seems to have included some kind of onstage access to the second performance level. The most distinct difference from the Elizabethan theatre, however, was a segregated seating area for unmarried or unaccompanied women, called the ***cazuela,*** at the back of the house facing the stage (see Figure 12.3). The existence of the *cazuela* was itself ironic, since actresses were performing on the stage. The history of theatre is littered with contradictions.

Like the Elizabethans, the Spanish practiced an episodic, almost free-form style in writing and staging their plays and showed no interest in neoclassicism until a much later date. Although many playwrights created popular *comedias*, which tended to be mixed in emotional tone and tragicomic in form, the work of two playwrights was especially important during the Golden Age and continues to be regularly revived, translated, and studied. Lope de Vega was one of the most wildly popular playwrights in theatre history. He wrote hundreds of plays, and his fan following could easily be compared to more recent pop phenomena such as the intense popularity of the Beatles, *Star Wars,* and the Harry Potter books. When he died in 1635, one theatre staged an apotheosis in which an actor playing Lope ascended into heaven like a saint. Most of his plays explore the very complex Spanish code of honor and feature love affairs, intrigues, awful villains, and restoration of honor after many tribulations experienced by the hero and heroine. *The King, the Greatest Alcalde* (c. 1620), for example, ends with the King of Spain stepping in and forcing a villain of noble birth to marry the peasant woman he violated, then executing the villain and giving his wealth to the woman as a dowry so that she can marry the man she really loves. Lope's most intriguing play might be *Fuente Ovejuna* (c. 1614), which features a **collective hero** (all the inhabitants of a village) who rise up against their evil overlord and kill him after he rapes and tortures an innocent village woman. No one among the brave and steadfast villagers will name a killer, even when tortured severely by the authorities. Their only answer, even on the rack, is the name of their village, Fuente Ovejuna.

Overlapping Lope's career was that of another prolific and remarkable *comedia* and *auto* playwright, Calderón de la Barca, who also explored the love and honor themes and was equally fascinated by philosophical questions. *The Constant Prince* (c. 1635) is a disturbing examination of self-sacrifice in which a prince captured in war refuses to allow himself to be ransomed. Calderón's most famous play, *Life Is a Dream* (c. 1636), explores illusion versus reality through the struggles of a prince who from birth has been kept imprisoned and ignorant of any social activity until he is grown. When released into the world as a prince once more, he believes that he is in a dream and, not surprisingly, often reacts with comic misunderstanding and deadly savagery. After the death of Calderón in 1681, the professional theatre continued, but no more great playwrights emerged for centuries; stage censorship after 1680 in Spain became quite severe. After the Golden Age, Spain (like England after its civil war) adopted neoclassicism.

FIGURE 12.3 Corral (Public Theatre), Ground Plan

A RECONSTRUCTION OF A SPANISH CORRAL on the site of a small theatre called the Almagro. It was rebuilt to allow and encourage modern performances of Golden Age plays. Note the two upstage doorways for entrances, second-level performance balconies, and a roof over the stage. Also, balconies for the audience extend on the sides of the performance space. The Golden Age theatres in Madrid and Seville were much larger than this one, but they were destroyed long ago. An annual National Classical Theatre Festival is held at this site every year.

2009 photo Corral de Comedias de Almagro.Wikipedia, by Antonio Levy

SEVENTEENTH-CENTURY FRANCE

While England and Spain were exploding with vibrant theatrical activity at the end of the 1500s, France was still struggling to find an artistic identity. Through the guidance and patronage of Cardinal Richelieu, the prime minister under Louis XIII, however, theatre and drama found prominent voices in the 1620s and well beyond. Avoiding the style of their enemy England, French theorists, artists, and playwrights found themselves attracted to the neoclassical model of drama and the Italianate models in theatre and scenic design. They endeavored to "out-Italian" the Italians, and in playwriting at least they were quite successful in their quest, so much so that many artists and scholars by the mid-eighteenth century began to identify neoclassicism with the French instead of the Italians.

The French were also attracted to *commedia dell'arte,* whose methods were especially influential on the development of French comedy after a *commedia* troupe took up residence in Paris in 1548. In the same year, Europe's first new theatre since the Roman Empire was built in Paris. The new Hôtel de Bourgogne eventually became the first home of French professional theatre companies. By 1641 Paris got its first proscenium theatre, the Palais Cardinal, built in the palace of Cardinal Richelieu. After his death, it became known as the Palais Royal and was ultimately the theatre of Molière, the premier actor and comic playwright of the era. Other theatres also quickly added proscenium arches, which became the European standard.

THE PALAIS CARDINAL, the first proscenium theatre built in France (1641). Here, Cardinal Richelieu, who commissioned the new space, attends a performance with his king, Louis XIII. The cardinal died soon after opening his theatre and willed the space to the king. Thus the theatre was renamed the Palais Royal, under which name Louis XIV made the theatre available to Molière, who presented his most famous plays there. This space was intended for court theatre, so it is small compared to professional proscenium theatres built in the eighteenth century.

From collection of Musee des Arts Decoratifs, Paris (Lalance).

Neoclassicism did not triumph in France without a bit of a fight, however. Pierre Corneille was the first of three great playwrights of seventeenth-century France. He tested the waters of neoclassicism in 1636 by writing and producing *The Cid,* a fascinating tragicomic tale inspired by Spanish history and drama. Although written in neoclassical form, the play features events that should really transpire over years, but Corneille forced the action into a single day. The play was popular, but Richelieu and many literary figures challenged the appropriateness of the play. The newly formed French Academy, created to standardize the French language, ruled that the play should have conformed more closely to the rules and spirit of neoclassicism. Corneille never wavered from neoclassical form again, but this early "irregular" play is his most admired and studied in our own time.

Jean Racine remains the most revered writer of tragedy in all of French theatre. He reworked famous plays and stories from Greek and Roman originals and in several cases produced the most profound versions. His tragic verse was written in rhyming couplets, making translation into English a monumental task. At the center of his plays is always a psychological struggle in which the protagonist (usually a woman) is given an impossible choice—a lose/lose situation. She is torn between her desire and her duty, and desire always wins. This triumph over duty is the heart of the tragedy. Racine's most enduring play in this vein is *Phèdre* (1677), a reworking of earlier tragedies by Euripides and Seneca in which a queen falls in love with her stepson and descends to despair.

In our own time it is the comedies of Molière from this period that are most frequently revived and studied. Unlike Corneille and Racine, Molière was also an actor and the manager of his theatre company, the most successful in Paris. Molière wrote farces and comedies of manners (depicting and satirizing upper-class society), but many of his plays feature eccentric central characters who are given to excess such as miserliness and hypochondria. The most popular of these are *The Misanthrope* (1666), which examines a man who hates humanity yet falls in love, and *Tartuffe* (1669), a satirical study in religious hypocrisy. Molière often took the leading male roles himself; late in his career, his talented young actress wife, Armande Béjart, often took the female leads.

The success of both Molière and his company was so great that when he died suddenly in 1673, the Parisian theatrical world was thrown into a tizzy (such as that sparked by our contemporary corporate raiding and scandals in the business world). The crown interceded and forced three professional theatres to combine. The new company was called the Comédie Française, and for many years it exercised a monopoly on drama in Paris. Although the monopoly is long gone, the Comédie Française continues still and considers itself the "House of Molière."

RESTORATION ENGLAND

When the monarchy was restored in England in 1660, the theatre was also revived after an eighteen-year absence. For the new actors, playwrights, and managers, the influence of France was more prominent than the memory of Elizabethan theatre practice. Many royalists loyal to the king had lived in exile in France along with the new king, Charles II. They became close to the French court and very conversant with professional theatre, which then featured actresses, Italianate scenery, and the neoclassical plays of Corneille and Molière. Once back in England, Charles II granted patents (official licenses) to new theatre managers to open professional theatres. Most theatre buildings had been demolished by the Puritans, and performance spaces had to be adapted from existing buildings such as indoor tennis courts. Once new theatres could be built, they featured proscenium arches and changeable scenery. Unlike other European theatres, however, the English spaces included functional doors just downstage of the proscenium arch

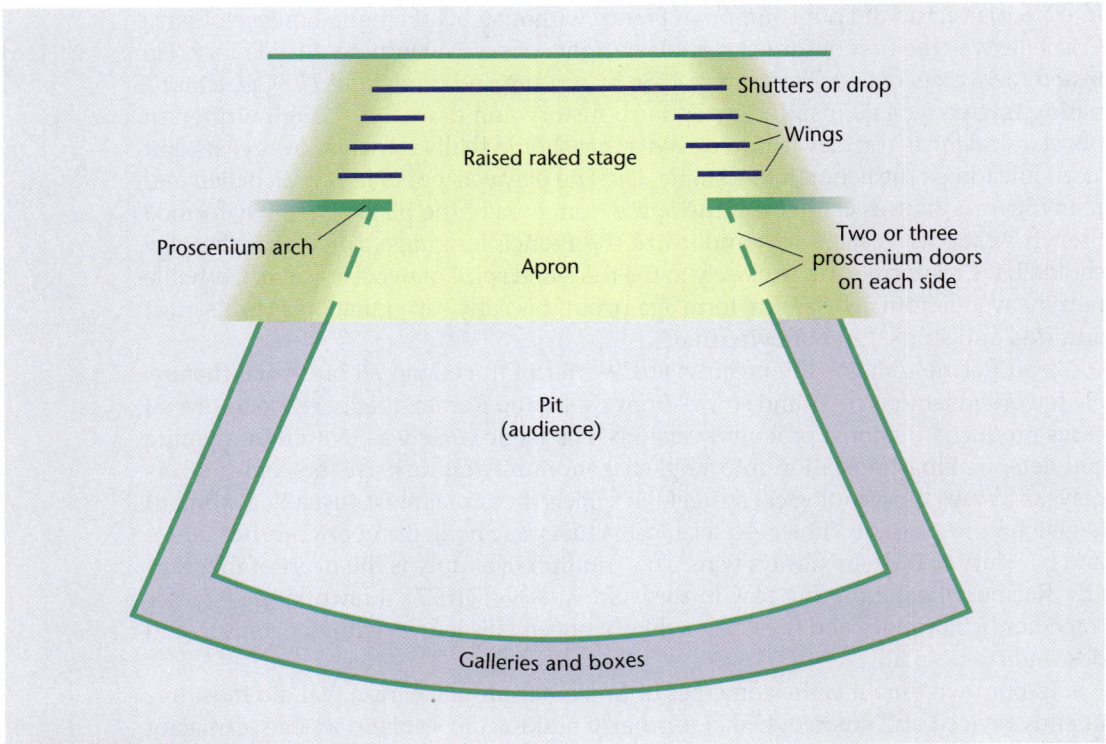

FIGURE 12.4 Restoration Theatre, Ground Plan

that the actors used for most entrances and exits (see Figure 12.4). This device (perhaps inspired by the memory of Elizabethan theatres) remained in place in Britain and British colonies or former colonies, such as Canada, Jamaica, and the United States, until the first decades of the nineteenth century (see Figure 12.5). Some proscenium theatres in our own time include variations on these proscenium doors.

FIGURE 12.5 Restoration Proscenium Doors, Audience View

Also in 1660 the professional theatres introduced actresses to the English-speaking stage. This novelty soon became the standard, and the second generation of actresses included very talented performers such as Anne Bracegirdle and Elizabeth Barry, who inspired playwrights to create roles specifically for them. The new actresses were the first women to play Shakespeare's famous female roles such as Juliet, Ophelia, and Desdemona, all of which had originally been played by boys or young men. A great male actor, Thomas Betterton, also appeared in the Restoration and created a tradition for performing Shakespeare's leading men that influenced a long line of classical actors stretching to our own time with the likes of John Gielgud, Alec Guinness, and Ian McKellen. Betterton also specialized in comedy of manners.

The comedy of manners reached a kind of perfection in the Restoration as upper-class characters were caught in a comic struggle between their own personal desires (often sexual) and prevailing social codes of behavior. In these plays, the most clever and intelligent people who could manage to control their emotions were always victorious over those who revealed their emotions too easily. Masterpieces of these comedies abound. *The Country Wife* (1675) by William Wycherley depicts a naïve young woman caught up in sophisticated liaisons; *The Way of the World* (1700) by William Congreve includes a famous wooing scene in which a couple desperately in love pretends indifference as they work out what might be the first prenuptial agreement in dramatic literature.

The Restoration period is also noteworthy for the earliest known plays written by professional women playwrights. Aphra Behn's intrigue comedies have found new audiences in our own time, especially her delightful romp *The Rover* (1677), the original

THE COUNTRY WIFE by William Wycherley. Actresses in late seventeenth-century England often dressed as young male characters. In this 2000 revival we see the famous scene where Margery Pinchwife (played by Tessa Auberjonois) is in disguise as a boy so that her overprotective husband will allow her to move freely in society. Other men, such as Horner (played by Leigh Lawson), are not fooled. Horner kisses Margery while pretending to believe that the woman is really a boy. The audience enjoys the joke on Margery's silly husband at the same time that sexual tension mounts. Directed by Keith Baxter; costumes designed by Robert Perdziola.
Photo © Carol Rosegg.

production of which featured Elizabeth Barry and Thomas Betterton. This play of chases and disguises was so successful that it led to a sequel. While securing a popular audience, Behn was adept at comically attacking the sexual double standard and the position of women in society.

Although British playwrights had embraced neoclassicism by 1660, they did so with a few variations that persisted until the romantic rebellion at the end of the eighteenth century. For the British, unity of place was defined not as a single location, as the French and Italians defined it, but as any set of locations that could be reached within a twenty-four-hour period. Consequently, the British had many changes of scene in the traditional genres, unlike the French and Italians. The British also maintained violence on the stage, with numerous sword fights, which their audiences seemed to admire but the French strictly avoided. Otherwise, the British stage was very neoclassical for about one hundred fifty years. The Restoration period, however, lasted a mere forty years. After 1700 the new plays in England and its colonies moved toward sentimentality, eliminated obvious sexual scenes in comedies, and more stringently followed the principle of teaching moral lessons.

EIGHTEENTH-CENTURY EUROPE AND THE AMERICAS

When looking back on eighteenth-century Western theatre now, we are often struck by similarities from country to country in terms of dramatic style, acting methods, theatre architecture, and scenic design. Of course, the subject matter and language of plays often differ dynamically, but nearly all plays follow the principles of neoclassicism. The plays of the eighteenth century that tend to be revived in our own period are comedies of manners, some of which enjoy popularity, especially in resident professional and university theatres. The tragic plays of the eighteenth century, although popular in their own time, rarely inspire us today.

From England, Oliver Goldsmith's *She Stoops to Conquer* (1773) and Richard Brinsley Sheridan's *The School for Scandal* (1777) have held the English-speaking stage since their creation. They continue to entertain audience members who still recognize incisive social criticism, duplicity of character, the dangers of gossip, and misguided attempts of elders to force their intentions on grown children. *The School for Scandal* inspired the most intriguing neoclassical play created in the new United States, *The Contrast* (1787) by Royall Tyler, a comic comparison of European and American society and values. In France René Le Sage wrote one of the most biting satires of social and economic cheating in any period: *Turcaret* (1709); the title character is a corrupt tax collector. It was Pierre Marivaux and Beaumarchais, however, who made the most lasting impact on later periods with Marivaux's comedies such as *The False Confessions* (1737), which center on characters surprised by their own love for another. Beaumarchais's *The Marriage of Figaro* (1784) introduced a remarkable level of democratization by focusing on servant characters

ROMEO AND JULIET. Mr. Barry and Miss Nossiter in the balcony scene, London, 1750s. Like all British productions of plays in this era, Romeo and Juliet are in eighteenth-century dress. Note the candelabra lighting the space. There would be many others as well. Juliet is probably at an onstage audience box situated near or above a proscenium door.

By permission of the Folger Shakespeare Library.

Mr. Barry and Miss Nossiter.
in the Characters of Romeo and Juliet.

throughout much of the action. Beaumarchais angered the authorities when he suggested that birth into a privileged class was not necessarily an indication of superiority.

Italy produced entertaining comedies through the efforts of Carlo Goldoni, whose reforms brought *commedia dell'arte* to an essential end by fully scripting plays for the Italian actors, beginning with the farce *The Servant of Two Masters* (1743/1753). Goldoni eliminated *commedia* masks and also created wonderful roles for women, especially in *The Mistress of the Inn* (1753). The heroine Mirandolina outwits all the men in the play and takes complete control of her life.

Female willfulness is also prominent in the English comedies of Susanna Centlivre, whose *The Wonder: A Woman Keeps a Secret* (1714) examined the themes of confinement and freedom as well as the concept of honor and held the stage for more than a hundred years. Shortly after the work of Centlivre, John Gay created a sensation in England by devising a satirical ballad opera (a musical with a comic story set to already existing popular music of the time but with new lyrics) about a highwayman and his gang entitled *The Beggar's Opera* (1728). It was not strictly an opera because it included much spoken dialogue. The play was so popular that it had more than one thousand performances in England alone in the eighteenth century. The ballad opera is one of several models that led eventually to the modern musical comedy.

It is very difficult to reconstruct acting methods for eighteenth-century theatre, but several things are clear. Actors performed in front of, not inside, the changeable Italianate scenery. Many theatres had a generous apron downstage of the proscenium arch, and it was on this open apron that most of the performance took place. Theatres were becoming quite large, with the result that actors needed to have great vocal facility. The gestures were probably quite expansive also. Actors often attempted to make very direct contact with the audience rather than interact directly with other actors (at least as the norm). This style of performance is often described as **rhetorical acting**—a "stand-up" actor or actress, whose big voice and grand gestures were intended to capture the attention and admiration of a fully lit and social audience. Many names and descriptions of actors and actresses have come down to us, but one is especially prominent. David Garrick of London is often singled out as the actor of the age. He was said to have had a "natural" style, but we should not read this as "realistic" in our sense of the word. He was subtler than his contemporaries, and he engaged in dynamic mimetic movement on the stage; Garrick was considered a genius of gesture and facial expression. He became internationally famous, which was most unusual for any actor before the nineteenth century.

Professional acting companies first came to North America from England in the eighteenth century. Professional theatre here is usually dated from 1745 in Jamaica and 1752 in Virginia, when first one and later several acting companies toured the colonies. Amateur theatre in English, however, appeared occasionally in North America from 1665 onward from South Carolina to New York. New England prohibited theatre for many years under its Puritan leadership. Amateur theatre appeared in French in Canada in the seventeenth century and in Spanish in the Southwest even earlier. Spanish religious plays were performed by conquistadors and Jesuits in many parts of the New World, including Central and South America. Mexico had active theatre based on the Spanish *auto* and *comedia* models from the 1500s and had practicing local playwrights, some of whom date to the late 1500s. In later years Spanish Golden Age plays would also find important homes in the Americas, in Mexico, and throughout much of South America. Of course Native American ritual and storytelling reenactments and theatrical activity throughout the Americas predate all of the European-inspired theatre.

As Europe and its colonies reveled in discoveries of the New World and rediscovered the glories of the Western classical past, they hurried to shuck off the sensibilities of the medieval world and express an enlightened attitude. In their

EXPLORING Collaboration

The Hallam Company in the American Colonies: A Family Affair

Although amateur theatre was practiced in the thirteen original American colonies from 1665, there was no attempt to create professional theatre until 1749, when a group of performers led by Walter Murray and Thomas Kean, with no apparent previous professional experience or training, declared themselves a professional company and performed in New York, Philadelphia, Williamsburg, Virginia, and elsewhere. This semiprofessional troupe lasted until 1752, when a bona fide professional company arrived from a small theatre that had recently closed in England. The actors hoped to free themselves from the Licensing Act (1737), which technically made their company illegal in England because of a monopoly held by two major theatres in London. They hoped to establish themselves in the New World. This London Company of Comedians was led by actor-manager Lewis Hallam and backed by his brother, William, who remained in England. The actors were on a **sharing system,** which means they split any profits after the day's expenses on the basis of how many shares each had invested in the speculative venture or had been granted by the manager depending on his or her duties and importance to the company.

The troupe was a family affair. Lewis played supporting roles. His wife (we know her only as Mrs. Lewis Hallam) played female leads in tragedy, and their children also performed and were trained in acting. There were other adults, some related to the Hallams, some not. Their oldest son, Lewis Hallam, Jr., within six years would graduate to the leading male tragic roles, resulting in odd casting such as playing Romeo to his mother's Juliet. By sometime in the 1760s Lewis was playing opposite his cousin Nancy Hallam in the younger tragic roles. His mother maintained the mature tragic leads until the American Revolution. The company first performed in Williamsburg and went on to towns in the circuit first played by the Murray and Kean company. Touring throughout the colonies was a necessity because no one town was large enough to support a permanent theatre company. When the first census was taken in 1790, the largest city in the new United States, Philadelphia, consisted of only 42,000 people. The actors often struggled to get local permission to play, since many colonists, especially

the clergy, Puritans, and Quakers, had prejudices against the theatre and often passed laws prohibiting it. Philadelphia was especially problematic, but the Hallams managed to get permission in the difficult areas by offering performances and giving all the proceeds to local charities. New England, with its Puritan leadership, was off-limits until the 1760s, and no serious inroads were made in that area until after the Revolution.

In 1755 the company left the American colonies and traveled to Jamaica, where a professional company already resided led by John Moody and David Douglass. While there, Lewis Hallam died. In 1758 the company reorganized and returned to the American colonies; Mrs. Hallam remarried and became Mrs. David Douglass, her new husband becoming the new company manager. Actors in the altered organization came from both original companies. Lewis Hallam, Jr., was now an adult and a reasonably accomplished actor. Under the leadership of Douglass, the company tried braver things. They ventured into New England with some success in 1761 and advertised that they were not playing "evil" plays, but moral dialogues and public presentations in the art of rhetoric and public speaking. Few people were fooled by this ruse, but Douglass continued in the Northeast by pretending not to be a theatre company. Under the Douglass leadership the troupe performed as far south as Charleston, South Carolina, and north to Rhode Island. Probably sensing the unrest in the colonies over British practices that culminated in the Revolution, the company renamed itself the American Company in 1763 even though all the actors were British. About this time Lewis Hallam, Jr., also joined the management of the company. Except for sojourns in Jamaica, he would remain an actor and theatre manager on the American stage until his retirement in 1806.

Douglass and his company built the first permanent structures intended from the beginning as theatres, first the Southwark in Philadelphia (1766) and then the John Street Theatre in New York (1767). These were the two most important American theatres until the end of the eighteenth century, when a new wave of improved theatre building got under way. The American Company continued to

Renaissance and post-Renaissance plays, whether it was through neoclassical idealism or comparatively free-form, mixed-tone dramas devised by the Spanish and Elizabethans, European theatre artists were simultaneously looking back at the Western classics and forward to a new world of exploration, discovery, and nationalistic zeal. The postmedieval world was more conscious of its national identity

A BRITISH PROVINCIAL THEATRE that likely bears a resemblance to early American theatre activity in the eighteenth century. Note the small house, box, pit, and gallery arrangement and wing scenery. This is assumed to be a production of Shakespeare's *Macbeth*.

Colored engraving by James or Joseph Wright, based on a drawing by W. H. Pyne, c. 1788–89.

perform until shortly after the Continental Congress forbade the performances of plays and other kinds of public entertainment in 1774 as a response to the growing conflicts with England. The all-British-born troupe retired to Jamaica during the Revolution. The actors returned after the Revolution as the "Old American Company" but without Mrs. Hallam-Douglass or David Douglass. The troupe eventually made New York their base of operations, but now there was a new Mrs. Hallam on the American stage: Eliza Tuke, the wife of Lewis, Jr. By the time he retired, Lewis Hallam, Jr., was the only link to the original 1752 company and provided valuable information to William Dunlap, a playwright, theatre manager, and the first person to write a history of the American theatre, in 1832.

INTERESTED? Check out

Don Wilmeth and Christopher Bigsby. *The Cambridge History of AmericanTheatre*, Vol. 1. Cambridge, UK: Cambridge University, 1998.

William Dunlap. *History of the American Theatre*. 1832. Introduction by Tice L. Miller. Urbana, IL: University of Illinois, 2005.

than any Western society since perhaps the Greeks of the fifth century B.C.E. As Elizabethan, Spanish Golden Age, and seventeenth-century French plays became themselves new classics, and as neoclassicism eventually played itself out in the eighteenth century, however, many artists were primed for radical change—and it came quickly.

CHAPTER REVIEW

Questions and Activities

1. The rules of neoclassicism were developed to produce a specific kind of play, similar to the rules for writing a particular kind of poetry (a sonnet, for example, always has fourteen lines). Choose some other forms of entertainment or art and list the rules. Some of these may be stated; others may be understood.

2. Imagine having seen plays performed only in a thrust configuration. How do you think the viewing experience would change if you attended a performance in which the actors stayed behind a proscenium arch and you viewed the action through a picture frame?

3. In Elizabethan England, women could attend and sit anywhere they could afford in the public theatre but could not perform on stage. In Spain during the Golden Age, women could perform on stage, but unmarried female audience members were restricted to seating in the *cazuela.* Discuss why these restrictions might have existed. What differing concerns might have led to the different types of restrictions?

Key Terms and Concepts

neoclassicism, p. 281
proscenium arch, p. 281
wing, p. 281
flat, p. 281
verisimilitude, p. 283
three unities, p. 283
decorum, p. 283
intermezzi, p. 283
masque, p. 283

commedia dell'arte, p. 283
zanni, p. 284
prima donna, p. 284
innamorata, p. 284
innamorato, p. 284
public theatre, p. 284
rolling repertory, p. 285
blank verse, p. 285
iambic pentameter, p. 285

chronicle, p. 285
wheel of fortune, p. 286
autos sacramentales, p. 288
comedia, p. 288
corral, p. 288
cazuela, p. 288
collective hero, p. 289
rhetorical acting, p. 295
sharing system, p. 296

For Further Exploration

See the list of sources at the end of Chapter 13 on page 320.

HOTEL CASSIOPEIA by Charles Mee (2006). A postmodern play and touring production directed by Anne Bogart. Scenic design by Neil Patel.

Photo © Michael Brosilow.

Revolutions

Romanticism to Postmodern Experiment

Once artists grew weary of neoclassicism, they found the form so entrenched that a revolution was necessary to dislodge it. **Romanticism,** a rejection of nearly every aspect of neoclassicism and a celebration of the natural world, was hardly itself a generation old when it came under serious challenge. In retrospect, the romantic rebellion seems to have opened a Pandora's box; as each movement wins acceptance, another is formed to rebel against it. Unlike neoclassicism, aspects of the romantic movement, as well as many other major movements to follow, continue to wield their influence on the theatrical professions that we currently practice and enjoy.

ROMANTICISM

The artistic and social movement of romanticism, which is so strongly associated with the nineteenth century, actually began in the eighteenth. It became the dominant style in both acting and playwriting in the first half of the nineteenth century. The first strains of theatrical romanticism can be found in Germany among young, rebellious theorists and playwrights who were sick of the limitations—the strict form and moral teachings—of neoclassicism. The rebels sought to overturn this monolith of art and culture. Preromantic playwrights who called themselves *Sturm und Drang* ("storm and stress") deliberately broke all the rules of neoclassicism. The *Sturm und Drangers* shocked their audiences with plays full of violence and forbidden topics such as teen pregnancy, rape, self-mutilation, and infanticide. One of the most successful and disturbing of these plays, *The Tutor* (1774) by Jacob Lenz, presents a young tutor who seduces his even younger student and later, filled with guilt, castrates himself. Heinrich Wagner's *The Childmurderess* (1776) begins with the rape of a girl by a soldier. The girl runs away, discovers she is pregnant, has the child, goes mad, and kills the baby.

These dramatic iconoclasts were soon followed by the romantics, led by theorist August von Schlegel, who wanted more than rebellion. The romantics wished to replace neoclassical structure with organic structure: Form should be dictated by subject matter, not classical precedent, they argued. The romantics were fascinated with the wild forces of nature, with the unexplainable, the gothic and mystical, and looked for correspondences between their beliefs and those of the Elizabethans, the Spanish Golden Age, and even the medieval world. Romantics championed democratic principles and dramatized emotion's triumph over reason. They found beauty in disorder and pleasure in expressions of characters divided against themselves. Their chief model from the past was Shakespeare, and the play of choice was *Hamlet.* Through the efforts of the romantics, Shakespeare (dead for more than 180 years) first became an international phenomenon and rose to the top of most evaluations of dramatic literature. The Germans, led by Schlegel, soon translated Shakespeare into their own language, and many other countries followed during the nineteenth century.

Romantic playwrights in Germany created both funny and disturbing works. Ludwig Tieck's fairy tale extravaganza *Puss in Boots* (c. 1797) is a comic **metatheatrical** play (a self-referencing play that presents the theatre as a theatre) in which the audience takes a major role as the characters argue romantic versus neoclassical principles before the play self-destructs. A haunting, disturbing vision permeates Heinrich von Kleist's plays such as *Pentheselia* (c. 1808) in which an amazon warrior on the battlefield eats out the heart of the man she loves. Later she suggests that there is little difference in biting and kissing; we often do one, she claims, when we mean the other. Although not fully romantic, Georg Büchner's *Woyzeck* (c. 1836) provided one of the earliest examples of a working-class antihero. Woyzeck loses his mind and kills the woman he loves because he not only is betrayed by her but also is the victim of an irresponsible scientific experiment. Büchner didn't find an audience in his own time, but his plays have been regularly revived since the early twentieth century and have had a powerful influence on modern theatre.

Two German playwrights, Johann von Goethe and Friedrich Schiller, who began their theatrical work with the *Sturm und Drang* movement, are associated with the romantic movement, although Goethe denied connections. What Goethe and Schiller accomplished with their playwriting and production work at the court theatre of Weimar is labeled Weimar classicism. They combined ancient classics and stories with romantic sensibilities and created remarkable interpretations of familiar work. Goethe's *Iphigenia in Tauris* (1787), a reworking of a Euripides play, focuses on inner turmoil and the need to listen to one's heart. In his most famous play, *Faust* (1808), the old story of selling one's soul to the devil for pleasure or power is altered to a search for perfection. Schiller, also a historian, dramatically revisited European history, as in the tragic political demise of the title character in *Maria Stuart* (1800).

France resisted the romantic movement for a time, remaining neoclassical under Napoleon and beyond while the rest of Europe succumbed to the intoxication of romanticism. It arrived amid great consternation in Paris when performances of Victor Hugo's *Hernani* in 1830 resulted in vociferous argument, demonstrations, and near-rioting in the audience, since the play deliberately violated every principle of neoclassicism. Hugo's romantic theory, which adds the idea of the grotesque to the romantic vision, is more significant than his plays. The character Quasimodo from Hugo's novel *Notre Dame of Paris* can stand as an image of the entire romantic movement: a beautiful spirit trapped in a grotesque body. Hugo's fellow romantic Alfred de Musset created haunting romantic conflicts in plays such as *No Trifling with Love* (1834), which mixed the comic and trivial with deadly events as a young on-again-off-again couple plays games with the emotions of people they don't care about.

Romanticism was very popular in the United States and found curious expression in many plays. *Metamora* (1829), a tragedy by John Augustus Stone, for example, featured Native American characters sympathetically at the center of the action. In the romantic language of the day any aboriginal race was portrayed as the "noble savage," a race destined, it was thought, to be removed or destroyed by the encroachment of "civilized" white settlers in ever-increasing numbers. Although a few evil Indians appeared in plays of the 1830s, it was not until after midcentury that Native Americans began to be routinely characterized as alcoholics and vicious villains in plays. Unfortunately, this stereotype has persisted to our own time.

Although few romantic plays in England left a lasting impression, the romantic actors of that nation created a new standard of performance marked by emotional overflow, athleticism, sudden outbursts, and mixed tone. Sarah Siddons (1755–1831), who was often painted in portraits as the personification of the tragic muse, was enormously popular for her instantaneous reversals of mood and her long-suffering portrayals, which set a standard for the century. Siddons, along with Edmund Kean (1787–1833), created a romantic style in both classical and contemporary plays. Kean erupted on the stage with such clamorous force that reports describe emotionally overwrought audience members screaming and fainting—responses not unlike those of modern audiences at the performance of an enormously popular rock star.

Beginning in the early nineteenth century, each country that boasted a popular professional theatre developed a

EDWIN BOOTH AS HAMLET, c. 1870. Booth is often remembered as the premier American actor of Shakespearean leading roles in the nineteenth century. He was very successful as an international touring star and had the misfortune to be the brother of presidential assassin and actor John Wilkes Booth. This studio shot is typical of nineteenth-century photos of actors. Although Booth is wearing his real costume, the photo was made in a studio rather than on the set of his stage production.

By permission of the Folger Shakespeare Library.

EXPLORING Historical and Cultural Perspectives

The Audience Has Its Say: Theatre Riots and Demonstrations

As long as the house remained fully lit during theatrical performances (from the beginnings until the late nineteenth century), there was always the likelihood of active, even vociferous audience response and interaction during performances of plays. Historical evidence suggests that beginning with professional theatre in the seventeenth century and continuing through the eighteenth and nineteenth centuries, audience behavior included talking back to the actors, sword and stick fights, and open demonstration and riots over actors, ticket prices, responses to a new play, and political issues. Descriptions of such theatre audience behavior sound more like contemporary disturbances and riots occurring throughout the world at popular sports events such as soccer, football, and basketball than like modern theatre audiences.

In 1809, when the popular actor-manager John Philip Kemble managed the Covent Garden Theatre in London, he created a firestorm of protest. Following a destructive fire, he rebuilt Covent Garden and made significant changes that favored wealthy patrons but angered theatregoers of the lower economic classes. To cater to the richer folk, for example, Kemble changed open galleries in the third tier to private boxes (which were more expensive than gallery or pit seating); the only remaining public gallery was so high above the stage that audience members could see little of the stage action. Kemble added insult to injury by raising the prices of admission to the pit by half a shilling (apparently to pay for his new construction and improvements). The price increase seems slight to us now, but many audience members took offense at the loss of good seats and higher prices and decided to attack Kemble's decision. The resultant audience response is called the Old Price (O.P.) Riots.

When the theatre reopened after its renovation, a large percentage of the first-night audience arrived with signs and placards demonstrating their displeasure with Kemble's unfair and greedy practices. Their jeers and catcalls were so loud during the performance that no one could hear any words delivered from the stage. Kemble attempted to ride out the storm, but he never had a chance. Soldiers were called in to control the crowd, but their efforts were unsuccessful. The audience not only demonstrated that first night, but essentially rioted (apparently without loss of life) and prevented any real performance for more than sixty consecutive nights. Kemble finally succumbed to the inevitable, offered a public apology, and restored the old prices.

Sometimes audience demonstrations were planned in advance. In France champions of the romantic movement held pep rallies and open demonstrations attacking the neoclassicists—for example, with the opening of Victor Hugo's *Hernani* in 1830. Sometimes, however, demonstrations were spontaneous. Audiences frequently talked back to the actors or, in the Restoration period, even tried to compete with actors for attention. On a number of occasions when a famous actor entered the stage obviously drunk, audience members would tell him to go home. The theatre did not close for the night, however; management would offer the audience a different play (most theatres operated a rolling repertory of plays with many possible productions in the repertory at any one time). In some cases the management had to negotiate with the audience to determine what play they wished to see. Sometimes, however, the results of theatrical disturbances were deadly, as occurred in New York with the Astor Place Riot of 1849. The number of casualties varies depending on the account one reads, but it appears that at least thirty-one people died in this conflict created by reactionary American attacks over feuding actors and what the violent demonstrators perceived as British and aristocratic elitism at odds with "American values."

number of touring stars—actors and actresses who usually toured alone and performed with local companies throughout Europe and North America. Actors such as the American Edwin Booth (1833–1893), one of the biggest stars of the entire century, toured internationally with both melodrama and Shakespearean tragedy. It was soon evident that the test of any male actor of the era was the role of Hamlet, although other tragic figures such as Othello, Macbeth, Lear, and Richard III were considered mandatory roles for most stars. This notion was so prevalent that even some famous actresses—Sarah Bernhardt (1844–1923) from France, for example, and Charlotte Cushman (1816–1876) from the United States—took on Hamlet. Although Cushman created the era's definitive Lady Macbeth, she also frequently played male roles, including a very successful Romeo played to her sister Susan's Juliet. The test role of the nineteenth century for actresses, however, turned out to be "Camille," the protagonist (actually named Marguerite Gautier) in Alexandre Dumas *fils's The Lady of the Camelias* (1852), a romantic tale of a courtesan (a high-priced prostitute) with a heart of gold who succumbs to tuberculosis and lost love.

Many audience demonstrations had happier endings for those involved. One in particular involved popular audiences siding with theatres against attempts by the U.S. Congress to raise ticket prices to increase revenue for the federal government. In January 1919, shortly after the conclusion of World War I, the government was searching for ways to pay for the enormous debt incurred by the war effort. Among the many taxes proposed by Congress was a 20 percent federal tax on professional theatre ticket prices (a 10 percent increase since the wartime theatre tax) to raise an estimated $80 million. Both theatre managers and audiences hit the roof, resulting in almost instantaneous public demonstrations both inside and outside the theatres, a flood of letters and telegrams to Congress, and petitions that gathered almost nine million signatures from well over two thousand cities in eight days. This unusual collaboration of actors, managers, audiences, and newspapers from different regions of the country orchestrated a forceful but peaceful revolt against government action. Overwhelmed by the public outcry over threats to theatrical entertainment, Congress backed down, and the tax increase was dropped. At the time a typical Broadway theatre ticket in the orchestra ranged from $2.00 to $2.50. The tax increase, if passed, would have raised the price range to $2.20 to $2.75.

INTERESTED? Check out

George Rowell. *The Victorian Theatre, 1792–1914,* 2nd ed. Cambridge, UK: Cambridge University, 1978.

Richard Moody. *The Astor Place Riot.* Bloomington: Indiana University, 1958.

Ronald H. Wainscott. *The Emergence of the Modern American Theater, 1914–1929.* New Haven, CT: Yale University, 1997.

"EXACTING A POUND OF FLESH THAT LIES VERY NEAR THE HEART." This political cartoon depicts theatre business threatened by the U.S. Congress, with Congress portrayed as Shylock in Shakespeare's *The Merchant of Venice,* demanding his pound of flesh. The public intervenes on the theatre's behalf, just as Portia comes between Shylock and Antonio in the play.

Published on the front page of the *New York Tribune,* January 19, 1919.

Staging and design in the romantic era introduced the **box set,** a scenic device that imitated the interior of a room with walls, furniture, and visual detail. This kind of scenery was very important to actors, moving their performances away from the apron and within the walls of the set. After a time actors were no longer playing just in front of the scenery. They were inside the box. We do not know who invented the box set, but it was popularized by actress-manager Madame Vestris (1797–1856) in England and North American tours beginning about 1830. Also associated with Vestris was the work of James Robinson Planché (1796–1880) who introduced **antiquarianism** (the creation of historically accurate costumes and scenery) to the stage in the 1820s. This idea of dressing characters and recreating locations as they would appear at the time indicated by the play was at first a novelty. For centuries actors had traditionally costumed themselves in clothes that were contemporary with their own time regardless of the age or time setting of the plays. Antiquarianism became a new model for design; historical accuracy obviously continues to be important to many directors, actors, and designers of our own day.

CHARLOTTE AND SUSAN CUSHMAN
AS
ROMEO AND JULIET.

CHARLOTTE CUSHMAN
was a remarkably powerful
actress in the mid-nineteenth
century who frequently
cross-dressed on stage, but
her approach was different
from the norm. Although
she also played female
roles, when playing a man,
she downplayed femininity
and seemed to wish to be
accepted on stage as male.
Here, she appears as Romeo
playing opposite her sister
Susan as Juliet. Such casting
today would be unusual
indeed.

By permission of the Folger
Shakespeare Library.

The romantic era also ushered in the first known professional African American theatre, the African Company (1821) in New York. Unfortunately, this troupe, which performed both Shakespearean and original plays, was harassed and chased out of town by white bigots. A young African American who might have been a member of that company, Ira Aldridge (1807–1867), soon left the United States and became a highly successful touring star in Shakespearean roles and romantic drama throughout Europe. The "African Roscius" never returned to the United States, and no African Americans, only white actors in blackface makeup, performed in the professional American theatre for a very long time.

NINETEENTH-CENTURY MELODRAMA

The dramatic form that dominated the nineteenth century and continues to dominate in television and film is **melodrama.** This form became the most popular application of romanticism and, later, early types of realism. Many variations of the formula for melodrama were created in the nineteenth century, and most of them continue to be reworked in our own time: disaster epics on land and sea (from volcanic eruptions to tenement fires to shipwrecks), crime and detective thrillers, supernatural horror stories, American West shootouts, tales of adventure in exotic locales, everyday domestic conflicts featuring love and divorce, reprieve from alcoholism, and an endless parade of villainous big businessmen, lawyers, and outlaws. Although melodrama was prevalent in nearly all Western theatre centers (and a few in the East such as Japanese Kabuki), those in England and the United States were exceptionally adept and prolific with the form. Planché in England popularized the monster with *The Vampire* (1820); Augustin Daly in the United States introduced the victim tied to the railroad tracks in 1867 with *Under the Gaslight.* Some people are surprised to learn that it was a man tied to the tracks; he was rescued by a woman. A successful actor and one of the best writers of melodrama, Dion Boucicault became an international phenomenon with his spectacular tales of Irish, British, and American struggles and hardships such as *The Poor of New York* in 1857. Five years earlier, George Aiken, followed by many others, adapted Harriet Beecher Stowe's abolitionist novel *Uncle Tom's Cabin* to melodrama, and this play was performed in the United States more than any other in the second half of the nineteenth century. The lists of popular melodramas are legion, but they are marked by similarities that are easily recognized regardless of language or spectacle or period or local references.

A very important change occurred during the reign of stage melodrama. In the 1820s, along with many other spectacular devices, gaslight was introduced to the stage; it quickly replaced candles and oil lamps even though it was volatile and dangerous. Gaslight produced greater intensity of light and could easily be dimmed up and down. Nighttime scenes could for the first time be dark and shadowy, blackouts were possible, and colored light using silks and glass could be projected in dynamic ways. It was also possible to put the audience in the dark, thus altering its behavior and making it quieter and more focused on the stage. Lowering of the house lights did not occur until late in the century, however.

Spectacle became very literal and was aided by remarkable inventions applied to the stage: conveyer belts that transported gliding ghosts and racing horses and wagons, hydraulic and electric lifts that created bridges and levels high in the air, three-dimensional scenery that replaced some of the flat painted scenery, traps in walls that enabled sudden entrances of vampires, collapsible scenery for earthquakes and fires. Many devices that we now associate with realism or special effects for film (from James Bond to Harry Potter, from *Mission: Impossible* to *Lord of the Rings*) were first developed for the spectacle of stage melodrama. The pod race in *Star Wars, Episode I,* for example, is an updating of *Ben Hur*'s Roman chariot race, but such chariot races were first done on stage, not on film.

Even parodies of melodrama did not seem to dampen the power of the form in the period. The team of W. S. Gilbert and Arthur Sullivan satirized melodrama in wildly successful melodramatic/comic operettas such as *H.M.S. Pinafore* (1878) and *The Pirates of Penzance* (1879). Although many musical forms appeared on the stage in the nineteenth century, the plays and music of Gilbert and Sullivan provide hints for the modern musical, which in the twentieth century frequently adopted devices and techniques from the operetta form. It was also in the first production of Gilbert and Sullivan's *Patience* that electric light was introduced to the theatre in 1881.

THE BELLS. In Henry Irving's famous production of this melodrama in the nineteenth century, he used a scrim and gas lighting to create a vision scene. The character is standing in a realistic box set, but the upstage wall of the apparent room is a scrim concealing a scene behind it until the lighting is added upstage and dimmed downstage. Traditionally, melodrama has utilized sensation and intense situations.

By permission of the Folger Shakespeare Library.

NINETEENTH-CENTURY REALISM AND NATURALISM

Realism was a rebellion against romanticism and melodrama, but at the same time a realization of what romanticism and melodrama had approached visually—a very detailed evocation of scenery and costume along lines of historical and contemporary accuracy. Whereas French melodramatic playwrights in the 1850s such as Alexandre Dumas *fils* were attempting to move the subject matter of plays in a more realistic direction, the first fully realistic plays are usually credited to Norwegian Henrik Ibsen. His influential *A Doll House* (1879) centers on a wife leaving her husband and children, and *Ghosts* (1881) broached the forbidden topic of sexually transmitted disease. Ibsen and the other realists were inspired by a scientific revolution that increasingly looked at the human being not as the center of the universe, but as another subject for scientific study. One of these scientists, Charles Darwin, in his *On the Origin of Species by Means of Natural Selection* (1859), created a firestorm with his version of evolutionary theory. For Darwin and other thinkers such as Herbert Spencer, the first sociologist to apply evolutionary theory to social development in the 1850s, the importance of heredity and environment was deemed critical to all animal life. Playwrights such as Ibsen began to use heredity and environment in their plays as strong determinants of human character and behavior. It was not just biological evolution that fascinated artists, but cultural and social evolution as well.

The importance of environment to character behavior extended to creating settings that were not just authentic in every detail, but also connected to the characters who worked or lived in them. Many of the physical trappings of realism had been developed earlier by the romantics through such things as antiquarianism and the box set, but the new realists labored to connect space to character and event both in production and in the written play texts. The realists insisted on creating conversational dialogue that avoided the poetic and included repetition, inane remarks, pauses, and imperfect responses to imitate the way people really speak and interact in everyday life. The subject matter of realism often disturbed audiences and critics the most: frank discussions of

EXPLORING Historical and Cultural Perspectives

Nineteenth-Century Women Theatre Managers in Britain and the United States

When Lucy Elizabeth Bartolozzi Vestris took control of London's Olympic Theatre in 1831, she publicized herself as the first woman manager. Technically, this was not true, since one German and several British women had managed companies, but Vestris was certainly the best known and most significant up to that time. The theatregoing public knew her as an actress and singer who specialized in **breeches roles** (male characters performed by women in costumes more revealing than the voluminous skirts of the nineteenth century). Sexual attractiveness was an important part of Vestris's appeal. Assuming the duties of a manager meant accepting many responsibilities that were normally considered masculine: hiring and firing, planning, and financial and artistic decision making. Vestris turned the small Olympic into a fashionable theatre and built a reputation for careful staging of productions using realistic props and scenery (the box set, for example). After leaving the Olympic in 1839, she teamed up with her husband, Charles Mathews, to manage the larger Covent Garden (1839–1842) and Lyceum (1847–1856) Theatres, producing several important revivals of Shakespeare and elaborate holiday entertainments. The middle-class audience had nearly deserted the theatre, but Vestris's attention to tasteful subject matter and audience comfort (meant to lure the middle-class patrons back) was widely noted and praised.

More women turned to management as the century progressed. Marie Wilton (1839–1921), also a popular breeches role performer, entered management at the age of 25. She turned a dirty theatre known as "the dust hole" into the elegant Prince of Wales's Theatre in 1865. Like Vestris, Wilton was complimented for bringing a domestic atmosphere to a public space, thus making theatregoing more acceptable to the Victorian middle class. She later married her leading man, Squire Bancroft (1841–1926), and the two managed the Prince of Wales's Theatre together until 1879, then the Haymarket Theatre from 1880 to 1885. In producing the plays of T. W. Robertson, they helped to further realism and ensemble performing in Great Britain and raised the status of actors with increased salaries. Sara Lane (1823–1899) managed the Britannia Theatre in Hoxton with her husband Sam until 1871. After his death, she ran it alone for over a quarter of a century until her own death. The working-class audience of the Britannia loved her, and she played the breeches role in the Christmas play until she was in her seventies.

Laura Keene (c. 1820–1873) had worked for Madame Vestris before coming to the United States as an actress to support her mother and two daughters. She specialized in ingénue (young woman) roles in eighteenth-century comedies of manners and Shakespeare's romantic comedies. Keene added management to her career, running theatres in Baltimore and San Francisco before forming a resident company in New York City in 1855 and moving into Laura

MADAME VESTRIS, a popular actress-manager in London, in a cross-dressing role, as Orpheus in *Olympic Devils,* 1831, Olympic Theatre.
By permission of the Victoria and Albert Museum, London.

Keene's New Theatre in 1856. Her strong company specialized in lavishly produced comedies that fit Keene's performance style. She gave up the New York theatre in 1863 and became one of the first managers to tour a combination company (one in which an entire cast traveled with all scenery and equipment). In 1865 Keene had the misfortune to be managing and performing the comedy *Our American Cousin* when actor John Wilkes Booth (brother of the famous actor Edwin Booth) assassinated Abraham Lincoln at Ford's Theatre in Washington, DC. She was arrested, along with her company, but was released, and the company continued its tour.

Although these women must have faced enormous challenges in a very male-dominated world, they were often successful and carved out specific identities for their companies, frequently at the forefront of innovative stage practice.

INTERESTED? Check out

Jane Kathleen Curry. *Nineteenth-Century American Women Theatre Managers.* Westport, CT: Greenwood, 1994.

William W. Appleton. *Madame Vestris and the London Stage.* New York: Columbia University, 1974.

George Rowell, *The Victorian Theatre, 1792–1914,* 2nd ed. Cambridge, UK: Cambridge University, 1978.

prostitution, adultery, and divorce; and treatment of monumental social problems in marriage, rights for women, and the plight of the working class. With realism the theatre became a forum for current, volatile social issues that could polarize the audience.

Unlike the romantics, Ibsen did not try to change everything at once in his plays but utilized easily recognized structure that remained popular throughout the romantic era (melodrama and the **well-made play**). At the conclusion of his plays, however, he did not provide an easy solution or a happy ending, thus throwing his audiences into a tailspin. When Nora walked out on her husband and children at the end of *A Doll House,* it was more than many audiences could stand; some even demonstrated and waited for Nora to return. Early realists, whose plays are still regularly revived, quickly followed Ibsen's techniques and challenged their audiences to face their own social and personal demons. August Strindberg in Sweden provided *Miss Julie* (1888), a study in both class and gender struggles in which a socially mismatched couple (servant and mistress) play sexual games that end in disaster and apparent suicide for the young woman; George Bernard Shaw in England wrote *Mrs. Warren's Profession* (produced in 1902), in which a former prostitute (now a madam) must explain her early life choices to her incredulous daughter—in effect defending logically her decision to become a prostitute in order to haul herself out of poverty. In the United States the title character of James Herne's play *Margaret Fleming* (1890) discovers that her husband has had an affair with and impregnated a poor woman whom he abandoned. Margaret shocked audiences by rejecting her husband and taking the orphaned baby of the wronged woman as her own. She even prepared to nurse the baby on stage—an act that for some audiences was the most shocking of all.

Unlike Ibsen, Shaw, and Herne, some playwrights wanted to throw out traditional structure as well. In 1880 Émile Zola in France called for **naturalism,** in which playwrights should create a "slice of life," following the actual pace of everyday life—in short, imitating novels of the period. Many playwrights, in fact, began to think of themselves as novelists of the stage. Such an approach was very difficult to take without boring an audience, but several playwrights came very close to the ideal. They avoided central characters and created a collective hero or focused the action on a group. For example, the Russian play *The Cherry Orchard* (1904) by Anton Chekhov follows the demise of a wealthy family when its members fail to recognize the social and economic changes going on around them. They end by losing the things that seem to mean the most to them, but they do nothing to prevent the loss. Similarly, *The Lower Depths* (1902) by Maxim Gorky, also a Russian, centers on a group, but this time a collection of down-and-out people at the bottom of the social hierarchy who live in squalor and slowly seem to fade away while no one notices. These and other plays, such as the German Gerhart Hauptmann's *The Weavers* (1892), dealing with starvation and labor problems, created a large array of eccentric characters requiring detailed psychological exploration and ensemble acting.

In the nineteenth and early twentieth centuries most productions of realistic and naturalistic plays were presented in independent theatres, which for a number of years operated outside the sphere of commercial theatre and government censorship. The first of these was the Théâtre Libre, founded by André Antoine in Paris in 1887. Antoine's work, and that of Konstantin Stanislavsky at the Moscow Art Theatre beginning in 1898, created a climate for a radical change in acting style as well as a love among many young and developing actors for the new realism and naturalism. The new acting model was not the romantic touring star, but the actor who worked in an ensemble and created character through close observation of real life, careful examination of character history and

SALVATION NELL (1908) by Edward Sheldon. Produced and directed by Harrison Grey Fiske and his actress wife, Minnie Maddern Fiske, who also took the starring role. Although the play was attempting some kind of social realism, it was structured in a melodramatic fashion with extensive local color. This setting is a good example of physical detail in early twentieth-century American pictorial realism. The setting was important for crowd scenes and displaying inner city street life and tenement activity in an overcrowded, economically challenged section of New York. Many of the upper-level fire escape landings and windows must be playable for the actors.

From *Mrs. Fiske and the American Theatre* by Archie Binns, 1955.

THE MOULIN ROUGE since 1889 has been a famous center of popular musical entertainment. Specializing in cabaret, dance (particularly the can-can, which originated here), music-hall entertainment, and variety shows, especially vaudeville, the Moulin Rouge was a precursor of Broadway revues of the early twentieth century and Las Vegas shows from the 1950s to the present. The Moulin Rouge continues to operate below Montmartre in Paris in a red light district. Much musical entertainment of the last century has often played on the edges of respectability with remarkable or glitzy spectacle.

Photo from early twentieth-century French postcard. Collection of the authors.

motivation, and psychological evaluation. This shift is the apparent beginning of actors psychoanalyzing characters as if they were real people. Urged to do so by directors from Antoine onward, actors created the impression that the audience was not present during the performance, creating an imaginary **fourth wall** at the proscenium curtain line. The change must have been startling. Much of what we associate with contemporary directing was created as a response to the need for careful control of the realistic presentation.

THE AVANT-GARDE FROM THE LATE NINETEENTH CENTURY TO THE 1960s

Two important terms that have been associated with theatre since the late nineteenth century sometimes lead to confusion, since they are used in various ways. *Modernism* and the *avant-garde* are closely identified with the twentieth century. **Modernism** in theatre is often used to designate the shift beginning with realism; throughout the twentieth century scholars noted that modern theatre and drama began with Ibsen. Many late twentieth-century scholars associated modernism with the type of theatre that rebelled against realism and naturalism. In this book we will use the term "modernism" to refer to both early realistic and much nonrealistic theatre from the late nineteenth century to the present day.

Avant-garde is also a complicated term and often is used synonymously with the term "experiment." Originally a French military term meaning *vanguard* (the front line of troops who are the first to engage the enemy), it was appropriated by artists to signify those who venture into new, unknown territory in the arts. By definition art that is avant-garde cannot remain so for very long. The work either fails or succeeds. If it fails, it usually disappears from practice as well as historical memory; if the art succeeds, it generally joins accepted practice and therefore is no longer at the vanguard. Technically, Ibsen was avant-garde for a few years, but his work then became a commercial standard.

The term "avant-garde," however, is typically a label for experimental work that rebelled against realism and naturalism. Beginning in the 1890s, nonrealistic and antirealistic theatre and drama appeared regularly in many different artistic movements and experiments, which continued almost nonstop through the 1960s. Sometimes the avant-garde shocked or surprised; it experimented with subject matter, dramatic form, and staging techniques. Experimenters challenged values and the moral order or often attempted to posit a new way of viewing the world. They were fascinated with dreams, the unconscious, psychoanalysis, alternative realities, the supernatural, and irrationality.

Symbolism in the 1890s and early twentieth century was the first major challenge to realism. Its leading playwright, Belgian Maurice Maeterlinck, created plays such as *The Blue Bird* (1908), a symbolic pursuit of elusive happiness. The legacy of symbolism is still very much alive in theatre for children, Disney films, and many romantic musicals such as *The Fantasticks* (1960), which presents a simple story of love found, lost, and found again with emblematic characters and imaginary scenery on a nearly empty stage. The Irish symbolist William Butler Yeats (1865–1939) encountered traditional Asian theatrical forms such as Japanese Noh and started incorporating similar methods into his stage work, using masks, open stages, folk music, and dance. Many in the avant-garde were fascinated with the possibilities of the relatively bare stage of some Asian theatre. This East/West fascination was a two-way street, with Asian practitioners appropriating Western melodrama, realism, and the proscenium stage. Touring companies from both hemispheres visited foreign theatres. Many classical Asian plays were first translated into English and other European languages in the first half of the twentieth century and became the subject of serious study and inspired periodic theatrical performances.

Also intrigued by Asian forms, August Strindberg in Sweden created not only realism, but also bizarre dramas such as *A Dream Play* (1907), which abandons causality as an organizing principle and substitutes dream or music as a model for form. Time and space shift suddenly in defiance of logic or causality, just as in our dreams. New directors such as Lugné-Poë (1869–1940) in France attempted to create an abstract stage focusing on color or substituting drapes for traditional scenery. Lugné-Poë directed plays by Maeterlinck, as well as one of the most famous outrageous plays of the avant-garde, *Ubu Roi* (King Ubu) by Alfred Jarry, a play that in 1896 seemed designed to offend everyone with its stupid antihero, scatological jokes, and runaway violence. The first word of the play (one that is subsequently repeated persistently) is "merdre," a fabricated word resembling the French word for "shit," which caused the first audience to erupt in a mixture of outrage and delight. Some historians see the notorious production of this play as the event that truly launched the avant-garde on its path to grotesque and sometimes shocking experiment.

Designers too joined the rebellion, and the majestic but simple designs of Adolphe Appia (1862–1928) and Gordon Craig (1872–1966) swept the theatrical world with their images of platforms, stairs, open spaces, and great, even impossible heights. A guiding principle was simplicity, avoiding detail and reducing a location to its most significant elements. In the United States this was called the **new stagecraft,** and it quickly made its way into commercial theatres; sometimes such scenery was used even for plays that were written to be realistic.

Experimental directors and designers took on Shakespeare and other classics anew and sought to return to a simple stage where the space could suggest any location without filling the space with detailed, realistic scenery. As Shakespeare had been the test for actors in the nineteenth century, his plays became the measure of directors in the twentieth. Harley Granville-Barker in England (in 1914) eliminated the traditional forest scenery of *A Midsummer Night's Dream* and replaced it with open platforms and diaphanous drapery. Many new directors were especially successful at combining classical plays with new, open stages. The Japanese revolving stage found its way to Europe in the early twentieth century and helped to revolutionize stagecraft. Even the Kabuki *hanamichi* was used in Max Reinhardt's German production

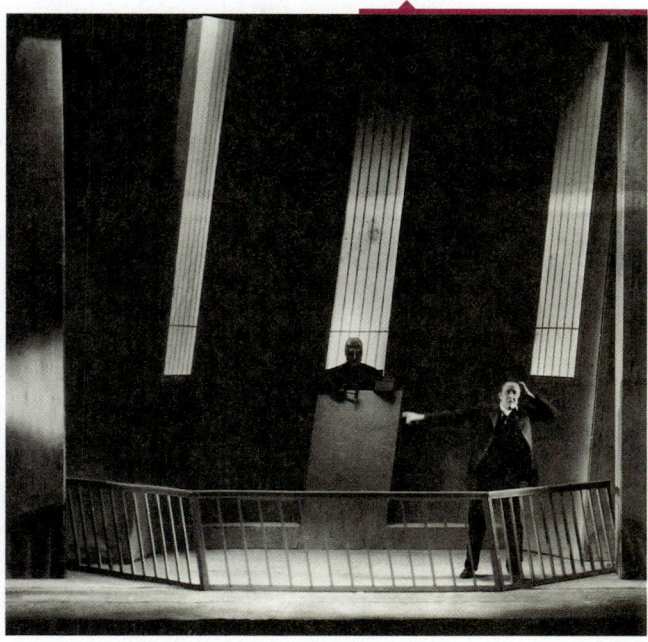

THE ADDING MACHINE (1923), an expressionistic play by Elmer Rice as produced by the Theatre Guild in New York in the original production. The anti-hero, Mr. Zero, played by Dudley Digges, is shown in agitation during his trial for murder. Note the mask on the judge and the angularity of the scenery, which was typical of expressionism in the period. Directed by Philip Moeller and designed by Lee Simonson, a new stagecraft artist.

Photo from Billy Rose Theatre Collection, the New York Public Library for the Performing Arts, Astor, Lenox and Tilden Foundations.

of *Sumurun* (1910), a tale of Arabian intrigues, which toured throughout Europe and the United States. The permanent architectural façade returned in the French work of Jacques Copeau (1879–1949), who sought to focus all of the audience's attention on the performer and the text, not on the scenery. The new directors were eclectic in their tastes and practice.

Early in the twentieth century, many Asian countries, especially Japan, would in turn borrow from the West and develop movements following European realism and then departures from realism. It was not long until Japanese playwrights and directors began to develop their own approaches to theatrical experiment. Theatres following a Western tradition, *shingeki,* and original experimental groups, *Shougekijo-engeki,* continue to proliferate in Japan and work alongside mainstream commercial productions and the classical forms of Noh, Kabuki, and Bunraku puppetry. As early as the late nineteenth century Kabuki adopted the Western proscenium to frame its classical productions.

German and American **expressionism** in the 1910s and 1920s dramatized the dehumanization or destruction of humanity at the hands of industry and war. Written long before Hiroshima, Georg Kaiser's *Gas II* (1920) presents an apocalyptic view of an entire culture wiped out by a superweapon. A principal effect of antirealistic theatre and drama was to dramatize and make concrete (objectify) an internal or figurative thought, idea, feeling, or imaginative event. Consequently, the antirealist might objectify a subjective experience. In expressionism what was seen on the stage, including the scenery, suggested the anxiety and mental breakdown of the central character. Eugene O'Neill's *The Hairy Ape* (1922) was first produced by the Provincetown Players, who were dedicated to American experiment. In the play, Yank, an animal-like ship's stoker, searches in vain for a place where he belongs. In *Machinal* (1928) by Sophie Treadwell, a young woman oppressed by the workplace and her mother—in fact, all adults in her life—finally cracks and murders her husband. The play ends with her execution in the electric chair. French **surrealism,** such as Jean Cocteau's *Orpheus* (1926), reconceived Greek mythology in an attempt to combine the dream world so completely with the real world that one could hardly distinguish the two.

Two avant-garde innovators, whose important work was created between the two world wars, had a profound impact on the rest of the century. Bertolt Brecht in Germany popularized Epic Theatre through theory and his Marxist plays such as *Mother Courage and Her Children* (c. 1939), an episodic journey in which the title character loses her children to the ravages of war and her own preoccupation with capitalist practice. **Epic Theatre** is anti-illusionist theatre featuring emotional detachment, narration, songs, and obvious theatricality; it has been adopted and adapted by countless directors and playwrights. In France, Antonin Artaud was not very successful as an actor and director, but his theory of **Theatre of Cruelty** from the 1930s (included in the collection of his work, *The Theatre and Its Double*) is still considered required reading by many avant-garde artists of the theatre. Artaud's theory is focused on personal rather than social change and advocates working on emotions by assaulting the audience's senses. He stressed process over product and visual imagery over text. Many avant-garde artists since the 1950s have created work inspired by *both* Brecht and Artaud.

World War II left artists disturbed by its horrors, especially the Holocaust and the atomic bomb. Artists of the avant-garde created a body of work dominated by plays centered on characters who are strangers to each other, trapped in a violent, meaningless world seemingly without design or purpose. Such plays are often dubbed **Theatre of the Absurd.** The bleak, existential, repetitious world of Samuel Beckett in *Waiting for Godot* (1953), a study of tramps on a road awaiting something or someone that never arrives, continues to haunt theatres around the world. Much of the almost random action of Act I is repeated with small variations in Act II. The manic absurdities of Eugène Ionesco, beginning with *The Bald Soprano* (1950), demonstrate the impossibility of meaningful communication among human beings. Although not strictly of the absurd style, the menacing plays of Harold Pinter, such as *The Homecoming* (1965), lack exposition, and many events seem random and disconnected. His characters are often savage to one another in language if not in deed. The audience often feels that it has been dropped into an ambiguous but clearly dangerous conflict.

EXPLORING Collaboration
Founding an Alternative Theatre: The Provincetown Players

At the outbreak of World War I, George Cram (Jig) Cook and his wife Susan Glaspell were writers from the Midwest who had moved to Greenwich Village in New York. They were also part of a colony of artists of all sorts—writers, painters, sculptors—who gathered in the summer in Provincetown, Massachusetts, to be near the sea, share ideas with other artists, and work on their craft.

It was apparently Cook's idea to create a summer theatre in Provincetown in 1915, a theatre based exclusively on new plays and very anticommercial in its approach. Nearly everyone Cook met became a candidate for dramatic author, as he seemed to invite any new acquaintance to join his revolution to create an important body of dramatic work for the American theatre. Cook wrote plays himself, of course, and emerged as the artistic director of what became known as the Provincetown Players, but his talent was not as an artist—he was a mover and shaker, an inspiration to others. Cook insisted that the playwright would be in charge of producing his or her own work, that the playwright's intent would always be followed precisely. The playwrights frequently directed their own plays, and they had the last word, an unusual power for a playwright to have in the modern era. The first play the Provincetown Players produced was *Suppressed Desires* (1915), a one-act play written jointly by Cook and Glaspell.

Susan Glaspell was the true artist of the two, and she wrote some of the most important one-act plays of the period, such as *Trifles* (1916), as well as a number of full-length plays such as *The Verge* (1921), the first produced American play to have significant expressionistic elements. The Provincetown Players first produced the plays of other dynamic members, such as *Aria Da Capo* (1919), the first American antiwar play after World War I, by the poet Edna St. Vincent Millay. The couple of Cook and Glaspell was the founding heart of this theatre, however, and when they were joined by the as-yet-unknown Eugene O'Neill in the summer of 1916, the Provincetown Players quickly took off as an influential force in the American professional theatre. By the fall of 1916 they had a tiny theatrical home in Greenwich Village that they fittingly called the Playwrights' Theatre. Even though they were amateurs, they regularly produced bills of one-acts and sometimes full-length plays that attracted the attention of major newspaper critics.

Under Cook's leadership, the Provincetown Players was a group effort. All of the members collaborated in all aspects of theatrical production: playwriting, acting, directing, scene painting, taking tickets. Even O'Neill, who was painfully shy, acted a few times. The results of production sometimes looked amateurish, in part because the group seemed willing to produce nearly any new play that the members wrote—good, bad, or indifferent. Yet the spirit of their artistic community was strong, and their commitment to experiment was enduring, even when the experiment sometimes proved silly.

The world of the Provincetown Players changed when it produced O'Neill's *The Emperor Jones* in 1920. Within a

THE EMPEROR JONES (1920) by Eugene O'Neill in its first production at the Playwrights' Theatre of the Provincetown Players. Many of the nightmare scenarios imagined by the protagonist were presented as near silhouettes. This tiny production moved to Broadway in 1921. Directed by George Cram Cook; designed by Cleon Throckmorton.
Courtesy of Billy Rose Theatre Collection, the New York Public Library for the Performing Arts, Astor, Lenox and Tilden Foundations.

month the play was on its way to a Broadway theatre, and it ultimately became an international phenomenon. Recognition of their work proved to be a mixed blessing for members of the Provincetown Players. Becoming professionals was ultimately devastating to the vision and efforts of Cook and Glaspell because they and their community of artists, many of whom worked only occasionally with the group, began to struggle with their artistic mission. By late 1922 this welcoming home of dramatic experiment dedicated to the vision of the playwright was at an end. In 1924 it was swallowed by the professional company Experimental Theatre, Inc., which was led in part by O'Neill but no longer with Cook, Glaspell, or the other visionaries who began their collaboration in a living room and an old fishing shack on a wharf in Provincetown.

INTERESTED? Check out

Robert Karoly Sarlos. *Jig Cook and the Provincetown Players: Theatre in Ferment.* Amherst: University of Massachusetts, 1982.

Susan Glaspell. *The Road to the Temple: A Biography of George Cram Cook.* (1927). Edited and introduced by Linda Ben-Zvi. Jefferson, NC: McFarland, 2005.

Helen Deutsch and Stella Hanau. *The Provincetown Players: A Story of the Theatre.* New York: Farrar & Rinehart, 1931.

Edna Kenton. *The Provincetown Players and the Playwrights' Theatre, 1915–1922.* Jefferson, NC: McFarland, 2004.

THE CAUCASIAN CHALK CIRCLE, written and directed by Bertolt Brecht and designed by Karl von Appen at the Berliner Ensemble. The heroine, Grusha, flees the war, saving the child of another. Her journey is depicted by walking in one direction while the revolve moves in the other. Notice the open, empty stage, except for the partially lowered billowing drop above her.

Photo by KaiDib Films International.

The 1960s also saw many disturbing experimental plays by African Americans: *Funnyhouse of a Negro* (1964) by Adrienne Kennedy is dominated by images and snatches of dialogue demonstrating a young black woman in conflict with her own feelings and all of her cultural and family baggage. *Dutchman* (1964) by Imamu Amiri Baraka presents a white woman randomly selecting and killing young black men on a train after ritualistically taking them through a psychosexual diatribe of insecurities and desires. These and many other African American plays continue to challenge and fascinate audiences and readers.

During the era of the Vietnam War the avant-garde in Europe and the United States was preoccupied with communal performance groups, environmental staging, and angry political messages. Jerzy Grotowski's Polish Laboratory Theatre became an international phenomenon with environmental productions such as *Akropolis* (1962), a stylized examination of survival and death in concentration camps. Grotowski led an ensemble of actors

ROCK 'N' ROLL (2006) by Tom Stoppard is a highly entertaining exploration of societal, artistic (especially in music), and political transformation during and just after the Cold War and fall of the Berlin Wall in Europe. In this ensemble piece the playwright examines the events both comically and incisively. Seen here is an extended family argument from the 2007 production in New York staged by Trevor Nunn who also directed the premiere in London.

Photo © Joan Marcus.

EINSTEIN ON THE BEACH
(1976), created and directed by Robert Wilson, popularized minimalist but theatrical images of contemporary life in this ground-breaking production. Wilson revived this production many times in the late twentieth century and helped to usher in a number of the elements so typical of postmodern theatre. In this image of a courtroom from a 1992 production, he combines static imagery, stylized event, repetitive movement, and glorious stage pictures.
Photo © T. Charles Erickson.

with a near-religious dedication to their projects. The Living Theatre in the 1950s and early 1960s was an **Off-off-Broadway** collective experiment led by Judith Malina and Julian Beck, but by the mid-1960s this company functioned as a group of radical expatriate Americans, wandering Europe with incendiary political productions such as *Paradise Now* (1968), which insisted on instant revolution. Some of the most fascinating group productions were created by the Open Theatre under the leadership of Joseph Chaikin (1935–2003). The Open Theatre production of *The Serpent* (1968) by Jean-Claude van Itallie combined the Garden of Eden, Cain's murder of his brother Abel, and the assassination of John Kennedy, all done with doubling of characters by actors and no reliance on scenery.

MODERN AND CONTEMPORARY POPULAR THEATRE

In the twentieth century many theatre artists found themselves both among the avant-garde and in the mainstream commercial theatre. Eugene O'Neill in the United States produced many experimental dramas between 1916 and 1934, but some of his plays, such as *The Emperor Jones,* were commercial hits as early as 1920. This was the first professional production (outside variety entertainment) to present a black actor with white actors on a Broadway stage. Inspired by Strindberg, O'Neill created both realism and nonrealism, but most of his late famous plays, such as *The Iceman Cometh* (1946) and *Long Day's Journey into Night* (1956), are strictly realistic.

The realistic trend has continued unchecked since Ibsen. We continue to create box sets and train actors in a realistic style; domestic family conflicts abound on the stage as well as in film and television. The realistic acting style, identified with Stanislavsky, made its way to other countries in the early twentieth century and received one of its most influential incarnations in the work of the Group Theatre in New York in the 1930s. This ensemble found its strongest expression in the Depression-era plays of Clifford Odets such as *Awake and Sing!* (1935), which depicts a hard-edged Jewish mother struggling to make ends meet and trying with little success to hold her family together. The Group Theatre disbanded in 1941, and from the ashes of the defunct company Elia Kazan and others created the Actors Studio in 1947. The Actors Studio was formed as a workshop for professional actors (many of whom, such as Geraldine Page and

A STREETCAR NAMED DESIRE by Tennessee Williams. This 2005 Broadway revival was directed by Edward Hall for the Roundabout Theatre Company at Studio 54. Natasha Richardson plays Blanche, and Amy Ryan plays her sister Stella. Costume design by William Ivey Long. Photo © Joan Marcus.

Marlon Brando, became household names). Other members of the Group Theatre, such as Stella Adler and Sanford Meisner, became acting teachers whose methods continue at the center of many acting programs.

Realism has persisted in the plays of famous and frequently revived playwrights. Arthur Miller in *Death of a Salesman* (1949) gave us the exemplar of twentieth-century tragedy. Some of the most unforgettable American characters fill the plays of Tennessee Williams such as *A Streetcar Named Desire* (1947). Director Elia Kazan and designer Jo Mielziner gave the first productions of both *Salesman* and *Streetcar* visual nonrealistic touches but maintained realism in characterization and action. This kind of modified realism (without all the traditional details of realism) has been common since the mid-twentieth century. You can see this approach in which realism dominates in the works of many playwrights: In *Who's Afraid of Virginia Woolf?* (1962), Edward Albee dramatizes in one night a catastrophic emotional breakdown in a dysfunctional marriage. In *True West* (1980), Sam Shepard presents the struggle of two brothers whose disparate lifestyles erupt in violence and role reversal. In *'night, Mother* (1983), Marsha Norman follows the final self-destructive path of a woman who no longer finds any meaning in her life. In *Glengarry Glen Ross* (1983), David Mamet demonstrates the business world out of control but presents it as a model for the American way of life.

The first nonmusical Broadway production written and directed by African Americans was *A Raisin in the Sun* (1959), a poignant and traditionally structured play by Lorraine Hansberry. The first production was directed by Lloyd Richards, who in the 1980s began directing the century's most popular and effective African American plays such as August Wilson's *Ma Rainey's Black Bottom* (1984), a conflict of race and power in the popular

MA RAINEY'S BLACK BOTTOM (1984) was August Wilson's first professional production and launched his cycle of plays exploring African American experience in the twentieth century, which he completed shortly before his death in 2005. Although all of his plays enjoy revivals, this one is more difficult than most due to the musical demands on the actors. Charles S. Dutton (who created the role of the jazz trumpeter Levee in 1984) is seen here reviving his interpretation on Broadway in 2003 with Whoopi Goldberg as the title character. Directed by Marion McClinton. Photo © Joan Marcus.

music world of the 1920s. Nearly all of Wilson's plays are realistic, and some, such as *The Piano Lesson* (1990), have an occasional touch of the supernatural and spiritual. In Wilson's final play, *Radio Golf* (2007), the playwright completed his ten-play trilogy on the black experience in twentieth-century United States. He creates a character running for mayor of Pittsburgh while trying to bury his past. Wilson is warning African Americans not to deny their ethnicity and not to assimilate so completely into a white world that their real heritage vanishes. Suzan-Lori Parks, the most recent Pulitzer Prize–winning African American playwright, challenges her audiences with difficult subject matter and experiments with dramatic structure and language in such plays as *Venus, Fucking A,* and *The America Play.*

The African continent became a major theatrical player in the late twentieth century, offering many new plays since the 1960s. Two playwrights especially have become international phenomena: Athol Fugard through realistic plays such as *Master Harold . . . and the Boys* (1982), a study in the issues of apartheid, and Nigeria's Nobel laureate Wole Soyinka with *Madmen and Specialists* (1971), which attacks political repression in Nigeria by depicting a bizarre power struggle during wartime. Soyinka incorporates ritual and ceremony in his plays, drawing on the ancient practices of shamans and tribal religion and performance from his African region. He even adapted a Greek tragedy, *The Bacchae of Euripides* (1973), as African ritual.

Without doubt the most popular theatre (in both economic and crowd-pleasing terms) of the twentieth century has been the modern musical, dominated at first by the United States but now generated in many parts of the world. England's Andrew Lloyd Webber gave us *Phantom of the Opera* (1986), Elton John and Tim Rice created *Aida* (2000), and *Les Misérables* (1985), by Alain Boublil and Claude-Michel Schönberg, originated in France. Musicals are sometimes categorized as a separate genre, but the musical is a play and can be of any genre (comedy, tragedy, melodrama), and most theatre before realism incorporated significant music, singing, and dance. The **book musical** (a play that tells a story and has spoken text as well as songs) was inspired by nineteenth-century operettas and has been dominant since the tragicomic, racially mixed *Show Boat* (1927) by Jerome Kern and Oscar Hammerstein II. The book musical peaked in sentimentality with the enormously popular efforts of Hammerstein and Richard Rodgers, beginning with *Oklahoma!* (1943). It then adapted tragic form with Bernstein's *West Side Story* (1957); incorporated rock music with Jerome Ragni, James Rado, and Galt McDermott's *Hair* (1967); experimented with development of the musical form in Michael Bennett's *A Chorus Line* (1975), which is dominated by dance because of the subject matter; reached some of its most sophisticated musical and structural efforts with Stephen Sondheim in such plays as *Sunday in the Park with George* (1984); and tackled contemporary social, racial, and sexual issues in *Rent* (1996) by Jonathan Larson, and *In the Heights* (2008) by Lin-Manuel Miranda and Quiara Alegria Hudes. Many of these accomplishments are hilariously parodied in *Urinetown* by Greg Kotis and Mark Hollman (2001) and *Spamalot* by Eric Idle and John Du Prez (2005). Although *Passing Strange* (2008) by Stew and Heidi Rodewald also makes fun of performance art, the play is really a wonderful rock musical and geographical journey through Stew's personal experiences with international touring in the rock world. With *Spring Awakening* (2006), by Steven Sater and Duncan Sheik, the past and the present are united in a remarkable theatrical expression that engages a young audience while resonating with the residue of nineteenth-century confrontational theatre and troubling cultural conflicts.

EXPLORING Historical and Cultural Perspectives

The Development of the Modern Musical in America

Although most theatre in most countries of the world since the ancient Greeks has been some kind of musical theatre, what we have come to label "American-style musicals" since the early twentieth century has become the heart of popular theatre in the United States. Many theatregoers prefer to see musicals, and some see only musicals. These are the most expensive plays to produce, and when successful, are usually the greatest moneymakers for commercial producers. The traditional sources for what we now call musicals range from melodrama (which uses strong underscoring and occasional songs) to black-face minstrel shows to European and American operetta. Quite popular in the nineteenth century, operettas include those by England's Gilbert and Sullivan (*H.M.S. Pinafore* and *The Pirates of Penzance*), Austria's Franz Lehár (*The Merry Widow* and *Friederika*), and America's Victor Herbert (*Babes in Toyland* and *Naughty Marietta*). The operetta form was probably the strongest influence on the rise of popularity of the book musical beginning with *Show Boat* in 1927 by Jerome Kern and Oscar Hammerstein. Each generation of musicals since the beginning of the twentieth century has typically utilized the most popular musical forms and styles of their time: the waltz, jazz, big band, and rock music, for example, and nearly all musicals are adapted from preexisting forms: short stories, novels, non-musical plays, films, tv shows, comics, and newspaper articles. Even plays of Shakespeare and Ibsen have been adapted to modern musical theatre. Although some musicals are created without a formal source, such as *Hair* and *A Chorus Line*, adaptation is the norm. Musicals are most commonly comedies and farces, but thrillers and melodramas, even tragedy appear on the Broadway musical stage.

One can easily expect a strain of the romantic in most musicals, either in the main plot or a subplot. Satirical musicals such as *Urinetown, Candide,* or *The Producers* typically have a love story prominently in place. And love stories drive the action in many traditional "golden age" musicals such as *Oklahoma!* and *Carousel* by Rodgers and Hammerstein, Cole Porter's *Kiss Me Kate,* and Lerner and Lowe's *My Fair Lady* and *Camelot,* most of which contributed countless famous love songs to the popularly described "Broadway Songbook." Even when the musicals are not in professional production, the songs continue to be performed in revues, cabarets, clubs, and on television. The wildly popular *Fiddler on the Roof,* with its serious story about persecuted Jews in Russia, and the more recent *Phantom of the Opera,* drawn from horror stories, revolve around romance. Surely this romantic element is a clue to the popularity of musicals.

Of course, the element of dance is prominent in most musicals, sometimes even driving and expressing much of the action as in the tragic *West Side Story,* the loosely structured but intriguing *A Chorus Line,* or the schematic triptych *Contact.* Despite our recurring expectations for what a new musical will bring us, we continue to be surprised by variations on dramatic structure, exciting new music, choreography and storytelling. Artists choose unusual sources to adapt, such as the remarkably inventive *Spring Awakening* that bridged issues from a nineteenth-century play with twenty-first-century style and psychology. The reconception of history

THE RECENT AVANT-GARDE AND POSTMODERN EXPERIMENT

Experimental work in the last several decades of the twentieth century has often been categorized as **postmodern,** which can be interpreted as work that is no longer "modern" in the sense that August Strindberg and Tennessee Williams were modern. The postmodern is not of the modern but comments on, satirizes, or reinterprets the modern. The postmodern artist is sometimes identified as artist and critic simultaneously. Some critics see it as an artistic style, hence postmodern*ism.* Others claim that it is a mindset, a point of view that looks back on the previous century of artistic work with cynicism or futility—and sometimes despair. In visual terms it is dominated by simultaneous action and electronic or cybernetic technology; structurally, it features repetition and deconstruction of masterpieces of the past.

The last several decades have witnessed considerable blurring of the avant-garde and commercial theatre, so much so that some critics argue that the avant-garde died in the 1960s and refer to experiment from 1890 to 1970 or so as the "historical avant-garde." We will continue to use the term "avant-garde" for noncommercial experiment but verify that experiment since about 1970 has been very different from that which occurred before.

In subject matter many experimental plays have focused on gay and lesbian lifestyles and conflicts, a host of gender issues headed by feminism, and the isolation

WICKED (2003) has proved to be a huge commercial success that continues to run in New York (well over 3100 performances in July 2011), London, and Australia, as well as on tour.

Photo © Joan Marcus.

century, he reinvigorated the operetta format so popular during the era of Rodgers and Hammerstein and challenged both his audiences and singer/actors with difficult lyrics, delightful storytelling, and risky structure in such shows as *Company, Follies, Into the Woods, Sunday in the Park with George*, and *Sweeney Todd*. His work has been on Broadway stages as well as all over the world from 1957 to 2011 and isn't likely to diminish in popularity in the foreseeable future.

Since the appearance of *West Side Story* in 1957, each decade or generation of youthful audiences has found one or two musicals to rally round and use as an anthem for problems and values important to the young. Among others, this can be said of *Hair* (1968), *A Chorus Line* (1975), *Rent* (1996), and *Spring Awakening* (2006). It appears that the musical, in new works as well as revivals, will maintain its prominence in the American theatre for some time to come.

in *Bloody Bloody Andrew Jackson* was startling and fun, and *The Book of Mormon* didn't just entertain an audience dedicated to *South Park*, but engaged a larger audience with its surprising moments of sincerity and fun without meanness.

We have discussed Stephen Sondheim earlier, but we should note here that in the second half of the twentieth

INTERESTED? Check out

Larry Stempel. *Showtime: A History of the Broadway Musical Theatre.* New York: W. W. Norton, 2010.

Michael Kantor and Laurence Maslon. *Broadway: The American Musical.* New York: Bulfinch, 2004.

of the individual in a self-centered world. Theatrical companies dedicated solely or primarily to gay and lesbian issues have been appearing since the 1970s. The company Split Britches, for example, deconstructs famous plays such as *A Streetcar Named Desire;* in *Belle Reprieve* (1991), a collaboration with the Bloolips Production Company, Stanley Kowalski is replaced by a lesbian and Blanche DuBois by a man in a dress. Gay material has been mainstreamed, of course, most notably with *Angels in America* (1991/1993) by Tony Kushner. *Angels in America* and many other plays since *The Normal Heart* (1985) by Larry Kramer have focused on the horrors and social fallout of the AIDS pandemic. *The Laramie Project* (2000), by Moisés Kaufman and his team of interviewer/performers, created a moving examination of an insulated but not uncommon society that spawns intolerance and commits violent, homophobic acts.

Kaufman's company, the Tectonic Theater Project, does not work exclusively with gender and sexual issues; in 2007 they explored a new play by Kaufman on the nature of genius (specifically Beethoven's), musical obsession, and the interweaving of nineteenth-century art with our own time in *33 Variations.*

Feminist issues have been a dynamic part of experimental work since the 1970s, when many women's acting companies and female playwrights proliferated in North America, Britain, and Germany. Audiences have been challenged by Caryl Churchill's comic and disturbing *Top Girls* (1982), a scathing examination of gender issues in the business world. Maria Irene Fornes dissects gender power struggles in Latin America in

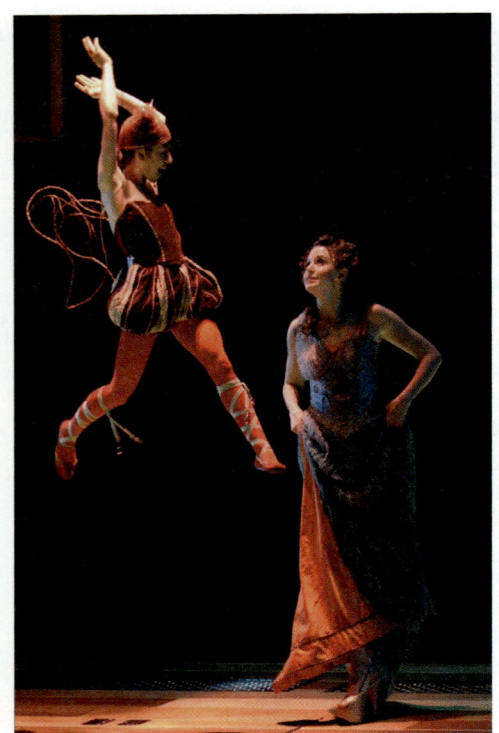

ARGONAUTICA (2007) written and directed by Mary Zimmerman, a revisitation of Jason and the Argonauts. Seen here at the Berkeley Repertory Theatre. Eros in flight (performed by Ronette Levenson) playfully encounters Aphrodite (performed by Tessa Klein). Photo © Kevin Berne.

The Conduct of Life (1985). Ntozake Shange calls her play *for colored girls who have considered suicide when the rainbow is enuf* (1976) a choreopoem; the poetic speech is delivered by a chorus of young women. In the 1990s, playwright Eve Ensler began performing *The Vagina Monologues,* based on her interviews with many women. The play initiated the V-Day movement in 1998 to stop violence against women and girls worldwide. These play-wrights, and others, have introduced new and exciting types of dramatic structures. Because so many artists have been preoccupied with gender issues in the last few decades, we have seen an explosion of cross-dressing on the stage—a whole new wave of gender-bending tied to sexual politics.

Sarah Ruhl's *The Clean House* (2006) is one of most remarkable American plays to emerge amidst postmodern work. It explores on a domestic front issues of intercultural and linguistic confusion, the mysteries of shifting romantic relationships, even in middle age, and the power and fears of confronting death and loss in the midst of telling jokes. The use of space is fluid, and at once austerely white made real by the proliferation of objects. At times the stage becomes something of a littering site. Ruhl's stage directions are also emblematic of the way the theatre is changing: She often indicates that many important discoveries or decisions are made in silence—between the spoken lines. Ruhl has also revisited Greek mythology in her *Eurydice* (2004), bringing this story into our own time and experience.

Many postmodern directors have deconstructed classics of the stage with startling revelations, imbuing old plays from Greek tragedy to Gilbert and Sullivan comic operettas with contemporary political contexts. **Deconstruction** in theatrical production means a radically reinterpreted famous play in which the original play may still be recognized. The new production, however, uses the written play as only a pretext and frequently comments on or negates the apparent intent of the original play. Peter Sellars (b. 1957), for example, directs postmodern interpretations of musicals, operas, and classical plays, often using collections of video screens, onstage cameras, and contemporary locations. In Germany Peter Stein (b. 1937) produces radical stage environments and unusual audience relationships for classics ranging from *The Oresteia* of Aeschylus to Ibsen's *Peer Gynt.* Sometimes the classics are so modified by the directors that they seem to become entirely new plays, as occurred with Ariane Mnouchkine's French production of *Les Atrides* (1990–1992), a Kathakali-like reconception of *The Oresteia.*

Wholly new work dominated by visual images, dynamic music and dance, or closely choreographed movement has become the hallmark for many **conceptual directors** such as Martha Clarke, who conceived *Vienna Lusthaus* (1986) with text by Charles Mee, Jr., and created a culture at the crossroads primarily through visuals. Clarke and Mee collaborated again in 2004 with *Belle Epoque,* an examination of the impressionist art and Parisian cabaret world of Toulouse-Lautrec. Robert Wilson is also a master of visual images and has combined minimalist and postmodern music (by Philip Glass and David Byrne) with remarkable designs and movement in vast projects such as *the CIVIL warS* (1983). Wilson has also reconceived famous plays such as *Woyzeck* by Georg Büchner in 2000 and the film *Dr. Caligari* as a theatre piece in 2002. One of the most intriguing postmodern artists is Tadashi Suzuki (b. 1939) from Japan. Suzuki combines different periods, cultures, and styles with international casts of actors trained in the martial arts for his experiments such as *Clytemnestra,* a reworking of Greek tragedy.

Prominent among postmodern trends at the end of the twentieth century was solitary work of performance artists, utilizing media and direct audience address. Karen Finley's one-person, semiautobiographical shows are confrontational and controversial, using nudity and strong political and social messages as in *We Keep Our Victims Ready* (1989). Spalding Gray gave his audience the convincing impression that his monologues such as *Monster in a Box* (1991) are entirely autobiographical and embarrassingly revealing of his psychological problems. Although Anna Deavere Smith often has performed alone (she also appears as a traditional actor in TV productions), she impersonates many different characters based on real people she has interviewed. Her *Fires in the Mirror* (1992) focuses on racial conflict in the United States, and *House Arrest* (2000) examines presidential politics.

In a post-9/11 world many theatre artists, not surprisingly, are preoccupied with terrorism and all of its potential fallout, from threats to personal liberty, to wide-ranging governments and freelance organizations that threaten to enshrine totalitarian practice and acts of programmatic suicide and genocide. The Cold War is long over, but many of its components have been resurrected, sometimes in surprising places. Many serious plays and theatrical events are centering on such practice and threat: the violent plays of Martin McDonagh, the political plays of David Hare and Michael Frayn, the troubling ethical plays of John Patrick Shanley and Suzan-Lori Parks, and the plays of Tony Kushner, Caryl Churchill, and José Rivera that plead for racial, ethnic, religious, and sexual tolerance.

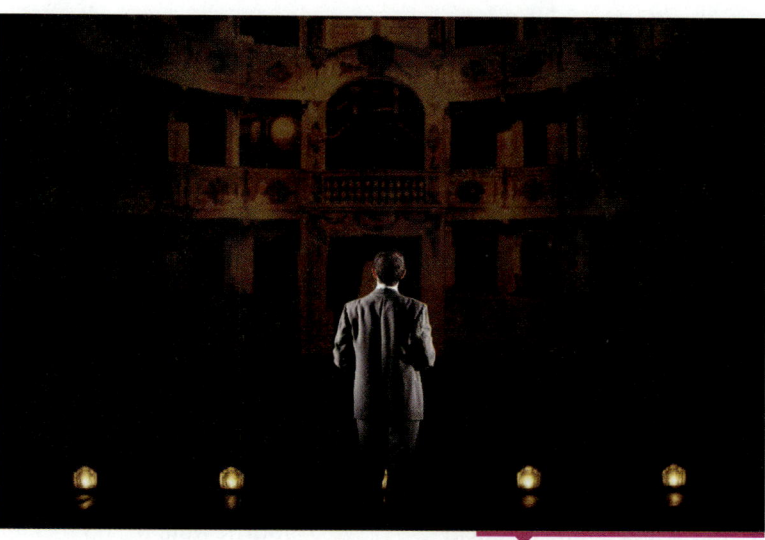

BLACK SNOW by Keith Reddin, adapted from a novel by early twentieth-century Russian writer Mikhail Bulgakov. A satirical look at the pitfalls and anxieties of writing for the theatre. In this image the fictional playwright, with his back to the live audience, encounters an empty Russian theatre created with projections upstage so that the real audience is looking at the seating area for another theatre, a mirror-like device that cannot be replicated in film or television. Directed by Evan Yionoulis; scenic design by Dustin Eshenroder. Produced in 2006 by the Yale Repertory Theatre.

Photo © Carol Rosegg.

Churchill's later work has often been more concerned with political and social problems than sexual, however. In *A Number* (2002), for example, she takes on human cloning, and in *Drunk Enough to Say I Love You?* (2006), she confronts the governmental regimes of the United States and the United Kingdom and their political relationship by reducing the global situation to two drunken men on a couch. Nilo Cruz, an American Hispanic playwright in his *Anna in the Tropics* (2003) explores poetically the dynamics of Cuban immigrants in the United States by selecting a pivotal historical moment, 1929, just before the Great Depression, and just as the social, economic, and employment issues of Hispanic immigrants were about to be irreversibly altered. Much of the pre-9/11 postmodern work was deconstructive of modernism, or simultaneously playful and anxious when commenting on contemporary life and contradictory lifestyles. Are we now moving beyond the postmodern? Are our cutting-edge artists once again redefining the avant-garde as well as the popular theatre?

The personal expression of some theatre artists comments meaningfully on the state of the world that many people find confusing or alarming. Neil Labute in *The Shape of Things* (2001) asks us to question the morality of exploiting others for the sake of art and of drawing focus to the artist rather than the art. Can or should the artistic expression outstrip the personality of the artist? Some performance artists claim that the body of the artist and the art are the same thing. Is such a point of view residue of a dying postmodern moment, or a verification of what theatrical experiment will become for the next generation? The theatrical future is all but impossible to predict, but historians and critics a few years beyond us will recognize the clues in our current practice—they lie in the new plays that we write and produce, in the plays from the past that we choose to revive, and in how we interpret those revivals. Although change is inevitable, it is equally certain that plays and performance of the past will continue to inspire new art and be themselves reworked and adapted to meet the demands and desires of future audiences. Some of you who are reading this book will be an important part of this change.

CHAPTER REVIEW

Questions and Activities

1. Class distinctions were considered important to a number of plays and events described in this chapter. Discuss the perceived relationship of social class to the current theatre and other forms of entertainment.

2. Theatres were the focus of artistic, social, and political conflict in the eighteenth and nineteenth centuries. What do you think could provoke a demonstration (or even a riot) in a theatre today? Consider plays, production elements, and management practice.

3. Selective realism has become a popular style: An actual location is suggested by realistic scenic pieces and props, but the audience is left to fill in the rest through imagination. The choice of what to include on stage becomes very important. Think about several different rooms or spaces that you know well. If you had to choose one item to suggest the space, what would it be? A second item? A third? Try this exercise with different kinds of spaces: a specific classroom, bedroom, living room, spot on campus, place in a city, specific store, and so on.

4. As a cultural institution, theatre is always a combination of using preestablished practices and reacting against them. Think of other areas of cultural change. How has your generation kept or changed what you inherited from the last? Discuss fashion, manners, vocabulary, and morality. How is film or television different now from what it was ten years ago? Twenty? Thirty? (Sometimes it is easier to notice differences. The similarities seem to be givens. Try to think of different ways in which things *could* have developed in order to see the similarities.)

Key Terms and Concepts

romanticism, p. 300
Sturm und Drang, p. 300
metatheatre, p. 300
box set, p. 303
antiquarianism, p. 303
melodrama, p. 304
realism, p. 305
breeches role, p. 306
well-made play, p. 307

naturalism, p. 307
fourth wall, p. 308
modernism, p. 308
avant-garde, p. 308
symbolism, p. 309
new stagecraft, p. 309
hanamichi, p. 309
expressionism, p. 310
surrealism, p. 310

Epic Theatre, p. 310
Theatre of Cruelty, p. 310
Theatre of the Absurd, p. 310
Off-off-Broadway, p. 313
book musical, p. 315
postmodern, p. 316
deconstruction, p. 318
conceptual director, p. 318

For Further Exploration

Oscar G. Brockett and Franklin J. Hildy. *History of the Theatre*, 10th ed. Boston: Allyn and Bacon, 2007.

Edwin Wilson and Alvin Goldfarb. *Living Theatre: A History*, 6th ed. Boston: McGraw-Hill, 2011.

Victor Turner. *From Ritual to Theatre: The Human Seriousness of Play*. New York: Performing Arts Journal Publications, 1982.

T. B. L. Webster. *Greek Theatre Production*. London: Methuen, 1970.

Richard Beacham. *The Roman Theatre and Its Audience*. Cambridge, MA: Harvard University, 1992.

Ronald W. Vince. *Ancient and Medieval Theatre*. Westport, CT: Greenwood, 1984.

Farley Richmond, ed. et al. *Indian Theatre: Traditions of Performance*. Honolulu: University of Hawaii, 1990.

Richard Beadle, ed. *The Cambridge Companion to English Medieval Theatre*. Cambridge, UK: Cambridge University, 1994.

James Crump. *Chinese Theatre in the Days of Kublai Khan*. Tucson: University of Arizona, 1980.

Benito Ortolani. *The Japanese Theatre: From Shamanistic Ritual to Contemporary Pluralism*. Princeton, NJ: Princeton University, 1995.

Roy C. Strong. *Splendor at Court: Renaissance Spectacle and the Theatre of Power*. Boston: Houghton Mifflin, 1973.

Barnard Hewitt. *The Renaissance Stage: Documents of Serlio, Sabbattini, and Furttenbach*. Coral Gables, FL: University of Miami, 1958.

J. R. Mulryne and Margaret Shewring. *Theatre of the English and Italian Renaissance*. New York: St. Martin's, 1991.

Gerald E. Bentley. *The Professions of Dramatist and Player in Shakespeare's Time, 1590–1642*. Princeton, NJ: Princeton University, 1984.

Lauren Shohet. *Reading Masques: The English Masque and Public Culture in the Seventeenth Century*. Oxford, UK: Oxford University, 2010.

Stephen Orgel. *The Illusion of Power: Political Theatre in the English Renaissance*. Berkeley: University of California, 1975.

Melveena McKendrick. *Theatre in Spain, 1490–1700*. Cambridge, UK: Cambridge University, 1989.

William D. Howarth. *French Theatre in the Neo-Classical Era, 1550–1789*. Cambridge, UK: Cambridge University, 1997.

Robert D. Hume. *The London Theatre World, 1660–1800*. Carbondale: Southern Illinois University, 1980.

Ronald W. Vince. *Neoclassical Theatre: A Historiographical Handbook*. New York: Greenwood, 1988.

Don Wilmeth and Christopher Bigsby. *The Cambridge History of American Theatre*, 3 vols. Cambridge, UK: Cambridge University, 1998–2000.

Brooks McNamara. *The American Playhouse in the Eighteenth Century*. Cambridge, MA: Harvard University, 1969.

David Grimstead. *Melodrama Unveiled*. Chicago: University of Chicago, 1968.

George Rowell. *The Victorian Theatre*, 2 ed. Cambridge, UK: Cambridge University, 1978.

Oscar Brockett and Robert Findlay. *Century of Innovation*, 2nd ed. Boston: Allyn and Bacon, 1991.

Roger Shattuck. *The Banquet Years: The Origins of the Avant-Garde in France*, rev. ed. New York: Vintage, 1968.

James Roose-Evans. *Experimental Theatre: From Stanislavsky to Peter Brook*, rev. ed. New York: Routledge, 1989.

Martin Banham, Errol Hill, and George Woodyard, eds. *The Cambridge Guide to African and Caribbean Theatre*. Cambridge, UK: Cambridge University, 1994.

Larry Stempel. *Showtime: A History of Broadway Musical Theater*. New York: W. W. Norton, 2010.

KEY THEATRICAL EVENTS

This timeline presents a chronological list of important theatrical events and plays mentioned in this book. The dates for plays are the first known production unless otherwise noted. (For example, we give the early-nineteenth-century composition date for the play Woyzeck because it was not produced until the twentieth century.) We also include a series of important historical and cultural events as points of reference for the context of the theatrical chronology.

THEATRICAL EVENTS AND PLAYS		HISTORICAL / CULTURAL EVENTS
Dramatized ritual at Abydos (Egypt, c. 2500–550 B.C.E.)	**2500 B.C.E.**	Egyptian pyramid building
	1100 B.C.E.	Trojan War (c. 1184–1174 B.C.E.)
	800 B.C.E.	Homer's *Iliad* and *Odyssey*. Public presentations of Homer and choral music— probable sources of Greek tragedy (8th century B.C.E.) First evidence of Olympics (776 B.C.E.)
	700 B.C.E.	
First known written dithyrambs (Greece, c. 600 B.C.E.)	**600 B.C.E.**	
Greek classical theatre period (534–336 B.C.E.) Athens reorganizes City Dionysia to include tragedy. Thespis credited with winning first tragic contest (Greece, c. 534 B.C.E.)	**530 B.C.E.**	
Contest for dithyrambs added to City Dionysia (Greece, 509 B.C.E.)	**510 B.C.E.**	Athens becomes a limited democracy (510 B.C.E.) Rome becomes a republic (509–27 B.C.E.)
Aeschylus begins competing at City Dionysia (Greece, 499 B.C.E.)	**500 B.C.E.**	

Comedy added to City Dionysia (Greece, c. 487 B.C.E.)

490 B.C.E

Wars between Greece and Persia (490–449 B.C.E.)

480 B.C.E

The Persians, Aeschylus (Greece, 472 B.C.E.)

470 B.C.E

Sophocles' first win against Aeschylus (Greece, 468 B.C.E.)

460 B.C.E

The Oresteia (Agamemnon, Libation Bearers, Eumenides), Aeschylus (Greece, 458 B.C.E.)

Death of Aeschylus leads to first play revivals (Greece, 456 B.C.E.)

Euripides begins to compete (Greece, 455 B.C.E.)

Peloponnesian Wars (460–404 B.C.E.)

450 B.C.E.

Contest for actors added to City Dionysia (Greece, 449 B.C.E.)

Antigone, Sophocles (Greece, c. 441 B.C.E.)

440 B.C.E.

Athenian Parthenon (c. 440 B.C.E.)

Medea, Euripides (Greece, 431 B.C.E.)

Oedipus the King, Sophocles (Greece, c. 430 B.C.E.)

430 B.C.E.

The Clouds, Aristophanes (Greece, 423 B.C.E.)

420 B.C.E.

The Trojan Women, Euripides (Greece, 415 B.C.E.)

Lysistrata, Aristophanes (Greece, 411 B.C.E.)

Hypsipyle, Euripides (Greece, 408 B.C.E.)

410 B.C.E.

Oedipus at Colonus, Sophocles (Greece, 406 B.C.E.)

The Bacchae, Euripides (Greece, 406 B.C.E.)

Fall of Athens to Sparta, but play production continues (404 B.C.E.)

The Frogs, Aristophanes (Greece, 405 B.C.E.)

400 B.C.E.

Plato's *Republic* (c. 373 B.C.E.)

370 B.C.E.

340 B.C.E.

Aristotle's *Poetics* (Greece, c. 335–323 B.C.E.) ———————— ———— Hellenistic period (336–146 B.C.E.)

330 B.C.E.

320 B.C.E.

The Dyskolos, Menander (Greece, c. 316 B.C.E.) ————————

Livius Andronicus performs tragedy and comedy ————
at the Ludi Romani in Rome (Rome, 240 B.C.E.)

240 B.C.E.

230 B.C.E.

220 B.C.E.

———— Great Wall of China (214 B.C.E.)

The Brothers Menaechmus, Plautus (Rome, ————————
2nd century B.C.E.)

200 B.C.E.

The Phormio, Terence (Rome, 161 B.C.E.) ————————

160 B.C.E.

150 B.C.E.

———— Rome conquered all Greek territory
(146 B.C.E.)

140 B.C.E.

The actor Roscius flourishes (Rome, c. 100–70 B.C.E.) ————

100 B.C.E.

First permanent Roman theatre (Pompeii) (Rome, 75 B.C.E.)

70 B.C.E.

60 B.C.E.

Theatre of Pompey (First permanent in Rome) (Rome, 55 B.C.E.)

50 B.C.E.

— Roman Empire (27 B.C.E.–c. 476 C.E.)

Horace's *Poetic Art* (Rome, c. 20 B.C.E.)

20 B.C.E.

Natyasastra and earliest evidence of Sanskrit plays (India, c. 1st century C.E.)

C.E.

— Ovid's *Metamorphoses* (c. 5 C.E.)

10

40 — Early Christian churches (C. 40 C.E.)

Oedipus, Medea, Seneca (Rome, c. 50–65 C.E.)

50

60

80 — Roman Colosseum (82 C.E.)

Tertullian condemns theatre and actors (Rome, c. 200)

200

The Little Clay Cart, Sudraka (India, 4th century?)

300 — Christians destroy much of the Library of Alexandria and copies of all plays produced at the City Dionysia in Athens (Egypt, 392)

— Roman Empire splits into East and West Schism remains until 1453 (395)

Shakuntala, Kalidasa (India, 5th century?)

400 — All actors denied the sacraments of the Church by Council of Carthage (398)

THEATRICAL EVENTS AND PLAYS		HISTORICAL / CULTURAL EVENTS

500

"Dark Ages" in Europe (c. 500–900)

Last record of a Roman theatre performance (Rome, 533)

900

Kutiyattum begins (India, 10th century?)

Hrotsvitha adapts six plays of Terence to
Christian principles (Germany, 10th century)

Evidence of professional theatre (China,
10th century)

1000

Quem Quaeritis, first record of performed
dramatic trope (Europe, c. 925)

Liturgical drama flourishes (Europe, c. 925–1570)

European Crusades to the East (1095–1291)

Gothic cathedral building begins (12th century)

1100

1200

Mystery cycle plays flourish (Europe, c. 1200–1550)

Islamic invasion of India

Beginning of Inquisition in Europe (13th century)

Yüan plays: *The Orphan of Chao, Romance of the Western
Chamber, The Circle of Chalk* (China, 1230–1368)

1250

Robin and Marion, Halle (France, c. 1283)

Aoi No Uye, attributed to Zenchiku
(Japan, c. 14th century)

1300

1350

Sotoba Komachi, Kan'ami (Japan, late 14th century)

Black Death, c. 25 percent of European population
dies (1348–1350)

Wakefield Cycle, *Second Shepherds' Play*
(England, 1375–1550)

York Cycle (England, 1378–1580)

1400

Kadensho and *Hagoromo,* Zeami (Japan, c. 1400)

Morality plays flourish (Europe, 1400–1550)

The Castle of Perseverance (England, c. 1425)

1450

Constantinople falls, much classical material "rediscovered" (1453)

Pierre Pathelin (France, c. 1470)

Gutenberg's printing press (1456)

Fulgens and Lucrece, Medwall (England, 1497)

1500

Columbus lands in North America (1492)

Mary Magdalene (France, c. 1500)

Everyman (England, c. 1500)

Valenciennes cycle flourishes (France, 16th century)

1510

Michelangelo paints Sistine Chapel (1508)

Martin Luther launches Protestant
Reformation (Germany) (1517)

Mandragola, Machiavelli (Italy, c. 1520)

1520

The World and the Child (England, 1522)

1530

Johan, Johan, Heywood (England, 1533)

1540

Serlio popularizes standardized, Italianate scenery (Italy, 1545)

Catholic Counter Reformation—Council of Trent (1545–1564)

1550

France bans cycle plays (France, 1548)
Hôtel de Bourgogne opens (France, 1548)
Commedia dell'arte flourishes (Italy, 1550–1650)

Queen Elizabeth ascends British throne (1558)

1560

First professional public theatre appears (England, 1567)

1570

Castelvetro outlines all major neoclassical principles (Italy, 1570)
Queen Elizabeth bans cycle plays (England, 1570)
First professional public theatre (*corral*) appears (Spain, 1579)

1580

Cysat's plan of the Lucerne Passion Play (Switzerland, 1583)

1585

The Spanish Tragedy, Kyd (England, c. 1587)
The Rose Theatre opens (England, c. 1587)
Professional actresses licensed in Spain (Spain, c. 1587)
Doctor Faustus and *Tamburlaine,* Marlowe (England, 1588)

The Spanish Armada defeated by England (1588)

1590

The Faithful Shepherd, Guarini (Italy, 1590)
Edward II, Marlowe (England, 1592)
The Comedy of Errors, Shakespeare (England, 1592)
Richard III, Shakespeare (England, c. 1593)
Opera developed (Italy, 1594)
Romeo and Juliet, Shakespeare (England, 1594)
A Midsummer Night's Dream, Shakespeare (England, c. 1595)

1595

1600

Much Ado about Nothing, Shakespeare (England, c. 1598)
The Globe Theatre opens (England, 1599)
Henry V, Shakespeare (England, 1599)
Hamlet, Shakespeare (England, c. 1600)

James I ascends the British throne (1603)

1605

Twelfth Night, Shakespeare (England, c. 1601)
Okuni's dances develop into Kabuki (Japan, 1603)
Othello, Shakespeare (England, c. 1604)
King Lear, Shakespeare (England, 1605)
First complete flat perspective setting, Aleotti (Italy, 1606)
Volpone, Jonson (England, 1606)
The Revenger's Tragedy, Tourneur (England, 1606)
Macbeth, Shakespeare (England, 1606)
Professional actresses onstage (France, 1607)

1610

The Tempest, Shakespeare (England, c. 1611)
The Duchess of Malfi, Webster (England, c. 1612–1613)

Fuente Ovejuna, Lope de Vega (Spain, c. 1614)

1615

Teatro Farnese (permanent proscenium theatre)
  (Italy, 1618)
The King the Greatest Alcalde, Lope de Vega
  (Spain, c. 1620)
Life Is a Dream, Calderón de la Barca
  (Spain, late 1620s)
Women banned from Kabuki (Japan, 1629)

1620 — Pilgrims found Plymouth Colony (1620)

'Tis Pity She's a Whore, Ford (England, c. 1630)

1630

The Constant Prince, Calderón de la Barca (Spain, 1635)
The Cid, Corneille (France, c. 1636)

Chariot and pole system (Torelli) (Italy, 1640s)
Palais Cardinal (later Royal) opens, Richelieu
  (France, 1641)
Theatres closed by civil war and Puritan decree (England,
  1642)

1640

1650

Theatres are restored, first women on English
  professional stage (England, 1660)
The Misanthrope, Molière (France, 1666)
The Miser, Molière (France, 1668)
Tartuffe, Molière (France, 1669)
The Hypochondriac, Molière (France, 1673)
Death of Molière and amalgamation of French
  companies (France, 1673)
The Country Wife, Wycherley (England, 1675)
The Rover, Behn (England, 1677)
Phèdre, Racine (France, 1677)
Formation of Comédie Française (France, 1680)

1660 — The Taj Mahal (1653)

— Restoration of English Crown (1660)

1670

1680

1690 — William and Mary crowned (Glorious Revolution)
  (1688)

— America: Salem witch trials (1692)

Women banned from the stage (China, 18th century)
The Way of the World, Congreve (England, 1700)
Kathakali begins (India, c. 1700)
Love Suicides at Sonezaki, Chikamatsu (Japan, 1703)
Turcaret, LeSage (France, 1709)

1700

1710

The Wonder: A Woman Keeps a Secret, Centlivre (England,
  1714)

1720

Caroline Neuber, first important woman theatre manager
  (Germany, 1727)
The Beggar's Opera, Gay (England, 1728)

1730

The London Merchant, Lillo (England, 1731)

Licensing Act (England, 1737)

1740

The Servant of Two Masters, first version, Goldoni (Italy, 1743)

Garrick becomes actor-manager of Drury Lane (England, 1747)

1750

The Comic Theatre, Goldoni (Italy, 1750)

Kumagai's Camp (Kabuki) (Japan, 1751)

Hallam company opens in Williamsburg (America, 1752)

Mistress of the Inn, Goldoni (Italy, 1753)

First revolving stage in the world (Kabuki) (Japan, 1758)

"Drame" introduced by Diderot (France, 1758)

1760

Drottningholm and Krumlov Castle Court Theatres open (Sweden and Czechoslovakia, c. 1766)

Southwark Theatre opens (first professional building), Philadelphia (America, 1766)

Gotthold Lessing, the first dramaturg (Germany, 1767)

British Stamp Act enrages Americans (1765)

1770

She Stoops to Conquer, Goldsmith (England, 1773)

The Tutor, Lenz (Germany, 1774)

The Rivals, Sheridan (England, 1775)

The Childmurderess, Wagner (Germany, 1776)

America: Revolutionary War begins (1775)

American Declaration of Independence (1776)

1780

The Marriage of Figaro, Beaumarchais (France, 1784)

American Revolution ends (1783)

The Contrast, Tyler (United States, 1787)

Iphigenia in Tauris, Goethe (Germany, 1787)

United States Constitution (1787)

France: French Revolution begins (1789)

1790

Puss in Boots, Tieck (Germany, 1797)

Napoleonic Wars (1798)

1800

Maria Stuart, Schiller (Germany, 1800)

Schlegel's romantic theory (Germany, 1801–1811)

Chinese music drama (Beijing Opera) (China, early 1800s)

Aqua drama (water tanks onstage) (England, 1804)

Pentheselia, Kleist (Germany, c. 1808)

Faust, part 1, Goethe (Germany, c. 1808)

1810

Prince Friedrich of Homburg, Kleist (Germany, c. 1811)

War of 1812

Gaslight onstage, Chestnut Street Theatre, Philadelphia
(United States, 1816)

The Scarlet Princess of Edo (Kabuki) (Japan, 1817)

The Vampire, Planché (England, 1820)

African Company in New York (United States, 1821)

Antiquarian productions (Planché) (England, 1823–1824)

1815

1820

1825

Metamora, Stone (United States, 1829)

Hernani, Hugo (France, 1830)

Madame Vestris uses box sets (England, 1832)

No Trifling with Love, Musset (France, 1834)

1830

1835

Masakado (The Demon Princess) (Kabuki) (Japan, 1836)

Woyzeck, Büchner (Germany, 1837)

Limelight introduced (England, 1837)

Queen Victoria ascends the British throne (1837)
Daguerre photography (1838)

1840

Tieck revives *A Midsummer Night's Dream* on an
"Elizabethan" stage (Germany, 1843)

Early minstrel shows (whites in blackface makeup)
(United States, 1843)

The Drunkard, Smith (United States, 1844)

Fashion, Mowatt (United States, 1845)

Astor Place Riot (United States, 1849)

California Gold Rush (1849)

1845

1850

The Lady of the Camelias, Dumas *fils* (France, 1852)

Uncle Tom's Cabin, Aiken (United States, 1852)

The Poor of New York, Boucicault (United States, 1857)

1855

Darwin's *On the Origin of Species* (1859)

Edwin Booth's *Hamlet* runs for 100 consecutive
performances (United States, 1864)

Lincoln assassinated by actor John Wilkes Booth
during performance of *Our American Cousin*
(United States, 1865)

Under the Gaslight, Daly (United States, 1867)

Peer Gynt, Ibsen (Norway, 1867)

1860

United States Civil War begins (1861)

1865

United States Civil War ends (1865)

1870

Saxe-Meiningen's company tours (Germany, 1874)

H.M.S. Pinafore, Gilbert and Sullivan (England, 1878)

A Doll House, Ibsen (Norway, 1879)

The Pirates of Penzance, Gilbert and Sullivan (England, 1879)

Electric stage lighting introduced (England, 1881)

Ghosts, Ibsen (Norway, 1881)

Theory of naturalism introduced by Zola (France, 1881)

1875

1880

329

1885

Théâtre Libre (Antoine) (France, 1887) ————
Miss Julie, Strindberg (Sweden, 1888) ————
Margaret Fleming, Herne (United States, 1890) ———— **1890** ———— Moving pictures (1890)
Hedda Gabler, Ibsen (Norway, 1891) ————
The Weavers, Hauptmann (Germany, 1892) ————

The Importance of Being Earnest, Wilde (England, 1895) ———— **1895**
Ubu Roi, Jarry (France, 1896) ————
Secret Service, Gillette (United States, 1896) ————
Moscow Art Theatre (Stanislavsky) (Russia, 1898) ————
Uncle Vanya, Chekhov (Russia, 1899) ———— **1900** ———— Sigmund Freud's *Interpretation of Dreams* (1900)
Appia's theory and designs developed (Switzerland, 1899) ————
La Ronde, Schnitzler (Austria, 1900) ————
Three Sisters, Chekhov (Russia, 1901) ————
Mrs. Warren's Profession, Shaw (England, 1902) ———— **1902**
The Lower Depths, Gorky (Russia, 1902) ————

———— Wright Brothers' flight (1903)

The Cherry Orchard, Chekhov (Russia, 1904) ———— **1904**
Riders to the Sea, Synge (Ireland, 1904) ————
The Art of the Theatre, Craig (England, 1905) ————
Man and Superman, Shaw (England, 1905) ————

1906

A Dream Play, Strindberg (Sweden, 1907) ————

The Blue Bird, Maeterlinck (Belgium, 1908) ———— **1908**
The Ghost Sonata, Strindberg (Sweden, 1908) ————

Sumurun directed by Reinhardt (Germany, 1910) ———— **1910**

Women restored to stage (China, 1912) ———— **1912**
Copeau creates open stage (Vieux Colombier) (France, 1913) ————

Pygmalion, Shaw (England, 1914) ———— **1914** ———— World War I begins (1914)
Granville-Barker's *A Midsummer Night's Dream* ————
   (England, 1914)
Founding of Provincetown Players (United States, 1915) ————
Trifles, Glaspell (United States, 1916) ———— **1916**
Yeats adapts Noh (Ireland, 1917) ————
Surrealism, Apollinaire (France, 1917) ————

1918 ———— World War I Armistice (1918)
Jessner's *Richard III* (Germany, 1919) ————
Aria Da Capo, Millay (United States, 1919) ————

The Emperor Jones, O'Neill (United States, 1920) ———— **1920** ———— Broadcast radio (1920)
Gas II, Kaiser (Germany, 1920) ————
Wedding on the Eiffel Tower, Cocteau (France, 1921) ————
Six Characters in Search of an Author, Pirandello (Italy, 1921) ————
R. U. R., Čapek (Czechoslovakia, 1921) ————

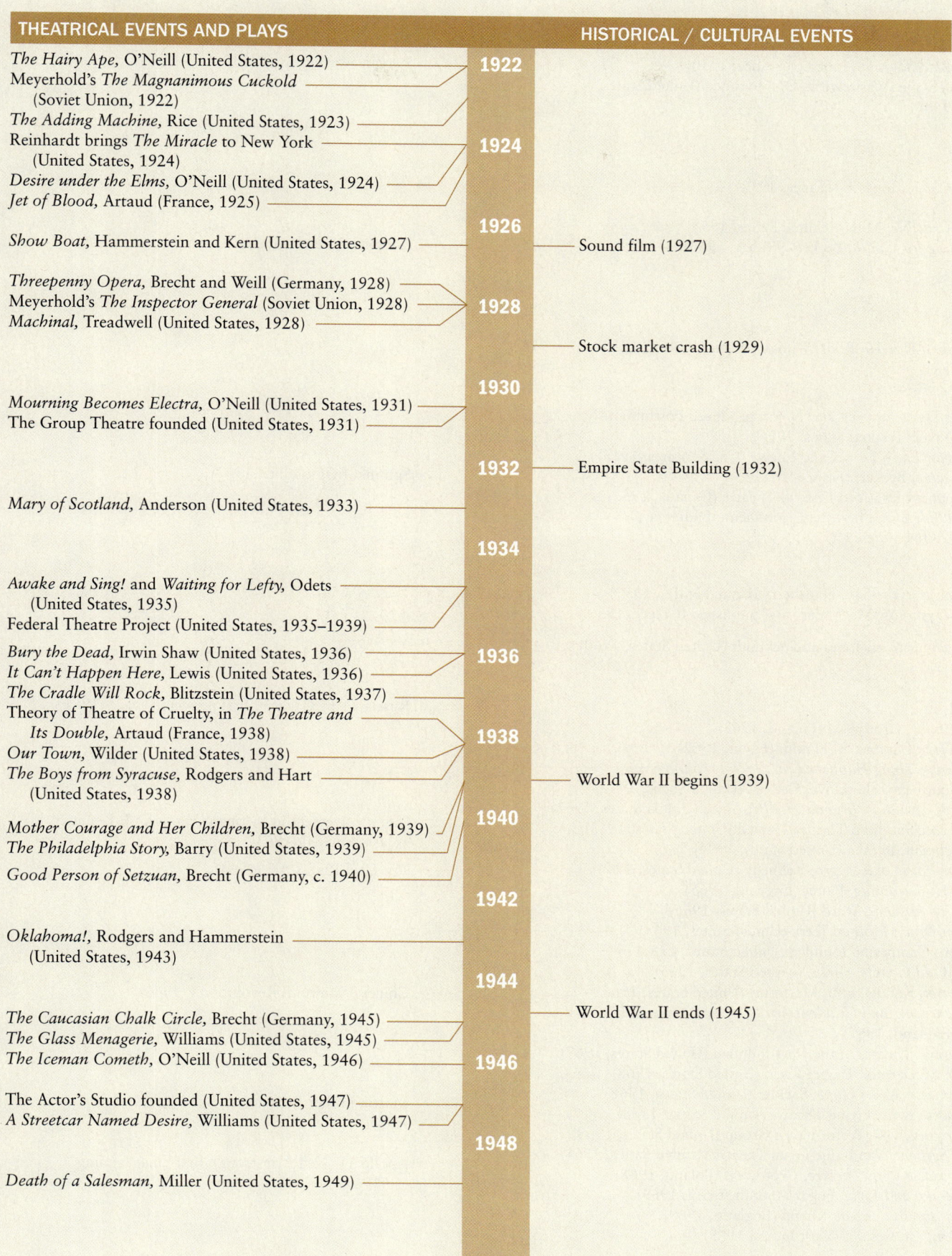

THEATRICAL EVENTS AND PLAYS		HISTORICAL / CULTURAL EVENTS

The Hairy Ape, O'Neill (United States, 1922)
Meyerhold's *The Magnanimous Cuckold*
  (Soviet Union, 1922)
The Adding Machine, Rice (United States, 1923)
Reinhardt brings *The Miracle* to New York
  (United States, 1924)
Desire under the Elms, O'Neill (United States, 1924)
Jet of Blood, Artaud (France, 1925)

1922

1924

1926

Show Boat, Hammerstein and Kern (United States, 1927) —— Sound film (1927)

Threepenny Opera, Brecht and Weill (Germany, 1928)
Meyerhold's *The Inspector General* (Soviet Union, 1928)
Machinal, Treadwell (United States, 1928)

1928

—— Stock market crash (1929)

1930

Mourning Becomes Electra, O'Neill (United States, 1931)
The Group Theatre founded (United States, 1931)

1932 —— Empire State Building (1932)

Mary of Scotland, Anderson (United States, 1933)

1934

Awake and Sing! and *Waiting for Lefty,* Odets
  (United States, 1935)
Federal Theatre Project (United States, 1935–1939)

Bury the Dead, Irwin Shaw (United States, 1936)
It Can't Happen Here, Lewis (United States, 1936)
The Cradle Will Rock, Blitzstein (United States, 1937)
Theory of Theatre of Cruelty, in *The Theatre and
  Its Double,* Artaud (France, 1938)
Our Town, Wilder (United States, 1938)
The Boys from Syracuse, Rodgers and Hart
  (United States, 1938)

1936

1938

—— World War II begins (1939)

Mother Courage and Her Children, Brecht (Germany, 1939)
The Philadelphia Story, Barry (United States, 1939)
Good Person of Setzuan, Brecht (Germany, c. 1940)

1940

1942

Oklahoma!, Rodgers and Hammerstein
  (United States, 1943)

1944

The Caucasian Chalk Circle, Brecht (Germany, 1945)
The Glass Menagerie, Williams (United States, 1945)
The Iceman Cometh, O'Neill (United States, 1946)

—— World War II ends (1945)

1946

The Actor's Studio founded (United States, 1947)
A Streetcar Named Desire, Williams (United States, 1947)

1948

Death of a Salesman, Miller (United States, 1949)

The Bald Soprano, Ionesco (France, 1950) ————
Arena Stage (Washington, DC) founded (United States, 1950)

1950

Korean War begins (1950)

The Chairs, Ionesco (France, 1952) ————

1952

The Crucible, Miller (United States, 1953) ————
Waiting for Godot, Beckett (France, 1953) ————

Korean War ends (1953)

1954

Cat on a Hot Tin Roof, Williams (United States, 1955) ————

Long Day's Journey into Night, produced posthumously, ————
    O'Neill (United States, 1956)
My Fair Lady, Lerner and Loewe (United States, 1956)
Endgame, Beckett (France, 1957) ————
Permanent Stratford Festival Theatre (Canada, 1957)
West Side Story, Bernstein, Sondheim, Laurents
    (United States, 1957)

1956

Sputnik, first satellite (1957)

1958

A Raisin in the Sun, Hansberry (United States, 1959)————
The Dyskolos (Menander) first published (Greece, 1959) ————

The Fantasticks, Jones and Schmidt (United States, 1960) ————

1960

Russian Yuri Gagarin, first person in space (1961)

Akropolis, Grotowski (Poland, 1962) ————
The Tree Climber, Al-Hakim (Egypt, 1962) ————
A Funny Thing Happened on the Way to the Forum,
    Sondheim, Shevelove, Gelbart (United States, 1962)
Who's Afraid of Virginia Woolf?, Albee (United States, 1962)
The Free Southern Theatre formed (United States, 1963) ————
Dutchman, Baraka (United States, 1964) ————
Funnyhouse of a Negro, Kennedy (United States, 1964) ————
The Homecoming, Pinter (England, 1965) ————
Day of Absence, Ward (United States, 1965) ————
Calm Down Mother, Terry (United States, 1965) ————
Teatro Campesino founded (United States, 1965) ————
The Odd Couple, Simon (United States, 1965) ————
Cabaret, Kander, Ebb, Masteroff (United States, 1966) ————
Rosencrantz and Guildenstern Are Dead, Stoppard
    (England, 1967)
National Theatre of the Deaf founded (United States, 1967)
Hair, McDermot, Ragni, Rado (United States, 1968) ————
The Great White Hope, Sackler (United States, 1968) ————
Paradise Now, Living Theatre (United States, 1968) ————
Dionysus in 69, Performance Group (United States, 1968)
The Serpent, Van Itallie/Open Theatre (United States, 1968)
Towards a Poor Theatre, Grotowski (Poland, 1968)
Boesman and Lena, Fugard (South Africa, 1969)
What the Butler Saw, Orton (England, 1969)
A Tempest, Césaire (West Indies, 1969)

1962

U.S. involvement in Vietnam War. John F. Kennedy
    assassinated (1963)

1964

The Civil Rights Act (1964)

1966

Chinese "Cultural Revolution" (1966)

1968

Martin Luther King assassinated (1968)

Apollo 11 (Neil Armstrong), first lunar landing
    (1969)

THEATRICAL EVENTS AND PLAYS		HISTORICAL / CULTURAL EVENTS
Brook's *A Midsummer Night's Dream* (England, 1970)	**1970**	World Trade Center completed (1970)
Madmen and Specialists, Soyinka (Nigeria, 1971)		
Sticks and Bones, Rabe (United States, 1971)		
A Little Night Music, Sondheim (United States, 1973)	**1973**	Vietnam War ends; Watergate (1973)
The Bacchae of Euripides, Soyinka (Nigeria, 1973)		
Equus, Shaffer (England, 1973)		
A Chorus Line, Bennett, Kirkwood, Dante, Hamlisch, Kleban (United States, 1975)	**1975**	
Death and the King's Horseman, Soyinka (Nigeria, 1976)	**1976**	
for colored girls who have considered suicide when the rainbow is enuf, Shange (United States, 1976)		
Einstein on the Beach, Wilson (France, 1976)		
Miss Margarida's Way, Athayde (Brazil, 1977)	**1977**	
Fefu and Her Friends, Fornes (United States, 1977)		
American Buffalo, Mamet (United States, 1977)		
Buried Child, Shepard (United States, 1978)	**1978**	
Betrayal, Pinter (England, 1978)		
Hamletmachine, Müller (Germany, 1978)		
Cloud 9, Churchill (England, 1979)		
Crimes of the Heart, Henley (United States, 1979)	**1979**	Iran hostage crisis (1979–1981)
True West, Shepard (United States, 1980)	**1980**	
Children of a Lesser God, Medoff (United States, 1980)		
Cats, Eliot, Webber (1981)	**1981**	AIDS pandemic identified (1981)
Master Harold . . . and the Boys, Fugard (South Africa, 1982)	**1982**	
Top Girls, Churchill (England, 1982)		
Glengarry Glen Ross, Mamet (United States, 1983)		
L.S.D. (. . . Just the High Points . . .), Wooster Group (United States, 1983)		
'night, Mother, Norman (United States, 1983)		
Tracers, Difusco and cast (United States, 1983)		
The CIVIL warS, Wilson (United States, 1983)		
Ma Rainey's Black Bottom, Wilson (United States, 1984)	**1984**	
Sunday in the Park with George, Sondheim, Lapine (United States, 1984)		
Largo Desolato, Havel (Czechoslovakia, 1985)	**1985**	
Les Misérables, Boublil, Schönberg (France, 1985)		
Fences, Wilson (United States, 1985)		
The Conduct of Life, Fornes (United States, 1985)		
The Normal Heart, Kramer (United States, 1985)	**1986**	*Challenger* space shuttle disaster (1986)
The Colored Museum, Wolfe (United States, 1986)		
Phantom of the Opera, Webber (England, 1986)		
Into the Woods, Sondheim, Lapine (United States, 1987)		
The Piano Lesson, Wilson (United States, 1987)		
M. Butterfly, Hwang (United States, 1988)	**1988**	
We Keep Our Victims Ready, Finley (United States, 1989)		Collapse of Soviet Union (1989–1991)

THEATRICAL EVENTS AND PLAYS		HISTORICAL / CULTURAL EVENTS

Assassins, Sondheim, Weidman (United States, 1990)
Mad Forest, Churchill (England, 1990)
Monster in a Box, Gray (United States, 1991)
Belle Reprieve, Shaw, Margolin, Weaver (United States, 1991)
Angels in America, Kushner (United States, 1991–1993)

1990 — Gulf War (1990–1991)

Fires in the Mirror, Smith (United States, 1992)
Marisol, Rivera (United States, 1992)

1992 — Bosnian War (1992–1995)

Arcadia, Stoppard (England, 1993)

The America Play, (Parks, 1994)

1994 — Nelson Mandela elected; apartheid officially ends (South Africa, 1994)

Blasted, Kane (England, 1995)

Rent, Larson (United States, 1996)
Venus, Parks (United States, 1996)

1996

The Lion King, John, Rice, Allers, Mecchi (United States, 1997)

Copenhagen, Frayn (England, 1998)
The Vagina Monologues, V-Day Movement, Ensler (United States, 1998)

1998

The Laramie Project, Kaufman (United States, 2000)
House Arrest, Smith (United States, 2000)
Aida, John, Rice, Woolverton, Falls, Hwang (United States, 2000)
Big Love, Mee (United States, 2000)

2000

Homebody/Kabul, Kushner (United States, 2001)
Topdog/Underdog, Parks (United States, 2001)
Mamma Mia! Andersson, Ulvaeus (England, 1999/United States, 2001)

September 11 attack on World Trade Center and Pentagon (2001)
U.S. invasion of Afghanistan (October 11, 2001)

The Lieutenant of Inishmore, McDonagh (Ireland, 2001)
The Producers, Brooks, Meehan (United States, 2001)
Urinetown, Kotis, Hoffman (United States, 2001)
The Shape of Things, LaBute (England, 2001)
The Coast of Utopia, Stoppard (England, 2002)
Avenue Q, Lopez, Marx, Whitty (United States, 2003)
Wicked, Schwartz, Holzman (United States, 2003)
The Notebooks of Leonardo da Vinci, Zimmerman (United States, 2003)
Democracy, Frayn (England, 2003)
The Pillowman, McDonagh (England, 2003)
Anna in the Tropics, Cruz (United States, 2003)

2002

U.S. invasion of Iraq (2003)

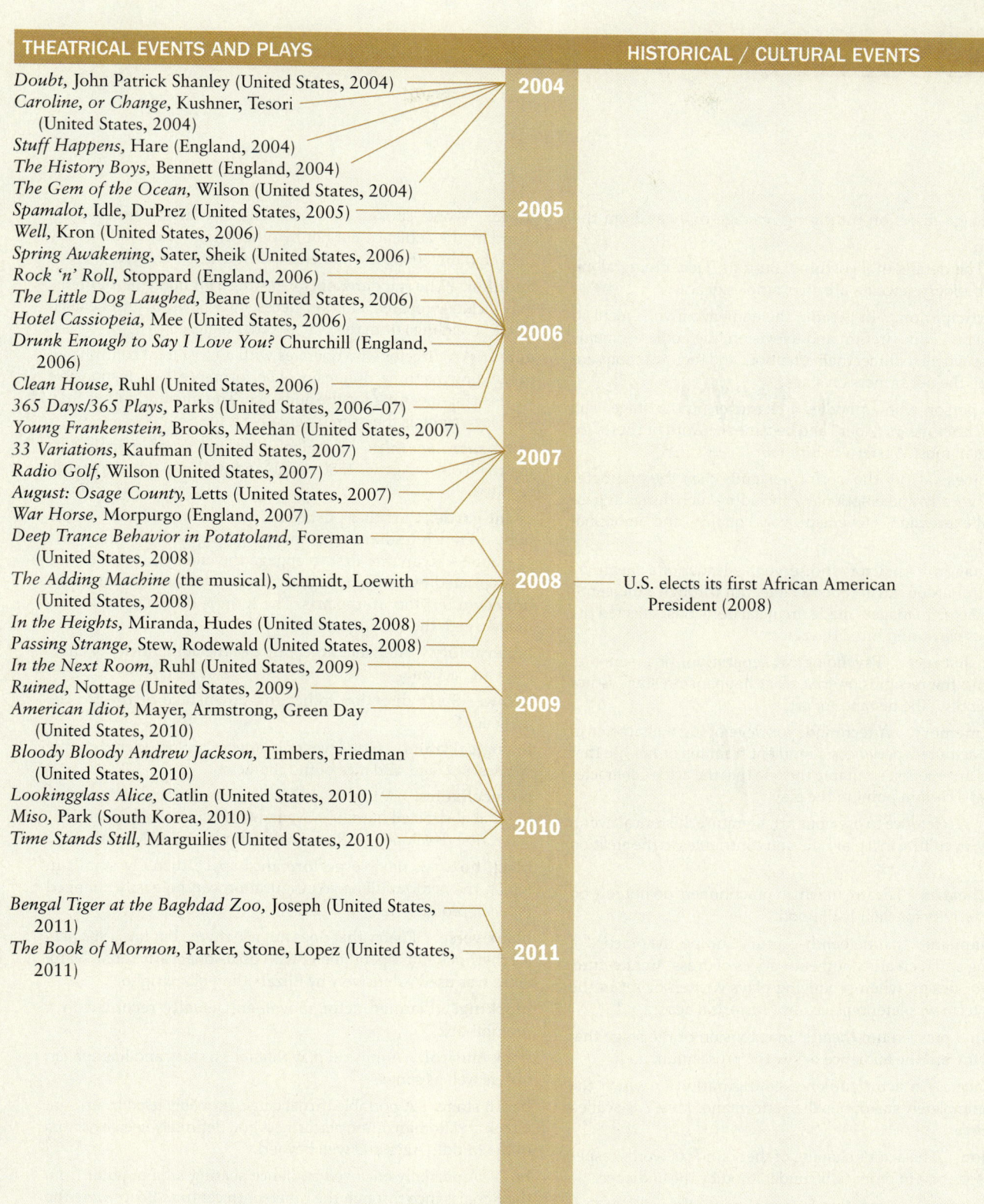

Doubt, John Patrick Shanley (United States, 2004)

Caroline, or Change, Kushner, Tesori
(United States, 2004)

Stuff Happens, Hare (England, 2004)

The History Boys, Bennett (England, 2004)

The Gem of the Ocean, Wilson (United States, 2004)

Spamalot, Idle, DuPrez (United States, 2005)

Well, Kron (United States, 2006)

Spring Awakening, Sater, Sheik (United States, 2006)

Rock 'n' Roll, Stoppard (England, 2006)

The Little Dog Laughed, Beane (United States, 2006)

Hotel Cassiopeia, Mee (United States, 2006)

Drunk Enough to Say I Love You? Churchill (England,
2006)

Clean House, Ruhl (United States, 2006)

365 Days/365 Plays, Parks (United States, 2006–07)

Young Frankenstein, Brooks, Meehan (United States, 2007)

33 Variations, Kaufman (United States, 2007)

Radio Golf, Wilson (United States, 2007)

August: Osage County, Letts (United States, 2007)

War Horse, Morpurgo (England, 2007)

Deep Trance Behavior in Potatoland, Foreman
(United States, 2008)

The Adding Machine (the musical), Schmidt, Loewith
(United States, 2008)

In the Heights, Miranda, Hudes (United States, 2008)

Passing Strange, Stew, Rodewald (United States, 2008)

In the Next Room, Ruhl (United States, 2009)

Ruined, Nottage (United States, 2009)

American Idiot, Mayer, Armstrong, Green Day
(United States, 2010)

Bloody Bloody Andrew Jackson, Timbers, Friedman
(United States, 2010)

Lookingglass Alice, Catlin (United States, 2010)

Miso, Park (South Korea, 2010)

Time Stands Still, Marguilies (United States, 2010)

Bengal Tiger at the Baghdad Zoo, Joseph (United States,
2011)

The Book of Mormon, Parker, Stone, Lopez (United States,
2011)

2004

2005

2006

2007

2008 — U.S. elects its first African American
President (2008)

2009

2010

2011

GLOSSARY

above. Stage direction indicating upstage or away from the audience.

accent. The details of a costume. Buttons, lace, piping along edges, embroidery, jewelry, are all examples of accent.

active participation. In theatre, the audience involvement in the live event. Unlike in film and television, the audience members choose where to direct their attention, and their reactions are shared with the performers on stage.

actor. A person who embodies a character on the stage. The Latin word *actor* meant "doer" and became the word of choice for performers in most Western traditions.

actor choices. How the performer embodies the character physically, vocally, and emotionally, including such things as gesture, facial expression, movement, vocal quality, and emotional expression.

actor-manager. An actor who served as leader of a theatrical company in Europe during the seventeenth through nineteenth centuries. Actor-managers made financial decisions, selected the repertory of plays, and hired the actors.

aesthetic distance. Psychological separation, or a sense of detachment; the recognition that what happens on stage is not reality; literally, "the distance of art."

affective memory. A technique for developing a character in which the actor reexperiences a moment from his or her life that stimulated an emotion similar to the one that the actor's character is feeling at a certain point in the play.

allusion. A reference to previous art, literature, historical event, geography, or culture in a play; allusion contributes to the creation of thought.

amateur theatre. Theatre in which practitioners do not rely on theatrical activity for their livelihood.

antiquarianism. In nineteenth-century Europe, the practice of researching and recreating authentic styles of dress, architecture, and interior design when producing plays written or set in the past. This term was later replaced by "historical accuracy."

apron. In a proscenium theatre an extension of the stage that continues toward the audience below the proscenium arch.

arena space. An actor/audience configuration in which the audience completely surrounds the performance area. Also called *arena theatre.*

articulation. The actor's shaping of the sounds of words (especially consonants) in order to be understood by the audience.

artistic director. In most professional nonprofit resident theatres (those that produce a season of plays) the staff member with primary responsibility for the artistic life of the theatre. The artistic director typically hires the season's directors and designers.

artistic intent. The purpose of a production, such as to entertain, to shock, to persuade, to comfort. In establishing the intent of the artists, an audience member can more effectively evaluate how well the production achieved its goals.

aside. Words spoken by a character that are intended to be heard by the audience but not by other characters. Traditionally delivered directly to the audience. Most asides are brief.

audition. The standard tool for casting a production. Auditions may include prepared audition pieces, interviews, or unrehearsed ("cold") readings from the play or other material.

auteur. A director who operates with almost total control and, in building the three-dimensional performance, feels responsible for creating meaning for the audience. The director, rather than the playwright, is the primary creative force.

autos sacramentales. Religious plays performed in Spain during the Golden Age (c. 1580–1680) and well into the eighteenth century.

avant-garde. Art that pushes recognized boundaries. Originally a French military term meaning *vanguard* (the front line of troops who are the first to engage the enemy), the term was appropriated by artists to signify those who venture into new, unknown territory in the arts. The term is often used synonymously with the term *experiment.*

believability. Audience acceptance of the authenticity of character and action.

below. Stage direction indicating downstage or toward the audience.

biological traits. First level of characterization, including the species, sex, age, and race of the character.

biomechanics. A highly energetic, mimetic approach to acting that abstracted human movement and created a very athletic actor, first developed by Russian director Vsevolod Meyerhold.

black box. A flexible performance space (usually small) in which the actor/audience configuration can be easily changed for each production.

blank verse. Poetry that does not use rhyme but has a specific, set rhythm (iambic pentameter with occasional variations). Blank verse was used extensively by Elizabethan playwrights.

blocking. Planned actor movement usually recorded in a promptbook.

book musical. A musical play that tells a story and has spoken text as well as songs.

booth stage. A portable thrust stage, probably used by ancient Greek and Roman mime performers and definitely used by actors in the Middle Ages and well beyond.

box. A partially enclosed audience seating area popular from the Renaissance through the nineteenth century. Boxes were the most expensive form of seating.

box office manager. Theatre staff member responsible for organizing and overseeing ticket sales, including supervising the staff members who deal directly with the public.

box set. Scenery that imitates the interior of a room with walls, sometimes ceiling, furniture, and visual detail, standard in Europe and North America after 1830.

breeches role. From sixteenth- to nineteenth-century Europe, a male character performed by a woman or a female character who disguises herself as a man.

Broadway. Both a particular area of New York (the theatre district bordered by 41st to 54th Streets and Sixth to Ninth Avenues) and the size of the house in New York commercial theatre (some Broadway theatres seat as many as 1,800 patrons). One Broadway theatre, the Vivian Beaumont, is housed at Lincoln Center on 65th Street.

Bunraku. Traditional form of Japanese theatre using large puppets (three-fifths the size of a human). The operators remain visible to the audience.

callbacks. A second or later round of auditions to which specific actors are invited.

casting. The selection of actors to play each character in the show; casting is usually the responsibility of the director.

casting director. A specialist in finding actors for specific roles who assists the director in some professional productions.

catharsis. A term used by the Greek philosopher Aristotle (384–322 B.C.E.) to describe the audience's emotional release at the end of a tragedy; a performance was designed to engage the audience's feelings and build in intensity so that the spectator felt cleansed or purged of strong emotion by the end of the play.

causal plot. Structure of a script organized by a cause-to-effect relationship of events; event A leads to event B, which leads to event C, and so forth. Without A and B there is no C. Most thrillers and comedies on film and television have a linear and causal structure.

cazuela. In the Spanish Golden Age, a segregated area for unmarried or unaccompanied women at the back of the house on the second level facing the stage.

center. In stage directions the space in the middle of the stage. Abbreviated C.

character. A person created to perform the action of the play; one of the six elements of a play identified by Aristotle.

character objective. Goal or intention of a character as defined by the actor; what the actor decides the character is trying to accomplish at any given moment of the play. Actors play character objectives that are important or logical to the character's action, needs, desires, and state of mind.

Chinese music drama. A form of classical Chinese theatre that is highly stylized with movement, dance, chant, and music. In the early 1800s Chinese artists combined forms of theatre that had developed in many different regions to create what is now known as *Chinese music drama,* also called *Beijing Opera.*

choreographer. Artist who stages dancing or stylized movement. A choreographer must work closely with the production's director; sometimes one person serves as both director and choreographer.

chorus. A group of performers working together vocally and physically. A chorus of approximately twelve to fifteen singer-dancers who interacted with and responded to the actors was an important element of ancient Greek theatre.

chronicle. A dramatic adaptation of historical events dealing with kings and frequent struggles for the crown, especially popular in Elizabethan England. Also called a *history play.*

cliff-hanger. A play with a causal plot that does not have falling action; the play stops at the climax and the outcome of the conflict is not shown.

climax. The emotional highpoint of the action in a causal plot; the conflict has reached a critical stage, and the outcome is finally decided.

collective hero. A group of characters serving together as the protagonist of a play.

color. An important design element in the theatre. Different colors tend to create different responses in human beings; designers think not only about the effect that a particular color will have on the audience, but also about the message that it sends about the world of the play. In lighting, color is created by filtering the light with color media or color filters.

combination company. Full productions (all actors, scenery, costumes, etc.) that toured throughout Europe and North America. The term was used in the nineteenth century, but the concept is applicable for touring companies today that transport all elements of production with them as they perform throughout the country or world.

comedia. A secular (not religious) play during the Golden Age in Spain.

comedy. A dramatic genre emphasizing humor, typically taking an objective (rather than emotional) approach to life.

comedy of character. A subgenre of comedy in which the action is driven by the eccentricities of its major figure.

comedy of idea. A subgenre of comedy organized around thought.

comedy of manners. A subgenre of comedy that explores the behavior of a particular segment of society; characters frequently find that their own desires are at odds with social expectations.

comic relief. Action that is created to ease emotional tension or contrast with a major event at strategic points within a tragedy, melodrama, or other genre that is not principally comic.

commedia dell'arte. Improvisational comedy that originated in Italy sometime before 1568. *Commedia* actors played conventional characters (some of which were masked) and planned the scenario and comic business ahead of time but developed specific dialogue and action as the show progressed in front of an audience.

commercial theatre. Shows that are produced to earn a profit for investors.

community theatre. Amateur theatre in which shows are created by residents of a particular area who come together without being part of a professional or academic institution.

company manager. See **managing director.**

composer. An artist who creates original music for a theatrical production.

concept. Artistic decisions meant to communicate a specific interpretation of a play to the audience. Concept is created visually and aurally with scenery, costume, lighting, tempo, line readings, movement, and composition. Development or the coordination of development of concept is a responsibility of the director.

conceptual director. Typically, a director who creates a production without an existing text or who chooses a text that then becomes a pretext for the director's conception. Such creative work is often dominated by dynamic visual images, music, dance, and carefully choreographed movement.

conflict. The central element of causal plot, two forces working against each other: Two or more characters (generally) want the same thing (money, power, a kingdom, love) or want different things to happen (escape or justice, revolution or consolidation of power).

constructivist set. A scenic unit that consists of exposed beams, supports, and sometimes movable parts.

context of performance. The place of performance that suggests audience expectations for a particular production; an audience member has a different set of expectations when attending a Broadway show with a high ticket price than a community theatre production, for example.

convention.　An agreement between the production personnel and the audience. A widely used convention in the twenty-first century is the dimming of the house lights, which tells the audience that the performance is about to begin.

corral.　A type of theatre that was popular during the Golden Age in Spain and featured a raised, roofed stage backed by a façade with doors and a discovery space, a second balcony level, three levels of galleries and boxes for the audience, and a pit (*patio*) for standees open to the sky.

costume designer.　The artist who creates costumes for actors to help define and express character.

costume plot.　A chart that records items of clothing worn by each actor in each scene of a play.

costume shop manager.　Staff member who coordinates the efforts of cutters, stitchers, and other personnel in building costumes.

critical research paper.　A paper examining how a play or production works that includes the ideas of other critics or historians as well as those of the writer.

criticism.　Analysis, interpretation, or evaluation of a play or production.

cross.　Actor movement of any length across the stage. Abbreviated as X.

crossfade.　Two or more simultaneous changes in lighting made possible by the creation of dimmers and lighting consoles in the twentieth century.

cue.　(1) A signal for a timed change in a technical element (light, set, or sound). (2) A signal for an actor to speak or move.

cue-to-cue.　A technical rehearsal in which only the parts of the play including cues are run; most dialogue or action in between is skipped. The stage manager organizes and runs the cue-to-cue.

cycle.　A series of religious plays (often called *mystery plays*) popular throughout Europe during the Middle Ages. Cycles (or cycle plays) were based on biblical stories ranging from the creation of the world to the last judgment and were performed outdoors in the vernacular (local language).

deconstruction.　A radically reinterpreted famous play in which the original play may still be recognized. The new production, however, uses the written play as only a pretext and frequently comments on or negates the apparent intent of the original play. Also called *deconstructed production.*

decorum.　The neoclassical concept of universality in morality and characterization, which led to characters drawn by playwrights according to current notions of what was most appropriate for behavior, values, and language in terms of characters' age, sex, social class, occupation, and economic condition.

deus ex machine.　"God from the machine." Originally a use of the Greek *mechane* or crane. Over time it came to stand for any contrived conclusion for a play.

dialogue.　Words spoken by the characters in a play.

director.　The person in charge of the artistic aspects of theatrical production. It is the director's job to guide the transformation of the play to live production. The director interprets the play and heads the artistic team, providing a focus and organization for the creative work.

discovery.　Something important is found, learned, or realized during the action of a play; an element of causal plot.

distribution.　An element of lighting design determined by where lighting instruments are placed as well as the types of instruments used. Angle is an important part of distribution since it affects the mood and appearance of the actors as well as suggesting time of day.

dithyramb.　In ancient Greece, a choric presentation sung and danced in homage to the god Dionysus.

downstage.　The stage area closest to the audience; on the raked stage of Renaissance theatres, the stage literally sloped downward as it got closer to the audience. Abbreviated D.

dramaturg.　A specialist in dramatic literature and theatre history who serves as a consultant for production. For a revival, the dramaturg conducts research on the play, author, or historical period. When collaborating on an original play (a script produced for the first time), a dramaturg reads the script, attends readings, attends rehearsals, and offers suggestions to the playwright and director. Such a specialist who coordinates a season of plays is often referred to as a *literary manager.*

dress rehearsal.　Rehearsal at which the costumes are worn by the actors. Several dress rehearsals usually end the period of rehearsal before the show is performed for an audience.

educational theatre.　Production of plays in schools at primary, secondary, undergraduate, and graduate levels. Production activity may be extracurricular or carefully integrated into classroom structure and pre-professional training.

elements of a play.　Plot, character, thought, language, music, and spectacle, identified by Aristotle in the *Poetics* (fourth century B.C.E.).

ellipsoidal.　Spotlight that creates a hard-edged beam and includes four shutters around the circular lens to further control its focus.

empathy.　Emotional identification. In the theatre empathy refers to a sense of participation—an identification with character. Empathy occurs when you feel along *with* the characters.

ensemble.　Actors who function seamlessly together as a unit rather than as individual performers.

environmental theatre.　A performance in which audience and actors share the same space. There is little or no separation of acting and observing areas, with the result that the audience members are physically part of the performance.

Epic Theatre.　Anti-illusionist theatre featuring emotional detachment, narration, songs, and obvious theatricality that was developed by German playwright, director, and theorist Bertolt Brecht.

episodic.　A structural term describing a play with an early point of attack; selected dramatized moments in the story are separated by breaks in the action. The playwright may indicate a passage of time between scenes through dialogue.

ethical choice.　A choice that a character must face about a moral issue; an ethical choice is often a defining moment for a protagonist, particularly in a tragedy.

ethical traits.　A level of characterization that includes the moral standards held by a character.

executive director.　See **managing director.**

exposition.　Information that is needed to understand the play but is not a part of the dramatized action. Although exposition may be introduced throughout the play, a great deal of information is typically conveyed in the first few scenes.

expressionism. A nonrealistic approach to production in which the subjective experience of the character is depicted on stage. Visual and aural aspects of production often suggest anxiety and the mental breakdown of the central character. German and American expressionism in the 1910s and 1920s dramatized the dehumanization or destruction of humanity at the hands of commercialism, industry, and war.

façade. An architectural background for the action of a play; a generalized standing or hanging structure, often multilevel, that may be neutral or decorated but always resides upstage of the action, creating a background that can suggest nearly any location, inside or out.

falling action. An element of causal plot; the events from the climax to the end of the play in which emotional intensity drops. Typically, loose ends are tied up for the audience and balance is restored, although something clearly is different than at the play's beginning. Falling action is also sometimes called the play's *resolution* or *dénouement.*

farce. A type of situation comedy that emphasizes broad physical action.

Federal Theatre Project. A nationwide effort representing the first time that the U.S. government directly subsidized theatre.

flashback. A scene that dramatizes an event that occurred prior to the play's beginning (point of attack) or at least earlier than the scene that precedes the flashback scene in performance.

flat. A scenic unit typically framed with 1 × 3 lumber and covered with canvas, muslin, plywood, or other material. Flats often represent a solid surface such as a wall but are actually lightweight and easy to move.

found space. A place that is used for production, indoors or out, that was never intended as a theatrical space when created or designed.

fourth wall staging. An approach to staging in which actors move and behave in the set as if it were actually the room represented and do not acknowledge the presence of an audience; the proscenium arch, if present, is often treated as the fourth wall of an enclosed room.

Fresnel. A spotlight that is used to create a soft beam of light that blends with others to create the appearance of an even area of light.

front elevation. Drafting of the set, breaking it into units to be built and showing each piece of scenery from the front.

front-of-house. Theatre operations that deal directly with the audience (such as ticket sales and assistance in finding seats).

gallery. Raised area of audience seating above the orchestra level in proscenium and thrust theatres since the Renaissance. Also called *balcony* or *mezzanine.*

genre. A classification of drama related to the kind of emotional response a play creates in the audience. The four major genres in the Western tradition are tragedy, comedy, tragicomedy, and melodrama.

given circumstances. Anything established by the playwright that distinguishes location, historical period, on-stage properties, time of day, and details about character that is not a matter of interpretation or opinion: where the character is from, for example, or the fact that he or she is highly educated, recently divorced, or terminally ill.

gobo. A lighting projection using a metal cutout like a stencil in front of the light source to block solid areas of light, casting shadows on the stage to suggest leaf patterns, prison bars, and so on.

grand drape. Front curtain in a proscenium theatre sometimes used to hide scene changes or to indicate the beginnings and conclusions of acts or scenes.

ground plan. A drafting of the plan of the set as seen from overhead. A ground plan shows where any scenic pieces or set props (such as furniture) are to be placed.

ground row. Low, flat, painted scenery at stage level. When combined with wing, drop, and border scenery, ground rows extended the line of the wing out toward center stage.

hanamichi. In Japanese Kabuki theatre, a stage-level ramp that passes directly from the stage apron down right center to the back of the house. This narrow path, which places the actor in the midst of the audience, is used for many important entrances and exits. Sometimes a secondary *hanamichi* is used down left as well.

happening. An event, planned or spontaneous, in which the audience watched or participated in the production of temporary art; popular in the 1960s and a precursor of today's performance art.

histrio. A Latin term for actor; the root of our word *histrionic,* by which we usually mean exaggerated human responses.

house. The audience area of any theatrical space.

house manager. The staff member who is responsible for the safety and comfort of the audience members during their time in the theatre. House managers coordinate ushers, make sure the audience areas of the theatre are clean and safe, resolve any seating problems, and deal with any emergencies.

hybrid theatre. Many theatres do not fit neatly into either the professional or the amateur category. The designation "semi-professional" is sometimes used for companies that aspire to professional status but currently are not well established enough to maintain the payroll of a professional theatre.

hyperbole. Use of overstatement as figurative language; for example, "I'm so hungry I could eat a horse."

hypokrites. Greek word for actor; the root of our words *hypocrisy* and *hypocrite.*

iambic pentameter. Set rhythm of verse in which there is a stress on each second syllable and five stresses per line (see also **blank verse**).

improvisation. A type of performance in which dialogue and action are not planned ahead of time and written down but are made up on the spot by the actors.

inamorata/inamorato. Female/male young lover. Stock characters in *commedia dell'arte.* Actors playing the young lovers were not masked and were cast in part for their physical attractiveness.

inciting incident. In a causal plot, an event that destroys the uneasy balance of the play's beginning and sets off the major conflict of forces.

intensity. Brightness of lighting on the stage; intensity is controlled by the number of lumens pumped onto the stage, which depends on the number of lighting instruments used.

interlude. A secular play (nonreligious drama) in the medieval period, sometimes presented between the courses of banquets. Interludes began to be written and performed by the 1200s. Most surviving interludes are farces from France and England.

intermezzi. Spectacular Italian pageants full of symbolism and allegory that were frequently performed at court between other entertainments or during the intervals between acts of a play or opera, popular from the 1400s to the 1600s.

International Phonetic Alphabet (IPA). A system of specific symbols representing individual sounds that helps actors to both analyze their own speech and reproduce a host of dialects and accents.

interpretation. (1) An audience member's intuitive response or subjective experience of physical action or setting; the meaning that the audience member assigns to what he or she has observed. (2) An artist's creation of meaning beyond what is literal or obvious in the text.

Kabuki. The most popular classical Japanese form of theatre, tragic, comic, and melodramatic in genre, featuring magnificent spectacle, colorful costumes, and the performance of female roles by men (see *onnagata*).

Kadensho. Japanese treatise on the theory of performance and composition for Noh theatre written by Zeami (1363–1444), which presents *yugen* as the central image of Noh.

Kathakali. A form of Indian dance-drama that is rooted in Hindu mythology, featuring dance and stylized gesture performed by men in elaborate, colorful costumes and makeup. Kathakali originated in the seventeenth century in Southern India.

Kutiyattum. A religious theatrical form from India based on ancient epics using music, open space, male and female performers, and colorful costumes.

language. The playwright's choice of words in a play; one of the six elements of a play identified by Aristotle. Language written for the stage must be capable of being spoken aloud. It is usually a heightened version of human speech.

levels of characterization. Qualities and traits assigned to a character by the playwright: biological, physical, psychological/emotional, social, and ethical. A minor character might be developed only through the first two levels; a full and complex character will draw on all five.

lighting console. A lighting control board with a memory system.

lighting designer. An artist who designs or affects all visual elements by controlling focus and mood with color, placement, and intensity of light.

lighting plot. A technical drawing created by the lighting designer showing where each instrument is to be hung, along with the type of instrument and color filters to be used.

linear plot. Organization of a play in which the action progresses forward and sequentially in time.

liturgical drama. Plays performed by the clergy in Latin as part of the worship service in Christian monasteries and cathedrals during the Middle Ages.

lyricist. An artist who writes the words (lyrics) for songs.

magnitude. The sense of importance typical of tragedy as identified by Aristotle.

makeup designer. An artist specializing in the design of realistic or stylized makeup for the characters; makeup is typically designed by the costume designer or the actors themselves if there is not a particular makeup designer assigned to a production.

managing director. The staff member filling the job of producer in nonprofit theatres. The managing director works closely with the artistic director to ensure the continuity and mission of the organization. The titles *executive director* and *company manager* are also used for staff members who hold producing duties.

mansion. A symbolic scenic unit indicating place in staging during the Middle Ages.

masking. Black velour draperies or flats hung or placed vertically and horizontally across the stage to cut off audience view of backstage areas.

masque. A poetic, extravagant court entertainment with dancing, often celebrating the monarch or a royal visitor to the English court in the sixteenth and seventeenth centuries.

master electrician. A staff member who works closely with the lighting designer and directs a lighting crew to hang, focus, and filter the lighting instruments and to set up circuitry, the lighting console, and sometimes sound equipment also.

melodrama. A dramatic genre featuring a conflict between good and bad characters, fast-paced action, a spectacular climax, and poetic justice.

metaphor. Figurative language equating two unlike objects to suggest a similarity between them; for example, "She was a rock during that difficult time."

metatheatre. A production or play that self-consciously comments on the play as taking place in a theatre.

mie. In Japanese Kabuki, an actor's showy pose and facial expression suggesting sustained emotion.

mime. (1) In ancient Greece and Rome, a "pass the hat" street performer; a kind of variety entertainment. (2) Today used interchangeably with "pantomime" and "pantomime artist."

mimesis. As defined by Aristotle, the artist's process of imitating character and action.

miracle play. European play from the fifteenth or sixteenth centuries that recounted the real or apocryphal lives of saints. Also called *saint's play.*

model. A three-dimensional miniature version of the set, built to scale (usually one-quarter or one-half inch to the foot).

modernism. The shift in theatre beginning with realism; throughout the twentieth century scholars noted that modern theatre and drama began with Ibsen. Many late-twentieth-century scholars associated modernism with the type of theatre that rebelled against realism and naturalism. In this book we use the term *modernism* to refer to both realistic and much nonrealistic theatre from the late nineteenth century to the present day.

monologue. (1) An extended speech heard by other characters in the play. (2) An extended speech used as an audition piece.

morality play. A play depicting humanity's struggle with good and evil using allegorical characters such as Good Deeds and Death, popular during the Middle Ages in Europe.

movement. See **orchestration.**

music. One of the six elements of drama as defined by Aristotle; music has been very important in the theatre of most cultures, and in many cases it has been vital.

music director. An artist who works with singers and orchestra in learning and performing the music for a play.

mystery play. See **cycle.**

National Endowment for the Arts (NEA). A federally endowed program that supports the fine and performing arts throughout the United States.

naturalism. A style of drama called for in 1880 by Émile Zola in which playwrights were to present a "slice of life" on the stage, following the actual pace of everyday life and avoiding well-made play structure.

Natyasastra. Sometimes translated as "Doctrine of Dramatic Art," a detailed Indian document by Bharata that appears to predate the most important surviving Sanskrit plays and outlines the principles of performance, staging, and dramatic form as practiced in India and applied to Sanskrit plays.

neoclassicism. A systematic approach to playwriting and production based on interpretations of classical Greek and Roman models of plays and theory. Neoclassical principles were developed in Renaissance Italy and popularized in seventeenth-century France.

new stagecraft. A term used for an approach to scenic design featuring simplicity, avoidance of detail, and reduction of a location to its most significant elements. New stagecraft was based on the innovative designs of Adolphe Appia and Gordon Craig with their images of platforms, stairs, and open spaces.

Noh. The first great classical theatre of Japan, developed in the court of the shogun in the feudal samurai system of the late fourteenth century. Noh features music, slow, choreographed movement, use of carefully carved masks, and all male performers.

nonprofit theatre. Productions from which no individual or organization realizes a profit from the investment in production; any money taken in at the box office or earned from other sources is funneled back into the arts organization to support other shows and programs. Nonprofit theatre may be amateur or professional.

nontraditional casting. The practice of casting actors of a race different from that of the character as written. Also called *colorblind casting*.

observation. Audience recognition of what is physically happening on stage: a change in the color of light, for example, or the sudden cross by an actor. The next step for an audience member is interpretation.

Off-Broadway. Commercial theatre in New York City with fewer than 500 seats in Manhattan, not located in the "Broadway District." The term dates from 1955.

Off-off-Broadway. In the 1960s, theatre in New York City that occurred outside the traditional theatre spaces of Broadway and Off-Broadway. Such work was typically experimental in nature and often occurred in alternative spaces—coffeehouses, church basements, warehouses, and private homes. Today, the term *Off-off-Broadway* is used to refer to professional or semiprofessional performances that are not Equity. While the term *Off-off-Broadway* originated in New York, this kind of theatre may exist anywhere. Such theatres in Chicago are known as *off-Loop* and in Los Angeles as *Equity waiver*.

onnagata. An actor who is a female impersonator in Kabuki theatre. The male performer attempts to create as complete and literal a transformation as possible through makeup, costume, movement, and gesture. In speech, however, the actor uses a falsetto voice that ultimately stylizes the presentation.

orchestra. (1) In a modern proscenium theatre the audience seating area at floor level immediately in front of the stage. (2) In ancient Greece a typically circular performance space, literally, "dancing place."

orchestra pit. In a proscenium theatre a sunken area between the apron and the audience that was traditionally used to seat musicians.

orchestration. In lighting design, a change of intensity, color, or distribution of light on the stage. Also called *movement*.

pageant. In the Middle Ages, wagons with scenery used in processional staging.

painter's elevation. A color picture showing the plan for painting each piece of scenery.

pantomime. A modern theatrical form in which a silent actor creates a scenario without words, relying only on physical expressiveness.

parados. In Greek theatre, an open space between the skene and the theatron that served as entrance and exit for the chorus and sometimes actors.

par lamp. A parabolic aluminated reflector; a type of lighting instrument used to create parallel rays.

performance art. Usually one-person or first-person shows that purport to make the artist the subject of the performance.

periaktoi. Prism-shaped, three-sided scenic units that could be painted and revolved, referred to in a late classical account of theatre architecture of Greece and Rome.

physical traits. A level of characterization that includes the character's stature, weight, hair and eye color, and facial hair. In the theatre such traits are filled in automatically by the actor playing the role and by changes made with costume and makeup.

pinakes. Flat, painted scenery, referred to in a late classical account of theatre architecture in Greece and Rome.

platea. In the Middle Ages in Europe, an open playing space in front of a symbolic scenic unit (mansion).

play. A written text indicating the dialogue the characters speak and some of the physical action. Also called a *script*.

play master. A man who coordinated and staged the cycles in Europe during the Middle Ages; a precursor of the modern director. Also called *prompter* and *ordinary*.

playwright. The author, or crafter, of the play.

plot. As defined by Aristotle, the organization of the action of a play. Plot is not a story or list of events, but an organizing principle: Plot is what gives a play its unity. Another term for plot is *structure*.

Poetic Art. A critical document by the Roman Horace (65–8 B.C.E.) that influenced the Italian Renaissance as much as Seneca and perhaps more than Aristotle.

poetic justice. A device typical of the end of melodrama: Good is rewarded; evil is punished.

Poetics. The first important examination of the tragic form, written by the Greek philosopher Aristotle in c. 335–323 B.C.E.

point of attack. In a linear plot, the point in the story at which the playwright chooses to start dramatizing the action. The story of the play may stretch far into the past, but the playwright selects one moment in that story to begin actually showing (rather than telling about) the progress of events.

postmodern. In the theatre, work that is no longer "modern" (in the sense that August Strindberg and Tennessee Williams were modern). The postmodern comments on, satirizes, or reinterprets the modern. The postmodern artist is sometimes identified as artist and critic simultaneously. Some critics see it as an artistic style, hence postmodern*ism*. Others claim that it is a mindset, a point of view that looks back on the previous century of artistic work with cynicism or futility—and sometimes despair. In visual terms it is dominated by simultaneous action and electronic or cybernetic technology, and structurally by repetition and deconstruction of masterpieces of the past.

poststructuralism. Dramatic work created after World War II that breaks down traditional causal structure. It may be impossible to figure out a logical story, since none is presented.

practical. A visible light source on stage that is often enhanced by unseen lighting instruments. For example, when a desk lamp or overhead chandelier on stage is turned on, light usually emanates from the practical, but accompanying instruments may "punch" the effect and help to imitate and perhaps intensify the light thrown by the practical on the stage.

presentational. A style of production that acknowledges theatricality and does not attempt to create the impression of "real life" on the stage. Presentational scenery, costumes, and lighting may suggest, distort, or even abstract reality. Presentational acting may include lines directed to the audience or other recognition of its presence.

preview. A performance of a show for a paying audience at a somewhat reduced ticket price before the official opening to which critics are invited.

processional staging. In the Middle Ages, the practice of moving wagons or pageants through the streets carrying actors and scenery to perform in various locations.

prima donna. The leading female role (performed without a mask) in *commedia dell'arte.*

producer. The person in charge of the financial and business aspects of a production. The producer usually negotiates the rights to a play and hires a director, who is in charge of the artistic aspects of production. In nonprofit theatres the job title is often *managing director.* One person may take on producing responsibilities, or they may be shared by a group.

production. The fully realized performance of a play with actors, sets, costumes, lighting, and props.

production manager. A staff member usually employed by a theatre company with multiple performance spaces who is in charge of scheduling (spaces, rehearsals, and production meetings) and coordinating stage managers for the productions, especially when two or more productions are running and/or rehearsing simultaneously; also called a *production stage manager.*

professional theatre. Productions created by individuals who make a living (or at least attempt to do so) in the theatre. The professional venue may be commercial or nonprofit, and many theatre artists and technicians work in both.

projection. (1) In acting, the process of making the voice loud enough to be heard by the audience in the back of the house yet still sounding conversational. (2) In lighting, an image thrown onto the stage using light.

promptbook. A notebook kept by the director and stage manager of a production containing the text of the play, detailed stage directions, lighting and sound cues, and notes on production practices.

prompter. In the days of rolling repertory, a staff member who sat at the side of the stage or in a special box down center to call out any forgotten lines or stage business to the actors.

propaganda. Material specifically designed to advocate a particular ideology or point of view.

props manager. A staff member who organizes the collection or building of all properties in a show.

proscenium arch. A large open arch that marks the primary division between audience and performance space in a proscenium space. The proscenium arch frames the action of the play for the audience and limits the view of backstage areas.

proscenium space. An actor/audience configuration in which the audience is on only one side of the performance area; all audience members face the same direction. Also called *proscenium theatre.*

prose. Language similar to everyday speech; not verse.

protagonist. The central character of a play.

psychological and emotional traits. A level of characterization developing the character's basic internal makeup. A character's psychological and emotional life provides the motivation for the action of the play.

public theatre. Professional playhouses in England and Spain in the Renaissance. In Elizabethan England, a three-story polygonal building featuring roofed galleries and a central pit (yard) open to the sky. Actors performed on a thrust stage backed by a façade with probably two doors and sometimes a curtained discovery space between them.

raked. Set at an angle. Early proscenium theatres featured a raked stage: The stage was elevated much higher at the back of the stage (upstage) than closer to the audience (downstage). Modern designers sometimes build a raked stage for a particular production as part of the design concept. When the audience area is raked, the seating is elevated toward the back of the house to facilitate seeing over the rows in front.

rasa. Mood; the organizing principle of Indian Sanskrit plays.

realism. A movement of the late nineteenth century championing the depiction of everyday life on the stage and the frank treatment of social problems in the theatre. The plays of Henrik Ibsen of the 1870s were important in establishing a dramatic style for realism. "Realism" continues to be used as a term for representational plays and production style.

rear elevation. A drafting showing each scenic piece from the back. Rear elevations are particularly important in constructing the scenery, since a rear view may show how each piece of scenery is to be built.

regional theatre. See **resident theatre.**

rehearsal. The period of work in which the show is made ready for the stage. A four- to five-week rehearsal period (six days a week, seven hours a day) is typical for professional productions. Educational and community theatres tend to take four to six weeks (five or six days a week, three to four hours a night).

rendering. A picture created by a designer to communicate with other production personnel. In costume design, a picture of each costume on an actor, ideally done in color often with appropriate swatches of fabric attached; in scenic design, a picture of the set, drawn in perspective from the audience point of view. The rendering shows what the stage will look like from the house. It is usually done in color and depicts the appearance of the set under lights.

representational. A style of production that attempts to represent reality on the stage. Representational scenery, costumes, lighting, and sound imitate precisely the kind of environment and details in which the action of the play would occur in real life. A representational acting style does not acknowledge the presence of the audience and uses techniques that result in a subtle, authentic style of performance.

resident theatre. A professional, nonprofit organization that maintains a constant presence in a community and produces an entire season of plays; sometimes called *regional theatre.*

reversal. In a causal plot, a line of action veers around suddenly to its opposite. The prime suspect in a murder investigation turns up dead, for example, and the detective must look for another solution to the crime.

review. A published account of a production giving information regarding where, what, when, and how to get tickets. An effective review gives the consumer enough information about the show to make an intelligent decision given personal tastes and priorities.

revival. Any production of a play that occurs after the original production.

revolve. A circular portion of the stage floor that can rotate, first developed for the Bunraku and Kabuki theatre in Japan in 1758 and adopted in the West in the late nineteenth century.

rhetorical acting. A style of acting that was popular prior to the coming of realism in the late nineteenth century. Actors often attempted to make very direct contact with the audience rather than interact directly with other actors (at least as the norm). A big voice and grand gestures were intended to capture the attention and admiration of a fully lit and social audience.

rhetorical delivery. In ancient accounts and well into the nineteenth century, the art of oratory and of any public verbal communication, including physical interpretation through gesture, posture, movement, and facial expression.

rising action. In a causal plot, small units of action following the inciting incident that build in emotional intensity to the climax of the play.

rolling repertory. A system of daily changes of plays. Maintaining many plays in the company's production season—any play can be performed at any time.

romantic comedy. A subgenre of comedy that follows the attempts of lovers to get together. It shares this basic structure with many situation comedies, but romantic comedies more often produce a feeling of well-being and sympathy at the end, rather than strong laughs.

romanticism. A movement of the late eighteenth and early nineteenth centuries that rejected nearly every aspect of neoclassicism, celebrated the natural world, and valued intense emotion and individuality.

royalties. Payments to the playwright made by the producing organization each time a play is produced.

run crew. Workers who maintain and execute cues for props, costumes, set, lighting, and sound during the run of a show.

run-through. A rehearsal in which an entire act or play is performed without stopping except at intermission breaks.

Sanskrit play. A play from ancient Hindu culture organized by mood, or *rasa*. Sanskrit drama suggested directions that later Asian theatre would take.

scene shop foreman. A staff member who oversees construction of the set by a crew of carpenters, scenic painters, and other craftspeople.

scenic designer. An artist who creates a visual home for the play on stage. Many people may help build scenery, but the designer envisions and controls the visual effect. Also called *set designer*.

scrim. A translucent piece of fabric. When lit from the front, the scrim appears opaque (solid). When the scrim lighting is extinguished and an object behind it is lit, the scrim seems to disappear, and the object becomes visible.

script. See **play.**

section. A drafting showing the vertical elements of the set and permanent theatrical elements and their relative positions (for example, the heights at which scenery, lighting, and masking are to be hung).

sense memory. The actor's recall of sights, sounds, touch, and smells from specific past events.

sensory imagery. The use of concrete language appealing to the five senses to bring the physical world of the play alive for the audience and help convey the character's experience of environment.

set properties. Large actor-usable additions to the setting, such as furniture.

sharing system. Financial organization of a theatre company that splits any profits after the day's expenses based on how many shares each had invested in the venture or had been granted by the manager depending on his or her duties and importance to the company.

sight lines. The set designer's determination of what the audience can and cannot see.

silhouette. The outer shape of a costume. Silhouette is particularly indicative of time period and culture. Also called *line*.

simile. Figurative language comparing two unlike things using *like* or *as*; for example, "Her cheeks were as red as roses."

site-specific performance. A production developed for and closely linked to a particular location.

situation comedy (or sitcom). A subgenre of comedy based on the humorous qualities of the situation in which the characters find themselves.

skene. In ancient Greece, a stage house upstage of the circular orchestra (our source for the words *scene* and *scenery*).

slapstick. Broad comic action; the term originated with *commedia dell'arte* actors and their use of a long, flat paddle with a flap that literally made a loud slapping sound when used for comic beatings.

social traits. A level of characterization that may include a character's job or profession, socioeconomic status, and/or religious or political affiliation.

soliloquy. A solo extensive speech that is intended for the audience but not other characters in the play. Often it is meant to convey the private thoughts of a character.

sound designer. An artist who creates acoustic and recorded sound for a production.

space and design choices. Choices made by the director and designers to create a specific effect for the audience.

spectacle. The visual elements called for in a play and added in production, including scenery, costumes, props, lighting, actor physicality, and movement; one of the six elements of a play identified by Aristotle.

spotlight. A type of lighting instrument that is used frequently in the theatre. Glass lenses create a focused and controllable beam of light and various shaped metal and glass reflectors affect the quality of light and shape of the beam.

stage directions. Written descriptions of physical or emotional action or physical appearance.

stage left. The actors' left as they face the audience. Abbreviated SL or L.

stage manager. A staff member who ensures that things run smoothly on and backstage. Stage managers coordinate a show during rehearsal and performance and keep the director's artistic choices intact during its run.

stage right. The actors' right as they face the audience. Abbreviated SR or R.

staging. Combining all elements of production to bring the text alive in three dimensions. Staging is ultimately the responsibility of the director.

structure. See **plot.**

Sturm und Drang **("storm and stress").** A preromantic movement that deliberately broke all the rules of neoclassicism. The *Sturm und Drang* playwrights shocked their audiences with plays full of violence and forbidden topics such as teen pregnancy, rape, self-mutilation, and infanticide.

style. The manner of expression and methods of onstage behavior as they affect composition and performance. Style is dictated by language—poetry, prose, and dialects. Style is identified by character movement and social manners and by changes and fashions in architecture, clothes, furniture, and decoration (on both low and high economic scales).

subplot. A secondary line of action in a causal plot. Conflict different from that of the major line of action is developed. Subplots may be entwined with the major line of action and reach a climax in the same scene, or they may develop independently and reach a climax at another time.

subtext. The actual meaning of dialogue behind the words spoken.

surrealism. Originating in France beginning in 1917, an avant-garde movement in which the dream world and the real world are intertwined and difficult or impossible to distinguish.

symbolism. Beginning in the 1890s in France, this avant-garde movement was the first major challenge to realism. Its plays were dominated by obvious symbolism and were often played in simple spaces with antirealistic scenery and acting styles. The legacy of symbolism is very much alive in theatre for children, Disney films, and many romantic musicals.

taste. The personal inclination and preferences of the beholder of an aesthetic experience.

technical director. A staff member who is responsible for the safety of the theatre space, for scheduling, for construction and equipment installation, and for making sure designs are executed according to designers' specifications.

technical rehearsal. A rehearsal in which light, sound, and set changes are added to a show. The term is also used for the specific rehearsal in which the stage manager, actors, and run crews practice putting all elements (except costumes) together in a complete run of the show. Also called a *tech run.*

technitae. An actor during the Hellenistic period; the term is probably related to the professional status of Greek actors in the fourth century and beyond.

texture. An element of costume; the feel of the fabric (fine, smooth, soft, rough).

theatre critic. A writer who specializes in evaluating production and sharing that viewpoint with the public.

Theatre of the Absurd. Post–World War II plays centered on characters who are strangers to each other, trapped in a violent, meaningless world seemingly without design or purpose.

Theatre of Cruelty. An approach to theatre developed by Antonin Artaud between the world wars emphasizing a breakdown of causality and stressing emotion over intellect. Artaud hoped to work on emotions by assaulting the senses of the audience.

theatron. The audience seating area (literally "seeing place") in the theatre of ancient Greece. At first temporary seating on a hillside, seats were set in stone permanently by the fourth century B.C.E.

thought. The ideas in a play; one of the six elements of a play identified by Aristotle.

three unities. Neoclassical guidelines for writing plays. These were unity of time (the action of the play should take place in twenty-four hours or less), unity of place (action should occur in one location), and unity of action (no subplots unless fully integrated with the central conflict).

thrust space. An actor/audience configuration in which the audience is on three sides of the performance area. Also called *thrust theatre.*

tragedy. A dramatic genre of plays that is serious and ends unhappily. Aristotle identified magnitude (importance) as a chief attribute of tragedy and noted that it evoked the emotions of pity and fear in the audience.

tragicomedy. A dramatic genre in which tragic and comic tendencies seem equally mixed.

trap. An opening in the stage floor for ascents and descents.

trilogy. Three related plays; ancient Greek playwrights submitted three tragedies—sometimes a trilogy—for the contest in honor of Dionysus in Athens.

trope. An exchange of dialogue in musical form in which the singers or chanters represented characters from the Bible, presented as early as c. 925 in the European Christian monasteries and cathedrals. The first recorded type of liturgical drama.

upstage. The area farthest from the audience. Abbreviated U.

unit set. A single scenic unit that is used to represent many different locations.

verisimilitude. A neoclassical concept that established that theatrical events as written and staged should be reality-based (events that could really occur in life).

verse. Poetry; heightened language that may have a rhyme scheme or just a specific rhythm. For many centuries stage dialogue was written in verse.

vomitory. An entrance to elevated seating for the audience that runs underneath the audience and comes up to empty out into the seating area.

well-made play. A category of drama in which a meticulous and involved plot takes precedence over all other elements. As perfected by French playwright Eugène Scribe (1791–1861), the well-made play featured an intricate pattern of causality, carefully controlled suspense, and misunderstandings and reversals, leading to an emotionally satisfying climax followed by rapidly falling action.

wheel of fortune. The notion that fortunes change if we wait long enough. In medieval and Renaissance art and literature, it is a literal wheel that carries a person to the top of good fortune before dropping him or her to bad fortune.

wing, drop, and border scenery. Flat pieces of scenery painted to look three-dimensional including flat painted panels on either side of the stage (wings), a large expanse of painted fabric up-stage (drop or shutters), and strips of cloth or panels hung horizontally across the tops of the wings (borders). This type of scenery was typical in Europe and beyond from the Renaissance to the late nineteenth century.

wings. (1) In a proscenium theatre, spaces offstage left and right for actors, crew, and scenery not yet in the visible performance space. (2) Changeable flats that could be pulled quickly on and offstage in grooves on the floor and at the top of the tall wings (in wing, drop, and border scenery).

zanni. Masked servant clowns such as Arlecchino and Brighella in *commedia dell'arte.*

NOTES

CHAPTER 1

1. Reprinted from Tracy C. Davis, "Questions for a Feminist Methodology in Theatre History," in *Interpreting the Theatrical Past*, edited by Thomas Postlewait and Bruce A. McConachie, published by the University of Iowa Press, 1989. Reprinted by permission.
2. "About the Healing Power of the Arts," February 13, 2011, www.artslynx.org/heal.
3. National Association for Drama Therapy, February 13, 2011, www.nadt.org.
4. The Broadway League website, February 13, 2011, www.broadwayleague.com.
5. League of Resident Theatres website, February 13, 2011, www.lort.org.
6. Professional Association for Canadian Theatres website, February 13, www.pact.ca.
7. Theatre Communications Group website, February 13, 2011, www.tcg.org.
8. Educational Theatre Association website, February 13, 2011, schooltheatre.org.
9. Association for Theatre in Higher Education website, February 13, 2011, www.athe.org.
10. University/Resident Theatre Association website, February 13, 2011, www.urta.com.
11. American Association of Community Theatre website, February 13, 2011, www.aact.org.
12. Steppenwolf Theatre Company website, February 13, 2011, www.steppenwolf.org.

CHAPTER 2

1. Peter Brook, *The Empty Space* (New York: Simon & Schuster, 1968), 9.
2. William Hooker Gillette, *Secret Service* (New York: Samuel French, 1898).

CHAPTER 3

1. For detailed analysis of audience reception and perception theory, various approaches to theatre as a system of communication, and case studies of the nature of performance and audience, see the Swedish historian and theorist Willmar Sauter, *The Theatrical Event: Dynamics of Performance and Perception* (Iowa City: University of Iowa Press, 2000).
2. William Hooker Gillette, "The Illusion of the First Time in Acting," *Papers on Acting* (Printed for the Dramatic Museum of Columbia University, New York, 1915).

CHAPTER 4

1. The term *crisis* is another term that is often used in discussions of dramatic structure. This contested term is used to suggest several different devices. Some use *crisis* to suggest a period of time after the conflict is defined leading up to the climax (which we call rising action). Some use *crisis* to mean the same thing as *climax* but also an identification of a series of secondary climaxes leading up to the big one. Some use *crisis* instead of *climax*, reserving the latter term to heightened audience response in causal drama. Some dramatic analysts prefer to avoid the term altogether.
2. Susan Glaspell, *Trifles* (New York: Washington Square Players, 1916).

CHAPTER 5

1. Shakespeare, *The Winter's Tale*, III, iii.57.

CHAPTER 6

1. Arthur Hopkins, *How's Your Second Act?* (New York: Philip Goodman, 1918), 26.
2. Charles L. Mee, "the (re)making project," May 24, 2011, charlesmee.org.
3. Meredith Kasten, "Interview with Mary Zimmerman," Second Stage Theatre website, July 23, 2002, www.2st.com.
4. George C. Wolfe. Public interview with Jonathan Michaelsen. The 2005 Ralph L. Collins Memorial Lecture Series, Indiana University, Bloomington, IN, March 29, 2005.

CHAPTER 7

1. See, for example Jason Robards in "Talk with the Players," *Newsweek* (Dec. 15, 1958), 63.
2. See Joseph Roach, *The Player's Passion: Studies in the Science of Acting* (Ann Arbor: University of Michigan Press, 1985).
3. Nineteenth-century review, quoted in Richard Moody, *Dramas from the American Theatre, 1762–1909* (Boston: Houghton Mifflin, 1966), p. 201.
4. Martin Sheen. Public Interview with Jonathan Michaelsen. The 2010 Ralph L. Collins Memorial Lecture Series, Indiana University, Bloomington, IN, April 19, 2010.
5. Steven D. Paola, Actors Equity. "The 2009–2010 Theatrical Season Report: An Analysis of Employment, Earnings, Membership and Finance." June 2, 2011. www.actorsequity.org.

CHAPTER 8

1. David Henry Hwang, quoted in Joel Hirschhorn, "Hearing a Different Drum Song: David Henry Hwang," *The Dramatist* (March/April 2002), 9.
2. "The Making of *Urinetown*," moderated by Gregory Bossler, *The Dramatist* (May/June 2002), 13.
3. Harvey Schmidt, "*The Fantasticks*," moderated by Richard Maltby, Jr., *The Dramatist* (May/June 2002), 27.
4. David Savran, *In Their Own Words* (New York: Theatre Communications Group, 1988), 157.
5. Alisa Solomon, "*Rent* Destabilized," *The Village Voice* (Aug. 12, 1997), p. 83.

CHAPTER 9

1. "Five Questions for Kevin Adams, Lighting Designer," Live Design BSMC, 2007. June 3, 2008, http://livedesignonline.com/mag/five_questions_kevin.

CHAPTER 10

1. Patrick Healy, "Broadway Banks on West End Pedigree," August 23, 2009, www.nytimes.com.
2. The Broadway League: The official website of the Broadway theatre industry, June 6, 2011, www.livebroadway.com.
3. The Broadway League, June 6, 2011, www.livebroadway.com.
4. Internet Broadway Database, June 6, 2011, www.ibdb.com.
5. Cleveland Play House website, June 6, 2011, www.clevelandplayhouse.com.
6. Jesse McKinley, "Picking Up a Broadway Tab," February 27, 2005, nytimes.com.
7. Ronald Wainscott, *Staging O'Neill* (New Haven, CT: Yale University Press, 1988), 98.
8. Zachary Pincus-Roth, "Ask Playbill.com: Broadway or Off-Broadway Part I," February 8, 2008, playbill.com; Patrick Healy, "*Spiderman* Frozen, and Actors Are Relieved," June 8, 2011, nytimes.com; Bill Marsh and Patrick Healy, "One Musical Succeeds. One Struggles. Discuss." June 19, 2011, nytimes.com.
9. Zachary Pincus-Roth "Ask Playbill.com: Broadway or Off-Broadway Part I," February 8, 2008, playbill.com.
10. Theatre Communications Group website, June 10, 2011. www.tcg.org.
11. Joal Ryan, "Cats: Broadway's Longest-Lived Show," E!online. June 19, 1997, www.eonline.com.
12. Les Misérables website, www.lesmis.com, October 2, 2002.
13. Patrick Healy, "Inside the Financial Wreckage of 'Lucky Guy'," June 6, 2011, www.nytimes.com.
14. Jesse McKinley, "Picking Up a Broadway Tab," February 27, 2005, nytimes.com.
15. National Endowment for the Arts, June 10, 2011, www.nea.gov.
16. Theatre Development Fund website, June 12, 2011, www.tdf.org.
17. Theatre Communications Group website, June 12, 2011, www.tcg.org.
18. The Broadway League, June 12, 2011. www.livebroadway.com.
19. The New 42nd Street website, June 11, 2011, www.new42.org.

CHAPTER 11

1. Pearl S. Buck, "China Faces the Future" Lecture, New York, October 13, 1942.
2. In medieval literature and practice, terms such as *mystery, miracle,* and *interlude* are often used interchangeably. Also, the terms often mean different kinds of plays depending on the country in which they occur. We have made choices here to avoid the overlaps and confusion.

BIBLIOGRAPHY

Adler, Stella. *The Art of Acting.* New York: Applause, 2000.

Allain, Paul *The Art of Stillness: The Theater and Practice of Tadashi Suzuki:* New York: Macmillan, 2003.

Appleton, William W. *Madame Vestris and the London Stage.* New York: Columbia University Press, 1974.

Arnott, Peter. *Greek Scenic Conventions in the Fifth Century B.C.* New York: Greenwood Press, 1978.

Aronson, Arnold. *American Set Design.* New York: Theatre Communications Group, 1985.

Astin, Elaine, and Elin Diamond. *The Cambridge Companion to Caryl Churchill.* Cambridge, UK: Cambridge University Press, 2010.

Ball, David. *Backwards and Forwards: A Technical Manual for Reading Plays.* Carbondale: Southern Illinois University Press, 1983.

Banham, Martin, Errol Hill, and George Woodyard, eds. *The Cambridge Guide to African and Caribbean Theatre.* Cambridge, UK: Cambridge University Press, 1994.

Beacham, Richard C. *The Roman Theatre and Its Audience.* Cambridge, MA: Harvard University Press, 1992.

Beadle, Richard, ed., *The Cambridge Companion to English Medieval Theatre.* Cambridge, UK: Cambridge University Press, 1994.

Beare, W. *The Roman Stage.* London: Methuen, 1964.

Beijer, Agne. *Court Theatres of Drottningholm and Gripsholm.* New York: B. Blom, 1972.

Benedetti, Robert. *The Actor at Work,* 10th ed. Boston: Allyn and Bacon, 2009.

Bentley, Gerald E. *The Professions of Dramatist and Player in Shakespeare's Time, 1590–1642.* Princeton, NJ: Princeton University Press, 1984.

Boal, Augusto. *Theater of the Oppressed.* London: Pluto, 1998.

Brockett, Oscar G., and Franklin J. Hildy. *History of the Theatre,* 10th ed. Boston: Allyn and Bacon, 2007.

Brockett, Oscar, and Robert Findlay. *Century of Innovation,* 2nd ed. Boston: Allyn and Bacon, 1991.

Brockett, Oscar G., Margaret Mitchell, and Linda Hardberger. *Making the Scene: A History of Stage Design and Technology in Europe and the United States.* San Antonio, TX: Tobin Theatre Arts Fund, 2010.

Brook, Peter. *The Empty Space.* New York: Atheneum, 1996.

Brook, Peter. *The Open Door: Thoughts on Acting and Theatre.* New York: Theatre Communications Group, 1995.

Brook, Peter. *The Shifting Point: Theatre, Film, Opera, 1946–1987.* New York: Theatre Communications Group, 1994.

Brown, Jared. *The Fabulous Lunts: A Biography of Alfred Lunt and Lynn Fontanne.* Bloomington, IN: Author House, 2005.

Canning, Charlotte, and Thomas Postlewait, eds. *Representing the Past: Essays in Performance Historiography.* Iowa City: University of Iowa Press, 2010.

Carlson, Marvin A. *Theatre Is More Beautiful Than War: German Stage Directing in the Late Twentieth Century.* Iowa City: University of Iowa Press, 2009.

Chemers, Michael Mark. *Ghost Light: An Introductory Handbook for Dramaturgy.* Carbondale, IL: Southern Illinois University Press, 2010.

Chinoy, Helen Krich, and Linda Walsh Jenkins. *Women in American Theatre,* 3rd ed. New York: Theatre Communications Group, 2006.

Cibber, Colley. *An Apology for the Life of Colley Cibber.* 1740. Reprint, Mineola, NY: Dover, 2000.

Clurman, Harold. *On Directing.* New York: Collier, 1997.

Cohen, Robert. *Acting Professionally: Raw Facts about Careers in Acting,* 7th ed. New York: Palgrave Macmillan, 2009.

Cole, Toby, et al., eds. *Actors on Acting: The Theories, Techniques, and Practices of the World's Great Actors, Told in Their Own Words,* 4th ed. New York: Random House, 1995.

Cole, Toby, ed. *Playwrights on Playwriting.* New York: Cooper Square Publishers, 2001.

Cole, Toby, and Helen Krich Chinoy, eds. *Directors on Directing: A Source Book of the Modern Theatre.* Indianapolis: Bobbs-Merrill, 1979.

Colin, Philip C., ed. *Suzan-Lori Parks: Essays on the Plays and Other Works.* Jefferson, NC: McFarland, 2010.

Conte, David M, and Stephen Langley. *Theatre Management: Producing and Managing the Performing Arts.* Hollywood, CA: Quite Specific Media Group, Ltd., 2007.

Cremona, Vicky Ann, et al. *Theatrical Events. Borders, Dynamics, Frames.* Amsterdam: Rodopi, 2004.

Crump, James. *Chinese Theatre in the Days of Kublai Khan.* Tucson: University of Arizona Press, 1980.

Curry, Jane Kathleen. *Nineteenth-Century American Women Theatre Managers.* Westport, CT: Greenwood Press, 1994.

Curtin, Kaier. *"We Can Always Call Them Bulgarians": The Emergence of Lesbians and Gay Men on the American Stage.* Boston: Alyson, 1987.

Davis, Tracy C. *Actresses as Working Women: Their Social Identity in Victorian Culture.* New York: Routledge, 1991.

Davis, Tracy C., and Thomas Postlewait. *Theatricality.* Cambridge, UK: Cambridge University Press, 2003.

Deutsch, Helen, and Stella Hanau. *The Provincetown Players: A Story of the Theatre.* New York: Farrar & Rinehart, 1931.

Duckworth, George, and R. L. Hunter. *The Nature of Roman Comedy,* 2nd ed. Norman, OK: University of Oklahoma Press, 1994.

Dunlap, William. *History of the American Theatre.* 1823. Introduction. Tice L. Miller. Urbana: University of Illinois Press, 2005.

Eccles, Christine. *The Rose Theatre.* New York: Routledge, 1990.

Ernst, Earle. *The Kabuki Theatre.* Honolulu: University of Hawaii Press, 1974.

Faber, Donald C. *Producing Theatre: A Comprehensive Legal and Business Guide,* 3rd ed. New York: Limelight, 2006.

Ferris, Lesley. *Crossing the Stage: Controversies of Cross-Dressing.* New York: Routledge, 1993.

Flanagan, Hallie. *Arena: The Story of the Federal Theatre.* 1940. Reprint ed. New York: Limelight, 1985.

Forsyth, James. *Tyrone Guthrie: A Biography.* London: Hamilton, 1976.

Fuegi, John. *Bertolt Brecht: Chaos According to Plan.* Cambridge, UK: Cambridge University Press, 1987.

Fuerst, Walter Rene, and Samuel J. Hume. *Twentieth-Century Stage Decoration.* New York: Dover, 1967.

Geis, Deborah R. *Suzan-Lori Parks.* Ann Arbor, MI: University of Michigan Press, 2008.

Gerould, Daniel, ed. *Theatre/Theory/Theatre: The Major Critical Texts from Aristotle and Zeami to Soyinka and Havel.* New York: Malden, MA: Wiley-Blackwell, 2007.

Giannachi, Gabriella, and Mary Luckhurst, eds. *On Directing: Interviews with Directors.* New York: St. Martin's Griffin, 1999.

Gillette, J. Michael. *Theatrical Design and Production,* 6th ed. New York: McGraw-Hill 2007.

Glaspell, Susan. *The Road to the Temple: A Biography of George Cram Cook.* 1927. Ed. and introduced by Linda Ben-Zvi. Jefferson, NC: McFarland, 2005.

Green, Stanley. *Broadway Musicals, Show by Show,* 6th ed. New York: Applause, 2010.

Grimstead, David. *Melodrama Unveiled.* Chicago: University of Chicago Press, 1968.

Guinness, Alec. *Blessings in Disguise.* Pleasantville, NY: Akadine Press, 2001.

Gurr, Andrew. *The Shakespearean Stage, 1574–1642,* 3rd ed. Cambridge, UK: Cambridge University Press, 1992.

Guthrie, Tyrone. *Renown at Stratford: A Record of the Shakespeare Festival in Canada.* Toronto: Clark, Irwin, 1971.

Hagen, Uta. *Respect for Acting.* New York: Macmillan, 1973.

Halleran, Michael. *Stagecraft in Euripides.* New York: Rowan and Littlefield, 1985.

Harrop, John, and Sabin R. Epstein. *Acting with Style,* 3rd ed. Boston: Allyn and Bacon, 1999.

Hayman, Ronald. *How to Read a Play,* 2nd ed. New York: Grove Press, 1999.

Henderson, Mary C. *The New Amsterdam: The Biography of a Broadway Theatre.* New York: Hyperion, 1997.

Hewitt, Barnard. *The Renaissance Stage: Documents of Serlio, Sabbattini and Furttenbach.* Coral Gables, FL: University of Miami Press, 1958.

Hidemark, Ove, Per Edström, Bengt Schyberg, et al. *The Drottningholm Court Theatre: Its Advent, Fate and Preservation.* Stockholm, Sweden: Byggforlaget, 1993.

Hill, Errol, and James Hatch. *A History of African American Theatre.* Cambridge, UK: Cambridge University Press, 2003.

Hirsch, Foster. *Harold Prince and the American Musical Theatre,* expanded edition. New York: Applause, 2005.

Hodge, Francis, and Michael McLain. *Play Directing: Analysis, Communication and Style,* 7th ed. Boston: Allyn and Bacon, 2009.

Hopkins, Arthur. *Reference Point.* New York: Samuel French, 1948.

Houchin, John. *Censorship of American Theatre in the Twentieth Century.* Cambridge, UK: Cambridge University, Press, 2003.

Howarth, William D. *French Theatre in the Neo-Classical Era, 1550–1789.* Cambridge, UK: Cambridge University Press, 1997.

Hume, Robert D. *The London Theatre World, 1660–1800.* Carbondale: Southern Illinois University Press, 1980.

Ilson, Carol. *Harold Prince: A Director's Journey.* New York: Limelight Editions, 2000.

Jones, David Richard. *Great Directors at Work: Stanislavsky, Brecht, Kazan, Brook.* Berkeley: University of California Press, 1986.

Jones, James Earl, and Penelope Niven. *Voices and Silences.* New York: Limelight, 2004.

Jones, Robert Edmond. *The Dramatic Imagination.* New York: Theatre Arts, 1941; New York: Routledge, 2004.

Kamimura, Iwao. *Kabuki Today.* Tokyo: Kodansha, 2001.

Kaye, Deena, and James LeBrecht. *Sound and Music for the Theatre,* 3rd ed. New York: Focal Press, 2009.

Kennedy, Dennis. *The Spectator and the Spectacle: Audiences in Modernity and Postmodernity.* Cambridge, UK: Cambridge University Press, 2009.

Kenton, Edna. *The Provincetown Players and the Playwrights' Theatre, 1915–1922.* Jefferson, NC: McFarland, 2004.

Keyssar, Helen. *Feminist Theatre: An Introduction to Plays of Contemporary British and American Women.* New York: Grove/Atlantic, 1985.

Kirby, E. T., ed. *Total Theatre.* New York: E. P. Dutton, 1969.

Krasner, David. *A Beautiful Pageant.* New York: Palgrave Macmillan, 2002.

Krasner, David. *Theatre in Theory 1900–2000.* Malden, MA: Wiley-Blackwell, 2007.

Kustow, Michael. *Peter Brook: A Biography.* London: St. Martin's Press, 2005.

Lamb, Andrew. *150 Years of Popular Musical Theatre.* New Haven, CT: Yale University Press, 2000.

Leacroft, Richard, and Helen Leacroft. *Theatre and Playhouse.* London: Methuen, 1984.

Magee, Byron. *Wagner and Philosophy.* New York: Penguin, 2001.

McKendrick, Melveena. *Theatre in Spain, 1490–1700.* Cambridge, UK: Cambridge University Press, 1989.

McKinney, Joslin, and Philip Butterworth. *The Cambridge Introduction to Scenography.* Cambridge, UK: Cambridge University Press, 2009.

McNamara, Brooks. *The American Playhouse in the Eighteenth Century.* Cambridge, MA: Harvard University Press, 1969.

Miller, Arthur. *Salesman in Beijing.* New York: Viking, 1983.

Moody, Richard. *The Astor Place Riot.* Bloomington: Indiana University Press, 1958.

Mulryne, J. R., and Margaret Shewring. *Theatre of the English and Italian Renaissance.* New York: St. Martin's, 1991.

Murphy, Brenda. *Congressional Theatre: Dramatizing McCarthyism on Stage, Film, and Television.* Cambridge, UK: Cambridge University Press, 1999.

Murphy, Brenda. *Tennessee Williams and Elia Kazan: A Collaboration in the Theatre.* Cambridge, UK: Cambridge University Press, 1992.

Nagler, A. M. *A Source Book in Theatrical History.* New York: Dover, 1952.

O'Connor, John, and Lorraine Brown. *Free, Adult and Uncensored: The Living History of the Federal Theatre Project.* Washington, DC: New Republic, 1978.

Orgel, Stephen. *The Illusion of Power: Political Theater in the English Renaissance.* Berkeley: University of California, 1975.

Orgel, Stephen. *Impersonations: The Performance of Gender in Shakespeare's England.* Cambridge, UK: Cambridge University Press, 1996.

Ortolani, Benito. *The Japanese Theatre: From Shamanistic Ritual to Contemporary Pluralism.* Princeton, NJ: Princeton University Press, 1995.

Palmer, Richard H. *The Critics' Canon: Standards of Theatrical Reviewing in America.* Westport, CT: Greenwood, 1988.

Palmer, Richard H. *The Lighting Art: The Aesthetics of Stage Lighting Design,* 2nd ed. Englewood Cliffs, NJ: Prentice Hall, 1994.

Parker, W. Oren, R. Craig Wolf, and Dick Block. *Scene Design and Stage Lighting,* 9th ed. New York: Wadsworth Publishing, 2008.

Pecktal, Lynn. *Costume Design: Techniques of Modern Masters.* New York: Back Stage Books, 1999.

Pendelton, Ralph. *The Theatre of Robert Edmond Jones.* Middletown, CT: Wesleyan University Press, 1958.

Pilbrow, Richard. *Stage Lighting Design.* New York: Quite Specific Media Group, 2000.

Rabillard, Sheila, ed. *Essays on Caryl Churchill.* Toronto: Stoddart, 1997.

Richmond, Farley et al., eds. *Indian Theatre: Traditions of Performance.* Honolulu: University of Hawaii Press, 1990.

Roose-Evans, James. *Experimental Theatre,* Rev. ed. New York: Routledge, 1989.

Rowell, George. *The Victorian Theatre 1792-1914,* 2nd ed. Cambridge, UK: Cambridge University Press, 1978.

Rush, David. *Building Your Play: Theory and Practice for the Beginning Playwright.* Carbondale: Southern Illinois University Press, 2010.

Sainer, Arthur. *The New Radical Theatre Notebook.* New York: Applause, 1997.

Sanders, L. C. *The Development of Black Theater in America: From Shadows to Selves.* Baton Rouge: Louisiana State University Press, 1989.

Sarlos, Robert Karoly. *Jig Cook and the Provincetown Players: Theatre in Ferment.* Amherst: University of Massachusetts Press, 1982.

Sauter, Willmar. *The Theatrical Event: Dynamics of Performance and Perception.* Iowa City: University of Iowa Press, 2000.

Savran, David. *Breaking the Rules: The Wooster Group, 1975–1985.* New York: Theatre Communications Group, 1988.

Savran, David. *In Their Own Words: Contemporary American Playwrights.* New York: Theatre Communications Group, 1988.

Scanlan, David. *Reading Drama.* Mountain View, CA: Mayfield, 1988.

Schechner, Richard. *Environmental Theatre.* New York: Hawthorn, 1973.

Senelick, Laurence. *The Changing Room: Sex, Drag and Theatre.* New York: Routledge, 2000.

Shattuck, Roger. *The Banquet Years: The Origins of the Avant-Garde in France.* New York: Vintage, 1968.

Shohet, Lauren. *Reading Masques: The English Masque and Public Culture in the Seventeenth Century.* Oxford, UK: Oxford University Press, 2010.

Sinfeld, Alan. *Out on Stage: Lesbian and Gay Theatre in the Twentieth Century.* New Haven, CT: Yale University Press, 1999.

Smith, Ronn. *American Set Design 2.* New York: Theatre Communications Group, 1991.

Spolin, Viola, and Paul Sills, eds. *Improvisation for the Theater: A Handbook of Teaching and Directing Techniques,* 3rd ed. Chicago: Northwestern University Press, 1999.

Stanislavsky, Constantin. *An Actor Prepares.* New York: Routledge, 1989.

Stebbins, Emma, ed. *Charlotte Cushman: Her Letters and Memories of Her Life.* Boston: Houghton, Osgood, and Company, 1878.

Stefanova-Peteva, Kalina. *Who Calls the Shots on the New York Stages?: The New York Drama Critics.* New York: Routledge, 1994.

Stempel, Larry. *Showtime: A History of Broadway Musical Theater.* New York: W. W. Norton, 2010.

Stern, Lawrence. *Stage Management,* 9th ed. Boston: Allyn and Bacon, 2006.

Strong, Roy C. *Splendor at Court: Renaissance Spectacle and the Theater of Power.* Boston: Houghton Mifflin, 1973.

Styan, J. L. *The Elements of Drama.* Cambridge, UK: Cambridge University Press, 1960.

Taylor, John Russell. *The Rise and Fall of the Well-Made Play.* London: Methuen, 1967.

Thomas, James. *Script Analysis for Actors, Directors, and Designers,* 3rd ed. Oxford, UK: Focal Press, 2005.

Turner, Victor. *From Ritual to Theatre: The Human Seriousness of Play.* New York: Performing Arts Journal Publications, 1982.

Viagas, Robert, Ed. *The Alchemy of Theatre—The Divine Science: Essays on Theatre and the Art of Collaboration.* New York: Applause Books, 2006.

Vince, Ronald. *Ancient and Medieval Theatre.* Westport, CT: Greenwood, 1984.

Vince, Ronald W. *Neoclassical Theatre: A Historiographical Handbook.* New York: Greenwood, 1988.

Wainscott, Ronald H. *The Emergence of the Modern American Theatre, 1914–1929.* New Haven, CT: Yale University Press, 1997.

Wainscott, Ronald H. *Staging O'Neill: The Experimental Years, 1920–1934.* New Haven, CT: Yale University Press, 1988.

Wainscott, Ronald, and Kathy Fletcher. *Plays Onstage: An Anthology.* Boston: Allyn and Bacon, 2006.

Webb, Duncan M. *Running Theaters: Best Practices for Leaders and Managers.* New York: Allworth Press, 2004.

Webster, T. B. L. *Greek Theatre Production.* London: Methuen, 1970.

Wetmore, Kevin J., Jr., and Alycia Smith-Howard, eds. *Suzan-Lori Parks: A Casebook.* New York: Routledge, 2007.

Wickham, Glynne. *The Medieval Theatre,* 3rd ed. Cambridge, UK: Cambridge University Press, 1987.

Willett, John, ed. and trans. *Brecht on Theatre.* New York: Hill and Wang, 1964.

Williams, David, ed. *Peter Brook: A Theatrical Casebook.* London: Methuen, 1988.

Wilmeth, Don, and Christopher Bigsby. *The Cambridge History of American Theatre,* 3 vols. Cambridge, UK: Cambridge University Press, 1998–2000.

Wilson, Edwin, and Alvin Goldfarb. *Living Theatre: A History,* 4th ed. Boston: McGraw-Hill, 2003.

Witham, Barry B. *The Federal Theatre Project: A Case Study.* Cambridge, UK: Cambridge University Press, 2009.

Worthen, W. B. *Drama: Between Poetry and Performance.* Malden, MA: Wiley-Blackwell, 2010.

Zarilli, Phillip B. *Kathakali Dance-Drama: Where Gods and Demons Come to Play.* London: Routledge, 2000.

Zarilli, Phillip B., et al. *Theatre Histories: An Introduction.* New York: Routledge, 2010.

Ziegler, Joseph Wesley. *Regional Theatre: The Revolutionary Stage.* New York: Da Capo, 1977.

INDEX